A PARLIAMENTARY AFFAIR

Also by Edwina Currie

Non-Fiction

Life Lines
What Women Want
Three-Line Quips (with others)

A
PARLIAMENTARY
AFFAIR

Edwina Currie

Hodder & Stoughton

LONDON SYDNEY AUCKLAND

An excerpt from 'The Hollow Men' in *Collected Poems 1909–1962*
by T. S. Eliot is reproduced by kind permission of
Faber and Faber Ltd.

First published in Great Britain in 1994
by HODDER AND STOUGHTON LTD

10 9 8 7 6 5 4 3 2

British Library Cataloguing in Publication Data

Currie, Edwina
    A Parliamentary Affair
    I. Title

ISBN 0 340 61815 9

Typeset by Keyboard Services

Printed and bound in Great Britain by
Mackays of Chatham PLC, Chatham, Kent

HODDER AND STOUGHTON LTD
A division of Hodder Headline PLC
47 Bedford Square
London WC1B 3DP

This one is for Ray, with love and thanks

All good books are alike, in that they are
truer than if they really happened.

Ernest Hemingway

Contents

Author's Note

This is a novel about modern British political life, today and in the near future. I have tried to make it as authentic as possible, to convey some insight and understanding of how we live and work. So the background is realistic, and I have even taken the liberty of fleshing it out with some real people, under their real names. But my plot and my central characters are all completely imaginary and no reference is intended to the real people holding their offices at the times in question, or to any other person.

Edwina Currie
London, February 1994

Who's Who

Unaccountably the following entries were omitted from the most recent editions of *Who's Who*, *The Times Guide to the House of Commons* and *Vacher's Parliamentary Companion*.

BOSWOOD, Rt Hon. Sir Nigel, PC, MP, Bart, Secretary of State for the Environment. Born 5 January 1934 in Hertfordshire. Tenth Baronet, cousin to the Earl of Cambridge. Sister Emily married to Marquis of Welton, *q.v.* Unmarried. Family background: publishing (Boswood & Boswood, Oxford). Evacuated to Canada in war; educated Eton and Trinity, Cambridge (Classical Mods). President, CUCA, and President of the Union. Toured USA with Observer Mace Debating Team, 1955. Short service commission in Dragoon Guards, 1955–8. Contested (Cons.) SW Islington 1959. First elected for Conservatives in by-election 1962 for Milton constituency (now Milton and Hambridge), Herts. Appointed government whip 1970, Parliamentary Under-Secretary at Department of Trade and Industry 1973–4. Opposition spokesman on small firms, technology and environment 1974–9. Minister of State, Department of the Environment (Local Government Minister) 1979–82; Department of Education and Science 1982–4; Privy Councillor 1983; Secretary of State, DES, and entered Cabinet 1984–9; Secretary of State, Department of the Environment 1989–. Clubs: Pratt's, Buck's, Garrick. Recreations: shooting, writing bad verse, politics.

CHADWICK, Martin. Civil servant. Born 1952. Educated Shrewsbury and Jesus, Oxford. Private secretary to Rt Hon. Sir Nigel Boswood, PC, MP, Bart *q.v.* Son of Sir Matthew Chadwick, CB, KCMG, former Permanent Secretary at the Home Office. Married with two children. Current residence: Sittingbourne. Club: Athenaeum. Recreations: writing Latin verse, collecting ties, wildlife conservation.

DICKSON, Roger, MP. Born 14 February 1952. Educated Wandsworth Comprehensive School, Wandsworth; AIB 1975; MA in Administration and Politics, OU and London University 1982. Tarrants Bank 1968–75. Chairman, Dickson and Associates, non-exec. director, Kyle Stewart Ltd 1975–85. Contested Hammersmith 1979, returned for North-West Warwickshire 1983 (majority 1,800). Joint sec., Conservative back-bench small business committee 1983–5 and chairman 1985–7. Trustee, Small Business Bureau 1985–7. PPS, Department of Trade and Industry 1987. Promoted whip 1990, senior whip (Lord Commissioner of Treasury) June 1992. Married Hon. Caroline Tarrant, *d.* of Lord Tarrant *q.v.*, May 1980; three children, Toby (1982), Emma (1984), Clarissa (1988). Clubs: Carlton, St Stephen's. Recreations: home, family, taking risks.

FERRIMAN, Frederick, MP. Born 1934. Educated Marlborough, Christ Church, Oxford; MA 1955, third class (Greats). Farmer. First elected 1974 for Northampton West. Chairman, secretary and treasurer of numerous Conservative backbench and all-party parliamentary committees and groups. Married, two grown-up children. Clubs: Carlton, White's, IOD. Recreations: welfare of the nation, playing the Stock Exchange.

MUNCASTLE, Andrew, MP. Born 12 September 1960, grandson of Sir Edward Muncastle, former Conservative MP for Horncastle *q.v.* Educated Harrow and St John's, Oxford (PPE). President, OUCA, and President, Oxford Union 1982. Contested St Pancras 1987. Retained Hampshire South-West for Conservatives April 1992. Businessman. Director and co. sec., Muncastle and Sons 1982–. Director, Scope Communications Management and Cray Electronics Ltd. Married 1986 Tessa Conlan; one child, Barney (1987). Clubs: Carlton, Hampshire CC. Recreations: cricket, family, politics.

QUIN, Keith, MP. Born 1952 in Manchester. Educated Bury Grammar School and Hull University (BA Hons History). Brother-in-law to Ms Josie Binn MP *q.v.* Lecturer in sociology and the sociology of history, Kingston upon Hull College of Further Education 1972–83. Retained Manchester Canalside for Labour 1983. Married to Councillor Mrs Edith Quin JP, Deputy Chairman, Manchester City Council; no children. Member various Labour backbench and all-party groups. Recreations: conservation of endangered species.

STALKER, Elaine, MP. Née Johnson. Born 13 October 1956. Educated King Edward's High School for Girls, Barham, and Barham University (BA Hons, History and Politics). Voluntary worker, adult literacy scheme, and part-time tutor, Open University 1982–6. Member

Barham Council 1985–91, Conservative spokesman on finance and deputy leader Conservative group. Member, West Midlands RHA 1986–90. Married 1977 Michael Stalker, senior pilot with British Airways. One child, Karen (1978). Retained Warmingshire South for Conservatives April 1992. Clubs: none. Recreations: family, home, domestic arts.

Election Results in Selected Constituencies

HAMPSHIRE SOUTH WEST   no change

Muncastle, A. D.	Conservative	40,202	61.9%
Lynne, Miss J. J.	Lib. Democrat	16,698	25.7%
Harris, N. H. A.	Labour	7,523	11.6%
Beesley, D.	Raving Loony	570	0.9%
	C majority	23,504	

MILTON AND HAMBRIDGE   no change

*Boswood, Rt Hon. Sir Nigel	Conservative	30,136	60.9%
Dowson, J. M. P.	Lib. Democrat	10,608	21.4%
Beadle, R. W. A. L.	Labour	8,781	17.7%
	C majority	19,528	

WARMINGSHIRE SOUTH   no change

Stalker, Mrs E.	Conservative	34,266	48.7%
Brown, N. P.	Labour	29,608	42.1%
Beckett, Mrs M. M.	Lib. Democrat	6,236	8.9%
Mercer, T. W. I. T.	Natural Law	291	0.4%
	C majority	4,658	

WARWICKSHIRE NORTH WEST   no change

*Dickson, R. N.	Conservative	34,110	52.4%
Airey, J.	Labour	20,863	32.0%
Davies, H. P.	Lib. Democrat	9,934	15.3%
Healey, Rt Hon. D	Raving Loony	202	0.3%
	C majority	13,247	

*denotes previous member

Part One

CHAPTER ONE

'Mr Returning Officer, Ladies and Gentlemen. Quiet, please!'

Major-General Johnny Horrocks cleared his throat, pulled down the bursting black velveteen jacket with its fancy buttons, wriggled his toes in the uncomfortable patent-leather pumps and wished he had taken his wife's advice not to wear full Deputy Lord-Lieutenant's regalia that evening to announce the general election result in South Warmingshire.

In the body of the hall Mrs Betty Horrocks patted her blue rosette for luck and eyed her lace-and-velvet husband with a grimace. The count had gone well and quickly and turnout had been high. What a shame to spoil it. The country would giggle at Johnny tonight as a puffed-up little peacock, once ruling the roost somewhere east of Suez and now Her Majesty's representative out here in Warmingshire, which was not exactly the centre of the universe. He was a good man, honourable and courageous. Britain once owed its splendour and world leadership to such officers. Pity he was such a fool.

Nicholas Brown, the Labour candidate, hugged his wife sadly. The television monitor now proclaimed a Tory victory despite all the pundits. Small, bedraggled and exhausted, his wife could hold back her tears no longer. The Browns were joined by women from his campaign team, arms around each other in mutual grief while their men stood around bewildered, examining the paper-strewn floor and shuffling their feet with no words for their anguish.

Jim Betts stubbed out a forbidden cigarette, tapped out a number on his portable phone and spoke urgently into the mouthpiece. Middle of nowhere, this was. Editor's revenge, no doubt, for his announcing he was leaving for a much better job on the *Globe*. London beckoned. No more tedium at magistrates' courts reporting poll tax and social security dodgers, no more penning sycophantic rubbish about visiting royals and local politicians. On the *Globe* he could at last write the truth, and show them all up for the hypocrites they were.

In a corner Tom Mercer, the Natural Law Party candidate, was rummaging in a cardboard box. Beside him his wife clutched a small chocolate cake and a box of matches. 'I'm sure I put it in here,' he hissed. 'Try your trousers, darling,' she suggested hesitantly. With an impatient gesture he thrust his hand inside a trouser pocket, found the white candle he had been seeking and placed it precisely on the cake. 'There! We're ready,' he breathed. Silently his wife prayed he would now go back to being a lowly clerk and forget about changing the world.

Liberal Democrat Miriam Beckett was dying for a cigarette and cursed the large 'No Smoking' signs hung around the echoing sports hall. A stiff whisky would have gone down well too. It was two o'clock on a Friday morning and she had been without sleep since the previous Tuesday. On the day before the election she had found herself with 3,000 freshly printed leaflets and only two exhausted helpers left out of the optimistic roomful who had nominated her. The three grimly spent the hours of darkness delivering to their best areas, falling over cats, disturbing a burglar, meeting an astonished milkman as dawn broke (got his vote, for persistence if nothing else) and cursing the collapse of the centre parties. It would be a relief to get back to teaching after Easter: normality, relatively, after all this.

At the BBC, a presenter was trying to get Sir Nigel Boswood to wind up so that the programme could catch the declarations from South Warmingshire, North-West Warwickshire and Hampshire South West. Boswood was enjoying himself hugely. His own result had come an hour earlier, with a comfortable 19,000 Tory majority. After a quick celebratory drink he dashed over to the studio, picking up the increasingly good news on the car radio, and was soon teasing the devastated Labour spokesman unmercifully. Regretfully he turned to the monitor.

What he saw pleased him very much. Dickson had made it back in Warwickshire; done well, a good chap. Boswood remembered speaking there in Dickson's first election campaign in '83, when a Labour majority of 4,000 had been turned by sheer hard graft into a Tory one of 1,800. Since then Roger Dickson had consolidated himself nicely. His reward tonight was a solid 13,000 majority. Not absolutely safe, but then no seat ever was.

Sir Percy Duff's old seat in Hampshire was as safe as houses, of course. Bit of a worry with a new candidate, this young chap Andrew Muncastle, but the result was splendid: over 23,000 majority. Boswood even felt a tinge of jealousy. And wasn't that old Sir Edward Muncastle hovering in the background? Must be Andrew's grandfather, surely. Thought he was dead.

The only marginal seat of this batch was South Warmingshire. Another new face there, someone a bit unusual.

In the sports hall Mike Stalker put his arm around his wife. 'We've made it, darling,' he whispered, and kissed her tousled blonde head.

4

She smiled up at him, tears in her eyes – of excitement, tiredness, gratitude, and a strange awareness that a part of their life was changing for ever. She stepped back from him, straightened his tie and adjusted the silky blue rosette so that VOTE STALKER was horizontal once more.

'Do I look all right?' she asked, and he nodded: 'You look lovely, as ever. Fresh as a daisy. I don't know how you do it – I'm bushed.' She glanced wistfully towards the platform. 'We'll have to get used to a different pace of life now, I guess. Hope we can cope.'

He squeezed her hand quickly. 'We will.'

Major-General Horrocks cleared his throat and stepped forward to the microphone.

'Ladies and Gentlemen. The result for the South Warmingshire election is as follows. I will announce the names in alphabetical order, as on the ballot paper.'

'You are a prat, Monty,' Mrs Horrocks muttered to herself. 'For heaven's sake get on with it.'

'Beckett, Mrs M. Six thousand two hundred and thirty-six.'

The only two people in the room sporting orange badges clapped vigorously. The counters, now seated at empty tables, looked round. Mrs Beckett had turned out to be pretty useless.

'Brown, N. Twenty-nine thousand six hundred and eight votes.'

The Labour candidate's wife smiled defiantly through her tears. A ragged cheer went around the hall from the red rosettes. Next time, perhaps.

'Mercer, T. Two hundred and ninety-one.'

A derisory booing rose from Labour supporters. The dotty parties who had enlivened matters for the punters made life much harder for those serious about politics. Had there been no third party, or fourth, Labour might have won, here and everywhere else.

The Deputy Lord-Lieutenant smiled ingratiatingly at the winner. It would do no harm to be in well with the new MP.

'Stalker, Mrs E.!' he boomed portentously.

Elaine Stalker wanted to remember this moment for ever. Her ears tuned in to the soft whispering noises in the expectant silence around her, to the sound of papers rustling, the jostling of blue-rosetted friends gathered by the platform, the hiss of the ventilation system overhead, the isolated pop of flash bulbs, the muted crackling of a policeman's radio, a train whistling faintly in the distance.

'Thirty-four thousand, two hundred and sixty-six,' Horrocks bellowed. 'I hereby declare Mrs Elaine Stalker to be the duly elected Member of Parliament for South Warmingshire.'

Unable to hide his partisanship any longer, he waved the paper over his head with a flourish, as if he were the winner and not the handsome woman in the Tory blue suit by his side.

5

Even the counters joined the applause, expressing not so much delight in her victory as a friendly welcome to their new Member of Parliament. All evening she had been the object of curious scrutiny. Would she win? Would she cry? Top marks for appearance: the lady would certainly make a splash with that good figure and golden blonde hair. Would she be strong enough, a woman? What did her husband think of having to play number two to his wife? She had a kid, too. Puts pressure on the family. Being a mother is hard enough without taking on a big job, away from home all the time.

Elaine Stalker was itching to get down from the platform to mix with the party supporters who were vigorously shaking champagne bottles to make the corks explode. Mrs Horrocks and her ladies, stalwarts all in blue, were jumping up and down in excitement and calling her to join them. Councillor Jennings was looking so pleased she worried he might have a heart attack.

Elaine was in a daze. She made a breathless little speech of thanks, then her beaten opponents made theirs in descending order. Now only one more candidate was left to take the floor.

Tom Mercer stepped forward nervously, put his mouth too close to the microphone and began to speak, reacting in cross-eyed bewilderment as it 'popped' back at him. Both Tory and Labour party workers were becoming restless. Mercer flourished the cake and began fumbling with matches. He seemed to take for ever. Mrs Stalker signalled the Labour man and the two edged sideways off the platform followed by the Liberal, leaving Mercer muttering a lonely incantation over the lighted candle.

Jim Betts, watching from the sidelines, took out his notebook. 'New Tory MP walks off platform at count,' he wrote crisply. 'New MP Elaine Stalker snubbed fellow candidates' – he would put in the names later – 'when she stalked off the platform immediately her own result was announced, ignoring the usual courtesies. Her own party workers commented adversely about her rudeness.' He would have to make up some suitable quotes. 'Mrs Stalker's behaviour augurs ill for her career in Parliament as South Warmingshire's new MP. Perhaps her future colleagues should be warned. This lady may have to be taken down a peg or two.'

He checked his scribbling. Not bad, really. More like the *Globe* than his current rag. Roll on Fleet Street; roll on fame as one of the country's best investigative reporters. The future beckoned brightly, and not only for the glamorous Mrs Stalker.

For the last month Parliament Square had been a graveyard. Now not only was Parliament back but it seemed everyone else – businessmen, lobbyists, media persons, tourists, all the invisible hangers-on of government – had returned to London as well. Cab drivers, brows furrowed in concentration, moaned and gesticulated with vigour. Traffic in the square was noisy and aggressive, vehicles zipping impatiently from one set of traffic lights to the next, honking at a lone intrepid cyclist who wobbled out of the way. Here only the nimble and quick-witted would survive.

At the square's south-eastern corner two sets of black ironwork gates stood open, leading to the House of Commons car park. Stolid London policemen like sheepish lions guarded the entrance, amiable but watchful. At the left-hand gate, Gerry Keown ran a finger around the stiff collar of his brand-new uniform, consulted a long list of new MPs and pulled a wry face. Behind him the great clocktower glittered in the afternoon sun. Big Ben was striking two.

'Rotten job, this. You have to learn every one.' Constable Robin Bell, a tall, cheerful man with bushy sideburns, was the doyen of the Commons rifle team. He had been a Commons policeman twenty-four years. It was the kind of job that kept people there for life.

'Not just their names and faces, all six hundred and fifty-one of them – and believe me some are very obscure indeed. Secretaries as well, and research assistants. And spouses, partners, even children. That's around two thousand people. Add the House's own servants – clerks and library staff and refreshment department and cleaners and a few others – that makes around four thousand on a busy day. You'll find staff all wear their ID badges religiously. The MPs expect you to know who they are and can get quite stroppy if you ask to check – even though it's them we're protecting. Got it?'

Gerry whistled through his teeth. An inch or two shorter than Fell and much younger, he had the glossy black hair and blue-green eyes of Irish ancestry. He was not a policeman but a former prison officer. A month ago he had joined the Metropolitan Police's own security force used to augment routine police operations around the Palace of Westminster.

'Bit different to security at Broadmoor. We didn't have nearly so many comings and goings.'

Robin Fell laughed. Keown would be teased many times about the obvious similarity between the nation's highest security hospital for dangerous nutters and some of the crackpots going through these portals. 'It can be a bit of a madhouse here too. Wait till the first day, the election of the Speaker: everyone will be in to vote, the lot.'

A jostling crowd, cameras and autograph books at the ready, stood on the pavement eagerly trying to spot famous faces. Gawpers and police eyed each other amicably enough. As each vehicle drew close its identity was carefully checked. Within very recent memory a plain white van had casually parked just down Whitehall. A police officer had begun strolling down to investigate. In a trice the roof slid back and mortar bombs were lobbed straight across the road at the Cabinet Office. Fortunately the aim was a fraction out. One exploded in the garden of Number 10, showering Cabinet and Prime Minister with broken glass and forcing them to take cover under the Cabinet table. The IRA again, an ever-present threat to all MPs and Ministers. Security was no laughing matter.

In one corner a battered blue car, still forlornly sporting stickers, was being packed by a disconsolate man in a tweed jacket. He was patted on the shoulder by erstwhile colleagues and then forgotten. Within a month he would sign on the dole and discover that nine modestly successful years as an MP qualified him for nothing.

A sleek grey chauffeur-driven Jaguar with two back-seat passengers paused briefly before sweeping inside and turning left into the shadows of Speaker's Court. The police knew its key occupant just by glancing at the number plate: the Right Honourable Sir Nigel Boswood MP, reappointed as Secretary of State for the Environment, his rubicund face looking jolly pleased with life, as well it might.

Nigel tweaked his distinctive bow-tie and amused himself by waving graciously from the elbow like the Queen. He was rewarded as two pressmen obligingly set off flashes in his face. At his side his private secretary, civil servant grade 5 Martin Chadwick, suppressed his annoyance. He didn't know why the fool bothered; tomorrow's papers would have no room for an old-timer probably in his last Cabinet post. Instead the front pages would be filled with pictures of the delectable new women appointees, the first into the Cabinet in over a decade, who had posed for the cameras all morning.

Nigel's cheerful demeanour concealed mixed feelings. A large number of seats had been lost. This was the hardest, physically the most crushing election he had taken part in since entering Parliament at a by-election thirty years before. He was getting too old for this game. Of course winning against the odds was wonderful: to retain power, to be asked to carry on, to gain the country's backing in these tough times. Thank heaven it was all over – things would improve now. That Britain in the uncertain nineties would be guided by people like himself made Boswood feel thoroughly comforted.

Roger Dickson was equally relaxed as he took the escalator from the car park. One hand stayed nonchalantly in his pocket; the other carried no more than a *Financial Times* opened at the page where its editor grovelled over his previous day's call to vote Labour.

The place smelled just the same, a mixture of dust and ancient stone and mildew and leather and fear and the whiff of an old cigar, yet it felt as if he had been away years, not a mere three weeks. He walked through the Members' cloakroom to see if the named pegs, for all the world like a school, had been reallocated yet. For centuries each MP had placed his sword here in a silken loop, for in this House issues were fought with sharp words. Modern loops, perhaps appropriately, were made of red tape. Then he turned left past vaulted damp cloisters where a dozen MPs would work cheek by jowl and took the stairs two at a time into Members' Lobby. On the way he glanced at faces, stopping to swap congratulations and anecdotes with MPs in his own party, while not neglecting to nod agreeably at the other side.

Dickson understood the arduous feat of memory facing security staff. If he were confirmed in his job as a whip he faced a similar task in getting to know all the MPs. Like the police, he maintained a private system based on acute and often irreverent observation. Already 'dirty fingernails' and 'concertina trousers' had appeared mentally beside two names, with 'pink wig' against a third. 'Hunchback of Notre-Dame' and 'looks mad' would follow. He needed more than their faces. Whips, the government's own policemen, had to become acquainted with all their supporters' foibles, preferences, proclivities and secret telephone numbers, their special friends, sworn enemies and lovers old and new, and know when and how to use this hotchpotch of information to the government's advantage.

Dickson did not expect to be hearing from the Prime Minister in the current reshuffle. He enjoyed being a whip, and had said so on the phone to the Chief Whip. This time he could expect promotion to senior whip with the fancy title of 'Lord Commissioner of the Treasury', a bigger desk and a respectable pay rise.

John Major once called the whips' office 'the last secure den in western Europe'. Whips were not appointed by the Prime Minister but by themselves in cabal, arguing wickedly about who would fit, who should be encouraged, who ignored. No woman MP had ever been invited to join them.

Dickson headed first for the whips' room off Members' Lobby. Years ago it was the fiefdom of flying men and colonels distinguished in the war, although the terminology – 'whippers in' – came from hunting. The atmosphere then was like an officers' mess, hearty, sharp, brutal and cunning. These days it was more like the prefects' study in a public school. Government whips must get the government's business through, by whatever means necessary, but no one forgot that there were carrots as well as sticks. The Chief Whip's other title is 'Patronage Secretary'. He it is who, using knowledge gleaned over months and years by his team, makes recommendations as to position, prestige and power – who should serve on important committees, who gets a better office, who goes on all-expenses-paid overseas trips ('jollies'), who gets promotion, who the sack. The Chief Whip will even help write appropriately oleaginous resignation letters, if the numbed signatory so wishes. In the Chief's room there is blood on the carpet, but far more under it. Nothing goes on in the Palace of Westminster that the whips don't know about; or, at least, so they think.

Thus Roger Dickson, temperament admirably suited to the task, was delighted to continue. He was part of the knowing aristocracy of the House. He had no desire just yet to become junior Minister in charge of stray dogs, mouthing trivialities in an empty Chamber at midnight and signing ministerial letters by the red box-load.

Dickson turned back into Members' Lobby. He recognised Andrew Muncastle, whose grandfather, Sir Edward Muncastle, had been a Member also, serving in Macmillan's government. Andrew was tall, fair, clean-shaven, pleasant-looking. Dickson searched for a distinguishing feature but found none; the man might be difficult to remember. No such problems with Elaine Stalker. Dickson had heard a lot about Mrs Stalker and was curious to meet her. That bright lively face had been instantly recognisable since her first fiery speech at Party Conference two years ago, before she was even on the candidates' list. He recalled the incident vividly. Pleading for more help for the former communist countries of eastern Europe, she took out a vast pair of scissors and shredded a Soviet flag, complete with hammer and sickle, to huge cheers and a standing ovation. To do it so effectively in the four minutes allotted for floor speeches must have entailed hours of practice. Delegates had loved every moment. Most of her future parliamentary colleagues quietly disapproved. Showmanship and headline grabbing, however valuable in a democratic society, were still regarded as talents rather beneath MPs. Especially since most were pretty hopeless at such skills themselves.

Elaine Stalker was the shortest in the group, even though wearing high-heeled shoes. She was striking in appearance, Dickson noted, almost conventionally good-looking with well-defined features and clear skin, an oval face with strong cheekbones, blonde hair in a great halo round her head – very well assembled. Pretty hands, emphasising her speech. Bold Butler and Wilson pearl earrings and a matching brooch on her smart blue suit piped in white, all saying emphatically, 'Tory woman MP'. Women's styles still bore the impact of Margaret Thatcher's tastes. It would be years before a woman MP could wear anything but a tailored suit and be taken seriously at the same time. Elaine Stalker would be in her thirties, a year or two older than Andrew Muncastle. A year or three younger than himself. In Roger Dickson's fertile brain the lady was promptly marked down as a new Member well worth getting to know.

'I'm Roger Dickson. I'm one of the whips. Welcome to Westminster, all of you.'

10

The little group turned to him respectfully. Members of the same party shake hands only once, on first meeting. After that, superstition sets in: if two members shake hands, one will lose at the next election. Roger told them the legend and was entertained as Elaine's eyes shone in disbelief.

'But that won't bother me. I would expect to kiss most of my colleagues, once I get to know them of course.' She looked up at him mischievously. She had hazel eyes, candid, friendly. 'Does the rule still apply?'

'I don't think so, but I should be careful who you start kissing around here!' Roger replied easily. 'From what I can see, the Labour people have really smartened up their act and look just like us these days. Make sure you know who you are cuddling up to, Elaine. Here endeth the first lesson.'

'I'll bear that in mind, and who gave it too, Roger.' Elaine fixed the name of this tall man firmly in her mind. Roger Dickson. An air of quiet effective power. Must go and look him up in the library – he would be in *Who's Who* already, whereas new arrivals would have to wait till the following year. She wanted the exchange to continue. 'Now tell us about the first day: what happens? Is it going to be exciting?'

There had been a slight atmosphere, just for a second. Andrew Muncastle, head bent, had been shifting his feet while the two had flirted so briefly and innocently. Dickson found himself slightly irritated by Muncastle. If that was all this alluring woman ever got up to, in the Lobby or elsewhere, she would do no harm and brighten many lives. Cold fish were far more trouble.

'Our first task is to elect our Speaker, who will then serve us for the whole of this Parliament,' Roger explained. The two new MPs were instantly attentive, like children on their first day at school. Dickson squared his shoulders proudly. 'It looks like there might be a real contest this time; you may even be voting, which hasn't happened in years. It's usually a member of the winning side. The problem is that there are five candidates on our side and none will stand down in favour of any other. Labour have settled on Betty Boothroyd, the Deputy Speaker. Their vote is solid. But the multiplicity of names means possibly more than one vote.'

How very gratifying. Andrew and Elaine were hanging on to every word, as was right and proper. Other new Members had gathered around to listen. Few recognised Dickson, who as a whip was little known outside the Palace of Westminster. Yet it was clear from his stance and manner, even from a distance, that he was a person of some importance. Long after this day every detail of their first contacts in this extraordinary place – who spoke to them, what was said, the strange schoolboyish atmosphere overlaid on the dazed pleasure at having made it here at last – would be burned in their brains. Roger was enjoying his appreciative audience no less. Nine years since first entering Parliament, he felt at last a veteran.

'The first nominated will be one of ours, but to make things easier for you all the first *vote* will be for or against Miss Boothroyd. Only if she fails to get a majority will we vote on anyone else. If she fails we go to the next one, and so on.'

Elaine Stalker was fascinated. 'Will she win?'

'Only if people like us vote for her,' Andrew Muncastle butted in. 'That's right, isn't it? She needs our support, and I for one am not starting my career by voting for a Labour Member.'

Roger allowed himself to sound worldly-wise. 'I do assure you that party whips are not applied for this vote, officially or otherwise. You may vote as you wish. We have of course taken soundings, as you would expect, but in terms of creating a unified front we got absolutely nowhere. Now if you have no more questions I must go and find my secretary and start answering my mail. You'll do the same if you have any sense.'

Andrew nodded stiffly and took his advice. People drifted away. Elaine watched surreptitiously, head on one side like a bird as Dickson's tall, broad-shouldered figure strolled down the library corridor. He walked as if he owned the place. It would be strange to be surrounded by men like that who meant to impress, men who checked their appearance in the mirror every morning.

Monday 27th April

The House being met; and it being the first day of the meeting of this Parliament, pursuant to Proclamation, the Members repaired to their seats.

A Commission having been read for opening and holding the Parliament, the Lords Commissioners directed the House to proceed to the Election of a Speaker, and to present him tomorrow for the Royal Approbation . . .

Elaine read her Hansard in puzzled appreciation. She had been warned but in the rush she had forgotten to come in early. She had no desire to share the gallery with the public on this special day for the election of the new Speaker, so shoulder to shoulder with a hundred other MPs she jostled at the crowded entry to the Chamber, at the spot she already knew was called, confusingly, the bar of the House.

It was immediately apparent that basic football-terrace skills were essential, otherwise she was in danger of being crushed or, at best, dwarfed by male heads raised above her own. With the aid of a judiciously sharp elbow and many gasped apologies she wriggled her way to the front. There at least she could see, even if her best new yellow suit was becoming crumpled and her feet beginning to hurt.

There was another unexpected hazard of such proximity to colleagues. Behind her, harrumphing to himself, an expression of aristocratic disinterest on his face, stood a Conservative Scottish MP of uncertain age. He was running his hand over her back, up and round, into the curve of her spine and then dangerously close to her rump, as if exploring a piece of prime Aberdeen Angus. When Elaine half twisted round to glare, the man offered an insolent leer.

'Load of bloody rubbish!' The remark came from a small man at her side.

'Beg pardon?' Saying anything politely in this heaving mass was difficult. Somehow she had expected her first few moments in Parliament to be more dignified.

Keith Quin, Labour MP for Manchester Canalside, gestured with a free hand. 'All this! Lords Commissioners, the Royal Approbation, doffing three-cornered hats, waves of the magic wand, Black Rod . . . all nonsensical flummery. The message is that the Lords, right up to Queenie herself, have to approve the appointment of the person who's the highest commoner in the land. This is a democracy. We need serious constitutional reform. It should all go.'

'Nonsense.' Elaine was intrigued at this, to her, new example of the political animal. 'It's all harmless and part of our history. And the tourists love it.'

'It's all a constant assertion that democracy here is a new arrival and on sufferance from those who really govern, the hierarchy, the inherited law-givers down the way, that bunch of chancers in fancy dress you've been gawping at.' The Labour MP glowered unconvincingly.

'And did you put all that in your manifesto?' enquired Elaine, feigning innocence.

'Might have done better if we had.' The man gloomily contemplated serried ranks of Tory Englishmen.

Behind her the exploring hand was at it again, lower down this time. Elaine bowed her head and considered her feet, took careful aim, and then quietly ground her high heel into the brogued foot behind her. She was gratified to hear a muffled sob as the pressure on her back eased.

'It's not as if anyone takes it all seriously,' she averred, as if nothing had happened. She was learning fast. 'After all, these traditions are all on the surface. It doesn't get in the way of running a modern country. Does it?'

In the absence of a Speaker, the Father of the House took the chair and called two distinguished Conservative backbenchers to propose their candidate, a popular Tory grandee.

Something jarred on Elaine. She was listening carefully, half leaning on Quin and heard him snort. What were Sir Michael and Sir Thomas saying?

'The office of Speaker, once secured, is all-powerful in this Chamber. Therefore, proposing who shall be the next Speaker is a perilous enterprise. I am all too well aware that if I get this wrong I may never catch the Speaker's eye again . . .'

That seemed a bit precious. Was that the approved style?

'The office of Speaker is the loneliest job in Parliament. Its holder is required to sacrifice that camaraderie which means so much to the rest of us. My Right Honourable Friend whom I am proposing today is steeped in the traditions of this place. He would bring dignity, wit and erudition to the exercise of the office and the stature to ensure firm handling of our often stormy debates . . .'

No, it wasn't that which jarred. These words were fine. She was listening intently. A hand on her waist squeezed gently, briefly. She looked around in annoyance again, then relaxed. It was Roger Dickson. His sharp eyes had observed her defending herself from the ruffian behind. Without any show or fuss, using whip's authority, he had moved the offender out of the way. Now he lounged unconcernedly, but close enough to protect her.

Sir Thomas was seconding the motion. 'My Right Honourable Friend would be impartial between the parties. He would make an admirable and excellent Speaker. Without wishing to sound impertinent, my Right Honourable Friend also looks the part. Indeed he is famous for his bushy eyebrows. His qualities will stand him in good stead . . .'

Looks the part? What does that mean? What is a Speaker supposed to look like? Elaine took a long hard look at the large, embarrassed, kindly man whose name was being put forward and who in a moment would be called to indicate his assent to nomination. Of course he looks the part. He's a bloke.

She turned her head and found her face a few inches from Roger's. He smelled faintly of Imperial Leather soap and wore no aftershave.

Suddenly she was angry. Looked the part indeed. Since when were eyebrows a qualification for anything? Her vote had been undecided up to that point. If Boothroyd impressed, however, Elaine would go into the lobby with Labour and hang the consequences.

Quin was snorting again as the Tory candidate rose to his feet.

'I am grateful to my Honourable Friends who have proposed and seconded me in terms much more generous than I warrant. Confronted with such a litany of perfection, I shall essay, but not achieve, the standard of humility set by King Lobengula of the Matabele, whose first loyal address to Queen Victoria began with the words, "We who are but as the lice on the edge of Your Majesty's blanket . . ."'

14

The House enjoyed that. The contest was far from over.

'My father entered Parliament when I was four years of age; he sat in both Houses. Both my parents sat in the Upper House. My first visit here was at the age of nine. My ancestor was Member for the City of London, which is part of my constituency, and was Speaker also. He lasted five weeks in the summer of 1554 in the reign of Bloody Mary before deciding that discretion was the better part of valour... A candidate must also be confident that his spouse understands what will be involved in the roles that both will need to play. My wife has experienced the life of a Minister's wife and has a willing understanding of the role that falls to a Speaker's wife...'

Quin and Stalker, standing shoulder to shoulder, mused on different aspects. 'All sounds like very good reasons for not electing him,' the socialist muttered. 'We don't want to encourage the impression that there are hereditary rights to the highest offices in the land.'

Elaine thought about the bewildered little boy the nominee must once have been. Only four years old when his parent became an MP. No one to say: You should not leave your child; he is too young. A wonderful wife who knows the role. Miss Boothroyd lacks this useful little extra. How nice it would be to have such a wife. Most of these men here had these priceless assets; she wondered if they were appreciated.

Roger Dickson leaned forward. It was comforting but also strangely exciting, having him close behind her like this. 'Now for some fun – it's Betty's turn to be nominated.'

The Right Honourable John Biffen, Tory, and the Honourable Mrs Dunwoody, Labour, championed their preference.

Then a handsome woman of sixty-two in a dark-red silk dress rose to her feet. On her appointment as Deputy speaker five years before, Miss Boothroyd had been asked by a cheeky Member, recalling her theatrical background, how she should be addressed. 'Call me Madam' was the acid rejoinder. At the bar of the House, Members shushed and nudged each other.

'I have been a Member for nearly twenty years. For me, the House of Commons has never been just a career: it is my life. I have never sought, and I have never expected to occupy, one of the great offices of government. I say to you, elect me for what I am, not for what I was born.'

Again Quin and Stalker reacted differently. The socialist whispered once again, 'Not for what I was born.' Not from birth, Betty. No birthright. Nothing taken for granted. No childhood spent in the gallery watching Daddy; her teenage years were spent as a Tiller girl, a high-kicking dancer on the West End stage, working in her spare time for the League of Labour Youth.

Elaine noted sadly a life devoted to politics – never marrying, no children. Was it really so impossible to be a woman MP and yet like millions of other women have a husband and children too? What had she let herself in for? Was she expecting too much of herself, and, if so, what was most at risk of failure – her career or her married life?

It was time: the division was called on Miss Boothroyd. Talking noisily and thrilled at their own importance, MPs streamed towards their chosen voting lobby as the bells rang. Roger was heading towards the 'Noes'. Elaine did not hesitate. Boldly she turned the other way. Looks, indeed. Bushy eyebrows, no less. Because she's a woman. My life. Not for what I was born.

It was an exhilarating relief to find she was not alone. Instead more than seventy Tories traipsed through the 'Ayes' doors, joining colleagues from all the other parties. By 372 votes to 238, the Commons elected as their 155th Speaker the first woman in all its 700 years' existence.

As the result was announced a huge roar went up. All the MPs, including the government, joined in a spontaneous and unprecedented standing ovation. Roger Dickson was on his feet, clapping and cheering lustily, looking pleased his side had lost. Reasserting tradition, the Speaker-elect allowed herself to be dragged laughing and feigning reluctance to the Chair, for seven of her predecessors had lost their heads opposing tyrannical monarchs and the job was still no picnic.

Smoothly the system glided into action and the real powers of the land asserted themselves. The first speech of congratulations was made by the Prime Minister, who had not voted. Backbenchers had had their moment of glory and attention; order was now restored. Prime-time television switched quickly from the glories of the Commons to *Neighbours*.

Elaine felt strangely empty as she turned away.

In the corridor outside the tea room Andrew was stopped by a great slap on the back which nearly knocked him flying. He returned a half-hearted greeting. Martin Clarke had been a prefect at Harrow School and Andrew his fag. In those days the little boy had been terrified of a clip around the ear if Clarke's shoes were not polished or the toast was burnt, but it reassured him now to be able to look down on his senior's sandy pate and note a growing bald patch.

'Well, I must say it's jolly good to see you,' Clarke began.

Andrew was less sure, but he relaxed and nodded. Clarke had entered Parliament five years ago and was a wealthy, cheerful lightweight.

'I have a proposition for you, Andrew old chap. Now you know that a lot of what goes on in Westminster doesn't go on in the Chamber at all, don't you? The real negotiations take place upstairs, or round the dinner table, in more salubrious surroundings altogether. Anyway, a group of us like to meet regularly. Support each other in debates, backbench committees, that sort of thing. We call ourselves the "Snakes and Ladders" – because of the ups and downs of political life, geddit? Dinner at the Beefsteak Club most Monday nights – good traditional nosh. Occasionally we'll invite a senior face to join us, all very private but useful. About thirty of us. You interested?'

'I'm not a member there. Would that be a problem?'

'No, no. We'll put you up for membership but it's not necessary. Oh, and females banned, so the talk is serious. Next Monday at seven thirty? If there's a vote at ten we arrange plenty of cabs to get us back, so we can drink too. I think you'll fit in very well. Welcome to the club, Muncastle. Good to have you on board.'

Mike Stalker was on the phone from New York. 'How did it go? We were watching it here on CNN. I looked for you but there was such a crowd. How does it feel now you've voted for the first time?'

'Oh, I can't tell you. It's all so big and noisy and pushy and competitive – not what I expected, yet a hell of a lot more wonderful. Physically it's a real surprise – everything is smaller, more cramped, more crowded than it looks on screen. There is always somebody breathing down your neck. And Mike, the working conditions are awful, a real letdown. The office I've been offered has hardly room to swing a cat, but it was made clear I was damn lucky to get one at all so early. If I want a bigger one I'll have to share. Worse than being at school.'

Across the ocean Michael Stalker, senior pilot for British Airways, tucked into a giant room-service steak. 'Talking of school, how is Karen? You heard from her? . . . The new term seems to have got off to a good start. Give her my love. Must go now. See you . . . when? . . . I have another trip to Lagos at the weekend . . . A week on Friday, then. Take care. Lots of love.'

Mike's transatlantic phone calls always sounded like rapidly written postcards or staccato conversations with air traffic control. Elaine yearned suddenly for a mature, intricate conversation with him. It was a pity he was not really interested in politics, though his loving indulgence towards her made up for lack of involvement. Most husbands would not have put up with her long absences and total preoccupation with work. My life. She picked up the phone again and dialled Karen's boarding school

Miss Karen Stalker, aged almost fourteen, unwound her legs from the common room's battered sofa, sauntered into the corridor and picked up the dangling receiver. She pretended nonchalance but in reality she was immensely proud and old enough to realise the extraordinary barriers her mother had leapt. Mum had explained the fascination of Parliament and why it was not enough, nowhere near enough, to stay at home as a councillor or a magistrate or chairman of the school governors.

Karen had been sour, and a little jealous. 'You'll have to do what the whips tell you. We've been looking at political parties in general studies at school. I had to write an essay on whether they work against democracy. I reckoned the answer's yes.'

It would have been more of a blow if her brainy, mixed-up daughter had been interested only in Slash and Megadeath and The Cure. If she was a bit of a rebel, a little critical and unwilling to take advice, those were modest faults she shared with her mother.

After exams Karen would be free for a few days. The school required her to find something useful to do which could be entered on her record as 'work experience'. Without a second thought Elaine arranged a Commons pass so that the girl could come and work for her. It was to be a fateful arrangement.

CHAPTER TWO

The best club in London was back in business. The Members' Dining Room, one of the grandest rooms in the dowdier Commons end of the Palace of Westminster, was beginning to fill up. Conservative Members seated themselves at small tables near the entrance under portraits of Pitt, Walpole and Speaker Onslow; Liberal Democrats disported around a single oval table in the centre, dwarfed by the cold buffet; Labour dominated the far end of the room, under the beady eyes of Gladstone and Disraeli. A few privileged servants of the House – the Serjeant-at-Arms in black knee-breeches and silver-buckled pumps, the Clerk bewhiskered, but without his powdered wig – were also sliding in, like family retainers permitted by virtue of age and distinction to eat near but not with the masters. The atmosphere, as always on a busy night with a three-line whip, was noisy, jovial, macho.

Most of the females in the room were black-skirted waitresses, scurrying around with plates of lentil soup and stuffed eggs, strands of hair escaping across damp brows. Elaine hesitated inside the polished oak doors leading from Lower Waiting Hall. Despite the fact that she was never timid about walking into a pub on her own, it was not easy simply to saunter in.

A hand on her arm made her jump. Sir Nigel Boswood's kindly face smiled down at her.

'This your first time here?'

She nodded, a trifle miserably. None of the faces was familiar, except from television. The thought of approaching such exotic strangers and perhaps being rebuffed left her unexpectedly shy. Obviously there were rules and expectations about the seating plan – but what? Her companion seemed to sense her discomfort.

'Well: I'm Nigel Boswood, and I would be honoured if you would join me. You're Elaine Stalker, aren't you? Congratulations on winning, and welcome to the madhouse. We don't save seats – not good form; we go to the nearest vacant, or start a new foursome. I suggest we do just that.'

19

He put a guiding hand on her elbow and led her to an empty table. As he did so Andrew Muncastle walked in, also hesitating on the threshold, but using his height to search for acquaintances. Boswood caught his eye and waved him over. One new boy or two, it was evidently all the same to him. The table was completed as Roger Dickson paused at the spare chair and asked if he might join them. Dickson was likely to be the government whip for the Department of the Environment in the new session and would be working closely with Boswood. The two established Members exchanged easy eye contact and a light smile, nothing too forceful, yet the authoritative style common to both announced clearly that these were important persons and to be treated with due deference.

A waiter hovered as Boswood examined the new menu and wine list.

'At last, my dears, we are repairing the ravages of Mr Maxwell,' Sir Nigel announced grandly. 'Respectable wines have at last reappeared. Do you know what that man did, may he rot in hell?'

Robert Maxwell had once been an MP and chairman of the Commons catering committee. Elaine tried the eye contact plus smile trick and was amused as Boswood winked back.

'Let me explain. Inevitably this place runs at a loss. Cap'n Bob cured the deficit all right, by the simple expedient of selling off virtually the entire wine cellar at knock-down prices – mostly to himself and his friends. He then resold what he didn't drink, and made quite a killing.'

Dead men can't sue. Elaine suppressed a giggle. 'But now, Sir Nigel, all is well?'

'Ah, yes.'

Nigel enjoyed talking to women and they warmed naturally to him, sensing in his courtesy that he sought nothing but friendship, and that he had no secret agenda. Minds and personalities mattered more to Boswood than gender or appearances. When he could choose, he had no truck with masculine games, be it with women or with men. Now, relief at winning the election was mingled with regret that this would probably be his last Parliament, the last time he could show off to a new intake.

'Indeed. The financial problems were resolved by putting the catering staff on the main payroll. All we have to pay for is the food. So we're in surplus at last, my dears!'

Elaine wryly sipped a slimline tonic. It had not occurred to her, tramping in the rain around South Warmingshire, that checking out a wine guide might have been worthwhile preparation for entering Westminster.

'It's very hard to explain to constituents why we should have subsidised canteens,' Andrew Muncastle murmured. He had been listening, and disapproving. He preferred a pint of bitter and was

20

unhappy at the conspiratorial way Sir Nigel was talking.

'Then don't try.' Roger Dickson sensed the man's unease. This chap would not be the first to start his career as an uninformed puritan. Reality usually intervened before long.

'They won't moan if you give them value for money, dear boy,' Boswood boomed. 'Just bear in mind that you would be substantially better paid in this year of grace as the manager of the Virgin Music megastore in Oxford Street. The nation has its priorities.'

His remark produced rueful guffaws and lightened the atmosphere. Andrew unbent a little, and began to tell a self-effacing tale of canvassing in his constituency. As polite attention turned to him, Elaine examined the menu. It was all in English, was indeed entitled 'Bill of Fare'; the *carte* at the Mother of Parliaments should not be in French, however much it irritated the chef. She relished the choices: grilled grey mullet with lemon and oregano, or braised quail on a bed of red cabbage with raspberry vinegar, or curry with basmati rice, or roast pork with apricot stuffing, all for £4 each. Swordfish steak with garlic and tomato concassé sauce came for £8.45, breast of guinea fowl with cranberries and brandy at £6. A sweet or cheese could be had for 85p, coffee to follow was only 20p. The linen was crisp and white, the cutlery only slightly smeared, the gold-crested crockery distinguished, the service slapdash but friendly. Value for money. No wonder the place was full.

'If you two are looking for advice, I would suggest you dine in here a couple of times a week, and certainly don't go a week without,' Dickson suggested as the starters arrived. Both he and Elaine had chosen duck terrine; Andrew Muncastle was sipping consommé, while Boswood tucked into a shellfish soup with yoghurt and brandy. The chef was certainly liberal with the brandy bottle. 'There are key places where you'll get all the gossip: here; the tea room; the Smoking Room next door, to some extent. The bars downstairs are always crowded. Avoid Annie's Bar unless you want to be a "Rentaquote" – that's the hang-out of press gallery journalists. If you're tempted to say something to them it's safer to pick up a private phone. If your remarks are likely to be hostile to the government I'd rather you say them to me instead. The Strangers' Bar, down by the kiosk, is dubbed "the Kremlin" since the clientele are mainly old-time northern socialists. It's the only spot in the whole Palace with decent beer – casks of Federation Bitter are trundled down from Newcastle-on-Tyne every week. They're a matey lot provided you don't mind a smoky masculine atmosphere.'

Dickson made the place sound more congenial, less mysterious. Elaine made a mental note to give the Kremlin a miss. He was watching her, head on one side, trying to assess her reactions. The conversation was evidently all part of an elaborate quadrille. She wished someone would tell her the rules.

She asked: 'That takes care of the evenings. What about lunchtime? If I accept all the invitations to lunch I'm receiving I shall be enormous in no time.'

'No such thing as a free lunch.' Dickson's plate was deftly removed and replaced with a generous helping of pork. Elaine busied herself with a fillet steak and salad. Muncastle, as if scared of the pleasures of the table, chose cold meat from the buffet. Alongside the other richer food the slices looked dry and forlorn. Dickson continued, gravely: 'Beware of organisations which ply you with smoked salmon, then tell you they're skint and need your help to lobby for more taxpayers' money.'

Talk languished as the diners concentrated on the meal. At last Boswood dabbed his lips with his napkin and burped very gently. He gestured at Elaine. 'And if you're the star at the lunch, as no doubt you will be before long, remember that even if you're not speaking you'll be performing. Be warm to people, make their day memorable for the simple fact of having sat next to you. You're always on duty – there's always somebody watching you.'

Watching her. Dickson was watching her, and not pretending. His gaze was disconcerting, yet not unpleasant. Her own reaction puzzled her. She felt an unwonted obligation to perform for the men at the table, directing her remarks at Boswood as the most senior, largely ignoring Andrew Muncastle but not avoiding Roger Dickson's eye. That would have been impossible: every time she raised her own eyes from her plate he was looking at her, as if it were his right.

Elaine mused, 'This job is rapidly metamorphosing into something quite different to what I imagined it would be. This place too.'

'But are you enjoying it?' Boswood looked like a benign Father Thames, ebullient, at ease. He was a little flushed after the wine, the bottle now standing empty.

'Hugely. It's just that it takes some getting used to.'

Muncastle agreed cautiously. Elaine regarded him more directly. It would help to tick his name off as somebody she had met, even though in manner and appearance he was, to say the least, unmemorable. Tall and fair, pleasant-looking but with a little frown-mark between the eyes: a mixture of formality and uncertainty. At that point Muncastle, who had declined coffee, rose to his feet as if the conversation were not quite to his taste and asked for his bill. He turned to Boswood.

'I don't think I want to know the tricks just yet, Sir Nigel. My voters already think I'm on the gravy train, simply by being here. I think I'd like them to stay wrong a while longer.'

Boswood heaved to his feet with a regretful sigh. 'I too must take my leave: my boxes await.' He bent over Elaine's hand and to her delight kissed it, then swept off with an elegant waddle.

'I like him,' Elaine said, nodding at Boswood's receding rump.

Dickson agreed. 'He's a lovely man. One of the old school. Got in because of his connections, got on because he was competent, still there because everyone likes him. He always turns in a thorough and reliable job. Yet a chap like that would have trouble these days getting past a selection committee.'

'Why? Skeletons in the cupboard?'

'No, not at all; his personal life is impeccable, as far as I know. His background, I mean. Essex man would be suspicious of a tenth baronet. Inverted snobbery fills this place with used-car salesmen and estate agents instead of men with class like Nigel.'

Elaine stirred her coffee. 'That's a remarkably snobbish remark, Roger. You surprise me. Aren't we the party of new wealth? Weren't we represented too long by chaps with breeding but no brains? Surely it all changed when Mrs Thatcher came in.'

'How short memories are, Mrs Stalker!' Roger enjoyed an argument. 'You forget that Ted Heath was the first party leader to be elected rather than emerging from that Smoking Room next door. Margaret didn't change anything: she just made self-made men proud. My point is that there is less room left for good, decent types like Boswood, men with no axe to grind, not on the make, who understand precisely what *noblesse oblige* means – that inherited position and the security of not having to earn a living confer obligation, in his case public service.'

Dickson's expression was friendly and encouraging. Under her lashes Elaine checked him out, trying to hide her interest, yet conscious immediately that he knew. His features were regular, the hair above the ears silvering slightly. In a fleeting examination she could not see what colour his eyes were, and chided herself for wanting to know. He wore a small signet ring, but no wedding ring; the cufflinks on a plain shirt were green and gold with the House of Commons portcullis. The effect was sober but stylish, and utterly masculine.

His manner suggested he was in no hurry either and would welcome further conversation. Elaine was not reluctant. To give herself time to think she played with her coffee. When she turned to the whip her expression was thoughtful and a little puzzled.

'You appear to be saying that, for most of us, there's a choice between being nice and being effective. But we can't be both. Is that right?'

'I'm not sure how to answer that. Of course it's possible, as Nigel himself shows. But he does seem to be an exception, which suggests there is a rule. Competence in politics, particularly among Ministers, requires hard talking and frequently unpopular decisions. If you're too soft to do that you're in the wrong job, period. You need ambition, not just for a sense of direction but to keep you going when times get rough. Promotions don't just happen, Elaine. This is a fiercely competitive

23

place. Yet there are unspoken rules, within these walls. For example: you're a clever girl, but take care not to show that you know it.'

Elaine raised an eyebrow and made as if to protest, then thought better of it. Dickson was toying with a spoon, turning it over and over, as if the words he wanted to say were written in the curve of its bowl.

'Don't take that badly. There's always a great deal of undeserved criticism, from the public, from the press, but worst of all from our own side. It can be very hard to take and perhaps a thick skin is essential, which can make the nicest person seem arrogant or insensitive. Yet you must go on feeling, somehow – about one constituent's little problem, or about some poor child dying in the desert ten thousand miles away; if you never bleed, how can you understand others who bleed?'

He stopped suddenly; he had been musing almost to himself. Elaine was silent. The staff were beginning to look at the clock. Dickson shrugged, as if shaking off a heavy hand on his shoulder. He put the spoon down and smiled at her sheepishly.

'Now then, Mrs Stalker. I will pass on the advice that wise old crow Attlee offered the young Roy Mason on his arrival in this place: "Specialise, and stay out of the bars." The glorious Miss Boothroyd, whom you so admire, was given different guidance by Labour Chief Whip Bob Mellish nearly twenty years ago: "Keep your trap shut, girl, and you will get on." No doubt you would bridle at such chauvinist suggestions. Betty certainly did, though on the whole she obeyed them. And, lastly, remember the three occupational hazards of being an MP: the three As. Do you know what they are?'

Elaine shook her head, eyes bright with amusement.

'Arrogance, alcoholism and adultery. As long as you succumb to only one, you'll survive.'

Roger Dickson still felt uneasy as he crossed the tiled floor of Members' Lobby to return to the whips' office. The light-hearted banter with Elaine Stalker troubled him, for it had quickly turned into a more probing discussion, and this in a place whose Members refrain from examining their motivations too deeply for fear of what they might find. Certainly there was a conflict between being nice and effective, for individuals, Ministers, governments. Politicians were required to make promises which could not be kept. They were supposed to know all the answers in a world of shifting uncertainty. The man who responded truthfully 'I don't know' would be sidelined very quickly. He compromised, daily, as a whip, and counted it a success to survive without ruffling feathers. But Elaine Stalker clearly did not think that was enough.

Roger sighed. Not only Nigel Boswood but the Prime Minister

24

showed it was perhaps possible to be both nice and effective. Now there was a chap who rose to the top not by eloquence or aggression but by infinitely patient persuasion. A man without enemies, at least in the heady aftermath of electoral victory, whose critics in the campaign had managed only to complain he was *too* nice. Yet the edge was there as well – for this was the man who had stopped returning Margaret Thatcher's phone calls, once he had firmly replaced her.

The Prime Minister had learned his skills through three years in the whips' office. That cheered Roger Dickson up: whatever his own prospects they were infinitely improved by service as a whip. He turned off Members' Lobby down the short flight of stairs and opened the door on his left into the lower whips' room.

Johnson was tapping away at a word processor, inputting details about his charges. Each whip covers a geographical area with perhaps forty MPs, as well as several government departments. Johnson was nearly six foot four, a laconic individual sporting a neat Van Dyke beard, unusual in a modern right-winger. It had been a form of protest, for Mrs Thatcher did not trust men with beards.

Without looking up from his flickering screen he greeted Roger. 'I saw you chatting that girl up. My God, Dickson, they're not here five minutes and you're already making a play. Should be ashamed of yourself.'

To his own surprise Dickson needed a moment to consider his response. He walked over to the stationery cabinet, found the scotch left from before the election and poured himself a couple of fingers.

Johnson grunted a refusal. 'Not for me. I'm on the front bench for the wind-ups in a minute; can't go breathing fumes at everybody. Come on, Roger, what's she like?'

'Smart, spunky and quite intelligent, I think. Going to find it tough here. Brightens the place up, though.'

Johnson was a bachelor with a long-standing girlfriend who adored him but could not figure out hcw on earth to make him marry her. 'Don't hedge. You know what I mean. She's much the best-looking of a rather poor bunch. There may be sixty females here now, but apart from the mouth-watering Virginia I wouldn't give you tuppence for any of them.'

Roger Dickson was surprised at his own distaste. Maybe he was getting too old for this sexist schoolboy joking. It no longer seemed funny. He wondered with a shiver if the women ever discussed their male colleagues in the same dismissive way.

'I disagree: several are quite pretty. But one can't, these days, just go round making passes at the women. They're a new breed and won't have it. You know the old saw: "I'm all in favour of more women in Parliament, my dear, as long as you're all attractive." I imagine if you

25

said that to the lovely Ms Stalker she would sock you one.'

'Ah! Now I might enjoy that.' Johnson triumphantly came to the end of his list, pressed 'Save' with a flourish and swung round to face his friend. 'I bet she's looking for it. Did she bore you with conversation about her husband? No? There you are. It might not be too difficult to find out more. She took quite a fancy to you, it was clear. So: a bottle of best champers to whichever of us lays that bright-eyed lady first. Failing her, one of the others. But Elaine Stalker looks as if she might be special. You on?'

Dickson raised his glass. He had little intention of pursuing the bet but even less of having a pointless row about it. 'You are a rogue, Johnson. Believe me it looks different when you're a married man. I'll attempt to keep you informed of her preferences. Now if you don't shift your butt the Chief will be on the warpath.'

The monitor on the wall pinged as the name of the person speaking in the Chamber changed from an obscure backbencher to the new Labour spokesman. Johnson cursed and fled. For a moment Roger Dickson stared into the golden dregs at the bottom of his glass. The multicoloured hue looked familiar, somehow. With a start he realised that Elaine Stalker's hair was exactly the same shade.

Upstairs alone in a small cramped room without a window, number T1-04 on Commons Court, Andrew Muncastle threw down his pen in disgust and tore up another sheet of Commons paper. To be tipped off that his early bid to speak had been agreed by Madam Speaker was wonderful. To have been warned that he was likely to be called, not in a few days' time, which would have been bad enough, but immediately after the front benches tomorrow and thus become the first maiden speaker – that was utterly terrifying.

There were ground-rules. He would not be interrupted, for the first and only time in his career. In return he was supposed to be non-controversial, though that tradition had been breaking down in recent years. It was *de rigueur* to pay compliments to his predecessor, and to describe his constituency in glowing terms. He would mention his grandfather, who was so proud of his grandson's ambition, so different from the dull despised son, Andrew's own father. Miss Boothroyd would call Andrew by name, a practice dating back to an earlier cross-eyed Speaker who, following the custom of merely nodding at the Member, had caused endless confusion; but for all other purposes he was referred to by the name of his constituency. That generated sentiments of continuity and duty which chimed well with Andrew's earnest character.

Christ, he was nervous. Dickson the whip had already given him firm guidance. He should time the speech for seven or eight minutes, no more. He was not allowed to read it out: the Commons had neither desks nor tables, and Members who read their speeches were catcalled: 'Reading! Reading!' In the days of Charles I, the King's spies crept around the Commons after hostile debates collecting scraps of paper as evidence of treason. More than one Member ended up at risk of his life. It was safer, therefore, to speak from the heart.

The national press, already tipped off, were desperate to get hold of him. Local radio in the constituency and both local television stations were primed to relay his contribution in news bulletins. He knew he should be thrilled and inspired by beating everyone else to the tape, yet instead he felt nauseous. There must be something wrong with him. Perhaps this whole idea of going into politics was a mistake.

Andrew took another extra-strong mint, picked up his pen again, and went back to work.

The morning dawned bright and clear. Elaine woke with a start, the rumble of traffic in her ears. It was all very well having taken a flat close to Westminster, but buses and taxis trundling along Victoria Street were not the most attractive dawn chorus. Gurgling from the bathroom reminded her she was not alone. Karen had bagged it first and would leave toothpaste all over the sink, hairspray on the mirror and wet towels on the floor.

Elaine's daughter was currently on holiday from boarding school. Mike was on extended service in the USA for the month – which precluded him yet again from childcare. Fortunately Karen had been keen to come and help out for a few hours, particularly when Elaine realised that she could legitimately offer pocket money from her clerical allowance.

In fact the office needed all the help it could get. Over 70,000 people had dutifully voted in South Warmingshire and it felt as if most of them had written to her since, with congratulations or moans or desperate problems needing the new MP's urgent attention. Half the constituency had always been safe; the other half had been Labour more often than not. The combination made the seat marginal. Those letters would have to be attended to promptly and efficiently or there could be trouble next time.

After two weeks as an MP the constituency post amounted to around fifty letters a day, but at present piles of advertising and bumf were adding to the heap, plus endless invitations to attend briefing meetings, seminars and pressure groups. Her spirits sank. She had not the faintest idea how to respond, nor how to put it all in priority order. The answer was to get somebody else to do it. Surrounded by newly printed notepaper, envelopes and file covers, with Karen struggling to keep the tide at bay with the letter opener, Elaine felt her most pressing task was to find a secretary.

Fate intervened. The phone rang.

'May I speak to Mrs Stalker?' A businesslike woman's voice.

Elaine was weary of being canvassed for specialised insurance or answering yet another opinion poll of new Members.

'May I ask who wants her, please?'

'My name is Diane Hardy. I used to work for a Tory MP who lost his seat and I'm looking for a job. I still have my Commons pass. Loads of references and all that . . . can work a word processor or electronic typewriter. I've worked at the House in all ten years. Do you think Mrs Stalker might be needing a secretary?'

'You bet,' breathed Elaine in relief. 'Where are you? Bring your CV and come and have a chat. How much do you want paying?'

Thus Diane Hardy entered Elaine's life. She was fat and frumpy and fun, endlessly inventive, a whizz at the typing, kind and gentle with fraught constituents, discreet about their tiresome foibles and deliciously rude about all authority. Her family background was more elevated and metropolitan than Elaine's. She had never married but sometimes had a man friend vaguely in tow. Long ago there had been an intense affair with a male MP, but she had sensed very quickly, being like most Commons secretaries smarter than her boss, that nothing would come of it. Ever since she had preferred to work for old buffers or for women Members. Diane lived with her cheerful mother and four contented cats in Battersea and was a power on the local Conservative ladies' committee. Rapidly she brought order to Elaine's chaos.

'Anything from other constituencies – and you as a woman will get a lot – we send straight to their own guy. That's what he's there for, even if he's a lazy beggar and they prefer to write to us. Anything on local policy gets sent to the council. The smaller the problem the bigger the fuss: we just tell them it's not a parliamentary matter. You got good councillors? No? If you want to save yourself a lot of trouble in future I should acquire a few, otherwise you'll be doing all the councillors' work as well. Don't touch planning applications with a barge-pole. If you take sides you'll only antagonise the other lot, who will never forgive you and will go and join the Liberals. Much Liberal Democrat support throughout the country comes from people bruised by encounters with the British planning system. Same with divorce cases – nobody will thank you and you'll lose more votes than you gain. Correspondence about current government disasters gets sent to Ministers. They thought up the sodding policy, so let them defend it. Campaigns about whales and deforestation and donkeys in Spain, we'll produce a standard reply; if a punter sends in a postcard or a coupon from a newspaper and can't be bothered to write a real personal letter, then neither can we. They're mostly Liberals too, you know, so don't get upset. Nasty missives calling you a slag and worse I will tear up immediately, unless you're masochist enough to want to see them. Likewise fan mail I can deal with and send them a signed photo, otherwise it will only make you vain. That will leave only a handful of proper letters and serious invitations you'll have to think about. Does that sound better?'

It was breathtaking, if a little cynical. 'I have an advice bureau every weekend too,' Elaine added weakly.

Diane rocked back on her heels. 'That is unwise,' she said severely. 'However much time you give, it will always be filled. Some people will just come to pass the time of day. Once a month is quite enough. And if you haven't already moved into the constituency don't, not if you ever want any peace.'

'It's too late – I'm there already. Actually I like it, but thanks for the advice.'

Elaine felt chided and vaguely cross, but was not about to dispute with her newly acquired treasure. Leaving Diane muttering at the heaps as Karen discreetly headed for the photocopier, Elaine walked down the corridor, trying to get her bearings.

It was all turning out much harder than she had anticipated. Why did everybody try to persuade her to do things differently? Never in her life before had her competence been so thoroughly and regularly questioned. It was like the first few weeks in the bottom class of a fast-moving new school. Did it make any sense to make new MPs feel so inadequate? Did everybody else feel the same, or was it just her?

CHAPTER THREE

Andrew Muncastle sat on the edge of his seat and waited. *This was it.*

Tubby Peter Pike, Labour front-bench spokesman on the environ-ment, wagged his stumpy finger one last time in mock fury at the government and settled back on the green leather to the ragged cheers of his supporters.

In truth there was not a lot for Her Majesty's Loyal Opposition to feel happy about, after losing another election. The greasy-pole game – who was out, who was in, which names were moving smoothly up, which into political oblivion – now dominated bars and tea room. The perfor-mances of the front bench, particularly newish faces like Keith Quin and Janey Irvine, were under close scrutiny. Such gossipy evaluation gave hope and a flicker of interest to both sides. There would be new leaders. There would always be another election.

There would always be new entrants waiting nervously at the starting gate. Andrew felt his mouth go dry as Speaker Boothroyd rose to her feet.

Betty Boothroyd looked splendid. She had dispensed with the wigs worn by her predecessors for hundreds of years, and in so doing had sparked off a debate among the judiciary as to whether the wearing of stiff powdered horsehair on one's head conferred more dignity on the wearer, or less. She fitted everyone's idea of a bright, formidable, no-nonsense north-country headmistress. It felt like a revolution.

Up in the gallery Tessa Muncastle held Barney's hand. Next to her, rigid and proud, sat Andrew's grandfather, now over eighty. In the car coming down Sir Edward had tried talking about his own days in Westminster but quickly sensed that Tessa, keeping half an eye on Barney and threading through unfamiliar London traffic, was not really interested. Women had better manners in his day. Lady Muncastle, the old duck, had probably been just as bored with his rattlings-on but at least she had pretended and been jolly supportive, at any rate in public. His granddaughter-in-law was a different matter. This pale, preoccupied woman would have a dismal time as an MP's wife if she really found the whole business a chore and couldn't be bothered to hide it.

Tessa screwed her lacy handkerchief into a ball. Her palms were sweaty and itchy. In recent weeks her eczema had flared up again. It was as if the tension found its way into her bloodstream and there turned to acid, so that her perspiration became a cruel, unstoppable dew attacking her sensitive skin in the worst places. It was starting again around her armpits and inside elbows and knees and under her breasts, and would be the devil to shift. Hot nights in London were the worst. She would wake up scratching, rubbing sore patches, trying to keep her hands away from the flaming skin down there between her legs, until at last she would give up and head for the bathroom and shudder as cold water touched the hot flaky flesh. Andrew regarded it dully as just one more reason why she didn't like him to touch her. It was hard to explain her anxieties. Initially sympathetic, he had lost patience little by little; it was simpler to leave her alone.

The Speaker knew where Andrew was sitting, had checked long before Pike sat down. Members opposite were heading off to the tea room but his own side had been primed that maiden speeches would be made, and stayed put. Cabinet Ministers smiled vaguely back at him, while the whip on duty was a familiar face, Roger Dickson. He at least knew what Andrew planned to say, for the two had rehearsed it with a stopwatch earlier that morning. Andrew had then copied it out by hand, in capital letters, on small sheets of House of Commons notepaper. Nobody would mind, should he dry up with nerves, if he referred to his notes, but in fact he knew the speech by heart. He felt comfortable with old methods familiar from school debating days; then he had done rather well. Nervously he patted his tie, checked his fly zip one last time and wished he was somewhere else.

Speaking in the Commons was not like making speeches from a platform, where the orator is at least able to see faces and tell by their reactions what impression is being made, so he (or she) can speed up, pipe up or – if the audience is asleep – blessedly shut up. Here he was confronted by a sea of backs, all dark-suited like his own, apart from the isolated dots of women in bold reds and yellows. The faces opposite were too far away to be useful and anyway would deliberately register disinterest or disapproval to put him off. It was no part of their brief to make encouraging noises at government new boys.

The hollow ache in the pit of his stomach intensified. Breakfast had been difficult, lunch impossible. He was conscious of being hemmed in. Members were twisting in their seats to look at him with curiosity and commiseration. Everyone else either had been through this or was worriedly awaiting his own turn. He gritted his teeth and checked his opening sentence once again.

Madam Speaker was looking at him, eyebrow raised. *Are you ready?* Nod, take deep breath.

'Mr Andrew Muncastle!'

To his surprise, everyone bayed 'Hear, hear!' before he had even opened his mouth. He rose, almost lost his balance, steadied. The Prime Minister had stopped chatting to Sir Nigel Boswood and was turning around. The PM's maiden had lasted fifteen minutes and was regarded at the time as unmemorable, worthy but boring. Look where it had got him barely a decade later. Maybe plod was better than splash.

'Madam Speaker. I start by paying tribute to my predecessor in the constituency of Hampshire South West, Sir Percy Duff, now Lord Duff, whom many Honourable Members will know. He served the area for twenty-two years and was highly regarded. His will be a hard place to fill.'

More rumbling 'Hear, hears'. I have just told my first lie in Parliament, Andrew noted with detached amusement. Now he was on his feet he was beginning to relax. If he had any ambition it was to make a better fist of being an MP than the lazy old sod who had been pushed out by an exasperated management committee, warned that if he did not retire pronto they would deselect him. Andrew glanced at the gallery. His grandfather appeared to be hanging on every word. The old man didn't say much. Barney was wriggling, Tessa looking anxious as usual.

'I am proud also to recognise the contribution in my life of my grandfather, Sir Edward Muncastle, formerly the Honourable Member for Hornchurch, who to my delight is here with us today.'

Everybody looked up, then back to Andrew with more respect. Roger Dickson opened the large blue folder, wrote Andrew's name in bold ink, and added: '3.42 p.m. Started confidently. Good speaking manner, pleasant.'

'It is normal practice, I understand, to say kind things about one's constituency, and in the case of Hampshire South West that is easy to do. We have the youngest population, highest rate of home ownership and lowest unemployment in all the area south of Oxford. We owe a great deal to positive economic change under recent Tory governments.' 'Hear, hear!' 'Yet this is no NIMBY area – not for us the cry, "Not in my back yard", for we have also made welcome the biggest biological waste disposal plant in Europe and generate from it three hundred megawatts of electricity which is sold to the National Grid.'

'Your shit is my command,' muttered a voice behind him. It was picked up by the microphone and could be clearly heard across the Chamber. Members smothered guffaws. Andrew coloured furiously, swallowed hard and decided to ignore the cherubic slob Ferriman sitting behind him who had scored a direct hit.

He had opted to concentrate on the issue dominating the press, the world conference on the environment at Rio de Janeiro. 'It is thus entirely appropriate that the Member for Hampshire South West should be concerned at the impact of human activity on the environment. On present trends the earth's surface temperature will rise in each decade of the next century by between nought point two and nought point five degrees Celsius. That rise is faster than any seen in the past ten thousand years and will make the globe warmer than it has been for a hundred thousand years. It behoves us all to take a close interest in the *hot air* being emitted by mankind.' *Hit back*; he smiled sweetly back at Ferriman, who chortled in delight.

'Success at Rio, and no doubt at summits to come, depends on trust between countries. We British can achieve nothing on our own. The United Kingdom must also make the point that not all the growth in deserts is due to global warming: much is due to simple population pressure in countries which have turned their back on modern contraception. That must change, or all our efforts will be nullified by increasing numbers of mouths to feed. I hope our own government will take a strong line in Rio on this matter.'

Tessa shrank back in her seat. She and her husband had one profound disagreement: her religion. Her heart sank and she uttered a silent prayer that he was not going to start attacking the Pope. She need not have worried. Andrew had said as much as necessary for a maiden and was coming to his peroration.

'This sovereign House has a role to play in environmental matters, even if we are concerned at encroachments on its influence.' More 'hear, hears', with feeling. The underlying battle of the 1990s which troubled MPs would not be the impact of hairsprays on the ozone layer but the steady erosion of their powers by the tides of Brussels.

'In these ways, Madam Speaker, I believe we can slow down the process of global warming, and hand on to our children and grandchildren an inheritance both worthy and intact. I hope our government can take a world lead in so doing. They have my full support in this important task.'

The clock showed he had been speaking for eight minutes exactly. It seemed to have gone in a trice, yet every second had been elongated, giving him time to observe his neighbours, the Clerk to the Parliament, still bewigged in black robes like an old judge, the gleaming gold mace dubbed a 'bauble' by Cromwell, Hansard's staff upstairs tapping silently on shorthand machines, pausing a fraction after he paused, the press gallery scribbling away, with the new chap Jim Betts from the *Globe* craning his neck over the balcony and the *Times* sketchwriter Matthew Parris in his corner seat watching the scene pensively, pencil in hand.

God, it was over. Andrew sat down weakly to encouraging murmurs. MPs do not clap, except on extraordinary occasions such as Miss

Boothroyd's elevation; their hallmark is restraint. Few, however, had made as workmanlike a job of their maiden speech as Andrew. He had been cool, well informed, clear-thinking, a little provocative. He had not crawled to his masters, not grovelled, nor had he broken any other conventions by being rude or hostile. He had not fallen over, lost his place, cracked a joke that wasn't funny, made a fool of himself. And he had had the courage to be first.

Roger Dickson contented himself with one further scribbled remark: 'Nervous, but plenty of self-control. COMPETENT.'

Andrew would never see it, but that would do nicely.

His snub nose came up to the level of the counter, so by standing on tiptoe he could just see the puddings. Luscious sultana cheesecake; five different kinds of fruit yoghurt; a vast, tempting piece of chocolate cake, bent over by the weight of its own sinful cream; slices of pale-green melon, little silver dishes of curved yellow peaches glistening in heavy syrup, tiny sweet mandarin segments. He looked up at his mother hopefully.

'I'm not really hungry, Mother. Could I just have dessert?'

It would be better to say no, to insist that Barney eat properly. Tessa felt panicky again. It would not do to risk a row here in Strangers' Cafeteria, in the very bowels of the Commons open only to Honourable Members and their guests, with Andrew standing beside her a touch impatient and jumpy after his great triumph, and Sir Edward already shakily paying for his tea. She nodded mutely. The child, eyes wild with delight, helped himself to the largest slice of cake, using both hands to carry the plate with solemn dignity to a table.

A handsome, well-dressed woman with a familiar face chuckled. Tessa Muncastle could never remember names: there had been so many new people to meet. The woman sensed her uncertainty and introduced herself, speaking equally to both mother and child.

'Elaine Stalker, South Warmingshire. You're with Andrew Muncastle, are you? Is he your daddy? Did you hear him speak just now? Gosh, you should be really proud of him.'

Barney nodded earnestly as they sat down. It was very cramped; the child's feet were knocking against Tessa's knees. The little boy picked up a spoon and fork and, concentrating hard, manfully tried to eat the disintegrating cake the way he had been taught. A dark chocolatey chunk slowly slithered off the fork on to his new shirt and best school tie. The small face began to crumple and blue eyes filled with tears.

Mrs Stalker leaned over diplomatically. 'If I were you, I'd try this way.' She handed him a large spoon. 'Nobody here has any manners and MPs are the worst of all, so you're in good company.'

35

Confidence and pleasure restored, the child tucked in gratefully. Elaine sipped her tea. Ten years ago, when Karen had been about his age, she had started exploring the idea of getting to Westminster. It had not been for want of trying that it had taken so long.

'Do you like being an MP?' Tessa was making conversation. She would have preferred to have taken Barney and Sir Edward straight home.

'Do I like it? Oh yes, this is what I've always wanted to do. It's all very bewildering at first. I expect Andrew feels exactly the same, though he's finding his feet quicker than most of us.'

Over on the far side of the room Andrew, cup in hand, was bending over a table talking to colleagues. He seemed almost to have forgotten them.

Elaine caught Tessa's wistful expression. 'It must be even harder being an MP's wife,' she suggested. 'After all, we make a choice but our families don't. We have the fun and privileges and you take all the hard knocks.' She didn't believe it, suspecting that in reality it was often the other way round, but it was a kindly flattery. The reaction took her back.

Tessa Muncastle, head bowed, was picking at the tablecloth and talking in a low urgent voice. 'I hate the whole business,' she was saying. 'Andrew says I'll get used to all the attention, but I've always been shy and I find it so hard. It's all right for him: meeting people and shaking lots of hands and being seen in public is all part of his job and he's good at it. I get the most awful sick butterflies every time. Now he's famous I'm being asked to draw raffles and give interviews but it scares me, Mrs Stalker. I'll make a fool of myself and say all the wrong things, then Andrew will be furious. It makes me so miserable. Most of all, I hardly ever see him. How am I supposed to manage when he doesn't get home till eleven at night? Then there's the child. He's only five. It's important for a boy to be close to his father. When is he supposed to see Barney?'

The words came out in a nervous rush. She was terrified that she was saying the wrong things. Andrew never seemed to listen and had rather given up helping her, particularly in the last few months when he had been so busy. It was easier to talk to another woman, especially one who might understand.

'There are moves afoot to try to change the hours,' Elaine explained gently. All the debate about the Commons' crazy hours, starting at 2.30 p.m. and frequently trailing on past midnight, had been about helping women MPs, particularly those with children. The benefits to male Members and their families had been ignored: in this workplace, New Men were thin on the ground.

Elaine doubted whether a crèche inside Westminster would encourage a single extra selection committee to risk a female candidate, but it would be a gesture. Improving the working of the Commons had her whole-hearted support for other reasons. A House which met at sensible hours might take a more sensible view of life. It might even be efficient and achieve more.

Tessa Muncastle pulled out a handkerchief and agitatedly blew her nose. The skin around her nostrils was red and sore. Without realising it she now put her finger on why change was unlikely.

'I hope they do change the system, though Andrew is so engrossed in politics that I doubt if he would come home any earlier even when there are no votes. Don't get me wrong – I do support him and I love him very much. I am sorry: I shouldn't be going on like this, but . . .' She faltered and attempted a watery smile. 'You caught me at a weak moment.'

Elaine had enough hard cases waiting on her desk. This one was for Andrew: better not interfere. Nevertheless her instinct to help reasserted itself.

'You should think of the political life as a bug which has invaded the bloodstream – for life, usually. We don't choose to be this way. Some are born with it in their genes or drink it with their mother's milk. With Sir Edward as grandad I expect Andrew is a bit like that. It must be harder for a person with a famous name – so much is expected of them. Barney here will be under similar pressures. But most of us were bitten long ago – at university, or listening to a great speech, or inspired by a Leader like Margaret Thatcher, or jolted into action by, say, Vietnam or the fall of the Berlin Wall. The point is, we can't help it. It takes us over completely. It's no accident that our ambitions sound vague and platitudinous to outsiders – "wanting to give people a better life", the sort of things we say in interviews – for what really drives us is the passion of politics itself. And it's like malaria: once it's in the blood the infection is lifelong. We suffer if we can't do it. You, our families, suffer if we do.'

Barney was now carefully wiping his mouth with a paper napkin. A stubborn bit of chocolate on his cheek threatened to wreck his efforts. Elaine leaned over and solemnly removed the offending crumb with her forefinger: engaging the child's fascinated gaze, slowly she popped it in her own mouth and smacked her lips.

'Now, young man, I have other people to attend to on the Terrace. And, I suspect, it's time to take your mother home and look after her. She's had a long, exciting day. I hope you'll forgive me.'

Barney nodded silently, and shook hands. For the rest of his long life he would be in love with Elaine Stalker.

The Terrace runs almost the whole 800-foot length of the building, its classic elegance disfigured by green and white marquees used as lucrative dining facilities. The Thames is high here, deep and green and greasy, with floating jetsam. Barges chug slowly to Tilbury and the Essex marshes followed by screaming seagulls. Pleasure craft crammed with tourists heave and toss in their own swell, amplified snatches of cockney commentary bouncing off the carved parapets. The client or constituent or cousin taken for drinks in summer on the Terrace enjoys an unforgettable experience, which also serves to confirm the host's evident superiority to the common herd.

So often had Elaine been shown around that it was a pleasure now to take Marcus Carey's arm, point out the kiosk with chocolates for his wife and settle him with a proprietorial air at a wooden table near the bar. To say Marcus was a friend from university days would be implying both too much and too little. He had been one of the crowd; brainy enough to be more than a hanger-on, yet too pliant, too eager to please, to join the leading group.

But there was something different about Marcus Carey. His name was being mentioned in higher places. He had been appointed to NHS health trusts and authorities and local government reviews. A period on the BBC's General Advisory Committee had followed. The list of appointments had grown longer and more illustrious and threatened to prevent him earning a living, so much time did they take. He had met, courted and married a local medical student. Marcus Carey, of medium height, slim, clean-shaven and well spoken, was not only well educated, intelligent, pleasant, ambitious and a loyal party member – all of which made him useful. There was one unavoidable aspect that made him truly special.

For Marcus Carey was black.

Very black. Heavy lips and flat nose and crinkly hair: not for him any Michael Jackson metamorphosis. That, however, was as far as his blackness went. Not a trace of an Afro-Caribbean accent revealed his ancestry. All the body language was faultlessly white, middle-class and English. Now he sat on the Terrace of the House of Commons in summer sunshine, stretched out his legs and sipped a Pimms. Surrounded by people for whom politics was no longer a hobby but a way of life, Marcus was exhilarated.

Politeness intervened and he turned to his hostess. A spell in Dublin on secondment to the Anglo-Irish talks had equipped him to talk animatedly and with enthusiasm.

'You should get involved in Irish business, Elaine. It needs people here, people with no axe to grind, to take an interest. It's about time that mainland parties and politicians made a bigger effort. The biggest problems there aren't sectarian but economic.'

'Hold on. You're not going to get new private investment over there as long as the security situation is dodgy,' Elaine replied. 'How many people did the bastards murder last month? In all honesty, how could I start persuading businesses in my constituency to open a branch in Armagh or County Tyrone?'

'Things are better than they were.' Marcus started quoting figures at her. 'And, Elaine, the only group that benefits from a continuation of problems there is the IRA. It wants to wreck the peace talks. We want to promote them. You could do yourself a lot of good.'

'I could get myself killed, more like. But let me have some of those stats you were quoting and I'll look at them. Now, Marcus, it was kind of you to write when I won my seat. At college you were thinking of a political career too. Is that still on the cards?'

There was a moment's silence as the man looked wistfully at the carved façade above them. A look of pain crossed the dark eyes. 'What do you think, Elaine? Of course I do. But for me it will not be easy.'

'Have you asked anyone for advice?'

Marcus shifted. 'My own MP, Martin Clarke, of course, but he was ... well, let's just say unfriendly. And I've talked to John Taylor, who fought Cheltenham. He's a decent sort but he couldn't help me himself. That's why I wanted a word with you.'

Elaine hid a feeling of unease. 'You're effectively writing your CV right now. You've done well so far – better than me at the same stage. You need to become better known nationally: speaking at Party Conference, letters to the press, TV, that sort of thing.'

Marcus cast her a sidelong look. 'I'm not sure about that, but it'd be useful gaining experience at the hard end here in Westminster. I put out feelers for an MP to work for, but in honesty I think I can do better than that. Say, working in a Minister's office. As a special adviser, helping write speeches and doing political research. You're very well thought of, Elaine, and you have lots of contacts. I was wondering if you might have a word in the right ears.'

If Elaine had indeed known whom to approach about such a valuable post a different name would have hovered on her tongue: her own. Not to become a special adviser, but to perform much the same tasks, as a parliamentary private secretary, a PPS, the first rung on the Ministerial ladder. Yet she had no such contacts. She eyed Marcus despairingly. He looked so longingly at her, as if she could open doors when in fact she had no idea how. He would not believe that; nor did she want to admit it. It was easier to hide her impotence. Again she asked for appropriate material, this time about himself. At last she could draw the conversation to a close and thankfully she ushered him down the steps to the exit.

* * *

Andrew Muncastle was hurrying on to the Terrace and nearly knocked her over. His tall frame looked thinner than on their earliest meeting in Members' Lobby that euphoric first afternoon.

'I'm so glad I caught you, Elaine. I just wanted to thank you for being so kind to my wife and son in the café. I'm sorry I didn't introduce you but I got a bit tied up. Tessa has taken him home now. You were a great hit – Barney is quite besotted with you and asked when he can have tea with you again.'

'I was very pleased to meet your wife.' Best not to respond to the invitation.

'Now, what's this, Mrs Stalker? Who is besotted with you?'

She jumped. The voice was very close. A male hand rested lightly on her waist. Roger Dickson might be a big man but he could move quietly and was developing a disconcerting habit of catching her unawares. He also seemed to take it for granted that he could touch her, though each time it was unobjectionable, unsexual and not unpleasant. He had picked up the tail-end of the conversation.

'I've been making a big play for a five-year-old boy, Andrew's son.' Elaine kept a straight face and pretended haughtiness. But Roger Dickson had another woman with him, standing very close.

Taller than herself, younger, on high heels, the woman was dark-haired, tanned and perfumed. A red silk jacket hung loose over firm shoulders, setting off a white bustier and short skirt. She looked stunning, whoever she was, with a mocking, knowing air. Elaine's heart skipped a beat. In rapid succession she felt alarmed, then cross with herself, then unaccountably angry with Roger. Was this Mrs Dickson? The style was all wrong for Tory ladies' tea parties. If not Mrs Dickson – was he a cheat?

Andrew was shuffling his feet again. He was clearly not comfortable in the presence of a man with a woman, or more than one woman, when a little sexual electricity was in the air. Elaine took refuge in a twinge of disappointment in both men: Andrew for being such a blushing dope and Roger, more so, for seeking the company of a bimbo.

Dickson turned to his companion with a proprietorial air. 'Miranda, I should like to introduce you to two of the best of the new intake. Andrew Muncastle here has won accolades today for his maiden speech, the first this Parliament. If he carries on like that he will be much in demand. And the lovely Mrs Stalker naturally needs no introduction.'

That remark, often said about her now, did irritate. It was so patronising and seldom well meant: it usually implied a snigger, a smirk hidden behind the hand. She *did* need an introduction and would have preferred it on straightforward political lines, similar to Andrew's. They were both MPs. Equals.

'And may I introduce Miranda Jamieson, a journalist from the *Globe*, one of the better of our tabloid newspapers?'

Miranda giggled. 'Roger, you do talk tripe at times.' The accent was loud and Australian.

Elaine's sense of disappointment intensified. If this were Dickson's lover she would rather not know. She shook hands frostily and quickly excused herself, controlling her temper. What with Marcus expecting miracles and now Roger Dickson flaunting his girlfriend, it was all too much.

Dickson looked at the retreating figure in puzzlement, then hooted with laughter, giving Andrew a conspiratorial slap on the back. 'I seem to have upset the prickly Mrs Stalker! My God, she thinks you're my dolly bird, Miranda. She must believe I'm some kind of sex fiend. Not that I would reject you out of hand, my dear, I hasten to add.'

He turned to Andrew. 'Now then, old chap. It is a good thing for bright sparks like you to get to know journalists and to learn how to talk to them without saying anything. The *Globe* asked the whips' office if they could meet a few of the new intake – I'm sorry Mrs Stalker has gone off in a huff. Would you be kind enough to entertain Miranda a while? I do assure you she is quite harmless. Just don't tell her any important secrets.'

Muncastle profoundly wished he were somewhere else, but good breeding and deference to authority were to the fore. In a few minutes Miranda Jamieson was perched on a high bar stool drinking vodka, showing off tanned bare legs in the evening sunlight to the assembled gathering. The miniskirt barely covered the essentials but Miranda seemed not to care. Andrew pulled in a few admiring friends and began to fuss over his charge. Given a task he was swift and capable, standing close to her protectively but not trying to impress her, yet in not trying succeeding. She was so used to men breathing over her and peering down her cleavage that it was an unexpected joy to meet this pleasant man with his impeccable manners. Not a wimp, either: he had been put in charge and had not hesitated. Interesting.

For his part, Andrew was fascinated. He had never met anyone like Miranda before. Cautious with his remarks, because she was press, he found himself making a considerable effort to entertain and look after her. Her appearance was a challenge to all his limited sensibilities. You could not call her a lady or even a girl; this was a *woman*. Yet no woman of his acquaintance ever dressed like this. Usually he would have run a mile. But Miranda was friendly and fun and undeniably good company. That was bizarre. How could a woman who paraded in such a blatantly sexual style, who recrossed her legs and smoothed her bare thighs with one hand and giggled as that fool Ferriman went pink also be so intelligent? Wasn't there a conflict here? Thoughtful women like his wife were not sexual creatures, indeed did not like sex much. Yet Miranda Jamieson, belying Roger's downbeat introduction, was not any old journalist but, he soon learned, had just been appointed deputy editor of the newspaper. She was an important person in her own right. Thus Andrew Muncastle fussed over her, and forgot his promise to phone home before Barney went to bed.

Eventually it was time for the wind-up speeches. Etiquette demanded that all backbench speakers should attend, as the Minister's office would have dug out answers to points made. Andrew regretfully made his apologies. He hurried through the Terrace door, turned right and headed up the stairs to take his place in the Chamber. As he got his breath back he glanced up at the gallery, where Tessa and Barney and Grandfather had sat. It had been a long day, a day of huge responsibility, and he was weary.

To his surprise Miranda Jamieson was settling in the front row of the gallery, accompanied by Freddie Ferriman, still pink-faced. Her legs were jammed up against the railing, making modesty difficult. Andrew also observed with a sharp intake of breath that she was paying her new companion no attention. Instead she leaned dangerously over the balcony, looked down and around. Then she caught Andrew's eye. To the amused nudges of his neighbour, she smiled at him, and gave a little wave of encouragement.

Getting up in the morning was never easy. Elaine envied people who so loved their work that as each day dawned they leapt from bed, showering and pulling on clothes, all in an excited frenzy. Not that many people of her acquaintance, friends or constituents, fitted that description.

Getting out of bed on a Sunday was a different and more pleasurable business. Mike was home and could be heard singing in the bath to the accompaniment of Classic FM. *Nessun Dorma* did sound better from the vocal chords of Pavarotti, but Mike was making contented noises, which made her smile affectionately. She carried a tray back to bed and began sucking an orange, stretching her limbs in unaccustomed luxury.

Mike came into the bedroom, dressed in a voluminous towelling dressing gown. Elaine was engrossed, and muttering to herself.

'What are you reading?'

'Mmm? Oh, an infuriating article which says that out of the hundred top jobs in Britain ninety-six are held by men. We are making progress, however. Twenty years ago it was ninety-eight. Funny country we live in.'

Mike was puzzled. Having achieved his life's ambition to be an international pilot he was at a loss when faced with the proposition that

42

someone else, equally well qualified, might be turned down on irrational grounds. The best people got where they wanted if they were determined enough. Promotion should always be on merit and nothing else. Those who missed out were simply not capable or gave up too soon. The fact that so many were women, or black, or north-country, was irrelevant.

'If it bothers you, I should read something else,' he suggested mildly, and headed back into the bathroom.

Elaine read bits out as Mike dressed. He should be keen to understand what annoyed her: she was, after all, his wife. She was aware that he was only half listening.

It was enough, Mike decided, to make appropriate noises. He brushed his hair in front of the mirror, fretting a little at the hairs which remained on the brush. With Elaine in this mood, golf and male companionship seemed very attractive. 'What's that?' Mike was being polite. 'What are you doing today, Elaine?'

His wife glanced up, a murderous glint in her eye. 'Me? Oh, I think I'll read a few more articles like this, and then maybe I'll just lie here and grind my teeth.'

Her husband was at the bedroom door, looking uncertain. 'Whatever you say, Elaine. Er... what time is lunch?'

'That's a wrap, Secretary of State. Well done, if I may say so.'

Martin Chadwick unrolled his lanky frame, rose from the conference table and focused through the windows at the remains of the afternoon sunlight. The flight home should be easy and comfortable. Satisfied, he shuffled the Minister's confidential papers first into a large red folder then carefully into a battered black leather briefcase and turned the key. The royal seal and 'E II R' in specks of gold were still just visible on the outside. The briefcase had been his father's: Sir Matthew Chadwick, CB, KCMG and a few more handles besides, recently retired Permanent Secretary at the Home Office, now serving on thirteen boards in the city and loving his well-pensioned freedom, while cherishing the thought that the brightest of his four children was climbing the same ladder, and faster.

'You mean we've finished. And not before time,' Boswood grunted. He made no effort to collect his own papers; security of sensitive documents could safely be left to Martin. He was tired after a grinding session. It irritated him that his private secretary so liked to show an awareness of the world outside the Civil Service as to use slang which made his superiors wince; that was the intention. In assessments an old hand would say, 'Chadwick? Isn't he rather . . . ah . . . slick? Wears wild ties? Is he quite ready, do you think?' Another, showing delicate discernment, in the same club as his father, would always add, offhandedly, that the chap's work was what mattered, and that was rather good. 'Just the type we're looking for, in fact.'

Chadwick coughed discreetly. 'Do you have any plans now, Secretary of State? Can I order you a car, perhaps?'

Boswood glanced at the ornate gilded clock, although he had been watching it with growing impatience for the last hour. Six o'clock was late to finish a meeting which had started at nine and crashed on with only a hurried lunch. Still, it had been a successful day. Agreement had been obtained with no concessions from the British. The French were looking gloomy; there would be trouble back at the Elysée Palace. The elegant, sandy-haired Dutch chairman was walking round the table chatting and shaking hands, looking relieved. One more feather in the cap of the Dutch government.

Boswood pulled himself out of his chair and shook himself to loosen stiff muscles. 'Thank you, Martin, but I have some plans for this evening. Can't let an opportunity of a few hours in Amsterdam go by. Got some friends here, so I shall be seeing them for dinner later. I can get a taxi – actually I'd rather: I can look after myself occasionally, you know.'

From the normally excessively courteous Boswood this was a curt dismissal. Martin looked anxious. It was not good practice for him to go straight back to London on the 8 p.m. plane, leaving his Secretary of State behind and alone. The Dutch secret service had been alerted but had simply shrugged; there was no terrorist activity in the area and their Ministers did not endlessly demand protection. Boswood was being difficult. Everyone on the British team, with the exception of the multilingual Forster who would stay to check texts and translations, was booked on the same flight home. Then last night, just as they settled down for a briefing session with the Ambassador, the Secretary of State had announced airily that he had decided to stay another night, and had changed the flight – himself! – to lunchtime the following day. Bloody nuisance.

Boswood smiled to himself. The Civil Service did not like to let anyone out of the cage, not for a moment, and certainly not for eighteen hours in a foreign city. Fortunately the Ambassador had not pressed him to dine. The feeling of unaccustomed revolt speeded his pulse. Tonight would be a good night.

Outside the conference hall he nodded briefly to Martin and noted with secret glee the ministerial boxes the man was now stuffing with an aggrieved air into the boot of the official car. He slung his hands in his pockets like a naughty schoolboy and strode off whistling in the direction of the Golden Tulip hotel. Chadwick climbed in the car and watched out of the back window. Satisfied but still uncomfortable, he turned to the driver: 'Airport, please. Quickly.'

As soon as the line of cars snaked away, Boswood changed direction. The clean fresh air of an Amsterdam evening ruffled his hair as he walked steadily along cobbled streets by the canal. First to a cash dispenser to get more money. The official allowance of £115 per day handed over on the plane by the ever-efficient Martin would not be sufficient for his purposes.

Then the porn shop. Just to look: one of these days he would go in, but for the moment he sated both curiosity and need by gazing into the shop window. You could not do this at home, just stop nonchalantly and stare at such a display. Photographs of women variously attired, sporting whips and handcuffs with a bored air; a life-size female model in scant lace underwear, bra pushing up and exposing the breasts, a large hole in the crotch; book titles, texts laid open for inspection like the girls on the wall – all drew the eye. In the centre of the window stood an enormous plastic phallus, all of three foot in height, erect and livid. At the tip some wit had drawn roguish piggy eyes and a grinning mouth with tongue hanging out and dripping. Boswood snorted, then a bystander might have heard him chuckle.

He glanced at himself in the window, smoothing his hair and straightening his tie. Not bad for fifty-eight really. Bit of a paunch, but better for not having had a huge lunch today. He should have no trouble finding what he wanted. Some people preferred a man who looked distinguished, who didn't try to be mutton dressed as lamb: just mutton, and plenty of it.

He turned into Regulierstrade in the heart of the old city. At this time of day it was quiet, with a few office workers scurrying for home. From outside, the small pink-painted café did not look anything special – just a large plate-glass window with a short handwritten menu. Two casually dressed young men, moustached with designer stubble, lounged against the wall by the doorway, gesticulating and laughing over a private joke. At the approach of a smartly dressed middle-aged man their conversation halted. Boswood ignored them. As he came close they shrugged, and bid goodbye to each other with a bear hug and a clearly audible kiss.

Nigel smiled to himself. In England men showing affection in public could find themselves arrested and charged with gross indecency. In Holland it was nobody's business but their own.

He walked in and ordered a coffee and a sandwich. The café was tiny and buzzing. White wicker chairs and small metal tables were crowded on the ground floor and a minute mezzanine, so close that customers not only had to share but even back to back were touching and getting in each other's way. But then that was the whole idea. Only the thin young man serving was completely disinterested, manoeuvring unconcerned and unnoticed between customers. British offhandedness was not possible; as Nigel found a corner seat away from the door he nodded amicably to three men already seated at the same table and gazed around with a heady mixture of total freedom and anticipation.

For the purpose of the pink café in Regulierstrade was unmistakable, once one had noticed the pictures on the walls. If the sex shop had exhibited the naked bodies of sleazy women in faded colour, a sight he could ignore, these black and white photographs were a different matter. All were of men in sado-masochistic poses. All were young and muscular, their oiled flesh curved and gleaming in the camera's gaze. Chains, whips and ropes sliced into buttocks, pressed tight across rippling pectorals, snaked up arms and hauled fists high over heads, so that torsos strained upwards to bursting point. One model in the nearest picture was Surinamese, black and brooding, with fleshy lips and Rastafarian dreadlocks and an angry look. And every single photograph concentrated on a long, fully erect penis, bound and cruelly restricted by metal and leather thongs, waiting to be let loose from its bonds.

It would have been bad form to stare at the pictures, as he had the first time. Still the tortured bodies cried out to him and he caught his breath: being here, not as a gawping tourist but as a customer, represented a crossing of some kind of Rubicon, a declaration of intent for the next few hours.

His neighbours were having a lively political argument in German. One was small, blond and young. The two older men were dark-haired, one Turkish in appearance; his German was simple enough for Nigel to understand most of what he was saying. Yes, Germany kept open borders for refugees and asylum seekers and that was good. Germany also tried to discriminate against 'economic migrants' like himself, but the country gained enormously from guestworkers and should grant them rights and protection under the law. The other man teased, pointing out that the law worked both ways: Kemal would have to register, pay his taxes and obey the law himself. That would restrict his activities somewhat.

Nigel ordered another coffee and sat quietly. It made a delightful change to be an observer instead of constantly the one under observation. It was a joy just to sit in this strange, dangerous café and listen to people arguing amicably, *not* seeking his opinion, *not* deferring to his experience or elevated position, *not* expecting him to take responsibility for all their complaints and woes.

The young blond man had said nothing for several minutes. Boswood became aware that he was being examined in a pleasant, inoffensive manner. He smiled encouragingly. The boy had blue eyes – very Aryan.

'*Sind Sie deutsch?*' the boy asked.

'No, no, English, sorry.'

'Oh, that's wonderful. Don't be sorry! It's so British to apologise, isn't it? I thought you might be. So am I. My name's Peter.'

Contact had been made. The boy had a reassuring Home Counties accent. He looked about twenty. His jeans were close-fitting, his shirt white, clean, the cotton sweater on top dark blue and emblazoned with the arms of the University of Utrecht, its pushed-up sleeves revealing slim, tanned forearms.

'I'm . . . er . . . Stephen,' Boswood said. He put both hands clasped on the table in an unconsciously supplicatory pose. 'I'm just here on business. Got the night off – don't have to go back till tomorrow. Grand feeling.'

'Been to Amsterdam before?'

'Oh yes, over the years, several times.' That would tell Peter all he needed to know. There would be no misunderstandings.

'Then you may know it better than I do!' The young man laughed. His teeth were white, slightly uneven. 'Have you been to that new place down the street? It's called EXIT. Bars, music, quiet areas too – if you like. The food's not bad either. How about it?'

There were lots of bars. In this area most were in converted warehouses. Proprietors would pay commission to good-looking young people like Peter to encourage custom; it would be better to take a look himself first.

'That sounds like a great idea, but perhaps I should go back to my hotel and change, if it's informal and there's going to be dancing. Shall I meet you there when things liven up a bit later?'

'Make it nine thirty.' Peter looked pleased and leaned over, putting a hand on his arm. Showing me he's not a junkie, thought Nigel, as he grasped the offered hand and turned it over. There were no needle marks. Eyes met again in mutual comprehension and Peter grinned. 'I think this could be a fun night for you, Stephen. Come on, I'll show you where it is, then we can meet there later. It's not open just yet.'

Back at the Golden Tulip, as he showered and changed into slacks, a polo-necked sweater and the grey leather jacket he had bought years ago for nights such as this, Boswood tried and failed to stop himself thinking about what he planned to do. At home it was legal – just; but never in a million years would the Prime Minister or the party accept as Cabinet Minister a man who was other than utterly heterosexual, all the time. Even to be excessively hetero was OK these days, as the survival of both Cecil Parkinson and more recently David Mellor, so far, had showed. It was so bloody unfair. When Paddy Ashdown's escapades became public knowledge just before the 1992 election his position in the opinion polls showed a 4 per cent improvement. But *gay*? That was still different entirely.

A gay man might have been able to manage as a private citizen, but the Right Honourable Sir Nigel Boswood MP, tenth baronet, cousin to an earl and related to the Royal Family, did not know what it was to be a private person. Since childhood he had been watched, his progress discussed, his moods and foibles noted and compared, his manners corrected, his beliefs laid bare, his companions carefully scrutinised and largely chosen for him. First by his family; then by family substitutes, guardians, nannies, teachers, friends of the family; then, when he became an adult, even at Oxford, by the endless, sleepless scrutiny of the press. That had always meant being ultra-careful, in word, deed, manner, even body language. Two dear college friends, erstwhile frequent visitors to his flat, had not been invited since his elevation to the Cabinet. It had eased the pain of seeing this couple together in harmonious amity; how he envied them their years of loving partnership. Had a love like that presented itself to him at the right time, he might never have gone into politics. But when Sir Nigel Boswood was young, homosexual love at any age was illegal and, further, regarded as twisted and evil. That was how he was brought up. He had learned to keep his feelings to himself. By the time the law changed it was too late.

So Amsterdam it was. A twinge of guilt assuaged him and he fought it down, like bile. Of course he should have exercised self-discipline and gone with Chadwick on that plane; gone home and spent the rest of a riskless evening with a large brandy watching *Newsnight* and catching up with his damned red boxes. Little did anyone realise the painful effort in maintaining an apparently blameless celibate life. At least he had avoided marrying and thus making some poor woman miserable.

So Sir Nigel shaved carefully, brushed his hair, cleaned his teeth and flossed them, tidied the hairs in his nose, dabbed aftershave on his handkerchief, checked his money and left papers, keys, ticket and passport in the hotel safe.

The boy would not be there, of course; but at least he had learned without having to ask the name of the latest place. It was dark now. A different crowd was milling about, young men and women in raucous groups, sizing each other up for a night out. Not a Saturday night: just a typical weekday. Not too crowded. Just right.

'Hi, Stephen! I thought you might not come.' The boy was there, waiting, leaning against the wall. His hair glowed red and yellow as neon lights flashed overhead; the sound of music and bursts of laughter floated around him.

Feeling genuinely delighted, Nigel slipped his arm round the boy's slim shoulders and leaned forward to kiss him. As he did so, Peter turned his babyface so that the kiss fell full on his lips. The boy then slowly, suggestively, licked his lips, eyes dancing. Nigel's heart leaped and started to pound. The great ache was screaming to get out.

'It's great to see you, Peter. You look lovely.' He felt a thrill of pleasure and hugged the boy to him. Together they went inside.

The big club was just filling up. It occupied the whole of a narrow, three-storey building. Downstairs and on the first floor were black-painted dance areas, throbbing with noise and flashing strobe lights. The lower dance floor offered sixties pop and rock; its clients were middle-aged, grey-haired, a little paunchy. Upstairs loud crashing heavy metal music attracted a younger crowd, dancers in leather. It was incongruous to see bikers and Hell's Angels jiving around and head-banging, then holding hands or cuddling in a corner. Nigel never really got used to the bizarre style of the Amsterdam gay scene and would dream wildly about it at home, waking sweating and gasping, the music still making his head spin. A bar area led off each dance floor where the sound was quieter and conversation possible. The downstairs bar was conventionally decorated in blue and silver, but upstairs the owners had encouraged a hard-up artist to use his imagination; so the walls had become green fields, peopled by Friesian black and white cows, brown eyes rolling and tails lifted suggestively.

At the entrance both men had been frisked and warned that no drugs were allowed on the premises: any trouble and the police would be called.

'If you did that in London or Manchester, the police would beat up every gay man in sight,' commented Nigel.

Peter laughed. 'In Amsterdam the police are just as likely to be gay themselves. The local police chief is gay and has been putting recruiting ads in our magazines. Some of his blokes are members here. Can you believe it?'

The boy nodded to a tall, bronzed man behind the bar. That, he explained, was Ernst, who ran the place with his partner Jan. So Peter was a runner for them. A student had to pick up extra money somehow. It looked a lively, friendly place and they were not overcharging for drinks.

A man without a regular lover may touch very few other human beings. Nigel feared being awkward as he bought drinks and made conversation, but the boy led him easily on to the dance floor, where alcohol and desire steadily took over. His dancing was clumsy and awkward but it did not matter. Nobody here was looking at them; everyone was doing exactly the same thing. Through the boy's shirt he could feel a taut body leaning sinuously into his own, the soft blond hair resting briefly on his shoulder. He felt happy, and thrilled, as the lights whizzed past, the music throbbed. The ache was concentrating itself in the pit of his stomach. Soon it would be time.

Peter seemed to read his thoughts. 'There's a room upstairs. Would you like to see it? You don't have to . . . you know . . . do anything, if you don't want to.'

It was as if the boy were the supplicant and he the provider instead of the other way round. Without another word Peter took his hand and led him like a child across the dance floor, nodding at Ernst and Jan on the way.

Behind a curtain it was all black. 'Mind the stairs, they're a bit steep,' whispered Peter. He pressed something into Nigel's hand: a condom. 'They're bloody strict here – quite likely to check up on us.'

Nigel swallowed hard and tried to sound light-hearted. His voice came out too British, almost a bray: 'Quite right too.'

At the top of the narrow stairs, in the eaves of the building, through another thick black curtain, all the doors had been removed, windows covered and all light sources painted out. The air was thick with the smell of sweat and sex. It was pitch dark and hot, but that the place was full of writhing bodies was evident from the slithering noises, grunts and whimpering. Boswood's mouth was dry and he was breathing hard. Stepping carefully, holding on to Peter and squeezing around corners, he found himself led into a narrow airless alcove equipped with a wooden bench.

And at last he let himself go, pulling the boy to him, kissing and holding him so tight it felt as if this slight body would break; but Peter was wiry and fit, fought back, pushing at him so he redoubled his efforts, panting hard. In a moment their clothes were in a heap, Vaseline and a towel appeared from nowhere, and with a cry Boswood joined the heaving groups of men on the anonymous blacked-out top floor of a Dutch warehouse, making love in desperation and anguish and pain.

'Oh God.' He was suddenly exhausted. His mouth tasted unpleasant and his head ached. His skin crawled, sticky and foul. He was immediately stone-cold sober and felt in need of a bath. Carefully, he eased himself up and stroked Peter's back, patting him in a gesture of thanks, as if the boy were a favourite pony remembered from childhood.

In silence they dressed, avoiding each other's space. Then Peter deliberately put out his hand into Nigel's. 'You were bloody marvellous,' the boy whispered. 'Thank you.'

Together they navigated the still writhing bodies, the feeling of distaste welling in Nigel's mouth. The stinking air lacked oxygen. Nearby a man screamed, twice, three times. Nigel was sweating profusely, his clothes stuck to his clammy body. If gays were part of a normal world, would any still come to places like this? Probably: some would want the ultimate excitement of not having privacy, of being surrounded by the sounds of sexual arousal. Some liked the feeling of taking part in an orgiastic activity. As he stumbled down the stairs

Nigel realised in a sudden flash of self-awareness that he also had strange needs: usually so fastidious, he *needed* to be sickened by what he had just done. Feeling disgusted afterwards was a necessary adjunct, this self-loathing the only thing that kept him under control the rest of the time. If it were too easy, as simple as just taking this pretty boy back to his well-upholstered hotel room, he would never be free of it, would never be able to curb or hide his queerness, his aching sin. For he had been brought up to believe all this was horrible and wrong. Anyone that way inclined was cursed. To prove to himself it really was evil, he had to come to an evil place, to do the necessary and exhaust himself, and to feel utterly sickened afterwards.

Oh, God in heaven.

Outside in the street he found he was weeping. 'What's the matter?' Peter was anxious. 'It's not your first time, is it?'

'No, but it's just such a terrible thing for me.' He wanted to be rid of the boy quickly now, get back to safe haven at the hotel. No names, no pack drill: no traces, no risks, no follow-up. He pulled out his wallet and peeled off 300 guilders. 'That's nearly £100. Is it enough?'

Peter's eyes widened. The pink tongue flickered over his lips. 'Oh, Stephen! Of course it is. Will you be OK? Look, shall I come back with you?'

But Boswood was already striding rapidly away, wiping his eyes on the perfumed handkerchief and gulping down sobs. It seemed an age before he walked quickly through the lighted lobby and headed for his room.

The sleepy night porter who saw him assumed that the English government Minister, usually so suave and full of bonhomie, a good tipper, had had a tiff with a secret lady friend. They came to Amsterdam for pleasure and were reminded only of their own despair. It happened all the time.

51

CHAPTER FOUR

Roger Dickson's eyes widened in pleasure and astonishment. Pulling up a chair he sat down expectantly. His three children, already seated and tucking in, ignored him.

'My! Bacon and eggs for breakfast! To what do we owe this delight, Caroline?'

His wife, tending a sizzling frying pan, grinned over her shoulder. 'Well, if you're going to be a lord you had better have a lordly breakfast. Mind, I shan't be doing this every day. Too busy. The children thought I'd had a brainstorm, especially with Nanny off sick. There's gratitude for you! Now how do you like your rashers? It's so long since I attempted this I've forgotten.'

'Crispy, please. Only one egg. And is there any chance of a piece of fried bread?'

Toby flicked hair off his forehead. 'What do we call you now, Dad?'

Dickson poured a glass of orange juice, sat back and contemplated the solemn ten-year-old. Out of the corner of one eye he was aware of Emma and Clarissa at the far end of the table fighting over the ketchup. Caroline was listening.

'I'm not a proper lord, you know. "Lord Commissioner of the Treasury" is the grand title, but all it means is senior whip. I share a better office. And I formally sign multi-billion-pound cheques – not my money, I hasten to add. That's about it.'

Caroline Dickson carefully ladled breakfast on to a plate and poured coffee. She was a solid, capable woman whose rosy skin and thick brown hair, tidied away under a hairband, revealed a preference for the outdoor life. Today she wore a green sweater over a check shirt, a silver pin of a fleeing fox at the neck and brown corduroy trousers. Although over forty she looked younger, with an air of ease and self-confidence. She sat and watched as her husband ate.

He paused, fork in air. 'Much appreciated. You not having any?'

'No. I had a grapefruit. Tiny Tim was labouring a bit over the stiles last week, so I have to get a stone off.'

Her passion in life was hunting and point-to-point. The weather was fresh and breezy so she would ride later. Roger was ignoring the newspaper, which meant he was happy to let the conversation continue. This morning he appeared to be enjoying the family chatter, though at times the children's exuberance would annoy them both.

She continued lightly, 'So that means I still can't call myself Lady Dickson, does it?'

Caroline was teasing. She knew her husband was pleased with this promotion, even though it meant little beyond the Commons. Nor was the former Honourable Caroline Tarrant, daughter of Viscount Tarrant, bothered about titles. Had England permitted the general accession of women, as was more common in the Scottish peerage, she would have become Lady Tarrant in her own right in due course instead of seeing the name and property passing to her younger brother. Then Toby would have become a peer in his turn. Their Lordships' House had considered such a change more than once, but being only marginally less male-dominated than the Commons had turned the idea down flat.

'Stick with me, baby,' Roger responded with a grin. 'If I get promoted out of the whips' office next time into a comfortable junior Minister's job, and if I make it through the ranks many years from now into the Cabinet, then on my retirement – around the year 2013, I imagine – I might just get a life peerage. If the House of Lords is still in existence by then, of course.'

'You don't think it's likely to be abolished, do you?'

The children were getting restless. Their mother sent them off upstairs to clean their teeth and fetch school satchels.

'No, not a chance. A second, revising Chamber is always useful. The fact that it is not elected is even more useful: if it talks sense, we act on its advice, and if it talks rubbish we overrule it. Who in their right minds would change that?'

'You still enjoy the life, don't you, Roger?' Her head was on one side. Spending so much time with animals gave her a sensitivity to how humans felt also, although despite mixing with articulate people she could not always explain how she knew.

'Why do you ask?'

'Because you look tired sometimes. And your description of the next twenty years didn't exactly zing with enthusiasm.'

'Being a whip is tiring,' Roger admitted. 'I seem to have landed late duties several times this month – staying till the bitter end. Naturally I wish I could make it all happen a bit faster but I'm not exactly a high flyer, you know. Been there almost ten years now and not got very far. People who started long after me are in Cabinet already. I may not make it at all.'

His wife picked up his dish, cleared the remains and placed it in the sink. The children were again clamouring for attention.

'Don't be silly. Of course you're a high flyer. Not done too badly for a man who left school at sixteen, have you?'

'Ah, my one stroke of luck was marrying you.'

'No, you did it yourself. False modesty doesn't become you. But remember, any time you want to stop there's always Daddy's bank. He adores you and you would have a great career there, out of the limelight, which would be a bonus for us all.'

'Spend more time with my family, maybe? Wouldn't you feel sorry if I left politics?' He was curious. In a moment the kitchen would be empty. He realised how seldom he talked about the future with his wife. Much was taken for granted in this easy-going household.

'Me? No, not at all. I'm easy. It's for you to decide.' She glanced up. Her husband looked a little upset. She shrugged, sorry she could not share his love affair with the political world; but he had always known that.

She explained, 'It wouldn't make any difference to my life. I should still support the local party, I should still spend most of my time in town ferrying children around – for the next decade anyway – and I should still be more interested in horses and hounds than in people. At least animals don't answer back. Emma, put that down and let's get going.'

Dickson half-rose, but she planted a quick kiss on his cheek and the children did likewise. Only the little one, his adored Clarissa, she of the dark hair and big sparkling eyes, scrambled on to his lap and gave him a proper hug. In a second the door had banged and the kitchen was quiet.

He poured another coffee and attempted to read the newspaper but was not concentrating. The unaccustomed conversation in the cramped town-house kitchen had disturbed his equilibrium. Some political families were a partnership of intensely like-minded people, who shared ambition and helped each other. Though tempting, having a wife in the Commons gallery taking notes would not have suited him and he would have disliked coming home to a post-mortem on every speech. And it was not her style. As a wife Caroline was supportive, certainly. No complaints on that score. Nor did she interfere. She kept her views to herself, if she had any, and had never been other than tactful and considerate to constituents. His passion for politics was tolerated with an amused, almost condescending good humour. But if one day he came home to tell her it was all over and he wished to return to banking she would have smiled and simply accepted his decision. Yet, he knew, she would have been secretly pleased.

The main whips' meeting was at ten; getting in early would do no harm. Caroline had taken the car so he would walk. It was pleasantly sunny out and the Commons was not far.

Early summer was the best time in London. All the plane trees were in full leaf, their green freshness waving over his head. He could almost smell the additional oxygen they had been pumping into the air all night. An early shower had left the streets newly clean. More people seemed to be walking; traffic was light.

His mind ranged over the discussion. Was Caroline right – was his enthusiasm waning? No, that wasn't it. It was in part the feeling that his own progress was taking so long which bothered him. Already there were two members of the new Cabinet younger than he. Several had entered Parliament after him. Years stretched ahead as a junior and middle-rank Minister before he could expect preferment; without special talent or luck, making the jump to Cabinet was by no means guaranteed. At the end he might be eased out, still largely unknown. A knighthood at best. Sir Roger Dickson. Caroline would become Lady Dickson, but so what?

Long ago as a small boy he had walked these streets near Parliament and wanted to touch the very stones. There had been no chance whatever of becoming an MP then. His family background was not exactly poor, but nobody in his household, in his street, stayed on at school or contemplated college.

But the leap had been made from that life of narrow horizons. Luck had played its part, certainly; and crucial support from wise old Lord Tarrant and his horsy daughter. Dickson had first understood himself to be ambitious when he was a boy on this pavement. For that reason he had rejected going into a factory and applied for a job at the head office of a small bank. The second whiff of it had come much later, in Tarrants Bank, when the boss's daughter had taken a fancy to him. A sense of shock had accompanied the realisation that he was capable of going about his wooing quite coolly. Tarrants had long since become part of an international banking conglomerate, but its office in the Strand still stood proudly and it had kept its name. It had also retained its reputation for quiet, responsible service. Rather like his wife.

He loved Caroline. Of course he did. That was not in question; that was not the problem.

Perhaps it was, in a way. He did not feel passionately about her; the marriage still had an air of a satisfactory arrangement. That passion was part of his nature he doubted, although when he contemplated his children, particularly the youngest, and the flicker of pain they generated in him, he knew that whereas he could survive losing Caroline – in a hunting accident, perhaps – and would remarry, the loss of a child such as Clarissa would break his heart.

It was reassuring that there was nothing much wrong with his emotional equipment. It had never been tested much. As a boy he had kept himself to himself, was a little distant with his older brother and sister, avoided falling in love, probably for fear of sentimental ties which might have chained him for ever to his background. That there was something cold-blooded about his make-up did not worry him. It did not make him a bad person. Indeed, for a political animal it could be a most useful attribute.

Perhaps all his emotion was reserved for the political world. It certainly took most of his energy. Caroline was possibly right that he was jaded. Thank goodness it would be recess soon.

He had arrived at the House of Lords end, but it was too early to go inside and his thoughts were still worrying him. On an impulse he turned right into the Embankment gardens, in the lee of Victoria Tower, then through the shabby iron gates with their long-neglected notices about park closing times. He strolled past the elegant small statue of Emmeline Pankhurst, down the path, to the grey stone embankment over the river itself. He folded his arms and leaned over, watching the muddy water.

Suppose he made a mental list of his faults and weaknesses as a possible future Minister, much as he might for another candidate considered objectively, and cheered himself up with a similar list of his strengths? Then he could consider how to diminish the former and augment the latter. At least it would give the feeling that he was taking his career in hand, regaining control.

Strengths? Some came immediately to mind. Plenty of money – at least, no money worries, no need to leave the relatively poorly paid Commons for the City for that reason. Being comfortably off gave him political independence of mind and judgement. Actually, it was Caroline's money, so personal independence was out of the question. A supportive wife and a happy home. Nothing rocky there. Good health, good character: both important. Too many careers had been jeopardised or ruined by a fondness for the bottle, for gambling and the like. A strong constituency and a first-class agent in Tom Sparrow, one of the old school, utterly loyal, fiercely competent. Part of his brain observed with detached amusement that his list was only appropriate for a continued political career: so he had not given that up, then.

Faults? Bit too easy-going. Ought to be more decisive. But that was because he could frequently see trouble coming and by taking small steps avoid it. He did love intriguing, which is why the whips' office suited him so well. And his adroitness meant he had few enemies and a reputation for getting things done without friction. He was unfailingly courteous, on principle: you could get much further with politeness than with a row. That was translated as charm, to his surprise. Not really a fault, then.

Yet it was. Being too content in the endlessly shifting world of politics was the main reason others were making progress faster than he was. He did not push himself, did not ensure that others knew of his successes. Never blew his own trumpet and, to be truthful, didn't know how. But fault it certainly was. If he simply tried to stay put he would find himself settling, neglected, in the middle ranks, as other layers slowly and inexorably piled on top, like a garden compost heap in which the richest bits may be deep down, but no one ever bothers to find them. To improve matters meant seeking and taking risks instead of avoiding them. As a youngster he had felt driven: somehow he had to recapture that need to prove himself.

The brownish water lapped gently at the foot of the stones. Piles of flotsam, bits of rotten wood, old plastic bags, an empty Perrier bottle bobbed past. What a mess the Thames still was. It was hard to believe that salmon swam up river these days. Must be mad, or brave, or desperate, or all three, to take such risks in such a murky environment. Just like anybody decent in politics.

This discussion with himself was turning out unexpectedly useful. Even as ideas flickered through his brain he recalled in the brief conversation with Caroline his use of the clichéd phrase 'Spending more time with my family'. That was a euphemism now widely used in British politics for a Minister who had resigned of his own accord, probably before being pushed. Yet the Cabinet Minister who had originally enunciated it had been nowhere near the push, and might well return to Cabinet before long. Maybe that chap had been serious. Perhaps his family had leaned on him. Dickson was sure Caroline would never do that. Was it thinkable that a man in Cabinet simply got bored . . . ?

Was that it? Was he bored with politics? No. Bored at the moment, then? He wriggled. It was not a word he used often. He had been bored witless at the bank in early days, but the job was a godsend and the money like manna from heaven. Once the promotions began he set to with a will. He had been bored at school because nothing happened – there were no stimuli, no challenges. His current feeling was somehow similar, though not as intense. A low-level sense of boredom and lack of challenge, then, but something exciting might reawaken that latent ambition.

There was a downside. If he were successful life would change. At the moment he basked in a total lack of public recognition. Other strollers in the gardens were giving him hardly a glance. How would he cope with being well known? Would the children suffer? He and Caroline would have to take steps to protect them. Not that there was much chance of media stardom for the moment. He was not a great orator, not by a long chalk. His radio voice was flat and dull and he had no idea how to handle television – the cameras made him appear cold and rigid. None of that so-called 'charm' showed on the screen.

The list of advantages and disadvantages was not too devastating. Having reached what felt like a natural break, Dickson started walking back, brow furrowed in thought. In front of the Pankhurst statue and gazing up at it was blonde woman in a blue suit. She did not notice his approach and stepped back as he drew near. A collision was inevitable; she yelped as he trod on her foot.

'Oh! I am sorry!' He began to apologise, and stopped dead. It was Elaine Stalker. She was rubbing her toes, shoe in hand. As she too realised the identity of her attacker, she hurriedly slipped the shoe back on and attempted to recover her dignity.

'My, but you were in another world,' she remarked. 'Lucky it was you, Roger, or I might have clouted you one. Penny for them?'

He was nonplussed. 'Pardon? Oh, penny for my thoughts. I was thinking about how to make myself famous for my bright, intelligent personality, just like you.'

She looked at him astonished, then warily. 'You're pulling my leg.'

He suddenly felt sheepish. 'No, I was serious. Here am I, a grey, dull old whip. There must be lessons I can learn in how to sparkle as you do. Ah, what you could teach me, Elaine!'

He meant it only as gentle flirtation, a way of leaving his moodiness behind, but her reaction was uncertain. Dickson sighed; he was not handling this too well. She seemed ready to move out of the gardens with him in the direction of Members' entrance. They fell in step together.

'I was thinking, that's all. I've been a whip some time now. Much as I like it, I don't want to spend the next ten years there. Nor, if I were being totally honest, do I want to spend ten years as a junior Minister either.' He was surprising himself, talking out loud like this. Those big hazel eyes were staring up at him with sympathy and concern. His youngest daughter had eyes like that, with a similar childlike openness and simplicity. Elaine's gaze invited confidences. He hoped she was discreet.

'I shouldn't think you have much of a problem, Roger,' she answered. There was a tartness in her tone which pulled him up short. 'At least your feet are planted firmly on the ladder. Look at me – I haven't started yet, and may never get the chance. Want to change places?'

Her remark restored the political geography with a clang, putting it reassuringly but dully back where it had been before he started the unaccustomed contemplation of his navel. He had been promoted, more than once, and should stop feeling sorry for himself. Other people saw him as a great success. He retreated into his official, cool professional mode.

'You should have no problem, Elaine, as long as you work at it. All you really need is patience. That's what I should call you, eh, as a reminder – Patience? How about it?'

Elaine was both annoyed and puzzled. Her sharpness had made this interesting man shut up, just as he was beginning to unbend. She cursed her quickness, and softened her tone.

'If you wish – or we could do a trade. Maybe, Roger, if I attempt to teach you how to "sparkle", as you put it, you'll teach me how to be patient.'

He laughed. 'Now that sounds an attractive proposition, Mrs Stalker. Allow me to consider it further. And to apologise for treading on your foot. I haven't hurt you, have I?'

She shook her head. Her toes were tingling but would survive.

'I wouldn't hurt you for the world.'

It should have been simply a good-natured remark, but it came out with some added significance. She was disconcerted, off balance. He was standing quietly in front of her; then he glanced at his watch.

'I must go. Goodbye, Patience. Don't forget.'

In the Commons cloakroom Elaine slowly took off her jacket and combed her hair in front of the mirror. Her toes twinged like a punishment. How she wished she had not halted those gentle musings by her roughness. At least she knew now that he was not such a cold fish.

And Roger Dickson, as he took the stairs to Members' Lobby two at a time, was exulting at a sudden lightness of heart. For in the last few moments one more weakness had pushed itself forcibly to the fore – a weakness which might also have the potential to turn into a strength. Instead of dismay it left a glow, an excitement and buzz long forgotten. Naturally nothing would come of it. Nothing could come of it: he was not that sort of chap. Nevertheless the very whisper of the thought – the flirtation with fantasy – presented a challenge, and a risk, and an answer to some of the problems of incipient boredom which had so scared him half an hour ago.

It was June, only three months since the election, which already seemed light years away. The last two weeks before the summer recess were a lazy time for MPs, who spent hours on the Terrace or queuing grumpily in the Thomas Cook travel office in the basement, arguing about plane tickets.

Roger Dickson and his fellow whips were busy. It was time to place friends and foes where it mattered. Select committees were set up in imitation of the powerful investigatory system of the US Congress, each shadowing the activities of a government department. Their political balance was giving rise to endless wrangling, for, with a tiny overall majority, in committee the government side had at best a nerve-jangling majority of one. Roger hoped that this Parliament would be remarkable for its lack of contentious issues, at least on the domestic front. He cursed those Members who craved seats on committees solely to make trouble. It needed only one misplaced pest for a Minister or civil servant to be pilloried for hours, often on television.

A glance at his list of available Members threw up Andrew Muncastle's name. The tall fair man whose anxious face he still had difficulty recalling had written an apologetic note indicating willingness to serve on a select committee. There was still a vacancy on Environment. Both Muncastle and Elaine Stalker and a couple of more nondescript new Members were after it, but Muncastle had already made a speech on the subject. The chap was also a pre-programmed government supporter keen to earn Brownie points. To clinch matters, Martin Clarke, whom Dickson owed a small favour after the defeat of a batty Euro-sceptic as chairman of the backbench Europe committee, had also mentioned Muncastle's name.

The lovely Mrs Stalker was a different matter. He pondered her letter for a long time. Putting her on the committee instead of Muncastle would be taking a bit of a risk. It would have been a different matter had there been two vacancies, but a choice was required. She did not have the same aura of dull dependability as Muncastle, perhaps because she was a woman, and a disturbingly pretty one at that. Her progress was slower than it should be. She would have to be reminded to get on with her maiden speech and not leave it till Parliament returned in the autumn. Until it was done she could not participate in debates or Question Time and was in danger of trailing behind scores of others who had followed Muncastle over this first hurdle.

So Muncastle it was. He congratulated himself on a sound choice.

An opportunity to assist Mrs Stalker's return to the fast lane soon presented itself. Year by year the Northern Ireland Act was renewed, usually at a quiet point in the summer. The debate covered the whole range of Ulster topics, not only security. A vote was not expected and few Members had put in to speak. Most, indeed, had paired and cleared off. Yet the subject matter was far from trivial.

Dickson found Elaine Stalker in the Commons library catching up on the week's newspapers. Elaine was dressed in a light-blue linen suit, its straight skirt skimming her thighs as her weight shifted from one high-heeled foot to the other. He halted for a moment at the narrow doorway and watched her as she stood at the old-fashioned reading desk, her back to him. Even from here in the small warm room he could smell her perfume – Chanel, he guessed.

Roger had not forgotten the moment in the Embankment gardens, but on reflection had put it aside as too foolish for words, or too dangerous. Looking at her now he felt the excitement flooding back, the buzz of something risky, different. Such a thing was not possible. A liaison between a whip and one of his own Members would be laughed out of court. It would diminish him for ever, stop his progress dead. Nevertheless he could look, and daydream. And consider how he might keep the implied promise made then, that he would try to help her.

Her hand turning the pages was square, not a delicate woman's hand but capable and workmanlike, fingernails short and practical, unvarnished. The golden hair was falling forward and she pushed it back from her face, revealing a big pale pearl earring nestling deep in the soft mane, like a naked body in a tumbled bed. Her finger caressed the long pearl, gently, rubbing it up and down. The innocent movement made him catch his breath.

She lifted her head, turned around and looked straight at him, her friendly gaze catching his confused reflections. So Roger Dickson noticed her in that way too, did he? He hadn't been the only one, of course. At least one colleague had made a quick pass and had been tactfully rebuffed. Elaine had not come to Westminster looking for a man. But it was flattering and, coming from a person as distinguished and important – and as attractive – as Roger Dickson, it was intriguing and not unwelcome.

'What are you doing here, Elaine?' he asked, and smiled at her. He kept his voice low, for chatter in the library was frowned on.

She explained ruefully she had not arranged a pair in time and had been frustrated by the scribbled notice 'No More Pairs for Thursday' pinned to the door of the whips' office. Greg Shepherd, the whips' clerk, keeper of those mysterious handwritten ledgers of approved pairs and absences, had shrugged sympathetically and shaken his head. He did not make the rules.

'If you have to be here, make the most of it,' suggested Dickson.

He told her about the Irish debate. It felt odd, talking lucidly to a person, making verbal contact with a brain and personality while secretly savouring her smell and minutely examining her physical being. Her skin looked fresh and alive, as if she enjoyed being a woman; she had acquired a modest tan sitting out on the Terrace each morning with Diane attending to her mail.

'There's a brief available. The debate is wide-ranging; almost anything you might say on Northern Ireland would be in order.'

Elaine was dubious, although her interest had been awakened by Marcus Carey's recent enthusiasm. Dickson pushed her a little, offering a whiff of flattery. 'The Secretary of State is dragging everybody in

Ulster politics to talks on its future. We must show some support. The more backing he can get from capable people like you, Elaine, the better. And if you do I won't forget it.'

It was not fair and he knew it. The debate was a formality. Its staged banalities would be widely reported in the province and ignored in the rest of the United Kingdom. On the other hand there would be no opportunities for big set-piece maiden speeches before the House recessed. Vaguely he felt he was letting her down. But for today he had his job to do, his duty to the front bench and the Chief Whip to deliver a well-managed debate. He was beginning to acknowledge to himself that he was drawn to her, not just as an arresting female or as an intelligent colleague, but as more than a mixture of both. In the autumn he could guide her career with a touch more finesse than he was showing now. A more hands-on approach, perhaps. Johnson's bet floated into his mind. Again, as at the time, he reacted uncomfortably to such arrant chauvinism, the sheer injustice of judging potential largely by sex. He had entirely forgotten his own assessment of her for the place she craved on committee.

'Okay, I'll give it a try. At least it won't be widely reported, which is a blessing, first time.' Elaine felt almost relieved to be concentrating now on her maiden speech, even on an unfamiliar subject. She turned to leave with Roger. An objective observer glancing at the two might have noted a preoccupied expression on the woman's face and a paternalistic, satisfied air to the man as he touched her on the arm and guided her towards the exit.

Deputy Speaker Dame Janet Fookes, regal and poker-faced, was in the Speaker's Chair. Clutching the data Marcus had sent, Elaine waited quietly until she was acknowledged, bobbed her head respectfully and asked to be called for her maiden speech. Dame Janet pursed her lips: another new Member got at by the whips. Elaine could expect to be called about 6 p.m.

Once committed Elaine could not shake off a feeling that speaking in that debate was a mistake. The place was empty. In itself that was not unusual. Most of the time the Commons Chamber was empty, a fact which always amazed visitors unable to contemplate that anything could be more alluring than speaking from the green benches. Most mainland Members, however, made a particular point of avoiding Northern Ireland business. It was too specialised, too tragic, too intractable to merit any of the soothing inanities which are most MPs' stock in trade. Thus the province and its activities remained a closed book to Elaine's colleagues, whose strongest reactions were helplessness at the outrages and a desire to be seen nowhere near such a debate.

Sir Patrick Mayhew, Secretary of State, shuffled his notes and put on record once again the policy of the government. His patrician accent, self-deprecating manner and languid stance were unintentionally but uncannily similar to all English forebears in this post, a throwback to less complicated times when the answer to such colonial problems was to send a gunboat or an extra battalion of Scottish regulars. Unlike them, he yearned not for dominance but for peace, for a glimmer of an end to the horrors and atrocities.

'What is our purpose in Northern Ireland? It is primarily to help the people there to secure a tranquil, just and prosperous way of life. It remains divided as a community, but I sense that increasingly there is manifested by ordinary people from each side a deep desire to see co-operation.'

Elaine felt out of place. There was no great ceremony today; nobody much was listening. She shifted uncomfortably on the hard bench. By teatime she was the only non-Ulster backbencher on either side and was wishing that she had taken no notice of Roger Dickson and his come-hither grey eyes. Her acceding so readily to his suggestion was a new and disturbing tendency on her part to wish to please those in authority, especially him. When Dickson asked her a favour, with that big head of dark hair with its whisper of silver at the side which made her want to stroke it, his easy manner and quiet baritone voice, it was getting hard to refuse. She should have said, 'You have to be joking, Roger', and removed herself like everyone else.

She rose at last with a dragging sense of anti-climax, cheated of a great event. Still, she must do her best. She pushed herself to sound forceful, energetic, positive.

'Madam Deputy Speaker: I hope I may help put right the complaints of Honourable Members opposite that the green benches are always empty for these topics. I can today only make a small contribution to the House's deliberations, but in my constituency of South Warmingshire we have a substantial group of people of Irish and Ulster origins who play a large part in local life. I believe they would want me to take an interest today.'

Most MPs could say that. She ploughed on. Her constituency deserved more fulsome description but the depressing atmosphere limited her inventiveness. Nevertheless she had started. Pity there was no one else here to watch – no Mike, no Karen. It couldn't be helped. As ever, once on her feet she relaxed a little and concentrating on the job in hand began to enjoy herself.

'We on the mainland take our nationality for granted, despite all the anxieties over Europe. We know who we are, we know our government, we rule ourselves. In Ulster forty per cent of the population feels it is governed by a hostile culture. The other sixty per cent wants to stay with the Kingdom but is terrified it may be abandoned. No one can feel secure or comfortable in circumstances like that.'

It was straightforward stuff, positioning herself as understanding both sides but taking neither.

'The province's economic performance is proving resilient during the recession. Although as the Secretary of State has admitted unemployment now stands at over fourteen per cent of the population, the rate of increase has slowed down in recent months and is below that of the UK as a whole. Similarly, even though output and employment have both fallen over the year, that compares with a UK average which has been falling nearly twice as fast.'

The numbers were culled both from the government's brief and from Marcus's tables. As she read them out she was acutely conscious that they did not exactly offer a tale of resounding success. She finished a little lamely: 'Taken overall, the past year has provided encouraging evidence of Northern Ireland's economic potential and capabilities.'

Mayhew was whispering approvingly about her to a fellow Minister, who leaned back to examine her. The whip was scribbling a note in his folder. Not long now.

Watching the clock, she addressed her remarks to the Secretary of State. 'It is impressive that so much progress has been made already by the talks on the future of the province. Of course we want to find a sensible, democratic solution. If we are to beat the terrorists, men and women of peace and goodwill must work together. The only gainer from any breakdown of talks would be the IRA.'

She took a deep breath. 'Madam Deputy Speaker. The path ahead is stony and we will stumble many times. But there is only one way forward, and I offer my Right Honourable Friends my full support on what I hope will be, at last, the road to success.'

Elaine sat down to murmured 'Hear, hears'. She was surprised to find she was trembling. The whip on duty entered a quick summary and the comment that she had done well in trying circumstances.

Later, Roger Dickson, reading the whip's remarks, reflected that Elaine must have worked hard to get her speech researched and written so quickly. She had genuine political talent, no doubt about that. He had not given her much help, had not even managed to come and listen. Maybe he should try and make it up to her before the recess.

Elaine was wrong in one respect: her assumption that no one was taking any notice of her that afternoon. Her words would be recorded in Hansard and her views noted, on this as on every other occasion she was to speak. But within a week her name would be entered on lists, in

London, in New York, in Belfast, in Dublin, in secret places and safe houses.

At Westminster itself nothing is ever missed or ignored. Two of her backbench colleagues read her speech in Hansard and were impressed in their turn. The Conservative backbench Northern Ireland committee needed a joint secretary. If she were willing a nomination and a seconder would be arranged. There would be no worries about a contest: that was all taken care of. Nor was there an enormous amount of work to do, just meeting an invited speaker each week and going for a drink afterwards. The whips felt it would be a good thing to have a woman involved, and had hinted it would be a shame if she came to the end of her first parliamentary term with nothing to show for her undoubted ability and staunch support. Elaine detected the protecting, threatening hand of Roger Dickson. And so it was done.

Meanwhile other backbench Conservative committees were also reorganising after the election. Around thirty such committees exist, replicated on the Labour side. There are no agendas, no apologies, no minutes, no action list drawn up at the end of each session. Instead these are private meetings in the House of Commons open only to those taking the party whip. Regularly the distinguished officers of a backbench committee will take tea and talk shop with the appropriate Secretary of State. These men and women, elected by their fellow MPs, are treated with extraordinary deference and given precedence in debate alongside adherents of the more formal House select committees. Key posts are strongly contested: by ex-Ministers, by would-be Ministers, by never-to-be Ministers looking for a little outcrop of rock to scramble to, a toehold on the foothills of the great mountain of state, affording at least a better view than the trampled, overcrowded undergrowth spread out below.

The backbench Environment committee presented a bigger battle than Northern Ireland. Andrew Muncastle found himself the object of considerable attention as his nomination paper, signed by Martin Clarke and another crony from the Snakes and Ladders Dining Club, appeared on Greg Shepherd's office wall. He had not expected to find himself in competition with several weighty former junior Ministers with friends in County Hall. Mostly their objective was to persuade Whitehall to subsidise council coffers more heavily in the run-up to county elections. The prospect of a bottomless pit for public cash, just as tax revenues were dwindling, filled the Treasury with alarm.

Andrew, confirmed government supporter and with enough friends in the right places, was duly elected.

The weather became sultry. It became too hot to sit on the Terrace in the mornings, baking in the sun, while a strange smell sometimes floated up from the river below. By contrast the evenings were cooler and pleasant, but there was no point in hanging around just for the sake of it; the whips were always on the lookout for under-employed manpower.

Elaine trudged back to her flat. Mike was in California, Karen still at school. The Commons would be finished in a week. The exhilaration and euphoria of the first days had worn off very quickly, as was to be expected. Not that any kind of disillusion had set in; the gap had been filled by a struggle to master all her new tasks. She needed to think through the mass of information being sprayed around. It all left her hardly any time to draw breath.

How much easier it must be for an Andrew Muncastle, with somebody knowledgeable – his grandfather – close at hand. Or for other new women MPs from a political background. Ann Winterton and Virginia Bottomley had been able to turn to husbands who had preceded them to the House. Not exactly a task for Mike, flying away God knows where. She wished she had someone – a guide, a mentor perhaps – at the very least, on a quiet night like this, a companion, to listen and to share.

It was not going to be an easy life.

When she had the flat to herself on evenings like tonight when there was no vote, Elaine had soon devised her own system of avoiding becoming too lonely. If there was nobody around, she would make the most of her solitude. A little uninterrupted pampering would be perfect, especially after a long, sweaty day.

She set about her task methodically. The small television set was moved into the bathroom and balanced on a stool. A generous measure of single-malt whisky went into a chunky crystal tumbler placed on the corner of the bath. Blue foam bath essence was poured into the running hot water. The little room filled rapidly with sweet-scented steam. Three large fluffy towels came out of the airing cupboard and formed a pink nest on the floor, the talc perched on top like a baby bird waiting to be fed. Faced with an hour or two to spare and the need to unwind, Elaine plumped for a lazy wallow in a hot bath.

Here, surrounded by rich foam perfumed by Nina Ricci, she could sing, soap herself, take a drink, rub the loofah wherever she wished, wiggle her toes with care up the tap and gaze down her nose at her glistening body with curiosity and modest pride. Not bad at all for thirty-five: not a wrinkle, not a sag, not a scar – not yet. Only a tiny mark low down on the right where the gynaecologist had entered to tie her tubes. More pregnancies were not on the agenda, or mornings remembering to take the pill. She smiled as she recalled interviewers, local and national, enquiring sympathetically about the sacrifices she had made to get to Westminster. Oh yes, she had made sacrifices. To become an MP she had sacrificed a load of undesirable activity, happily giving up both housework and morning sickness in return for a job she loved.

Fuzzily through the steam she examined the half-moons of her breasts and their small pale nipples. Then the hillock of her belly and its navel, like an extinct volcano, the suds forming a white mountain top, slithering down the sides like an eruption. She took another large sip of whisky, hummed merrily and piled more foam in the hollows between belly and hip-bones. Only in the bath did they stick up now: she would have to diet during the recess. Some hope.

It was nearly ten o'clock. Elaine turned on the television set and lay back, waiting for the nightly news and comment. The foam swished around her shoulders, wetting her hair and covering her chin like a man's beard, hiding her body in sparkling white like the hair on a great warrior's chest. In the bath she could pretend to be male, but still intensely enjoy being female. She giggled and blew bubbles off her nose. The whisky warmed her inside, making her drowsy, suspended in time, independent of gravity, no longer subject to the stifling restrictions at Westminster, the unsmudged make-up and ladderless tights, the immaculate expensive outfits and unrelenting public scrutiny.

She moved her hand slowly over her breasts, caressing, curious and entertained as the nipples rose and hardened under her fingers. Much too good to be wasted.

What a pity Mike isn't here. If he goes on neglecting me like this I shall have to get a boyfriend. He wouldn't even notice, I'll bet.

The television pictures swam gently before her unfocused eyes as the producer chose a long shot of the Commons in session. Elaine's fingers slithered down her belly and involuntarily, because it was such a delicious feeling and because it was such a long time since Mike had been down there, began very gently, almost without noticing, to flicker up and down, up and down, in the moistness between her legs.

One tall figure standing at the bar of the House turned to face the camera. With her free hand she raised her glass in mocking salute. He seemed to look straight at her, to know what she was doing. It was nonsense, of course: this was a recording, a piece at random. He was not there. He could not see her.

She wished he could.

It was Roger Dickson.

She sat up, startled, pulling her hand away, flesh tingling. The remaining whisky spilled into the bath, its alcohol mixing with the steam. Suddenly the place smelled lascivious, like a brothel. She coughed and spluttered as the foam with a life of its own found its sinister way into her mouth and nose. The water sloshed dangerously around and she felt herself slipping, unable to get a grip.

What on earth was she doing? Thinking? Not thinking, more like. The man was married. Happily, for all she knew. *Do Not Touch; verboten.*

Dickson had made no move of any kind, overt or subtle. He had shown nothing other than a fraternal, professional interest. His pushing her to make her maiden speech in that ghastly Irish debate was no evidence that he saw her as anything special – rather the opposite. Other people had lost their parliamentary virginity weeks ago. His suggestion of a nickname had been a game to relax her, nothing more. If he were taking a shine to her she was resolutely unaware of it.

Yet there had been something wistful in his eyes in the library. And in the gardens. Surely she was not imagining that.

Elaine sat for a moment in the subsiding sudsy water and tried to think with more clarity. Dickson was a deeply attractive man, of that there was no doubt. There was no harm in admitting that. But he was a formidable character, vital to her further progress as her whip, and absolutely not to be trifled with. Misjudging him could lead her to make a complete fool of herself.

Or was it so crazy?

A parliamentary colleague would have as much reason for keeping quiet as she would have herself. An outsider might be tempted to tell the tale for money. Outsiders would not understand, could not share the joys and misfortunes of this exotic political world. An insider like Dickson would grasp all that in a trice, and would have as many reasons as herself for discretion. An affair with a colleague, if indeed she were planning an affair at all, might be better, safer and more exciting than an affair with almost anybody else. If she could be cool and self-controlled about it, the question demanded her consideration.

Roger's face had appeared only fleetingly. Doubtless she had imagined it, or it had been some other man. She pulled out the plug and felt her previous certainties ebb down the plug-hole with the grey frothy water. A cool flicker of air was coming under the door, chilling her wet skin.

The trip to San Francisco was in the nature of a few pleasant days off. British Airways ran its most profitable routes to California; it was comforting in a recession, Mike Stalker noted, to be employed by a cash-rich company, and one so compulsively determined to beat all its rivals.

His wife was engrossed in the Commons and Karen was safe, if bored, at his mother's. Thus Mike had joined Linda the stewardess and one of the stewards, Simon Williams, and jumped at the chance of a few days on the West Coast.

The city always gave him pleasure. Its sweeping blue bay with the breathtaking bridge, its sea breezes which kept the air fresh and sweet, the wooded hills and delightful jumble of old houses, all styles and colours, colonial and Spanish, the waterfront now handsomely restored after the fire, the Japanese garden and its windmill overlooking the bay, and most of all the climate: he could well understand its inhabitants believing themselves living in paradise.

Linda had taken herself off almost immediately to see cousins. Mike found himself an evening later out on the hotel terrace sipping an old-fashioned Tom Collins and chatting with Simon.

'I can't understand how anyone can leave this place,' Mike mused. 'If I were to be born again, I hope it will be here.'

'You could always move,' suggested Simon. 'You would get a pilot's job anywhere.' He was a slim, fair-haired man, younger looking than his thirty-four years. Although Mike was only a year or two older, his appearance was much the more mature, with a touch of silver already in his brown hair.

'No, that's not possible. Working for BA means staying British; and Elaine's job . . .' His voice tailed off. It was the first time it had occurred to him that his choices were limited. That he might have to defer to his wife's needs was a new and slightly uncomfortable thought.

'How's she getting on?'

'Fine. Seems to love every minute. Made her maiden speech last week. I was sorry I couldn't be there, but it came up while we were flying over the Golden Gate. Couldn't be helped.'

It was a warm, soft evening. Birds twittered and fluttered, perching on the eaves and railing, preparing for rest. From the two men's position looking west over the bay the sunset would be clearly visible. Mike settled down to enjoy the vista.

'I may have to move soon,' Simon remarked quietly.

'Really? Why?'

'Oh, it's a long story.' Moodily Simon clinked ice in his glass.

'Well, I'm your team leader, in a manner of speaking. I'm supposed to know if any of my crew are unhappy. And if I can help I'd be glad to.' Mike Stalker was well-liked as competent and professional, though a little distant.

Simon Williams took a deep breath. 'You know I'm gay, don't you? Quite a lot of the stewards are, so that's not news.' He paused.

Mike was alarmed. 'You haven't—'

'Got AIDS? No. Nothing like that. Fernando and I are very careful. Safe sex and all that. I shan't be visiting any dives on this trip, I can tell you. Real stairway to heaven, that sort of lark.' He shifted. 'But the trouble is Fernando. I think you met him at the Christmas party?'

70

Mike Stalker squinted at the dying sun and tried to remember. With an effort he recalled a darkly good-looking young man who had hovered shyly behind Simon. He nodded.

'We met in London, where he's a postgraduate student at King's. He's a Cuban-American. His family are based in Miami. Very proud of him. We set up home together two years ago, and I think it's for keeps. The trouble is, he can't stay in the UK.'

'Why not?'

'Because he has no right of residence. The UK laws on immigration are extremely strict, and when his time is up as a student he'll have to go home.'

'Can't you apply for him to stay?'

Simon's laugh had a hollow ring. 'Oh, we have. Now if he was a Cuban-American girl we could marry, and provided we filled in all the correct papers and were patient he would almost certainly get permission. But because he's a bloke our relationship isn't recognised. So he has to go back.'

Mike was astonished. 'Surely there's something you could do? Would you like me to have a word with Elaine about it?'

'We've tried MPs,' Simon said bitterly. 'Our own wasn't interested at all. Suggested we might like to find ourselves girlfriends instead. Our lawyer wrote to a couple of dozen who were supposed to be supportive of gay rights, but apart from sympathetic noises we got nowhere. You can see why – it's not their pain. Being in a stable relationship with a gay man in Britain doesn't count for anything at all. We could have been together ten years, twenty, living abroad perhaps, but we don't exist in official texts as a couple. And yet I can't leave him: he's my life. We want to stay together. That means I must give up the land of my own birth and try to join him in the States.'

'I am sorry,' Mike offered sombrely. 'I didn't know about all this.'

Simon warmed to his theme. The light from the setting sun touched the side of his smooth face, turning it to flame. A small gold earring, which he did not wear on board, gleamed dully.

'We couldn't live easily in Florida near his people – not that I fancy it anyway, too humid and hot – so this area may well be a possibility. Fernando has been applying for jobs at Berkeley and we're hopeful. Then, all quiet, I'll apply to emigrate to the USA too. We've learned a lot about what to keep to ourselves. At least in San Francisco nobody thinks we're nutters or freaks.'

'You sure he's the right one for you?' Mike was hesitant. The expectations and etiquette of homosexuality were a closed book. Perhaps it was not unreasonable to talk to Simon as he would to any lovelorn member of his staff with more ordinary cravings.

'Yeah, I'm sure. Before him I was just fooling around. He's great to look at, as you know, and I was drawn to him at once: not quite love at first sight, but not far off. He's clever, very deep. With him, my life has some meaning. I'm not giving him up.'

'Would it help to tell me more?' Mike suggested. 'I mean, you must have some choice in the matter. I'm so pig-ignorant about all this being ... ah ... normal myself.'

The man opposite him suddenly lost his temper. '*I* am normal!' he spat out. 'For heaven's sake! You're as bad as all the rest, Mike. Look: nobody chooses to be gay any more than people choose to be straight. Don't you think I would rather have made my parents happy, married and produced children? And Fernando the same? We have no choice. God, that is cruel.'

Mike frowned. He felt the need to fight back. 'What do you mean, cruel?'

Simon looked around exasperated, as if for inspiration. 'All right, I'll tell you. You know that steward on the Lagos flight, the one you chided for having such a long face? Do you know what that guy was putting up with, while you were moaning at him? His lover had just died of AIDS. They'd been together ages – oh, about eight years. He had spent the last eighteen months nursing him, every spare moment he had got. He would have given up work but we told him not to – they needed every penny. Then, when his partner died, the family turned up and insisted on taking the body and giving it what they called a decent Christian funeral. They wouldn't let him come and won't even tell him where his lover is buried – or cremated, more like. He has no rights in the matter *whatsoever*. There was even a will leaving him a little money but the family ignored it. If he wants to challenge them he has to go to court, besmirch the boy's memory and drag his own name through the dirt. He won't do that. And you moaned at him for looking miserable!'

Mike sighed. 'And if his lover died of AIDS, then he must be HIV positive.'

'For God's sake! That's all you lot ever think about,' muttered Simon angrily. 'Can't you get it into your head that the problems facing gays are not just a question of disease? When you look at a hetero couple' – he gestured around at the little knots of people sitting languidly on the terrace – 'you don't immediately think of gonorrhoea and syphilis, do you? You think of love, romance, and people building things together, looking for a partner for life. Why shouldn't we be the same?'

Mike was silent. Never a particularly thoughtful or introspective man, he was unused to challenges outside flying packed jumbos to the ends of the earth. The hardest choices facing him, week after week, concerned getting his craft down safely in rush hour at Heathrow. That was enough. There was already one politician in the family who relished looking for trouble.

Simon relented. 'I'm sorry, Mike, for yelling at you. But you asked if we have any choice and the answer is no. Most gays just know they are different. Some experts think most of it, maybe all, is inborn. We don't know how, or why, and there isn't much work being done on it. Did you know that the identical twin of a homosexual has an odds-on chance of being gay too even if they were brought up separately? That implies there are influential genetic factors involved. The idea's gaining ground in scientific circles that being gay is like being left-handed. Just as "normal", as you put it, but *different*.'

He looked out over the bay. The sun had shrunk to a faint, hazy red spot on the horizon, where it shimmered like a distant drop of blood. On the terrace lights were being switched on, attracting tiny glowing flies which moved and zizzed, unable to overcome their attraction to the artificial energy source which would eventually kill them.

'I can't tell you what a relief it is to find that it's my genes and not my mother's potty training. That's why Fernando and I want to make a go of it, and try to make each other happy for the rest of our lives.'

He sat in silence for a moment as Mike fetched more drinks. The anger had passed, the anguish remained. Mike Stalker found himself shivering and pulled on a sweater.

'Are you sure Elaine couldn't help? I'll speak to her if you want. She isn't prejudiced. At least, I don't think so.'

Simon shook his head. 'No, I think we've tried everything. Most people would be as shocked as you at the level of institutionalised discrimination which goes on, nearly all of it pointless. I couldn't join the air force, for example. Why not? Do they think I'm going to rape every piece of trouser that brushes past me? Bloody ridiculous.'

Simon took a great gulp of his drink, then banged his glass down on the table. It gave a protesting scream and broke, gin, ice and juice running out, dripping forlornly down the table leg. A waiter armed with a cloth came hurrying over. Simon looked up, his eyes full of despair.

The waiter twittered at them; Simon and Mike rose to go, leaving a generous tip. Mike felt distinctly embarrassed. The waiter behind them was obviously camp, handling the broken shards of glass with a woman's delicate care. Was it also obvious to knowledgeable onlookers that Simon was gay, and would it then be assumed that he was also? He paused at the lift

'I hope things work out for you and . . . er . . . Fernando, Simon,' he said formally. 'It's just waking-up time over there so I'll go and phone my wife. She will be interested in your story.'

Simon bit his lip. 'If you could encourage anyone to take the matter on board in the House of Commons . . .' His voice died away. He did not want to break down in front of Stalker, who seemed such an emotionless man. How could he be expected to understand? '. . . though I doubt it.

Very old-fashioned place, it always seems to me – way behind the rest of us.'

'Or perhaps unable to do much: lots of show but not much substance,' Mike commiserated smoothly.

The lift arrived. Mike was glad more than one other guest crowded in. He held himself to one side, so as not to rub unwittingly against the bronzed half-naked bodies. At his own floor he nodded a curt farewell to his colleague, headed quickly for his room and shut the door.

CHAPTER FIVE

'In my humble estimation, there will be no more votes tonight.'

It was hard to tell whether Frederick Ferriman was indulging in wishful thinking or making a statement of fact. His large, florid face exuded irritability. Before him in the Members' tea room cowered a cup of tea and a small white sideplate with the distinctive Commons green border; on the plate, dripping gently, were two large bacon sandwiches on thick toasted white bread. Ferriman was a farmer whose main purpose in life, it seemed to Elaine, was endlessly to demand more subsidies to prop up the production of precisely the kind of fat animal product in which he was now indulging, and for which most people had less taste year by year.

The butter was dribbling down his chin. Elaine eyed him with amused distaste. A Member for eighteen years and generally regarded as a jolly good sort, Freddie Ferriman was available to speak at blue-rinse-and-pearls fundraising lunches in any constituency within driving distance of his own, even at relatively short notice if the local MP had better things to do. On arrival he would chat affably with the gathered ladies; after lunch, as apple-pie crumbs were brushed discreetly from Jaeger skirts, he would entertain them skilfully, talk only briefly of current politics, speak gruffly and well of the local Member and of the Prime Minister of the day to a round of enthusiastic applause, tell genuinely funny stories, flatter the lady chairman, pull raffle tickets with a flourish, urge greater efforts and leave all present feeling proud to have met him.

'Do you know, or are you guessing?' Elaine asked. 'If you really think we're finished for the night, why are you still here?'

'Missed a three-liner last week. Got to show willing. Daren't budge until my whip says I'm free to clear off.'

He offered her a roguish wink. Playing a naughty but contrite schoolboy rather suited Ferriman. Elaine wondered if there were any brain in there at all, or if ever he had been slim, keen and ambitious, making well-researched speeches on the defence needs of the Rhine Army and hoping for preferment.

'Ah! Here he comes.' Ferriman shovelled down the rest of his sandwich, wiped his mouth hurriedly and sat up straight, like a neglected dog on the approach of its master.

Roger Dickson strolled into the tea room carrying a cup of tea. 'Delighted to see you still here, Freddie, old chap. Are you planning to speak in this debate?'

It was not a question meant to be taken seriously. A dusty annunciator screen showed that the Chamber was engrossed by the Urban Areas (Amendment) (Scotland) Bill. One of the government's few loyal Scottish backbenchers had been on his feet killing time for forty minutes. Ferriman was not noted for speaking these days on anything except farming, the iniquities of the Common Agricultural Policy and occasionally, when neither pet topic was running, the immorality of the government's campaign against AIDS.

'Very funny, Roger. I am as ever here to support the government, should my efforts be required. The question is, are they, or can we go?'

Dickson chuckled and arranged his legs more comfortably under the table. Elaine observed him under her eyelashes, staying out of the exchange. Spooning sugar, he stirred his tea and took a sip, apparently ignoring Elaine but playfully watching Ferriman throughout. His victim shifted, discomforted.

'That depends, as you well know. This is an important government bill. It will put another forty-five million pounds of taxpayers' money into the decaying inner cities of Scotland. Its objective is to turn slums into attractive and desirable homes which will be purchased in large numbers at huge discount by the grateful inhabitants, thus breaking socialism's hold on some fifty constituencies north of the border. The beggars on the other side who currently represent those seats might actually vote against it. You wouldn't want us to lose, now would you?'

All this was delivered in a deadpan voice, as if by the Chief Whip himself. The accent was faintly North London but the manner and style patrician. Not Eton or Harrow, Elaine guessed; and there was no flamboyance. Ferriman looked round miserably. They were seated in the far room, which would usually be occupied by government supporters, of whom only a scattering remained. Tables closer to the tea urns and ginger cake were traditionally the fiefdom of the Opposition. In the distance by the far wall a committee clerk, double first and languid with it, sat sipping Earl Grey and reading the letters page of *The Times*. The place was dead.

Ferriman grumbled: 'There's nobody else here but us. If there was going to be a vote in a hour's time the place'd be packed.'

Dickson decided not to push his luck. Ferriman's whine irritated. If he could be persuaded to clear off there might be a chance to talk to the table's only other occupant, who was altogether more interesting.

There was no point in antagonising backbenchers so early in the session. A small majority might mean genuinely leaning on this jerk, but not tonight. He gestured towards the door. Ferriman scraped back his chair and was gone.

Roger was not the only person to seize the day. Elaine quickly sought an acceptable official excuse for staying. Her whip might be persuaded to talk, show off a bit. She cast around for a subject. Compared with many new Members who had worked as parliamentary research assistants and knew their way round, she felt at a constant disadvantage. At the very least here was a splendid opportunity to learn more about the unwritten rules of her new job. But she did not conceal, at least from herself, a secondary and altogether more powerful motive. More than two weeks had passed since she and Dickson had spoken together alone. It might be possible here in solitude, for just a few moments, to recapture the intimacy of that peculiar exchange in the Embankment gardens, under the silent chaperoning of Mrs Pankhurst.

'Is there any good reason, Roger, why we can't agree in advance when the votes are going to be?'

Immediately he put on his senior whip's face and looked authoritative. 'We do, more or less. At least, the whips do. We are what is known as "the usual channels". The whips' offices on both sides establish how their Members want to vote, or anyway what they're willing to go along with; when to pull out all the stops for a three-line whip – say on the Budget, of course, and the Queen's Speech, but also on second readings of important bills, of which tonight's is not one; or when there's trouble.'

'We have a majority, don't we? Why can't we pair more often, provided we can keep up the majority?'

She leaned forward and looked for the first time into his eyes. There was hardly anybody around, and no reason why not. People in public life frequently have to focus on other faces and often reduce the intensity by fixing their eyes at a point midway between the brows. Elaine did not take this easy way out: she looked straight into Roger Dickson's grey eyes, with a slight smile, and let her lips pout slightly at the word 'pair'. It worked. She sensed him jump, then bring himself back under control.

Dickson was not ready for her. His unannounced appearance in the tea room had indeed been prompted by Elaine's presence; he too had hoped it might be arranged that, released from obligation, she would not dash off at once. But the message seemed to be passing to her too fast. He needed more time. He raised an eyebrow and decided to tease her a little.

'Sloping off already! You'll not learn much about this place, my dear Patience, unless you're physically here and in the Chamber as much as

77

possible. However much you see it on TV, it's never the same as being here.'

He looked at her coolly. Elaine Stalker was waiting. He took a deep breath and continued as if unperturbed; two parliamentary colleagues chatting casually at a tea table littered with sticky remains and uncleared plates. But the world was spinning more slowly, and his words were coming out as if in a dream.

'Why are we whips so mean to you all? It's our own lot who give us headaches. There are always a number of Members over whom the whips' office have virtually no influence; mavericks and fanatics who think they know better than Ministers. Everyone outside thinks whipping is inimical to good governance but that's wrong – there'd be chaos if we could never get a consistent series of votes through. We don't lightly slap on a three-line whip. But when we do, dear Ms Stalker, that's when – if you have any ambitions to go further – you turn up and vote. On a three-liner you vote or you're dead.'

He emphasised the 'Ms' with a sly look. Ms: as if to say, I know you are married, *Mzzz* Stalker, you don't need to remind me; you are not Miss, but not fat frumpish Missus either. Not, however, divorced or separated, or even a merry widow. I know a lot about you. It is my job to know, and I have made it my business to find out. I know you are clever and beautiful and provocative and brave and ambitious and a little forlorn. I know you are impatient and restless and frustrated and, yes, a bit lonely. I see you are in no hurry to leave this table. I know you are fascinating, and tender and kind and vulnerable, and that you are sorely afraid to show these qualities for fear that they would be derided. And there you're damned right. I know, moreover, that you inspire in me an unprecedented longing to lower my barriers and talk about myself, my ideas, the troubles which pursue me too, to share my doubts and fears and to ask for comfort and encouragement, in a way impossible with my wife, who suspects that all politicians are quietly crackers. And there she's right, but neither you nor I would ever choose to be otherwise. I know you would understand as no outsider could.

Dickson was acutely conscious that the emotions tumbling so suddenly through his brain were a million miles from the cool, cynical words flowing from his mouth. As Elaine watched him, he tried to see inside those hazel eyes. She met his scrutiny steadily: she was as strong as he. Now the question he had been trying to suppress surfaced and forced itself on to the tip of his tongue. With a massive effort he reminded himself that he was fantasising, creating from thin air his perfect woman, and that he knew this flesh-and-blood person sitting a few feet from him hardly at all. Yet there it was.

. . . Most of all, I guess that as a very attractive and highly successful modern woman you may faintly be interested in a modern man, both of

78

us with impeccable reputations and every reason to keep them that way.

He could simply put it to her, like that, and see what happened. Should he have made a big mistake she would correct him instantly. Either she would start flirting like mad, in which case he would back off politely and make a small note, later, in the secret black book he kept on all Members allocated to him; or she would freeze and look frightened, in which case he would apologise gallantly. She could shake her head and chide him gently, and they might continue friends and there might be another opportunity. Or she might respond and push the boat out, a little further. He wondered with a vertiginous feeling in his stomach which it was to be.

Everyone else in their part of the room had taken the hint of Freddie's rapid exit and left. The place was deserted. Elaine Stalker had certainly caught the *Mzzz* and the unspoken question it contained: what kind of woman are you? She fingered her pearl earring self-consciously. He was studying her, trying to get under her skin. Normally self-protective and cautious, even hostile to male examination, from this man she found it exhilarating. She listened as he talked, but let her mind play over the unasked questions.

What kind of woman was she? Was she the kind to challenge the rules? Certainly: that was proven by her being here. Was she the sort to take a risk? Naturally – she would find life much duller without. What kind of risk – the risk of making a fool of herself? No problem, she did that all the time. The risk of hurting somebody else's feelings? That too was a necessary concomitant of the job. Of being hurt? She was getting used to that. Playing for high stakes? Sure, why not? She was hardly a tea-lady in Lyons these days. Playing around with somebody else's husband?

Elaine blinked and pulled up short. It would be better not to play this game at all; or, if she continued, not quite according to his assumptions. It was all going a great deal too fast.

Dickson was observing her with mocking appreciation, much as he had done on her first day. He was too wary and ultimately too engrossed in politics to make a practice of infidelity, but he understood President Jimmy Carter's tortured confession of having committed adultery many times in the mind. On more than one occasion he had walked away from an open chance: some deep seriousness militated against the shaming triviality of one-night stands. If he were to take the plunge it would have to be something worthwhile, from which he could gain and to which he could give a small part of his deepest self. That meant seeking a matching need to his own. A soul-mate as well as a bed-mate.

He took another sip of tea, still sizing her up. His own self-control amazed him.

Elaine pushed away the debris of other people's snacks and folded her arms on the table. She was wearing a short-sleeved jacket and had put a dab of scent inside each elbow; he would catch a faint whiff of it. The bare arms, the Chanel Number 5, all said: *I am. Notice me.* Her motives did not bear thinking about too closely.

'I do not understand, Roger,' she enquired as coolly as possible, 'how anyone can stand for Parliament for our side, go through all the hassle of getting selected and then elected, and then not support the government.'

'Now that is naive and you know it,' Dickson chided. 'If you want to become a media star the easy way is to oppose your own side. The press and TV will be falling over themselves to give you prime time. If truth be told there's nothing much I could do to dissuade you. It's the old Andy Warhol syndrome – any fool can be famous for fifteen minutes, though here it can last for years. There's no future in it, of course, but then most people here have no future anyhow. It makes life more exciting for them, and they feel important. In reality they're nobody.'

With a swift movement he drank the rest of his cooling tea, watching her over the rim. She seemed a little nonplussed, sombre, confused. Maybe he had gone too far, talking to her like . . . an adult, puncturing the euphoria and innocence which were entirely appropriate in these first few months. She would discover soon enough the bleak impotence of the back benches. With a bit of luck and good management – perhaps on his own part? – she might never discover it, and instead head straight up the ministerial ladder. The diminutive Mrs Shephard had gone from maiden to Cabinet Minister in a single Parliament. A good woman could certainly do it, if she were keen – possibly more quickly these days than an equally good man.

Or perhaps he had pushed her too far over . . . the other matter. Ms Stalker was certainly a looker. Splendid figure, not too much of it. Well turned out, clever understated make-up – though he was uncertain what was real and what artifice. It would be entertaining, if nothing else, to find out. Golden blonde hair, not too stiff or formal, in a great cascade around her earnest pretty face. A few freckles on her nose he wanted to trace with his finger. Enticing, enquiring eyes, with darker long lashes lowered virtuously as she examined her unpainted nails. He suddenly realised she was indeed flirting with him – gently, subliminally almost. Maybe he had not misjudged her. Perhaps she was open to being impressed. Time to show off a little.

'It's harder with a big majority, Elaine. In the last Parliament some of our Members got the message they weren't needed. One chap disappeared altogether. He told us he was in his constituency, and told them the whips were being beastly and keeping him in Westminster. In reality he wasn't in the country at all.'

Pause for effect. Elaine's eyes widened. Both had stopped pretending they were staying merely for refreshments. She was on board once more.

'Where was he?'

'Oh, in Jersey, running a somewhat shady business. Picking up his salary and allowances here at the same time, naturally. Eventually we tipped off his constituency chairman and he was warned to retire or he'd be deselected. There was another who became known as the Member for Southern California. He'd been here years – had been a Minister, in fact, but not got very far; too bone idle. Then he was invited to do a lecture tour of the USA, met up with a pretty woman in Berkeley who just happened to be the dean's daughter and decided to stay in the sunshine. The inconvenient fact that he was still a Member here was a minor irrelevance, of course.'

Elaine giggled. Roger wondered if she would object if he lit a cigar, since it appeared to be story-telling time, and decided against. He hoped to God nobody was checking up on the two of them, but didn't dare turn round to look, for fear of breaking the spell. Whatever was happening, the chance was not to be missed, or muffed. This woman was not going home alone tonight. He carried on talking easily, for he had told the tale many times before.

'He organised himself very well. He'd come back once every six weeks or so to speak or ask an oral question. His secretary handled all the constituency cases – very competently indeed; the locals never guessed. The technique was simple. She put down written questions at his behest and issued a press release as the question appeared on the order paper – "Bloggs MP demands government action", that sort of thing; and again as the answer came up: "Bloggs MP pleased with government response." He'd even do interviews for local radio over the phone from the West Coast. They hadn't the foggiest idea where he was.'

Her mouth opened in disbelief. Roger finished with a flourish:

'So he was in the local papers all the time, his punters thought he was a jolly good MP and his majority never wavered.'

She was hooked. Now was the time.

'Look, Elaine, I shouldn't have kept you. Your voting record so far is fine: there are no votes tonight. You're free to go.' He paused, almost imperceptibly – but not to her. 'If you want.'

She stretched like a cat, keeping her eyes on his face. A woman who wore perfume, no less, even in the Commons tea room on a dead night. A woman who liked being with a man.

'Just as I was enjoying our conversation, too. You know, Roger, for us new Members this place is a bewildering morass of rules and manners and Spanish practices. I feel I need lessons: it's like having a musical instrument without instructions. Learn how to play and you'll produce sweet music – but attack it blindly and the result is cacophony. Teach me to play just a little longer, will you?'

'Certainly, but not here.' He felt suddenly apprehensive. He rose to his feet and made gentlemanly motions to hold her chair. She did not object. 'My home is just round the corner. We've finished here. Why don't you come round for some decent coffee, or a drink? A brandy perhaps?'

'I'm a malt drinker.' Archly, a challenge.

'How about Glenfiddich?'

'Thank you, that'll do nicely.'

'With or without ice?'

'Without. You don't spoil good whisky.'

'Good – that makes my life easier. I think my kids had all the ice. Meet me at Members' entrance in ten minutes. I have to tidy away some papers and tell the Chief I'm off. It's only a few minutes' walk.'

It was done; the invitation issued. Plus a cooling-off period: Elaine could always excuse herself before they left together. So could he.

The next few minutes were like an hour, as Dickson found pretexts for dawdling. In truth he had no clear idea what he expected to do, apart from vaguely getting to know Elaine Stalker better. Such an approach, unplanned, unpremeditated, was reasonably safe on a quiet night with no curious observers. Nothing would come of it, of course, but even if something did happen they were both sophisticated adults. No one was about to jump off Westminster Bridge if either had made a mistake. On an impulse he quickly phoned his home in the constituency. Just to check.

Dickson might not have been surprised that much the same considerations were running through Elaine's head. She made her way immediately towards the Lady Members' room on the bottom corridor, stood in front of the long mirror, straightened her skirt, brushed her hair, applied lipstick, blotted it carefully, picked a stray golden hair from her jacket and struggled with herself. She was reasonably sure she was not about to be made a fool of; some reserve in Dickson told her that whatever might occur he would keep tonight strictly private. Had she any doubts on that point it would be best to abort the mission right now. He had not touched her in the tea room, not been crude or leered or peeped at her legs, nor made any inappropriate remarks. The quiet thoughtful man in the garden had asked her to come to his home, that was all. She trusted him. She had no choice. She was not about to insult him by turning down an innocent invitation to a drink. Male MPs had drinks with each other all the time: perhaps Roger was conscious that she felt excluded from that camaraderie. It was kind of him to ask.

Dickson appeared at Members' entrance exactly on time with a curt 'Ready?' and opened the side door for her. He had a folder in his hand but no box or briefcase. She shook her head as he offered to carry hers, for it was empty.

Outside it was still daylight, just, as the late sun caught the western face of Big Ben. As the two crossed over by St Stephen's entrance she glanced back. Sir Charles Barry's great clocktower was quite beautiful, its carved gilded stone gleaming and tranquil. Starlings wheeled and squabbled over roosts for the night. A few tourists straggled, taking photographs. It was a few minutes after nine.

Roger led her down towards Millbank and turned right at Great Peter Street. They were in an area of eighteenth century speculative development, houses which would be on offer at £600,000 or less, but which fetched up to a million at the height of the 1980s boom. Teresa Gorman owned two such properties in Lord North Street near Jonathan Aitken's, Alan Duncan one in Gayfere Street, in the basement of which the most recent bid for the Leadership had been successfully plotted. At 4 Cowley Street the Liberal Democrats had their headquarters. Conservative Central Office was round the corner in an ugly modern building in Smith Square, with Transport House, erstwhile home of the Labour Party, right opposite: the concentrated political hinterland of Westminster.

Roger Dickson stopped at a black-painted fence and unlocked a small door. He felt his mouth go dry.

'I'm lucky to have this house,' he explained. 'I hope it's not too much of a mess. During school holidays with three kids running round it gets to be a bit of a pigsty. You're not to start tidying up.'

'I won't. I'm not that kind of lady.'

He chuckled. 'No, I can see you're not.'

She felt a twinge of disappointment, then guilt. It sounded as if the family were in residence. It would be easy to misread the signs with someone you'd only just met. The back garden was tiny and untidy, but full of old climbing roses, lilies and tubs of pink and red geraniums and fuchsia. There was a woman's hand here, casual about appearances but full of natural life. The sun fell on the garden all afternoon; walls and terracotta pots were warm to the touch. On a pocket-handkerchief patio stood white-painted wrought-iron chairs and a table, while a ragged hammock was slung between an old tree and the wall. Dickson walked past and unlocked the french window, standing aside to let her in.

'These are the children's quarters. The kitchen is just here. We can make coffee and then have drinks up in the living room – that's on the first floor.'

He was right – the kitchen was a mess. Used crockery filled the sink. Judging from the gummed-up remains, nothing had been moved since breakfast hours earlier. A dirty tea towel graced the draining board. His wife was not a keen housekeeper, Elaine noted primly. Roger fished out a small pan, rinsed it under the tap and started heating milk. The coffee machine was half full of cold black liquid, but short of covering all the dirty dishes in old coffee there was nowhere to empty it. Roger looked helpless.

Elaine laughed and came to his rescue. 'Just put on the kettle. I'm perfectly happy with Nescafé.'

They carried two milky mugs of coffee carefully up the uneven narrow stairs, negotiating a way around toys and a pram. Roger opened a door into what was evidently a smarter living room where the children were not admitted. A dark-red Wilton carpet made it immediately comfortable. By the window an elegant chaise-longue upholstered in deep-yellow silk offered a friendly invitation. Books lined the walls; a red leather Chesterfield looked well used; an untidy pile of weekly Hansards and hunting magazines gathered dust by its side.

Roger poured drinks and motioned her to the chaise-longue. Elaine thought for a moment. She had other ideas. She sat down on the floor with her back to the window, so that she could gaze up at her host. If his wife came in at least they would not be sitting on the sofa side by side.

When Roger turned round from the drinks cabinet he caught his breath. The woman was curled up, legs tucked under her, in a posture which could be interpreted as wanting to sit at one's feet, to drink in wisdom, to look up and *admire*. It was so unbelievably flattering. Sensual, too. Making clear who was to be the dominant animal in this room, as the dust danced in the warm air and the sunbeams meandered across the glowing carpet.

'Are you the hunter?' She pointed to the magazines, realising how little she knew about this man.

'No, not my scene. That's my wife's passion. She went up this morning and no doubt will have been out hunting twice by the time I get home tomorrow night.'

The news hung between them, floated softly from the man to the woman. She sipped the dry whisky as he sat on the chaise-longue and watched her.

'Aren't they home? I was hoping I might meet your . . . children.'

'Oh, you will, no doubt. But not tonight. Caroline took them and the nanny up to the constituency first thing this morning; much better for them in July, though as you can see I have to fend for myself when I'm on my own, and I'm not very good at it.'

So he *was* alone, and he had invited her here knowing his wife was absent. The mess downstairs indicated that he was no Lothario making a habit of casual liaisons when his wife was away. His evident inability to master the disorder made him vulnerable, endearing.

She did not move, except to incline her head so the blonde hair engaged the lazy sun, and sipped her drink. She held the glass up and watched the light swirl through the liquid, break and scatter, bronze and golden and yellow.

Roger was rolling a tumbler slowly in his hands. She could hear the crystal click against his signet ring. Somewhere in the room a clock was ticking softly.

'I've often thought it must be even harder for the women Members. You have a child, haven't you, Elaine?'

'I had two, but one was handicapped and died.' That was not the reply she usually offered. Her *Who's Who* entry did not mention two children, only one. Jake had lived two years. The child's jerky smile swam into her thoughts but she pushed the memory back down again. Her face darkened sadly. 'He was one reason why I was determined to go into politics. I was so appalled at the way we were treated as if his disability were all our fault, and we were nuisances for insisting on reasonable facilities for him. But we have a daughter, Karen. She's now fourteen, taller than me! If your question is who looks after her while I'm busy prancing around being an MP, the answer's that she's at boarding school. During holidays I have exactly the same problem as you. At the moment she's at her grandmother's in Hereford and not enjoying it very much.'

'And Mr Stalker? There is a Mr Stalker, I gather.'

I gather. Been checking up. Was this just his style, to know everything possible about his charges?

'Mike? Right now? Somewhere over the Atlantic, at a guess. Otherwise at home. In the Midlands. He's an airline pilot. We have always had to check our diaries to figure out when we could get together, so I don't expect any extra difficulty.'

Her glass was empty. She giggled.

'I think you gave me a double.'

'And would you like another?'

'Yes, but not quite so much.'

Roger obliged, the bottle neck clinking on the glasses. Hidden from her his hand was shaking. The coffee, hopelessly bland, stood forgotten on a side table. Then he asked:

'Are you warm enough? Would you mind if I take off my jacket?'

'Go ahead. It's your house: you can do what you like.'

He looked at her sharply, took the suit jacket off, hung it over a chair and sat down again. She had moved closer to the chaise-longue and was leaning against it, pretending to be a little drunk, playing with her shoe, demure. Slowly she took off her shoes and placed them to one side. Her feet and legs were silky and bare. She was extraordinarily beautiful. He leaned forward.

'I can do what I like in my own house, can I? Now what exactly does that mean?'

She shifted again, just an inch closer. Her hair was almost touching his knee.

'You must not tempt me, Elaine.' But the tone was teasing, playful. She turned slowly to him, her lips slightly parted. He looked into her face; her amused, inviting expression mirrored his own – more than meeting him halfway. It was not clear who was leading whom. He had thought he was in charge, but it was obvious that Elaine also knew what she wanted.

'And you, Mr Whip, should not invite strange women into your house when you are all alone.' If we are going to do this, she was saying, we're both equally responsible, equally guilty, making equal choices.

He spoke quietly now. 'Me? Did I force you against your will, then? I might ask you, what exactly are you doing in my house?'

Elaine finished her drink. Her head was buzzing. Before leaving the Commons she had dabbed her perfume, not demurely on her wrists, but between her breasts, under the soles of her feet, on her belly below her navel. In the warmth its sweetness shimmered delicately in the air, mixed with the powerful masculine aura of the scotch. Dusk was gathering. In a respectable household lights would be going on. But not here.

Her hair lay against his knee. Silently he stroked it, as he might have one of his children. Slowly she ran her right hand up his calf – slowly, yet it was like making electrical contact. Then she kneeled up in a swift smooth movement until she faced him as he sat, legs apart, a dazed look on his face, on the yellow sofa. Holding his gaze as he had held hers over the teacups, she put one hand on each of his thighs and slid her fingers up the inside of his legs to his crotch, as a man might do to a woman. He gasped; his body moved under the fabric, as he caught her hands just in time.

She held her position. 'Just wanted to make sure you weren't having me on,' she whispered.

'Having me, more like . . .'

And then he kissed her, bowing towards her from the yellow sofa, taking her in his arms as he had wanted to since the first moment he saw her. She responded joyously, pulling back and laughing. Then he came at her again, more urgently and hungrily, pushing his tongue down far into her mouth, reaching for her, clutching her body. He pressed her hand where it was placed on his crotch and she could feel him growing harder. Her fingers searched for the zip and she slid her hand inside. There was no stopping now. He groaned and whispered her name. The carpet under her knees rubbed and chafed and her thigh muscles ached and still he kissed her with great longing, eyes closed, not daring to know what she was doing. The physical position she had put herself in – kneeling upright between his legs, reversing the traditional male-female roles – made the next step almost inevitable. She moved her face away from his, and bent down.

When it was done, panting, choking a little, she laid her head on his knee, like a faithful dog. He sat back, breathing huskily, stroking her hair.

'My God! I don't believe this . . . Are . . . you all right?'

Her voice was not under control. This was not quite what she had expected, but he was not to know. The chance had presented itself and she had seized it boldly. She swallowed hard to get rid of the salt taste. 'I think I could do with another whisky.'

He flopped back in the chair, pulling off his tie, and gestured weakly at the cabinet. 'Help yourself. Bring the bottle over here. I could too. Merciful heavens!'

The room was almost dark. The drink settled her. He looked down at himself in sheepish appreciation.

'Well, you made a bloody good job of that, I must say. I think you should know, Elaine, that I don't make a habit of this. You've caught me unawares – with my trousers down, in a manner of speaking.' Both were giggling now in a conspiracy of illicit enjoyment.

'Neither do I. But you're a fine-looking man, and I can now confess I've fancied you since I set eyes on you.'

He was startled at her girlish slang. 'Fancied me! Maybe I should start a new career, as a public heart-throb? How does the adorable Ms Stalker think I would get on?'

'Extremely well, if that equipment is anything to go by.' She indicated his untidy crotch. He moved to cover it modestly with a handkerchief, but she stopped him. 'No, let me have a look. You should be proud of what you've got. It certainly gives a different meaning to Honourable Member.'

'I don't believe this. My God, I think I'm being raped.'

Obediently he removed the handkerchief, watching her in delight as she ran her fingers over his penis, tenderly but with increasing rhythm. It throbbed back into life as he gasped again with pleasure. With her free hand she undid the nearest shirt button and slipping her hand inside began making little circles on his belly; the small hairs there also began to rise and his skin shivered in anticipation.

Then suddenly he was serious, standing up and pulling her close, warning her not to make too much noise, covering her in kisses. With firm authority he propelled her into an untidy bedroom, tossed slept-in pyjamas on to the floor, pushing her down on to an unmade bed. Afterwards she could not remember undressing, only that it was in haste as if tearing down barriers between them, and that he, struggling out of shirt and trousers and plain blue underpants, was both shy and aggressive and in great need of her . . .

87

Burying his face in her, in all of her, as his wife would not let him do; holding on, leaning back and looking at her, exploring her, curving his hands over her breasts to remember their shape, touching her nipples, loving the sweep of her body, tracing the line down from her navel, tentatively at first, then plunging his hand into her, playing with her inner tenderness as her husband never bothered to these days, till she squealed and had to grab a pillow to stop herself shouting out ... and she caught his head and held it and smelled his hair, and held him tightly as he shuddered, and was at last spent.

It was dark. He felt as if he had emerged into a secret place with no name. A place for Elaine and himself, nobody else, which they could create with a landscape entirely of their own making. The prospect filled him with both delight and terror. He said nothing: to put any feeling into words would be instantly to destroy it. He was not about to start declaring undying adoration, not yet. If ever.

Nose to nose, panting and sweating, the man and woman wondered what they had done. There was no undoing it.

'That,' she said at last with an air of great satisfaction, 'that was absolutely fucking marvellous. Thank you very much.'

The incongruous mixture of polite and obscene language, schoolgirl and whore, made him laugh out loud. 'You're a basket-case, Elaine, do you know that? Do you make a habit of going around seducing strange men?'

She gazed ruminatively at the ceiling. 'It's taken too much energy getting to Westminster – every spare minute of my life, so far, so the answer is no. I'm always too exhausted when I get home, and so is Mike a lot of the time. Anyway, if you live in a small town and start playing around somebody will let on, sooner or later. Not a great idea if you want to be selected for a parliamentary seat, man or woman.'

He agreed. 'I haven't enjoyed it so much in a long time.' That was not a criticism of his wife; nor an admission of his own frequent failure to make such an effort. Elaine's description of the preoccupation and single-mindedness necessary to arrive at Westminster was entirely familiar. It had genuinely not occurred to him that it might be the same for a woman.

Elaine rolled over and looked at him, being careful not to stain the crumpled sheets. 'Being married is different, isn't it? But this was fun.'

Roger decided to leave it at that. 'Come on, it's getting late. I'll walk you back to your flat. It's in Morpeth Terrace, isn't it?'

'Have you been checking up on me?' she asked archly, as she leaned over and fumbled under the bed for her underwear.

'Naturally. All part of the service. We have bets on in the whips' office as to who is going to lay the new women MPs.'

Alarmed, she sat up quickly and began to pull on her clothes. 'You don't intend to start telling people about this, surely, Roger?'

He stood stock still. Teasing might be in order. It had worked with her before. 'Aha! I've got you worried. Now what exactly would you do if that was the idea?'

She jumped up, fixing buttons, suddenly edgy. Then the twinkle in Roger's eye made her stop short and laugh. This was going to be a complex relationship, whatever else.

'I think, Mr Whip, that I should hint that you did try, but were absolutely hopeless at it. Couldn't get it up at all, perhaps?'

She would at that. Elaine's expression had a wicked glint. Roger had no doubt that the lady was perfectly capable of protecting herself by turning the tables and making him look the fool. There was still extraordinary tension and charged sexual energy between them, but carrying on further tonight was unwise. Both needed to break away, to consider, to absorb the events of the evening and to prepare for the next time. Should there be a next time.

He caught her hands, opened them palms upward and gently kissed first one, then the other. Then he held her face in his hands in a protective, parental gesture.

'If you doubted me that much, Elaine, you wouldn't have come.'

She bent her head in mute apology, and he held her close. It was time to leave.

'I'll walk you back to your flat.'

'No, I'd rather you didn't.'

He did not argue. Her independence was a great asset. 'Will you be all right?'

'Sure. I can look after myself. I need to be alone now.'

With dignity he led her down the stairs and out into the darkened garden. In the orange glow of a London night only a couple of intrepid stars were visible. Overhead, house-martins settled twittering under the eaves. A burst of music from a nearby pub reminded them of the danger of discovery. Pausing before the black door, they looked once more at each other in wonder and gratitude. Then he unlocked the door and she stepped quickly into the street.

CHAPTER SIX

As September dawned the Prime Minister again made a spirited but lonely defence of Europe's latest treaty. Then the boys in red braces, dealers in billions, refreshed from more exotic vacations, switched on their VDUs and began to toss around world currencies like so much confetti. Sterling seemed to collapse, in retrospect, quite quickly. News and political editors were summoned hastily from weekend retreats and the nation stirred. The economics editor of *The Times* waxed ecstatic. And Parliament was to be recalled for an emergency debate.

Elaine prepared to pull out of South Warmingshire Conservatives' annual dinner, which had been so cautiously booked for the recess. Some in her constituency shared *The Times*'s joy; manufacturing companies and exporters poised for new orders rubbed their hands in glee. Meanwhile high overhead circled the modern vultures, insolvency lawyers and accountants, looking forward to another excellent year.

A huge crowd was standing on the pavement in front of the Houses of Parliament, being pushed back by PC Robin Bell and Gerry Keown, as car after car swept inside. To the staff, being recalled from leave for a two-day emergency session of both Houses was a mixed blessing. Since the announcement it had been all hands on deck as carpets were rolled back, ceilings refitted, wiring reconnected, toilets hurriedly scrubbed, boxes of library books unpacked – all to be redone the following week as annual maintenance resumed. On the other hand, the overtime was very useful.

Scaffolding hid the Cabinet Office and other Whitehall edifices behind huge sheets of white and blue plastic. Extensive building work was under way, improving protection for the Prime Minister and senior civil servants. The street looked like a house shut up for the summer, furniture in dust sheets, startled that the family had returned unexpectedly early, ashamed of being caught in a shambles, its grandeur hidden in shrouds.

Even at 10 a.m. the underground car park was packed. Elaine bumped into Andrew Muncastle as both headed up the escalator. They

91

contented themselves with 'Well, well, well' and 'Quite a turn-up for the book', neither too sure whether the other was referring to the sudden disappearance of a well-known donor to party funds or the sickly state of the currency. In Members' Lobby dozens of MPs stood greeting friends and gossiping. The whole place was buzzing; like flies clustering on rotten meat, politicians are drawn to the smell of trouble.

As 2.30 loomed Elaine, Andrew, Roger, Sir Nigel Boswood and two hundred other government supporters were packed and jostling in their places. The Opposition benches were as well covered. Back in her office the Speaker adjusted her lacy jabots, took a last drag at a cigarette, pulled on new buckled shoes and checked her grey curls. The door was opened. Off she went in stately procession preceded by an usher in court dress, her black and gold train held in one practised hand by the appropriately named Mr Lord, the whole looking like a bunch of dignified king penguins. Uniformed police cried, 'Hats off, Strangers!' – and with a flourish whipped off their own helmets and stood to attention. The crowd gaped and MPs bowed as the Speaker passed.

Division bells clanged throughout the Palace of Westminster and in offices, halls, clubs and restaurants nearby, where a hundred grey-suited men looked up, wiped mouths hastily on linen napkins, proffered apologies and hurried away, leaving their companions to pick up the bill.

The bells rang again, insistently. The Speaker was at prayers.

The event is never televised or broadcast. Outside hover non-believers and those too late to get in, for the way is barred by respectful doorkeepers until the ceremony is over. Elaine listened as the chaplain intoned: 'Let us pray.' Then with all the other Members she turned around to face the wall, backs to the enemy. And this is how MPs say their prayers: heartfelt pleas for divine wisdom may pass their lips but no hostile glances can be directed towards the benches opposite, only down at their well-polished shoes and into their own murky souls.

'Prayers over!' policemen shouted; bells rang again; doors swung open; annunciators pinged proudly, 'Speaker in the Chair'. Elaine sat down quickly and smoothed her skirt. Not only were her devotions done. The main purpose of attending prayers was accomplished: she was guaranteed this seat for the rest of the day's business. The whole event had taken only four minutes.

Sir Nigel Boswood settled his substantial frame between Sir Patrick Mayhew and Nicholas Scott. The three gentlemen resembled Toby jugs on a mantelpiece. Roger Dickson lounged by the back of the Chair. Opposite Boswood sat an intelligent thin-faced woman in pink, Labour's newly elected Deputy Leader. Two rows behind her Glenda Jackson glared, a modern Medusa. A pensive Neil Kinnock looked discarded and old.

Elaine was seated three rows up with a splendid view of the back of the Prime Minister's head. Elaine liked the man, but could not fathom him. Naturally a consolidator, he kept his own views and passions deeply hidden. By instinct he sought to please everybody, but in practice he succeeded in satisfying relatively few. Perhaps the former was the cause of the latter. Elaine was not the only MP to wonder if a more vigorous approach mightn't work better.

One fact was indisputable: the Prime Minister was no orator. There had been constant interruptions and a rising drone of chatter. The troops were becoming restless and bored.

The new Labour leader also knew the importance of this debate. Cultivating the slightly condescending manner of a Scottish family solicitor, John Smith was no more a crowd-mover than the man he challenged, but he had thought through his material with greater care. Soon he was poking fun at the Prime Minister's forlorn ambition, outlined in the *Sunday Times* a few weeks earlier, of making sterling the strongest currency in Europe.

Even Elaine had to admit it was well done. His own side rocked with laughter, the press gallery scribbled furiously, while Tories sat chins in hand, silent and unhappy. Behind Elaine a figure rose attempting to intervene. The Labour Leader squinted up. It was only one of the new Members; let him have his moment of glory. Smith shrugged and gave way.

'Mr Andrew Muncastle!'

'Does the Right Honourable and Learned Gentleman not concede that it would be an objective of his – a worthwhile objective, and right for any British parliamentarian – to want to make the pound a stronger currency than the Deutschmark, or anything else?'

Of course it was. There was nothing to mock in the Prime Minister's longing for greatness. All that was missing was the wherewithal. Smith fumbled and turned pompous.

'The Honourable Gentleman will understand the purport of my comments in a minute or two . . .'

The rest was drowned by a howl from the Tory benches. The purport of my comments? Will understand? He was not getting away with that. Freddie Ferriman dug Martin Clarke in the ribs. The two took a deep breath and, turning puce with effort, bellowed: 'ANSWER!!'

Smith looked up in surprise. He had lost the point by prevaricating. He sighed and conceded: 'Of course, any sensible person wants a strong and stable currency in this country.'

All around people were slapping Andrew on the back. By sheer courage he had hit a seemingly invulnerable target. The black hole at the centre of Smith's approach, as Andrew had correctly surmised, was that he agreed almost too much with the government. It was not enough to claim that Labour would have avoided all these problems: had the election result been different the currency crisis might only have come sooner. But then, with a Labour victory, Kinnock would have been Prime Minister and Smith would not have been Leader of his Party. He could afford to fudge the issues for a good while yet.

As the front-bench speeches ended Elaine slipped out towards the tea room with half a hundred other gloomy colleagues. Roger was standing at the entrance to the Ministers' corridor, talking with a junior Minister at the Home Office. He motioned to her with a casual glance to wait. A few moments later the Minister disappeared and Roger turned to face her, put his hands in his pockets, leaned back on his heels and looked down with an appraising smile.

There was no reason why an MP should not talk to her whip. From a few yards away their body language indicated only that two colleagues, male and female, one more senior, were having an enjoyable brief conversation; that they liked each other but were not entirely at ease. Their eye contact hinted at wariness, darting glances indicating that this discourse would be broken off the instant anyone might come close enough to overhear.

'And so, beautiful Mrs Stalker, have you had a good summer?'

'So-so. It would have been better if we had not had to return in such inauspicious circumstances.'

'You're not the first to say that, as you can imagine. Apart from politics, are you well?'

'Very. Never felt better.' She stood upright, shoulders straight, hands behind her back, and flashed him a smile. She wondered if he would refer to their brief intimacy; there had been no contact since. Perhaps it was just a fling, over. That would have been a shame but not altogether unexpected.

'I'm pleased to hear that. And are we still friends?' His voice was lower.

She swallowed hard and held his gaze. 'Yes. I hope so. Are we?'

If he looked closely he would see the pulse jumping in her throat. She hoped she was not blushing under those damn freckles. He was asking, can I sleep with you again? She was saying, yes please.

He breathed what sounded like a sigh of relief, relaxing visibly. 'I really feel, Mrs Stalker, that we will need to explore again those issues you raised with me in July. I do hope you haven't forgotten how completely your arguments overwhelmed me on that occasion. I still have not entirely recovered my composure after your skill and audacity.'

This was a new game. She folded her arms with a mock frown, pursing her lips. 'Yes, I did rather overdo it. I'll just have to keep my big mouth shut next time.'

Roger raised his eyes to the ceiling and suppressed his mirth with difficulty, a flush suffusing his temples. 'Indeed, Mrs Stalker. We may well have to explore other parts of the body politic. I should be glad to do all I can to assist, but there will not be time during this short recall of Parliament. Will you be at Conference?'

'Sorry, no. Can't afford it this year.'

'Ah, that's a pity. On our return in October, then. I really feel we were only scratching the surface last time. There's a great deal more to be exposed and explored properly, don't you think?'

Elaine was longing to laugh out loud. 'I really do agree, Mr Dickson. We must tear off the covers and discover how far we can go.' She added softly, 'I shall look forward to that.'

Then, without waiting to be dismissed, she headed down the corridor, catching Ferriman and Martin Clarke and greeting them warmly. The tea room's post-mortem beckoned. Her friends noted that she alone was uncommonly cheerful.

The passenger on the 10 a.m. express from London's St Pancras station to Derby smiled benignly and settled his substantial pin-striped bulk into the faded velour of the Intercity seat. With a trim beard and well-cut suit, his appearance suggested a prosperous Dutch or German businessman. In front of him lay half-read copies of *The Times*, *Financial Times*, *The Economist*, *Investors Chronicle* and *The European*, and a Hansard of the previous day's emergency debate. In a briefcase at his side nestled papers for the forthcoming session of the European Parliament in sleepy distant Strasbourg, of which he had been a Member for nearly ten years. In his stomach there rumbled a full English breakfast as served at his club. He could afford it, and was pleased with life on a tax-free Euro-expense account amounting to £75,000 a year.

Tim Marks was in good time for the journey to Derby, where he was to speak to the local Chamber of Commerce on 'Britain's role in Europe'. If there was uncertainty in the public's mind on that topic it did not affect him. Unlike Westminster MPs he did not expect or hope to be recognised on the train, and that suited him fine. Only briefly had he considered standing for Westminster, long ago when the new European assembly was in its infancy. Once, however, the ballot boxes opened in 1979 for direct elections to Strasbourg he was up and running, and was elected at his second try.

An attractive, smartly suited youngish woman was standing at his shoulder. She looked closely at him, then held out her hand.

'Tim Marks, isn't it? The Euro-MP? Hello, I'm Elaine Stalker.'

Elaine did not need to explain further. Her assured demeanour, the whispered glances from other passengers and her recent appearance on London Weekend TV jogged Tim's memory. He half heaved himself to his feet, murmuring welcome, but she waved him back and settled herself opposite. She was heading for home, she explained, and would be changing at Leicester in an hour or so. Tim resigned himself to making no further progress with the newspapers.

No sooner was the train moving than yet another MP was standing beside him, clutching a heavy leather briefcase and panting. Marks groaned inwardly. One could have too much of a good thing.

Andrew Muncastle had decided to save the taxi fare and taken the Underground via Victoria in the morning rush hour. The Tube carriage had been packed and uncomfortable, but all was well until it stopped dead in a tunnel near Oxford Circus and the lights went out. Andrew found himself jammed between the door and a large black lady going home after hospital night duty. The carriage's occupants swayed and sweated in the glimmer of emergency lighting; the nurse leaned on him, snoring gently, as Andrew tried desperately to prop her upright and shift her weight off his back. At last power was restored. The nurse woke up with a startled look, evidently surprised to find herself still on the train, and a dishevelled Andrew was regurgitated like Jonah from the whale's belly on to the litter-strewn platforms of St Pancras.

Marks and Stalker clucked in sympathetic amusement as he told his harrowing tale. 'I should walk next time, old man' and 'You could have shared my taxi' were their only helpful remarks. The coffee trolley restored his equanimity as the train slid past Luton.

There were plenty of topics of conversation – the emergency debate in the Commons, the spectacular collapse of the government's economic strategy, the desperately narrow 'yes' vote in the French referendum on Europe the previous Sunday night.

Elaine was in gloomy mood. The adrenalin of the previous ten days had receded, leaving her tired and flat. 'I confess to feelings of helplessness,' she said. 'We capitalists believed we were doing the right thing, freeing up international capital markets all over the world, removing exchange controls. Then the dealers go haywire, billions flying around the world non-stop, twenty-four hours a day, like a multi-headed monster that never sleeps, devouring the next weak currency as if we were all wild-eyed rabbits, and – hey presto! first the krona, then the lira and suddenly sterling slip out of our control. And it doesn't stop.'

Andrew was scanning the inside pages of Tim's *Financial Times*. 'Perhaps we should have stayed floating all the time and sod the speculators. It looks as if the Bank of England has spent half our foreign exchange reserves, or more, to prop up the pound. All to no avail.'

He was chided by Elaine. 'You didn't say that in the tea room yesterday. You were giving the government full backing and urging us back into the system as soon as possible.'

Tim Marks folded his substantial arms and quoted softly: '"Those at the back cried Forward! And those at the front cried, Back!"' With detached enjoyment he watched the two new MPs wrangle as the train rattled north at 125 miles an hour.

For a fleeting moment Muncastle allowed a sly look to cross his face. 'That was in public. Today I take it we are musing in private, three intelligent, well-informed people, members of the same party. Where does a supportive MP stand in all this? What are Britain's long-term interests, and our short-term ones too for that matter?'

'Keep inflation down, compete in world markets, generate enough capital for investment,' Elaine offered primly. 'Those are our objectives, and a good choice, in my view.'

Andrew said, 'What about getting unemployment down?'

There was no answer. Somebody pays the price for international economic ineptitude – people who can only dream of riding first class up and down the line to important jobs in London.

Tim Marks leaned forward. 'The fact is, Parliaments have never controlled economies. That isn't our job. Economic decisions are taken by business men and women around the world with a little nudging from central bankers and governments, and are seldom influenced by backbenchers in debating chambers. What Parliaments do frequently is make matters worse. The Italian lira is weak because Italians can't afford the welfare state they've created for themselves, particularly given their lackadaisical attitude to paying taxes. Germany reunited on promises of zero pain and no increase in taxes, and it can't be done. Everyone is being so bloody unrealistic. Parliamentary assemblies around the world, under pressure from the voters, vote to increase spending without the means to achieve it. UK parliamentarians are just as bad – our government's budget deficit is simply horrendous. Then you wonder why currencies collapse and you feel so helpless.'

He prodded a finger at Elaine, who had been a prominent supporter of increased allowances for MPs, and leaned back in his seat. His remarks were accurate enough to make the other two squirm.

'We might as well all go home?' she enquired. His argument niggled. Governments had pleaded for hair-shirt policies before but electorates failed to support them. When nasty decisions had to be made, at least Parliament was recalled, and informed. Afterwards. As a courtesy – a formality.

Muncastle was regretting his momentary indiscretion. The best defence was always attack. Marks might be older, and have been in politics far longer, but that smirking face irritated him.

'You presumably wouldn't claim that the European Parliament has any more influence than we have, particularly after the chaos of the last few weeks.'

'Ah, but there you're wrong, old man.' Tim Marks leaned his bulk forward, as if he could physically fill the empty space between them where the government's policies should have been. 'Whatever happens for the moment, the Single Market is almost complete. When we get Scandinavian and Alpine countries joining later this decade, we're nudging 400 million people. Already the EC is bigger in population than the USA and Japan combined. Europe, my dears, is the greatest association of free nations the world has ever seen and is not about to disintegrate or disappear.'

Face flushed, he was warming to his subject. Nearby heads half turned to listen as his voice rose and boomed over the electric hiss of wheels on rails. He was dominating the two young MPs almost without effort. 'Nobody is going to dismantle it. Nobody is going to withdraw, start putting up barriers again: that way lies economic beggary, as in the thirties. And if we're to have rules for good behaviour, some kind of checking up and reporting and chasing miscreants, then the Commissioners have a job. As long as the Commission and pan-European activity flourish, then so does the European Parliament, slowly making national parliaments less significant. The shift is inevitable. Sorry, chaps, but that's how it is.' He sat back, triumphant.

Elaine felt as if she were a small child defeated unfairly in a complex argument by a wordly-wise adult. Marks had ignored the question whether the European Parliament had much influence either. His manner was infuriating, his arguments insulting. She counter-attacked.

'What about subsidiarity? It's in the Maastricht Treaty, one of the best bits we negotiated – that decisions should be made at the lowest level possible. Member nations should be responsible for everything that can be better done at national level. Or something like that,' she ended lamely. No one had quite articulated the formula properly, though everyone thought they knew what it meant.

'Oh yeah?' Marks was dismissive. 'Huge new role for national parliaments in there, and I don't think. Even when Maastricht is ratified, all it would do is drive home the message that the institutions of Europe are superior: if it works, the Commission, the Councils of Ministers and the Parliament will be responsible not for the trivia but for all the issues member states cannot manage by themselves. In my submission, that means all the big things: economics, the Single Market, international transport, infrastructure, energy, regional development, environment and pollution, farming subsidies, countryside policy, equality law – that includes what age we all retire at, remember? – oh, crime busting, aid, AIDS, great chunks of foreign policy and a host of other subjects besides. By all means toddle around in Westminster. Enjoy yourselves. Learn your craft. But don't be surprised if your feelings of helplessness increase over the years. The really important, juicy matters affecting the lives of hundreds of millions of people are being debated and decided elsewhere.'

It was a brutal judgement, delivered across the swaying table with driving conviction.

Elaine sat back listlessly. 'I hear what you say, Tim. But I should feel happier if it were democratically elected politicians who were taking those decisions, not faceless bureaucrats in Brussels.'

'Fine: I concur entirely, although the bureaucrats are very able and may make sounder choices. But in that case you should be arguing for the European Parliament. National parliaments don't have the constitutional power to do what you are wanting. Suppose the Italians employ child labour in shoe factories, and put Clarks out of business. Can Westminster blow the whistle on them? No, but I can. Are the Greeks admitting Pakistanis with dubious entry papers, giving them access to anywhere in the Community including Bradford – and they are – and do you in Westminster know about it, and can you pass resolutions ordering Greece to desist? No, you can't, but I can. Are the French subsidising their car industry illegally – can you stop them? No, but I can, and do, and have. The British Parliament can't tell the Germans what to do, any more than the Assemblée Nationale in Paris can tell the Spanish, or the Dutch censure the UK. It doesn't work like that. But the European Parliament, young as it is, can tell each and any of these countries when they're breaking the rules, and demand via the Commissioners that something be done.'

Marks's rhetoric petered out as he caught up with the two stony faces in front of him. He relented a little. 'I grant you the system is imperfect. Poke fingers at me by all means and you would have a point. But I am elected just like you, and outside Britain a lot of people care that the European Parliament should function properly. So if and when you get fed up debating the Cardiff Bay Barrage Bill, or how many toilets there ought to be per prisoner in Strangeways, let me know and we'll bring you over for a few days. Then you can see how a great chunk of the future is working.'

Marks leaned over and dropped his voice. The whole carriage had been listening to this big determined man, speaking in a normal English accent but perhaps not quite British.

'You will get people asking why we need Europe, why we can't manage by ourselves, standing alone, not joining in, not sharing any power or responsibility or – what is that buzz word? – "sovereignty". Some like Margaret Thatcher proudly remember 1940 when we stood alone as the rest of Europe collapsed under the German jackboot. We spilled British blood rescuing continentals, foreigners, from the shit they got themselves into. Oh yes, I've heard all this. But the idea that we can or should stand alone again is ludicrous. Britain by itself is an offshore island, relatively poor and increasingly unimportant. If you need an answer to a bloody-minded questioner, Elaine, just remind him that there is indeed a country in Europe which turned its back on the world, refused to trade, kept its boundaries tightly closed, believed its people could manage entirely self-sufficiently without outside contacts. The result shows what happens when nationalism dominates over any kind of economic sense. You know where I mean?'

Both Elaine and Andrew looked puzzled.

'That country is Albania.'

The train was slowing down for Leicester. Elaine, feeling deeply troubled, saying nothing, reached for her bag and jacket. Marks looked a little crestfallen, as if he knew he had overdone it and had upset his parliamentary colleagues, to no real purpose. As the train halted and she opened the door to step out, Elaine felt burdened by the sense of unpleasant revelation which the conversation had induced and for which she was quite unready. It was like discovering that God does not exist.

Her connection was not due for twenty minutes. She sat on a platform seat, feet and knees neatly together, contemplating her face reflected in her shiny black shoes, and wondered about the future.

Eventide Rest Home, 28 September

Dear Mrs Stalker,

I am writing to tell you that our oldest resident, Mrs Dorothy Holmes, will be 100 years old on Tuesday 20 October. She is a great fan of yours and always watches you whenever you're on television. We will be giving a party for her that day. If there is any chance that you could attend, I know she and her family would be delighted.

Yours truly
M. Swanson RGN (Mrs), Matron

'Blast!' Elaine consulted the diary. 'It's midweek. We may be required to vote. Yet I would like to go. I gather Dorothy is quite a character.'

'Go and see her the weekend before,' suggested Diane, looking up from a pile of correspondence. 'Offer to go on the Saturday morning before – that's ... wait ... October the seventeenth. You can have a civilised conversation with her without loads of visitors. Tell the local press; a hundredth birthday is good news. Don't forget to take postal vote forms. She could still be around at the election and you need all the votes you can get.'

'Good idea. Anything else I should deal with now?'

Diane handed her a sheaf of faxes. 'Only four more requests for television chat shows. You could become quite a star if you wanted – queen of the light entertainment circuit.'

'Not quite what I was expecting when I came to Westminster,' Elaine confessed. 'I'm not sure how to handle it. Why on earth do I attract so much attention?'

Diane considered. 'All the women MPs do: it's not just you. But you've the added advantage of being young and attractive, and with a good tongue in your head. Most of your colleagues in front of a microphone are useless. They sound like Colonel Blimps or Central Office clones mouthing slogans. You at least think about what you say and it's interesting. On TV your appearance is a huge bonus. So you'll keep getting these invitations. If I were you I'd accept from time to time. You'd be surprised how many people will vote for you because they've seen you on *Celebrity Squares*. The nation's at heart trivial about its politics.'

Elaine was silent. Diane continued, 'Just remember this: if your constituents don't know who their MP is, that's your fault, not theirs, Elaine. If they need help any time, they must know who to turn to. Politicians have no choice but to use the media. It's a blessing you're good at it, and talk more sense than most.'

Elaine parked the car behind Eventide Rest Home and sat for a moment listening to local radio news. A bus had crashed into a bridge at Whittington and fouled up traffic for two hours; Mrs Horrocks would be on the warpath. South Warmingshire Women's Institute Christmas Carnival Committee was appealing for more helpers. 'It is the same people every year and we are all getting too old' came the plaintive voice of the organiser. 'I'm the youngest on the committee and I'm seventy-five.' A rapist up for sentencing had been let off lightly because the elderly judge said the young lady had been provocative. 'That does not give him the right, even if it were true,' Elaine commented savagely to the dashboard. She picked up the car phone, angrily called the radio station, and soon heard her own voice promising to raise the matter urgently in Parliament. Still muttering crossly to herself she locked the car and headed for the home's entrance.

Mrs Swanson was a tubby, motherly woman with a soft Irish accent and a ready smile, her Registered General Nurse's badge prominently displayed on a dark-blue dress. Elaine liked her immediately, appreciating the mix of professionalism and kindliness. Tea in the best china was brought into the tiny cubby-hole which served as her office.

'The photographer is on his way, and if you don't mind we'll take a few snaps of our own too. When you've finished with Dorothy would you be kind enough to come into the lounge and meet a few of the others? Most are not really up to it, but one or two would be pleased to shake hands. If I let you go without introducing you I'd never hear the last of it. It's not often we get an important visitor.'

Eventide was a new home, neatly built in red brick by a consortium of three local Asian doctors. Modern stained glass with iridescent parrots, galleons and irises graced double-glazed windows, their garish colours reflected on pale-grey wall-to-wall carpets, set off by magnolia paint and apricotvelvet curtains. Familiar prints of landscapes, dogs and chubby children hung cosily over pseudo-marble fireplaces. Baskets of bright artificial flowers made the place look more like a hotel, while Muzak floated from small loudspeakers perched high out of wavering reach. To most of the old people gratitude was obligatory, yet an air of resentment and unhappiness pervaded the lounges. On the other hand, here were no illusions and the whole place functioned on professional lines. Its plush style and remarkable cleanliness were reassuring to distant relatives paying the bills.

Elaine commented favourably on the immaculate condition of the home. Mrs Swanson agreed: 'Thank you for noticing. It's the doctors. They insist there should be no smell of urine in here. Bad for business, you know. Our job is to banish the reality of old age, not bow down to it. I would get the sack.'

The bedrooms were equally pristine. Elaine and Mrs Swanson paused at the threshold of one room. How clinical, how aseptic: even though more flowers filled this room and chased each other over the wallpaper in merry profusion, despite frills and fringed lampshades, the effect was of a nun's cell, devoid of the life and mess of real human bodies. It was as if denial of the process of normal physical disintegration could postpone mortality for ever.

The matron led Elaine to Mrs Holmes's bedroom, which she shared with another resident, 'young enough to be her daughter – only eighty-one, but blind. The two boss each other about.' As they knocked and entered, a solidly built but diminutive figure in a dark-green tweed suit struggled to its feet, leaning heavily on a stick and waving a beringed hand.

'Aah! My dear! So you have come to see me!'

Dorothy Holmes was not at all what Elaine had been expecting. It was not the strong, tough face with its intelligent eyes and smudged lipstick which startled her so much, though the blonde wig, slightly askew and held on with two large hairpins sticking out at the back, was striking enough. Nor was it the vigorous personality, after the glimpse of vacant faces in the lounges. It was Dorothy's voice that was her most arresting feature: broad, rich, fruity, whooping and flirting with vowels, running its tongue in delicious satisfaction over consonants, making the most of every note. She was increasingly deaf and was aware that she talked too loudly. From this arose a greater duty to be good company.

'I've come to wish you Happy Birthday for Thursday,' Elaine began formally, handing over a large card and a box of House of Commons mint chocolates.

Dorothy seized the box with cries of delight. 'How wonderful, Mrs Stalker! That will impress my sons no end, I can tell you. You are most kind, my dear, most *kind*. Now I will put them *here*, on the table where all my visitors can see, and I will deny myself any at all, until the great day.'

Music hall stars and primadonnas must have talked like that. Dorothy turned 'kind' into a word of half a dozen syllables, while there was an octave difference between 'self' and 'day'. The rheumy old eyes caught hers and winked.

There was a knock on the door and Mrs Swanson ushered in the local newspaper's photographer, a middle-aged and permanently harassed man with whom Elaine was already familiar. The photographer fussed and flashed as Dorothy leaned on both her stick and Elaine's arm, grinning on command like a Cheshire cat. She was heavy but her head came barely up to Elaine's shoulder.

'How tall are you?' Dorothy hissed at one point as the film was being changed.

'About five foot six,' Elaine replied.

'Are you? I used to be even taller than that. Shrunk, you know. Crumbling away. Awful, isn't it? Don't get old, my dear.'

When at last the man had finished and left, the old lady settled herself in a high-backed chair and examined her visitor for a moment without speaking. Satisfied, she pointed to a cupboard with her stick.

'Now, my dear, you will join an old lady in a drink to celebrate. Sherry? Of course. Can you reach the glasses and bottle? Let's have a chin-wag, a real heart-to-heart. I have been looking forward to meeting you.'

She pronounced 'sherry' as if its sweetness were already rolling pleasurably around her tongue. Elaine's unasked question as to whether the voice owed its origins to any terpsichorean links was partly answered as she obeyed Dorothy's instructions. The cupboard held a jumble of ancient books, records and sheet music of long-forgotten comedy numbers, with modern cassette tapes on top. There was no time to glance through them all. On a black-lacquered tray sat six assorted crystal glasses and two enormous opened bottles, one cream sherry, one Irish whiskey.

'The hard stuff is for the men; most of my relatives are Irish,' Dorothy explained. 'Unless you would prefer . . . ? Fine. Bring two big glasses. I have decided to be tipsy between now and the great day or I will never survive all these unctuous congratulations.' 'Unctuous' journeyed around the old mouth, slithering out slowly, onomatopoeically. 'You're to start me off. Good girl' – as Elaine poured two tumblers of sweet sherry.

'Do you like being here?' Elaine asked, looking around.

'Me? No, of course not. Would you? I have no choice: can't manage by myself at all these days. It is ghastly being old, my dear. I suggest you pop off around seventy, before the aches and pains set in. Well, what am I to do? My sons and their wives are pensioners themselves. They couldn't look after me. My grandchildren have their own lives, one in America, one in Brussels – that's the clever one, George. He works for Mr Delors – you should hear the tales he tells of what goes on! No, I'm better off here.'

The gnarled fingers drummed restlessly on the wooden arm of her chair. It was not home. Then the old lady brightened.

'Now you tell me about yourself. Far more interesting than me. Do you like being an MP? Is it as exciting as it looks on television?' Like millions, the old lady was an avid watcher of the live broadcasts of Prime Minister's Question Time twice a week and was familiar with many of its regular performers. Her comments were observant and unorthodox.

'You were pulled up by Madam Speaker in Question Time recently, weren't you? May I call you Elaine? What was that for?'

'Yes, I was. We're not allowed to make any kind of demonstration in the Chamber – not supposed to wave banners or placards, or even newspapers. That's the reason we wave order papers: all that's allowed. One Kent MP, a very distinguished knight of the shire, was hauled up for eating an apple when making a point about Kentish agriculture. It's all in the interests of good order. On the occasion you mention, I was seated next to David Amess, the young Basildon MP, who's a pal of mine. He was planning to ask a question about his constituency, so I waved a car sticker saying "I Love Basildon" as he rose to his feet. It was a very *small* car sticker, but the Speaker had a fit.'

Dorothy gurgled with delight. 'I suppose you have to watch what you say, too?'

Elaine nodded. 'Yes and no. We have parliamentary privilege: we can say whatever we wish without fear of being sued. I've used that very sparingly – only once, in fact, to accuse a local councillor of being a crook. He is, too; the police are investigating him. I couldn't have exposed him any other way. But we do have to watch our language. Since we are all "honourable members", you can't call someone a liar, for example. Do you remember Churchill getting around that by accusing an opponent of "terminological inexactitude"?'

'Rather! These days you would say he was being economical with the truth, isn't that right?' Dorothy's eyes were gleaming with pleasure. She gestured at the sherry bottle. 'I'll have a little more, if you please.'

Elaine settled in and told more stories, glad of an appreciative audience. The old lady hung happily on every word as the sherry slopped over the glass. 'Well, my dear, you seem to be making a great success of it. I'm so pleased that there are more women there now. Do you know, I couldn't vote until 1918 when I was thirty? We were all regarded as too stupid before that. A man could be a drunken layabout, but he could vote. I was a fully qualified nurse, but I couldn't. Power to your elbow! I'll drink to that!' And she did, with a shaky hand and a mischievous grin.

'But you were interested in music hall,' Elaine commented. Dorothy raised an eyebrow. 'The sheet music in your cupboard.'

'Oh, that!' The old woman was dismissive. 'Only amateur, my dear. Nursing was as close as I could get to freedom, and that was quite a fight to persuade my parents. There were so many things young ladies couldn't do in those days. You have a much easier time of it now, believe me.'

'Were you a suffragette?' Elaine asked, curious.

'A bit,' the old lady confided. 'I went on a few marches before the war. I never had the courage to do what some of those poor brave women did, going to prison, the hunger strikes and forced feeding and all that. Ruined their constitutions for the rest of their lives. Asquith has a lot to answer for – wicked, cruel man.'

The clock was ticking away. Dorothy spoke more urgently. 'Listen to me, Elaine. You stick to your guns, you hear? You're representing a lot of women like me who didn't get your chances. Make the most of them.'

There was a lump in Elaine's throat as she began to gather jacket, handbag and briefcase. So often was she just a symbol to people; so frequently did she herself relegate those she met into categories. Dorothy was vividly real and her humanity touched her visitor.

'Now you are to come and see me again. I may look like a stupid old woman but there's nothing wrong with my brain and I admire you enormously. I expect you have lots of family of your own, but if you would enjoy popping in for a chat you would brighten an old lady's day. And you can rely on me: I can keep secrets. Some of what this old duck has got up to in her life would bear telling too, believe me. Will you come?'

The two women looked at each other, one anxious, one hesitant. A growing wave of sympathy and affection swept over Elaine. She bent and put an arm around Dorothy's shoulder.

'I feel I've found a friend, Dorothy. Yes, I should like to come again.

I'll bring more booze next time, shall I? From the House of Commons, the kind we drink ourselves. You look after yourself till then.'

Elaine kissed the soft cheek. Close to, instead of the smell of decay she had been steeling herself against, there was an unexpected whiff of lavender. Dorothy's face had wrinkles everywhere and the skin was so fine the little blue arteries and veins were clearly visible. Her strange wig was now quite lopsided, a few sparse, fine, silver hairs escaping from underneath. Elaine realised she must be nearly bald.

The old woman put a hand on Elaine's sleeve, detaining her. 'I had a daughter, you know, Elaine. She died of diphtheria when she was seven. I was a nurse: I watched her die.' Her eyes were filmy with tears. 'I had to hold her down on the kitchen table as the surgeon cut open her throat to help her breathe, but we couldn't save her. I still miss her after all these years.'

'And I had a son,' Elaine said softly. 'Perhaps I'll tell you about him. Next time. Take care, Dorothy. And God bless.'

She touched the old lady's face. It was as if she had touched eternity: still warm, the blood faintly flowing, yet this soul was already turning towards the light. Dorothy recovered herself, blew her nose noisily on a lavender-perfumed handkerchief, dashed off the remains of the sherry and gamely waved her stick in farewell.

CHAPTER SEVEN

An unwelcome noise reverberated through Tessa Muncastle's brain. On the bedside radio a few inches from her ear John Humphrys and Brian Redhead, professional and laconic, were talking about Bosnia. A reporter at the front line in Sarajevo crackled in, fear raising the pitch of his voice. From the comfort of her bed in London Tessa wondered what to do with her guilt feelings about the daily diet of misery on the radio. Not that she felt in any way responsible or involved in these atrocities: quite the reverse. She wanted desperately to switch off, or at least start the day with music or something more cheerful or trivial. Her selfishness was wicked, especially since those people had so little while she and Andrew had so much. She resolved to go to mass in Westminster Cathedral later in the day. It might help. It would certainly help her.

Andrew was whistling in the bathroom. Downstairs Barney was getting ready to go to school, teasing the au pair, spilling milk on the kitchen tablecloth, picking raisins out of the muesli and leaving them in a neat line by his plate. In a couple of years the child would be off to prep school as a boarder, under the care of Andrew's old headmaster, living in a dormitory with ten other boys, far from London and home. Andrew said Barney's separation from his parents would not be a problem; he would get used to being away and would enjoy himself in the company of lots of friends. To Tessa it seemed cruel, but both Andrew and Sir Edward were adamant that a similar pattern of parental deprivation had done them no harm and a great deal of good. She was too shocked at the prospect to fight them effectively. Because of her pleading it had been agreed that the child should only be a weekly boarder, could come home after Saturday-morning school or around 5 o'clock following afternoon games if he won a place in a team. Tessa felt rebellious against this cold upper-class English style which still insisted on sending children away. Something warmer in her own blood, Irish maybe, or Italian from a grandparent, said Barney should be with his mother.

It had to be admitted that the au pair was far more efficient at getting the boy to school on time properly and tidily dressed. Here Tessa was, still listlessly in bed, wondering what to do with the day. She forced feelings of inadequacy to one side. It was better for children to be with their mother: of course it was. It was certainly better for the mother. A wave of bereavement and self-pity overwhelmed her, and she buried her face in the pillow.

The bathroom door was opening. Quickly she wiped her face on the sheet and blew her nose on a tissue. By the time Andrew entered the room, towel around his waist, she was sitting on the edge of the bed reaching for fluffy pink mules and pretending to be bright and breezy.

'You're up early, darling. It's not yet seven thirty.'

Andrew was looking preoccupied. 'Where's my ankle protector, Tessa? You know, the elastic-webbing one. Last week my foot turned on the Powerjog machine. I keep forgetting I'm not an athletic kid any more.'

He started to rummage in a cupboard, pulling clean undergarments and woollen socks all over the floor. Tessa quickly reverted to duty and gave up her bed. She rose and pointed to a large carrier next to his briefcase.

'I packed all your gym things last night. It's in there. I hope you're getting some benefit from all this early rising. Makes me feel groggy even to think of it.'

Tessa's fluttery tones failed to irritate him this morning. Now that the House had returned after recess he was looking forward to his twice-weekly visit to the Commons gymnasium, pumping a little modest iron, nothing too dramatic, enough to keep encroaching thirties flab at bay. His reward so far, he noted with satisfaction, was the loss of eight pounds in weight and a definite firmness of waistline, chinline and step. Over time the effort might increase his stamina – useful for late-night sittings and the grind of travelling.

Maybe something else too. He watched Tessa tying the belt of her all-enveloping pink dressing gown. Apart from her head and neck, now bent, all he could see was the narrowness of her Achilles tendons spreading down into fleshy heels half hidden in the slippers, concealing everything important elsewhere.

'How is the eczema these days, Tessa?' No harm in asking.

A haunted look told him everything. 'Still bad, I'm afraid,' she apologised, rubbing her arm absent-mindedly.

He reached over and lifted her chin, forcing her to concentrate on the question really being put to her. His naked chest, his skin, the smell of his talcum powder were too close and made her shrink back. She pulled the dressing gown tighter. One distracted fingernail started scratching at her palm. A flush of angry colour spread about her neck.

Why couldn't he leave her alone? Did he realise how miserable it was, being pawed and entered and hurt, feeling humiliated and disgusted and unclean afterwards? Why were men like that, even decent men like Andrew? They could do it, just do it, and put everything away afterwards, see *it* all shrink and subside, until the next time. It was dangling there under his towel right now, animal and hungry. To men, sex was separate, an appendage. Women could not react in the same way: for women, intercourse was a violation of their very being. The thought of opening up again to her husband, of somehow relaxing, as the doctor had suggested to her, lying on her back with her legs open and her privacy all gone, made her shudder. If he did it anyway, as he used to before the eczema provided an effective barrier, the raw ache was not a figment of her imagination but stayed deep inside all day, a reminder that men were always in the ascendant, had to be obeyed, and women would suffer.

A woman in her social class was of course expected to marry, and to be a helpmeet to her husband. In everything else she did her willing though not very competent best. Had she known before the wedding day exactly what was entailed in marriage she might have chosen a different life. It had been worth it for Barney, but now they wanted to take even him away from her. Maybe the nuns in her convent school had had the right idea, lying in their crisp white night habits between clean sheets all alone, hands crossed protectively over their breasts, loving only in the spirit and married only to Christ. Jesus was not likely to come pestering late at night after a hearty House of Commons dinner. She caught her breath at her own blasphemous thoughts. Mass would have to be preceded by thorough confession to Father John – maybe watered down a bit, to save the poor man embarrassment.

The gymnasium was busy as Andrew signed in. Abba music blared over the loudspeakers, covering grunts and gasps and clashing machinery, the sounds of the overweight hurling sweating flesh against metal and mortality. He recognised several policemen and security staff, for whom fitness was an obligation. That formidably brainy lady from the enquiry desk in the Commons library was here too. Nicholas Baker in white shorts was pounding away at the exercise bike reading *The Independent*. Dapper little Jerry Hayes, his gingery hair and curly beard making him look more than ever like a miniature Caligula, was on the step machine. No wonder Mrs Thatcher used to doubt whether such a chap, apparently more suited to picket lines and student activism, was indeed 'one of us'.

The gymnasium's manager Vicki Rose was demonstrating the pec deck to Elaine Stalker. Andrew found himself looking at both women appraisingly. Vicki was in her twenties and recently married. She had that ripe happy look of a girl who loves every minute of life. Mrs Stalker was in her mid-thirties, mother of a teenage daughter, trim-figured but just starting to get solid around the hips. She didn't talk much about a Mr Stalker, though there was one; Andrew was fairly sure he had never met him. There was no hint of divorce or separation either. Maybe this was one of those private marriages, contented and productive at home, never paraded outside, a personal matter, not a parliamentary affair. Many parliamentarians protected their family life by refusing to bring its members into the limelight at all. Given Tessa's hatred of attention, maybe that was wise.

He paused on the rowing machine as Elaine passed and nodded agreeably to her. He set to, bent himself, back and forth, as flickering numbers measured time elapsed and distance travelled. They had all come a long way since their first days as new recruits. There was something different about Elaine even now. Andrew looked closer. Surprised, he noted the same happy light in her face as in Vicki's eyes. Maybe she was in love too; how lucky for her if she had that kind of marriage. He felt almost disappointed – and it was not simply a twinge of jealousy but a faint sense of loss that Mrs Stalker was clearly already spoken for. The idea that he might be attracted to her himself was really too silly. For his own taste she was a bit old and far too domineering, at least in reputation. If he fancied anybody, it would be a younger woman, and not a blonde: a woman with thick dark hair and laughing eyes, who enjoyed going to bed with him.

Then Andrew Muncastle realised that for the first time he was raising his eyes from Tessa's dismal bed and beginning, just beginning, to look elsewhere.

'Good morning, sir!'

Despite the weather, Gerry Keown was enjoying his first morning on duty outside 10 Downing Street. The wind blew leaves in skittering gusts from Whitehall, found chilly gaps in his well-buttoned uniform and whistled down the narrow passageway to St James's Park. A hint of rain was in the air. Umbrellas nestled in ministerial cars drawing up outside the famous door. Keown's radio crackled fitfully. Journalists on the pavement opposite stamped cold feet and pulled their jackets closer at the neck.

The Secretary of State for National Heritage arrived early looking pleased with himself as usual. The Chancellor of the Duchy of Lancaster and Minister for the Citizens' Charter, despite his grand title, was ignored by the press. The Home Secretary strode up, cheerily aware that the significance of a Cabinet job is in inverse ratio to the length of its title. Sir Nigel Boswood beamed as he hauled himself out of the big car, nodded to the policeman on duty, adjusted his bow-tie and fastened his double-breasted jacket with a flourish. Old friends and comrades stood around in the tiled hall of Number 10 chatting amicably. Most, however, having been thoroughly briefed at their own departments, had a sense of foreboding.

The Cabinet Room is light and airy, surprisingly small, and is decorated in warm yellow and cream. The famous polished wood table is not square, nor oval, but more angularly ellipsoid, so no one is hidden or can hide. Red leather blotters inscribed 'Cabinet Room 1st Lord' greeted each place. The Prime Minister was already seated facing the window in the only chair with arms.

Official business was dealt with briskly. Decisions had previously been reached in Cabinet committees of Ministers and civil servants. Cabinet would confirm those views, resolve disputes and hear briefings on foreign matters or forthcoming summits. Minutes were taken and carefully checked before confirmation and burial for the next quarter-century. All present adhered to Cabinet responsibility: once a decision was taken all were committed to it, all would defend it. At least until the next U-turn, or their memoirs.

As the formal proceedings closed, the Cabinet Secretary tactfully left the room, to be replaced by the Party Chairman and his deputy. The atmosphere hardened. Chairs were drawn a little closer and twenty-five well-groomed heads came together. Nigel Boswood cleared his throat and reached for a glass of water. He hoped he would not be required to contribute to the discussion. Under the last Prime Minister one could stay quiet apart from grunting sagely at strategic points, but this one had a disconcerting habit of going round the table and listening attentively as every single participant was put on the spot. The thought made his easy-going soul quiver. It was so difficult to equivocate afterwards about one's position. It made taking sides easier for those with an itch to do so, and these did not include Nigel. Next to him the gaunt Leader of the Commons looked desperate for a cigarette, forbidden in this beautiful room. Well-known faces, troubled, sardonic, wise and vacuous, glanced around.

'As you know, we are confronted with adverse conditions necessitating some quite difficult decisions,' the Prime Minister began. No wonder he had such a reputation for understatement. Briefly their Leader summarised what everyone present already knew. Phrases such as 'substantial unplanned devaluation' and 'budget deficit around one billion pounds a week' floated into Nigel's consciousness. The numbers were so huge his brain refused to grasp them. He recalled the suggestion of an old schoolmaster that it was not worth worrying about matters which appeared to have no solution. It was a comfortable thought, but a cop-out.

'We also have a trade deficit of around a billion pounds sterling *a month*,' the Prime Minister was saying. Nigel forced himself to listen. He did find economics so unfathomable. 'We expected the recession to improve matters there, but it hasn't. Actually we expected the recession to be over by now, but it isn't either. So we have to take some action.'

Things ain't going too well, Nigel translated to himself, so we have to *do something*. The question is, what?

The President of the Board of Trade sounded more cheerful. 'One effect of the devaluation is a fall in the prices of our goods sold overseas,' he pointed out. 'So there's a wonderful opportunity for exporters. I propose we have a big multi-million pound advertising campaign to promote British exports.'

Visions of the incumbent off on the first plane, dining with expatriate managers in the far outposts of the trading world, filled the minds of all present.

The Chancellor answered sourly, 'I'm afraid there will be no advertising or campaigning budgets in your department or any other. We no longer have the money to buy time. Just get yourself on the box, dear, and do it for free.' There was no love lost between these two.

Nigel Boswood was a natural optimist. All this doom and gloom unsettled his stomach. Given a task he could tackle it with a will, even a hopeless task: he would gladly put his finger in a crumbling dyke for the sake of the country, the government, the party. What he hated was the ineffectual discussion now trudging round the table. It all seemed too reminiscent of a small-town Micawber waiting for something to turn up. Maybe in the end the economy ran itself. Maybe in future it would be run by the Brussels Commission, or by international businessmen. If things went wrong it might be run on the instructions of the International Monetary Fund, as in the seventies. This Cabinet seemed an increasingly small and irrelevant cog in a swirling machine. Not the way he was brought up, when a quarter of the known world was British and subject nations did what they were told. He wondered quite what he was doing there.

Nigel allowed his mind to wander. There might be time for another little trip across to the continent before all these budgets were chopped about. More than once in recent weeks he had found himself absent-mindedly rubbing the skin on the back of his hands or needing to touch and fondle after a bath; last night he had had a wet dream about a desirable young blond boy, a sure sign that relief was needed before too long. He leaned his elbows on the table and rested his chin on his hands.

There was no need to fake a look of concern. If the country came through the next year without rises in prices, interest rates or taxation, and probably in all three, it would be a ruddy miracle. It all felt very bleak. Thank God the election was behind them.

Johnson was tapping away at his computer again and driving everyone in the upper whips' office mad. His analyses were always entertaining and useful, if disturbing. Gloomily he munched a sandwich and explained to anyone who would listen.

'We have no majority, I keep telling the Chief that.'

To express solidarity Roger Dickson came and perched on Johnson's desk. For several minutes the bearded whip explained, scattering crumbs over his keyboard in agitation. The other whips had heard it all before and drifted off until only Roger was listening.

Dickson muttered despondently as he grasped what was likely to happen. 'That means we'll have to rely on votes from other parties to get our business through. The Liberals or Ulster Unionists, heaven help us.'

'Worse than that.' Johnson was grateful for an audience. He did not like what his calculations showed. 'Labour as well. Can you believe that? We may have to persuade them to clear off and abstain. The Labour MEPs are our best allies. They won't allow their people here to do another about-turn on Europe.' Johnson looked miserable. 'And if some of our nutters get into bad habits of voting against us, we could have an uncomfortable time right through this Parliament.'

Dickson laughed nervously and glanced longingly at the door. 'If you keep playing with that machine of yours, Johnson, you'll talk us all into a depression. Allow me to change the subject. How's the love life?'

His friend shrugged, fiddled for a moment and switched the computer off. 'Not so good. She's determined to walk me up the aisle somehow. I'm scared rigid she'll take it into her head to get pregnant. Then I'll have to marry her.'

'What's wrong with that?' Johnson's live-in girlfriend was uncommonly pretty and totally devoted to him.

'I like being a bachelor. Like playing the field. Not the sort to be dandling babies on my lap.'

Slowly and with a heavy sigh he rose and stood, hands thrust deep in pockets. The prospect of being outwitted by his lover seemed to trouble the man even more than the distinct chance of the government being defeated.

Roger put a fatherly arm around his shoulders and mocked gently. 'But you don't play the field, old chap. You talk about it, but you're as faithful to that girl as if you were long since in holy matrimony.'

Johnson's face broke into a rueful grin. 'That's not true. I do get around. But I don't boast about it like some. What about you, then? How did you get on with the lovely Mrs Stalker? The bet's still on, you know.'

With a twinge of alarm Roger wondered if anything had got out. What on earth had possessed Johnson to mention her in that context? He scrutinised his friend but there was no knowing wink. Maybe it was just a chance remark. He decided to play it long.

'Now then! Unlike you I am married, and unlike you I don't go playing the field, as you put it. As for Elaine Stalker, I think she's as engrossed in politics as the rest of us. She's certainly not here for a pick-up, that I have ascertained. I rather admire her, I must say – she has to put up with a lot of ribbing and gossip behind her back, none of it with any foundation as far as I can tell. I can't say I find her attractive, though, come to think of it. There is a Mr Stalker and they've been married a long time. You might understand a bit better if you let your charming lady persuade you into wedlock.'

Johnson eyed him mournfully. 'Fate worse than death.'

'Well, I'd rather you play with the girl than with your confounded number-cruncher. Go and get married. And if you have any sense, leave Mrs Stalker out of it.'

Johnson laughed ruefully and the atmosphere lifted. As the two men walked out into Members' Lobby Roger reflected with a profound sense of shock how far he had travelled already. He was no longer prepared to hint about Elaine to a friend – not that Johnson or anyone else in the whips' office could be trusted for one minute. She was not a conquest, a proof of masculine success, but a secret. How easily the casual falsehoods had tripped off his tongue. Perhaps she was right when she complained about how women were spoken of in that place. It had not occurred to him before.

It was not so easy, however, to arrange a meeting. Suddenly Roger decided that he wanted to see Elaine, to be with her; the discussion with Johnson had brought her powerfully back into his mind. There were issues to be resolved between them before the affair went any further. To his surprise the thought of talking to her did not lighten his mood but darken it.

The opportunity came on the committee corridor as the weekly Thursday backbenchers' meeting known as the '22' came to its end. Although the private session had lasted barely twenty minutes there had been a bad-tempered row about the government's handling of contentious business. The Prime Minister's troubles meant unusual press interest and the chairman, a cocky little Yorkshireman ousted years before from ministerial office, was only too happy to oblige. The whips stood by watchfully; for the moment there was nothing they could do.

Roger waited impassively as the chairman gabbled away to scribbling hacks. Then he saw Elaine, hovering on the edge of the group as if hoping to catch his eye. He motioned her over.

'This will take a few minutes. If you would like a lift, wait for me at Members' entrance.'

It was a simple exchange in a dusty crowded corridor between a whip and a transport-less MP he felt obligated to help. Elaine marvelled at the coolness with which Dickson compartmentalised his life. For a brief moment she wondered if he had changed his mind about her. Perhaps a lift was all she was going to get.

It was raining hard and pitch-black outside as the dark-blue Rover drew up at Members' entrance. By the time Dickson had extricated himself from the chairman's clutches and reported back to the Chief Whip, most MPs had disappeared and the taxi queue had dwindled. Elaine was profoundly thankful despite the long wait. For all its seeming innocence, being seen getting into Roger's car, especially if it became a regular occurrence, would excite comment. The place was alive with eyes.

The car radio was on, stuttering inadequately about misery in Somalia, troops stealing and looting emergency food supplies as children lay dying of starvation. Roger concentrated on moving smoothly out into busy traffic in Parliament Square as Elaine began to give him directions. He cut her short brusquely.

'I know how to get to your flat.'

She was startled at his tone. 'How do you know?'

'I'm a whip. Of course I know.'

She subsided, flattened. As they drove down Victoria Street he gesticulated at the radio, now offering the chirpy voice of the '22' chairman.

'Sorry. I'm still seething about him and his alternative society. Now we'll have to arrange for the Prime Minister to go to the same meeting next week and insist on some sense. Forgive me if I sounded a bit rattled.'

Elaine offered soothingly, 'It requires a change of behaviour all round.'

If Roger wanted to talk seriously that was OK by her. Being with him was like standing outside a lighted window and drawing the curtain to glimpse the inner worlds of real politics and decision-making, of government, after the empty posturing of the Commons. It looked so exciting from outside. That being indoors was not cosy at all was a discovery made within days of appointment by every junior Minister, but hidden from everyone else.

She continued: 'The government mustn't decide policy in Cabinet without consulting anybody, then hand it over to the whips' office to force through. That won't work any more.'

115

He did not answer. The Rover turned into her narrow street and edged past parked cars. Elaine noted the easy grace with which Roger used the power steering to slip the big car noiselessly into a parking space.

'Maybe we should follow Matthew Arnold's suggestion,' she said softly, as Roger turned to her.

'What's that?'

She had learned it at school, long ago, for an examination, had copied it out and pinned it on the wall in her study at college, marvelled at its bitter-sweetness, found repeated comfort in the thought that Arnold was much too pessimistic by far, that things were never that bad. And, if they were, at least the poet was offering a solution.

> 'Ah, love, let us be true
> To one another! for the world, which seems
> To lie before us like a land of dreams,
> So various, so beautiful, so new,
> Hath really neither joy nor love nor light,
> Nor certitude, nor peace, nor help for pain;
> And we are here as on a darkling plain
> Swept with confused alarms of struggle and flight,
> Where ignorant armies clash by night.'

The radio was chattering of ignorant armies in Bosnia, of struggle and flight in Sarajevo, as Roger switched it off. That did the trick. He laughed, gently, glanced quickly around to ensure they were not observed, leaned over and kissed her softly on the mouth.

'Ah, love. What a good idea. A little comfort in a bad world. Come, Mrs Stalker, show me what you can do.'

In silence they climbed the stairs to her flat, which she had left warm, tidy and well provisioned. There were clean sheets on the bed and the radiator was full on, clean towels in the bathroom and new soap and plenty of hot water. It was a conscious contrast to the disorganised mess of his own home, but also a deliberate statement that as a woman she could be an all-round success.

She did not switch on the lights, not yet. Inside the door Roger took off his coat and hung it up, then held her quietly in his arms for a long moment, her head on his shoulder, stroking her hair, which in the light from a window opposite was silver and spun gold. She slid her hand under his jacket and could feel his heart beating strongly after the climb. For months she had imagined a wild passionate scene on his return, but it was not like that at all. He spoke quietly, as if from far away.

'Now why are we doing this, Mrs Stalker? We had better establish some ground-rules.'

She ruminated for a moment. She really did not want to get too serious. Life was tough enough without ponderous philosophising.

'For fun?'

He laughed. 'Yes, I think that's a good enough reason. For pleasure, and for mutual satisfaction. No more, no less. How does that sound?'

She nodded, and ran her hand around where his back was pressed against the wall, and kept her hand moving, moving, this time.

He continued, as if he had rehearsed and was working his way through a mental list: 'I am happily married, and not looking to change partners. I assume the same is true for you. If you have any other fantasies or intentions, Elaine, you had better play them out with somebody else.'

She murmured agreement. This was nothing to do with Mike. The conversation she and Roger had shared in the car, the intimacy and trust of the last few minutes, were way beyond her husband's taste or abilities, but nor was that Mike's fault. She had not married him for his political skills. Of course she loved Mike. Roger was a bonus, not a substitute.

'I have no plans to change my arrangements either. Don't worry.'

'And if anyone ever challenges us, we deny and deny and deny.'

'Too bloody right' – with feeling.

'That's all right, then.' The negotiation appeared to be over, and he moved his own hand down over her breast, bending to kiss her neck and slide a warm wet tongue into her ear.

'Hey, this is a bit one-sided!' she protested. 'I have a condition too.'

He stood upright, startled. 'Really? Now what can that be? That I don't wear my socks in bed, perhaps, or never eat curry or garlic before coming to see you?'

'No, you prat.' She dug her knuckles into his solar plexus and he grunted, grabbed her wrist, held it. 'I don't want you to embarrass me. Flirting with other women, I mean. I can't help it, but I don't want to feel I'm just an accessory. Do you know what I mean? Like you did with that stunning-looking woman journalist on the Terrace. You were teasing me. Please don't; it hurts. If you want to have other women at the same time, that's your business, but count me out.'

Roger grinned. 'You were jealous, were you?'

Elaine was affronted. She withdrew her arm, putting distance between them. Roger pulled her into the living room and sat her down like a naughty child, kissing her, then held both her protesting hands and talked urgently.

'Listen to me, Elaine. I do *not* make a habit of this sort of thing. In fact – well, never mind, but I do assure you that you are the only one. You rather laid yourself open to a bit of teasing, but I hadn't realised that under that tough exterior beats a sensitive heart. I am truly sorry. I

117

wouldn't hurt you for the world – surely you know that by now.'

He touched her face. Then, consciously, he changed his tone.

'Now I think that's enough intensity for one night. What were you telling me about having some fun? Isn't it about time we had a demonstration . . . ?'

He motioned her towards her bedroom and she moved without resistance, holding his hand like a child. And so they made love for the sheer joy of it, released briefly from both certitude and pain, exploring each other's warmths and secrets, flesh upon flesh, tongue inside mouth, entering and holding and crying and moving as one joined organism, a special secret world of escape and abandon and exultation and longing . . .

He was taking his time, luxuriating in not having to hurry, driving her as she panted close, closer, until she seized him and yelled at him to come, now, now . . . and still he played with her, and held off . . .

And, eventually, a great rush of satisfaction, a whoop of triumph at one thing well done that day, that week, as both lay spent and sweaty and gurgling and happy on the tousled bed.

'Oh, Elaine. You are marvellous.'

Great gasping breaths came from deep inside him as he slithered clear and flopped down heavily beside her. She wriggled and stretched, familiar now with his body. Her head with its damp matted fringe of blonde hair fitted snugly on to his shoulder, but for a moment she wanted to gaze at him. She propped herself up on one elbow.

His body was solid, but boyish and almost hairless, to her surprise, for his forearms were hairy and he had persistent trouble with a five o'clock shadow. She ran an index finger lightly down the line of his cheekbone, rubbing at the rough stubble going silver at the edges. It seemed to have grown even in the hour he had spent with her. His upper body was strongly muscled, as were his thighs. She let her fingers stray wistfully down over his abdomen, but he caught her hand quickly and prevented her going further.

'Not tonight. You seem to enjoy it so much, Elaine. You really get going, don't you?'

Elaine was startled. Didn't every woman? 'Doesn't Caroline?' came out, involuntarily.

His look darkened. He rolled off the bed and stood up, but spoke softly. 'We are not going to spend our time together discussing my wife. Remember the rules? And now I must be off.'

A wave of regret, as if she had burst a beautiful bubble, washed over her. When he returned from the bathroom she was still lying motionless and quiet in the same position, half covered by a duvet.

He touched her shoulder and bent down to kiss her. 'I'll let myself out. See you at the House, no doubt. I don't know how often I'll be able to do this, Elaine, but don't expect too much. No notes or phone calls, mind.'

She shook her head. He didn't need to tell her. His caution was impressive; it suggested he was settling in for a long affair. That pleased and comforted her. It wasn't only the physical stuff. Knowing him made the Palace of Westminster less of a mapless maze. At the very least she could pick his brains. At her most altruistic she could give him some support. That he was a whip could surely not hinder her own progress up the greasy pole. In fact, it could only help. She felt slightly guilty at even considering using her feminine wiles to assist her career. That was not the reason for her attraction to this man, although honesty insisted that it was not entirely absent.

At best this affair could offer a lot of welcome, even innocent, pleasure and a great enrichment to her life. She spoke sleepily.

'Understood. Roger, and out.'

CHAPTER EIGHT

The year had flown. High Street shops were full of diaries and calendars, red-coated bearded men, fractious children, tinsel, holly, mistletoe, Christmas trees real and artificial and tinny carol-singing. Marks & Spencer were doing a roaring trade in frilly knickers and flowered tea towels; foodstores were crammed with customers, their trolleys laden with turkeys and liquor. In cold churches women dusted pews and clucked at the price of altar flowers, while ministers and priests hoped forlornly for peace in a troubled world and congregations numerous and generous.

Elaine managed to get her shopping done early, with most of her gifts purchased through mail order. There was no time to do it any other way. Three full Saturdays had been occupied signing 300 Christmas cards: everyone, from the lowliest councillor to the new Deputy Lord-Lieutenant himself, expected one. Just in time she remembered that Mrs Horrocks at Whittington had been recently widowed – a card addressed to the dead did more harm than good.

The last days before the holiday were a busy time for Mike Stalker also, as thousands of Brits headed for skiing holidays and Florida. He was, however, rostered free for the rest of Christmas week. For the first time since summer Elaine would be spending time alone with her husband and daughter. The prospect filled her with unease. She was dog-tired. There would be endless cooking and clearing up, hours sitting around falling asleep in front of old films on television, more hours down in the village pub pretending merriment; no chance of shifting a heap of paperwork, no hope of persuading Mike to don wellies and jacket and come for a cheerful muddy walk – and no contact for several weeks with Roger.

Not that politics was to be absent from their lives for the whole recess. On the contrary: at Mrs Horrocks's suggestion a function had been arranged at the Stalker home for Boxing Day. Key party loyalists were invited to a buffet lunch prepared by Elaine as thanks for their successful exertions on her behalf during the year. Mutual-aid workers

121

from other constituencies, including Roger Dickson's in Warwickshire North West, would be coming too. Paradoxically, although it involved an enormous amount of avoidable work, Elaine felt almost enthusiastic. With these functions, unlike family events, she had both choice and control. Feeding eighty friendly people with minimum effort and modest expense was more challenging than stuffing an unwanted bird to satisfy tradition, and wondering what to do with the remains. The lunch was all planned. She had even programmed time for a bath, washing her hair and make-up; she would be on show, performing, in her element. By contrast the family would expect her to revert to being Mum, or to an ideal of motherhood in a steaming productive kitchen which she had never completely achieved, nor aspired to.

Before that came duty to the rest of the relations, however forced it might feel. Elaine's parents had divorced when she was a child and her mother had died when she was at college. Her relationship with her father, who had long since remarried, was perfunctory and polite. He was content with a phone call, was indeed pleased to boast about her telephoning to his friends: his little girl. Far more insistent and demanding were Mike's parents and his sister Christine, who, following a brief unsuccessful marriage, lived with them in a damp household completed by an ancient, smelly wolfhound called Paddy which got too little exercise.

It was not that Elaine Stalker was hostile to family life. She held most strongly that the traditional family was the heart of western civilisation. Marriage meant a great deal to her, and in her marriage until quite recently she had found much of the warmth missing during her earlier years. There were, however, distinct problems. The first stemmed from her preoccupation with politics, which increasingly excluded normal conjugal and parental activity. The hours were so daft, the demands on her so exhausting. Finding time to care for Mike and Karen was not only tough but emotionally draining when she had already given her all dealing with constituents' pressures. Their hurt feelings on the matter might remain unexpressed, yet that fact itself added to the burden she was tempted to push away and ignore. This was why Roger filled the gap so effectively: he was fun, he was satisfying and he was brief. He understood the need to use their limited time as fully as possible. He demanded nothing of her, yet the affair was already doing its damage. It fitted more neatly into her political life than did either husband or child.

There was also the tricky matter of the role Mike still expected her to play. It was not simply that he had failed to adjust to her new-found importance, but rather that for Elaine there was the feeling, every time she entered Parliament, of that being her real home. Whenever she thought about the conundrum she felt dimly guilty, but postponed any serious consideration of what to do. Most of the time she did not think about it at all. Only at Christmas, when Mike's family would expect her to revert to the doting submissive wife they believed she always had been, did her gorge rise with resentment.

Their attitudes were plain. Never an introspective bunch, they were clearly puzzled why Mike's wife should be in the least interested in politics, let alone keen to go through the whole peculiar business of being elected an MP. It was hardly a respected or well-paid profession, like, say, being a solicitor. It dragged Mike and Karen unwillingly into the public eye, which was unforgiveable. It boasted of conceit and arrogance, unacceptable qualities in a Mrs Stalker. It was *weird*. Had Mike given Elaine an ultimatum at any time, that she must choose between this strange malady and himself, he would have received the applause of his family. And they would have expected her immediately to capitulate and go back to being a normal spouse. Had there been a spark of good nature in any of them, or a willingness to listen, ask questions and ruminate over the answers, she might have tried to explain, but the worst part of the whole miserable business was that Mike's family were awful.

Elaine resisted any suggestion of eating Christmas dinner in their joyless home. The distance of over eighty miles and the poor health of both Mr Stalker senior and the dog precluded the in-laws travelling to Elaine and Mike's, for which she was profoundly thankful. After protracted negotiation it was decided that Mike, Elaine and Karen would spend Christmas Day together at home in Warmingshire and most of Christmas Eve at the parental abode three counties away.

Mike's big BMW was duly laden with gifts. Would Christine like the colour of the Hermès scarf? How would Mike's mother react to the Teasmade for her bedroom – would it hint that she ought to take to her bed and stay there? Mr Stalker had angled helpfully for an electric seed propagator and its bulky form now filled the back seat jammed into Karen's thigh. He was the only one Elaine looked forward to seeing, though his tendency to vanish at the least hint of trouble made him an uncertain ally.

Old Mrs Stalker was waiting at the door, Paddy flopped at her feet panting wetly, as the car scrunched up the gravel. Elaine was always startled at how wealthy Mike's family were, conscious of their view that he could have married better. Not that they knew how to enjoy their money. The old lady was grumpily enduring her seventies with the help of chocolates and the remote control on the television set. She was heavily overweight and moved ponderously in her flowered-print dress and cardigan. Her sloth had not affected either mind or tongue, which responded to increasing immobility and frustration by becoming sharper every year. Mike's older sister was standing next to her, a skinny grey-haired woman with an expression of permanent discontent. Christine's arid routine would be put out for ages by the arrival of Mike's worldly bunch, especially Elaine, who would want to watch the news instead of *Come Dancing*, and would ask about parish council affairs and have opinions and infuriatingly know everyone on the front pages of the newspapers. Christine would have bridled at any suggestion that she was jealous of her sister-in-law, whom she regarded as a jumped-up interloper. It was with malicious satisfaction that she noted a slight coolness, a lack of cosy familiarity between her adored brother and his wife as they climbed out of the car.

After a meal of dark-brown dry roast beef and salty packet gravy Elaine found herself in the cheerless lounge trying to make conversation. Mike was strolling around a sodden garden, the dog moping at his heel, bored and half listening as his father pointed out winter brassicas and the depredations of slugs. Karen had disappeared into the library and was seated on the floor surrounded by old books, tolerably happy and keeping her young head down. Elaine was irredeemably stuck for at least a couple of hours with the ladies of the house.

'Enjoying the political life, are you?'

Mrs Stalker was sitting bolt upright in an overstuffed easy chair. Her huge thighs and the arms of the chair were identically rounded. Too many tight rings squeezed flesh on podgy fingers. Her unsubtle gaze examined her daughter-in-law. Dark circles under eyes. Bit pale. Overdoing it, no doubt. Neglecting herself and her family. Not a job for a woman, not at all.

'Oh yes, very much. It is hard work, but very worthwhile. I feel like I've been doing it for years, not just a few months.'

She was aware she was gushing. Talking to the forbidding figure on the other side of the room necessitated raising her voice as if addressing a meeting. The armchairs were arranged almost at the edges of the carpet, as if the owners were afraid of contagion.

Elaine was reasonably sure the failure was not all on her side. Most old ladies she met were friendly and keen to chat or even give her an affectionate kiss and cuddle – Dorothy Holmes, for example. Or they had problems and were tearful and needed her advice: even then, the relationship was clear and unequivocal, with some sharing of the human condition. With Mike's mother there were no bridges and no understanding.

It was coffee-time. Christine carried the cafetière towards her as if it were a machine-gun. The water had not been boiling and the resulting brew was gritty and unpleasant. Elaine refused the sugar cubes, opting instead for a sweetener from her handbag. The act of rebellion was observed icily. She shivered.

'Cold?' Mrs Stalker looked triumphant.

'A little. It is chilly for this time of year.'

Mrs Stalker smiled glassily, showing stumpy yellow teeth. 'The heat doesn't come on till five, I'm afraid. Would you like to fetch a sweater?'

Elaine, subdued, shook her head. She felt defeated. Christine and her mother engaged in chat about members of the family and their doings, people Elaine barely knew and could not recall clearly. Mixing with so many vibrant personalities at Westminster made it harder to endure such small talk. The conversation switched to medical matters as mother and daughter discussed Mrs Stalker's forthcoming hip operation an the doctor's outrageous suggestion that she should lose three stone first. Long waiting lists at the local hospital caused them no anxiety. By going private they could demonstrate the family's superiority to all and sundry.

A blast of wintry air with the sour whiff of dog signalled that the garden tour was over. Mr Stalker had spent long periods of early life abroad in the colonial service and had learned on his occasional returns to stay out of his wife's way. He rather liked Elaine and recognised the sparkle that first had attracted his son. It seemed subdued at present; he hoped vaguely that all was well. Of course there would be strains with Elaine's new job, and Mike was pushing for promotion too. Couldn't be easy for either of them, especially for her: as an only son and younger child, Mike had been rather spoiled. Mr Stalker had known absolute power, had ordered beatings and imprisonments and deaths in Africa. In his own home it suited him to be powerless and thus comfortingly without conscience or responsibility. If Elaine and Mike were having difficulties, if his wife spluttered out her disapproval of Elaine over the teacups after the family had left, he would grunt noncommittally. It was none of his business.

The hands of the clock on the mantelpiece crawled round as winter gloom seeped into the lounge. Paddy was banished to the kitchen, where he left large muddy pawprints and a smell of bad breath and rotting leaves. More food appeared, thin scones and grey tea; for next Christmas, Elaine sighed, she would buy them an electric kettle which switched itself off only *after* the water boiled. Under a pile of *Woman's Own* magazines Mrs Stalker's open chocolate box remained resolutely unoffered.

It was an enormous relief when at last the clock struck six, the earliest hour at which it would be polite to move. The journey back would take nearly three hours on winding roads. More presents were loaded in the boot, fewer this time, for Mrs Stalker preferred to give small envelopes with cheques and save herself the bother of considering the personal preferences of recipients. Elaine kept smiling as she roused Karen, gingerly patted Paddy while averting her face from his powerful breath, kissed the old man with as much genuine warmth as she could summon after seven hours in his wife's unrelenting company, offered a perfunctory peck to Mother and Christine, and headed with an aching need to escape into the car and away.

In the back Karen yawned, opened her envelope, nodded approvingly at her grandmother's cheque and quickly slid down into sleep. Classic FM filled the empty silence as Mike drove. Elaine wished to God she could find some way either of breaking down the family's coolness towards her or, failing that, of not seeing them at all. Visits like today's did not help either family relationships or her edgy nerves. Worst of all, she was beginning not to care: not to hate the miserable old bat as she had done for much of her married life, but simply not count Mrs Stalker and by extension the appalling Christine as real people at all. Indifference was a protection. It meant she felt no obligation to change, adapt or bend. The Stalkers' own hardness had shut her out for ever. She could simply ignore Mike's family while feeling a little sorry for old Mr Stalker. None of them could now elicit the warm friendly response that even her lowliest constituent could command.

She saw Mike glance in the mirror at Karen. The girl was slumped in her seatbelt, breathing deeply.

'You might have tried a little harder, Elaine.' His voice was low but full of suppressed anger.

Good job he could not read her thoughts. It was not worth a row, not after her self-discipline all afternoon. 'I'm sorry, Mike. It's just that I don't click with your mother. I don't know why. I have tried, but nothing I've ever done seems to satisfy her. I'm fond of your father, but he doesn't exactly assert himself, does he? And she seems to be getting worse. I've been part of her family for fifteen years. Can she still not accept me?'

Mike Stalker watched the road. It was beginning to rain, making visibility poor. 'She's getting old and that hip causes her a lot of pain, though she won't admit it. She's a very strong woman, Elaine, like you. I'll admit Christine can be a sourpuss, but she was like that even when I was a little boy.'

'Christine was probably always destined to be a dried-up old spinster. She should never have married – it's merely confirmed her unhappy view of life.' It did not seem appropriate to add, 'Not like us.'

Mike continued, self-justifying, half pleading: 'It's not as if we see such a lot of them.'

'That's not my fault. You could if you wanted.'

'Elaine, be realistic. I have a job to do.'

'So have I.'

No more was said. It was an unsatisfactory conversation and left ends trailing. Even if her fling with Roger Dickson was nothing more than a bit of fun, a friendship at work, it seemed to be affecting the way she responded to her husband. By contrast with Roger he seemed dull and one-dimensional. It took longer when she and Mike were together to re-establish worthwhile contact, to find again the private gentle words of married people, that way of signalling affection which leads to intimacy. His willingness to put up with his family and to defend them and his insistence that filial duty overrode other considerations – including his responsibility to her – seemed to her more a weakness than a strength.

That night, as rain sleeted down and rattled the windows, she and Mike slept back-to-back, not touching. She lay awake for a long while, and wished defiantly that she were in Roger's bed instead.

By the evening of Christmas Day it was clear that this would be the worst Christmas they would ever spend together. She overslept and woke with a headache. The turkey had taken so long to defrost that it was not cooked till after three o'clock. Both Mike and Karen were so ravenous by noon that they demolished half a loaf of bread and destroyed their appetites. Mike opened a bottle of Clos de L'Echo 1991 red wine and declared it too young; but that did not stop him drinking most of it and falling asleep in front of the Queen's Christmas broadcast. Karen played records in her bedroom all morning, then commandeered the telephone for long calls to friends. In clearing the kitchen table of its usual layers of papers and junk in order to lay for lunch, Elaine knocked her pocket dictating machine on to the tiled floor and smashed it. A pretty crystal bowl full of paperclips, a wedding present, had followed soon after. She consoled herself with a large glass of sherry, and then another.

By the time the food appeared it was good but unappreciated. No one wanted Christmas pudding and not for the first time Elaine wondered if the rest of the nation like herself bought it as a talisman and eventually dumped it cold and uneaten in the bin. The Belgian chocolates Mike had brought her were prettily wrapped but she ate too many and felt slightly sick.

Then the pretence disintegrated with a vengeance. Karen announced that a friend would be picking her up at five to go out; Mike said he would not be needing supper and would spend an hour or two at the pub; and that left Elaine alone, sitting marooned and slightly drunk at the bedecked table still littered with substantial remains, picking at an unwanted tangerine, wondering what was on television and slowly starting to cry.

It had to be possible to be a good mother and wife and good at her job too. *It had to be possible.* Lots of other people managed it. Margaret Thatcher had been appointed to the Cabinet when her children were the same age as Karen, and she had had twins. Astonished civil servants still

127

told the story that at five o'clock one afternoon she had dashed out of a meeting to go and buy bacon for Denis Thatcher's tea. It must be easier now. Prejudice against women had been much greater in those days, and Mike was not the sort of chap to demand dinner on the table at set hours. Indeed, given today's performance maybe he did not want dinner cooked by her at all. Enough: next year she would book them all in at the Dog and Partridge Special Christmas Grill and Carvery instead.

The phone rang and made her jump. She wiped her nose, drained her glass and reached for the handset.

It was Roger.

'Hello, Mrs Stalker. A very Merry Christmas to you and yours!'

'Oh, put a sock in it. I can do without Christmas and all that false merriment.' She noted, her spirits rising, that he sounded a little merry himself. There was childish laughter in the background. 'To what do I owe the pleasure?'

'Nothing in particular. I merely longed to hear your wonderful voice. Yes, there is something. You're having some of my people over to your house tomorrow, isn't that right? I wanted to thank you. You'll meet my agent, Tom Sparrow. Be nice to him – he doesn't approve of women MPs, other than the Blessed Margaret, but if he did he'd quite approve of you. As I do. I've told him. Hope it all goes well . . . Bye.'

Abruptly he rang off, as if someone had interrupted him. It was fortunate Mike was not there to ask who was calling her on Christmas Day. What he did not know would not hurt him. She shook her befuddled head, collected the dirty plates and with a heavy sigh headed back into the kitchen.

Tom Sparrow stood at the door of the big airy study which Elaine had converted into a buffet, noted the beautifully decorated table groaning under the food and nodded in appreciation. He was a tall, upright man in his mid-fifties, grey-haired and moustached with sharp eyes and a military bearing. Tom had so enjoyed National Service that he had signed up and completed twenty-two years in the British Army, rising through the ranks of the Royal Fusiliers to warrant officer. Eventually an old cartilage injury had put an end to his modest career. Thus in early middle age, armed with a substantial army pension and with no ties, he had been looking for a job. Sparrow had always used his service vote, though he was scrupulous not to inquire too closely into the intricacies of policy affecting wherever he happened to be serving, in case it reduced his effectiveness as a soldier. While mooching around testing the employment market he attended a rally addressed by Opposition Leader Margaret Thatcher and was hooked. On asking how he might help ensure her victory he was directed to North-West Warwickshire, then a key marginal seat close to his home. The election set every bone in his body tingling, even though the seat was retained by Labour. He knew he had found his *métier*, with its extraordinary combination of teamwork and leadership, hard slog and downright cunning. As soon as possible he trained as an agent and was appointed to the post, just as the Boundary Commission changed the boundaries in their favour and Roger Dickson was adopted.

Elaine slapped the last hot quiche down on the table, smiled sweetly at Tom, took off her pinny with a flourish, strode into the crowded main room and clapped her hands for attention.

'Ladies and gentlemen! First of all, Mike and I would like to welcome you all to our home, and particularly those who have come a long way, as you did nine months ago to ensure we won this seat. You will be delighted to hear there's no charge today' – muffled cheers from long-suffering party workers who were accustomed to dipping endlessly into pockets for the cause – 'no raffle' ('Hooray!') 'and no speeches' ('Hear, hear!'). 'I just want you to enjoy yourselves, and thank you all very much. Lunch is now served.'

It was graciously done. She stood to one side and ushered her guests in, accepting their compliments with satisfaction. Mike was at the bar unpopping sparkling Saumur, a respectable substitute for champagne. British Airways had phoned that morning and rostered him to fly the following day in place of a sick colleague; he had not seemed devastated as he told her. Karen was wearing black tights and a black velvet miniskirt she had bought in a sale, too short in her father's view, her long legs seeming to start from her ears. The child was already taller than her mother. With a start Elaine realised that the girl was turning into a woman. She felt almost panicky – that should not happen before she had talked to her more, warned her about the pitfalls of a world so cruel to women and yet so full of opportunities. Not today – there was no time today: it would have to wait.

'We're grateful to you for your help.' Mindful of Roger's warning, Elaine spoke formally to Sparrow, whose bearing and demeanour did not invite informality. He bowed slightly, though she half expected him to come to attention and salute.

'Did you do all this yourself?'

'More or less!' Elaine laughed. Why, she had taken pride in doing all this herself, apart from the booze, which was Mike's fiefdom. 'Sainsbury's provided the cold pies, specially ordered last week and collected first thing this morning. Everything else is mine own fair hand, though the secret is to get the maximum result out of the minimum effort. Just like politics.' She gave him a conspiratorial grin: the look which had so captivated Roger.

129

Dickson had mentioned Mrs Stalker more than once. Sparrow was a man of the world and had been in politics long enough to know that anything was possible. He examined the lady with professional interest, hoping she was not setting her cap at his MP. That would lead only to trouble.

The event was a great success and more than made up for the unmitigated disaster of Christmas Day which Elaine put resolutely behind her. Four women insisted on staying behind to help clear up and filled the kitchen with bustle and companionship. By the time all the spare Stilton had been cut into chunks and given away, butter restored to the fridge, the remaining trifle guzzled and the empties removed to the garage her house was looking tidier than for ages and she was feeling a lot happier. She kissed Mike goodbye and waved him off without a twinge.

When the phone rang with Roger once more on the other end she was vastly more cheerful and composed. A slight buzz suggested he might be using his car phone.

'You sounded so blue yesterday. Did I catch you at a bad time?'

'Ummm, yes; I don't think I am going to succeed at my ambition of being a combination of Sheila Kitzinger and Eve Pollard.'

'What?'

'Earth mother and career girl. I think I'm better at the latter. I seem to tackle work with more enthusiasm and more . . . talent; I'm better at my job than most people, but pretty mediocre in the household stakes. Any advice?'

'Sounds exactly like me and most of your male colleagues. We all face precisely the same problem, yet most men don't trouble themselves over it.' Roger was reassuring. 'Why do women want to be good at everything? From what I hear, however, you've excellent domestic skills. I just spoke to Tom Sparrow and he's singing your praises.'

They chatted for a bit. The international news was gloomy, the recess might be cut short. She sensed that he was building up to something and cut in, making the offer herself.

'Roger? It's lovely talking to you but we aren't secure on the car phone. If you had a few minutes perhaps you could pop over. Mike is on duty and Karen is at a disco with friends. She was afraid I'd make her clear up so she skedaddled sharpish after the party this afternoon and may stay over. Could you come?'

She had read his mind correctly, for he was parked on the brow of a hill barely a mile away and had been watching her house in the wintry sunlight even as he dialled her number. Ten minutes later his car was neatly in Mike Stalker's place in the garage with the door closed. Ten minutes after that he was firmly in Mike Stalker's bed, the glass of

French fizzy on the bedside table warm and flat and forgotten as he made love, slowly and with the greatest pleasure, to Mike Stalker's wife.

Elaine had missed him and told him so. Both had spent too long with their families, getting bored and fidgety, aching for serious insider conversation. Now they indulged, talking through the poor state of the economy, the atrocious performance of key Cabinet figures, the perils of steering the government's programme through the Commons. All around them husbands and wives were falling out after the holiday, stomping off and heading for the solicitor's, for more couples break up at Christmas after concentrated exposure to failed relationships than at any other time of year.

He lay at last on his back, tucked her head on to his shoulder and pulled the duvet over them both. The evening was quiet.

'Why are we like this, Roger? Why are we so driven by our outside lives, so that we can't function for five minutes without them? There are times when I can't imagine how I would live without my work. Honestly, I love my family, and in particular dread the day when Karen will have grown up and left. I'm not sure how well Mike and I would get on without her to cement us together. I also adore being an MP and I want to do it well and be recognised as competent – and be promoted. At times that's a much more powerful pull. I'm beginning to feel torn in two.'

'You will be promoted!' That was what she wanted to hear. Roger eased his arm, which was going numb. 'You just have to be patient, that's all. Haven't I told you a dozen times?'

'I get scared my ambition will damage my family. Perhaps it already has: I'm less patient with them, especially my ghastly in-laws. Once I used to make an effort but on Christmas Eve I sat there seething the whole time we were at their house. If I could find some way of never going there again I would – isn't that awful? Or perhaps it's because I meet so many lovely people these days that my relations seem even worse by comparison.'

He hugged her silently. It was wiser to say nothing. Being in love with his job was taken for granted, by both himself and society generally – and certainly by his spouse. He could well fathom that for a woman it might be a lot trickier. If Elaine were to add to her obsession with politics a substantial affection for another man, her marriage might prove fragile indeed. He hoped firmly that that was not the case. An affair was one thing; a love match something else. One might withdraw easily if regretfully from a sophisticated casual encounter. Love, on the other hand, involved obligation. Both had enough obligations already to last a lifetime.

Dickson rolled over and turned on the bedside light. Regretfully he

131

checked his watch then started to extricate himself from the tousled, inviting bed.

'I said I was visiting a constituent with an emergency flooding problem,' he explained gently. 'I am expected back. Your own daughter may return at any time, or your absent husband's plane may be cancelled. Much as I adore you and enjoy your inestimable company, getting caught *in flagrante delicto* is not part of the game plan – for you or for me.'

She watched him appraisingly as he dressed.

'I think I'm falling in love with you,' she said quietly.

He sat on the bed with his back to her, pulling on socks and shoes, returning to normal. She could not see his face, flushed and working as he struggled to regain control. A soft, expectant silence filled the warm room. It was a long time before he spoke.

'Don't, Elaine. It isn't wise. Now I really must go.'

He bent and kissed her on the mouth, resisting her entwining arms almost roughly. Soon he had left her. She heard him reverse his car into the path, grind his gears uncharacteristically and then roar away. She rolled over and contentedly buried her face in the pillow still warm from his head, a stray precious Dickson silver hair tickling her cheek. The bed smelled of him, of his soap, his sweat. She would have to change the sheets.

But not yet.

CHAPTER NINE

Diane Hardy looked up from her cluttered desk and spoke severely. 'It would be *very* helpful if we could sort out your diary. You've got thirty-two unanswered invitations to speak next month. Even if you attempted one each day you'd have some left over. There's a Chief Inspector Collis needs half an hour: I think he's Special Branch. Probably routine – they talk to all the new MPs. The BBC wants you for *Any Questions* again; you were quite a hit last time and it looks as if you're going to be a regular. Central TV are after you for *Celebrity Squares*. No? I warn you, they don't give up easily. Or there's *Central Weekend Live* this Friday night for your views on grunge fashion – and they'd like you to model some.'

Elaine was staring out of the window. Her tiny office, perched high in Commons Court building, gave out on to a grimy inner courtyard of the Palace of Westminster. Opposite on three floors were similar offices into some of which she could see clearly. A number were far more of a mess than her own, with piles of yellowing papers all over desks, floor and chairs. At least in hers movement was possible, if difficult. Diane was ruthless in filing the minimum and throwing out everything else.

She motioned her secretary to come and look. Down a floor and to the left Freddie Ferriman's office was visible. He was sitting talking to a pretty, long-legged girl with a notebook on her lap who might have been a researcher. Unaware that he was being observed he was sliding his hand up her skirt.

'Dirty old bastard,' grunted Diane. 'It's only ten o'clock in the morning.'

Elaine was unsure how to react. Perhaps the girl was a willing partner, had sought a job at the Commons hoping to land herself a glamorous MP as a lover or potential husband. In that case she was barking up the wrong tree with Freddie, who was not known for commitment to any woman other than the unsuspecting Mrs Ferriman. It was, however, depressing to be obliged to be pleasant to men who saw women purely as sex objects: worse, it was demoralising. A more introspective person than Elaine, who was inclined to scoff at other people's fears, might have recognised that it was thoroughly intimidating.

Diane took a different view, fearing the pressure on young female staff whose continued employment might depend on their co-operation. It had been put that way to her – once. By comparison, working for Elaine Stalker was a treat. But if that kind of pressure were to be combined with a little charm, excitement and skill – and neither watcher doubted Freddie could manage all those when he was so minded – then the girl was in no position to argue. Only the very brave would scream blue murder. If she was an American, as many of the Commons researchers were, she might find herself on the next plane back to Houston in disgrace. Better to smile sweetly, run the tongue over the teeth in a frozen smile and hitch up the skirt.

Elaine and Diane argued amicably for several minutes over the scene. Despising such characters, calling them names and dismissing them, as Diane could readily do, was not enough for Elaine. There were too darned many like that. Individually such men were insignificant. Collectively there were enough to preserve the intensely masculine aura of the House of Commons. She felt a compulsion to try and change matters, somehow. The notion that women had specific roles in life and that serving men was the most important of these was so outdated. Millions of men no longer reacted that way. Yet in the overwhelmingly male Commons it was men like Ferriman whose style predominated, and who might be the last to disappear from the place, some time in the next century – if ever.

Across the way Ferriman drew the curtains. The two women bent their heads and concentrated on the post. Among the letters were several from Northern Ireland, including a request from Unionist MP Sir James Kilfedder, an incorrigibly good-natured man who usually sat and voted with the government, that she might like to meet his supporters on her next visit. A couple of days were duly set aside for a trip to Belfast.

'Marcus Carey has been on again. He's back in England next week and asks if he can take you for lunch. He wants your advice.'

Elaine pulled a face. 'I don't know why he keeps asking me. He has far more friends in high places than I have.'

'I suspect you're one of the few people who's genuinely nice to him,' Diane suggested quietly. 'The rest ignore him, don't return his calls or, worse, patronise him.'

'Book a restaurant near my flat and tell him we're going Dutch. OK?'

Peter Manley combed his blond hair nervously, tucked the *Evening Standard* under his arm, jumped down from the red 77 bus and stood gazing with open mouth at Big Ben. He had never been this close before. The place was so startling, so dramatic, so *big*. It looked just as it did on television, yet far more awesome.

Gerry Keown was on duty and watching him. Peter was confident he would pass muster in his grey suit and polished shoes. A haircut that morning irritated his neck and he ran a finger around his collar. He hoped to be taken for a City dealer, like those red-braced fanatics frantically making money and boasting about it on the telly, but with the self-deprecating manner which always worked so well. As a result he resembled the stylish, impecunious young men who work as political assistants for all parties, blandly handsome and falsely modest. The long queues waiting for Prime Minister's Question Time had dispersed. Peter had deemed it prudent to come when the rush was over. Like shoplifting it was easier to escape attention at the end of the day.

A long way from Swindon. The memory made him wince. Still, it was in Swindon, in the Mayblossom home run by the local council, that Peter had first learned the importance of appearance. It was not their fault that he and his sister had been brought into care when their mother collapsed for the umpteenth time with serious psychotic illness. Dad – or the man who had most recently answered to 'Dad' – had long since disappeared. Mum would turn up on Wednesdays doped to the eyeballs and leaning heavily on the arms of sturdy psychiatric nurses who stood by watchfully. Later she came to Mayblossom by herself, a mass of shawls and boots and clanking jewellery, clutching bags of presents bought with money provided by the latest lover, and weep over her embarrassed children. Gradually, as her spells in hospital diminished, so did her visits, until one day Peter realised that she had not been for over a year and that it was getting difficult to remember her face. Aged twelve, he was growing from a pretty child to a delicately fine-looking boy. He knew because the warden Jack Hudd had told him so.

At first it was just a bit of touching, not unpleasant or frightening at all, in exchange for sweets or an illicit cigarette. He grew three inches that year and supposed that the attention might even be doing him good: it made a change from the usual casual neglect. When at last he was almost as tall as Jack Hudd, he tasted his first wine one Saturday night in Hudd's room and liked the woozy happy feeling very much. Cautiously he responded to the man's hesitant approaches. He slid his own hand in a caress over Jack Hudd's bald head, and bent down and kissed him. Curious as to what Jack was up to, Peter stood passively as buttons were undone and his shirt was pulled slowly off, then the rest of his clothes, all folded in a neat pile, as if to compensate for the abnormality to come. The room was warm and he did not shiver. It hurt a bit, then, even though Jack apologised and cuddled him afterwards, but it was the first of many times.

135

Peter knew the other children mocked Hudd behind his back but responding to Jack's need and making someone else happy did not seem to him so dreadful, and there was no duress. In the absence of any other love, why not? The girls around him were all dirty tarts with too much lipstick and cheap perfume, reminding him of his mother. Girls might tease him if he wasn't very good at it. Jack would never laugh at him, just talk dreamily while the boy half listened and fought off sleep. It wasn't that he couldn't imagine sex with girls: he could imagine it all right, having heard it all too often grinding away through his mother's bedroom walls with drunken laughter and worse, bangings and shouts and screams, and black eyes and swollen faces in the morning. That was not, never would be, his way. That he was being corrupted and engaged in immoral or illegal activity did not cross his mind. A clear distinction between right and wrong had never been offered to Peter through either pre-scription or example. Like most of the nation, he reckoned, if he bothered to think about it, that if he enjoyed something and hurt no one it couldn't be that bad. Not wicked, like killing was wicked. Not anti-social like thieving. It was enough that somebody treated him with gentleness.

All went well until he was fifteen, at which point Hudd was promoted to another home out of the area. The new warden was a cretin who accepted as gospel truth all the children's lies about being allowed out at night. Before long Peter discovered that Jack Hudd was not the only man who found him attractive. Hudd had given him small sums of money – not enough to arouse notice or jealousy – without comment or explanation, until it seemed normal. Yet the first time a casual lover had stuffed a twenty-pound note in Peter's pocket he had been confused and scared, not sure he dare try to cash it. Swindon led to Soho, and thence to Belgium and the Netherlands. The name 'Manley' wasn't his own; but it had a fine ring to it. He'd seen it on a letter from the council once, and liked it.

Quickly Peter came to specialise in older men whose agonised fumblings betrayed a terrible guilt. Often they were married, or had been. Even with Holland's liberal laws the stigma still existed. Lacking any sense of shame, Peter was able to help. While relieving their desperate need, he was gentle and reassuring. Several in Amsterdam had become regulars. He was quite proud of his ability to earn a good living providing a necessary service.

The visit to London was nothing out of the ordinary. As usual he touched base with his sister and dossed down in her cramped boxroom in Stoke Newington, his head jammed against unpacked suitcases and boxes. Since her second marriage and acquisition of teenage step-children, his presence, though welcome, was no longer particularly

convenient. Either he would have to find somewhere more comfortable, preferably conducive to work, or by Friday he would be back on
the plane to Amsterdam. That was why he had bought the newspaper's
first edition halfway through the morning. Finding little to tempt him
among the short-term lets, he had flicked over the pages and come
across a familiar face.

'Stephen', wasn't it? He opened the newspaper and looked again.
False names were nothing new in his game but he was reasonably sure
that the florid features smiling back at him were the same. A quick
check in the public library had revealed the man's full name, title and
constituency, Milton and Hambridge. The map at the back of the
reference book showed it was not so far from where he grew up. There
was no harm in trying.

A tall, black-haired policeman bent and listened to Peter's request,
then pointed him towards St Stephen's entrance. The boy chuckled as
he heard the name: so that's where 'Stephen' came from. Up three
steps, he explained himself once again: 'I've come to see my MP.'
Already he had picked up the jargon: 'I'm going to put in a green card
for him.'

A short flight of stone stairs led to the south end of Westminster Hall
under an enormous stained-glass window. Sunlight filtered obliquely
down, turning the dun-painted security hut gold and red and blue,
improbable hues blending and shifting as clouds moved across the
source of light.

Peter was carrying no baggage so his progress through the screening
system was swift. Now he was in Central Lobby. The sheer scale of it
took his breath away, as indeed it was designed to do. It was like a great
cathedral, a place of worship of Victorian self-confidence, but far busier
and noisier than any church. All around people were waiting, talking,
voices echoing, or sitting on nearby green benches clutching bags and
papers and petitions. A well-dressed group were filling in gallery passes.
One tubby MP was expansively bidding farewell to a constituent – or
was it a client? – shaking hands effusively and propelling him towards
the exit. Several women sporting large lapel badges for some minority
cause were waiting disconsolately. Police guarded the entrance to the
House of Lords to the right. To the left, surrounded by supplicants,
stood a wooden upright desk. Peter approached, took a deep breath and
asked to see Sir Nigel Boswood MP.

A green card was handed to him to fill in. All that is required is the
name of the MP summoned, the name and address of the summoner, a
brief purpose for the visit and the time. No identities are checked, no
references required. Parliament has repeatedly reaffirmed the ancient
liberties of the people to badger their MPs any time the House is sitting.
It was an easy matter for Peter to think up an address in Hambridge. He

hesitated about the reason for the visit, then wrote 'Personal – Amsterdam' underneath.

The card was taken from him and shunted into the inner sanctum of Members' Lobby a few yards away, to the noticeboard where phone messages were also received. It was from there a few moments later that Sir Nigel Boswood retrieved it himself, on his way to the tea room.

For a minute Nigel was nonplussed. The word 'Amsterdam' reminded him he had been meaning to book a flight for Bank Holiday weekend. His brain was reluctant to make the connection between the city and anybody he knew. Perhaps this constituent had business there and needed advice. There were a few minutes to spare. He hurried into Central Lobby, showed the summons and waited impatiently, tweaking his bow-tie as the police officer on duty called out the name.

Peter rose from a side bench and moved smiling towards him, hand held out in greeting.

'Hello, Sir Nigel! Do you remember me?'

Nigel felt the blood drain from his face.

It all came back in a great mixed-up unhappy rush. He grabbed the boy's arm, gritting his teeth in a welcoming smile, and pulled him into the nearby corridor where narrow green benches line the walls. The two sat, knees nearly touching.

'What are you doing here?' Nigel tried to remove all menace or alarm from his voice. This was no private place, only marginally less public than Central Lobby. The corridor was ideal for giving a nervous constituent the illusion of concerned intimacy, but that was all. They could easily be overheard. Their body language might betray them, as might snatches of conversation to anyone passing.

'I saw your picture in the paper, Stephen, and I only wanted to say hello now I'm back in London.' The boy piled on the charm but ensured no touching. The use of 'Stephen' served as reminder and warning – and offer. He turned his head slightly like an enquiring puppy, looking at the older man with clear blue eyes.

'Are you here for long?' Nigel was controlling himself with difficulty. The boy was so *beautiful*: so clean, tidy and fresh. He had just had a haircut, almost too short, giving him a fragile, vulnerable air. The image of razors and sharp steel scissors on Peter's blemish-free flesh, the danger of drawing blood from that tanned neck, made Nigel gag and swallow hard.

The boy smiled. He could guess the tumult in Nigel's brain. 'No, not long. I came to see my sister, but there's no room in her house for me. Then I saw your picture and wondered if you could help, or at least advise me. Is there anywhere central I could stay? So many of the hotels round here are flop-joints, really horrid. I'm looking for somewhere quiet and respectable.'

He lisped slightly on 'horrid', just a little, like a choirboy, reinforcing the impression of childish innocence.

Nigel felt helpless. 'There are lots of hotels – Royal Horseguards, St Ermin's in Caxton Street . . .' His voice trailed off into a mumble, as he realised he only knew expensive places.

Peter said nothing but was gazing at him quietly, head on one side.

'Do you need money?' It was a challenge really, a way of pushing the boy away, of identifying his true purpose. A blackmailer, if that was his intention, would always ask for money. At that point, even risking a scene, Nigel would rise with dignity and ask the boy to leave. Lots of people were led away from Central Lobby yelling accusations and blasphemies; since the rules allowed anybody to enter to summon an MP, even loonies, it happened all the time. There would be sympathy from the police and head-shaking from the crowd. The perpetrator would be dumped unceremoniously on the pavement, and the incident forgotten.

'Oh, Stephen, you must know me better than that.' Peter looked reproachful, his eyes huge in the gloomy light. Nigel's heart turned over. 'I have enough money. That's not the problem. I need somewhere to stay for a few days, that's all. Somewhere quiet, private and clean. Where I'll be safe – do you know what I mean? London can be unpleasant for a young man trying to find a place to stay. There are young boys sleeping in doorways all the way along Victoria Street. It's awful at the moment.'

Nigel Boswood shuddered. Peter pressed home his advantage. 'The truth is, Stephen, I'm a little scared. I don't really know my way around London. Can you help me?'

A strangled noise came from Sir Nigel Boswood's throat. He sat tense, hands clasped tightly together as if he did not trust them unleashed, arms thrust between his knees. For a moment he did not speak but stared hard at the floor, trying to think. Orderly words of polite refusal would not come. Only necessity and hunger nagged, and fear of what might happen if he sent the boy away. If Peter had to sleep rough, or had to go to a hostel: with such a lovely face, the danger of attack by hard men tumbling him in the dark and stifling his cries was all too apparent. Nigel had only the most limited acquaintance with the shady world of London low life and had no desire to know more, but homosexual rape he could readily visualise. He groaned again, cleared his throat, pulled out a large handkerchief and wiped his mouth.

This would never do. He made up his mind and spoke quickly, to keep ahead of the niggling voice of common sense. 'Look, I don't know if this is any good to you, but there's a basement in my house in Ebury Street which is going begging at the moment. It's fully furnished, central heating and all that. I have to be very careful who I allow in there –

security, you know. But if you only want it for a couple of days I can't see any harm in it. We certainly don't want you on the streets, do we?'

Peter smiled his broadest, most delightful smile and bounced up and down like a happy infant. That would do very nicely indeed.

'That's wonderful!' he said quickly. 'When would it be convenient? I have to fetch a few things from my sister's but it won't take long.' Feigning concern, he added: 'You must let me pay you. Rent, I mean. I can afford it. I don't want to take anything from you.'

A look of misery crossed Nigel's jowly face as the memory surfaced of the previous time money had changed hands with this boy. As with all his sexual adventures there was a terrible moment when anxiety and self-disgust soured the pleasure to come. Controlling himself with an effort he consulted his diary.

'There are no votes tonight so I plan to be home about nine. You can't get in before then. Here's the address.' Nigel wrote on the back of the green card and handed it back to the boy. 'Wait around till I'm safely inside and my car and driver have gone, then knock. That would be safest. Don't worry about rent – we can settle that when I see you. Will you be all right till then?'

The boy nodded, smiled with pleasure and rose to leave. The gentlemanly suit hung well on those young shoulders; he looked like a male model. Nigel heaved himself to his own feet and formally shook hands. At last their eyes met.

'Thank you so much for coming,' Nigel said, a little loudly.

'Thank you for being so kind, sir.' Peter was unsure of the appropriate style for speaking to MPs and plumped for a similar mode of address to a wealthy customer in a gents' outfitters. It seemed to work. Nigel beamed and showed him back to the Lobby.

Sir Nigel Boswood watched as the boy headed off down St Stephen's Hall towards the street entrance, one hand in his pocket, lifting the flap of his jacket to reveal a neat flannelled posterior, swinging the slim hips just enough to make his sexual orientation unmistakable. Nigel allowed himself a moment of dismal longing. It had been a long stretch since Amsterdam.

It was like sitting in Rapunzel's tiny cell at the top of her tower and wondering how to get out. Alternatively, this could be a basement chamber, for there were no windows. The claustrophobic cubby-hole was in one of the oldest parts of the Palace, its mouldy walls lined with numbered black files and red manuals. Above were unusually large hooks hung with black leather jackets, belts, gloves, handcuffs and ancient weapons. Souvenirs of crime, mostly. Opposite her chair were charts of mugshots and a collection of curling photographs of a woman's dismembered body. The air was redolent of old sweat and fear. Under her chair the rug was sticky. Elaine was fascinated but apprehensive.

Chief Inspector Collis was grey-haired, clean-shaven and taciturn. He could sense the scared curiosity in the pretty woman sitting opposite. The room had been a police post since the days of the Bow Street Runners, when murder had been foul and the penalty death by hanging. Better, really, that she did not know too much about the blood-stained hammer nailed over the door, or who exactly was pinned up on the wall for him to remember. The reality of modern terrorist crime was far worse. His job was to protect the public, and VIPs like Elaine Stalker, from finding out from their own experience.

'I must impress on you, Mrs Stalker, the necessity of checking underneath your car. Keep a newspaper with you and put it on the ground before you turn a key in the lock; get down on your knees and have a thorough look. Don't be embarrassed about it – better sheepish than in smithereens. Next time you take it in for service, ask the garage if you can get in the pit underneath, and try to memorise what your car looks like from below. You're more likely then to spot something unfamiliar. If you do, don't touch it – and don't let anyone near it. Call us immediately.'

'Are we all targets? All MPs?' Elaine wanted to salvage something from this stony man in his horrific cavern.

'Yes, but some are more at risk than others. Members of the government, of course, especially the Home Secretary and Lord Chancellor. Judges, high-ups in the armed forces. Anyone that has anything to do with Northern Ireland. Now: have you got a proper alarm system at your home – one wired up to the local cop shop? I'll put the chaps in your area in touch with you. Your local Special Branch sergeant is a woman, you'll be pleased to hear. Whatever else you economise on, get the best system you can afford. You especially, Mrs Stalker. In the end, however, your best protection is common sense.'

She was troubled. 'Why me?'

The chief inspector sighed. They all said that, these arrogant MPs, making his job almost impossible. They all believed themselves protected with a cloak of invisibility inside which speeches and attacks on the IRA could be made with impunity.

'You're just a name on a list, Mrs Stalker.'

'Am I really on a list, or do you do this for everyone?' She had sensed he did not want to tell her too much.

'We do this for everyone – at least, all those who take it seriously and will listen . . . and, yes, I am afraid you are on a list. A real one. I have to tell you, Mrs Stalker, that your involvement with this backbench committee on Northern Ireland is putting you into a higher-risk

141

category. Everything you say is noted and gives offence somewhere, you know. We found your address on a piece of paper in the dustbin behind an IRA safe house in Winchester not long ago.

'Terrorists in Winchester?!'

'Certainly. Why not? Ideal place. These blokes – and there are women too – could be anywhere, even in this building. It's a good job Mr Gerry Adams never took his seat in the last Parliament – his mates could all have had passes to get in here, legit. Then there are sleepers. It's long-standing IRA practice to put sympathisers into sensitive jobs and leave them there, absolutely clean as a whistle and above suspicion, with exemplary records, for years, until the time comes. Cleaners in army barracks, porters in hospitals, waiters in clubs, that sort of thing. Very hard to discover unless we have a tip-off. The best approach is to take no chances whatsoever. The bastards make progress every time someone else is blown to kingdom come, and you, Mrs Stalker, have placed yourself in the firing line by your political involvement with the province.'

Elaine felt annoyed at the inference that she had been foolish, then calmed her flicker of temper. Whatever she might inadvertently have done, this policeman was on her side. He must have seen terrible things.

'Have you worked on this for a long time?' she asked, more gently. He looked weary.

'Me? Yes, about fourteen years. I was first on the scene down in the Commons car park when Airey Neave was blown up. He was still alive when we got to him, but we couldn't identify him from what was left of his face till we picked up some papers blowing around. You be careful, Mrs Stalker, you hear?'

That was enough. Collis rose and showed her the door, nodding curtly as she left. He sat down heavily again in his den and tried to wipe from his mind the memory of the mess they had made of the old war hero. It would not fade, even after all these years.

Elaine rested her head against the cold stone. No one had told her on the selection weekend that she must prepare for a life of caution, of looking over her shoulder and under her car, of looking askance at parcels with an Irish postmark, of poising her finger above the record button in case a sinister voice came over the telephone. Over a hundred people had been killed by the IRA on the mainland, most of them innocent civilians. Most, including dead children in Warrington and elsewhere, had no idea they were targets: yet she knew.

Slowly Elaine found her way down the stairs and out into daylight. The mysterious smell had permeated her hair and left her queasy. If it ever happened – if she woke to find a gun in her face, or if she crawled away having seen something underneath her car – she hoped she would react with bravery and dignity as well as cunning. With a whispered prayer to whatever deity had guarded her this far, she hoped never to find out.

Stephen – as Peter still thought of him – was late. Lounging under a street lamp, he had been waiting nearly half an hour, pretending to read the *Evening Standard*. Already he had been propositioned by two men in cars, and warned off by a transvestite prostitute in fishnet tights and a miniskirt. It had been hard not to laugh at the over-rouged cheeks and false eyelashes, even while offering nervous assurances that, seriously, he was waiting for a friend. He hoped Stephen – Nigel – had not played a dirty trick on him, given the wrong address perhaps. Time to call him Nigel now: no need to pretend any longer.

Peter Manley was not entirely sure what he wanted from this arrangement other than a comfortable bed and a soft touch in return for the usual. He had not been brought up to plan more than a few weeks ahead. His work so far had depended on fleeting contacts, perhaps repeated, certainly, but had anyone asked where he expected to be in a year's time he would have been genuinely hard put to answer. A lot depended on money. There was plenty in the bank now, dollars and guilders and marks, giving a feeling of security. His needs were meagre: no mortgage, no bank loans, no insurance, no dependants, no car. It suited him to acknowledge the role of his clients – let them pay, let them take him out, fetch him, send a car for him. Buy him clothes, gifts, a good watch, gold cufflinks. They could afford it. He had no time for freeloaders. Life was too short for love, and anyway it had never found him, so far. Such largesse did not get in the way of the relationship – rather the contrary. The clients felt marginally less anxious when asking for something in return, which not everyone else – perhaps no one else – could provide. It was a business arrangement involving value for money and payment for services rendered, nothing more, nothing less.

Peter was debating whether to head for a nearby pub when at last a sleek Jaguar slid to a halt on the other side of the street. A chauffeur in government-issue grey peaked cap got out and held the door open for Sir Nigel Boswood. Two red boxes were removed from the boot and deposited with their owner inside the lighted hall. Sir Nigel glanced briefly outside as the car pulled away, and shut the door. A light in a red shade went on in an upstairs room. Peter counted to fifty, crossed the road, mounted the whitewashed steps and rang the bell.

'Who is it?'

He spoke his name, quietly, and the door opened to let him in. Nigel had removed the bow-tie and jacket and pulled on a frayed cardigan missing two buttons. In the doorway, alone, he seemed a forlorn figure. In his own way Peter had been fond of Jack Hudd and in Nigel, despite the famous name and bonhomie, he recognised the same aching need. That made the man a sitting duck.

Inside the hall Peter put his bags down and stood expectantly. There was a smell of fresh wine on Nigel's breath. It had not taken long for him to uncork a bottle and gulp down a glass, for courage. Dutch courage.

One of them had to make the first move. Peter put his hand to Nigel's face and gently stroked the cheek, rough with an edge of evening stubble. The boy himself scarcely needed to shave, his skin luminous like fine china. Nigel placed his own big hand over the boy's and, moving it palm upwards to his mouth, kissed it slowly and repeatedly, smelling soap and the leather handle from the suitcase. The boy moved cool fingers to Nigel's throat, sliding under the shirt, and watched the older man's pleading gaze, blue eyes urging him to wait. There was plenty of time tonight. Then he raised his other arm and with a single movement entwined his fingers behind Nigel's neck and slowly pressed his firm young body into the old sweater and soft belly. He pulled Nigel towards him, whispering, until suddenly there it was: a full, passionate embrace, mouth to hot mouth, tongue to searching tongue . . .

Holding the boy in one arm Nigel leaned over, turned out the hall lamp and slipped the latch down on the front door. Pink light filtered down the staircase. Nigel indicated the direction. When he spoke the words came out hoarse and hungry: 'Up there.'

Peter nodded and moved to the foot of the stair, his slim silhouette outlined against the light. Then with confident grace he started to undress, there and then. Nigel stood rooted to the spot, sweating hard, compelled and frightened. The boy removed his clothes with concentrated solemnity, keeping his back turned, folded the garments neatly and laid them over the banisters. As he finished he took a step up and turned to face his host.

He was sporting a splendid erection, framed in fragile blond curls, hair which caught the pink light, like spun sugar, like candy-floss in the fairgrounds of his youth. Nigel cried out, a great cry of anguish and longing, as he realised for the first time that the boy was offering whatever he wanted – active or passive, male or female, above or below, oral or anal, or whatever fantasy he fancied: *anything*. He began to tug frantically at his own clothing, his breath coming in short gasps. The boy smiled ethereally and turned again, the light gleaming rose and gold on his shoulders and buttocks, an Adonis, a Persian boy to his Alexander. Slowly, slowly, each tread creaking its unheeded warning, the ghostly figure mounted the stairs.

And beckoned him to follow.

CHAPTER TEN

'Why, hello there! It's just great to meet you!'

Nobody but an American could sound so enthusiastic, so *thrilled* to make one's acquaintance, Andrew reflected drily as he shook hands with the Honourable Walter Shoesmith III, Ambassador of the United States of America to the Court of Her Britannic Majesty. The effusion might even be sincere. The ambassador was over middle height, loud and a little paunchy. His bald head glistened under the lamps in the tiled hallway of Winfield House, the official residence in Regent's Park, where he stood with his wife welcoming new Members of the British Parliament and other guests for a Fourth of July supper.

The ambassador's wife was also in her element. A small, florid woman in an orange silk dress and too much jewellery, Maud Shoesmith had given up her own career to support her husband and had pushed him relentlessly, hoping Walter might stand for the Senate as her father had done and maybe some day for the supreme post of the nation. She reckoned she'd have made a fine First Lady. But Walter Shoesmith had no taste whatever for the political front line, preferring to exercise an influence behind the scenes bolstered by hefty donations – with loyalty rewarded by his surprise appointment not long before. Maud promptly resolved that her husband should make the most of the job once held by President Kennedy's father. There was always the chance that the glamour and hobnobbing with the great might rub off on Walter IV, currently a lankier, pimplier version of his father.

Cradling a glass of Californian red wine, Andrew moved to one side. The main room was already half full. Freddie Ferriman was holding forth in his capacity as Secretary of the All-Party Parliamentary Group for North Atlantic Trade. That meant he could fly off to the USA or Canada whenever he fancied at the expense of the non-parliamentary affiliated members, mostly companies keen to promote trade with the USA. Freddie bartering with reluctant Congressmen could sometimes be very useful. What it cost the companies was buried in their accounts. All it cost Freddie was a bottle of duty-free perfume to keep Mrs

Ferriman happy; and sometimes her fares were paid too. Not a bad life.

Andrew used his height to crane over the room. It might be fun to do a little female watching in such a smartly dressed gathering: nothing serious, but his newly awoken awareness was an increasing and delightful distraction. A trim figure in a bold yellow outfit caught his eye. Elaine Stalker was in the middle of a crowd, blonde hair brushed back and secured with a spangled tortoiseshell comb, chatting merrily. Andrew wistfully envied her that sparkle which made her presence so magnetic. He grasped only too clearly why she did so well, particularly on television. She was a lively, even aggressive speaker – unusual in a woman – with occasional flashes of an originality which, try as he might, always escaped him. Her manipulative use of the vernacular, her Midlands accent and her body language helped make her points instantly understood. All so different from his own unbreakably county vowels and self-effacing dullness.

In such a gathering nobody is left alone long. A young woman staffer approached Andrew, unsure which of several new MPs he might be, asked his name, flashed a toothy smile and firmly steered him towards a suitable group, where a slim man with a wily clever face was listening politely as Freddie Ferriman, glass in hand, held forth on the British economy.

'I agree it's not entirely Germany's fault,' Freddie was saying sagely. 'But we went into the ERM too high against the Deutschmark. Our interest rates were tied to yours. And that knocked our businessmen sideways.'

His Excellency Baron Hermann von Richthofen, Ambassador of the Federal German Republic, bowed slightly. He had heard the argument many times before. The weakness of British business, its inability for years to sell more goods abroad than it purchased, was somebody else's fault, naturally. All that changed from time to time was the excuse.

'I think you may find we are all suffering as a result of the weakness of the US dollar,' he suggested, deftly creating a 'European' feel in the group. 'We too face cheaper imports from dollar areas including Taiwan and Korea. But in Germany we still face enormous problems following reunification.'

Another voice chimed in. Freddie received support from Keith Quin, the stocky little Labour MP for Manchester Canalside. Quin was a bit out of his depth. Despite that, he would issue a press release the following morning based on what he told both Richthofen and Shoesmith, if the latter would ever stop shaking hands long enough to be buttonholed.

'I always said the government should never have joined the ERM in the first place. I didn't agree with it at the time. Pity our government has made such a hash of things since.'

Quin pronounced it 'guvvermun' and repeated the word like a mantra.

Andrew decided to join in. 'The sterling crisis was forced on us. Yet every time the British have a choice between modernising industry and debasing their currency, people like you, Keith, prefer the latter.'

The German Ambassador smiled indulgently. When he was a student after the war, one pound sterling bought nearly 12 marks. That morning the rate had been less than 2.50 and falling. He assessed the group. Quin had been a college lecturer in sociology; Freddie had studied classics in a desultory way at Oxford and had scraped a third; Muncastle had read philosophy and politics. All had struggled and failed with maths; none had ever wrestled with economics. This was the legacy of imperial complacency. It was a fair bet that none of the Englishmen could tell a catalytic condenser from a can of Coke, in a nation which still depended heavily on quality engineering for its economic well-being. No wonder the country was full of Japanese.

Walter Shoesmith, face shining, finished greeting latecomers and clapped his hands to announce supper. With the help of the toothy staffer, Andrew found himself seated American-style, alternating male and female, round a table of ten. Ferriman was on the opposite side and gave an encouraging wave. To Andrew's right sat a pretty Chinese woman; her husband next; then Elaine Stalker, still chatting animatedly. He wondered if she ever stopped – it must annoy her husband sometimes. At least Tessa was quiet. Perhaps that was why Mr Stalker was seldom in attendance.

The chair on his left was empty and he looked around with curiosity; then peeped at the name card. Ms Jamieson, it said. The name rang a loud bell and his heart jumped as he pictured the woman journalist on the Commons terrace. He had never contacted her afterwards, though she had dropped the hint and called him once. The summer recess had intervened and three months later he was too busy, and emotionally still distracted by Tessa. With a jolt he realised it was almost a year since.

Miranda Jamieson: how splendid! His for the next hour, if she turned up. Quickly Andrew straightened his tie, checked the handkerchief in his breast pocket and wished he had worn aftershave. A little innocent dalliance with that lady might make the evening vastly more enjoyable.

'I'm Miranda Jamieson, hi.'

There she was: he scraped back his chair in welcome.

'Andrew Muncastle MP. We have met – do you remember? I was trying to recall which paper you work for, Miranda.'

What a striking woman. Deep red lipstick, and lots of it. Dark glossy hair lightly grazed her shoulders. His eyes strayed to her tanned breasts, which, he noticed, were heavily freckled. She wore a tight lacy black body-stocking and a black velvet skirt with a gold belt and a sequinned jacket. Her legs were bare. The overall effect was stunning.

'I'm with the *Globe*. Deputy editor, these days.' Miranda had noted the methodical nature of his rapid once-over. There was no harm in returning it; perhaps this time he would not run from her like a frightened rabbit. A year in Parliament might have matured him. An undistinguished grey suit, light-blue shirt, modestly flowered tie. Face clean-shaven, trim-jawed, clear blue eyes. Tall, not thin, not well built either; looked athletic – cricket, at a guess. Less forward than most of her escorts. More polite by half. Made her feel safe. Almost.

'I never know what to wear at events like this,' she confided, trying to blush. 'If you dress too upmarket the hostess gets annoyed; too casual and the other women guests who've taken a lot of trouble go spare. Difficult, isn't it?'

Miranda certainly outshone the other women in the vicinity and was the recipient of cold disapproval from the Chinese lady. Elaine was sufficiently self-confident and good-looking in her own right not to care. He was remembering now: Elaine had been cross with Roger Dickson that day, thinking Miranda was his girlfriend. Perhaps she was; they had all become a lot less innocent since those early days. To his acute embarrassment Andrew caught Elaine watching him. She winked conspiratorially as if wishing him luck, and returned to her own conversation.

'I think you look very nice, Miss Jamieson,' Andrew offered gravely. He raised his glass in salute and it was immediately refilled by an attentive waiter. He had always resisted attempts to tutor him in how to chat women up, recoiling instinctively from that game; now he wished he had taken more notice.

She threw back her head and chortled. 'My, you sound just like the Prime Minister. Is that style catching?'

He inclined his head. 'I'm a supporter of the Prime Minister, you know, so I think I'll take that as a compliment. I hope you'll accept my remark in the same way.'

Miranda considered his buttoned-up manner: it might be interesting to find out more. With a grin she acknowledged him. Immediately he had the sense of being admitted to a charmed circle.

Etiquette required that Andrew divide his time between the ladies on each side. It was easiest to allocate them one course each. So Miranda received Andrew's engrossed attention during a peppery clam chowder, which made him thirsty, while she chatted about seafood and argued about the chances of a woman ever becoming Prime Minister of Australia. To his right Mrs Lin also turned out to be more than merely decorative. Andrew felt almost deferential as he learned she was a Member of Hong Kong's Legislative Council, virtually an MP in her own right. Half flirting, half seriously pumping her for information and practising his new-found worldliness, he found the lady an engaging conversationalist through the tournedos, French-style in cooking but American in size, which quickly defeated her tiny appetite. Sandwiched between two beautiful, wordly-wise, non-European women, both so different to his wife, Andrew Muncastle was becoming deeply conscious of more than his lack of travel experience.

By the time an enormous slice of pumpkin pie arrived, Andrew had drunk several glasses of wine and was feeling full and happy and a little careless. Miranda Jamieson's powerful presence a foot away was making it hard to concentrate. Looking across the table to where Ferriman was equally deep in conversation with an attractive young American, Andrew suddenly glimpsed how and why so many colleagues played around. Miranda, Mrs Lin, that American junior diplomat opposite – all were graduates, all ambitious, all eager to please, to entertain, to learn, to make a big impression, on a man's level, in a man's world. Only briefly at university had he come across such a dazzling collection. He was reasonably sure it was not just the wine addling his brain. Had Tessa been here she would have commented sarcastically on the woman flaunting her body so blatantly. Had Tessa been there the talk would have turned to children and school holidays; but Tessa was not there and none of these women, he realised with a slight shock, had children or any comparable preoccupations. Miranda wasn't married, he had established that. Guiltily he caught himself wondering if she had a regular boyfriend. She had not mentioned Dickson at all, so probably he could be discounted. Some other journalist, probably: her world was as incestuous as his own.

Women without children were a different breed, especially if they were young and lovely and smart. Andrew hesitated, then considered why, and how. There were no distractions; no energy dissipated changing nappies, fetching to and from school, sewing on name-tapes, doling out pocket money and going without to save for school fees; no attendance at parents' evenings and prize-givings, no tearful examination days or post-mortems, no anxiety over chickenpox or whether that headache might be meningitis or if the kids were safe on their bikes. Such women had time to read serious newspapers and *The Economist* and *L'Express* and *Die Welt*, and good novels and the latest literary biography; time for the theatre and art galleries and cinema, and not only Walt Disney. Their bodies, too, were more under their control, with time and money to work out or have a massage or play tennis or go skiing – no sagging breasts or stretch marks, no caesarian scars; no miscarriages. Abortions, maybe, as the punishment for carelessness, but early abortions left no scars. Their money could be spent on themselves – no wisps of hair turning grey, no spreading girth, no

149

fingernails broken from weeding. Women without children – provided singleness was a matter of choice, not of anguish – looked and smelt and sounded different. To Andrew they did, at least. Most of all, if it were their intention, such women could make the man of their choice feel truly special.

It was time for coffee. The ambassador's guests had polished off several cases of Opus One from Robert Mondavi, king of the Napa wine industry, and the atmosphere was noisy and jolly. Among them Andrew was slowly losing his shyness. Clearly well in with at least two handsome women at his table, he was earning envious glances from other men nearby.

Andrew left Mrs Lin supporting her husband in heated discussion with Elaine, and turned his whole being over to Miranda. The wine had brought a soft pink flush to her skin. He could almost feel her body moving under her clothes. A renewed urge to touch her forced itself into his consciousness.

'You're young to be deputy editor of a big paper, aren't you?'

'Not really. I'm nearly twenty-nine. People get promoted fast in journalism and I'm almost ancient compared with some. How old are you? Forgive my asking, but had I known I was sitting next to you I'd have looked you up in *Who's Who*.'

Andrew offered up a prayer that he was not being made a fool of. 'I shall be thirty-three in September. I suppose our professions are exactly the opposite; in my job it doesn't do to be too young. You're regarded as a bit of a pipsqueak if you're aiming for Parliament before thirty. On the other hand, we mustn't leave it too late; trying to get a winnable seat past forty is doing it the hard way, while after fifty it's nearly impossible.'

Miranda found the self-effacing manner terribly English and appealing. 'That might explain why there are so few women in Parliament – taking time out to care for families means being older and at a disadvantage by the time they start, I guess.' Miranda had researched the subject, interviewing would-be women MPs from his party who were bitter at the many barriers.

'Part of the problem is that selection committees have a fixed idea of what an MP should be like,' said Andrew. 'Male, of course, preferably married, with the regulation two children. White Anglo-Saxon Protestant, if possible; blond and bland, I'm afraid. But as long as we're more successful than the Labour Party at the hustings there's no great pressure for change. I'd like to see more good female candidates coming forward – that's not flannel, I mean it – but it's said to be the women on selection committees who aren't keen. They and the voters – women voters too – persist in seeing it as a man's job. We're still some way from equality in this country.'

He was conscious that he laughed a little nervously. Chairs were being scraped back as guests began to leave the tables. The two of them stood up, suddenly, found themselves physically close, forced together by the tangle of chair-legs and tables. He almost put out his hand to guide her – Ferriman would not have hesitated – but drew back. Miranda was almost his own height. Her dark eyes were large, skilfully made up. If he kept his own gaze studiously away from her breasts it was difficult to avoid looking into those slightly mocking eyes. He felt uncomfortable and a little scared.

Miranda's response was robust. 'Don't apologise! Australia's far worse. At least here you do believe women should have every opportunity. Down under we've the original Neanderthal Man, and lots of 'em. Neither Les Patterson nor Crocodile Dundee is entirely fictitious – I know guys just like that. Makes it bloody hard. That's why I'm here.'

Walter and Maud Shoesmith moved tactfully back under the hall lamp. It would not do for the party to carry on too long as the ambassador was still expected to show his face at the embassy staff celebration. Coats were being collected; a line was forming to say goodbye. Andrew took a deep breath and turned to Miranda.

'How are you getting home?'

Ever the gentleman, she reflected, amused. Perhaps taking a taxi alone was not on the agenda tonight. She noted the implication that he wanted to be involved whatever method she chose. The main door was open, letting in a gentle breeze. It was a fine night.

'Do you have a car? No? That makes two of us. Anyway we'd get nicked for being over the limit. My God, your drink-driving laws are ferocious! Good thing, I guess. It's dry, so why not walk for a while through the park, past the mosque and the boating lake and come out down near Baker Street? Then we can catch a cab. How does that sound?'

Their conversation had lasted nearly two hours without flagging. She had a roguish, almost masculine style about her, swashbuckling, piratical; she didn't actually say, 'Coming?', but pulled the shimmering jacket around her shoulders and set off into the warm night, then waited a moment, looking back over her shoulder. Andrew scurried quickly after her. Nothing ventured, nothing gained. If Tessa wouldn't come to events like this, then she, not he, was to blame if he walked a lady home.

Miranda would have resented any description of herself as promiscuous. True, had she bothered to list all those men she had slept with, the numbers might have troubled her and left her wondering what risks she might thereby be running. But never so far had an encounter left any unpleasantness, for she was choosy and careful. The usual problem was that a man got too keen, but she had developed kindly ways of turning

151

passion into undying friendship, such that her amorous path was littered with devoted men who thought the world of her.

The men she was attracted to came from a variety of backgrounds, but were mostly strong-minded types with large bank balances and bigger egos. She was not interested in their money, or even in the power they wielded, though both put such men in a category with which she felt quite at home. Once, she had taken a fancy to a young garage mechanic but he had become quite besotted, almost impossible to deter; putting him off had been an unhappy business which had probably marred the poor lad for life. From then onwards Miranda restricted herself to charming successful men with limited emotions and some inkling of where to stop. Not one, however, had touched her heart. Secretly she wondered if anybody ever would, and whether, as she approached thirty, she would now recognise the great romance if it ever appeared.

Andrew matched her step for step. A lacklustre fight with his conscience had been abandoned between the second and third glass of wine, in the middle of an uproarious anecdote from Miranda on the goings-on in the upper echelons of the *Globe*. Briefly he consulted the oracle of his upbringing but found there nothing but encouragement. A little philandering was par for the course, provided it was kept private and upset nobody. The key was not to take it all too seriously; not to get involved with a close friend's wife; not to be a marriage wrecker. With Miranda there was no such impediment. Yet she was like no one he had ever met before. The learning curve felt like a roller-coaster, with his former dim self wringing its hands at the top, too terrified even to try, just as the new Andrew let go and started an exhilarating descent.

The two were deep in conversation as they walked down the Outer Circle road and past Clarence Terrace. The Regent's Park mosque loomed on their left, its gold dome resembling nothing so much as one of her breasts now hidden under the jacket. So to Baker Street Tube station. Miranda had not really meant to walk far but the air refreshed her and helped clear her head. She started to think hard about what she intended to do with the man now talking animatedly by her side.

It did not seem such a foolish idea, once they arrived at the brightly lit station, to take the Tube the rest of the way to Victoria instead of hunting for a taxi. Deep in the tunnels there was nobody to recognise them, no one to chide. Both, a little light-headed, felt like children let out of school. Sitting beside Miranda in the scruffy carriage surrounded by drunks on their way home, Andrew felt protective towards the woman at his side. Tentatively he put an arm behind her, across the back of the seat. Heads turned in their direction: a pair of toffs after a party, no doubt. Miranda wriggled into the corner and smiled at him. His eyes strayed helplessly downwards. She pulled the jacket back over her cleavage, meeting his look with an embarrassed shrug and a grin.

'Can't help it, I woke up like this one day when I was thirteen. I do assure you it's all mine.'

He did not answer. He felt uncomfortable, not really knowing what to do, palms moist and pulse quickening. A wild kind of jubilation was already jumping in his brain.

At the Wilton Road exit from Victoria station Miranda paused and bought copies of the first editions off the newsstand, glancing quickly through them. 'Our first edition won't be out for at least an hour,' she confessed. 'We're lucky even to be mentioned with the other papers at the end of *Newsnight* each evening. Makes me wild.'

Then they stood uncertainly in the street, avoiding honking taxis and theatre crowds fresh from *Starlight Express* and *Buddy*. For several moments they chatted as traffic lights changed from red through amber to green and back again, twice. Still they did not move. The summer wind blew rubbish and bits of old newspaper down the road. Neither wanted to end the evening. His earnest lack of pushiness could be a handicap, Miranda noted. On the other hand, his English manners might be turned to good purpose. She gestured down the street.

'My flat is in Rochester Row. Now would you please be a real sport and walk me there?'

She had given him the key. Now he felt completely free. A decent chap could not ignore a girl's reasonable request: it would have been gross to refuse. Gravely he offered his arm. 'May I?'

Nobody talked like that in Australia. Miranda stood back in amazement for a split second, then slipped her arm through his.

This time they walked linked, matching stride to stride. Her hair streamed behind her in the breeze coming off the river. Her perfume seemed potent and sensual; his heart was beginning to thump.

Miranda's flat was on the first floor of an old brown house not far from Vincent Square, close to the *Globe* office in Vauxhall Bridge Road. Nothing was said as they climbed the carpetless stairs, only a giggle of shushing conspiracy as she tried to put her key in the lock. He put his hand on hers to steady it. Both were trembling slightly, their breath coming in short bursts.

Miranda stepped inside the doorway and stood with her back to the wall near the phone stand, looking sidelong at him. He closed the door quietly. As he searched for the light switch she shook her head; there was enough light coming in from street lamps beyond the window. Her hands were pressed flat against the wall, her back arched. He stood completely still, not daring to take hold of her, not yet. Now he could stare, openly, without pretence or subterfuge.

Slowly the brilliant jacket slipped from her shoulders. Sequins flashed at him – blue, silver, flame, lifting softly up and down as she breathed.

153

The jacket slithered to the floor. She nudged it to one side, kicked off her shoes and rubbed her bare toes slowly on the carpet.

With a shake, like a dog after swimming, she tossed her dark hair back; then ran her tongue over her lips, eyes crinkling with suppressed laughter. He moaned and passed a hand across his face, but smiled back at her, sharing her own pleasure in her body. Slowly first one shoulder, then the other emerged from the black lacy top. Andrew leaned against the closed door only two feet away, and watched, feeling himself harden and begin to throb, as first with her left hand and then her right she stripped the top down to her waist.

She was tanned all over – no swimsuit line. Her breasts were big, womanly globes, the aureoles large and dark, like an Italian's. Light from the street lamps fell softly on her so that the nipples stood out clearly; he watched them change from soft to firm, and clenched his fists to hold himself in check.

Those huge amused eyes did not leave his face, but the hand movement and the swelling in his trousers did not go unnoticed.

'Time enough. In a minute – don't be impatient.'

The gold belt and skirt joined the sequinned jacket and then the whole body-stocking. She seemed to be moving in slow motion, teasing him, mocking the involuntary crude nature of his own reactions. Then she stood before him in her panties, nothing but a wisp of stretch lace, still back to the wall.

'Enjoying watching me, Andrew?'

He nodded, stammering. 'God, you're beautiful! I feel I want – I want to eat you.'

'Then watch some more, if you like.'

She cupped her hands around her breasts, rolled them together, began making a rhythmic sigh, and took her nipples between finger and thumb. Cradling her breasts in her left arm she moved her right hand down across her navel and belly, then slipped her hand between her legs, making soft noises in her throat. She turned her face again, mouth open, towards Andrew.

He was sweating hard now and felt as if he would burst. Quickly he pulled off his own jacket, tie and shirt, fumbling with buttons and losing one in his haste. Her eyes were glazing over as he struggled to undo his trousers, but at the sight of his erect penis she called his name.

'Andrew . . . Andrew . . . come on . . .'

She reached over and handed him a condom from the drawer of the phone desk. His hands trembled violently as he tried to remember how to put it on. Never before had he wanted sex so desperately. He stepped forward and pressed her up against the wall for all the world as if she were a dockside whore. She pulled down the panties, stepped out of them and wrapped one leg round his waist. Her judgement was accurate

– she was just the right height to make it easy to perform standing up. Memories of trying to do this once behind the sheds at a school dance came back to Andrew fleetingly: it had not been a success and the girl had laughed at him. This glorious ripe woman was instead yelping with merry delight as he pushed himself into her, as if all lovemaking was supposed to be like this. She was not ashamed or fearful – she was with him, thrust for thrust, cry for cry, carrying him along. She was bloody well enjoying it!

In a moment he was done, gasping and panting, and she collapsed into his arms with great gurgles of pleasure, clutching him, embracing him, her kisses mixed with sweaty chortles.

'I guessed right, didn't I? Under that English exterior you're really something else, Andrew. That's the best – the biggest, I must tell you – that I've had in years.'

The compliment pleased him and he eased himself gingerly out. Tessa complained that he was too big and hurt her. At home he only tried once and was usually repulsed. Better put Tessa firmly out of his mind.

Miranda was weaving a different spell on him. To his own surprise he was far from finished. His trousers, concertinaed unceremoniously around his ankles, made him giggle helplessly. He removed the rest of his clothes, put them methodically but quickly over a chair, looked around and found the bedroom. Then, with an echo of his earlier courtesy, he led Miranda there by the hand.

The bed was in an old-fashioned style with brass rails, a white duvet and loads of frilled lacy pillows – startlingly feminine. This time he turned on the bedside lamp and satisfied his desire to look more closely at her, running his fingers all over her body, kissing her lightly. She leaned back and stretched luxuriously, curling her hands around the brass bars of the bedhead.

His sexual experience was extremely limited, if truth be told. In any case, his wife's cold disapproval of any foreplay or games implied his sexuality was somehow evil, a rough side of an otherwise docile character. To her it was original sin – *the* original sin – though for the life of him Andrew could not imagine what kind of cruel God could make something potentially so wonderful the same time sinful. He had tried everything he knew to get Tessa to relax, but after Barney was born she lost interest entirely. Although she denied it she probably had never liked sex and, now she had produced an heir, it appeared she no longer needed to pretend any more.

Most of the time his wife's lack of enthusiasm did not matter; sublimating sexual energy into his political career had proved useful and effective. Harold Macmillan, long cuckolded by Robert Boothby, had done exactly the same. Meanwhile here he was, naked on a lacy bed, having just removed a used condom from his still engorged penis, next

155

to a marvellous woman, her mouth and legs moist and slightly parted, an open invitation to have another go. And he was in no mood to stop.

Carefully he wrapped the condom in a tissue from a box under the lamp and disposed of it in a waste-bin. Miranda was watching him with an amused expression and he grinned back at her. She understood without words. From somewhere near the bed Miranda produced another condom, tore the wrapper off and held it in her lips so he had to kiss her to get it, wrestling her, arms held above her head on the soft bed. The thin rubber tasted of strawberries.

'Bloody hell! Have you got these secreted all over the flat?'

'Just about. Why – do you prefer to take the risk of catching something nasty from me?'

'Get through a lot, I imagine, a wonderful woman like you.'

'Don't ask, Andrew, if you don't want to know.'

She was right – it was none of his business. If Miranda did not take lovers on a whim he wouldn't be here now.

Now he took his time, playing with her, caressing her breasts with the pleasure of possession, kissing her long and deep. She was close to climax again when with a swift action he moved down the bed and bent her legs back and buried his face in her, thrusting his tongue as far as it would go, nibbling her with his teeth; no other woman had ever allowed him to do that. She was aching for him and cried out, caressing his head between her legs.

He glanced up through the sodden bush of her dark pubic hair, past her curved belly through the valley of her breasts to her throat. Her head was thrown back and she was panting hard, holding the bedstead, calling his name urgently. He could see everything glistening, ready. With his forefinger he traced tiny circles on her clitoris, then started rubbing her hard with his fingertips until her body began to arch and rock on the bed. If she liked to come almost to climax before he entered that was OK by him. He made a decision and continued with his fingers, pushing her back on the bed, holding her down on her belly with his free hand as she yelled an obscenity at him. He would show her who was master in the sexual act – maybe Tessa was right and he was in his deepest nature bestial. Maybe all men are, or are capable of so being. *He did not care.*

Suddenly she cried out as the orgasm shook her; its ferocity startled him. Quickly he moved his body up and thrust deep inside her. He lifted her legs as she protested and draped them over his shoulders, bending her almost in two. And – now, now, now – he came to his own climax, as she shuddered and writhed beneath him, until at last they both were uone.

She lay beside him trembling all over. Protectively he rolled an arm around her and cradled her head in the crook of his shoulder. All her bravado had gone. For a few minutes both drifted off into an exhausted doze.

When he opened his eyes she was looking at him, her expression troubled. 'I think I could fall for you, Andrew Muncastle,' she was saying. The words seemed to come from far away. 'You're too damned nice to be a good fuck and yet you're a prince at it. Where did you learn? Or would it be rude to ask?'

Andrew lazily drew circles on her thigh. 'Here,' he said softly. 'You're teaching me. You seem to . . . to like it so much.'

'You mean I make a helluva noise about it.'

Tessa put up with sex in a long-suffering silence. His natural caution began to reassert itself. 'As long as we don't wake the neighbours.'

'Pish! What if we do? They'll think some lucky bugger is having a good time.'

'And they'd be right.'

It was long after midnight. A sound at the door heralded the *Globe*'s first edition being pushed through the letterbox by a messenger boy. Andrew felt alarmed; this was no secret place, not really. This reminder of duty brought Miranda also back to her senses. She nudged Andrew in the direction of the bathroom. When he returned she was sitting in a dressing gown flicking over the pages; the interlude was over.

He retrieved his clothes and dressed quickly. Sitting on the bed as he pulled on his socks, he asked, 'Can I see you again? Or was this just a one-off?'

She put the paper down and looked thoughtful. He had given her a love-mark on her breast and she touched it with a finger, looking this way and that in the mirror.

'That will cramp my style for a day or two! . . . I was afraid you were going to ask me that. Which would you prefer it to be?'

'If I can trust your discretion then I'd like another opportunity. Many opportunities. But I'm a married man, with a child, and a career in which playing around is disapproved of. Do we understand each other?'

Miranda was no fool. 'If you had any doubts about me you shouldn't have come, so I guess you think I have an honourable face. No, don't worry: if we're to be friends, Andrew, you can trust me. I don't want my name in the papers any more than you.'

They parted at those words, with Andrew promising to call her the moment he knew the voting pattern for the following week. He did not need to tell her how to contact him, and hoped good sense would guard against her phoning him too obviously or too often.

His head was spinning and his mouth dry. As he walked the half-mile to his own flat Andrew Muncastle knew his world had been blasted apart and reassembled, with vivid fluorescent colours in place of the former drab grey, its structure changed for ever. His muscles ached but his spirit shouted with joy and exultation. If this was damnation, this consummated marriage between his body and his human soul, then St Paul was mad and he, Andrew, was all in favour.

It was beginning to look as if he could have his cake – his career in politics – and eat it, in the form of Miranda's forbidden fruit, at the same time. An affair with a woman like that, who relished her freedom, with no strings and no obligations, would be no threat to his public life, nor to his marriage. On the contrary: it would make coping with Tessa's tearful coolness a great deal easier.

He walked on, whistling.

CHAPTER ELEVEN

The narrow entrance to Overton's can be surprisingly difficult to find, unless the searcher knows to look out for the six-foot shrimp painted alongside. Immediately opposite Victoria Station, the restaurant was established in the earliest days of the railway, bringing to the heart of London lobsters, crayfish, oysters, eels and other produce packed in ice straight from the coast for the capital's working men and women. Today it is the customers who come by train, in crumpled pin-striped suits on the 7.40 from Brighton, while the fish goes to market at Nine Elms in refrigerated lorries, arriving in much better condition.

The establishment clings to a narrow ridge of space at the curved edge of an old building ripe for redevelopment. Downstairs is an oyster bar; the main restaurant is upstairs. On the top floor is a poky kitchen, its greasy windows half hidden behind a vast advertising hoarding. The surroundings may be unprepossessing, but inside is an older, slower world.

Marcus Carey was waiting at a table in the corner, anxious and early. As Elaine entered he rose, a smile on his face, his manner hovering between friendliness and deference. He wore a charcoal-grey suit, the handkerchief in his breast pocket matching his tie, a small carnation in his buttonhole. Marcus was genuinely glad to see her.

Elaine for her part greeted him warmly, shaking hands and deciding against a peck on the cheek. She wondered why he wanted to see her again. He was not that close a friend, really. His philosophy of life left her uneasy. There were times at university when she had wanted to shake him, to shout into his face that he shouldn't be so conciliatory, should be proud of being black. He should neither pretend to be whiter than white, as if to erase all signs of difference, nor ignore the dismissive sniggering that went on behind his back from those whose manners he sought to ape. His earnest vulnerability had stopped her. There were parallels in her own life. She was aware that loudly proclaiming a feminist viewpoint in a masculine world was no way to break down

159

barriers or bring the Freddie Ferrimans to heel. It was all about being effective, which might involve saying things you did not believe, smiling sweetly when your heart was not in it – and having lunch when you did not feel like it with people you would rather avoid.

The two bent their heads over the menu as black-coated waiters fussed around. Marcus and Elaine were seated by a window above the traffic scurrying around the station. Despite the illusion of light and space created by long mirrors facing the windows, it was remarkably cramped.

'So how has the first year been?' Marcus was in cheerful mood.

The crab cocktail was so fresh he could smell the sea. Elaine was relishing a ripe avocado smothered in prawns and pink sauce. A white Macon was going down nicely.

'A year already?' Elaine was startled. 'I'm not sure, to tell the truth. A mixed picture. On the positive side, I'm settling in well in Warmingshire, though I still have to fend off adulatory fables about my useless predecessor. And I like my constituents. They've a lot more shrewdness and a greater understanding of politics than all the leader writers put together.'

The plates were cleared as Marcus reflected: 'You don't agree with those MPs who say living in the patch is a pain, then?'

'I can understand their point of view, especially in London. Some people will never give the MP any peace. Any notion that one might have a family or a private life is forgotten. My area has several huge advantages. I can only realistically get up there at weekends, and that enables me to compartmentalise my life – national politics all week and local at the weekend; and they are darned intelligent, most of my punters, so listening to them isn't just a duty, it's useful to boot. It means when I talk on TV or radio I get the language right: that makes me a better communicator.'

Marcus was envious. 'It's good to hear you talk with such enthusiasm, Elaine.'

'There's a down side, though. I didn't expect to have to work so hard – such long hours. One of the whips told me it was even worse when Margaret Thatcher was Prime Minister. The average time – the *average* – the House rose one session was 12.47 a.m. She didn't believe MPs or Ministers were doing their utmost unless they were prostrate with tiredness.'

'But it'll never be a nine-to-five job.'

'No, but working late becomes a habit, you know. A bad and unnecessary habit, in my ill-informed new-girl view. Officially the finishing time of the Commons is ten o'clock, but often we push on till midnight or beyond, without thinking whether it's a good use of our time. It leaves you whacked.'

Marcus smiled. 'At least you're there, on the inside.'

It was a signal that it was time to talk about him. He was toying with a grilled Dover sole, fiddling with bones carefully, like a maiden aunt. A vast platter of 'Seafood Victoria' was sitting in front of Elaine, chunks of fish and crustacean poached in chablis, basil and cream, with a puff-pastry shell at the side. Working in central London, for all its rush and relentless pressure, offered compensations not available in Warmingshire.

She heard Marcus's remark but ignored it for the moment: she needed to try out ideas. Roger had been so busy of late.

'What bothers me, Marcus, is that it suits those in high places to keep the Commons up late and getting tired. If we're all shattered we think we must be working effectively, but it isn't true. We even attract the admiration of our constituents – there's nothing like phoning the local radio station at the end of an all-night sitting and telling them you have not yet hit the hay. Nobody dares say that it's not admirable but *barmy*. If we had more time to think and a little more energy, we might ask more searching questions altogether. We might, in other words, be better at our job.'

'I shouldn't worry. It won't be long before you're a PPS or a Minister. Then you'll be glad the backbenchers are kept at bay.'

'Very flattering, Marcus. I doubt it. I'm beginning to suspect they've a thing against women. I could be there years before anybody gives me a job.'

Half a bottle of white wine had gone. A crème brûlée appeared for her, perfumed sorbets for him. The bill was mounting and would reach over £60 with coffee: still modest by London standards, but even her share would cost more than a meal for two in the Strangers' Dining Room. Next time she would let her companion choose the place and pick up the tab. Like all the other MPs.

'Your turn, Marcus,' she said briskly. 'You didn't suggest lunch solely for the pleasure of my company. What are your plans?'

He stirred his coffee thoughtfully. 'I have to make a move soon about finding a seat. That's still what I want to do – indeed, talking to you makes me even keener. Retirements begin to be announced from halfway through a parliament. Good seats come up that way. There may be by-elections too, so I have to be ready.'

To give herself time to think, Elaine looked away. Down on the pavement two young blacks were talking animatedly. The girl was tall and slim, her light-chocolate skin glowing, her hair a mass of tiny frizzy plaits. She wore a fitted tartan jacket over red leggings. The young man was taller and glossy beetle-black, his hair cut tight and asymmetric around the crown; he stood lithe on the balls of his feet, at ease with his body. A white shirt and bright tie were tucked into narrow-waisted trousers, whose knife pleats fell in elegant lines over well-polished shoes. These two were leaders, of fashion at least.

She snapped her attention back to the trim grey Englishman sitting opposite and tried to concentrate. The man and woman outside invited admiration on their own terms; with Marcus she felt irritated and sad.

'You shouldn't go in for by-elections, Marcus. They're horrendous, and you in particular would find one very tough.'

Of course that was correct once his colour was taken into account. That was not the way this man wished to function.

'I was thinking I might fight a Labour-held one, for the experience, and to show willing.'

'Still unwise, though I can see your point.' If he was refusing to discuss the issue, she wasn't going to press him. She decided to try a different tack. 'With your background you should try for winnable seats. You'd get a lot of backing from the party.'

He was eyeing her slyly. 'Do you remember saying you'd put in a good word for me? Did you make any progress?'

It had slipped her mind entirely. Maybe subconsciously she had not wanted to help, fearing what happens when ambitious heads are popped over parapets, particularly when they are more than usually visible against the light.

Time to lie. 'I did, but I got nowhere. You're still interested in being a special adviser? Perhaps the best I can offer is to have a word with my own whip and mention your name. All right, Marcus, I shall see what I can do.'

He looked pleased and relieved. As he insisted on paying, she felt ashamed of herself for letting him, not just because of the hypocrisy of believing in sexual equality and not practising it, but because it felt like a little bribery and corruption. The meal was bought and so was she, and both knew it. The green Amex card on the saucer created an obligation. Yet the dangers of pushing Marcus Carey and his wife and his colour into the limelight left her uncomfortable and dismayed.

Outside on the narrow sidewalk they shook hands and exchanged pleasantries. And then, because she was a good-hearted woman, Elaine Stalker kissed Marcus Carey quickly on the cheek, squeezed his arm and wished him luck. He gazed wistfully after her as she walked away.

'Might I have a word?'

That was their signal now. Elaine turned smartly on her heel and smiled at the man who was her lover. Totally innocuous though the phrase might be, when she heard anyone else use it, it made her jump and feel suddenly guilty, but thrilled too. For other people it signalled the start of a brief private conversation, the contents of which were to remain confidential. For her it meant Roger had checked his diary, gained his freedom from the evening's rota, ensured that his spouse was occupied elsewhere, and wanted to know if the same was true for her.

Early euphoric days had given way to a busy routine, as Elaine had expected. More than a year on, she had now spoken half a dozen times in the House, each time competently enough but with little recognition. She made more progress outside. Her voice and face were increasingly well known in the media, on serious matters including Northern Ireland, but more often for personality pieces which often started irritatingly by asking what it was like being a woman in a man's world, as if she and the other women MPs were unwelcome interlopers.

Another baptism had occurred. Along with a dozen colleagues she had spent hours upstairs in Committee Room 10 serving somewhat reluctantly on the Education Bill. It had taken weeks before she admitted to herself that the minutiae of legislation, this line-by-line discussion of detail, did not exactly capture her imagination. In committee, ministerial offerings were merely scrappier versions of the set-pieces in the Chamber. Opposition spokesmen harangued, filibustered and nitpicked hour after hour. Interventions from government backbenchers were frowned on by their whips for prolonging the debate. The public filed in and sat at the back on hard benches, some studiously with notepads and pens, acting for various interests; others, often schoolchildren, lounged bored and puzzled before trooping out to seek ice cream on the Embankment.

When she and others grumbled, Johnson, the whip, explained the convention of waiting till sixty hours' work had passed in committee before he could request a timetable motion, a 'guillotine', to bring its efforts to a speedy conclusion. For the life of her, Elaine could not figure out why such a proposal was not regularly adopted in the first place. Sitting at the back of the stuffy committee room, resigned to following proceedings in attentive silence while getting on with her post, she felt that games-playing at Westminster went quite a lot too far.

It became her practice to make mental notes of such questions, for the next time she would see Roger Dickson. He liked being put in a position of authority; and now, trusting her, he had begun to tell her his real views, not merely the agreed line which she could obtain from any junior Minister. He appeared to be a middle-of-the-roader with little sympathy for the impassioned fringes. Pragmatism pervaded most of his remarks. Elaine, by nature one who sought commitment, applauded his practical approach but wondered aloud whether one shouldn't, at base, believe in *something*. That made Roger look thoughtful.

He seemed happier, more secure, explaining the intricacies of the parliamentary system. Steadily she was learning how Westminster and Whitehall functioned. She read Bagehot and Trollope, and reflected that precious little had changed in a century, except that no aristocrat could now become Prime Minister. Those fictional intrigues, the pettiness, the ambition and double-crossing sounded depressingly familiar, especially once Roger regaled her with some of the juicier moves played out on the Chief Whip's chequered carpet.

So now she took a few steps and stood closer to him, face upturned. At once it was as if a warm protective cloak had encompassed them, not to be sensed by anyone else but themselves. He could smell her scent, see her freckled nose. She could feel his quickened pulse, sense the hairs rising on the back of his neck at her nearness. Neither could stand so close for long, not on an open corridor of the Palace of Westminster at the back of the Speaker's Chair. A conversation held like this could last only a few seconds.

'After the guillotine debate tomorrow night, there'll be no other whipped business,' Roger told her rapidly. 'Are you free?'

She pretended to consider, raised an eyebrow, but sensed he was in no mood for teasing. 'Fine. What time?'

Not 'What time should I expect you?' Nothing like that. It had to sound as if a public engagement was being arranged. Maybe she was to speak to his businessmen at a dinner in Dining Room A, or chat to his party workers at tea on the Terrace. Quite innocent.

'About eight? Usual arrangements?'

She nodded, smiled and left him. The invisible cloak vanished, replaced by a cool chill from an open window.

It was not only her political life which had fallen into a steady routine. So had her activities with Roger. Although the affair had started in his home he never again invited her there. She pondered, but did not ask him why not. Perhaps his wife had spotted something incriminating, as a woman might: perhaps she, Elaine, simply made the bedroom smell differently. That was certainly possible, for despite the risk she always liked to wear perfume for Roger. And there was the tell-tale linger of sex in a room.

By contrast, there was no one at her flat to spot any unusual signs. Mike's absences were both frequent and predictable; Karen might not have guessed anyway. The flat had no awkward associations of family or domesticity, no toys or pictures of children gazing down reproachfully. Her flat was part of her professional life.

There was a set of unwritten rules about the flat too. Too tidy, too much effort, and Roger would remark on it, hinting that she was trying too hard. He did not want any signs that he was an important part of her life. She sensed that he did not wish to be faced with any decisions at all about her, other than whether to make contact that week. A bunch of daffodils in spring or roses from her garden were fine, since she might easily have done that for herself. Brand-new towels in the bathroom or a toothbrush still in its packet left casually in the mug – this was going too far.

Yet she strove to avoid routine. And that night, as she walked home in the evening sunshine, a new idea had sent her to the last fruit stall down by Sutton Ground. Two big punnets of strawberries and an aerosol can of cream now sat on the low table. There were no plates or dishes, and no spoons.

The phone rang. 'All clear?' he asked. His voice lifted with suppressed excitement. He was still in the House, on a deserted corridor, his mouth close to the phone.

'Of course. See you in a minute.'

She glanced at the clock. It would take about ten minutes for him to fetch his Rover from the car park, drive the half-mile to Morpeth Terrace, find a place to park, check he wasn't seen, then stroll casually to her front door. You could walk it almost as fast. But after he had seen her he would climb back in the car and drive home, with no need to explain the missing couple of hours. It worked a treat. And a treat was what she had in store for him.

The entryphone buzzer sounded. She picked up the handset on the wall as her heart leapt. 'Yes?'

It would never do to greet him by name. The bell could as easily have been pressed by a journalist. Carelessness cost careers.

'It's me.'

She pressed the button releasing the street door, left her own front door ajar an inch, returned to the sitting room, switched the television on low and started eating the strawberries, holding each delicately by its green stalk. She counted his footsteps on the stairs. The climb made him pant slightly. He stood just inside the doorway and took off his jacket, hanging it on the hook on the back of the door. As Roger entered the room she was apparently engrossed in the programme and unconcerned at his arrival, so that he had to call to her softly.

Once she had been making coffee in the kitchen and had teased him, refusing to budge when he entered. Then he had been obliged to search for her, and had taken her from behind, hands firmly on her breasts and squeezing her almost angrily until it hurt. Turning her bodily around he had kissed her hard and desperately, till at last she broke free, tears in her eyes and a sob in her throat from the longing he had unwittingly revealed.

He never put it into words, never said, 'I love you.' The shutters would come down if she attempted to say it to him.

'God! What are you watching?' He gestured at the television set.

'It's quite interesting.' She pretended to be defensive. 'I'll switch off and try to concentrate on you, if you prefer.'

'Quite right too!' He pulled her to him, entwining a fistful of her hair so that she could not move her head, and kissed her.

Outside came the noise of cars parking as neighbours returned from work, a few late theatregoers, friends calling to each other. Sometimes they went into the main bedroom, but tonight Roger lay back on the single bed in the living room which was covered with a woven rug. He gathered a pile of cushions behind his head, and lounged long-legged on the bed, pulling at his tie and kicking off his shoes.

That was fine by her. Elaine knelt at the side of the bed and tugged off his socks, then leaned over and started to undo his trouser belt, deliberately fumbling so that he covered her hand with his own and helped her. The two chatted all the time, almost inconsequentially as she calmly removed piece after piece of his clothing, folding them in a neat pile in humorous imitation of the acts of a nanny. She had long since sensed that he found the contrast between her gentle prattle and sensual actions intensely erotic, and so now did she. All the while his other hand stroked her hair, caressing, with loving anticipation.

It was warm enough to lie unclothed, for the evening was still sunny. When he was naked, lying splayed out on the little bed, she stood before him and slowly took off her own garments, one at a time, dropping each item into a tumbled heap. As she pulled off a sweater, arms and hair tangled and her face momentarily hidden, he ran his fingers over the delicate skin on the inside of her thighs, and looked at her with hunger in his grey eyes.

She leaned backwards and picked up a punnet of strawberries and the can of cream. He looked down at his erection with a raised eyebrow, and then at the strawberries.

'Shouldn't those wait?'

'No,' she said firmly, and placed the first strawberry in his navel, and then two at the root of his penis and the next two in the smooth hollow of his almost hairless chest, and the biggest in his mouth, so he could not protest and had to chew or choke. Suppressing laughter, she then took the can, shook it and spread mounds of whipped cream over the strawberries. She shoved another large strawberry determinedly in his mouth, then balanced the smallest fruit gently on the very penis tip where it wobbled dangerously. After a thoughtful pause, she then covered this last one with a whirl of cream, and sat back to survey her handiwork.

'I've always wanted to eat you, Roger Dickson, and lick you all over. That's exactly what I'm going to do,' she announced softly.

'Oh, my God,' he moaned ecstatically. 'I don't believe this. Elaine, careful with your teeth! I can't get a replacement . . .'

Pulling her hair back with one hand, she balanced with the other, and ate the strawberry and cream from his chest, running the tip of her tongue into each crevice of his skin, lapping up every trace of white foam. She moved down and performed the same action on the fruit and cream in his navel. He wriggled, chortling with delight, his eyes fixed firmly on her face. Then it was the turn of the red fruit in his groin, her tongue moving like a cat's as he muttered at her, not daring to move, gurgling with sheer pleasure. The tiniest strawberry trembled, but with a flick of her tongue it was in her mouth. She examined the untidy dollop of whipped cream remaining and licked that off too, making a thorough job of it, particularly the most sensitive area right at the tip, leaving him moist and sticky. Then in a swift movement she was on him, her hand guiding his penis deep inside her, and she cried out as he began urgently to move.

When it was done they collapsed in a clammy heap, skin clinging to skin. He held her tightly and could not stop laughing.

'Heavens! You make it such glorious fun. What a talent! Well, Mrs Stalker, I'll never be able to see strawberries and cream on a menu again without breaking into a cold sweat.'

'That was the idea,' she said matter-of-factly. 'I wanted to ensure that throughout your life, whatever else may happen, you'll never forget this night with me.'

She uttered the words lightly, but his eyes clouded for a moment. She took advantage of the pause to fetch a flannel and wiped him carefully, then settled herself by his side, tucked on to the narrow bed, snuggling close, ready to talk.

'You expecting to move in the reshuffle?' she asked.

'I don't know, to be truthful.' He was eating the remainder of the strawberries. 'I've said I'd like a move from the whips' office, but that guarantees nothing.'

'Don't you like being a whip?'

'Oh yes, very much. You find out everything that's going on. But it's destructive, in a way.'

Long ago she had learned how to arrange herself, her voice and manner, so that he felt free to muse out loud. As he might have spoken to Caroline, had she been interested. As once Mike had talked to her, when Jake was dying, the tears streaming down his face. She shut out that picture quickly, and concentrated on Roger.

'How do you mean?'

'Well...' He shifted his position. 'A whip's job is to get the government's business through, by hook or by crook. Even the most reliable Members have to be hooked from time to time, persuaded that their vote matters and their views are of value. They can be harder to deal with than the devils who are being awkward, some of whom you just have to write off. So I spend an inordinate amount of my time stroking people – being nice to nuisances I can't abide; listening to little schemes, tolerating insults with a smile, fixing here, arranging there, balancing everywhere. There are days when my face aches from smiling and I feel like hitting somebody. I thought I was going to be an honest John when I came here, but it doesn't work out that way.'

'You don't have to lie, though, do you? I mean, not outright?'

'All the time: lies are our stock in trade. I tell you, it gets at you eventually.'

'Perhaps you get hardened to it.' She ran one finger slowly down his face. As it reached his lips he caught it, sucked for a moment, let go, then sighed.

'Probably. And I don't like that. Churchill said it was easier to tell the truth: then you don't have to remember which lie you told last time. Anyway I'd feel happier in a job where I was creating policy instead of coercing the troops into supporting it. And I've had enough of working so hard and still being a complete unknown, as far as the nation is concerned.'

How easy it had become to lie as a matter of course. Elaine would have preferred a good marriage and no lies. But if love and joy were not available with honest behaviour, she for one did not bat an eyelid at lying to get them. She shivered as a night breeze stirred the air. She leaned across him, letting her breasts brush his face, to close the window.

'You'll have to do more TV and radio,' she remarked. 'Have you had any training?'

He shook his head. 'A bit, locally, that's all.'

'You probably don't need any advice, Roger. In fact, you give it to others now. But, for example, if you're speaking on TV or radio, you need to be crisp and natural.'

'Go on. I'm always interested in hearing from an expert, and you're very good at it, Elaine. Almost as good as you are at eating strawberries.' He grinned.

She sat up, using her hands to demonstrate. 'It's easy, really. Listen to the words ordinary people actually use: simple, informal words. There's a difference between how we talk and official language. Don't use long words. Say "bollocks" instead of "damnation", if you like! "Wrong" instead of "incorrect", "rot" instead of "inappropriate". It'll make your remarks vivid and instantly understood.'

His eyes rounded. 'I get it – bonking instead of intercourse.'

She threw a pillow at his face in mock irritation. 'Prat instead of idiot, more like. But you're right – that's what makes the *Globe* headlines so memorable, whereas *The Times*'s aren't. And decide first what message you want to get across: if it's important, keep saying it in the same words, over and over again. If you say it often enough it'll stick. But if the message is "No comment", keep your head down and refuse to make any comment at all. Eventually they'll give up and go away, and find some other mug.'

Roger folded his arms behind his head and listened intently. Elaine had not been taught these matters any more than he had, but she understood them instinctively. He knew other things she might never learn: how to win over a group of angry colleagues, how to keep his temper under control, how to flatter his companions instead of competing with them.

Elaine was engrossed in her lesson. He watched her while absorbing her advice, enjoying the way her breasts bobbed as she moved her arms, the curve of her belly.

'You're not listening!' she accused.

'I am! But I'm gazing at you in adoration as well. Don't stop. I'm taking it all in, I promise.'

For a moment she had lost rhythm. She eyed him dubiously, but he was waiting for her to continue.

'All right. I've almost finished. All speeches are composed of three things: message, medium and mode. Message we've done. By "medium" I mean you must know who the audience is and exactly what are the circumstances. Are you speaking live or recorded? First or last? Live is always best, as you can't be edited, and if you're determined enough you can usually get the last word in. If your opponent or interviewer becomes angry or aggressive, so much the better. You should sound mildly shocked: that puts the other one in the wrong and you'll get the sympathy vote. Try out your expressions in front of a mirror. Listen to your own voice – practise with a tape recorder. Learn what it sounds like, and how to make it sing.'

'Ye . . . es,' he admitted slowly. 'My voice always sounds so flat and toneless. I'll try that.'

She nodded, content. 'Lastly is the mode, by which I mean you should back up your message with real knowledge and not waffle. Always be well prepared. If you make a point, have some evidence. A few well-chosen facts will stick, and make your critics sound stupid and wrong. Thus Roger Dickson is always convincing.'

He was beginning to stir again. Almost absent-mindedly, she rubbed her palm in slow circles across his abdomen, gently willing him, for she was nowhere near spent. Outside, the street had fallen quiet.

'I meant to ask you one thing, Roger,' she said.

'Umm? . . . Don't stop, that's lovely.'

'I promised a character I know called Marcus Carey that I'd put in a good word for him. He's on the Anglo-Irish joint talks at present, but he wants to get back into mainstream politics. I think he'd like to be a special adviser of some kind. I've told him I can't really help, but at least now I've kept my promise.'

'I know him. Tell him I'll pass on his interest . . . Ah, look what you are doing to me! Now before we make love once more, O most delicious and tantalising Elaine, are there any other suits you wish to put?'

She hesitated. 'Only my own, really. It's fifteen months and still nothing, while I see others getting on. Are there any chances for me in this reshuffle, do you think?'

Her voice was wistful. He took her hand and kissed it, and turning it over kissed the palm, using it to hide his expression. For he too wanted her to rise in the hierarchy, if that was her desire, but he doubted whether she was made of the right material, and he did not dare use his position to help her. The sparkle which so attracted him hinted at a lack of gravitas. The sharp observations and wry comments with which she lightened his life raised dullard eyebrows in the tea room and made her enemies. Her very femaleness in that male environment was not fresh and welcome, but an intrusion and a threat.

'Goodness only knows, Elaine. If a chance comes, I'll put in a good word for you, too. But don't count on it. You must just be . . .' His voice tailed off, but now his eyes were merry, for her hand had moved back to caressing him and he was ready to make love once more.

'Patient! I know.'

He grabbed her and tumbled her on to her back, and with a whoop pinned her arms above her head, and entered her with the full vigour of a man in the prime of life with the woman he adored; and this time their two bodies clung together and became as one, as one, as one, till at last night fell, all unnoticed, in the darkened room.

She lay on her back, the ceiling hidden by his bulk, the world shut out by his profound dominance. She put her hands to his shoulders, pushed him off her a little and looked into his eyes. She wanted to win, tonight, a reward for all the lessons. She wanted to tell the truth to him, to be one person who did not lie to him, with whom there were no lies.

'I love you, Roger Dickson,' she said softly, 'and I believe I will love you till I die.'

A sigh came from his lips, but she could not see his face clearly in the darkness. He moved his head slowly from side to side, and seemed to be saying, 'No . . . no . . .' but no sound came out.

He let his weight down on her, then rolled away, but still held her close, stroking her hair, making strange guttural sounds in his throat. His eyes were shut tight. The street light caught the corner of his eyelid, and there was a wetness, which rolled slowly down his cheek on to the pillow.

He lay still for a long time, then opened his eyes, and instantly old straightforward Roger was back inside his skin. He sat up and stretched.

'Ah! My dear Patience. All good things come to an end. I am afraid I must go. Pass me my clothes, please.'

170

Carrying the little pile he headed into the bathroom, staggering slightly. The blue underpants fell to the floor. She picked them up and hurried after him, then stood in the doorway watching calmly as he began soaping himself under the shower.

'Next time, let me do that,' she offered.

He laughed: 'After what you got up to with the strawberries? What instrument would you propose using on me – the backbrush, maybe?'

His teasing tone restored the lighter atmosphere. She smiled at his face in the mirror as he concentrated on his task. She had no warning of his next question.

'Do you believe in God, Elaine?'

'What? Oh, yes, I think so. Why?'

'And heaven?'

'I've no idea. What an odd question. Yes, I think there must be something after all this life, and I hope it's enjoyable.'

He fastened and smoothed his crumpled shirt, then his tie. He pointed at the mirror, at the strange Magritte image of the man and woman together, disturbing and exciting, he dressed, she still naked, her skin warm and flushed from their lovemaking.

'That's heaven, the only one we're likely to get,' he said. 'So let's just make the best of it, and not think beyond that, OK?'

There were to be no more words that night. She pulled a big bath towel around her, twisting it over her breasts to make it stay put. Fully dressed, he took her face in both hands and kissed her forehead, as if he were a priest blessing a child. Then he was gone.

Peter stood in the basement flat and jingled the bunch of keys. It was several weeks since he had led Nigel Boswood upstairs, receiving these keys, it seemed, in return. Boswood had questioned him closely about money, and when satisfied that he was not destitute told him gruffly that there would be no question of rent and that if he wanted milk he should put a note out for the milkman.

For all that, money had changed hands. Not cheques, naturally. A little wad of ten-pound notes nestled on Peter's pillow one evening when he returned from a visit to his sister's. He took it as a hint that his services were requested that night, and he had been correct. The sum was not large – about £100 – but useful. No words had been exchanged the next day, the money never mentioned. A fortnight later the same thing happened again, then at regular intervals, enough to make other clients unnecessary. When, almost out of curiosity, Peter commented on how expensive London had become during his long absence in Amsterdam, the sum increased substantially. It felt like hitting the jackpot: as easy as falling off a log.

That night he had slept in Nigel's bed, curled close, one hand flung across his lover's chest, and had been awoken in the morning with a murmured kiss. Thereafter he took to knocking gently on the door soon after Nigel had gone to bed. The man was often stuck doing his wretched boxes and would wryly shake his head. Sometimes, however, the boxes were finished, or done before leaving the office, and the two would lie abed, holding hands and half watching the news on the television set on the dressing-table.

It was an undemanding existence. Peter realised that Nigel's detective knew of him; the chauffeur also pretended not to see him behind the net curtains in the mornings. But Peter was practised at disappearing into the background and giving no trouble. For the moment this was a very pleasant life. At the least hint of problems he could always take the plane to Amsterdam.

'Thank God, recess soon.'

The Prime Minister poured a mineral water and a weak whisky and soda, handed the latter to the Chief Whip and settled himself uncomfortably in a low, chintz-covered sofa. Margaret Thatcher's taste up here, in the diminutive private flat under the eaves of 10 Downing Street, was more than a little suspect. His wife's check jacket hung loosely over a high-backed chair near the small desk she used for her own correspondence. Tonight she was presenting the prizes for Children of Courage. Time and space to clear urgent business.

'It has been the worst year in my parliamentary career,' the Prime Minister continued, passing a hand over his face. Both men were clean-shaven but showing five o'clock shadows. Here in trusted company he could remove his spectacles and rub his eyes. The Prime Minister was very short-sighted, far too much for contact lenses. He peered blearily into middle distance. The fog in front seemed clearer somehow than the impenetrable future. Beneath the glasses the eyes were surprisingly dark brown and gentle. The face was drawn and a little pinched. His bad leg ached. He felt very tired.

The Chief Whip waited sympathetically. The management of a tiny majority was a new and unpleasant exercise after the overwhelmingly favourable odds of previous Parliaments. It was also grinding hard work, long tedious hours with two hundred recalcitrant backbenchers, persuading, cajoling, commiserating. Previously something might have been offered in return for firm support, a little log-rolling not unknown in other countries, a new road or a new government project in the constituency; but, with public-spending budgets already rising five times faster than inflation, all bets were off. Nor did arm-twisting work. With what could he threaten a man whose constituency was facing 15 per cent unemployment? For such Members, trying to force the government to change tack seemed not a disloyalty but a duty. Deselection could seem like a relief.

The Prime Minister sighed, replaced his spectacles, swallowed a little of the tepid water and reached for a sheet of paper underneath the table lamp. He resumed a brisk manner.

'Reshuffle time, Chief. There aren't a great many vacancies, I'm afraid. So many moves recently, under both Margaret and myself. A little stability would be welcome. Anyway I hate moving people just for the sake of it.'

The Chief did not entirely agree. Moving people kept everyone on their toes, especially new boys waiting for their chance. It improved behaviour, pure and simple. It was not only the troops who were badly affected by inertia. The prevailing philosophy in the Cabinet that keeping heads down and not causing any fuss was also the best policy was having a seriously damaging effect. Far too many Ministers were effectively faceless, silent, anonymous. Several made far less impact than in their livelier backbench days. A few were utterly useless. He wished the Prime Minister would use the knife.

The Chief ventured a comment: 'Department of the Environment needs beefing up, though.'

The Prime Minister agreed. 'I'd expect Boswood to retire before too long, but he's so reliable that I'm reluctant to move him. Shall we put in a stronger voice as number two? Who might be suitable for Minister of State?'

Various names were bandied about. The Chief had his own preferences. The best way was to offer someone senior from the whips' office, then promote within the office to fill the gap, taking in a new boy straight from the back benches, an apprentice to train up. That route left control of the inflow of Ministers almost entirely to the whips, for they alone decided who should join their number. New *boy*, of course. No room for any women. No need to change that.

'Might I suggest Roger Dickson? He was Environment whip and has been in the whips' office three years, long enough for anyone who's not a career whip, and he isn't. He's very capable, and has been hinting recently that the time has come to move on. His seat is in the Midlands, which is helpful – too many chaps from the south aren't good for the image. Pleasant, sensible, got his head screwed on. With a bit more exposure could do well on TV – just the sort to appeal to the ladies. How about it?'

'Any skeletons?'

'The ladies? Sorry, I meant the twinset-and-pearls brigade. Happily married, as far as I know. Not a whisper of any problem, apart from increasing frustration with the whips' office. He hides it well, but you can feel a tension underneath. It's time to move him on. I can recommend him without reservation.'

Consciously the Chief Whip used formal language as if he were writing a reference. The Prime Minister noted the offer.

'All right, if you say so: Minister of State at Environment. Now, Chief, what on earth am I going to do about the Chancellor?'

Roger received the news just before lunchtime the next day from the Chief Whip at Number 12. He walked through the connecting door to Number 10 away from prying eyes. A handshake, a smile, a quick drink with the PM, and that was it.

The front door of Number 10 opened as Dickson walked out into the dull summer day. A few flashbulbs popped, but he was barely known and of no interest. A slight bespectacled figure approached in a grey chauffeur's uniform. The man introduced himself as Alec Vinson, his new Ministry driver, and indicated the two-year-old Rover car. Whips do not have an official car allocated to them by name, but Ministers do: wonderful! Roger started to laugh. Yet he needed a few moments to think. Courteously he declined the offer of a ride and began to walk rapidly towards Marsham Street and the Department of the Environment.

What a relief. And it would be a pleasure working with Boswood. Roger had noted that the Cabinet Minister had been looking a little troubled recently, a mixture of excited irritability and unusual moroseness. A man his age was probably beginning to suffer from rheumatism or a queasy prostate. This life was notorious for wear and tear on the bodily fabric. He resolved to watch Boswood carefully, and offer help to relieve the burden.

Roger would be the most senior Minister after the Secretary of State in a much slimmed-down department. The DoE used to be a lot larger; at one stage there had been ten Ministers including the Lords. Now that one spate of pointless reform in local government was finished, indeed substantially reversed, a smaller team was preferred. Thank God he would not have to take a new poll tax through Parliament; messing around with finance systems was over, it was to be hoped, for at least a generation. On the whole Roger preferred to interfere as little as possible.

Martin Chadwick was waiting at the lift on the fourteenth floor to greet him. The two men were about the same age and height and appraised each other calmly.

Dickson saw a tall slim man with a loud tie, a public servant from a background wholly traditional to the Civil Service. Public school, Oxbridge, a bow-windowed cottage in Sittingbourne bought wisely

174

before the boom, a plain dull wife in Jaeger skirts, two offspring heading in the same direction as their father, a love of expensive opera subsidised by the state, a single acceptable eccentricity – lepidoptera? an extensive knowledge of Icelandic sagas? – all coupled with a haughty disdain for Brussels and a preference for holidays in Tuscany: this was Martin Chadwick. Whatever his lamentable lack of knowledge about the workings of commerce or science and engineering, however snooty his view of Birmingham, Manchester and all places north of Watford (and of course Watford itself), his sense of public service was profound and all-pervading.

In Chadwick it extended to keeping his own political opinions firmly to himself; only his wife knew how he voted. His job was to serve the government of the day to the best of his ability, not to decide policy or impose his personal view. As a form of self-protection over the years Chadwick had so subsumed his private beliefs that now he would be hard put to dredge some up if challenged. His opinions of his masters the Ministers were another matter and often, as the head of the Secretary of State's private office, discreetly sought. How on earth such appraisals might be transmitted to the Prime Minister or the Chief Whip was a closely guarded secret. A favourable review of Chadwick himself, who was overdue for promotion, was probably even now sitting on the Perm Sec's desk, behind which some day Chadwick himself no doubt hoped to be seated.

Further, Roger reflected wryly, such people were not swayed by the usual influences. Chadwick would have been genuinely disgusted had anyone ever tried to offer him a bribe. Had he smelled corruption it would have been his duty to speak to his superior and put his worries on record. That the administration in many other countries was run entirely on backhanders would cause the man real grief, especially when he tried ineffectually to explain during training sessions with puzzled and incredulous trainees from Third World governments at the Civil Service College in Belgrave Road. It was a kind of trust. Their reward was a job well done. And, of course, the knowledge that with absolute certainty, as night follows day, their unknown names would eventually be duly honoured. Roger could already picture Chadwick at the palace in morning dress, cradling the stunning jewels of a KCMG nestling in a white silk-lined box in his gloved hand, the lady wife holding on to her hat and simpering. By then a handsome inflation-proofed pension would be augmented by generous directorships arranged by ex-civil servants who had gone before. Nothing arduous. Nothing not lucrative. Not corrupting at all.

Chadwick shook Dickson's hand formally and introduced himself. As the Secretary of State's private secretary he took precedence over Dickson's own staff, to whom the new Minister was then introduced.

Flora Murray was to be his own private secretary; not a dogsbody, not a PA, but a career civil servant in charge of his office. Flora was thin, red-haired and very Scottish. His other staff included Jane, the diary secretary, a bouncy youngster from Liverpool. Winston was in charge of correspondence, another equality appointment, for he was a six-foot-two Rastafarian with dreadlocks hidden under a red, green and black striped woolly hat, the colours not of Britain but Jamaica. Lastly there was the trainee, Sharon from Leytonstone, a podgy mouse with lank hair and terrified eyes. As Roger glanced over her desk littered with the remains of her lunch, Sharon blushed furiously and swept the papers away, knocking a plastic cup of coffee over in the process. Flora pursed her lips; Jane looked at the ceiling in disgust. Roger wondered how such a disparate bunch in these cramped conditions could function smoothly, if at all.

The phone rang: it was the Secretary of State's office three doors away, asking if the Minister might be available in ten minutes to see the Secretary of State in his room. Used to the easy informality of the whips' office, Roger could see that life as a Minister would be distinctly different.

Boswood greeted him like an old friend and shook hands warmly. Over a drink and a sandwich the two men fell to discussing the department's programme and likely problems. Roger would be fortunate to have Boswood as boss in his first ministerial job, for behind the bonhomie was a shrewd brain and consideration for those working with him. The complexities were daunting. Roger squared his shoulders and concentrated.

'You'll need some help of course,' Boswood pointed out. Each senior Minister was entitled to an unpaid political assistant, an MP who would rejoice in the cumbersome title of parliamentary private secretary, or PPS. The place was awash with secretaries, none of whom could type or take shorthand. The incumbent would be expected to do his master's bidding, be his eyes and ears around the Commons, help with speeches and questions and those letters of a more political nature than Winston could be entrusted with; carry Roger's bags and coat and papers, except those secret files which would be Flora's responsibility. It was the first step on the ladder, a much sought-after post.

Temporarily back at the whips' office to collect his personal effects, Roger checked which MPs were currently on the secret list of those judged ready for preferment. He pondered, paper in hand. Elaine's name was there, at the bottom, in pencil. That implied she had only recently been added: the scribbled impermanence suggested hesitancy, that others were firmly regarded as more suitable. It would have been quite easy to appoint her. And fun. A Minister would expect to see a great deal of his PPS. It would add spice to life, especially given that strange collection in the outer office, to have her around, sharing lunch, bringing coffee the way he preferred it, commenting in that quirky wise way of hers. There would be no difficulty arranging evening rendezvous – afternoons, even. It would, however, cause gossip, even though Roger was certain no one had an inkling. He would be teased about her, asked how 'private' the relationship was; jealous rivals would watch like hawks. It might be awkward if they fell out, even temporarily – just suppose if a row in bed were to interfere with departmental business. The body language might be tricky. The Civil Service were sharp and cynical, would spot a longing look, might overhear a snatch of conversation. Altogether, asking for Elaine, even though she was desperate for promotion, would not be a good idea.

He ran his finger up the list and alighted on Muncastle. He was pleasant and earnest and hardworking. His achievements so far were quite impressive – the man seemed to have done all the right things. In the end, a PPS job was either a first step up or it went nowhere fast. It was up to the incumbent. Muncastle offered no threat, no risk, no challenge, no fear.

Muncastle it was.

Part Two

CHAPTER TWELVE

'Conference time, everybody! Conference. Let's get moving.'

Nick Thwaite, the paper's news editor, stuck a dishevelled grey head around the door of the editor's office and yelled down the corridor. Morning editorial conference at the *Globe* was already late, today as yesterday; the place was beginning to fall apart. Not surprisingly, he thought grimly, given the pressure from their owner to cut costs, the features editor's defection last week to a rival, the sports editor in hospital facing a charge of drunk driving, a collapse in advertising revenue and a raging recession. He was feeling foul.

To be fair, the *Globe* was not the only paper forced to confront a slowly falling circulation. Newspapers were going out of fashion. These days the punters got their news from television. Given the state of the country's education system it was amazing anybody under thirty-five could read at all, let alone buy a paper other than for topless girls and Spot the Ball. The *Globe*, like more than one other, would be lucky to survive the next year.

Thwaite called out once more. Behind him the editor, Steve McSharry, waited, quiet but impatient. Doors flew open and bodies appeared, brows furrowed anxiously, arms full of notebooks, proof photographs, page layouts, text, sheets torn from press agency tapes. Thwaite nodded curtly as each entered. He loved the tension, the possibility of creating each time the best edition, of beating competitors to a story, of taking an original line.

The paper had a short but distinguished history. Thwaite had been there from early days when in the wake of the introduction of new technology the then proprietor decided to take on the trade unions. Thwaite had been the only senior journalist willing to support him. Once the row was won the proprietor had a well-earned heart attack and sold out to a mysterious Australian. Nick Thwaite had hoped to be promoted but the coveted editor's post had gone to the softly spoken Steve McSharry, who moved from a Sunday tabloid. The two men got on well and warily liked each other. The editor had ideas for the *Globe*, but was constantly hampered by lack of money. The new owner left them alone as long as the business was making a profit, which at present it most definitely was not.

A dozen men and women were now settling around the big table. The editor himself was in his forties and dark-haired, donnish and bespectacled. Miranda Jamieson, his breezy young deputy, was a complete contrast. Reputedly she had simply caught a plane from Melbourne and turned up one day as a reporter. Thwaite knew what wasn't his business and had carefully not enquired how she had come to know the owner.

As Miranda entered the room, Thwaite winked at her, a friendly, avuncular gesture, which she returned with a wry wave. Despite her smart dress she was looking distinctly bleary. The computer links to the printing presses had crashed halfway through the first edition in the dead of night, and Miranda had personally had to input much of the second edition line by line through to the print setters, writing chunks of it from her imagination and press agency tapes as she went along. Around 100,000 copies had been lost, but the fact that there was a paper at all on the news-stands was entirely due to her. Thwaite envied her: with guts like that, she would have her own editor's chair before long. She already outranked him. This was the new generation.

Five senior staff sat round the table helping themselves to a large pot of real coffee, the only concession to hospitality. An outer concentric circle was by mute agreement reserved for lesser breeds obliged to peer over shoulders as the page layout was discussed. Should they want to make a point it was necessary to stand up, reinforcing the atmosphere of a headmaster's study. On a good morning there were chocolate biscuits. Not today.

McSharry and Thwaite listened, prodded and questioned as the photographic editor showed displays from war zones in three parts of the world. The fashion editor was tossing her red hair petulantly, itching to catch a lunchtime plane to Milan. Late, as ever, came Andy Mack, the paper's shambling, bearded political editor. He grabbed a coffee and pulled out his notebook.

'Just been to the Prime Minister's press conference,' he announced, as if to justify his existence. 'Great news on the – wait for it! – Citizens' Charter! It appears that real success is being achieved over at British Rail. Instead of only seventy-five per cent of the trains arriving on time – that is to say, within ten minutes either way, folks – it's anticipated that next year eighty-five per cent will! That will be achieved by the simple expedient of cutting the number of trains on the least reliable routes, mind you, including Network Southeast.'

Journalists dependent on the worst railway in the world for getting to work groaned. Only senior editors had car park places. Thank goodness they were not in Canary Wharf.

The conference lasted about forty minutes. Nick was impressed as ever at his boss's light hand, chairing rather than instructing, summing up, obtaining agreement, giving leads. The man operated through a practised mixture of cajolery and encouragement. At last staff were sent on their way.

'Nick, a moment.' McSharry motioned him quietly to close the door and sit down again. Miranda hovered, hand on hip, sucking the blue pencil used for layouts. 'More coffee?' It was nearly noon.

Nick Thwaite took his fourth cup of the morning. Miranda started to speak, as if McSharry found it too painful.

'We're still slipping. The board are concerned about our position.'

On the wall a poster advertised the latest promotion, £100,000 bingo. It didn't compete with the *Sun*'s Million Pound Madness, but then the *Sun* was slipping too, more expensively.

'There's a critical mass for our advertisers, as you know. We don't have much of a business section, so we have only limited attraction for insurance ads and the like. We carry no personnel advertising, unlike the *Guardian*, who have created a niche especially in media jobs. Nobody much is buying houses, though we've kept up that side. Nevertheless we pay our staffers and contributors the usual over-generous tabloid rates, which we cannot afford. The fact is, we are more dependent than most of our rivals on income from the cover price.'

'So what's new? I know all that.' Nick wondered what was coming.

McSharry took over. His voice was cool, almost lifeless. 'Last night's loss of circulation was £35,000 down the drain. That's two junior members of staff, so I would be grateful if you could decide who you can do without by the end of the month.'

Thwaite swallowed hard. Once news staff were laid off, the effectiveness of the paper started to slide. On the other hand, there were few other areas where cuts could quickly be made.

McSharry was still speaking. Thwaite had heard he practised transcendental meditation in secret: that could account for the steady gaze, the lack of tremor in his voice. An editor without histrionics was rare – and creepy.

'And we're being asked to do what we can to increase circulation. There's precious little on the political front at the moment, but I'd like material ready for when Parliament reassembles in the autumn. I'm afraid it's dirt-digging time again. Would you discuss with Andy who might be vulnerable – losses at Lloyds, financial scandals, fingers in pies, hidden assets, funny friends not declared on the register of Members' interests, that sort of thing. Don't neglect sex, of course. Take a look at some of the up-and-coming stars and find out what you can about them. Get somebody on to the new women MPs – how did they get where they are? Which is the sexiest? That sort of thing.'

Miranda, standing behind her editor, pulled a face but said nothing. Nick caught the slight movement out of the corner of his eye. Despite the dark circles under her eyes she was spectacular to look at. If it was true she had slept with somebody to get where she was, he was a lucky chap and his identity was likely to remain a secret. Only two groups were reasonably sure their private lives would be ignored, mostly, by the tabloids: libel lawyers and senior staff in their own newspapers.

Nick Thwaite sighed, made a note and headed for his own room. He threw off his jacket, called in Thompson and phoned Andy. In a proper office he would have a secretary who could ring around, and who might also make decent coffee. A proper secretary might even be worth having a fling with – fat chance here when he had to share an elderly temp with three other editors. 'Somebody organise sandwiches for four, now please. Where's Jim Betts? Go and get him for me.'

Within minutes the *Globe*'s news and political brains were hard at work. None of the men round the table cared a damn that their victims might get hurt. Politicians were public property. Anyone conceited enough to hand in nomination papers should expect such scrutiny as his or her due. Most of the time the electorate was not interested in issues but in personalities: the world was a giant soap opera, filled with princesses, pop stars and politicians, morons every one. Nick Thwaite's scruples ran as far as insisting on accuracy. The paper could not be sued for what was true, at least not successfully.

Seated opposite the news editor and making rapid notes, Jim Betts munched soggy prawn mayonnaise sandwiches on brown bread, sipped bad coffee with vegetable creamer from a polystyrene cup, and longed for a pint with pie and chips. Being brought up in Liverpool meant food wasn't wholesome unless it was hot and greasy and doused in vinegar, ketchup or HP sauce. He picked a bit of lettuce leaf out of his teeth and examined it mournfully. Eating this rubbish would make him grumpy all afternoon.

He was thirty, and educated fitfully at Quarry Bank School, whose proudest boast was John Lennon as a former pupil. His apprenticeship on the *Liverpool Echo* was uneventful but thorough, a fact for which he would be perennially grateful. By contrast the Warmingshire interlude had been tedious in the extreme. He was of medium height with pale skin. A ragged moustache, sharply pointed nose and sandy hair made him ferret-like – as, he felt, befitted an outstanding investigative reporter on a great national paper. It was only a matter of time before everybody agreed on the former estimation, if not the latter.

The discussion continued in a desultory fashion until Thwaite had exhausted the possibilities. Armed with a list of suitable targets Betts headed out into the corridor with a swagger. For this job he could have a pool car and could draw out-of-London expenses as much as he judged necessary, provided he brought home the bacon. Jim Betts turned a corner, humming to himself, to find Miranda barring his way.

Although only a year or two older than Miranda, he was acutely conscious that he was not in her class. For a start she was several inches taller, bringing her bosom uncomfortably close to his nose. It was impossible not to look down her cleavage, but watching it heave up and down made him almost seasick. It put him at a serious disadvantage, while she regarded him with amused disdain.

'Jim! I hear you're on the dirty MPs job.' A half-smile. Surely she didn't want to come too.

'Uh-huh.' Non-committal.

'Can I see who you've got? I might be able to point you in the right direction for one or two.'

He produced the notebook and ran through names. He had volunteered to take the second half of the alphabet, more or less, starting with M.

'Mmm, Muncastle,' murmured Miranda. 'I wouldn't bother with him, Jim, not if you value your job here.'

Betts pricked up his ears. Miranda leaned over, holding her thick dark hair with one hand, indicating that she wanted to speak privately, close to his ear. Obediently he bent forward.

'I hear he has some link to the owner. There could be trouble, even if he's clean as a whistle. Get it?'

Betts nodded and put a line through the name. That Miranda had some link with the owner was a widespread whisper, probably resulting merely from the coincidence of accents and origins. If, however, there was any truth in it then her suggestion that one of the duller names in his notebook might be best forgotten was fine by him. Others on his list were far more promising. Time to get on with it.

It had been a splendid day's shooting; the birds had flown fast and free, the dogs had been faithful and his eye was still true. Nigel Boswood positioned himself, whisky in hand, in front of the painting of a distinguished ancestor who had been Foreign Secretary, and awaited his guests. He glanced at the picture behind him wistfully. He would have loved to have become Foreign Secretary himself, but that was never to be.

Indeed, he was likely to see more of his Scottish shooting lodge, and his friends, in future. For Nigel planned to tell the Prime Minister, when the time was right, that he would not be standing again for Parliament, and that he therefore expected to relinquish his Ministry post within the next year or so, at the Leader's convenience. He would be sixty in January and had first joined the front-bench team as a junior whip in 1970 – a generation ago. A year or two on the back benches being helpful to the government would secure a couple of useful City directorships, each paying more than a parliamentary salary – not, of course, that money was a problem. At the conclusion of his time in the Commons a peerage, reflecting over thirty years' service and the attainment of Cabinet rank, would be his certain due. As Lord Boswood he could enjoy a happy, useful and comfortable old age.

The voices of his guests as they changed for dinner floated down through the ceiling. For entertainment as he waited, Nigel debated different names and titles. Lord Nigel-Boswood, perhaps, like Lord George-Brown? Or Lord Nigel, like the former Labour MP Cledwyn Jones who became Lord Cledwyn of Penrhos, quietly forgetting the proletarian Jones? Maybe something altogether fancier. Perhaps he should consult his cousin the Earl. There was plenty of time to decide.

One huge area of relief beckoned: his personal life would at last be private. If he chose to fly to Amsterdam or San Francisco or Haiti or Bangkok, or even sample a discreet gay bar in London, that would be his own business. Of course, if Peter decided to stay on in the basement, no such trips would be necessary. What a pity the boy had demurred at coming here. Didn't fancy it, he said, preferring to be dropped off at Gatwick so he could go to visit friends in Germany.

He knew Peter would come back. That fact, at least, made returning to London and announcing his decision easier I bear.

'Mike? *Mike.* Can I talk to you for a minute?'

There was silence. It was irritating to have to ask in the same wheedling tone a child uses for a neglectful parent. This was her husband, sitting slumped in front of the television, a half-finished glass of beer at his side, head lolling with tiredness. On the screen energetic young men with muscled thighs and mercenary faces darted about, artlessly kicking each other and punching the air. Around the nation ten million men slumbered in armchairs. It was a typically British Saturday afternoon.

She tried again. 'Mike! I have to go out in a minute. I need to know whether you're planning to come to Party Conference, so I can book a hotel and reply to invitations. If you are, you must fill in the forms this weekend to get your security pass. You can't decide at the last minute – it causes an awful fuss. Will you come?'

The last sentence was delivered in a softer tone. Elaine was troubled at the multiplying number of occasions at which Mike's absence was noticed. Despite a long-standing promise never to drag him unwillingly to a political event, in return for which he never insisted that she attend interminable airline dinners as his dutiful spouse, she wanted him to come. Or, rather, she wanted him to want to come, whether he came or not.

It was not unreasonable to ask. Conference was far more than wall-to-wall politics. Most people would jump at the chance of rubbing shoulders with the famous and the infamous, or goggling at every kind of oddball exhibitionist parading both inside and outside the conference centre, or the sheer intoxication of seeing news in the making. Then there were splendid parties and receptions galore where a protective male companion at one's side would be most acceptable. For anyone who enjoyed politics the week was a heady cocktail, a whirl of colour, noise, alcohol, endless arguments at the tops of voices, lapel badges, pockets stuffed with leaflets, crowded hotel lobbies, expensive food, sore feet, exhaustion and exhilaration. For the hangers-on, there was ample to do, whether laughing at the late-night antics of the *Blue Revue* or pottering around stalls or buying yet another signed Jeffrey Archer or just listening to the party's stars. He could find ways of enjoying it if he wanted.

Mike Stalker rubbed his eyes. 'Sorry,' he mumbled. 'After all these years you'd think I wouldn't suffer from jet lag, but it hits you sometimes. I must be getting old.'

Elaine sat on the armchair and ruffled his hair. Even though Mike irritated her profoundly sometimes, her main feeling towards him was still affectionate. 'No, not yet. Maybe just a little – did you know you have a few silver hairs already?'

He was yawning and staring at the screen again, mesmerised by the flitting figures. She slipped around on the carpeted floor in front of him, interposing herself between the set and his heavy-lidded eyes. It was as if she spoke from the television itself.

'Mike, I need to know. Party Conference or no Party Conference? It's at Blackpool in October, which doesn't compare with Honolulu or Singapore, but it will be lively this year and I'd be delighted if I could be on my husband's arm. I like showing you off – you're easily the best man there. Otherwise I get snide remarks about where you've got to.'

The compliment was not just flannel. Whenever she bothered to look carefully at her husband, love and remembered desire came back. Not flooding perhaps, but trickling: Mike was good-looking, successful, decisive and (when he wished) charming. All those qualities, which had so attracted her to him in the first place, had not diminished over the years. Not even recently. Her involvement with Roger did not change Mike, should not interfere with her regard for him. She did not even feel particularly guilt-ridden, but rather marvelled at the ease of hiding her delicious secret. Her increased sexual activity was making her keener, not less so, to have a successful parallel life with Mike. She was faintly ashamed that she took her husband for granted, but annoyed whenever it was grumpily drawn to her attention. She was sorry that the demands of a busy life led her to neglect him; she was not conscious of how often she simply forgot all about him.

Mike sat up and yawned. 'They elected you, not me, Elaine. I don't find it exciting, being your appendage. The parties are an effort; normally I wouldn't waste five minutes on idiots like your bad-breathed acquaintances who find salvation in a free gin and tonic, a mini-sausage on a stick and a brief conversation with Norman Tebbit.' The effort seemed to tire him further and his shoulders sagged. He stared at the television and she wondered what incident, if any, he was recalling. 'If I speak my mind, you have an instant problem. If I stay away, likewise it creates difficulties for you – I understand that. It's just not my style. I am not a wife: sorry. For me it's a real switch-off. Count me out.'

She sighed but was satisfied. The question had been put fairly, and answered. She would miss him. Yet he would not be missed.

'Right, so now I know. I'll go on my own. Save money, that's a bonus. Now I'll be back about eleven; there's steak and ice cream in the freezer, salad in the fridge, potatoes for microwaving in the cupboard by the sink, if you're hungry. I'm tolerably well organised this week. Will you be all right?'

But answer came there none. Mike was asleep.

'Ah! Mrs Stalker! How good of you to come. Come in, come in!'

Light bulbs flashed to a smatter of applause and excited chatter, as Elaine stepped over the threshhold of Vane Hall for the annual buffet supper of Andrew Muncastle's Conservative Association. A hundred and twenty noisy people in formal dress, men stuffed into tight trousers and jackets that no longer fastened over midriffs blessed by the god of plenty, the younger women in Frank Usher black dresses, the older ladies in jersey lurex and real pearls, surged forward until Elaine feared being knocked over. The air was redolent with the smell of cigars.

The house's owner Mr Townsend, now bouncing before her on the balls of his well-shod feet, was the proud proprietor of Townsend's Stopovers, a string of late-night garages. He grabbed her hand in both of his and pumped it up and down as his sharp-eyed wife hovered at his side. Andrew and Tessa Muncastle greeted her, then melted courteously into the background.

'Are you alone? Surely not.' Mr Townsend was concerned. 'Did you drive yourself?'

'Certainly.' Elaine smiled, but was vaguely irritated. She could guess what lay behind his enquiry. 'We MPs may have generous allowances but they don't run to a personal chauffeur, you know.'

'But you found your way all right? You didn't get lost?'

'No problem. You can thank Andrew here for giving me excellent instructions. Why should I get lost?'

'But a woman! You shouldn't be driving yourself. My wife gets lost all the time.'

I bet she doesn't, thought Elaine drily. Women who let men think so, though, are more of a pest than the fools who believe them.

'I'm here now, and jolly glad to be.' Avoiding the temptation to be cutting, Elaine turned her attention graciously from host to hostess. 'What a crowd! Mrs Townsend, your house is lovely.'

Mrs Townsend was a narrow-hipped woman with small dark eyes and tightly drawn skin from a recent facelift. She had supported her erratic husband through thick and thin over thirty years, ignored his philandering, hoarded his money, paid off his gambling debts, run his business whenever it was in trouble and brought up his three children to successful lives of their own. She took Elaine's arm determinedly.

'I just want you to say hello to my daily. She's dying to meet you. Then there's Lady Wooster – bit old and gaga now, but so generous . . .'

The daily stood holding a tray of champagne. She dimpled with delight as the two women bore down on her. 'Saw you on telly last night, Mrs Stalker!'

Elaine had been on a chat show, endeavouring, in between silly questions about her life in Parliament, to inject a modicum of serious discussion. Here was a chance to discover if she had succeeded.

'Really? Was it all right?'

The daily was flattered. 'Very nice. Very interesting.'

'But did I make sense? Did you agree with what I said?'

'Ah, I wasn't really listening. I was peeling potatoes and our lad called me in to see. You looked lovely, I must say.'

Elaine smiled ruefully. Perhaps Lady Wooster might be more forthcoming. The dowager, a skinny wreck in a shimmery fabric and diamonds, was holding forth in a corner. As Elaine approached, holding out her hand in greeting, the woman fixed her with a gimlet stare and raised a quavery voice.

'I don't hold with this equality, Mrs Stalker. I mean, are all these working women really happier?'

The old lady was clearly used to winning arguments, but Elaine resolved to disappoint her. 'Yes, I believe many of them are. It's nice not to have to ask your husband all the time for money for the things you want.'

The crone fingered a diamond earring, her mouth working. When she spoke again in a hoarse whisper there was a look of triumph in her eye. 'Huh. We used to get what we wanted from our husbands – and lovers – and *without* having to go to work for it, either.'

The two MPs began to circulate smoothly around the crowded rooms, spending time with everyone: nobody must be missed. Between them they worked a room, starting at opposite sides, having a few words with each person, face to face; pausing a moment here, sitting for a minute there by a disabled lady, speaking respectfully to a retired colonel, listening to the deputy mayor on refuse collection, quizzing his blushing son about school results. It was part of the job and both were soon totally absorbed by it.

Tessa slipped quietly away down a darkened passage and pushed open a heavy panelled door. The bright light inside made her blink. It was the kitchen. Two middle-aged men in chefs' white aprons and hats, one tall and skinny, the other short and fat, were waving ladles and arguing fiercely with each other. She began to apologise and back out, but they pulled her inside, delighted to have such an important visitor.

'I'm Brian, and this is Clarence,' the tall one announced. His face never stopped moving, jerking and twitching as he glanced down affectionately at his red-faced partner.

'He's the stupid one,' said Clarence with a thumb jerk upwards. 'We keep the Clarendon restaurant – d'you know it? Left the sous-chef in charge tonight.'

'Should be quiet there – all our regulars are here!' Brian hooted happily at what was clearly an old joke.

'Come for our game pie, see.' Clarence pointed the ladle in the direction of five magnificent pies on a rack. Their pastry was thick and golden and now cool to the touch. 'Five kinds of game: hare, grouse, partridge, duck and a little venison. We've just finished ladling in the jelly – our own recipe. Then half an hour or so in the fridge, and hey presto!' He slapped Brian's lean stomach, all he could easily reach.

The kitchen was warm and homely, with plates and pots full of butter and fresh herbs; the double sink was cluttered with dishes. An innocent joy, based on a knowledgeable love of well-made, wholesome food, pervaded the air. The two men had no desire to talk politics but were pleased at her interest and began to scribble down recipes in a spirit of shared delight in good cooking. Tessa found herself at ease in their company. Brian and Clarence spoke in turns, each carrying the story forward, each watching the other speak, anxious to understand, to please, to pick up the tale the moment it was let go, like two ball players long used to each other's rhythms. They touched constantly, hand on arm, fingers to elbow, lightly, as if needing repeated reassurance that the other was still there.

Tessa was intrigued. She, a good Catholic, might normally have felt repulsion at these two ageing queers. Instead she found herself laughing at their jokes and enjoying their performance, though the swaying ladles as she had entered suggested they were like that all the time, even without an audience. Centuries ago they might have been monks, running a straw-strewn monastery kitchen, abjuring the sins of the flesh, or most of them. Even now each had his counterpart in a priest of her acquaintance, a blasphemous thought quickly banished from her mind. At least neither was going to make a suggestive remark to her, or try to pat her bottom. Quite suddenly she felt safe.

'Have you been together long?' she asked, for all the world as if she were talking to a married couple. Brian was instantly wary and moved protectively close to Clarence, but Tessa was not about to make fun of them. They looked at each other and giggled.

'Too long!'

'Thirty years. Isn't it a gas? Never thought I would put up with him for thirty minutes. Such awful habits he has . . .' And they were off again, teasing, poking fingers in the air and gurgling with contented laughter.

Tessa smiled with them, leaning against the closed door, recipes clutched in her hand as if maybe they contained the secret of marital happiness. Of course gays could stay together as devotedly as any hetero couple: her common sense told her that. Famous names sprang to mind – Britten and Pears, Noel Coward and his Gerald. She had simply never met any before and was captivated.

Suddenly essential tasks were remembered. With a great flurry and anxious cries, pies were carried into the big fridge and arranged meticulously on shelves. Knives flashed as salads were chopped, four creative hands in long-accustomed unison, two mouths chattering, Brian, Clarence, Brian, Clarence, like rapidly alternating pistons driving their efforts.

'I envy you,' Tessa said softly, but the men were once again absorbed in their work and she was an intruder.

Brian spoke as she opened the door. 'Thank you for popping in to see us, Mrs Muncastle. Much appreciated. When you get back to Westminster, would you say hello to a friend of ours? Sir Nigel Boswood. We used to know him years ago, but we've lost touch. If you get a chance. Give him our . . . our love. Just say Brian and Clarence, he'll know.'

'I will.'

Mike was in the same armchair, glass empty, ruefully rubbing his stiff neck. Evidence that he had moved at least once was provided by the evening newspaper draped across his middle and the greasy wrappers from the fish and chips which had formed his supper. He examined the disorder surrounding his armchair and felt faintly ashamed. He was not bored or lonely, just tired. The thought of joining Elaine at that evening's beanfeast had not seriously occurred to him, but doing so would have been similar to joining passengers in the arrival lounge after a long flight:

unexpected, unnecessary and wearing. The punters wanted to see and hear Elaine, not him. Mike was vaguely proud that his wife was successful in her chosen occupation, as long as she did not insist that he be involved. His presence would, in fact, have been a distraction to her, just as if she had turned up to sit on the flight deck. She would be glancing at him anxiously, particularly at his glass, trying to guess how many he had had. If the argument got heated, she would try and pull him away just as he was winning his point. The body language between himself and Elaine had to be perfect too: there was quite a skill in promoting the right messages. What a pain such evenings could be.

He gazed mournfully at the empty glass and debated heaving himself out of the comfortable chair to fetch a refill. Elaine used to do that for him, once. Wistfully, he would have preferred Elaine as she used to be: her life and thoughts revolving around him. She'd tried hard in the early years of their marriage and he had failed to respond, leaving her alone for long weeks with two small babies, one handicapped, yet she had expressed no resentment. The reserves of spirit and energy she had summoned to deal with Jake hadn't vanished after the child's death, but had been directed outside the family into her burgeoning career. He had neither the right nor the urge to criticise. His reaction to Jake's suffering had been to roster himself secretly on to longer flights without telling Elaine. He had left her to her own devices, denied her the warmth and intensity promised in their courtship, and without rancour she had simply developed away from him and their home. What she wanted in life did not come through her husband, but she got it nevertheless. Another marriage might long since have disintegrated, though of course Elaine had strong reasons for not challenging him too hard: a woman MP would face hurtful accusations of failure over a divorce. Splitting up would always be seen as the woman's fault for being too ambitious.

Mike yawned, shook his aching shoulders, cracked his fingers one by one, reached for the remote control and changed channels. It was nearly midnight; Elaine had miscalculated again. Still, she might prefer it if he were waiting up for her, slightly reproachful, a dutiful spouse. He smiled at his own acquiescence as her car came up the drive. A moment later his wife, looking weary, was entering the room. He spoke first.

'Had a good evening?'

'Not bad. Thank heaven there'll be no election for a while yet.'

'You sure?' The press was full of speculation.

'Uh-huh. As long as we can maintain our majority in crucial debates we'll survive. Only strong governments with big majorities, who are well ahead in the polls, call early elections. Don't worry.'

Mike pulled a face. 'I'm remembering what happened to the last Labour government. Hesitated till the last minute, then lost, badly, and the next three elections too. Not a good precedent.'

Elaine took off her jacket. 'Given the highly dodgy nature of my seat, I just hope the election is a long way off.'

Mike shrugged. 'You could lose anyway, even if the next election is a roaring success.'

She was irritated again. Her husband's political antennae were almost non-existent. 'That's the equivalent of me telling you that one of these days your plane might crash. Thanks a million.'

He was chastened and muttered an apology. Somehow the evening had come to an unsatisfactory end. Neither had intended it that way; there had been no row, no big disagreement. No meeting of minds either. A vague feeling of a missed opportunity pervaded the air, but each was too tired to pursue the matter or express concern at the fact that most of their evenings now were spent apart, and most of the remainder, like this one, ended in stalemate.

CHAPTER THIRTEEN

'Your fan club's at it again.' Diane Hardy's voice on the phone sniffed disapproval. 'Mr Sutton is inviting you to tea during Party Conference. What do you want to do?'

Crouched on the floor of her flat surrounded by scribbled reminders, Elaine cradled the phone between chin and shoulder. 'Which one's Mr Sutton? Isn't he the retired newspaper chap? What does he say?'

Diane snorted. 'Pin your ears back. "My dearest darling Elaine. I do hope you had a very happy birthday – your own day: congrats! What joy, when you wrote and thanked me for my card in your own dear hand. Well, my beloved Elaine, I was so thrilled. I shan't forget your kindness to me with this beautiful gesture." It goes on like that for four pages. You want me to read it all?'

'Makes a change from some of the letters we get. What does he say about the conference?'

'Um . . . Ah, here it is. "As you know, my darling Elaine, my poor wife died in 1976 and October 10th would have been our wedding anniversary, so it will be a sad time for me. It would cheer me up so much if you would consent to have tea with me, when you are nearby at your party's conference in Blackpool. You have been writing me such kind letters . . ."'

'How sweet!' Elaine giggled: 'We just acknowledge the steady stream he sends us.'

'". . . for two years now and yet we have never met. I watch for you on television all the time and it makes my day when I see you there, looking so lovely . . ." and so on. It's a bit difficult to read, the handwriting is so shaky.'

'Poor old sod. Well, why not? We don't often get a chance to make someone happy. How old d'you think he is?'

'Search me. But from the feebleness of the writing and the fact he's been on his own and retired for donkey's years, he could be nearly eighty. Sounds very lonely. He's certainly pursued you with energy; the file of his letters is an inch thick.'

'Fine. Then let's invite him to tea at my hotel. Make his day.'

Diane sniffed. 'I don't think you should. But if you're determined then I'll arrange it. And I'll tell the local press – no, don't argue – it's a human interest story. At least then you'll get something out of it too.'

Elaine put the last touches to her hair, fixed the large pearl earrings which Roger liked so much, carefully applied a bright pink lipstick, checked her tights back and front for holes, slipped her feet into newly polished black patent high-heeled shoes and took a long hard look in the mirror.

How nice it would be to have a day off and slop around in jeans and an old stained sweater. How wonderful not to have to bother with her hair, to dispense with the monthly hairdressing appointment necessary to keep her hallmark blonde. Its real colour was a mystery now. Greyer than last year, certainly. Elaine agreed with Margaret Thatcher, a brunette at her first election, who chided a woman friend for going grey; and so the Iron Lady's hair wavered between gold and corn, depending on the seasons, her mood and her standing with the electorate, until the week after her fall when like her face it turned ashen.

The face this morning had to be impeccable. Anne Cook, doyenne of Fleet Street's lady columnists, was coming to her house to do an interview for the *Herald*.

'A personality piece, darling,' the throaty old voice had grated down the line. 'It's about time! You've hit the headlines more than once, dear, and our readers are asking about you. I want to know all about your life as a high-profile new MP. We'll bring a photographer, then we can have a nice cosy chat.'

Fastening her jacket, Elaine tried to shake off her feeling of unease. Most colleagues didn't get the chance of a full-page spread in a national newspaper. Most would demur modestly, but in secret would give their eye teeth for such publicity. Ministers in particular would be chary of such an invitation. Personality pieces about individual Ministers suggested ambition, and, being British, that would never do. Some simply did not trust the press, alleging that only bad news would be printed. Elaine was scornful of such attitudes. If MPs and Ministers were more media-wise they might be better at explaining themselves, their policies and beliefs to the people who chose them.

Yet Elaine believed with rare passion that press freedom was just as important as political freedom. Britain's investigative journalism, at its best, was the best in the world. All the more pity that quality reporting lay cheek by jowl with bare breasts and buttocks and endless sleazy interest in the private lives of public people. This is the price-tag of freedom of speech: that the press can say what they like.

Elaine drew away from the mirror, still apprehensive, and checked the kitchen and living room. If the interviewee were a man, piles of Hansards littering the sofa would produce indulgent remarks about devotion to duty. If a fine smell of roast beef emanated from the kitchen his choice of competent caring partner would be praised. It was different for her. A woman never gets the benefit of the doubt. Any mess would imply incompetence at the monumental twin tasks of running a home and a career, and that she was foolish to try. Dinner in the oven, proper cooked dinner, would suggest an obsession with trivialities. A pile of unwashed laundry hidden at the back of the washing machine would be gleefully spotted and quoted as evidence of sloth. Either way, tidy or disorderly, the implication could be drawn by a grumpy journalist having a bad day that she was a pushy bitch who did not love her husband or children. For, if she did, how could she leave them behind?

Female feature writers were the worst. Often the top females in journalism had become embittered with their own struggle; few had successful private lives and simply did not believe it was possible to manage both. Anne Cook was better than most, but even she assumed there must be cracks in the edifice on show, and that it was her job to find them.

The train slowed near Ratcliffe power station's giant cooling towers and turned west. Anne Cook folded her newspaper, put out her cigarette regretfully – it could be the last for hours – retouched her lipstick and reached for her coat. A tall woman, once handsome, with wide shoulders and thin hips, she wore a green wool jacket with black revers and massive shoulder pads over a tight black skirt, slit at the side, revealing veined flesh in shiny dark stockings. Today's expedition to the sticks was in the nature of a day out. She was not looking forward to the winter. Forty years' hard slog was giving way to drifting fears of old age. Not retirement; old journalists never retire, they just grow old and mad, until the last deadline is missed and the phone rings no more.

Outside the station a convoy of run-down blue and white taxis waited hopefully, their cheerful Pakistani drivers chattering in heavily accented English. No one seemed to have heard of her destination. A noisy conversation in Punjabi ensued with much gesticulation and finger-pointing, everyone pitching in with advice. Nor was there a map. With a sinking feeling Ms Cook realised she had travelled way beyond A-Z maps. Clutching her coat, bag and briefcase she tried again.

'It's Elaine Stalker's house. The MP. Does that help?'

It did. The leading driver's face broke into a mass of smiles. Why hadn't she said so in the first place? As the cab moved off Cook reflected grimly that similar systems exist as far afield as downtown Tokyo and upstate Bangladesh. A postal address is for banks and the taxman; to arrive physically at a destination you give the name of the occupant and the approximate location, describe both briefly, and off you go. She hoped to God the house had modern plumbing.

The two women greeted each other warily on the doorstep, both overdressed for the event, both unduly bright and effusive. Cook's glance took in all the artificial effort at once. Both realised this contest mattered far more to Elaine than to Cook.

The agency photographer, driving from Leicester, telephoned that his van was broken down and he would be late. It was decided to continue without him. Anne Cook settled herself at the kitchen table, politely accepted a cup of instant coffee and studied her notebook. Younger writers used a tape; she prided herself on her spidery shorthand, written without once taking her eyes from her subject's face. It was an extraordinary talent. Elaine found herself distracted and disconcerted. It gave the woman a creepy air, like an automaton, the furiously scribbling right hand working quite independently of the rest of the taut, concentrating body, the gaze connecting permanently with her own face, the head nodding slowly to a completely different rhythm.

'Now, Elaine – may I call you Elaine? – what first took you into politics?'

Elaine had been expecting this one. 'My family were an argumentative bunch and my father was always very interested. And I was at university in the mid-1970s – there were two general elections in quick succession while I was a student, plus the end of the Vietnam War and Watergate and Nixon's impeachment. I found the whole thing totally absorbing.'

'When was that?'

'I was at college from 1974 to 1977.'

'And you were married soon after?'

It was a question, not a statement. The facts, the bare bones of her life, were all in the *Who's Who* entry which she had written and vetted herself, as all entrants do.

'Mike and I were married the day after we finished exams.'

'Was there any particular reason for that?' The voice was bland, noncommittal, the mouth squeezed into a smile. A flake of red lipstick disfigured the distinctive Cook front teeth.

'Not really. We wanted to get married and felt it was best to wait until the exams were over.'

'Did you have to get married? I mean, were you pregnant?'

Elaine gasped. Bloody cheek. She looked closely but the face opposite her was expressionless.

'No, but we were unusual in other ways, I suppose: most of our friends thought we were very old-fashioned getting married at all.'

'Ah, I see. Highly commendable. Is that because you were sleeping together?'

Elaine stiffened. 'I'm really not sure that's any of your business.'

'But everybody did in those days.'

'I think we had better move on to the next question.' Elaine hoped she sounded frosty.

Cook turned a page and spent a moment studying her notes. 'Do you enjoy being an MP?'

'Oh yes, enormously. It's a fascinating job and I am particularly lucky to be representing South Warmingshire. People here have been very kind to us as a family, and as you can see it's a lovely place to live.'

That was a fairly standard answer. Cook shifted restlessly. 'It must be difficult being one woman amongst only a handful of other women, surrounded by all these men in the House of Commons?'

Elaine sipped coffee. She was going to have to be extremely careful. 'It is difficult, yes. I would much prefer there to be a lot more women. It would be good for the country, apart from anything else.'

'And what does your husband think about your activities? It can't be much fun for him.'

Elaine winced as she realised that she and Mike had not had a serious conversation for months. That Christmas fiasco had put a serious dampener on everything, so almost by mutual consent they had spent relatively little time together since. Still, she was not about to air any personal worries in the press. Too late: the journalist had noticed her hesitation and slight frown.

'Mike has an important job in his own right, you know. He is not in politics himself but I find that helpful. I wouldn't want a post-mortem on every speech the moment I came home.'

'Of course.' Cook spoke smoothly, with a reassuring smile. The tongue flickered and transferred more lipstick. 'Now, let's return to the strange life you lead, surrounded by all these male MPs. Do you find the men attractive?'

'*What* did you say?'

'Do you fancy any of them – your male colleagues?'

The woman was waiting for an answer, her eyes glittering. Elaine felt an angry flush spreading across her neck.

'I don't think that's what I or they are there for, frankly.'

'So you don't fancy any of them. Aren't they attractive? Some of

199

them must be. What about the Prime Minister – do you think he is attractive? A lot of women do. They say he gets the women's vote. Would you agree with that?'

Elaine allowed herself a prim look. 'I wouldn't know. Most people voted for him in my view because they saw an honest, decent, capable, caring *person*. And that's what he is.'

Cook turned the page. Most of the article was already written in her mind, but a little local colour was always helpful. Pity Elaine wasn't rising to the bait more.

'Why do you think there are so few women MPs?'

Elaine was tempted to say, because we have to put up with crap like this and most capable women have far more sense. Instead she pretended to think deeply for a moment.

'It has a lot to do with most people's image of an MP as a chap in trousers aged thirty-three with a wife and two children,' she answered. 'Women at that age are tied down with children, even if they are working as well – the priorities are different. By the time most women interested in politics get started they're already in their forties and a long way behind. That makes it harder. Apart from anything else it affects their confidence. And I think women also find it straight-forwardly objectionable to have to leave families behind, which is in the nature of the job and unavoidable. The men don't like it either, but they'll put up with separation, whereas women often simply refuse to contemplate it.'

'It must be hard for the men MPs too, with their wives away. Would you say that?'

'Yes, I would. The problems are exactly the same for male MPs as for women. Everyone forgets that.'

'Does it tempt them into affairs?'

'Possibly. I wouldn't know.'

'But do you think the separation makes these men MPs vulnerable?'

'Probably. Why don't you ask them?' The interview *stank*. Elaine was getting very angry.

'Well, then, I'll ask you. Do you have affairs?'

'*I beg your pardon?*'

'Do you have affairs with your male colleagues? There you are, all thrown together, attractive men and women – you've admitted that you find the men attractive – spouses away, the MPs will play. Haven't you ever been propositioned?'

Elaine leaned forward, a grim smile on her face. 'Well, if you really want to know . . .'

Cook licked her lips. The beringed hand paused, hovered, trembled.

'. . . I have. We all have. By about three hundred of them. All in one week. And we accepted. There are two brothels in the basement of the

House of Commons, all decked out in red plush velvet and staffed by the women Members on both sides. We charge the blokes through the nose and give the money to charity. We do it as a public service so they go home to their wives happy. We're very good at it. Does that satisfy you?'

Cook put down her pencil, annoyed. 'I was asking a serious question, Elaine.'

'Come on. If I had, would I tell you?'

The journalist noted the offhand answer as significant and persisted. 'I heard a story that somebody sent you a bunch of red roses to your desk a month or so ago in the House of Commons. Is that true?'

Elaine cradled the near-empty cup in her hands and appeared to contemplate. 'Yes.'

'Who might that have been?'

'I know who it was.' Elaine leaned back and folded her arms. She had conceived a total hatred of the woman opposite her, sitting in her kitchen, drinking her coffee and asking her impertinent and intrusive questions.

'Will you tell me? Off the record, if you prefer.'

'Certainly. You may do with the information whatever you like. It was a really gorgeous chap, a distinguished professional man, older than me. Married, I'm afraid.'

'Who?'

Elaine pointed at the photograph on the wall. 'Him. He goes by the name of Mike Stalker. It was my birthday. And now, Ms Cook, if you have no more "serious" questions, I think we had better draw these precious moments to a close. I have work to do.'

The pencil was waved dismissively in the air. Cook was not leaving yet. 'I just had one or two questions about your family. It is of great interest to our readers that you are a mother. Now, how many children do you have?'

Elaine slumped back in the chair. 'I have one daughter, Karen, who was born in 1978, a year after we were married. Before you ask, there was no reason to wait. She is fifteen now and doing GCSEs this coming summer. Very grown up for her age, taller than me.'

'At the local school?'

'Not exactly. As there's no one at home to look after her she goes to a nearby boarding school.'

'Fifteen, you say. What sort of advice do you give her?'

'We've told her she can do what she wants with her life and we would encourage her in most things, but we're keen to ensure she completes her education by going on to university. She is capable.'

'Would you advise her for or against going into politics?'

201

'That's up to her. If she wanted to try I'd give her all the help I could. I wouldn't push her, though, it's a hard life.'

'Would you give her advice about sex?'

'Of course. I am her mother.'

'What would you tell her?'

By now Elaine was controlling herself with every remaining shred of self-discipline at her command. 'When the time comes, to behave with care and consideration. I hope she will be like that anyway, in all her dealings with other people, not just sex.'

'Would you give her condoms?'

'I have had no reason to do so. They do receive sex education in school now, you know.'

'Would you, though? Make sure she was using condoms?'

For a brief moment Elaine considered picking up her interrogator by the lapels of her vile green jacket and throwing her out of the house. Anne Cook would make a wonderful crumpled heap on the gravel, stockings torn, hair awry, papers and notebook scattered, scrabbling around in the dirt for a lost earring and expensive contact lenses. And those lipstick-covered false teeth.

The doorbell rang. It was the photographer, flustered and apologetic, clutching four bags of equipment. He was a local man, delighted to get a lucrative national assignment. He knew Elaine from previous work but nevertheless was startled to be kissed heartily by her on the cheek with a whispered 'Am I glad you're here!' He wondered what had been going on.

For the next half-hour Elaine had the satisfaction of watching an increasingly tetchy Anne Cook working for a living as a photographer's assistant, holding lighting reflectors, kneeling at her feet under instruction from the earnest photographer trying to ensure that the right quality of soft white illuminated the shadows on Elaine's face. Cook for her part gritted her teeth and concentrated her mind on the double gin and tonic with ice and lemon to come from the train buffet. Not a good day.

At last it was done. Elaine held out her hand to both. The photographer would take Cook to the station – which relieved her victim of any obligation to offer a lift, or that awkward wait for a taxi, when no one is quite sure what to say and whether it is still on the record. As the battered van trundled down the path Elaine wished heartily it would break down again, preferably not here but a long mile or so from the station so the ghastly Ms Cook would have to walk. She was filled with foreboding at the article to come.

The Blackpool hotel was old and scruffy and miles from the conference centre but was all that was available. The best rooms were bagged months in advance. Elaine dumped her suitcase heavily on the hotel bed, opened it, shook out and hung up her best two blue suits and carefully pressed matching shirts, as well as a new silk jacket and black evening trousers for Wednesday night's drinks party, arranged her cosmetics the right way up by basin and bedside, sniffed at the stained bath and searched for a drink. Out here beyond the edge of North Shore it seemed no one had ever heard of hotel minibars, or had figured out why, given the whisker of a chance, the British prefer to stay in almost any country's hotels other than their own.

There would be plenty to drink later. Her first appearance would be at the Midlands Area reception in the Imperial Hotel, home base for the duration of the Prime Minister, Cabinet and top party officials, and location of invitation-only social events. It would be a noisy, cheerful affair of 500 or more comrades celebrating the survival of another year and greeting each other over-loudly. The following morning would be her first taste of the conference itself.

It seemed an age since she had last attended, before the election. Mike might watch on television; he would probably see more of the debates than she would. As an MP she would be expected to circulate, to chat dutifully with delegates drinking execrable coffee, to stroll among commercial, political and charitable stalls collecting unwanted leaflets and lapel stickers, and generally to put herself about. Choosing instead to listen to a debate, luxuriating in intellectual argument (such as it was), would have been the height of bad manners. Conference, like most other aspects of her life these days, was not what it seemed.

The Imperial was a hive of activity. Additional staff above and below stairs had been vetted and hired. Several were members of Special Branch, now disporting themselves as waiters, kitchen hands and cleaners. For a month the hotel's guests had been subjected to unusual scrutiny, their antecedents checked, baggage discreetly searched. During conference itself the Imperial became known as Fort Knox. Getting into the hotel was comparatively easy for Elaine as a recognised face, but still she was required to queue alongside journalists and hotel guests for security clearance. In front of her she recognised the upright figure of Tom Sparrow, Roger's agent, who had attended her Christmas party. The interminable checks would be repeated on every entry to the combined hotel and conference centre complex, rapidly becoming irksome. By the end of the week tempers would be wearing thin.

Once she was inside, the picture changed completely. The majestic foyer, its stucco and architraves fresh with paint and new varnish, heaved with a great barrage of smartly dressed people, brightly lit by television lights, the din making the crystal chandeliers shake and judder. At the bar, tall young men waved fifty-pound notes and attempted to buy overpriced champagne. At the reception desk harassed clerks were trying to accommodate additional VIPs wearing pained expressions; there were always some who turned up late, insisting that reservations had been made, openly offering backhanders to be booked in. In the kitchen a perspiring chef cursed guests who wanted real mayonnaise on a night when the eggs were curdling. Behind a glass door on the terrace BBC technicians prepared a makeshift studio among the potted palms, their cables criss-crossing the floor like liana vines in a jungle, waiting to trip up unwary studio guests. The breakfast broadcasts would beam to the nation a dismal view of storm-tossed seas beyond Blackpool esplanade to the chagrin of the town's tourist officer.

Elaine headed towards the largest reception room. Under the lights the noise was deafening as a crowd of delegates greeted each other with unfeigned affection. Quickly she availed herself of a large orange juice. Mr and Mrs Townsend were standing inside the doorway and pounced on her, talking at the tops of their voices and demanding her return to Vane Hall. Mrs Horrocks and several South Warmingshire ladies waved a welcome from the far side of the room. Elaine gestured helplessly as the crowd pressing in prevented her moving. Half listening to the Townsends' insistent chatter gave her a chance to look around.

With relief she spotted Roger. Sir Nigel Boswood was present too; as a Cabinet Minister his more agreeable duties included doing the rounds of as many area receptions as his constitution would allow. Andrew Muncastle, his new PPS, was nearby, Tessa beside him.

'My dear Elaine!' Boswood boomed, and kissed her heartily on the cheek. He was looking more rotund and contented than ever. She smelled good red wine on his breath, and, remembering Roger's approval of him, responded warmly: had he had a pleasant recess? Was he looking forward to the new session?

'Ah, I fear we may have a hard time in the coming months.' Boswood's assessment was delivered in a low voice. What was to be shared between fellow MPs was to be hidden from the delegates. 'I'm glad you're on board. Could do with a few more like you.'

'A few more like you, Sir Nigel, and we would have fewer difficulties.' Elaine raised her voice and nearby guests nodded agreement.

The remark was sycophantic but none the less true. Too many Cabinet names had been bandied about in the press recently as plotting in secret with supportive backbenchers. The objective was to force the Prime Minister to sack Ministers from the moderate centre of the party, who could be trusted to give him their faithful backing, and replace them with men of less certain loyalty and views more to the plotters' taste. It was a disreputable business and Boswood would have none of it. He raised his glass in graceful salute and moved smoothly away.

Elaine waded over to greet the Muncastles but found Andrew caught by several elderly female fans, leaving Tessa somewhat lost on the edge of the group. She was wearing a short-sleeved pink dress which set off her slim figure quite well; her expression had a faint air of petulant resentment. Elaine frowned, recalling the exchange in the Strangers' Cafeteria eighteen months before and the tinge of hysteria then in Tessa's voice.

Lightly she touched Tessa's arm. For a moment the woman was unwilling to respond and appeared preoccupied, but Elaine was already speaking, breaking the ice.

'Hello; Elaine Stalker, remember me? How is your little boy – Barney, isn't it?'

Tessa shook herself out of her reverie and held out her hand. 'Thank you, Mrs Stalker, he's fine. You were so nice to him that day with the chocolate cake.'

Elaine gestured at the packed room. The heat was making her perspire. Her voice was sympathetic. 'Do you still find all this difficult, or are you more used to it by now?'

'Still uncomfortable, I'm afraid. I'm not very good at all this.' Tessa's hand flew to her neck and rubbed at a sore spot behind her ear. 'Andrew is very sweet about it, but it's a life which suits some people and not others.'

Elaine sought for some way of reassuring Tessa that she was neither alone nor beyond the pale. 'Andrew's lucky. At least you come; he must appreciate that. My spouse doesn't turn up at all. He has a living to earn, of course, but it must be nice to cuddle up warm in bed with someone you love after all this hullabaloo.'

To Elaine's surprise Tessa blushed bright red and looked at the floor. Her discomfiture and unhappiness were plainly visible. But whatever was wrong here was none of Elaine's business. Becoming a confidante of the distracted wife of an MP was not in the game plan; if she had to choose, Elaine's instinctive empathy was with her colleague, not with his partner. She knew which side she might be on in this conflict and it was not Tessa's.

'Sorry. Did I say something wrong? Forgive me. Anyway, have a nice evening.' Rapidly she made her escape.

Roger Dickson was at her elbow. His sudden presence made her jump and her pulse began to race. Before she could open her mouth he announced formally, a warning light in his eye: 'I don't believe you have met Caroline, have you?'

She froze. Till now it had always been easy to avoid meeting Roger's wife. Caroline Dickson came hardly at all to the Commons; her time was spent in the constituency where she was now a successful and well-liked Joint Master of the Hunt, which guaranteed contact with virtually all the influential supporters of the local party, including puppy walkers and hunt followers who after a good day's outing returned home flushed and happy to their council houses.

'No. I'm delighted to meet you.' Elaine shook hands with the strongly made woman standing before her.

Anyone less like the pained misery of Tessa Muncastle could not be imagined. Caroline was slightly taller than Elaine. She wore a dark-green velvet suit which fitted well across her broad shoulders, a blue silk shirt and real pearl earstuds. A matching velvet hairband wound with gold and small pearls kept her brown hair off her face. The style was slightly old-fashioned, Sloaney, timeless; the effect casual, friendly, stable, normal. Her skin was tanned and even weatherbeaten, her eyes bright blue and candid. Caroline looked healthy, bold and confident, unfazed by all the noisy clamour around them. A complete person, at ease with herself, as absorbed in her own life as Tessa, as Elaine even, yet more content than either. Caroline would have no doubts, no anxieties, other than Toby's getting into Sandhurst or a fallen horse or the summer fête. Her approach to life would be shrewd and perennially positive: politics was Roger's job, and she was happy to leave the thinking to him, though of course both he and the constituency could count on her reassuring presence as required. She would not hassle him for promotion but would offer automatic, vague encouragement whatever he chose to do. This was the rival, then. That Caroline had no suspicions of her was immediately apparent in her open grin as they shook hands.

'Whew! Bit crowded in here. Do you enjoy all this, Mrs Stalker? I bet you do.'

'It's all part of the job. Got to support the troops.' Elaine found herself imitating Caroline's hearty manner. Despite herself she liked the woman very much; it was impossible to feel any jealousy. It dawned on her that Roger needed them both, fulfilling different roles, both peripheral to him, with himself firmly at the centre, the bright sun around which both moons orbited, attracted by the same magnetism. Only a man could think or function like that, could take for granted that his own needs came first. There was no chance whatsoever that one affection could replace the other, that she could ever take this steady woman's place at the heart of Roger's life. That was plain in the protective way Roger stood by Caroline, a hand on her elbow, like those Victorian photographs, Roger the paterfamilias, Caroline the strong yet subordinate wife, mother and helpmeet.

Having made the introduction Roger deftly moved Caroline away. For a moment Elaine felt bereft. Goodness knows when she might talk to him again, in circumstances where flirting could take place, with the gentle skirmishes which re-established contact. Humbly she recognised that she had a little too much in common with Tessa Muncastle's mixed feeling of regret and anguish at not being at the centre of her man's universe. Not that Elaine wanted to function by being the centre of any man's life. What she achieved she did herself. Yet it was not comfortable being on the receiving end of such a brusque reminder that, should Roger ever have to choose between his wife and his mistress, like most politicians he would choose his wife.

Her musings were interrupted by being bumped hard from behind. Freddie Ferriman had been to two receptions already. He was red-faced and talkative and not quite in control of his limbs. Hanging on his arm was a lissom young woman, with a long neck, lightly tanned skin, a mass of tumbled mid-brown hair and a vacant look in her eyes. Freddie was contrite.

'Elaine! So sorry. Did I knock your glass? Here, let me get you another one. Orange juice, is it? But the drinks are free. Look, you chat to Marlene here and make her feel at home.' He headed unsteadily towards the bar.

Elaine was embarrassed. She had a feeling that she had seen this girl before. 'I'm Elaine Stalker MP. And you . . . ?'

'Marlene Weisacker. I'm Mr Ferriman's research assistant.' A Texas accent accompanied a flashing double row of perfect teeth. Elaine made one more comparison between the women present tonight and reflected drily that no one could be more different to Caroline Dickson. Since Roger's taste apparently ran to real women, intelligent women, he was unlikely ever to take up with a dumb bimbo like this. Elaine decided to tease, gently.

'That must be so interesting for you! Mr Ferriman is a wonderful man. So well thought of.'

'He is?' The girl sounded doubtful. Not so dumb, then. Elaine's expression was studiously neutral. The girl readjusted swiftly. 'Oh, yeah! You're so right. I'm here for a year as part of my studies at the University of Austin, Texas. I'd like to go into politics myself, so this is valuable experience.'

I'll bet, thought Elaine. 'Which branch? Are you thinking of standing for Congress some day?'

'Oh, I'm not sure yet, Mrs Stalker. Maybe I'll join a lobbying organisation. We have a lot of those in Washington these days.'

'It would give you plenty of opportunity to exercise your talents,' Elaine offered sweetly. She had just remembered where she had seen those long legs before. Ferriman was returning clutching three glasses. 'Your research assistant is a very special and interesting young lady, Freddie. I congratulate you.'

He puffed out his chest with pride as if the compliment had been paid to himself. Marlene stood beside him, her face unreadable.

The party was breaking up as dinner-time approached. At last Elaine was able to make her way to Mrs Horrocks and her cronies. Since Major-General Horrocks had died, all but one were widows, the exception being married to a retired gentleman who hated politics and preferred to spend the week golfing at nearby Lytham St Anne's. Courteously the women explored whom she was with (nobody) and her plans for the rest of the evening (nothing much). Shrewd Mrs Horrocks had come to the tentative conclusion that her MP's home life was not all it was cracked up to be, but was discreetly sympathetic. An invitation to join the ladies for a modest meal was pressed. Elaine accepted with alacrity.

Boswood tapped on the bedroom door, once, then twice close together, then once more, a code worked out with Peter on arrival. There was silence, then a shuffling sound from within.

'Who is it?' A hoarse whisper.

Boswood bent his face close to the door. 'Me. It's all right. Are you decent? Let me in.'

Down the corridor a woman secret service officer, dressed as a hotel maid, paused by her trolley full of cleaning materials and observed Sir Nigel Boswood talking to the door of his own room. Somebody else was inside. She had tried to gain entry earlier with her pass key but had been thwarted by the door being bolted on the inside. Her respectful request to turn down the bedclothes had been met with a brusque 'Go away!' Like any other guest Sir Nigel was entitled to share his bed with whomsoever he pleased. Her job, however, was to check names and faces against lists. Unidentified visitors left her and her boss feeling jumpy.

The door opened a crack on the chain. Peter checked suspiciously, muttered, 'Oh, it's you', and let Nigel in.

'You sure you want me to stay the night here, Nigel?' he said uneasily. 'The place is crawling with fuzz. I can smell them a mile off.'

'Certainly,' Nigel answered, making his voice sound brisk. He had a headache and his throat was hurting. He hoped he was not about to come down with a cold: Friday was too important. 'You're my official parliamentary research assistant; why not? You stayed doing some work on my speech and it was too late to go back to your digs. So you kipped the night on the sofa here. What could be possibly wrong about that?'

The younger man was still troubled. 'Can't stand this place, that's all,' he muttered. 'If it's all right with you, Nigel, I'd like to go back to

London tomorrow morning. More my scene.'

'What about my speech on Friday?' Nigel sounded hurt.

'I'll watch it on telly, and make notes for you. Better than hovering around on the fringes of the conference with a not very convincing story. There are police here from all over, even the Met. I could be recognised, do you realise? I've no desire to be arrested for loitering.'

It gave Peter a twinge of satisfaction to see his lover wince. Increasingly, partly as a way of reasserting his own independence, he reminded Nigel of how he earned his living. That usually produced some useful cash as a disincentive to further pick-ups, but paradoxically it reinforced Nigel's own strange need to be disgusted with the liaison. Had Peter talked about leaving this life and becoming respectable, going to college perhaps, Nigel would have pulled out all the stops to help; but the relationship would have lost its power and excitement, and the boy would have become no more than a neutral acquaintance. Peter had long since worked out Boswood's psychology. He had no intention of letting go yet.

'I'd almost certainly have to watch on TV anyway and I'd feel happier doing that in the flat. I won't miss, I promise. Please?'

The boy sidled up to Nigel. He placed a long-fingered hand on the man's chest, on the shirtfront under the jacket so that his young flesh was separated by only a few strands of cotton from Nigel's body. Peter gave his blue-eyed little boy look, long perfected, capable as a wizard's wand of guaranteeing most of what he asked for. It worked this time too. Nigel sighed heavily.

'If you must, then. Tomorrow, after breakfast – don't go dashing off at dawn, they really will arrest you then. Now we need to tidy up in here. In about half an hour my new speech-writer is coming and Roger Dickson, the new Minister, to go over this debate for Friday. Have we got any aspirin? Do you know I haven't made a conference speech for four years? I feel quite anxious about it. Be a good lad and sit quietly in the background. Fill their glasses but don't say a word. I know you won't let me down.'

Peter felt irritated. The need to be free of entanglements was beginning to reassert itself. He was fond of Nigel, but then he had been fond of Jack Hudd, and thought with intermittent affection of Hermann and Gustav and one or two others, and there would always be fresh faces on the Amsterdam scene. Being with the same person all the time, even one as generous and caring as Nigel, was becoming a bore. Having to behave in company not of his choosing was an imposition, yet Nigel had failed to notice his peevishness. A bad sign. More than anything else he would not be taken for granted.

Further knocks on the door produced Roger and Marcus Carey together. With a word in the right place from Roger, Carey had what he wanted and had slipped into his new post a month before. The arrivals were formal and reserved with Peter, whom they had not seen before. Then they stood in the doorway of the room gazing around with more than a little envy. As a senior Cabinet Minister Boswood was entitled to a fine suite. The lavish bathroom was crammed with miniatures of soap and cologne, the large sitting room furnished with big sofas and plush Wilton rugs, its mahogany writing-tables and an enormous leather-topped desk surmounted by a huge display of fresh flowers and foliage, pot plants in brass holders and oversized ashtrays. Its exotic chintz fabric was not to their taste, but the television was wired for satellite and CNN, a distinct bonus. A large beribboned basket of fruit was half eaten, mainly by Peter, who after a vague introduction from Boswood played at being the helpful assistant and then lounged in the background munching a pear.

'By Friday the delegates will all be feeling pretty jaded, and really are waiting for the Prime Minister's speech, so you have the most important job of all this week – the warm-up.' Roger was teasing his boss. He liked the man's self-deprecation, which was based on genuine surprise that a steadfast devotion to duty should have propelled him to one of the highest offices in the land. 'The speech therefore needs some funnies to get them going on a cold morning, a knock at the opposition, and a clear statement of our own policy. Have we any new initiatives to announce?'

Boswood looked askance. 'New initiatives? You have to be joking. It has been heaven's own job holding the budgets together at all this year. The new Jerusalem will have to wait.' He pulled a face and turned to Marcus Carey. 'I'm glad you could make it. Now: what have you come up with?'

Marcus pulled out a sheaf of notes from his briefcase and began chattering a little too enthusiastically. Roger caught Boswood's eye and suppressed a half-smile. For the next hour the three put their heads together, trying out phrases, rummaging for synonyms and euphemisms, soaring with hyperbole, searching for a suitable quote from Shakespeare or Burke or Churchill or somebody else the audience might possibly have heard of. As a good phrase occurred, Boswood would jump up and stride round the room, waving his arms, booming and gesticulating, testing its timing.

Marcus marvelled at the skill with which his mentors used words both to convey and to conceal meaning. Some Ministers speak well before enthusiasts at Party Conference but are truly terrible in the Commons. Others are useless on the platform, but come into their own in parliamentary debate. In a world dominated by television, old-fashioned oratory still mattered, but Boswood, Dickson and Carey all knew that in the twenty-five-minute speech what rated most was the crisp sound-bite of two or three sentences. Boswood needed to go out on a high; this could be his conference farewell. He intended to make a workmanlike job of it.

From the shadows Peter entertained himself by observing Boswood's two companions, sizing them up. Dickson was masculine and at ease in his skin. A sensual man, Peter guessed, but with a preference for bold handsome women, not boys or men. He could picture Roger as a well-muscled young student, playing rugby or cricket and drinking jocularly with male friends, but always withdrawing politely and without rancour at the slightest sexual approach from one of them. Carey was a different matter. Peter watched him silently for a long time and was amused that Marcus was uncomfortable at being examined. The smooth-shaven black face was eager to please; his well-educated mind and literary turns of phrase were placed doggedly at the service of the two older men despite the faintly patronising way they treated him. The body language was submissive, like the pictures in old history books drawn by Victorian explorers of the native bowing the knee in subjugation. There was a mixed-up psyche in there somewhere. Peter entertained himself briefly with a daydream of seducing Carey, knowing that his chances of ever finding out if the man was gay were slim. He would not have been interested anyway. He didn't like blacks.

That both Carey and Dickson were married would not have surprised him nor stilled his imagination. Many of his clients were married. Some were bisexual, some genuinely homosexual but hiding in an apparently straight relationship. There was only one group of homosexuals whom Peter never met – the gay man in a contented long-term partnership with another gay, where discovery presented no problems. Along with many heterosexuals, Peter would have scoffed at the notion that such couples exist. It suited him that homosexuality, even where legal, should carry a powerful stigma. If gays could live in tranquil happiness, he and his ilk would be out of business.

At last the three were satisfied. Marcus would phone through the agreed text to Central Office and have it faxed back for checking. A speaking copy typed in phrases would come up in the red ministerial box. Once out on the wires and on the autocue on Thursday night, it would nestle in the hands of bored hacks on Friday morning as Boswood spoke. The smarter ones would notice any changes and write clever pieces on the turn of a single word.

Boswood was looking tired. Roger wished Carey would stop gabbling so they could leave. He could sense rather than see the shifty impatience of the blond young man seated in the corner, legs crossed, hands in lap. Boswood's personal tastes were not unsuspected, but having a boy in one's room was taking a risk. Perhaps the bloke was getting demob-happy: that could be dangerous. At last Dickson rose, nodded a dismissive goodnight in Peter's direction and a more genuine one to

Nigel, grabbed Marcus's elbow and shepherded him firmly out of the room.

Andrew Muncastle picked up a toothbrush and methodically began to clean his teeth in preparation for bed. Peering into the mirror he caught his wife's dismal face, and with a sigh turned to her.

'You might *try*, Tessa. It's becoming very noticeable.'

His wife sat miserably in her night clothes on the edge of the hotel bed, twisting a damp tissue in her fingers. 'I *do* try,' she said defensively. 'I'm fine in the constituency, with people I know. It's mixing with strangers I find so awkward. Please, Andrew, do I have to be here? Couldn't I go home?'

Andrew hesitated. Keeping Tessa on track was a wearying business. He suspected she needed psychiatric help but was at a loss as to how to broach the subject. He walked over to her in an effort to be more gentle and took both her hands in his own. Turning them to examine her palms he exclaimed in astonishment.

'Your eczema is back with a vengeance, isn't it? Look, Tessa, don't you think you should have a word with Dr James? You've always been tense, but it seems to be getting worse.'

She pulled her hands away, hiding the sore patches. At least in a long-sleeved cotton nightgown the flaming areas by her elbows, under her arms and in her groin were not visible.

'You haven't answered my question. Can I go home, please? It might be best. Then you wouldn't have to worry about me.'

Andrew pondered, then shrugged. 'All right, if it'll make you feel better. But on two conditions. First that you go and see Dr James. Please, for all our sakes. Second, we're on the platform Friday morning. If you felt able to come back in time for that, I would appreciate it. Alec, Roger Dickson's driver, is driving up first thing Friday to bring the boxes and to give Roger a lift home. You could come up with him. Would that do?'

Tessa nodded dumbly. At least it would mean the rest of the week in peace.

Long after Andrew's regular breathing assured her he was asleep, Tessa lay awake, staring at the ceiling. She needed to understand, but had neither insight, experience nor vocabulary to express her fears. Educated by nuns, she had been taught from an early age to despise her body and to pray to be free of fleshly desires. The priest preparing them for marriage had quietly given her a booklet. Once alone, she dutifully glanced through it, then threw it away in distaste. It was impossible to believe that Andrew expected her to do all that and like it.

The night of their wedding had been a nightmare. Fortunately both she and Andrew had had quite a lot to drink; enveloped in a haze of blessing she had quite enjoyed the woozy tumbling about on the bed, until Andrew had returned from the bathroom, much as now, naked except for his underpants and with a towel around his neck. He looked so silly she had started to giggle, and was still laughing as he struggled to undo hooks and eyes and buttons on the long white lacy dress, so much that she rolled over and did it all for him, tossing the crumpled garment on to the floor and kicking her satin shoes after it. It was only then that she wondered what he was doing, but she was drunk enough not to struggle, just to gasp and cry out with surprise. Andrew was no great lover, had no finesse to prepare her nor any recognition of the state of her ignorance. Once he climaxed he had kissed her happily, rolled over and fallen asleep.

Months later she timidly broached the subject with her mother, who grimaced and admitted that she did not enjoy it either, but that it was a wife's duty. Thus Tessa never knew the sheer joy of sex, and quickly came to hate and fear it. Before long, however, she was pregnant with Barney.

Barney's birth was the most terrible thing Tessa had ever known. Labour was long and painful and not helped by her own tension and terror. In the antenatal clinic the doctors and midwives seemed so secure in their knowledge that she had nodded whenever she was asked if she understood the implications of 'natural' childbirth. Instead the pain blasted all human dignity out of her, until in the final stages she was screaming and begging to be allowed to die. After that, all Tessa could remember was Andrew's frightened eyes above a surgical mask, matching her own humiliating horror as the sweating obstetrician worked feverishly away under the canopy formed by her green-tented legs, strapped so helplessly into loops hung from poles. The baby's face, when he was laid at last in the crook of her arm, was purple with bruising from the forceps and streaked with her own bright blood.

It would not happen again, not ever. Her version of the healing process meant closing in on herself. At first Andrew was openly sympathetic, for she had had a hard time. It was months before it dawned on him that normal relations would not easily be resumed. Tessa had never been responsive in bed before; now she told him it hurt her. Her lack of interest and adroitness at finding polite excuses fended him off, especially as he was working flat out at politics, nursing the seat, frequently arriving home dog-tired, content to give her a peck on the cheek and turn in.

After the election he had gained a new lease of life and complained bitterly. For the moment, however, he seemed more sensitive and had not pressed her for ages. Perhaps he too was losing interest; in time, if he was kind, she might be able to respond once more. Nevertheless the idea of sleeping alone the following couple of nights filled her with relief. She looked at his head on the pillow, as his chest rose and fell with his steady breathing. None of this was his fault.

'I'm sorry, Andrew,' she whispered, but he was dreaming, and could not hear her.

It was raining. Elaine had suddenly remembered the tea party with Mr Sutton. The old chap would be worried.

She pictured him as she hurried along the windswept front. The spidery handwriting suggested someone slight and frail. For some reason she attracted the devotion of several lonely old gentlemen, complete strangers, whose interest in her activities was intense and well informed. One sent her all the press cuttings featuring her name or picture that he could lay hands on, every week. Having fans was highly flattering to her ego, especially when few Ministers could claim the same. It also troubled her, for it was as if her own being was disappearing, being subsumed into the powerful images on the screen. Parliament was becoming a giant soap opera, a happening for the benefit of the watching public, its personalities existing only as long as somebody had the set switched on. It made her shiver.

Mr Sutton was her most persistent correspondent. He had tried to invite himself to lunch in the House of Commons more than once. In one letter he had mentioned heart trouble. Elaine did not want to be responsible for his having a heart attack on the long train journey south; anyway, he was not her constituent. The tea party proposal was a more appropriate alternative.

As she rushed into the hotel lounge, shaking her umbrella and tossing her damp coat over a chair, several people rose to greet her. Two photographers and two journalists, one from the local radio station, introduced themselves. A reunion between pen-pals intrigued their editors, especially when one correspondent was the famous Elaine Stalker and the other a local resident.

Elaine looked round for Mr Sutton as she apologised for keeping them waiting. A large middle-aged man, a very large man, enormously obese and huffing heavily, moved slowly out from behind the journalists and held out his hand.

'My darling Elaine,' he began, 'don't apologise, please: waiting for you has been so worthwhile. I am so thrilled to see you at last. After all this time . . .'

The man towered and swayed over her. He was built like a Sumo wrestler and it was all fat, nearly 300 pounds at a guess. A large grey mackintosh like a Scouts' badly erected tent, flapping and frayed at the edges, covered faded corduroy trousers and a scruffy sweater. He waddled as he came towards her, trouser fabric rubbing in loud protest between overlapping thighs. His face was flushed, with fine beads of sweat standing on the brow. From the smoothness of his skin and his mousy hair he could not have been more than fifty.

She stood stock still, rooted to the spot. Mr Sutton grabbed her hand in a huge paw, squeezed it till her bones crunched and pressed it to his fleshy lips, kissing it loudly. The action dragged Elaine close to him as light bulbs flashed. She fought to control her distaste as a powerful wave of cheap aftershave emanated from the pink cheeks. If he came any closer he was going to lunge and kiss her on the face. That was clearly his intention. With an effort she pulled free and backed off, quickly putting space between them. His chest heaved and he looked sad.

'Yes, well, er, Mr Sutton . . .'

'Call me Jack. You must, I beg you.'

One of the girl journalists was having a fit of giggles. Sutton looked around offended and poked her hard on the shoulder.

'This is a very special occasion for me. My beautiful Elaine has asked me to tea. She is the most wonderful politician, the best MP in the whole country, in the world. You are not to make fun of her, do you hear?'

The hack looked up at the huge bulk and glaring eyes and subsided, mouth open.

The man did not seem simple, but was definitely strange. Elaine could not put her finger on it. The event posed several conundrums: how to extricate herself from it (and the overall relationship, such as it was) with the minimum pain to the peculiar Mr Sutton; how to avoid a row or appearing ungracious in the presence of the press; and her own curiosity – always a danger – to find out what made this oddity tick.

For the moment she had to behave as if nothing untoward had occurred. Elaine ordered tea and seated herself warily on the other side of the low table while Sutton squeezed his bulk into the biggest armchair, which sagged protesting under his weight.

'You told me you were in the newspaper profession.' It seemed a suitably anodyne remark.

He shuffled his feet and gazed down at his vast belly, brow furrowed. 'No . . . o, not exactly. I'm retired now, as I told you, on invalidity benefit. Oh, please forgive me, Elaine. I so admire you. All I did was sell newspapers at a kiosk until ill health prevented me from carrying on. I thought if I put it like that you would never write to me.'

He had a point. 'And I had the impression, Mr Sutton, that you were a little, well, older,' Elaine said weakly as she poured the tea. 'You must have been very young when you lost your wife.'

The man put a paw on each knee and examined his hands solemnly, first one, then the other. The fingers flickered up and down, as if divorced from the slothful body. With a ponderous sigh he answered:

'Yes, she was only thirty. She was a very beautiful woman, Elaine, just like you. Same blonde hair, same lovely figure.'

He raised his eyes a little, lower lip thrust out, and stared at her legs. Quickly she hid them under the chair and handed him a plate of fruitcake and a cup of tea.

'What happened to her? Would it help to talk about it to me?'

Whatever the story, she would do her best to be kind to him for these few minutes.

Mr Sutton looked mournful. 'It was in all the papers,' he intoned, and picking up the piece of cake devoured it in a single bite. Elaine was puzzled.

The older of the two photographers paused in changing a film. 'Sutton? Round here, was it? I remember. Nasty murder, that. Never caught the bloke, did they?'

The young journalist opened her mouth again, then, moving around behind Sutton's back, began scribbling furiously. The man shook his head morosely and stared at the carpet.

'Don't want to think about it all now. Gives me a bad headache. Not now I've got my beautiful Elaine with me.' And he groped forward, trying to reach her hand. A gleam of malevolence lit up his face. 'You want to be careful about these people, Elaine,' he muttered, waving his lumbering head in the direction of the journalists. 'Write lies all the time, they do. They write terrible things about you, don't they? If you ever want them sorting out, tell me. I'd do anything for you. You look so pretty. I am thrilled to see you at last, to touch you.'

A mental picture of Mr Sutton sorting out Anne Cook entertained her fleetingly. It seemed wiser to bring the exchange to a speedy close.

'I'm afraid I have to get back. I have constituents waiting for me – they are my first responsibility, after all.'

She started to rise, a paper napkin fluttering to the ground, her cup of tea half full. Anxiety crossed his pudgy features.

'Oh no, not yet. We've only just started. I wanted to have such a nice chat with you, Elaine. I was hoping we could stay here for a couple of hours, and then you would let me take you out to dinner. I have money; I could take you somewhere really nice. And then bring you back here – this is your hotel, isn't it? And I could look at you, and you could talk to me, just like you do on the television. Please, Elaine – Mrs Stalker – don't go yet.'

Time to be extremely firm. She hoped he was not planning to hang about in the lobby for her. She turned to the press.

'Happy? Got all you want? Good. Would you forgive me, then? I'm sure Mr Sutton would be delighted to answer any further questions you may have. I must go. Goodbye now.'

Formally and rapidly she shook hands with the assembled crew, then turned to Sutton, who was struggling to rise from the low chair. A look of anguish played over his purple face. Firmly she pushed him back down again. 'No, don't get up. I am so sorry. Goodbye, goodbye.' And patting him quickly on the shoulder, avoiding that crunching handshake or any danger of another attempted embrace, she gathered up coat and umbrella, and fled.

How had this happened? The biter bit, indeed. Then she understood. Television is a one-way medium. If programme-makers could observe the audience, the unimaginable millions watching, they would know all human life is there in its batty, misshapen glory. Those faces in the flickering dark are only data on a survey sheet and are not real entities at all to the broadcasters, not picturable, until occasionally like Mr Sutton they switch off the set and appear, alarmingly, in front of their idols, and demand to be loved in return.

Elaine hastened through the swing doors back out into the rain, knowing that the next edition of the local newspaper would splash the pictures of herself and the fearful Mr Sutton, with perhaps more stills from long ago, of Mrs Sutton, poor woman. Presumably the police had investigated. Maybe he had only gone nutty since, through loneliness. With any luck he would now pursue somebody else – Selina Scott, maybe, or the Princess of Wales. She had enough complications in her life without him.

The bedside alarm roused her from fitful sleep. It was 6.45. She rolled over and opened one eye. She had deliberately left the curtains open in the hope that daylight might make waking easier, but outside was still dark, with a fitful wet wind hurling black gusts at the window. How she hated Blackpool, with its tatty frontages and tight-lipped landladies, its gaudy illuminations and clanking trams, its faded air of long-forgotten rumbustiousness, the all-pervading smell of vinegar. The place seemed out of time, as if the fair had moved on or long since closed down, with only the memory of pre-war laughter and the tinny music of dancing horses still hanging on the air.

The room had a stained plastic kettle, two sachets of instant coffee and four teabags, with four tiny containers of UHT milk and ten sachets of sugar. Northern businessmen, the room's usual occupants, liked it strong and sweet. She stumbled sleepily across the room and switched on both kettle and television. Better take a quick look at the papers and then get moving.

Page 5 of the *Herald* brought her up short. The photo taken at her home was fine, though it made her simper. The headlines and the first words of Anne Cook's page were a different matter.

217

'I DON'T FANCY ANY OF THEM!' SAYS NEW GIRL ELAINE.

Just who does Elaine Stalker think she is? Elaine, 37, hit the headlines for the first time shredding a Soviet flag for the cameras at the Tory Party conference three years ago. Newly arrived at the House of Commons last year she quickly made her mark. Mind you, in a dull intake of grey-suited men that would not be difficult. It appears that the controversial Ms Stalker thinks so too.

Publicity-mad Elaine invited me . . .

'I did not!' the victim snorted.

. . . to her fabulous £300,000 home in Warmingshire, where she ostentatiously lives in her constituency . . .

'Makes us sound like ruddy plutocrats. It's not worth half that. And if I didn't live there you'd still moan.

. . . with her long-suffering husband Michael, a pilot with British Airways, and their daughter Karen (15). The family have shunned local state schools for Karen who attends posh £10,000-a-year St Augustine's where efforts to turn her into a little lady are failing badly. 'She is quite a handful at times,' says Mrs Mary Carter her teacher . . .

'I made no such remark, Mrs Stalker,' the teacher explained later. 'This reporter asked me to talk about Karen and I refused. Then she asked wasn't she a bit of a handful at times, and I said of course, as all children are. That's all.'

. . . No doubt we'll be hearing more of Karen in future.

The private lives of MPs are much in the news. Modern marriages, they say, are more open these days. Elaine knows all about modern marriage. She boasted to me of her belief that sex before marriage is a good thing. 'We were a bit old-fashioned getting married at all,' she told me, looking pleased with herself. It makes you wonder why she bothered. Perhaps it has to do with Tory selection committees, who no doubt would disapprove of hopeful applicants actively undermining the family.

As we sipped lukewarm ersatz coffee in her expensive kitchen, I looked around. We were surrounded by the latest imported gadgetry from Neff and Bosch. Mrs Stalker seems to have a penchant for German goods.

'Cheek! The kitchen was like that when we bought it. So what, anyway?'

Her admiration for the Prime Minister knows no bounds. With an eye on possible promotion next summer she declared, 'He is an honest, decent, capable, caring person.' Tell that to the 3 million unemployed, Mrs Stalker.

She told me her frank opinions about her male colleagues. Mostly her views are uncomplimentary. 'Attractive? Them? No, I wouldn't say so,' she sniffed. No wonder she is so disliked by male MPs.

As we settled down to a long chat, Elaine Stalker revealed to me her innermost thoughts. 'It is hard for the men with their wives away,' she confided in hushed tones. 'The separation makes them so vulnerable. I have no idea how many of them have affairs, but it is a lot.' But when pressed she admitted that she and other women MPs had been propositioned in the House of Commons. She thought it was funny. I doubt if their wives would agree.

Last month a huge bunch of red roses appeared at her desk, with a card with love from a secret admirer. Who would know where to find Mrs Stalker's office? Only an insider. All she would tell me is that he is gorgeous – and married. Answers on a postcard please.

But Mrs Stalker really gets going on why there are so few women MPs. Her views should have all the sisters up in arms. 'Women are tied down with children and lack confidence,' she informed me, as if that were all their own fault. 'They simply are not up to the job. By the time most women get started in politics they're a long way behind.' That's true, but what is Elaine Stalker doing about it? Not a thing. With friends like that, girls, who needs enemies?

Speaking freely to the *Herald* about her own teenage daughter she told me the astonishing advice which serves as parental guidance in the Stalker home. 'We told her she can do what she wants. We encourage her to try everything, as long as she gets to university. Anything goes is our motto.'

Mrs Stalker talks sex to her 15-year-old daughter but would not answer when I asked if she advises her to use condoms. Since that is the advice peddled at public expense by the government she supports, we may take it as read. Nor does the Honourable Member see any difference between sexual relationships and any others. What happened to innocence?

The *Herald* takes a strong moral line on these issues. We know from readers' letters that you agree. This woman is dangerous. She is not alone. Our future is in the hands of people like Elaine Stalker. You have been warned.

Elaine felt sick. Slowly she sat down on the edge of the bed, spilling coffee unheeded, and read the article again. It was a hatchet job. The tone suggested that it was always intended to be so. That its sneering was inconsistent, lurching from painting her as not helpful enough to women to being too liberal with her daughter, was the least of its faults. Her refusal to answer stupid questions had been turned into coyness, her careful explanations of the wrongs of a system which limited the advance of women transformed into criticisms of womankind in general. She had been deliberately misquoted and words put into her mouth; even her quotes had been distorted. The advice she tried to give to her daughter – and thinking about what she had said to the journalist she could find little fault with it – had become an implication that Karen was to be led by her mother into a life of sexual extravagance. The truth of the red roses didn't fit Anne Cook's purpose and so had been ignored. Most of all it made her out to be trivial, sex-obsessed and unpleasant, and turned her from public servant into a parasite.

She should have followed her instinct and thrown Cook out. How could anyone do this and live with themselves afterwards? Didn't the woman care at all for journalistic integrity? Of course not: Elaine knew the answer herself. Could she challenge it? The slurs were serious, almost certainly libellous. But a court case would cost thousands she did not have, would take months or years, and would require the repeated resurrection of an article she would much rather bury – along with its author. Given Roger, a libel case would have been taking an impossible risk. It was out of the question. Her affair, which gave so much comfort and fun, had inadvertently robbed her of the protection of the law.

Elaine tossed the paper on the floor and allowed herself to feel something painfully close to despair. The faces on the television screen swam before her eyes. My God, what a life.

CHAPTER FOURTEEN

Mary Bristow hoped her feet would last out. Balancing the tray of drinks on a plump forearm, she shifted her weight from one foot to the other, slipping off each battered black shoe in turn and wriggling her toes. Her doctor was right – being twelve stone did not help. Still, needs must. The poor were ever thus: eat what you can when you can, grab a plate of chips doused in salt and ketchup, seek comfort in a bag of crisps and a big McDonald's creamy milkshake. She could just do with one of those now . . .

Mrs Bristow, forty-five years old, divorced, with grown-up children, dressed in black with a clean white apron and her frizzy greying hair as tidy as she could get it, stood patiently with two others inside the door of the redecorated Thatcher Room, on the first floor of the Imperial Hotel. Chandeliers glittered and noisy conversation flowed around her as the room rapidly filled and the drinks were poured. This party would go on into the small hours.

What a blessing tonight's guests were recognisable, interesting and not too plastered. As Mary Bristow told her friend Mavis afterwards, there were lots of politicians there as you might expect, and well-known faces from the telly. She loved *Spitting Image* and was surprised to see how much like their gawky puppet caricatures some famous people contrived to be.

She recognised Kenneth Baker. He was very tall, towering over the assembly, exuding jovial smoothness. In the warmth his face seemed oiled, as if centrally lubricated, like a well-made machine.

The face of a smaller man nearby also glistened, but with energy and sweat and pleasure in his own cleverness. His Scots voice was telling a joke at somebody else's expense. They said Matthew Frank was a young man yet he looked a weatherbeaten fifty. Maybe it was something to do with that fast lifestyle; it didn't do to have too many girlfriends, as well as editing the nation's most successful newspaper and having your own radio and TV programmes. An attractive, dark-haired young woman, a head taller than Frank and well-endowed in a low-cut red dress, had arrived with him. No better than she deserved, sniffed Mrs Bristow, then switched her attention back to Mr Frank. There was something wrong with his hair. Mrs Bristow gazed fascinated and wondered if it came off at night. Well, she was never likely to and out.

The place was packed now, people literally rubbing shoulders with each other. A man with a piggy face and gimlet eyes was standing in front of her, staring. She jumped and nearly dropped the tray, recognising the lugubrious features of Sir Nicholas Fairbairn. Her heart beat faster, knowing his reputation with all sorts of females; he wouldn't care that she was fat and going to seed, he would see the real woman underneath. The MP for Perth and Kinross was bizarrely accoutred in a tweed jacket, tight tartan trousers and matching waistcoat, a gold watch and chain draped theatrically across his middle. A deerstalker hat with a large golden pheasant's feather completed the outfit. Rumour had it he designed and made his own clothes.

He gestured at the empty glasses and spoke in an extraordinary gravelly voice, rolling the words round. 'Now, my dear, you are not doing your job properly. How can you look after a man if there's not a single full glass of whisky on your tray?'

Mary Bristow was covered in confusion. He had spoken to her. She galloped into action and headed for the bar.

Fairbairn's mocking tones floated after her. 'I will be waiting for you right here, my dear. Make it two, or a double, or best of all two doubles, d'you hear?'

Panting, she was soon back and offered him his drink. He looked deep into her eyes, and winked.

Another hand took a whisky from her tray – one of the women MPs, Mrs Stalker, looking smart in black trousers and a silk jacket and big dangling earrings peeping out from her blonde hair. Very nice effect, almost like a film star. Arrived on her own but soon chatting nineteen to the dozen with one of the blokes Mrs Bristow did not know, a tall chap, good-looking if you like that sort. Giving him a real 'come-on' look. Makes you wonder what they get up to in that House of Commons, when the cameras aren't on them.

'You look stunning tonight. There's no other word for it.' Roger Dickson raised his wineglass to Elaine in mock salute. She giggled and found herself blushing. He bent lower. 'Don't worry; I've been drinking. It loosens the inhibitions, I'm told. It's good to see you, Elaine.'

'So where's Caroline?' she replied archly, her head on one side, flirting openly. It was that kind of party.

A dismissive hand was waved gaily towards the door. 'Not here; gone to a field sports dinner at the Metropole. Tedious people, but she likes them. Not gone home, either, so I'm sorry, but I can't ask you back for a little drink, much as I'd like to.'

His face was flushed, with a slightly silly smile and an air of thoroughgoing well-being. Standing too close. His body language, usually so impeccably correct, had become endearingly but dangerously affectionate.

'I've never seen you like this before,' she protested. 'You have had a couple, haven't you? It's really rather comical. Be careful what you say, Mr Dickson. You might start making all sorts of propositions to me, and I might be tempted to accept.'

It was her signal to start the ritual, the elaborate verbal foreplay which preceded their lovemaking, the reminder that they were not a married couple, that neither was to be taken for granted. Since the private occasions were so rare, each moment was precious; the preparation had to be meticulous. Even if nothing came of it, getting the tone right mattered. Married people and long-term partners have their rituals too, a special phrase, a pet name, a caress, a smile across a room. Sometimes through long practice the signals become so abbreviated as to have almost disappeared – a touch on the arm, a single word. Those marriages may be in trouble if the magic has vanished along with the ritual. But married people who love each other can afford to get it wrong sometimes and misunderstand a mood, for there is another day. Secret couples have no such second chance. The opening skirmish which invites as it reassures must be right first time; an aborted approach may mean a long lonely wait.

'Tempted? Of course I'm tempted, Ms Stalker, when you walk in here all alone, dressed to kill and clearly in need of a man's protection. I offer myself as a gentleman to a lady, Ms Stalker. Within the limits of what I am permitted to offer, naturally. Let me look after you. Can I get you another drink?'

He was fooling around and it dawned on her that he was not quite as drunk as he was pretending. Damn Caroline; damn having a hotel so far away. She held out her glass.

'This isn't the first party you've been to tonight, is it?'

He shook his head. 'No, but it's the first I'm welcome at. I've just been down the corridor to Jeffrey Archer's. He has a champagne and shepherd's pie bash during every conference. Top notch: Cabinet, newspaper editors and suchlike only.' He helped himself hungrily to a slice of pizza from a passing tray. 'Nigel Boswood gave me his invitation. He's not feeling too chipper and went to bed early. So there I am, a distinguished member of Her Majesty's government – I am distinguished, aren't I, Elaine?' (She nodded agreement.) 'Yes, I think so too. Where was I? Ah yes. So this angry little man comes up to me and pokes me in the stomach. In a loud voice, he says, "Who are you? I didn't invite you to my party!" So I tell him who I am: Roger Dickson, Minister of State. "Oh really!" says this little chap. He is little – I had to bend down to him. "Well, whoever you are, you're not important enough to be here!" And he insisted I leave.'

'You're kidding!' she laughed.

'I'm not. Serves me right for gatecrashing, but still! I therefore downed my glass of champers, polished off another for spite, and that's why I'm no longer quite myself. And enjoying every minute.'

Nodding agreeably at her over the rim of his glass, Roger was happy and relaxed, more than she had seen him for a long time. She put her head on one side and listened appreciatively to the tale of Lord Archer's selective hospitality, then as he finished, dropped her own voice:

'Roger, you look marvellous when you're tiddly. I mean it: listen to me. Usually you seem a little fierce, a bit forbidding, as if your authority depended on distance. Maybe it does, but you have the sweetest smile and you should use it more often.'

In response Roger pulled a face and made her laugh again, but it occurred to her that he might have been practising in front of a mirror as she had recommended him to, for his manner and stance were definitely more assured than before the recess. It left her feeling a little uneasy; sometimes the pupil outgrew the teacher.

The two talked and flirted a while, and then he glanced around the noisy room and checked his watch before turning to her: 'Are you staying here much longer? Or may I walk you to your hotel – which is it?'

'No, it's quite a long way. But you could walk with me along the seafront until we see a taxi. That I would appreciate. It's a bit dark and wild out there.'

Mary Bristow watched the tall man and the pretty blonde woman move away, collect coats, walk together down the stairs. The party was still in full swing; nobody else made a move, though one or two people watched them leave. How she envied them, these famous, glamorous people. Of course they were all very wealthy too, which helped. Not that she would know what to do with a lot of money. People made utter fools of themselves when they won a million pounds on the pools. It didn't buy happiness. For herself, she would like just a bit more, though it was best to be satisfied with what she had.

Miranda had been more than pleased to accept Matthew Frank's invitation. He was an old friend but not a current lover; for the time being, at least, there was only one.

A cheery wave of fresh arrivals followed the end of another boisterous party nearby. Miranda had put a message on the board at the conference, telling Andrew where she would be. Her attachment to her rather ordinary Member of Parliament still took her by surprise, she who was always so in control. Her heart jumped as he came hesitantly into the room, accepted a drink, spoke to another MP, then detached himself from the group and approached.

In the weeks since the American Ambassador's dinner she and Andrew had managed to get together several times. The follow-up had involved her leaving a phone message, quite simply, on the Commons message board, just as any other journalist chasing a story might; only the call-back number was for her flat. He called so quickly that there had hardly been time to tidy up. The amazing events of that first coupling had been repeated. His unaccustomed mixture of courtliness and sexual dominance was turning him into a lively and adventurous lover. Even as he walked towards her now, that slightly sheepish half-smile on his face, she could feel herself pulsing and going moist, her body sending out signals of readiness to him.

'Hi.' She kept her voice casual, as if this consorting was entirely coincidental. Her arms stayed at her sides but her hands modestly smoothed the tight ruched fabric of her dress down a little. He refrained from touching her. A close observer might have noted far more reserve in her overt behaviour with this man, and wondered at it.

'Hello. Has it been a good party?' Andrew always seemed taller than she remembered. He was thinner – no, trimmer – than in the summer and it suited him.

It was an effort to keep his voice steady. He could smell her – not just the heady perfume, not only the expensive conditioner in her glossy dark hair, but something else, a deep sweet odour, so faint, so obvious. Andrew caught his breath.

It made sense to dispense with niceties. After all, she had summoned him.

'Miranda, I'm on my own. My wife has gone back to look after our child. Might I offer you a drink somewhere more private?'

She threw back her head and laughed, the dark hair fanning back in a wave. 'Oh, you take the biscuit,' she chuckled. 'You're so formal, Andrew. So bloody English! Considering what you're planning, that is really funny.' She dropped her voice. 'The answer is, sure. I'm ready to go now if you want.'

'You're under no obligation,' he said stiffly. He felt offended that she had laughed at him in public.

Miranda was contrite. 'Sorry,' she whispered, touching his arm. Producing Andrew's po-faced look had been unintentional, but it was handy. To any curious onlooker, it suggested she had given him a gigantic brush-off. 'Tell you what: you flounce off as if you're very put out. Just take your coat and go. I'll meet you outside in a couple of minutes. OK?'

Once outside, the collar of his new wool coat turned up, he was moving into the windy dark as she caught up and thrust her arm into his, snuggling close. That was their signal for intimacy, as it had been the first evening outside Victoria Station. Tessa never allowed him to hold her hand or take her arm in public – not that she allowed it now in private either. He took a lungful of the sweet air surrounding her and his mind began to race, as it always did, with how and where on her body he would start their lovemaking.

As for Miranda, no man she had ever met before, except perhaps her father, had bothered to behave with such good manners, to dignify her with such an old-fashioned honouring of a woman, so that her need to lean on him in the biting wind was an advantage, a restatement of their bond as strong male and weaker female.

Oh, she loved it: how she loved it. Having Andrew was a wonderful addition to her life. The power and kindness of him filled her with amazement and gratitude. His ardour had not cooled, but then that was no surprise, for Miranda was accustomed to men pursuing her long after the moment of passion had passed for her. The puzzle, which she relished, was that she was still keen on him, more so each time. She felt genuinely apologetic for hurting his feelings. As soon as they found themselves behind closed doors, she would make it up to him.

The party was ending; it was past one o'clock. Ignored by the myriad visitors, a slight figure in a thin raincoat huddled inside the Imperial's portico and considered packing up for the night. Jim Betts had been scribbling notes all evening, observing who arrived with whom, and, more important, who left with whom – often not the same person – and in what state of inebriation or otherwise. Already half a dozen stories suitable for the gossip column had been gleaned, though so far nothing leading to the major piece demanded by Nick Thwaite.

That Miranda Jamieson had arrived earlier on the arm of dapper Mr Frank was no surprise – and no use to the *Globe* either. From time to time he perked up, then crouched and wrote, and dreamed of a warm bed. His fingers were freezing and a dripping nose was defeating a grubby handkerchief. Whoever thought the job of an investigative journalist was glamorous should try it for real.

The emergence of the newly promoted Environment Minister Roger Dickson with Elaine Stalker, of all people, had aroused his curiosity. He remembered her from his Warmingshire stint, though she arrived there just as he left. Anne Cook had done a terrific job on her that morning in the *Herald*. Might be worth following up.

Betts was making ready to pursue them when he caught sight of a more familiar face, his own deputy editor's. In truth he heard Miranda's noisy laughter pealing down the lobby first, but it was her all right, her black jacket open, flaunting herself, she who thought she was too good for an ordinary working journo like himself. Humiliating that stuck-up bitch would be a pleasure. Who the devil was she going home with this time? Pulling up a scarf around his face he turned away so she should not see him.

Not Matthew Frank. Taller, better-looking. Another bloody MP! Feeling frisky tonight, obviously. It did not take Betts long to place Muncastle, and to observe the unduly friendly and familiar way in which, arms linked, the gilded pair headed off down the promenade. No wonder she had warned him off. Bloody nerve. Not that she would stop him: she was not a censor, not the arbiter of all that was fit to print. Press magnates were swapping around so fast that she might not be his boss for ever. A little illicit knowledge was always useful.

Betts hesitated, chewing his moustache. His ears were white and numb: that wind would freeze the balls off a brass monkey. He was torn. The Stalker combination was also prime material, well worth following. Probably better, because both were MPs, and one a Minister. He licked his lips in anticipation and sniffed hard. Pulling the scarf around his mouth and cursing Thwaite, Miranda, the *Globe* and the unrelenting hunt for unvarnished truth, he set off at a fast trot in the direction of the receding figures of Stalker and what, if his luck was in, was her paramour. It would make a fine story.

It would have been possible to have called a taxi from inside the hotel and to have waited in the glowing warmth. Both Roger and Elaine knew that; instead by mutual consent both wanted to walk and talk, away from prying eyes and company. For a moment they were silent, heads bent into the wind. Then both spoke at once:

'Roger, what did you think about the *Herald* this—?'

'I was sorry about that awful article—'

The unity of their thoughts made both laugh, comforted. They walked on. Gusts of cold wet air blew eddies of sodden litter around their legs. A late tram clanked in the distance, its lights jerky and unreal. By this hour most of the illuminations along the sea walk had been turned off, those that remained casting garish green and red neon over their backs.

Dickson stopped and leaned over the metal railings and looked out at the invisible sea, hearing it roar in the distance. In intervals when the wind stilled he could smell seaweed and brine. At this point the esplanade was dark and deserted. Elaine came to his side and he pulled her close, his arm round her protectively. From behind they could not be recognised.

'It was a horrid article. I don't know how you put up with it.'

She was grateful, but shrugged. 'What option do I have? If I sued it'd take years, with no guarantee of winning. I don't have the spare cash to risk. I have to remember that these pieces are only written because I'm getting noticed, which I suppose is a good thing, isn't it?'

'It's a high price to pay for fame.'

'It'll happen to you; just watch. When you become better known and are a target worth pillorying. I mean' – she corrected herself hastily – 'you are worthy of attention now, so you should be careful.'

He wanted to kiss her very badly. Their position was some way from the main hotels, whose lights twinkled behind them. Out on the black horizon a fishing vessel lay at anchor. Her body was close to his, so close it made him ache with longing and regret. With an almost involuntary movement they clung together for comfort, as animals will in a warm stable when all is cold outside. He could feel her misty breath filling the air between them.

Slowly she turned to him, for these days she could almost read his thoughts. Her head tilted back, her earrings tinkled. She opened her mouth, showing bright teeth gleaming in the dark, and smiled. She spoke for him:

'I love you so much, Roger Dickson, and I want to go to bed with you, right now. I'm thinking lewd thoughts about you, all mixed up with honey and sweat and the very taste of you. I would like to take you deep into me, and make love to you all night.'

He spoke softly as if from far away. 'It isn't possible. If we were to go to a hotel we'd be open to blackmail. You know that.'

'I know. The danger is exactly the same for me as it is for you. However, there's one chance. If you kiss me, properly, now, I will return to my virginal bed content. For the moment.'

What choice did he have? There in the northern chill night he bent his head and complied, tongue upon tongue, grasping her tight, reaching under her coat to feel her breasts, getting as close as he could in substitute for what he so desperately wanted, remembering that first time when she took him into her mouth, in a gesture so simple, so audacious, so submissive that he still cried out with the shock of its recall. He could not say to her, 'I love you.' Not now, not ever. Not just because he belonged to a wife – Elaine understood that, and it would not of itself have stopped him – but because to say it implied a commitment to Elaine, to this affair, that he could not give.

What had started as a bit of fun had slowly turned into a central part of his life, but he was not about to abandon everything he had worked for to plunge himself and his family straight into a divorce. That had been ruled out absolutely at the beginning and was still ruled out. Caroline did not hold a candle to Elaine, but Caroline was an excellent politician's wife, competent, friendly and self-effacing; he had nothing to reproach her for, nothing at all, no case he could or would make against her. To be frank, as he admitted to himself, Elaine would have made a pretty hopeless political wife. She would have been competing all the time, laying demands for the right to have her own opinions instead of dutifully supporting him as he needed. The idea was ludicrous, considered only briefly and as quickly dismissed. If his wife ever wanted a divorce, that might be a different matter. Dickson was perfectly aware that he would not have stayed unmarried for long, would soon have been saying 'I love you' to some female. He shut out of his mind the thought that, even in these circumstances, Elaine would still not have been suitable.

Yet he was caught: for the trouble was, he did love Elaine. That did not mean he had taken leave of his senses. He loved her dearly, and he was never going to tell her.

At last the embrace was spent. Roger said gruffly: 'I'll find you a cab. The hotel over there'll have a phone, or a rank. Come on.'

It was so cold. She slipped her gloved hand gratefully inside his. Walking quickly away from the promenade, the two failed to notice Betts a hundred yards away. But he had noticed them, and was smiling.

At the moment of waking Boswood knew he was in trouble. Every joint and limb ached. His eyes were sticky and hurt when he rubbed them. As the alarm buzzed, he tried to roll over, only to fall back in misery at the crashing sounds of a noisy building site at full pelt inside his head. Slowly he eased himself into a sitting position, desperately running fingers over his feverish forehead and tried to clear a dry rasping throat. A bout of flu had been threatening all week, but regular doses of aspirin had kept it at bay. Now it was back with a vengeance.

Carefully Nigel slid his feet to the edge of the bed and felt for his slippers. By now his head was pounding hard in syncopated rhythm with his heartbeat. Damn Peter for leaving him in a mess. There must be a doctor in the Imperial somewhere. He reached for the phone and dialled the desk. As a languid young man answered, Boswood realised with a groan that he could not respond.

His voice had gone. Kaput, finished. This morning's orator was silent. He could produce only a painful whisper. At the other end of the phone an irritated voice was asking him to speak up.

'I can't!' he almost shouted. What came out was a strangulated squeak. 'I've lost my voice! Boswood here, room 312. Can you get me a doctor, quickly?'

Elizabeth Murless had cold thin hands and humourless steel-blue eyes. Small, slight, fair and rigidly Scots, Dr Murless had trained in Glasgow and not been best pleased to find herself as a GP trainee south of the border in the wilds of Blackpool. She surveyed the stricken Cabinet Minister with an unsympathetic air.

'You have laryngitis, Minister. Nothing serious. I should make less fuss about it if I were you. I'll give you a prescription. No need to stay in bed unless you're feeling really poorly. Just don't talk much. I know that's hard for a politician, but it's the only cure, do you hear?'

'But I have to make a speech,' Boswood whispered miserably.

'Not today, you don't.' Dr Murless was firm. 'If it's that important, somebody will have to read it out for you. Sorry; but, if you try, your voice will give out in no time and you could strain your vocal cords. Is that understood? Won't do you any harm to rest quiet for a few days. Most politicians, in my opinion, talk too much anyway.'

So do doctors, Boswood reflected murderously, but decided against using precious breath on the woman.

As soon as she vanished he was on the phone again. Within half an hour, during which he showered gingerly and dressed, Roger and Andrew were in the room, anxious expressions on their faces.

'You'll have to do it, that's all,' Boswood croaked, thrusting the speech into Roger's hand. 'We will all be on the platform as planned. It's your big chance. Good luck.'

Dickson began to protest, but Boswood was right. It was much too late to cancel the morning's debate. The simplest damage-limitation exercise was to do as Boswood suggested. It was not all bad news; the goodwill engendered by his boss's plight might smooth the way for Roger's introduction.

Fortunately the Environment team were not the first on duty. By 10.30 Sir Nigel Boswood, blowing his nose vigorously and trying not to look sorry for himself, was assembled with the rest of his team at the side of the enormous blue-draped platform, as a debate on Sunday trading drew to its usual inconclusive close.

From his vantage point, half hidden, Roger surveyed the conference with mixed emotions. The old-fashioned hall contrasted oddly with the ultra-modern ziggurat of the podium. Behind the speakers a thirty-foot envelope wall, almost to the height of the gilded ceiling, carried a suitably anodyne slogan and the party's symbol so hugely and elaborately portrayed that it was only recognisable as a flaming torch from far away, or on television, which was the intention. That the platform took up space which might have been filled with several hundred more seats for delegates was unimportant. The whole edifice was awe-inspiring to those nearby and quite terrifying for speakers from the floor, and fulfilled its purpose of making all Ministers seem godlike.

Roger watched as the party workers, now filling the hall, laid claim

to the best places and determinedly shoved cameramen and photographers out of the way. These people would be judge and jury on him.
By lunchtime, if all was well, he would be fêted and congratulated. He
in turn warily admired the delegates, those volunteers who gave time
and money year after year without thought or hope of reward except to
see their side win. Democracy could not function without their efforts,
yet many harboured furious anti-democratic urges. Roger reflected
with a shiver that anyone who contemplated granting the British people
a referendum need only spend an hour or two in the company of Mr
Bloggs from Darlington or Mrs Bloggs from Dartmouth to know how
dangerous it might be. Dickson agreed with Attlee's view that such
devices were for demagogues and dictators. For the moment, to its
credit, the party was led by neither.

All too soon it was the turn of Boswood's team, which trooped on to
the platform as the chairman shook hands. A swell of noise filled the hall
as delegates shifted, yawned, changed seats, read newspapers, headed
for the loo before the next session. Behind the Ministers and party
worthies were rows of seats filled with portly councillors and area
chairmen. Tessa was there in a dark-blue dress, a simple gold cross at
her neck. Next to her Caroline Dickson looked hale and hearty in fine
tweed, her long muscular legs gracefully crossed. Alison Carey sat on
the other side, wearing an almost regulation outfit of blue suit, dark
tights and black patent shoes. Alison had checked the Secretary of
State's health a moment earlier and ascertained that he was not likely to
pass out on the platform under the glare of television lights; his pulse
was shallow and fast and his temperature a little too high, but there was
no sign of heart distress.

'Provided you behave yourself and don't get too excited you should
survive the next ninety minutes without disaster,' she had whispered to
him severely. Boswood decided glumly that he did not care for this
fearsome new breed of women medics. He preferred the days of
bumbling old fools with whiskers who knew nothing and dispensed only
worldly wisdom which could then safely be ignored.

Once ten feet up on the platform, watching the swirl of noisy
movement, Roger became aware of how dramatic and overpowering is
the main hall of Blackpool's Winter Gardens in the full flow of Party
Conference. He found himself staring at a sea of upturned faces. He felt
sick at the pit of his stomach and swallowed hard to steady himself. Not
for years had he felt nerves, not since his maiden speech in the House. In
a few minutes those thousands of eyes would be fixed in one direction.
All the cameras would be glaring at him, not at Boswood, staring up his
nostrils, trying to detect a glimmer, whether terror or disagreement or
pretentiousness or boredom: anything interesting or unwonted in his
facial expression, for tomorrow's inside page. Once the media interest

started it would never stop. Never again would he be able to relax completely.

Roger was genuinely sad for Boswood, who had wanted to go out on a bright note. So many younger Ministers were pushing for an opportunity. The party was ruthless in sloughing off the old and changing its colours and style to suit the new: that was how it retained its hold on power so long. Dickson had no serious doubts about doing a competent job in Boswood's place. It was not as if he were unfamiliar with the speech, which would come at the end of the debate. He had written large chunks of it, based on Marcus's technical suggestions, though Boswood's wily brain had supplied much of the line of attack.

The chairman, a moderately distinguished Midlands businessman who knew Roger and Caroline well, murmured a welcome. Chairs were quickly swapped around, names scribbled in and crossed out. The changeover was smoothly and quickly completed. Responsibility and authority passed silently and permanently from the flushed and coughing older man to the tall, quiet heir-apparent now instinctively smoothing his greying hair. An imperceptible shift in power: as if an invisible mantle had been lifted softly from one set of shoulders and floated down to rest on another's.

The chairman rose at the microphone and called the hall to order. He welcomed the platform party and explained the change. A groan ran around the vast building, for Nigel was held in high esteem and well loved, a familiar reassuring figure and a bit of a character in a dull world. All eyes settled in curious anticipation on his replacement. The chairman announced the motion and called the proposer, Mrs Davies, a nervous young woman from Leamington. They were off.

The debate itself was a serious matter. Most of the floor speakers would offer only barbed and conditional support. Expressions of outrage and accusations that Ministers were not listening or not prepared to act on the advice of ordinary mortals such as themselves would be cheered to the echo. Had the leadership listened in the past there might have been no poll tax, no recession, no split over Europe (and probably no health service or end of empire, either). With hindsight anything is possible. That Conference would also shortly greet in rapture the same Ministers who had just been so roundly abused did not seem odd to anyone present. The conundrum remained as to why the nation's free press continued to report it all in such hostile terms.

Councillor Mrs Davies tearfully overran her time. A dozen more hopefuls sat scattered around the body of the room clutching notes. All, without exception, would try to speak for more than their allowed four minutes. Not one had timed the speech; not one had allowed time for nervous fidgeting at the beginning or titters or a burst of applause. All came to the penultimate page in increasing panic as the red light flashed under their noses. Not one had practised as Roger had done in front of a mirror, checking facial expressions, marking the text for pauses and breathing and timing. Yet the speeches from the floor were important: herein lay the summation of the party's current political thinking, a hint of preferred or abhorred directions. Roger listened carefully, nodded, clapped politely, and waited, heart thumping steadily, for his own turn.

The chairman checked he was ready. The great chamber hushed.

At the back of the hall Elaine leaned against a pillar and was glad the attention was all on the platform and not on herself. A great lump came to her throat as she watched the tiny figures in the distance and their multi-magnified selves, left and right, on the wall behind. The sight of Roger's face ten feet tall, every movement jerky and inhumanly oversized, was creepy and startling. Reality was being reversed. It was as if the minute person now rising to his feet were a mannikin, a puppet being manipulated by his own giant televised enlargement.

Most people were watching the image, not the human figure. By the end of the next half-hour Roger Dickson would be recognisable to millions but would no longer be in control of his public persona. Soon he would have a nickname and a regular cartoon character. Her intimate knowledge of him, so unique, so precious, would rapidly be overwhelmed by this overpowering official version which was *not the same*. In time she would struggle to remember the special sound of his voice as he entered her room, or his private half-smile, or the cry as he came to climax, or the sweet smell of his white body afterwards, or the tender fumbling of his large clumsy hands. Instead she would hear only a measured, self-assured voice uttering twenty-second sound-bites, see only the soberly attired body with tie, hair and wristwatch neat and straight, that the television editor permitted to reach the world.

'Mr Chairman, ladies and gentlemen: may I begin by introducing our team. Sir Nigel Boswood you all know well. It seems very strange to be introducing my boss to you all, but it gives me a most welcome opportunity to say, Sir Nigel, on behalf of all your Ministers, how we hold you in the highest affection and regard, and offer you our best wishes for a speedy recovery.'

Boswood was suddenly embarrassed and emotional, his face reddening. He reached for a handkerchief to blow his nose, as delegates courteously applauded.

'The motion before us this morning speaks of the concern of the British people for the quality of our environment and urges us to do more to protect it. It may of course be true that these issues are not uppermost in people's minds at a time of economic recession. But as our economy starts growing again, environmental questions – planning permissions, green belt, derelict land – will once more rise towards the top of the political agenda.'

The conference sat listening. It was unnerving. Roger ploughed on. 'We have a proud record. Conservative governments have initiated all the legislative landmarks, from the Clean Air Acts of the 1950s to the Control of Pollution Act in the 1970s, the Wildlife and Countryside Act in the 1980s and the Environmental Protection Act in the 1990s.'

Getting his tongue around that lot was not easy. There had been no time to practise on the autocue. He was conscious of failing to make eye contact with his respectful audience. With an effort he looked up and fixed his gaze on a small figure at the back of the hall, leaning on a pillar. With television lights dazzling him he could not see clearly who it might be. Not that it mattered.

'*We* are the pioneers: with the Prime Minister in charge, *we* lead the way!'

That was a cue for applause. The audience relaxed and obliged. Roger took a sip of water. Time for more political stroking.

'The concept of inheritance is at the heart of our political tradition. It was Edmund Burke who reminded us that we belong to a partnership between those living and those yet to be born. "The ends of such a partnership cannot be obtained in many generations," he said. Up and down the land it is you – and people like you – who provide the backbone for so many environmental groups – the National Trust, the Royal Society for the Protection of Birds, and so on.'

The chairman nodded ruefully. The party's falling membership was a closely guarded secret but its overdraft of over £19 million was not. It would be almost the date of the next election before the last one was paid for. The Labour Party faced similar problems. Meanwhile, Greenpeace rejoiced in over 400,000 subscribers while Friends of the Earth could claim 230,000. The RSPB, non-political, gentle and effective, had over 800,000 supporters and the National Trust had a membership of over 2 million. Credibility was the key. Obliged to choose between the veracity of Friends of the Earth and Environment Ministers, most people preferred the former. Politicians were a declining and derided breed. Roger was wise to recognise the power in the militant innocence of the pressure groups.

The audience were warming to him. Time for a ritual crack at the opposition.

'Then there is the Labour Party's much-vaunted support for public transport as opposed to road building. That needs to be handled with care, Mr Chairman. It is a complex issue. Our bypass building programme is at its largest for decades – that reduces congestion and pollution, as any village dweller can tell you.' Applause, heartfelt, rippled around the hall. 'And we are investing more in rail services than ever before, with privatisation on the horizon.' The enthusiasm was a little more subdued. 'Yet when the Labour Party went to its conference last week, did it travel on the bus?'

'No!' yelled the Tory Conference, which hadn't either.

'Of course not. The car park was packed out. Plenty of Renaults and Fiats and Volvos there, and a few larger cars too. I am delighted about that. I am pleased that Labour Party members can afford cars. They never could under a Labour government!'

Loud laughter greeted this sally. Roger dropped his voice and wagged an admonitory finger. 'So it ill behoves them to criticise us, or to claim that they are the greener party. They are not: *we* are, and so we intend to stay, with actions not words, with respect for our land and with care for our planet.'

Time was getting short. If he edged into lunchtime, delegates would start to slip away. Roger skipped the next two pages and moved smoothly into his peroration, head high.

'Today I want to chart a new way forward. I want to make it worth people's while to help the environment, instead of harming it. I believe we can do that best by putting in place incentives and deterrents – carrots as well as sticks. I want to make *market forces* work for the environment.'

It was a bizarre notion that government intervention, in this field as in any other, was about making market forces work. Still Roger could obfuscate along with the best. The audience expressed its approval. The tiny figure at the back was clapping vigorously. Five thousand pairs of hands were in action. He raised his voice, cutting into the applause, not waiting for it to end, an old manipulative trick much used by skilful orators such as Arthur Scargill.

'We have come here this week as the party of government. We have been crossing a stormy sea, but we in the Tory Party stand as a rock. We seek a Britain ahead of its critics, strong and proud, a Britain caring for the environment and proud of its achievements, conscious of its responsibilities.'

Dickson drew himself up to his full height. Above him the colossus of his image stared down at the populace, steady, wise and strong. Hands at the ready, handbags tucked under seats, papers grasped by the knees, delegates held their breath.

'With your help we can achieve these goals. For ourselves. And – for – our – children.'

It was done. To tumultuous acclaim Dickson sat down. Dimly he became aware that members of the audience were rising to their feet. The chairman, sitting next to him, rapidly assessed the mood and rose majestically, signalling to the rest of the platform. A standing ovation – he had done it. Roger rose slowly to his feet and waved, and suddenly there it was – a big broad smile, lighting up his face, a smile which spread across the television screens, wide and happy and wonderful.

A sigh flew around the conference hall. A new star was born. The whole conference was on its feet now, the clamour and cheers lasting several minutes, a highly gratifying result for a first appearance. Everyone would go off to lunch content.

Down behind the platform photographers were grabbing at Dickson and the ailing Boswood, but were swatted away. Nigel was looking groggy; no one wanted photos taken of him in that state.

In the distance Elaine smiled agreement with adulatory comments from nearby ladies: 'Isn't he good? Taking over at such short notice! Most impressive!' How fine Roger had looked up there, upright, capable, smart, in control. Her eyes misted. Something had happened on that platform, during that speech. He no longer belonged exclusively to her.

CHAPTER FIFTEEN

'I think you should know,' Diane Hardy said with mock severity, 'that your postbag's now touching two hundred letters a week. And that's in a *normal* week. What are you going to do about it?'

Elaine sat back helpless. 'I've no idea. We get such a lot from outside my seat, too. Why don't people write to their own MPs?'

Her secretary sniffed. She had worked for too many MPs not to know the answer. 'You're too well known, Elaine. It would help if you started saying no to all the requests for TV appearances. Otherwise you'll be a prisoner of your postbag for ever.'

'They pay well,' Elaine muttered defensively. 'We voted ourselves no pay rise this year, remember? All to set an example to the rest of the nation. Doesn't help with the mortgage, though.'

'If you ask me, half the British public is mad and the other half's daft. At least if your letters are any guide.' Diane had been up half the night with a sick mother. She was not about to admit any weakness to Elaine. A certain grumpiness of manner was all she would permit herself.

'Not the constituents. They usually write sensibly.' Elaine was daydreaming and looking out of the window. A weak sun sent shafts of light into the stone recesses of the inner courtyard, making it seem less forbidding. She wondered what Roger was up to.

'I wonder sometimes if people read the stuff they write to you.' Diane was not yet ready to stop grumbling. 'Look at this one.'

Dear Mrs Stalker,
 We are students at Oxford Brookes University who have started a new society called 'The Achievers'. The aims are to make people aware that they can achieve anything they set their mind to. The society holds no political or religious views; our view is that the only thing preventing someone from succeeding is themselves.

'Ouch! Grammar!' Elaine grimaced.

As you are viewed as one of Britain's most successful achievers we would like you to be one of our guest speakers. We realise that your time is precious both as a family and businessman . . .

Elaine snorted. 'Do you think they know I am female?'

Diane laughed. 'Don't be too hard on them. Your own colleagues are much worse. This one was on the board for you this morning.'

From JON OWEN JONES MP, HOUSE OF COMMONS

Dear Elaine,

The provision of public conveniences is certainly far from adequate to meet the needs of most people. A large proportion of the public, women for example, have difficulty in finding good toilet facilities in our Towns and Cities. For many people this is not just an inconvenience . . .

Elaine winced as Diane read this out but was flapped into silence. 'Ssh! There's worse to come.'

. . . it can cause real difficulties, embarrassment and even suffering. As the vast majority of MPs are male you are unlikely to have had the experience of looking desperately for a suitable toilet whilst menstruating and needing to change the clothing of a bawling infant . . .

'Oh yes I have. The nerve!' Elaine was annoyed. 'You sure it's addressed to me personally?'

Diane checked. 'Oh yes, topped and tailed by hand.'

'Am I right to feel insulted?'

'He wants you to sign a motion calling attention to the fact that the Public Health Act 1936 discriminates against women because they have to pay for the service whereas men do not.'

'I'd have them all pay. Then we might have decent public toilets.' Elaine turned around from the window. 'I hate getting letters like this, patronising us as women, talking about us as if we are all weak and frail; and then having the gall to assume that all MPs are male, and that the few who aren't won't mind if we're treated as honorary men.'

'You sound as if you're demanding "politically correct" language.' Diane was teasing. Conversations like this with her employer helped clarify her own feminist leanings.

'No, the PC people go too far.' Elaine ruminated. 'For example, I disapprove of calling the mentally handicapped "people with learning difficulties". It's so unfair to them. "People", certainly: they're not inanimate objects, or helpless creatures devoid of feeling. But they have more than learning difficulties to cope with. They'll have serious problems all their lives – these poor souls are handicapped, mentally, and I don't see why we shouldn't face that. It's the same with calling disabled people "physically challenged". If we try to negate the negative by renaming it, in reality we belittle the genuine problems they face, and we may forget to provide practical help at all. But I do object to "authoress" as if the female of the species were a lesser breed, and if actresses prefer to be called "actors" that's fine by me. I prefer "police officer" and "ambulance crew" and "firefighter" because they aren't all men now, not by a long chalk. Have you noticed that there's no problem with "solicitor"? That's because they always were blokes. Now, almost overnight, nearly half our law graduates are female and the women are sliding into practice without having to kick down any barriers of nomenclature.'

'Still waiting for a woman Law Lord,' Diane averred. Her uncle was a Crown Court recorder and a keen supporter of more female appointments.

'"Businessman" is the worst,' Elaine sighed. 'How blithely we dismiss the millions of women in business. D'you realise we have no suitable word in English? We have to dive into French for "entre-preneur". Drives me wild.'

Diane turned back to the pile of correspondence with a smile. 'Anyway, tell me what to do with this lot. And remember, while it may be grand for you being a model professional lady, it just results in more hard work for the other woman in your life.'

'Sorry!' Elaine grinned. 'Tell the students no, nicely, and put Mr Jones's peculiar letter where it deserves.'

'Bin?'

'Bin.'

Mike Stalker took off his uniform jacket and hung it askew over the back of a kitchen chair. He glanced at the clock. Karen should be home soon for the weekend, bouncing in as usual clutching hockey stick and homework, with Elaine and a bulging briefcase not far behind.

He felt exhausted. There had been trouble on board that last long flight from Bermuda. All had seemed well as he started his talk-down, then three miles out of Heathrow the main undercarriage jammed. His heart had leaped into his mouth, for that could be one of the nastiest of mechanical failures. He had circled carefully to lose fuel and repeatedly shoved the control stick into gear. He could hear the faint uplift of alarm in the laconic voice from the control tower ahead. The passengers had known nothing, for after resisting for an infinity – probably all of ten heart-stopping minutes – the gear caught the offending notch and with a squeal of protest the wheel descended. Then the landing went without a hitch. One passenger even moaned the plane was early.

His arm still ached with the effort. A strained muscle in his shoulder would give hell tomorrow. Wrestling with the risks of landing a packed jumbo on two out of three wheels was not his idea of fun. Stress was all part of the job, but he wondered at what age a pilot decided enough was enough.

The clock ticked quietly. In the distance a dog barked; probably Barbara's, the woman next door. A jar of fresh flowers stood on the table: roses, picked a little too full. A shiny brown earwig sheltered in one yellow tea rose. Mike flicked it off with his finger. The blooms seemed to have no fragrance, only prettiness. How empty the house was. It did not help that a new steward was on duty now that Simon had gone.

Suddenly Mike felt angry. A man with a stressful job like his should not return to an empty house. There should be a cheery wife and laughing children running to hug him, to make it all seem worthwhile. There wasn't even a dog to keep him company, shoving its wet nose in his hand and wagging its tail in delight: only a bloody earwig, and that was an interloper. In his ideal home the kitchen would be full of the smell of cooking, as it once was, in the early days of his marriage. He remembered how Elaine used to bend over as she took out the dinner, offering a curvy rump to be patted. The family would sit down to eat together. It was not a fantasy; it had happened.

Nobody, and certainly not the Stalkers, sat at the table to eat with friends or family any more. Conscious of being very tired, Mike moved a little further into his reverie. There was a time – more than a decade ago – when all present would listen enraptured as he told his adventures, the dreadful dangers he had endured, the unique skills he had brought to play. He had been warmly appreciated. They used to love and admire him, and count themselves lucky that he was safely home.

'Some chance, some chance,' ticked the clock. 'Poor you, poor man,' sighed the net curtains in the gentle air. The earwig scuttled across the floor and was gone.

There was a knock, and a face at the back door, peering in at the window. A woman's face, pleasant, kindly, a bit vacant.

'All alone, then?' The neighbour, Barbara, stood uncertainly on the threshold.

Mike gave her a cursory glance. She was wearing a sloppy sweater, cotton slacks and white sling-back high-heeled shoes. Probably she expected to be asked in. That Barbara didn't bother much with her appearance, in the way Elaine always did, was readily apparent. Her earnest desire to please grated on Mike in his irritation that she wasn't his wife and family. He was not sure whether Barbara was a widow or divorced or even whether she had children.

She had no job but did not seem short of money or time to waste. Mike did not interest himself in trivia or gossip. He did not want to know anything much about his neighbours, particularly the females. However, it paid to be polite. He turned stiffly, shook off his weariness and smiled.

'Yes, but they'll be back soon. Can I help?'

The woman hesitated, put one foot over the step, then withdrew it. She would be about his own age. Her expression of amiable docility made her seem older, a different generation. It was none of his business, but it was a pity when a woman still quite young neglected herself.

'I was just checking if everything was all right. Elaine – Mrs Stalker – asked me to keep an eye on things.' She pointed at the vase. 'I brought some flowers in from the garden earlier. To make it nice for when Mrs Stalker gets in.'

Presumably Barbara knew the silver BMW in the driveway was his car. She was just being nosy. And there were two important breadwinners in this house, not one. His bad temper intervened.

'That's very kind of you, Mrs . . . er. I will tell Elaine you popped in.'

His cold smile suggested dismissal. Barbara pulled back rapidly, started to speak again, thought better of it and left, looking a little sad.

Instantly Mike regretted his rudeness. The silly woman meant well. She had no man to wait for, not enough to fill her life, in all probability. Sucking up to the famous family next door was pretty harmless, and it was useful having somebody to keep guard on the house during their long absences. He cursed his hasty reactions, his defensiveness. He had never been like this before Elaine became an MP and spent so long away, before Karen went off to boarding school. If Barbara was all the welcome home he was going to get, at least he could have been friendly.

He had almost made up his mind to stroll after her to apologise when another car scrunched up the gravel. Elaine had been to fetch Karen for the weekend. The Stalkers were a family at last. He found himself still grumpily wishing they had beaten him to it, in the house to welcome him instead of the other way round. His smile was tight as his wife and only child entered.

Karen was dressed in a highly personalised version of school uniform: grey skirt down to her ankles, black tights, heavy black shoes (Doc Martens?), shirt hanging out, tie askew, blazer too big and hanging lazily off her shoulders, as fashion models wore their jackets in magazines. She seemed to have grown taller in the last month. She had started to stay at school over most weekends: she claimed there was so much to do and all her pals were there. In reality there was no pull to the house. It was a battle to persuade her to come home at all.

He watched her with puzzled pleasure. How like her mother she was – in personality at least, feminine and bright and wilful and all the more delightful for it. Not in looks, for Karen was dark where her mother was – well, blonde, officially. Mike could remember when Elaine's hair was a muddy brown. At college she had experimented with different hair-dyes until the day when he had exclaimed in surprise at the startling yellow newness of her hair. To be truthful he had liked it just as well in its natural colour, but without doubt going blonde had done wonders for her looks, as it had for Monroe and Madonna and a million others. She would stay blonde now. It was her trademark. A return to her old colour would have made her unrecognisable. It did not occur to Mike that the original was now streaked with grey, as was his own. Married people don't always notice change in each other.

Karen was taller than her mother, slimmer and more athletic, though Elaine seemed to benefit from her visits to the Westminster gymnasium. The girl was at the turning point, changing from teenager into young woman. Too fast, surely: she was only fifteen. In some girls that age means gawkiness and wretched shyness, braces on teeth like a batsman's face-guard, acne aflame and period pains and knees all knobbly, their virginity guarded like a silk-lined secret, negotiating to let a favoured boy touch a breast, enough to send a chap crazy but no further. At least, that was how girls were when he was fifteen, before the pill and abortions and AIDS. He shivered. Maybe he was getting old, or simply out of date.

'Gawd!' Karen exclaimed as she planted a cursory kiss on his cheek.

Mike was instantly disappointed, for he had not seen her for a month and yearned for a proper cuddle. He checked himself quickly. A man could get into trouble for loving a daughter too much. She was not a little girl any longer.

'Sorry, Daddy. Got to get out of this awful kit!' And she was off up the stairs, making the whole house shake. Bangs and thumps issued from her bedroom, then loud music and tuneless yodels in casual accompaniment to the group Madness, apparently this week's favourites.

Left in a vacuum, Mike and Elaine tested each other's mood. She was pleased with life, for Roger had phoned at the office. A few minutes' conversation had brightened her day, even though contacts in recess would always be difficult. Long after she had replaced the receiver and headed for school to pick up Karen the pleasurable sensation persisted; she would be friends with everyone, all weekend, including her husband. Quickly she put an arm round him and kissed him, on the cheek.

There was a chicken casserole in the fridge, and a salad ready made. Mike felt doubly guilty as Elaine explained that both had been prepared by the neighbour, who was aware of all the problems a family such as theirs faced, and was anxious to help. She mistook Mike's scowl for disapproval. So it was; but mostly he felt inordinately cross with himself. That neighbour had her uses and should not have received such a curt rejection.

Conversation across the table was stilted and formal. As a family they had never been great communicators, but repeated absence was causing them all to lose the little verbal touches which re-create and confirm closeness in people who love and need each other. Elaine could put over almost any point or message in her work: that was her job. But to tell her family out loud that she was glad to see them was somehow much more difficult. The logistics were also horrendous. To get all three together at home, especially as Mike's schedules became ever more erratic as he was promoted, required comparison of timetables and diaries months ahead. Yet Elaine needed occasions such as this to concentrate on her husband and daughter, or the two would play no part in her emotions at all.

'What are we to do with you, miss, at half-term?' Mike wanted to know of their daughter. Karen was wolfing down the casserole; the surviving child in her ensured a healthy appetite. 'You planning to stay with friends again? We must owe everybody you know umpteen holidays in return.'

Karen, fork in hand, was avidly reading a magazine collected *en route* at the village shop. She looked up and brightened. 'Oooh, could I invite Marie and Catherine to stay here for half-term? We'd behave and keep the place tidy, honest we would.'

'No!' Elaine spoke sharply. She had no half-term holiday as such, though a few days could be wangled. It would not go down too well if she had to ask the whips for time off to look after her daughter and friends. Another reason for not promoting Mrs Stalker, as if she needed any more. 'I would rather you stay in the flat in London, where I can keep an eye on you,' she said. Another tack occurred to her. 'Would you be interested in earning some money?'

In her childhood Karen had had her fill of washing dishes and tidying up for peanuts. The greatest event ever in that household was the arrival a couple of years back of a large dishwasher. Dad liked it so much he happily loaded it all by himself. Suited her fine. The alternative, a visit to her grandparents, was to be avoided at all costs. There she would be given the worst chores to do without argument or reward, and have to watch boring TV programmes other people chose, for there was only one set. No fun at all. However, if negotiation brought more interesting work from her mother, with a near-adult rate for the job, she was prepared to haggle. She put her head on one side and eyed her mother.

'Doing what?'

Elaine caught her coyness immediately. 'You could come into my office and help Diane. Open the mail, answer the phone, fetch and carry, do the photocopying, and send off the signed photos, raffle prizes and standard notes. Plenty to keep you busy.'

'How much?'

'You want paying by the hour? Well, now. It means you'll have to be in the office when Diane is, in the morning at nine. No mooning about in bed till two in the afternoon.'

'Fine, I can do that.'

Elaine and Mike exchanged parental glances, amused and astonished.

Elaine tried a figure. 'Two pounds fifty an hour?'

'Huh. That's below old Wages Council rates. We had to do a project on minimum wages for economics GCSE. I know all about that.' Karen gave a triumphant look of mock belligerence.

'Then you will know that young workers under twenty-one were not protected by Wages Councils, even when we had them,' countered Elaine in mock fierceness. 'Don't trifle with me, miss! Only one of us is the politician. I will pay you two pounds fifty an hour while you learn the job. You'll need a full pass for the Commons. If you're any good – *if*, mind, for there'll be no nepotism in this family – you can expect a pay rise next time.'

Karen grinned. 'That's OK, Mum. I hoped you would say that. I'll start on the Monday. By the way, what's nepotism?'

Her mother had to go out again; her father settled to the evening paper and a spot of reading. Upstairs Karen stretched out on the bed, absent-mindedly cuddled an old teddy bear and flicked through the latest batch of teen magazines.

A pile of recent copies lay scattered over the bed. She had entered a couple of competitions, got nowhere, but wanted to check the answers. The despised school uniform lay in a discarded heap on the floor. It had been replaced by tight black jeans and a black sweater, scoop-necked, so that, when she bent to check her socks, down its front her breasts showed round and pale in their low-cut black bra.

She sat up and examined herself critically in the mirror. Not bad, these days. Still too many spots, but the Biactol seemed to be working. Ears too big, real Prince of Wales's own. Mum would not let her have surgery to pin them back. Hair awful, still. Uncertain how to style it, she had ended up having it done once too often and now it was too short. Boys liked it, though.

Around the mirror, from the limited number of posters Mum would allow to adorn her walls, men and boys looked back at her, hungry, moody, half-naked. Most were pop or film stars in standard publicity shots with smouldering eyes, silver lashes, semi-developed pectorals above smooth stomachs, faded blue jeans undone at the waist, hands thrust inside belts as if to check that something in good working order lurked down below. Half the faces had cigarettes hanging, in defiance of official bans. Cigarettes were smart.

Had Mike leaned over Karen's shoulder to read his daughter's magazines with her, he might have been even more alarmed at her generation's heedless flirtation with rampant sexuality.

'SEXY! The *Mizz* readers' sexiness survey results' was among the more harmless. Asked 'Which bum would you most like to grab?' the answer came: 'Brad Pitt had better watch out. Our poll shows that, given half a chance, three out of ten of you would happily pinch his pert little bot. Could the lone Birmingham fan who voted for Prince please explain how she could possibly fancy such a scrawny bum?'

'*More!*' screamed another title. Karen liked this one: it was more sophisticated. 'She's got sex appeal: a siren of style, this girl dresses to cause a reaction. No novice in the flirting stakes, she wears provocative clothes to show off her sexy figure. She seeks attention and loves glamour. This is a girl who knows her assets and knows just how to FLAUNT THEM!' In illustration, a pretty dark-haired girl sat at a café table before a tempting ice cream sundae. A dribble of cream ran down the side of the glass. Sensually, eyes half closed, the model was licking ice cream off a cherry, tweaking it by its stalk before her pouting lipsticked mouth.

Another copy of *Mizz* caught her eye: while the face on the cover could have been thirteen or thirty, the headlines pulled no punches. 'How to snog a celeb!' on one side vied with 'Boys you fancy (who fancy your Mum!)'. A *Mizz* reader's true story was headed 'My Mum gave me condoms'. Further down the pile, *Just Seventeen* highlighted 'Ten Lies Boys Tell' and 'Readers' Bedrooms Revealed!' with most of the readers featured aged fourteen or fifteen. Karen's friends reckoned *Just Seventeen* was aimed mainly at twelve-year-olds, with tell-tale signs the competition prizes of two nights at a horse-riding centre and M&Ms sweets dispensers. *Mizz* went one better, with 'Boys in their bedrooms: what are they like when you're not looking?' and 'I snogged my best friend's boyfriend . . . in front of her. YOUR WICKED SINS INSIDE!'

Karen turned to *More!*, at £1 every two weeks well within her pocket money. The lady at the village newsagent's handed it over to her without even a glance. It was more meaty than the other glossies. Editor Fiona Gibson asked, 'How often have you made the mistake of spying a hunky-looking bloke in a club, giving him the come-on and then, when he is glued to your side and it's too late to escape, discovered you've made a horrible mistake? That, in fact, he's got the charisma of a slug?' Karen pulled a face. A chance would be a fine thing. She sighed and turned over, and settled happily for 'Sex Special! Laugh him into bed . . . and put a smile on *your* face!' This was more like it.

Karen chewed her thumb reflectively. So much to know about: so much to come. The world which beckoned so tantalisingly, so near, was one in which sex clearly played a huge part, far more important than exams and college entrance and careers. These magazines were as crammed with useful information on how to please men as ever her mother's had been. But this time not with good cooking.

She read on quietly, a half-smile on her face.

Elaine opened the jar of face cream and began to remove her make-up. Her skin was beginning to lose its springiness. In another year or two crow's-feet would appear.

Mike pottered about at the other end of the room, unpacking his overnight bag, methodically heaping underwear and crumpled shirts into a laundry basket. Years in a cramped cockpit had made him abhor mess. He glanced at Elaine absent-mindedly and stood up, rubbing his shoulder. Both had strong reasons for seeking a good night's sleep. Both were wondering, almost as a matter of course, or out of a remote and accustomed politeness – and each knew the other's thoughts, almost automatically – whether the other was feeling sexually aroused and whether a performance was expected.

Both waited for a signal, somewhat stoically. Neither felt like energetic activity; and no signal came.

Mike yawned as he pulled on his pyjamas. As she brushed her hair Elaine avoided looking at him, as she had avoided kissing his mouth. With a twinge of anxiety she realised it was quite a long time since he had put the question, or reached out for her across their orderly bedroom; even longer since she had taken the initiative, as once he had loved her to do. She toyed with the idea briefly, but it was clear that Mike had had a hard day, though he said nothing.

Supposing she leaned across and touched him on his belly or buttock, stopped him pulling up those striped cotton pants. They were the old-fashioned sort with a white pyjama cord, whose knobbly ends straggled down inelegantly. He might grumble and give in with a bad grace, to do her a favour. With Roger in her life there was no longer that need. Or he might snap at her, yank himself away from her outstretched hand, turn his back. Nobody in this room was desperately seeking rejection. There was more to marriage than sex. She got into bed and pulled the duvet up to her chin.

The trouble was, without the sex the mortar between the bricks of their home was slowly drying out and losing its strength. Marriage was not just friendship either, nor a sterile compilation of shared experience and responsibility. There was no obvious sign, yet each failure to connect allowed hairline cracks to appear, and the edifice was weakening a little more each time.

She lay quietly near her husband but not in contact with him. He wriggled and groaned at the painful shoulder. Sympathetic, she leaned across and lent him her pillow, tucking him in as a mother might a child.

If he did not want to talk, maturity and familiarity suggested letting him be. More than ever Elaine understood what it meant to have a pressured job. If he did confide, she would have to listen and concur, might even have to take some action, cancel engagements to be with him, perhaps feel obliged to arrive home occasionally before he did. How inconvenient that could be. There was the forthcoming fact-finding trip to Sweden, for example, with a group of MPs: she did not want to miss that. Fleetingly she realised that it seemed easy for her to find time for that, yet not for Karen or Mike's needs. He had looked cheesed off when she and Karen had come home. Perhaps that was part of the problem. If so it might be safer not to enquire. In truth, if it meant changes to her way of life, she did not want to know.

Within a few moments, back to back, breathing quietly, both were asleep.

'May I see your pass, please, Miss?'

Gerry Keown was on duty again at the main gate leading to Members' Entrance. A chill wind was blowing down Whitehall. The nights were drawing in; the previous weekend the clocks had been put back, a sure signal that winter was on its way.

'Of course,' Karen Stalker responded proudly, holding up the brand-new pass which hung on a chain around her neck. 'Here.'

A new name. Keown examined the pass with care, his eyes moving from the photo to the bright young face above it, which smiled back at him cheekily, thoroughly enjoying the examination. On her way down Victoria Street the Army and Navy store had beckoned. Karen strolled fascinated through their cheap jewellery department. The result, her new silver-gilt earrings, dangled and twisted in the wind, drawing attention to the sparkle in her eyes and her slim neck. Long legs stretched out from under a black miniskirt. The fashion editors said calf-length skirts were in; but they also said to flaunt one's assets.

'Stalker? Would you be Mrs Elaine Stalker's daughter?'

Karen subsided, deflated. She twiddled an earring. The last thing she wanted was to be known as her mother's daughter: she, Karen, was a person *in her own right*.

'Yes, I am, as it happens. Does it matter?'

'No, no. It's our job to know everybody who comes in here, pass or no pass.'

He was looking at her again. Not waving her through, and not indifferent. His lilting accent was definitely not London, though she was too inexperienced to place it. Her spirits rose. Head on one side, making the earrings dance, she smiled up at him again. He had dark, almost black hair, eyes not an English china blue but a sort of sea-greeny, mixed-up colour. Maybe mid-twenties. Clean-shaven – a point in his favour; beards and moustaches did not appeal. None of the magazines explained what you did to avoid getting all that spiky hair in your mouth. Of medium height – he was easily topped by that older policeman standing nearby, the one with the cheerful face and sideburns; but this one stood straight, hands on hips, mouth puckering into a sardonic smile. Keown became aware that he was being examined almost as intently, and flushed. He was not used to female attention.

'I'm sorry if I said something which offended you, Miss Stalker.'

'No, no, you didn't. And it's Karen, anyway. What's your name?'

'Me? I'm Gerry – Gerry Keown. Pleased to meet you.'

The two shook hands, formally. Karen felt a little silly. She would have to get used to shaking hands if she were to merge into the background working here.

'Watch out, miss!' the other policeman called out to her, as a Jaguar leaving the Commons cruised to a halt, impatient, wanting her out of its way. A stern-faced chauffeur in a peaked cap glared. In the back a rotund figure in a bow-tie smiled benignly and mouthed apologies.

'That's Sir Nigel Boswood,' Gerry explained. He seemed in no hurry to move her on. 'You coming to work here, then?'

'Yes, just for half-term. Earn a bit of pocket money.' As soon as the words were out of her mouth Karen could have bitten her tongue. How childish, to talk about 'half-term' and 'pocket money'. If anything branded her still a child, that would.

Her discomfiture had been observed, and smoothed over. 'Yes, lots of MPs' children do that. It's very good practice. You should enjoy working with your mother. She takes an interest in Northern Ireland, doesn't she? That's where I come from too.'

'I don't suppose I shall see much of her this week.' Karen began to relax. This man was easy to talk to. His self-assurance seemed tinged with shyness; he was not forward or aggressive like some of the boys at home. 'This morning she flew off to Sweden on a trip, so I shall be on my tod. Her secretary's here, of course,' she added hastily.

Gerry had been considering rapidly. He had no girlfriend at present. Anti-social rosters and his permanent need for discretion mitigated against picking up just anybody in a pub, while clubs and dives were not to his taste. He'd seen too much as a child in Belfast. Life now had meaning and purpose – and a lot of emptiness and dull hours alone, if truth be told.

'So what would you be a-doing after work this week, then?' He allowed the Irish lilt to open up. A reputation for blarney could come in useful with a young lass.

'What, me? Watching TV at home in the flat, I expect. I don't know many people in London and I promised my mother I wouldn't go off on my own.'

'Well, now.' Keown shifted his helmet, showing his glossy hair and emphasising his status. He put his hands on his hips again. 'What would your mother say if I were to ask you out to the pictures tonight? Would she have any objection?'

He really meant, would you come? Her 'No, no' was the affirmative answer he'd hoped for.

'Good: I'm off at six, so we could have a pizza or something beforehand. Would you like to meet me at Members' Entrance, just over there?' He pointed out the glass canopy where Members wait for taxis.

Karen looked dubious. 'Won't you need to go home and get changed, or am I to go out with a policeman in uniform, like I have my own bodyguard in tow?'

That was clearly not a pleasing proposition. Keown laughed and shook his head. Behind him PC Bell was half listening, silently amused. Mrs Stalker's daughter was a lively little madam.

'Don't worry. We don't go walking around the streets in uniform unless we're on duty. It'll only take me a few moments to change. You look at a paper and choose what we go to see. Is it a date, then? See you at six.'

Waiting for the lift up to her mother's office, Karen felt inordinately pleased with herself. Her first real date, with a complete stranger, and somebody highly respectable at that. She would be safe with a policeman. If he suggested a pub after, even that would be all right, provided she stuck to orange juice.

Choosing the substance of the evening was a bigger problem. The *Evening Standard* listings, pages and pages of them, were an Ali Baba's cave to Karen. Column after column of movies in and out of town jostled with theatres, fringe happenings, pub entertainment, street events, exhibitions. At home in Warmingshire hardly anything ever happened. The nearest cinema complex was twenty miles away; she had been once in six months. Some of the cinemas here showed films she had missed. Her eye roved across the page. Then she found it.

It was obvious: *The Bodyguard* with Kevin Costner and Whitney Houston. Something for both of them to gawp at, and a talking point too – whether that was how bodyguards operate, or what points of technique Gerry might spot which were incorrect. That would pay him the obvious compliment of putting him in a position of seniority: obvious, yes, but then she did not anticipate that a Metropolitan policeman would be a man of great brain and learning. Good thing too, if she were to keep up without making a complete fool of herself.

She was late. Quickly she headed through the main archway, across Commons Court, and cursed as the lift eluded her. It was nearly 9.15 before she poked her head sheepishly around the office door.

Diane was waiting, tapping away at the typewriter rather crossly; the keys clicked in disapproval. Elaine's secretary had never learned how to use a computer and now felt herself too old to try. A rapid and accurate typist for whom the correcting mechanisms of a modern word processor were almost unnecessary, she did not believe claims that computerisation saved paper and space. Not if other MPs' rooms were any guide.

Without stopping, Diane nodded to a large bundle of mail still tied with string. New hands could be a nuisance, requiring to be told everything.

'If you'd like to get that lot opened, staple letters together so we don't lose any pages and paperclip any other bumf, then sort into piles. Pick out all the constituents' letters – there's a map on the back of the door if you're not sure – and put them on top. Your mother's reputation rests on our getting it right for her voters. Everything else is optional.'

'Will it all help on election day?' Karen asked, eyeing the heap warily. She reached for the paper-knife and waste-paper bin.

'Who can say?' Diane did not take her eyes from her typing. 'Your mother has a highly marginal seat. Even the best MPs get defeated, if the swing's against them. Still a good Member has a better chance. Or so we all like to believe.'

Diane's refusal to acknowledge Karen as a person, other than as a presence in the room, was beginning to grate. Her grumpiness did not arise out of malice or jealousy; but, since Diane had no children and not much to do with young people, it would not have occurred to her that her behaviour was discouraging.

Karen sensed that she was expected to sit down quietly and get on with her allocated tasks. It would take a good hour to open this lot. For a while the two worked without speaking. The Commons was relatively quiet, for the excitement of the party conference season was behind them and the new session had yet to begin. After half an hour Diane had finished typing one batch, yawned and stretched.

'I could use a coffee. Coming?'

Time to be equally standoffish. Karen shook her head. 'Thanks, but I'll get on with this lot. Taking me longer than I expected.' She was about to say, 'It's boring, isn't it?', as she might have done at school, where all adult activity was 'boring', but thought better of it.

'Suit yourself.' Diane shrugged. 'I won't be long. You can answer the phone while I'm away. Take any messages – don't let them go without saying who they are.'

Without the older woman's tap-tapping, the small room was hushed and Karen made progress. The heap of unopened envelopes shrank satisfactorily. Thoughts of her unexpected night out flitted through her mind. What might he expect on a first date, a sophisticated Londoner? Wait – he wasn't a Londoner. What should she wear? Would dashing home to change seem too eager? He was a policeman; he would be sure to notice. She decided against it. Mustn't look too keen. Anyway, he might be awfully dull and not worth seeing again.

The phone ringing in the stillness made her jump. It was a man's voice. For a split second she imagined it was Gerry about to cancel, then realised that the soft Ulster accent was missing. This voice was faintly familiar but one she could not place.

'Sorry to trouble you. Is Mrs Stalker available please?'

'No, she's not here. She's away.'

Not the smooth, sophisticated secretary yet. She should at least have said 'Good morning.'

'Ahh.' The voice paused. 'Where might I find her – in London, or at home?'

'Neither. She's in Stockholm. She went this morning.' Maybe telling this person was unwise. Karen felt a bit scared.

'I see.' The voice sounded disappointed. 'She did mention her trip, come to think of it, but I must have got the dates wrong.'

'She will be back next week. Can I take a message?'

'No . . . yes.' Karen sensed from his hesitation that the caller realised this was not the ultra-efficient dragon who normally looked after her mother. 'If you're in touch with her, just tell her I was asking after her and send my best wishes, and hope she has a lovely trip.'

Karen scrabbled for a pencil, mindful of Diane's last instruction. 'Who shall I say called?' Got that bit right. Sounded much more sophisticated.

'Just say Roger. She'll know who.' The phone went dead, leaving Karen puzzled and troubled. Roger who? She looked at the handset for a moment before putting it back.

By the time Diane returned there had been three more phone calls, all requiring immediate action. In the resulting flurry of activity Karen forgot to report the first call. It had not seemed significant, yet the voice had been expectant. He had wanted to see Mum, wanted at least to speak to her. He hadn't said casually that his business could wait till her return, nor that it wasn't important. He hadn't left a number or even his full name, so Mum must know him very well. He had sent his good wishes, sounding apologetic and regretful, just as Daddy might if he had forgotten the time of departure and rung up too late. A warm, caressing voice, very manly. Very sexy. Who was he?

Instinctively the conversation left her uncomfortable. Mentioning it to Diane did not seem right somehow, though it could have easily been Diane who'd answered. Perhaps the man would not have said anything at all to Diane. Why did she suspect that he had been a little more open with her, a new presence? 'Have a lovely time . . .' How odd.

Then a cold hand took hold of her. 'Roger . . .' Her mother's voice, speaking quickly and lightly, using the phone on the hall table at home, before it was moved into her study. It was indeed someone her mother knew well, whose number was known by heart. He had phoned her in Warmingshire sometimes, when Daddy was away. She always sounded pleased and excited to hear him, though the calls were brief. Karen had no way of knowing whether it was the same voice. At home most phone calls were politics, so she never bothered to answer, even when it would have been helpful to do so, for example if her mother was in the bath or outside. It was one way of entering a grudging protest at the domination of their lives by her mother's job. Who was Roger? Another MP? She reached for the *Vacher's* directory but it was out of date. Somehow she knew who it was.

The niggle of anxiety stayed with her all day, as bits of those hurried phone conversations came floating back. Mum always seemed so happy when he called. The 'Roger' on the other end then had been her whip, she had said once. Tomorrow the Commons library might be able to help. Was it the same man?

Six o'clock and time for her date with Gerry. The phone call slipped from her mind. Karen brushed her hair, tweaked the earrings, smoothed down her skirt – was it too short? – applied fresh lipstick, bolder than her daytime shade, and headed downstairs.

Out of uniform the man waiting for her looked more Irish, dark-haired and slim. He wore grey slacks, a check shirt and a light-blue pullover under a big navy donkey jacket. Not exactly a raver, then: not the sort to draw attention to himself. Not good-looking enough to be a film star, but pleasant manners, a bit stilted. She got the impression that he didn't often take girls out. She wouldn't let on that she hadn't been out on dates, much. Unless he were to change radically later on, he didn't seem the type to jump her.

Her faint worries about being out in London alone with a stranger began to dissipate. His behaviour was a model of decorum. She relaxed, showing off a bit, determined to be fun to be with, though clearly he wasn't fooled. Once or twice she caught him looking at her with a slightly sardonic smile, as if he found her trivial.

The pizza was ordinary, but there were no pizza parlours near home, so sharing a large juicy mouthful with a new acquaintance in the crowded Pizza Hut was more like a kid's treat than a first date. Both were nervous to begin with. The movie, however, was perfect for an evening out. Both could enthuse, she at the singing, he at the action bits. There was to be no hand-holding, it seemed, though Karen would have raised no objection. He did not take her hand or touch her, even in the sexy bits on screen. She kept her own hands busy eating popcorn. A sidelong glance found Gerry apparently watching the screen in rapt absorption, arms folded across his chest, the donkey jacket over his knees. Irish. Maybe Catholic – a bit religious? No harm in that, of course. But it was not very *exciting*.

As the movie finished and the audience rose to leave, Gerry commented appreciatively. 'That was great: thank you for suggesting it. Now in the normal run of events I would ask you for a drink, but I gather that you are a bit young for pubs – would that be right?'

'How the devil – how do you know that?'

'I looked you up, of course. Your pass application is on file in the security office. Needed to know who I was spending the evening with!' He chuckled.

Karen felt annoyed. Bloody nerve. So that explained the hands-off approach.

'Now, if it had bothered me, I would have cancelled our date, wouldn't I? But you're good company and I've enjoyed myself, better than for ages. Done me good, that has. I was turning into a bit of a monk, I suppose. But I don't take too many chances on breaking the law – it's more than my job is worth, quite literally.'

He waited. She was extremely pretty as she pouted in annoyance. No doubt with a few drinks in her she could be quite a handful. Lucky the man who bedded that one in a year or two.

'Maybe I could take you out again towards the end of the week?'

She did not answer. That he had checked up on her was *infuriating*. Still, going out with him was better than nothing. Maybe he would make more effort if she played harder to get now.

'I'm not sure at the moment that I know what I'm doing later,' she answered loftily. 'Right now, since you're not going to take me for a drink, perhaps you would see me home?'

Gerry took her arm, laughing. There was an edge about that laugh, as if it was all he would allow himself. He was intriguing. Maybe he had been hurt long ago, and that was why he was mainly solitary these days, why he took on that tedious old security job. She had sat with him through four hours this evening but not got to know him at all. He had told her bits about working at Broadmoor and the loonier patients, but had not been forthcoming about himself. Another mystery.

Gerry didn't bother to hide the fact that he knew the flat's address and location, walking her there steadily. She understood the irksome feeling of the woman character in the film, watched constantly, as an object, all in a day's work. It was a dry evening but he did not suggest taking a taxi, as her mother would have done: he earned a lot less than an MP, nor did he have her pressing need always to save time.

At the door he paused and shook hands again, awkwardly. If there was to be a kiss, Karen was going to have to take the initiative. Oh, blow him. Time enough for that next time, if there was to be a next time. It would have been better with a couple of drinks inside her. Still, she was not yet ready to give up on him. She fished in her bag for the door key and smiled at him sweetly.

'Thank you. You've fulfilled an ambition for me.'

'Really? What was that?' He was just being polite. Spending all night with a kid must have been hard work. She felt suddenly contrite and childish, and very tired.

'I've always fancied telling my mother that the police brought me home one night, and then watching her face.'

That was an elegant dismissal. It solved a problem for the young man also, who nodded and grinned, turning on his heel, half hoping the lass would take up his offer. 'You take care now, and let me know when you're free.'

CHAPTER SIXTEEN

Jim Betts put the phone down with a sigh, ears still ringing from the curses at the other end, and pulled at his moustache. Why did people get so cross when he asked a perfectly ordinary question, like the identity of a companion at the dinner table on Monday night? Nobody in politics would ever give a straight answer, even if the circumstances were entirely innocent. Which in most cases, of course, they weren't.

Betts rubbed his face and concentrated. In his view politicians weren't as good or as bad as the people they represented but much worse: rogues and liars every one. The exposure of such hypocrisy was not a crime, nor an intrusion into private lives. All claims to privacy had been abandoned when first they poked their vain heads over the parapet. In other words, publish and be damned. Let the buggers sue *afterwards*.

He pushed his chair away from the untidy desk and stretched. The Commons press gallery was a mess even in recess. He had been on the phone researching stories for an hour, with virtually no progress. Time to try a different tack. Perhaps his notebook would help. Turning back pages he contemplated the squiggles for several moments. Yes, this lady was promising material, though his call to Warmingshire had drawn a blank.

He flicked through the Commons phone directory and dialled Elaine Stalker's number.

'Mrs Stalker's office, good morning.' A pleasant voice, young.

'Er, good morning. My name is James Betts – I'm a journalist. Is Mrs Stalker there, please?'

'I'm afraid she's away at present. I'm her daughter, Karen. I'm looking after the office while she's away. Can I help?'

This could be valuable. 'I'm not sure, Karen ... ah, Miss Stalker. I used to work in Warmingshire on the local paper – long time ago. I've been commissioned to write an article on the pressures on MPs and their families – you know, the problems of having spouses and children a long

255

way from Westminster. But it sounds as if Mrs Stalker has her family all round her. Still, maybe you could provide the rosier side of the picture for me?'

Karen prevaricated. It would have helped to hand the phone over to Diane, but the secretary had been called home early to help with her sick mother. As Diane's confidence in Karen had improved during the week, it seemed no problem to leave the girl briefly in charge. That now posed Karen with an unresolved question. She knew she had to be careful with the press, but Mum had always made a point of being co-operative. She decided to play for time.

'Where are you from, Mr Betts? You have a funny accent.'

'Me? Oh, you're right. I'm not a Londoner, I'm from up north. Find London a bit hard going, to tell you the truth. Especially when an editor is chasing you.' He lifted the tone of his voice to make it sound younger.

'I was born up north too. We live in the Midlands now where my mother has her constituency. London can be a pain, can't it?'

Betts couldn't believe his luck. 'Especially if you're on your own in your first job,' he ventured. 'Everything that's on, you feel you need someone to go with, don't you?'

Karen agreed. She liked the sound of this voice.

'Look, it would help me very much if you could tell me a bit about what it's like, being the daughter of a famous MP. It can't all be hard work, manning the fort when your mother is away. It must be fun sometimes. And I wouldn't ask you anything unpleasant. I'm not that kind of chap – just want to write a light-hearted piece.'

She wasn't sure. 'I don't know . . .'

He pressed his advantage. 'The editor has given me an expense account, so I could take you somewhere if you like. A restaurant – a really nice one. What would you say to that?'

Betts's instinct was correct. Gerry had been all right but a bit dull. Being taken to dinner sounded much more like it. It would be in public, so nothing could happen. If he was horrid she could simply get up and leave. Even if the bloke wasn't much, the food might be good. Better than egg on toast alone in the flat.

After negotiation they decided on an Indian meal; Betts arranged to meet her that evening in Dean Street in Soho, at the Indian restaurant known as the Red Fort.

As she put the phone down Karen felt excited and pleased with herself. This time she would change and put on something more alluring. There were a few more jobs to deal with and then she could call it a day.

Her mind on her date, she slit open the remaining second-post letters quickly and began to sort them. It was not till halfway down the last letter, handwritten on House of Commons notepaper, that she realised she had made a mistake, and was reading material intended for her mother's eyes only.

Puzzled, she fished the envelope out of the waste-bin. It was also made of characteristic cream Commons paper with the green portcullis crest on the flap. The front was addressed to her mother, but it was marked 'Personal'. Its tone suggested a friendliness that was surprising. And it was signed 'R'.

It was him again. She sat confused for a moment, trying to think. Then the clock reminded her to get a move on. She put the letter back in its envelope, started to return it to the pile, hesitated, and then put it in her pocket.

Elaine stifled a yawn and bent her head to make a note. It would not do to let her hosts see that she was bored, but, however fascinating Sweden might be to the Swedes, it held no excitement for her.

What a pity the team leader was Freddie Ferriman and not a colleague with more intellect or drive. Freddie's best earnest style was on full display, but the vacant expression on his face suggested that he too had lost the gist of the argument and that his mind was elsewhere. Ten minutes ago he had asked the Minister for External Affairs to explain why Sweden wanted to join Europe. The explanation was taking a long time.

Nevertheless she must make the best of these few days. The following morning there would be a trip north to reindeer country and a promised stay in the hotel boasting the largest mixed sauna in Europe. Freddie had become quite flushed at the thought. Elaine would have preferred different company.

She wondered if all was well at the office, then dismissed her worries. Diane was more than capable of running the whole caboodle virtually indefinitely without her intervention, and she had Karen to help. It would do the girl good.

It had settled to a fitful grey drizzle by the time Karen arrived at the restaurant a few minutes early. Despite its address in the heart of Soho, the Red Fort was larger and smarter than she had expected. For a fleeting moment she was alarmed. Inside, the plum-red décor was exotic, inviting. Thick carpets softened all sounds. The uniformed waiter, small, dark-skinned and friendly, settled her in a wicker chair in the window, brought a Coke and a bowl of Bombay nibbles and flashed her a big smile.

Betts had been home, showered, shaved, cleaned his teeth and changed. It had not occurred to him to suggest more esoteric food from the extraordinarily diverse range available in London: Spanish, say, or Japanese. Like much of the British population, Betts had been weaned on Saturday night takeaways from leaky aluminium containers and his preference was curry.

Appearances mattered tonight. He wanted to pretend he was about five years younger than his real age; if she asked, he would claim to be twenty-four or twenty-five. The more uneven fragments of his moustache were now clogging the wash-basin plughole in his flat and he was wearing aftershave – not too much. Better to be innocent, gawky, but doing his best. That would put Miss Stalker at a serious advantage, when she might talk more freely.

Outside it was already dark. Several men and women were seated with menus in the pre-dinner area, but only one was alone and looking at him invitingly. Betts's spirits rose as he examined Miss Karen Stalker surreptitiously as he struggled, with the waiter's help, out of his damp mackintosh.

Long-legged, long-necked, short dark hair, pretty. Big sophisticated dangly earrings. Got up all innocently in a black stretch tube outfit which started several inches above her knees and clung all the way up. Nice-looking bird. Bit of a surprise; it had been such a rush he had not had time to look up the family details properly. As she rose with a hesitant smile from the low chair, she looked very fetching indeed. This evening might do more than fill his notebook.

Formally he shook hands and exchanged pleasantries, asking her to call him James, as if he were some kid trying to make the big time, all most respectable, needing her help. Choosing from the enormous red menu was difficult, but glorious smells of coriander and cumin from the kitchen downstairs whetted appetites and increased confidence. Karen kept her eyes demurely down; partly to conceal her disappointment that tonight's companion had a moustache and was shorter and not nearly as nice-looking as Gerry. She was, however, also doing her best to hide her enjoyment at being so pampered.

'They don't use curry powder in a place like this,' she whispered. 'You sure you can afford it? I don't fancy having to do the washing up.'

Got her where I want her, thought Betts. He established that she was only helping her mother out temporarily and was planning to go to college the following year. Persuading her to share a bottle of wine was unexpectedly easy, as he ostentatiously placed a small black tape-machine on the tablecloth. Its ruby light winked steadily, as if it were a chaperone, watchful but indifferent.

'Now I have to do my job, Karen, so while we're tucking into this excellent chicken tikka kebab – a very good choice if I may say so – let me ask you about your mother. I must say I admire her. Do you and your father see much of her?'

Karen fiddled with the candle as she spoke. 'Not a lot. I see more of my mother than my dad. He's away even more. At least Mum is home most weekends. I mean, she sleeps in the house, though often she complains that in winter she never sees it in daylight – last in, first out.'

'Would you say it was a happy home?'

'Oh yes. I mean, I don't plan to leave.'

'Your mother never complains about her lifestyle, never says she wishes she were doing something else? Doesn't she ever say, "I wish . . ."?'

Karen fidgeted and considered. This James bloke was being so sweet, not pushy at all, but his editor would expect something. And keeping to herself matters she did not understand, with no one to consult, was an uneasy burden. She ran her finger around the top of the wineglass.

'Well – I think she would like my father to be around more and to take more interest, but he says politics isn't his style. He supports her, but it's not like the men MPs with a wife, is it?'

Their main course was placed before them and for several minutes Betts concentrated on his plate. The saffron lamb was bloody good, and a lot cheaper than some English places where he might have taken her. It was a stroke of genius to have suggested Indian. The glasses were refilled, the tape turned over.

'Your mother has become famous quite quickly, hasn't she? Has that created any problems for her?'

'She's just good at her job.' Karen sounded defensive. Her face was a little flushed. The curry was mild but still its pungent flavours made her thirsty. 'It's not right when the papers say she isn't popular with her colleagues. A lot of that is only jealousy. She has lots of friends, close friends.'

'Is it easier to be friends with somebody in politics than someone outside?'

The girl paused and swirled the red wine, watching scarlet, silver and black form and break up in the flickering candle flame. Her crowd drank lager or cider, not wine. She was silent.

'Would you say she has anyone special in politics – someone she might especially confide in?'

The girl drained her glass, pursed her lips and looked straight at her dinner companion. Her eyes were troubled. Betts leaned over and switched the tape recorder off. He held her look and spoke softly.

'You know there are stories circulating about your mother, don't you? That she is especially close to one of the other MPs?'

Karen swallowed hard and looked down at her plate. Betts put down his fork and took a deep breath.

'They were seen together at Blackpool. It's Roger Dickson, isn't it?'

She said nothing, but bowed her head. She was very still.

'Look, I won't say anything. The machine is off. All you have to do is tell me it's not true, and I'll believe you.'

Big, dark-ringed eyes lifted. She was not crying, but neither was she entirely in control. Her mouth trembled. 'I don't really know what to do. There was a note from him. Said how marvellous it was to see her at Conference and hoped to see her again when the House returns. It was marked "Personal". Diane, Mum's secretary, had gone home. She told me that anything marked "Personal" I shouldn't touch. I didn't mean to.'

Betts was cheerful, reassuring. 'That doesn't sound much! I don't suppose it means anything at all.'

The boot was on the other foot. He had obliged Karen to try and convince him.

'But, James, if there was nothing in it, why bother writing? After all, lots of MPs saw each other in Blackpool, and they will all see each other when the House resumes. And why mark it "Personal" if it was so innocent? It wasn't, anyway. He finished it, "Thinking of you". That's a bit much. And there's more – he phones; he phoned the office the other day, and he calls Mum at home. I've heard her talking to Roger Dickson several times.'

'Maybe he has a good reason to talk to her?'

'Oh, I could understand that he might if he was her whip, like last year. But the library told me he's a Minister now. Why should a Minister be phoning a backbencher at home during the recess, and sending her notes marked "Personal" if there wasn't something funny happening?'

Bingo, thought Betts. That's how it happened – when he was her whip. That meant it had been going on some time, wasn't just a quick fling at Party conference.

'I don't suppose you kept the letter, did you?' Casually. Don't sound too interested.

Dumb pain showed on her face. 'I really didn't know what to do with it. Diane doesn't know about it and of course Mum hasn't seen it yet. It's so unfair. I think he's leaning on her – he's so much more important and experienced than Mum is. I wish he would stop.'

To Betts's amazement she reached in her handbag and handed him the letter, still in its original House of Commons envelope. Elaine Stalker's name was written in Dickson's distinctive hand.

HOUSE OF COMMONS
LONDON SW1A 0AA

1 November

My dear Elaine,

I am so sorry I missed you when I called your office today – like a fool I had forgotten your trip to Sweden. As usual I have some urgent business which might interest you on your return, so do contact me at yr convenience.

Have a good trip – thinking of you.

Yours,
R

Betts could just imagine what 'urgent business' Dickson had in mind. That sentence was almost the standard formula with which a Minister might contact a backbencher on his own side, in order to impart particular knowledge which might be politically useful – the start date for a new bypass, for example. Almost but not quite. That sort of thing happened only once or twice in a Parliament – not often enough to justify 'As usual'. A top barrister, George Carman say, could have a field day with that. The 'R' instead of a proper signature didn't matter; all that would be needed in a libel court would be a sample of Dickson's handwriting, which could be requested right there, in front of the jury. Betts's eyes gleamed at the prospect.

Now the problem was how to retain the letter. He thought for a moment, then took hold of the envelope in a theatrical gesture between finger and thumb as if it were infected.

'I think there's only one thing to do with this, don't you?'

He put the letter back into the envelope. Slowly and deliberately he tore it in four pieces and put them in the ashtray.

Karen was looking distressed; it was time to cool it. He replaced the tape-machine in his pocket and leaned across the table, patting her hand.

'I am quite sure – *quite* sure – that there's nothing in all this and that you are imagining things. Your mother and Mr Dickson are grown-up responsible people and we shouldn't really be talking about what is, after all, their business, not ours. I will leave her out of my article and we'll both forget about this letter. That's a promise. Now: it would be a shame to waste this nosh. Let's just have a good time together. How does that sound?'

An audible sniff. The girl fished in her handbag for a tissue. He waited as if sympathetic as she blew her nose. Karen appeared to share several characteristics with her mother. The same hazel eyes; the same unguarded friendliness; the same willingness to look on the bright side and not stay miserable for long. The same liking, apparently, for male company. In a few moments the sniffing stopped. Karen smoothed down her skirt and nodded. She picked up her fork again.

For the next hour Jim Betts gave a passable imitation of an

ordinary bloke out with a special new girl, watching her every move with pleasurable admiration, solicitous of her welfare, keeping her glass filled, ordering dessert and coffee, offering her a cigarette, which after a moment's hesitation she declined. He flicked ash on the remnants of the letter but was careful to leave them unsinged.

It was past eleven when Karen, swaying slightly, rose and looked around hazily for the Ladies. Mr James Moustache had given her a good night out, much better than Gerry Keown. Spent some money on her: about time somebody did that. She patted Betts on the shoulder and gave him what she hoped was a conspiratorial wink as she sashayed across the room, her black ribbed skirt riding up over her thighs.

Betts was not entirely sober either. He had been considering his next move, but even while maintaining his deception he had helped Karen Stalker put away a bottle of wine. What might a normal healthy bloke do with a fair bit of skirt after such a night out? He was not too sure about this baby, but it would wrap things up nicely to find out.

When Karen returned to the table Betts was already on his feet and the bill paid. Almost as an afterthought he picked the pieces of the letter out of the ashtray, scrunched them up and casually put them in his pocket. 'Can't have anyone else reading this, can we? Mustn't take chances.'

In the taxi she was talkative and snuggled up to him invitingly. It would have been easy to kiss her there and then, but with an effort he restrained himself and instead merely took hold of her hand. Snogging in cabs was undignified, and unnecessary if you had somewhere more comfortable to go. The rain had stopped.

At the door of her block he got out of the taxi with her and paid it off. The cold air hit his face and made his eyes water.

'Of course I'll see you up to your flat. Anything can happen in London, young lady. There might be somebody lurking on the stairs and I should never forgive myself.'

Roger Dickson signed the last letter with a flourish, slipped it back into its official green folder and shut the red box with a snap. He was not looking forward to the return of Parliament, what with all the additional hundreds of parliamentary questions which would surge his way for written answer night after night. Even their Lordships had started that game now; once they had left probing questions to the awkward squad in the Commons, but not any more. He still had to check that consistent replies were given in both Houses, or there might be trouble.

Still, while recess had its advantages, stimulation wasn't one of them. He had to confess to a feeling of lassitude. There was plenty of work to do, naturally, but, as his department were not engaged in any heavy legislation in the autumn, he could expect a relatively straightforward year. All being well, there would be plenty of time for spending with Elaine. He checked his watch and wondered what she was doing now, on her freebie to Scandinavia.

Her hotel phone number was tucked in the smallest pocket of his wallet. He debated if it would be safe to call her, but decided against. That new girl in Elaine's office had sounded distinctly suspicious. It would not do to get careless, not now just as his career was beginning to take off.

It was natural to invite James Betts in. He had given her a great night out. He had not touched her in the taxi. He had been jolly nice about Mum and that awful man Roger Dickson. They both had drunk a bit – well, a lot, for her, really: her head was spinning as they climbed the stairs and she had to hang on to the banister. She needed a coffee. Nothing wrong with asking Mr Moustache up: nothing at all. And if he kissed her, so what? Maybe it was time to find out what that spiky wet hair really tasted like. Curry, in all probability. Karen giggled.

Betts stood in the doorway and looked around, journalist's eye to the fore. He longed to take out a notebook but thought better of it. The flat was small, only two diminutive bedrooms, a bathroom, a larger living room and a minute kitchen set into an alcove. Even so, being close to the Commons it must have set the Stalkers back £100,000; the mortgage would be costing Mrs Stalker more than half her parliamentary salary. And no tax relief, for this was a second home.

The living room was simply furnished. A large carved desk with a green leather top, possibly a family heirloom, dominated most of one side, a word processor and old printer on top. Bookcases were filled with a mixture of political biography, parliamentary papers, modern novels and P. D. James. He pretended an interest as Karen fussed with coffee. She peered out at him.

'That one – *A Taste for Death* – is about an MP who gets killed,' she informed him. Making the words come out was evidently proving difficult. 'It's good but makes you think all MPs are wealthy aristocrats with Lady Something as their mum, and fancy labels to their names and Rolls-Royces in the garage. They're not. Most MPs are very ordinary.'

'Yeah, I know.' he said under his breath. The flat was warm; he took his jacket off and hung it on the back of the door, patting its pocket with a smile. Karen had her back to him, chattering as she struggled ineffectively to open a new pack of ground coffee. Her fingers would not do what she wanted.

He turned to take a good look at her, and whistled through his teeth.

The girl was standing, her weight on one foot, her buttocks outlined under the close-fitting dress. As she talked she shifted to the other foot and the curves rolled provocatively. It was a long time since he had had a woman.

Time to get a return on that dinner. He walked over, planted his hands on her hips, then slid his arms around her waist from behind, clasping them tight and pulling her in towards him. She was about the same height and her body smelled good.

'Forget the coffee. That's not what I've come for. Time for a little kiss.'

Karen giggled and swayed, half knowing what to expect. Of course he had a hard-on; she was gorgeous, wasn't she? At a suitable moment she would tell him he would be more attractive clean-shaven.

Betts adjusted his position until he was rubbing himself against her bottom. Pushing his face under one jangling earring he nuzzled her shoulder, nibbling the firm flesh under her ear, then moved his mouth around till his tongue was gently licking the nape of her neck, just on the point of the bone.

'Take your earrings off, they're getting in the way.'

As she reached up obediently to do so, his hands moved up to her breasts. The nipples were taut and the girl murmured as he brushed his fingers over them. The earrings tinkled on the kitchen counter.

His hands were moving all over her breasts and shoulders now, producing in her a mixture of sensations. There was still the smell of curry clinging faintly to him, a reminder of the lovely evening he had given her, and for which she was appreciative. He began to squeeze her breasts. Yes, she thought, that was what bosoms are for; that is what men like. In a minute she would turn around and kiss him.

Then those hands slid down her front, still holding her hard against him from behind, down quite fast towards her crotch, not all the way, pressing her abdomen and giving her butterflies, then up again. His erection was pressing hard in the small of her back. Of course, it was quite natural. Time for that grotty moustache. She turned around, opened her mouth as in all the magazines and movies and let him kiss her hard.

It was rotten being fifteen – knowing what was supposed to happen and never getting a chance to try it. All those glossy magazines, *Just Seventeen* and *19* and *More!* and *Mizz*, were full of how to capture the man of your dreams and what to do with him when you got him; agony columns discussed *exactly* where to put your tongue, when to take a breath. Even how to put on a condom, not that she had ever seen one. She knew from *19* magazine that coming on strong could turn a boy off – but this one seemed keen and, apart from the taste of curry, which no doubt he was getting from her too, he was reasonably acceptable. What did that article say? 'When you're overwhelmed by a desire like this you

264

feel helpless.' Helpless was precisely how she felt, so she must be doing everything right.

Karen could not believe she was being kissed with such aggressive determination and she kissed him back, laughing with excitement. Her head was spinning with the wine, but with more than that, with a heady delight in her own unexplored sexuality and her power to turn this daft bloke on.

The kisses obliterated control for Betts. He hadn't had any for too bloody long and now was his chance. The girl was responding, thank God. For a moment he'd worried that she might be a bit prissy, but she appeared to be participating willingly. Feverishly he pulled down the fabric of her top.

She leaned back invitingly, as in all the magazine photos. He took a deep breath and began kissing her breasts, tugging at the fabric. His moustache was tickling, but it helped her keep tabs on how far he had got. Must show him I'm enjoying this, she thought woozily and caressed his head as he moved down. She gave herself up so completely to being held and kissed that it was a moment before she realised he was nuzzling her nipples and not so gently, sucking at them and making her gasp. Twisting her hand up behind her back, she quickly discarded the redundant bra before he tore it. Is this how it was supposed to happen? Oh, heavens . . .

He was rubbing up and down the inside of her thighs and muttering about tights being a bloody turn-off. Obediently she pulled them down and kicked them away, and, since it was now ruched up around her waist and it seemed the appropriate thing to do, wriggled out of her dress too. It lay like a reproach, an unwanted skin, on the floor.

He grabbed her hand and pressed it on his penis, hissing at her to touch it, to grip it through the trouser fabric, then to slide her clasped finger and thumb up and down it, not too fast. She obeyed as much out of curiosity and heard him moan with pleasure. If that's what he wanted . . . It was larger than she expected, longer and firmer; he sniggered when she told him so. He was whispering something she couldn't hear. Karen sensed herself crossing a barrier. Wait till she told the girls at school about this – none of them had been this far, with a proper bloke, not some hairless schoolboy.

Betts put his hand firmly between her legs, touching the fabric of her panties and the moistness beneath. He was starting to feel in a hurry and pressed his fingers into the gap. Then he began to rub her.

Suddenly he knew he had made a mistake. She yelped and pushed him away, eyes blazing. 'No! You can't do that.'

'Oh, come on. If you want me to stop, just say so. You're so beautiful, Karen, and you've really turned me on.' Panting and helpless, he looked at her like an appealing dog.

She wrenched herself away from him, but the sight of her standing there mother-naked except for the bikini-style pants, young breasts thrust at him, made him nearly frantic. It was not going to stop there.

'I think you're ready,' he announced, and started to unbutton his shirt.

Karen looked at him aghast. 'What do you mean – go the whole way? But I've only just met you. I can't . . . no, no.'

'Look at yourself. Look at the state you've got me in! You can't fucking say no now.'

'I can and I do.' Karen was doing her best to be firm. Reality was establishing itself in her still fuddled brain. She tried to step back but was jammed up hard against the kitchen counter. Betts fumbled at his belt and started to take his trousers off. He reached for her panties and yanked them down, shoving his hand between her legs.

'You said yes the moment you let me do that,' he ground at her. 'And I'm bloody well having it, do you hear? What are you – some kind of cock-teaser? If you didn't want it, you shouldn't fucking well have asked me up here.'

He was drunker than he had realised but she had really got him going. There was no way he could simply pick up his jacket and leave. Damned women – there was only one way; he'd show her who was master. He held her tight with one hand and unzipped his fly. Grabbing her right hand with his free one he shoved it inside and closed her shaking fingers over his penis. She was rigid with terror. Too bad: that was her problem, not his.

Karen tried to push him away but he kept her hand tight and lunged towards her, kissing her hard on her mouth. That would shut her up. The two swayed in a fitful embrace, then the girl lost her footing and slipped, almost fainted, down on one knee; there she found herself looking straight . . . at *it*, huge and red and wrinkled and horrible with an opaque drip on the end a few inches from her face. Betts gave her a push and she sprawled on the floor, half in and half out of the kitchen. The packet of coffee went with her and burst, scattering everywhere, its aroma filling the air.

He worked quickly now, ignoring her protests. There was no time for a condom – she would wriggle away while he was fiddling. His face was set in a grimace as he pulled off her panties and his own trousers and underpants and laid himself on top of her, using his greater weight to counter her struggles. With one hand he pinned her arms over her head; the other he held near her face.

'Now, if you don't want to get hurt, you'll open your legs like a good girl,' he grunted. Eyes wide with fright she shuddered. 'Yes, you will. Otherwise you will get a wallop. I mean it.'

Spangles of red and white exploded in her brain and she screamed as he hit her very hard, once, across the mouth.

'Keep quiet, you little bitch! You just keep your knees wide open and your mouth shut, you hear?'

She could not get away. He drove himself into her hard, pounding brutally. It had not crossed his mind that she might be a virgin, not in that tight mini-dress and the provocative way she had wiggled in the restaurant and in the kitchen, with that come-on look. He cursed her for a stupid slag. Ten years ago he had been one of a gang of four boys that had held down a girl on Wavertree Common one summer evening, stuffing her knickers into her mouth to stop her screaming while they all had a go. She had been a sobbing heap when they had finished, but one of the older boys had told him comfortingly afterwards that the reason for all the blood was not because they had been particularly rough, but because she was a virgin. Virgins were harder work. Best to ignore her stricken expression and get on with it. In a moment he was spent, and sagged, panting, over her.

'Right! I'm done,' he said in a matter-of-fact voice. 'That wasn't so horrible, was it?'

He picked up her panties and wiped away the blood smears from himself and from between her legs. 'Sorry about the mess.'

She found her voice from somewhere, a long way away. She was sober now if he wasn't.

'You shouldn't have done that. I'm only fifteen.'

He was astonished. 'What? But you said you were going to college next year.'

'Right, I am.' She sat up wearily. 'But to do A levels, not a degree, not yet. I was fifteen on the first of June.'

Gathering up his clothes he looked at her uncertainly. There were coffee grounds in her hair, some in his mouth. He spat them out in distaste.

'I shall say you asked for it. You would have to explain why you invited me in.'

'I said no, and I meant no. What if I go to the police?'

Betts thought as rapidly as ever in his life. Then he got it. 'I should tell my editor what I know about your mother and Mr Roger Dickson. I bet they did it here; I can describe it all now.' He looked around at the disorderly flat. 'On the sofa, maybe, or there on the carpet. Where do you think I should put them, two naked people rolling around among the Hansards?'

Her eyes widened in confusion and horror. 'No! You mustn't! You promised! You said you wouldn't say a word about all that.'

'That was before you started howling about fetching the boys in blue.' He was gathering up his things, zipping up his fly. He had to get out as quickly as possible.

'Right, then, Miss Karen. I want a promise in return. This little incident is between you and me, right? You don't tell anybody, not your mother or anyone. After you've had a bath you'll feel better. It happens to every woman sooner or later if they're not to die old maids, so you could say I've done you a favour. Not a word to anybody, or your ma and her boyfriend will be all over the front pages. Is that a deal?'

Karen cast around for an alternative and, finding none, nodded dumbly. Her body was stiffening up and she longed for hot water, flannel and soap. The side of her face throbbed. The flat was in a filthy state – it would have to be cleaned up before she collapsed into bed tonight.

What a God-forsaken mess. She felt a terrible sense of loss: whenever she had dreamed of this moment it involved some wonderful Adonis on a grassy bank under a blue sky, sunlight filtering through his hair from behind scudding clouds. Not a drunk, foul, ferrety man with a rough Liverpool accent and brutal hard hands and the odour of curry, cigarettes and bitter coffee on his breath, in her hair, on her skin.

Later she would cry, but right now she refused to give him the satisfaction. With as much dignity as she could muster, she stood up and put her dress back on, pulling it down as far as it would go.

'It's a deal. I won't say anything if you won't. Now you had better clear off before I change my mind. Shut the street door as you go.'

Betts felt almost jaunty as he walked into the night air. She was certainly a pretty girl and of course it had all been her fault, leading a man on like that. Still, a court case could be nasty. Even if they believed him it might cost him his job. How was he to know she was so young? She didn't look it or act it. He should have looked her up in her mother's *Who's Who* entry – a basic precaution, forgotten in the early heat of the chase. Rape, it was; sex with a minor. Karen weeping in the witness box. Maximum penalty, he knew: automatically, life, which meant ten years. Just for a bit of nooky. Didn't bear thinking about. Have to keep his promise.

Stopping by a refuse bin he fished out of his pocket a used phone card, two old Tube tickets, several sweet wrappers, an empty cigarette packet, a grubby tissue and the crumpled bits of letter. Then he hesitated: he must be mad. No investigative journalist would ever discard a useful piece of incriminating evidence. These little scraps might help pay the rent some day.

Tossing the rest of the rubbish aside but shoving the particles of letter back into his pocket, he went on his way, feeling better than for ages. And whistling.

CHAPTER SEVENTEEN

Betts knew something was wrong. Last time he had sensed an atmosphere like this had been in a police morgue after a nasty shooting incident involving five children. Today he had crashed his way noisily through the street doors at the *Globe* as usual, its chief investigative reporter touching home base after a fortnight chasing a story up north. The reception area brought him up short.

Behind the desk there no longer sat a pretty young girl filing her nails but a tough-looking uniformed black man with hard thighs and cold eyes.

'May I see your ID, sir?' The man was correct, polite.

'What? Here it is. Where's Dolly?'

The guard examined Betts's grubby NUJ card. 'No, sir, your ID for this building, for the *Globe*.'

Betts was becoming irritated. 'And who the hell are you?'

'Jarman Security, sir.' A steely half-smile. 'Now if you'll let me see your ID, *sir*, or I'm afraid I can't let you in.'

Betts fidgeted with increasing incredulity and impatience while the grubby plastic card was examined and his name checked against a list. Satisfied, the guard nodded and motioned him away. As Betts walked on, puzzled, the guard sat immobile and watchful, a glossy copy of *Body Builder* in his lap.

Betts headed for the stairs. The main editorial and journalist offices were one floor up. Disorientation increased as he pushed open the door to the main corridor. The place was so damned *quiet*.

Several unlocked office doors swung open at a touch. The rooms inside were empty, papers scattered, files opened and tossed on desks. Sodden polystyrene cups littered the floor. On one wall was pinned a recent inside page of the *Globe* showing the proprietor at a party, Miranda grinning on his arm. Across his face was written 'SHIT' in red felt-tip.

Betts found Thwaite at last, at his desk, inputting text rapidly and swearing under his breath. An overflowing ashtray meant trouble. Betts, who had wedged his foot with impunity in a thousand reluctant doors, chewed his moustache a moment, then knocked, softly.

'Mr Thwaite, sir. May I ask what's going on? Where's the reception girl? Where's Dave, and Susie, and Nick the Greek? Where *is* everybody, for God's sake?'

Thwaite swivelled round in his chair, reached for his cigarette packet and lit up. There were dark circles under his eyes, damp circles under his armpits. He slid over the packet. Betts accepted it in mute male comradeship.

'Got the sack. This morning, first thing. Forty of them. That'll save a million quid a year in salaries, more in expenses. All they got was a phone call – the earliest at seven last night after the board meeting, the last around seven this morning. Told to collect their cards, clear their desks by eleven. All gone.'

Thwaite's tone was sardonic but his eyes were wild. 'We're the lucky ones, you and I. The features editor isn't being replaced and only sport is more or less intact. That tells you something about the future direction of the *Globe*. All contracts have been ended that can be ended, but mine has a clause that means that as long as there's a *Globe* I'm here till I'm fifty-five, if I want. I insisted on retaining three reporters. You're one. Together we have to write the whole bloody newspaper.'

'You're kidding. How can we do that?'

'Not so difficult, now the paper is to be thirty-six pages instead of forty-eight. Not that we have the advertising to fill much more. We have one page of politics – Andy Mack and Thompson are still here, but then they've been our entire political staff all year anyway. We have two other pages of news which it is our job to fill, plus the leader to write. When we're stuck we'll use agency tapes and the phone. You and I are going to be writing a lot, ourselves, fast. And we're to keep our mouths shut. No whingeing, or no job. Understand?'

Betts nodded. He realised he ought to feel grateful and patted his boss on the shoulder. It was not as if Fleet Street was crawling with jobs. Even if it were, there would now be forty more journalists chasing each vacancy.

'Where does McSharry stand in all this?'

'Our esteemed editor?' Nick Thwaite allowed himself to sound bitter, then stared morosely at his cigarette, letting the ash fall on to the table. 'He had to do the fucking telephoning. Came back from that board meeting white as a sheet and started. All he would say to me was "If twenty main board directors, not one of whom has ever worked on a newspaper, were deprived of their twenty chauffeur-driven cars, we'd save that million easily and still have a newspaper." Right now he's putting tomorrow's edition together with Miranda. She's still here.'

'Friend of the family, her. Untouchable.' A meaningful glance passed between the two men.

'Skate over that, young man, if you intend to eat breakfast tomorrow at the *Globe*'s expense. The question you should be answering is, how are you getting on with your checking out of MPs with their trousers down? McSharry says he's still interested. There's still a budget for that. If we can't use the material, one of the other papers in the group can.' He did not need to add: *If we fold in a few weeks' time.*

Betts concentrated and flicked through his battered notebook, discussing what he had found. First, murky finances. Freddie Ferriman had bought shares in four names at the last privatisation sale: that could mean prosecution. Martin Clarke had wept as he wrote out a cheque for a million to cover his losses at Lloyd's with more to come. The charitable doings of the Hon. Rosemary Arbour MP had attracted police attention, after most of the money raised at a big charity ball seemed to have disappeared. Any of these events could result in bankruptcy, and, as Jeffrey Archer found, even the threat thereof could force a Member with a great future out of Parliament.

Thwaite chewed on a biro. 'Freddie's good for a run, but the bugger won't resign. None of them ever do these days. We'll have a word with Steve about Lloyd's – that might be a goer. And just check with the Met if they are anywhere near charging the horrible Hon. Rosemary. Can't stand the bitch; that woman's voice is like metal on glass. Isn't daddy a distinguished member of their Lordships' House? Have you spoken to her yourself?'

'Not yet. I'll try the usual – "If you don't talk to me, I'll write it anyway, so you might as well pre-empt all the nasty lies and get the truth in first." They always sing after that.'

'There must be something about your charm that makes them confess, Betts, though it escapes me. What about sex, or are they all celibate these days?'

'No-o-oo.' Betts took a deep breath and chewed his moustache. 'Though the new intake seem a bloodless lot. More interested in *Geld* than girls. Gelded by ambition, you might say.' He paused for effect as Thwaite grimaced. At least the man was now smiling, or nearly. 'Seventeen of them are suspiciously still single, so I shall keep my beady eye on them. Keith Quin is having it off with Dr Janey Irvine – but then they're Labour. On the Liberal benches we have wee willie wonder Gordon McDonald, who's rumoured to have a lady friend in the BBC. It'd be more exciting if the whole Lib Dem bench would simply climb naked into a London taxi together and let the rest of us watch.'

Thwaite chuckled. 'Too many of them, these days. Go on.'

'I have six who are bedding their secretaries, but the besotted cows won't talk; I've tried every one. We'll have to wait till the chaps start complaining about the coffee stains on the typing – then the fur may fly.'

Betts had run out of steam. Thwaite brooded, sighed.

'They're all too bloody normal. What we need is an MP who is rogering his dog, for heaven's sake, or a real eccentric who likes being whipped while five in a bed with black women who can take razor blades out of their anuses.'

'Come back, Madam Cyn, all is forgiven.'

'Too right! I think we need bigger quarry, Jim. Let's go through the Cabinet. What about our saintly bon viveur, Sir Nigel Boswood? There have been whispers about his . . . proclivity . . . for years. Do you think there's anything in it? He must be coming towards the end of his wonderfully distinguished and overlong career. Maybe he's ready to come out, as they say?'

Betts shrugged. Thwaite had a nose for possible stories and a theory, frequently proved correct, that a man could not deny his nature for ever. The eerie silence was getting on Betts's nerves; it was time to get out on the road again.

'No idea, but might be worth trying. He lives down Ebury Street – Eaton Square way – doesn't he? I remember doorstepping him over that row about imported nuclear waste, the *Karin B*. He never lost his temper – offered us all a glass of dry sherry, would you believe? Anyway, leave him to me.'

The house had belonged to Sir Nigel's aunt. A tall, white, narrow terrace, returned to its original purpose of a gentleman's town house, it was within walking distance of the Commons on a fine night, elegant for small dinner parties and comfortable enough to live in all the year round.

Betts was whistling as he examined it from the other side of the street. Its white stone was set off well by purple and pink asters in window-boxes. The first frost would kill them, but frost was rare in central London. A nearby estate agent's window had valued such a house at half a million. That Boswood was wealthy Jim Betts did not doubt; the calculation started off with this chunk of real estate, a modest mansion in his constituency, and that shooting lodge in Ayrshire. Worth at least a couple of million altogether, or more. He made a note to find out more about the place in Scotland, maybe by phoning a mate on the *Glasgow Herald* who owed him a favour.

It was time to put flesh on the bare bones. He climbed the steps to the front door and rang the doorbell.

Boswood did not keep living-in staff. Mrs Perkins came in mornings,

272

tidied up, watered the plants and was available to help if guests were expected. He preferred his privacy. Betts rang again, long and loud this time.

The basement door flew open and a tousle-haired youth poked his head out. He was naked to the waist down and was rubbing wet blond hair with a blue towel. Betts's eyes widened.

'Can you cut out that racket? If you're looking for Nigel, he's not here. He's at the House of Commons.'

Nigel. Betts pricked up his ears and smiled encouragingly.

'I'm so sorry to bother you. Actually I'm from the council and we've had complaints about smells from the sewers down this end of the square. I wonder if I might just check? Could I come in?'

'I guess so. Wait a minute – got to see your ID, Nigel said.'

For the second time that day Betts flourished his union card. This time it worked.

'Front door's locked so you'd better come in this way. Sorry about the mess but I've only just got up.'

Hardly believing his luck, Betts sauntered down the steps. The basement flat was dark, for the curtains were still drawn; an unmade bed appeared recently occupied and the bath was still full of soapy water. A wardrobe hung open, clothes were tossed on the floor. The place had a stale body smell as if not frequently cleaned. Betts made a pretence of checking around taps and outlet pipes and peering down sinks, as the boy dried his hair and pulled on sweater and jeans in the bedroom. It was three o'clock in the afternoon.

'Live here, do you?' the journalist enquired. If Boswood really was a queer then he was taking a hell of a chance. If he wasn't, then who was this bloke sleeping in his basement in broad daylight? Memories of the goings-on in Norman Lamont's basement stirred in Betts's brain. Even though the ex-Chancellor had let the rooms entirely innocently, the activities of a temporary tenant, a rough-looking female with a penchant for suspenders and whips and a curriculum vitae including appearances in porn films, had provoked much ribaldry.

'Sort of,' the boy said.

Betts was making mental notes feverishly. Very young; very good-looking – that fine bone structure, those high cheekbones would photograph superbly. The blond hair had some help from a bottle, perhaps. Nice body, what he'd seen of it – tanned even in November. Looked after himself. What for? Who for?

'Ah – have you noticed any strange odours? Anything untoward? Have you been here long?'

''Bout five months. Nigel lets me doss down because I've nowhere else to stay. If it's a bit whiffy in here it's probably my fault – I don't get round to changing the bed too often. Sorry.'

'Mind if I smoke?'

The boy shook his head and indicated an ashtray. He was combing his wet hair carefully in the mirror, slicking it with gel. Betts seated himself politely on the edge of the scrambled bed.

'I suppose I really ought to ask What's-his-name' – consulting his notebook – 'Mr Boswood? Would you be a relative of his?'

'It's Sir Nigel, and no, I'm not a relative. Just a friend.'

Betts was already writing the first paragraph: *Just good friends, says boy lodger*. His eyes glittered.

'Oh, I've heard of him. What's he like? Nice bloke? Must be to let you stay in his house like this.'

The boy was defensive. 'I told him I'll pay rent when I have the money but he said it wouldn't matter. Yes, he's a good sort. Been good to me, anyway.'

Peter glanced curiously at the sandy-haired man seated awkwardly on his bed smoking a cheap cigarette and chewing a tattered moustache. The council certainly attracted grotty types – not his sort at all. It would be fun to make this twerp envious.

'He's going to take me skiing after Christmas,' the boy boasted. 'Switzerland – Davos. With the House of Commons and House of Lords ski team, against MPs from the Swiss Parliament. He goes every year. The Swiss beat us every time but we might do better this winter because I'm quite good. Officially I'm his research assistant. Bit of all right, that.'

'Ye-e-s, I can see that, Mr . . . what did you say your name was?' The notebook came out again.

'Me? Oh, just Peter. Everyone calls me Peter.'

Betts rose and moved to the door. It was time to be out and making rapid phone calls.

'Well, Mr Peter, you've been most helpful. Thank you.'

'Don't you need to look at the rest of the house?'

'No. If there's a problem, it'll be here, in the basement. And everything is all right, as far as I can tell. Fine, just fine. You have been most helpful. Thank you.'

Peter circled the room, putting himself between the door and Betts. He put his head on one side and contemplated the nervous man now shifting uneasily from one foot to the other.

'I don't think you're really from the council.'

Betts's mouth went dry. His brain, already working at a furious rate, went through his story. If there were trouble, he would say that he had shown his press card and been admitted. That much was true. He had made no false claims to gain entry, none at all.

'What makes you think that? I showed you my ID and you were satisfied.'

'Soap in my eye. I didn't look properly. Don't worry, I won't tell on you. You press?'

Warily: 'What would you do if I were?'

Peter laughed. It might be fun to play cat and mouse with a stupid journalist.

'It would depend what you wanted. I've nothing against people like you – you have a living to earn. But if you're expecting me to say anything nasty against Nigel, forget it.'

Betts breathed easier. There are many varieties of fools in the world but the best, the most easily tripped up, are conceited fools. There are no secrets a good investigative reporter can't winkle out by a combination of bribery, blackmail and flattery, and the latter was always the cheapest.

'I would expect you to speak well about your landlord. You seem like a mature, intelligent sort of person. To tell you the truth, I didn't realise this was Sir Nigel's house; I'd been told to look at homelessness, and compare the hostels with high rents charged for flats and bedsits round here. I don't suppose you can help me much with that, Peter, though you did mention you had had nowhere to go: your experiences would be of interest to our readers. There's a pub round the corner. May I buy you a drink? All off the record, of course. No names, no pack drill. It might even help other people in London who are sleeping on the streets tonight – get the government to take the matter more seriously.'

Peter considered, then shrugged. 'Yeah, why not. Glad to help out a fellow creature. Nothing else on this afternoon. I'll just get my jacket and lock up. Can't be too careful, Nigel says.'

'Start, please.'

Mrs Mary Carter's eagle eyes swept across the hall as fifty young girls prayed silently and turned over examination papers. Regally the teacher walked up and down the long columns of desks, tidying away a bag here, glancing intimidatingly at scribbled sheets there. At last she mounted the platform. Seating herself rigidly at a table from which all the desks and examination candidates were clearly visible, she crossed her legs, arranged her skirt decorously over her knees, and opened a large file behind which was hidden Jilly Cooper's novel *Polo*. She lowered her eyes and began reading. From time to time, her mouth twitched.

The examination paper was a collection of hieroglyphics. It was supposed to be English literature, and it was only a mock, in preparation for the following summer's. Nor did it matter much, for course-work made up the bulk of the marks and Karen was confident that her project work was satisfactory. She was familiar with the set-pieces. Why, then, did the words coalesce into meaningless blobs? The very paper shimmered in front of her eyes. She was feeling sick again.

Mrs Carter sat upright and still, apparently engrossed in her bulky file. From time to time she would glance up, eyes darting around the room like a hawk's. Karen reflected grimly that the teacher cultivated a reputation for not missing much, but couldn't spot calamity sitting right under her nose.

Karen sat quietly trying to make sense of the paper. Nearby girls were scribbling furiously, or staring at the ceiling, lips moving, seeking inspiration. Only at her own desk was there as yet no action. With a sigh she abandoned the effort and settled instead to chasing the tangled thoughts in her brain, at least for a little while.

After Betts had left the flat, she had dully cleaned up. There were coffee grounds everywhere. The mess had been so phenomenal that the task had taken over an hour and had started her bleeding again. The bath had been too hot and the bath salts stung; at last she had allowed herself to lie in the sudsy water, and cry.

The dress and underwear were rolled up savagely into a ball and shoved into a black plastic bag with all the other rubbish. On an impulse the silly earrings went in too. They had sent out all the wrong signals; she would not take another chance with them.

Karen made herself think hard about the whole incident. Of course he should have accepted 'no' as 'no'. That was the law, whatever old fools in legal wigs and gowns might say. A refusal was precisely that and should have been respected. It was his fault, his wrong: of that she was certain. The thought was barren but comforting.

Yet she had led him on, asking him up to the flat when he was so far gone – drunk, and sexually. Her inexperience meant she was not to know that, but she might have *guessed*. She wasn't *stupid*. Though the outcome was stupid, and too terrible to tell anybody. Least of all her mother.

So did she carry any responsibility? That was a hard question, not least because every fibre of her being wanted to scream, 'It wasn't my fault!' Believing that, however, gave her no practical protection. The same thing could happen all over again, if she had been foolish in some unseen way. She shivered miserably and forced herself to concentrate once more. It was essential to figure out exactly where it had all gone wrong, and where in future she might behave differently.

Perhaps men couldn't help it – all men, or at least a certain type. Once they got so far, there was no holding back. Maybe they were all ruled by their willies, as some feminists alleged. Betts himself seemed to think so. Yet that seemed to her generous spirit a confession of failure, an expression of crude prejudice as blatant as any misogynist claim that all women were ruled by their wombs. One article in a magazine had argued that it was insulting to suggest that men were simply carried away like that. Men were not crude, unthinking animals any more than women were. Any man, given a moment to think, could control himself. That suggested Betts also had had a responsibility not to put himself in a position where there was no going back. It came down again to his fault, not hers.

He wouldn't have done it had he realised her age. Even he had confessed that much. Yet if that was significant why didn't he ask? The thought made her smile ruefully. Oh yes, she could just hear the conversation in the restaurant as the wine waiter lovingly cradled a bottle in front of them. 'By the way, Karen, I am thinking of having my way with you tonight. Before we go any further and I get carried away, could you just confirm that you have reached the age of consent?'

He didn't ask because she didn't look under-age. Every day she strove to look not fifteen but older, to ape girls – women – in their early twenties. Her body was fully adult. If you have got it, flaunt it. Yet that deliberate flaunting was an invitation.

No, it wasn't. A feeling of indignation arose. She was entitled to dress any way she wanted, and still say 'no' and have that respected. Short skirts were fashionable. Stretchy, clingy outfits were normal wear, for millions of girls. Perhaps all the designers were trading on sex; that wouldn't be a surprise, given its role as the most basic urge of all. She wouldn't change her style; or at least only a little. No wearing long skirts like Mrs Carter, not till they were really in. He didn't know what she looked like when he asked her out (but then he had other motives, she now realised). It was her choice to dress sexily. It was her choice for that sexy style not to be confused with an open invitation. Had he stayed sober he might have realised. Had she, he wouldn't have got near.

Being ruled by her womb.

That was a different matter entirely. That morning she had been sick into the sink. Alarming new fears which had not entered her head surfaced, in a feeling of terror and panic. Supposing she were pregnant?

A woman of the world, however shocked the day after, might have summoned the courage to go to her doctor and ask for help or advice – the morning-after pill, for example. But Karen had no doctor in London. The thought of chatting gaily to the kindly old family doctor in the village about a potential pregnancy, asking him about abortions, was ludicrous. She would not know where to start. The school doctor, a lady, might be a better bet – she must have come across this sort of thing before, would know what to do, be discreet. It would cost money, mean a few days off school, need an excuse. Her mother would have to know, but perhaps no one else.

Perhaps she ought to get a pregnancy test kit and try herself, before springing it all on an incredulous world. But where? There was no chemist near the school, which was deliberately set in the middle of nowhere, to protect young ladies from temptation. Any nearby pharmacist would give her a funny look if she asked for a pregnancy kit. It might be different in London or other big cities where pregnant girls were more frequent customers. It would have to wait until the end of term when she could get into town; but by then it might be too late.

Karen had only the haziest knowledge of the law on abortions. That she could get one easily, soon, if necessary, she was reasonably sure from her magazines. Something to do with the physical and mental health of the girl, wasn't it? She could scream blue murder if necessary. She felt like screaming right now.

That abortion would be even more easily obtainable for a rape victim was a consideration she pushed firmly out of her mind. The first hint of the word would have the police panting hard, hot on the trail in minutes. It was not the shame or anything like that. She did not feel ashamed, only foolish, and sick, and angry with herself. She, a modern woman, had let a man take her most precious gift: she was taller than Betts, she should have kneed him in the groin, made him think twice before trying that again, ever. Yet what stopped her examining the consequences of rape was there, all the time, at the forefront of her mind: that he would then betray her mother.

Karen did not doubt now that her mother and this Roger were involved somehow, though it still seemed preposterous that her own mother, the brilliantly successful Elaine Stalker, should dream of wasting her time taking lovers. She was married, and Dad loved her. They'd been married a long time. What on earth was Mum playing at?

The only way to find out would be to ask. That would require a confrontation of sorts. Karen's loyalty to her mother made her shy away: Mum had more than enough on her plate without prying questions from her kid. Being Mum, and being clever, she might well dig out of Karen exactly where she had obtained this incriminating information. The girl could not clearly envisage her mother's reaction should she understand the circumstances. Would Mum yell for the police? Or would she deal with it all discreetly? One thing was for certain: Mum would not let it rest once she knew that her only daughter had been violated. Any sense of control Karen had, however scrappy, would vanish entirely. That bit Mum was not to know.

If a termination were necessary she would simply say it had been an accident and keep her mouth shut. That's what most girls would do. And be more careful – a helluva lot more careful – next time a man poured her a glass of wine. Maybe even say no to that, too, loud and clear. And never be alone with a man anywhere near a bed unless she was ready. Which was unlikely to be for a very long time.

Mrs Carter had been watching her intently for several minutes. Karen shifted uncomfortably, bent her head, read the first question again. Her head was spinning and a wave of nausea rocked her. Breakfast had been impossible; now cramps gripped her and her mouth salivated. She was going to be sick again.

Unsteadily she rose to her feet, white as a sheet. 'Mrs Carter, I don't feel . . . well . . .' she began timidly. Then with a crash she slumped to the floor.

Karen came round to the murmuring of concerned voices, and kept her eyes shut to listen for a moment. The nurse and Mrs Carter and the nice school lady doctor were discussing whether to phone her mother. Gingerly she moved her head; the headache seemed to have subsided and she just felt woozy. Maybe the doctor had given her a shot of something. Her gut still hurt. She opened her eyes and managed a weak smile.

'No, there's no need to bother my mother. I felt faint, that's all. Exams, you know.'

The three women stopped talking and gathered around the couch, anxious faces peering down on her. The doctor felt her brow.

'Feeling sick still?'

Karen nodded. 'A little.'

'Do you want to go to the bathroom?'

'Yes, please.'

Groggily she rose to her feet and was helped into the cubicle off the nurse's office. It had no lock on the door.

There was blood on her pants.

Blood on her pants? Her period! She wasn't pregnant!

Then tears came, in great floods, sobs of relief and delight and exhaustion, as she sat in an undignified heap, grabbing handfuls of white toilet roll to stem the weeping.

Nurse was peeping uncertainly round the door, guessed, and handed her a towel. 'Bad one, is it? Often happens at exam times, dear. You sort yourself out and then come and have a lie down till the cramps go.'

The doctor was a sharper individual. She stood over Karen as the girl gratefully took tablets and water. When the nurse had left the room and Mrs Carter had returned to her duties, the woman glanced over her shoulder, then spoke very quietly.

'You look a lot happier than a few moments ago. Now if you've been silly, young lady, you have also been very lucky. If you want to try and avoid trouble in future, you come and see me first, you hear?'

Karen did not move. Her eyes opened wide and she made her face expressionless.

'Absolutely confidential. I don't tell your parents, or school, or anyone. If you're old enough to get pregnant you're old enough to have an entirely private relationship with your doctor. I'd rather anything than have to start arranging abortions. Do I make myself clear?'

Karen nodded mutely. The doctor turned to go. The girl put out an arm.

'Thank you,' she said sombrely.

Down in the Lord John Russell, Peter was knocking back tequila sunrises and chatting amiably to Jim Betts. It was long after Betts should have phoned in copy, however anodyne, for the following day's paper, but this was too good to miss.

Betts had slid nonchalantly into the role of host, plying the boy with drinks in mimicry of what he guessed might well be a familiar scene, if he was correct in his suspicion that Peter's link with Sir Nigel derived originally from a gay pick-up. Lull him into a sense of false security and loosen his tongue with liquor – it usually worked. No point in taking notes or taping the conversation; that might have scared the little poofter off. Softlee softlee catchee monkee.

Jim Betts's own attitudes to homosexuals were equivocal. In the treeless terraced streets of Wavertree, Liverpool, where he grew up there had been prostitutes of every kind, mostly blousy women doused in cheap scent keeping the tallyman at bay. If you wanted something better or out of the ordinary, a narrow-hipped tart or a Chinese or a queer, you had to go down near the Pier Head, or tip the head porter in certain hotels. A mate from school had plied his trade down there occasionally when business was slow. Most gays that he had met in that sad grimy port had been more desperate and more diseased than this and he had felt some pity. Peter, young and highly presentable, would make a tremendous subject for a double-page spread. With his co-operation, or otherwise.

'You spoke well of Sir Nigel.' Betts lit another cigarette. It was time to turn on the charm. 'I liked that, Peter. Not often these days anyone has a good word to say about politicians.'

Peter had put away four drinks on an empty stomach and was feeling light-headed. Talking to a journalist was almost fun; the chap opposite was so pleasant and not pushy, he made it easy. Peter was not unaware that his own vanity was being flattered, and liked it.

'He doesn't keep me, you know. I work. I paint. It's just that I haven't managed to do much since I've been in that flat. No room, see. And paints are so bloody expensive.'

'Doesn't Sir Nigel give you anything? Not even for looking after the house? It must deter burglars having you around.'

'Yeah, I hadn't thought of that. No, not a penny. He should, shouldn't he? I'll have to ask him. Tell him a newspaperman said I should.' The blue eyes were not focusing properly. An attempt at a smile didn't quite work and emerged as a leer.

'No, I shouldn't do that, Peter. He might be a bit upset that you've had a drink with me. Probably wouldn't understand that we were just ... friends, you and I.' Then, warily: 'You could make money out of him if you wanted to, of course.'

The sentence hung on the smoke-filled air, coiled around Peter's head. Dreamily he let his gaze rove around the room, then rested them on Betts's face and giggled.

'You mean if I talked about Nigel, don't you? No, I wouldn't do that.'

Betts took a chance. Stubbing out his cigarette: 'That wouldn't be enough, anyway. That's not the sort of story I would work on, of course – I do this social awareness stuff, homelessness and the like. But if you wanted to earn a lot of money from selling a story, you would need dates, times, details. You would have to be prepared to tell everything. And you'd need photographs.'

'What do we mean by "a lot of money"?' Peter asked. Knowledge like that was always useful to a working boy.

Betts considered, taking his time. 'Well, like I say, I have no experience of that kind of reporting myself, but you could ask ... ah ... twenty-five thousand pounds. If it was with someone famous. And you had some decent photographs. You need proof, see, that you're not making it all up.'

He allowed his own eyes to rest on Peter's face in his best imitation of a straightforward honest look. It was a long time since he had felt so in control of an interview.

'I am not going to encourage you in any direction, Peter.' Betts tore off a piece of paper from his notepad and scribbled his own name, the office phone number and, as an afterthought, his flat number. 'That number is for late at night only. If I can be of assistance, phone me. In fact I'd say don't do anything without phoning me. Even if all you want is some advice, there's no charge. I can put you in touch with the right people who would value your story highly and look after you properly, should you ever want to tell it.'

He rose to go, patting the boy on the shoulder. With some satisfaction he noticed a disconsolate look. Being the boyfriend of a busy Cabinet Minister must be a lonely occupation.

'In cash? Could it be paid abroad?'

'Anywhere in the world. Don't forget, phone me.'

At the pub door Betts turned. A thought had occurred to him. 'By the way, Peter, how old are you?'

'Me? Nineteen last birthday.'

'Really? Illegal, isn't it?' A conspiratorial grin.

Peter's pretty face was flushed. He smirked: 'I'm old enough. It's sixteen in Holland. Anyway, what does it matter?'

How odd, Betts thought fleetingly, that, whereas age with the too young Miss Stalker was a prohibition, with this boy it offered an opportunity. He waited till he was out of sight of the pub before kicking his heels and breaking into a run. Only one activity in Britain was still illegal till the age of twenty-one. It mattered all right.

Roger and Elaine made love that night in silence, needing comfort, sharing their yearning for each other. Outside it was raining hard. The persistent shushing sound of heavy rain lingered in the air as a steady stream of dirty water sluiced down the window. Roger's overcoat, hung near a radiator, steamed gently and smelled of winter.

As they lay together on the double bed a feeling of greater warmth at last stole over them, so that they dozed, and yawned and stretched, and began to smile. He consented as she leaned over and turned the bedside lamp on. There was no rush; Caroline was out of town, happily cleaning mud off her boots in a brightly lit kitchen at home after a grand day's hunting. He could stay the night if he wanted, though the two red boxes waiting in the hallway suggested he would eventually leave to sleep alone.

He opened a sleepy eye. 'God, this is nice. I wish it could go on for ever.'

She made no answer, but raised herself on an elbow and stroked his face with a caressing finger. The frown line between his eyes was deepening. His handsome face was half hidden in shadow and his mood seemed reflective and sombre.

'Penny for them?' she asked quietly.

He hesitated. 'I was only reflecting how very much harder government is in reality than those on the outside believe. Whichever way you look at it, it's been a dreadful year. Yet I don't think we made many mistakes, things we ought to change. The problem is to get people to accept what needs doing, all of which is unpopular.'

Elaine wriggled down closer to him. Her voice had the slightest edge. 'Since I'm not a member of the government, I've not been obliged to consider such questions. What is the view of Her Majesty's Ministers, sir?'

'Well . . . persuading the voters to accept short-term pain for longer-term goals requires two things we don't currently have in abundance: firstly, skills in communication, which would give us the power to orate and inspire, if you like.' Roger paused, half smiling.

She picked up the bait. 'And the other?'

'Since you press me, my dear Elaine, a clear idea of what those long-term goals are.'

She was shocked. 'You shouldn't talk like that, even to me. You're a member of this government, and likely to be an even more important member of it in future. You can be a major contributor to thinking ahead, Roger. What's the point of being in power otherwise?'

At that he was silent.

There was no clock in the bedroom. Elaine made a point of hiding the radio alarm under the bed before Roger came, to give him no reminders of passing time. Their encounters were events suspended in time, non-existent: recorded in no diary, measured by no instrument, referred to outside in no dialogue. Should he want it, his watch was on the table in the living room, but he made no move. Supported on her elbow, her finger slowly traced the hollows of his face.

'You seem more than usually contemplative tonight, my darling. Do I detect a fatal faltering, a lack of confidence?'

His reaction was to laugh ruefully. 'I could muddle through, keeping my head down and staying out of trouble, but that's not enough. You're absolutely right that I'd like to make a greater contribution. The twist is that I don't feel, unfortunately, that I have the capability.'

'Rot!'

Now she sounded like Caroline and he grinned up at her. Maybe all his women were right and he should simply shake off moods like this.

'Look, Roger, you are, first, one of the best-looking men on the British public scene. And an exceptional lover. Outstanding, unbelievable! If that wasn't true, you wouldn't be anywhere near my bed. Furthermore, you're one of the most thoughtful, most intelligent people in the House. Your colleagues, the most critical audience in the land, think well of you and that's no accident. You're rapidly improving as a speaker on TV and radio – getting really good at it; all that woodenness has disappeared. Most of all, you come across as honest and sincere. That's no surprise. In my humble view, my love, your public reputation accurately reflects your superb personality.'

'More! More!' Dickson was grinning broadly.

'Well . . .' She had been saving this thought for a suitable moment. 'For a person who left school at sixteen you haven't done badly.'

In normal conversation Roger would have murmured self-deprecatingly that he owed everything to his wife. Financially that was certainly true. However, as he climbed further up the greasy pole, he was prone to say it less often. On one occasion an opponent had remarked tartly that in that case perhaps they should have elected his wife.

'Roger, most of the top jobs are still held by public school and Oxbridge types. I know how highly you think of Nigel Boswood, but you should be asking why we don't bring on more people similar to yourself. And more women, too. This country can't afford to continue in the same old way. People like you can help make the changes we need. It's the top you should be aiming for, Roger Dickson. By the end of this Parliament you'll be in the Cabinet, and you should keep going.'

'Oh, nonsense. I shall be lucky to survive in this job. Half of what's on my plate I don't understand at all. Environment is heavy-duty stuff, a lot of it horribly scientific. The other half consists of endlessly stroking interested parties, and arm-twisting at Westminster to get measures through. I learned that in the whips' office.'

She prodded him. 'You're not going to divert me. I think you should be chock full of self-confidence, and as ambitious as hell. You're as capable as anyone currently in Cabinet and you've come a lot further than most already. Something must be driving you onwards, or you would be . . . just running a shop, or whatever.' Elaine searched her lover's face. 'So what makes you tick, Roger Dickson?'

It was the question he never dared ask. As a young man his motivation had been clear – to begin with, a hatred of having his horizons limited by the ignorance and acquiescence of his family, teachers, peers. Then the need to make money, to create that bedrock of security so lacking in his early days. Running away from his past, of course. Nothing wrong with that. But now that those objectives had been achieved he was on a plateau. To go further required a clear grasp of why: what did he seek *now*?

'It's easier for someone like Nigel Boswood, Elaine.' That seemed an easy entrée. 'He was brought up to it – to govern, to expect office. That gives him a thick skin – he expects the slings and arrows and ignores them. He has a whole class of people like himself – a clan, almost, who act as support and friends. His clubs, for example. The invitations he receives, the country house parties he attends. As long as he does his job well, he's invulnerable.'

There was no need to explain to Elaine that his comments were not motivated by jealousy. He continued slowly, 'I always felt it's not my place to push myself forward, even to dream of taking a top job. When I was a child, ambition was seen as . . . wicked, dangerous – as courting disaster. Staying at home, settled for ever in the same street or area, was soothing and safe. To counteract that fear, to dig it out and get it to the surface and destroy it, is the hardest thing I have ever done. It means leaving friends behind – I have already. When I meet people I was at school with, we hardly communicate at all – we have nothing whatever in common. Worst of all, they think I'm a traitor.'

'It means knowing what you want to do and why, Roger. I suspect you do know, but you're reluctant to seem disloyal to Nigel. You should be planning and plotting like crazy, if not to replace him eventually, then at least to get as close as possible. I mean not just Nigel – the very top.

Don't argue! If you were in Cabinet, and stood for the leadership next time, you might not win it but you'd have put down a marker.'

She sat up and looked down at him. 'You should want the top job, like the people who climb Everest, because it's *there*.'

He had to play devil's advocate, to find the right way. 'To have any chance of success I'd need to build up a backing, a group of followers. I don't quite see how I can do that as a Minister of State. That really would be disloyal.'

He was thinking out loud. Her heart skipped a beat as she realised that some of these thoughts were not new to him. It was one thing to seduce a whip, her whip, and to engage him in sexual badinage, for fun. A whip more than anyone knew the risks and, having assessed them, minimised them. Having a lover on the inside was infinitely safer than pursuing one on the outside. It was quite another matter sleeping with a senior Minister: like playing dominoes with sticks of high explosive. Even if all the fuses and detonators were safely locked away in a lead-lined box, with nothing loose or unconsidered to cause an accidental explosion – yet what they were playing with was still dynamite.

Both thrived on the risk. Both fought off boredom and loneliness and ordinariness as greater evils. And, she suspected, their lovemaking, so successful, such an opportunity for honesty, for loving support, was becoming steadily more important to them both, even as the struggle to find time for it intensified. A desperate longing came over her sometimes in the House when she watched him at the dispatch box, head up, hammering away at his points, refusing to give an inch. Of course she wanted him to succeed. But as he rose higher in the hierarchy, where would it end? If he were to spread his wings and fly, would there be room in the sky for her?

'I think you should be as ambitious as hell,' she repeated firmly. 'Some of the other Ministers are: look in their eyes. They want to be Leader, they burn to do it. So should you. I'd rather see you there at the top than anybody.'

He laughed, and rolled over easily. The frown on his brow had cleared and he gazed at her appreciatively. 'I don't know what I'd do without these fireside chats.' He was teasing but his tone was serious. 'You cheer me up immensely.'

They were silent for a while, digesting their own confused thoughts as the rain pattered on the window. His mind at least was much clearer. He glanced towards the doorway and sighed heavily.

'In the normal course of events, I would now place my hand in supplication on your luscious bosom and beg you to make love to me once more. But if I do that I'll fall asleep afterwards. Then I and my untouched boxes will have some explaining to do tomorrow. So I must go.'

The warm bed was abandoned with reluctance. Roger dressed meticulously as usual. Outside the rain eased to a soft drizzle, reducing his excuses for staying. As he knotted his tie they chatted, the topics moving from the intense to the mundane, as if both were slowly being beamed back to the real world.

'And how are you, my lovely Elaine? We haven't talked much about you tonight.'

She shrugged, pulling a dressing gown around her shoulders. 'OK, I guess. My husband is as ever – not there a lot, and not very communicative when he is. I don't think it's in any way your fault, Roger. We'd probably be drifting a bit anyway. I must make a bigger effort – he is, after all, my home and the father of my child. I wouldn't be the first woman MP to find that her husband couldn't cope. And my daughter Karen is back at school but is very quiet – I think she's worrying about exams.'

He lifted the still damp coat, pulled a face and placed it over his shoulders.

She continued, hastily, not wanting him to leave. 'Yet to be truthful, Roger, I resent the constant pressure on me. There are double standards at play here. Why should it always be me that has to try harder? Why should the woman have to carry the burden? That sounds so selfish – but I could do with more love and support from my family, week in, week out. I get it from you, but that's uncertain, and dangerous.'

'Too right.' There was no need to elaborate. It was respectable for a male MP to seek solace from his family, to demand uncritical support. Many didn't get it, but none was thought selfish for expecting it.

He took her face in his big hands in his farewell gesture, and kissed her forehead, her eyelids, her cheeks. Then his mouth was on hers, hard and longing, but he pulled brusquely away from her with a grunt, touched his forelock in a sad, ironic movement, picked up his boxes and was gone.

CHAPTER EIGHTEEN

Question Time. Roger reflected ruefully that far more work goes into First Order Questions than meets the eye. It was his turn – or, rather, the department's – on Tuesdays every four weeks. The Prime Minister had to face the music much more frequently, twice a week on Tuesdays and Thursdays, but for fifteen minutes only, whereas the Boswood team's ordeal would last three quarters of an hour. The questions had been put down in their hundreds by MPs a fortnight earlier and shuffled in an electronic ballot. Forty now appeared on the order paper. Only the first twenty or so would be answered today. He was not looking forward to it.

Once Commons officials in the Table Office accepted a question as in order, it had to be answered as quickly as possible. In the previous session nearly 2,400 questions had been answered orally at an average cost of £202 each, with over 16,000 put down for written reply at around half the cost. In an election year the numbers could soar to over 50,000. Nevertheless it was all value for money, considering how much material could be dug out by curious or campaigning MPs. Hansard the following day would thus be dominated by the Department of the Environment in all its glory, as scrutinised, prettied up and censored by Minister of State Roger Dickson and his colleagues.

The whole team was on show. All morning Roger and Sir Nigel Boswood had been closeted with officials and other Ministers, worrying over tricky points. The pitfalls lay with possible supplementaries called by the Speaker. Provided MPs referred however vaguely to the topic, their queries would be allowed. Point-scoring was the game. Boswood's team could not expect an easy ride, even from their own side.

Madam Speaker was in the Chair. Prayers were over. An expectant rustle filled the air as Members and press turned to their order papers. The atmosphere was businesslike.

Nigel sat stolidly on the front bench, the first of two imposing red folders in his lap. Most of it he knew almost by heart. Thank heaven for

287

a good memory. A brand-new polka-dot tie graced the fleshy Boswood neck. He wriggled his bottom to get comfortable. No doubt about it, he was putting on a bit of weight. Came from being contented with life. A faint image of Peter's blue eyes, blond hair falling fetchingly over his forehead, came hazily into view, and was regretfully pushed away.

Roger was joking with the whip at his side but felt nervous. The experience of First Order Questions was still too new to have become routine. Opposite, a remote-controlled television camera swung its black eye at him. That there was no human being standing behind it, no face or skin, only that gaping black hole impassively examining him, possibly in close-up, was horribly unnerving.

Elaine's encouragement had been timely. He had been feeling more uncertain than he would admit, even to her. To ask openly for advice was not in his nature; accustomed to keeping fears and failings to himself, he would normally have denied there were any problems. Her shrewd understanding had led her quickly to a correct guess without his spelling it out. Nor did she think of herself as she responded unselfishly, only of how to help him. Their lovemaking did wonders for his ego too. He was vaguely aware of a paradox. Whatever her overt views on the role of women, which increasingly he acknowledged, Ms Stalker played certain of the traditional parts very well indeed. If that caused her any queasy moments, it was not his fault. And not really for him to resolve.

He glimpsed Elaine for a heart-stopping second as she entered from Members' Lobby. She bowed to the Speaker and took her place out of his direct sight. That meant she intended him not to be distracted by seeing her, instead of concentrating. He felt grateful. What Elaine had urged was all very well, but confidence-boosting in this job came in the end from performing effectively. Every public event was a test to be fluffed or conquered. There was no room for mediocrity or hesitancy or waffling or mistakes.

He took a deep breath to calm the thumping of his pulse, shut Elaine firmly out of his mind and signified readiness to the Speaker. For the ever-present camera, he lifted his head and smiled sweetly. As if angry or embarrassed at being so manipulated, the alien eye turned away with a faint whirr.

Seated directly behind Dickson, Andrew Muncastle was also jumpy. He would be on screen as a mute background to his masters every time they were on their feet. To be more precise, since his head would be cut off the picture much of the time, his midriff and groin would be on show. Quickly he fastened his jacket buttons, checked his fly and sat up straight.

Question Time is supposed to be an occasion for careful Commons scrutiny of Ministries, not an extension of pre-planned party politics.

However, two weeks before, on the day for putting down Environment questions, Andrew had scurried around the tea room with a conspiratorial air, offering a fistful of suitable enquiries, answers to which would draw conclusions favourable to his masters. Nothing in Westminster is quite as it seems.

Andrew's job this day included passing rapidly scribbled advice back and forth from the Civil Service bench behind the Speaker's chair. He turned and checked. Officials were entering, getting their bearings, clutching black briefcases. In charge was Martin Chadwick; next to him sat Marcus Carey, who was glancing wistfully at the languid man by his side. Perhaps he hoped the Chadwickian manner of dignified English coolness might be contagious.

Ferriman and other supporters were in their places. So were many not so friendly faces, including the Labour MP Keith Quin, whose name was on the first question, which Roger was due to tackle.

At last the preliminaries were over and Madam Speaker was on her feet. 'Order! Order!' she bawled. The House subsided. 'Questions to the Secretary of State for the Environment.' The first questioner, eager and composed, was in his place. 'Question number one – Mr Quin.'

'Number one, Madam Speaker.' Keith Quin, MP for Manchester Canalside, did not need to read it out. The question was printed for all to see, asking whether the Secretary of State planned any new measures to reduce the number of homeless people sleeping rough. He resumed his seat and waited.

Roger rose solemnly. 'Madam Speaker: the government are providing more than six million pounds in grants this year to voluntary organisations throughout England which give direct help to homeless people. The primary responsibility for assistance to people sleeping rough rests with local authorities.'

It was a long time since he had strolled home on foot, late. The ministerial car and Alec were always waiting by Members' entrance, engine purring. Special Branch would have had a fit had he tried. The memory was fading of doorways in Victoria Street crammed with muffled sleepers. But he knew they were still there.

Swiftly gathering the red folder in his arms, Dickson sat down. Quin was on his feet, speaking politely but with pointed force. 'Will the Minister consider increasing those grants to voluntary bodies? I refer him to the annual report of the Salford Centre, a charitable hostel in my constituency. In the past year they have helped over four hundred clients and most had slept rough at some point recently. I urge the government to do more.'

Dickson checked his notes before replying and rose to his feet. 'According to the census in April, only six people were sleeping rough in

Salford. I believe the assistance we are giving is . . . ah . . . effective' (the briefing said 'sufficient', but Dickson's compassionate side rebelled) 'but I shall look with interest at the figures cited by the Honourable Gentleman.'

It was a Tory's turn. Ferriman was up, hands clasped together across his middle like a country rector from a well-fed parish. 'Would I be right in thinking that the government has allocated not six but more than *eighty-six* million pounds to this problem in London alone, to cover the next three years? Somebody's getting a lot of money to deal with this problem. Where's it going? Should not Labour-controlled local councils' – he glared across at Quin as his voice rose – 'which fail to collect rents or do repairs, thus keeping *thousands* of properties empty through sheer *incompetence*, take much of the blame?'

Dickson was benign. 'My Honourable Friend is absolutely right,' he acknowledged graciously. Of course he was; Andrew had given Freddie the information just before Prayers. 'At the last count there were over seventy-four thousand vacant properties in the hands of local councils, far more – *far* more – than the numbers of homeless.'

A rumble of 'Hear, hears' came from the back benches. Dickson, already well known and liked for his handling of his former role as whip, was winning further approval.

The Speaker felt that one had been flogged enough. 'Mr Roy Hughes!' she called.

'Number two, Madam Speaker,' came the reply from the dark-haired Welshman, and the House moved on.

Twenty minutes into Question Time the event was assuming an air of routine. It was going reasonably well. Dickson fought back complacency. The next question could always mean trouble. As Boswood dealt with a tricky issue with graceful aplomb, Roger thanked the lucky stars which had brought him to Nigel's side. Plenty of Cabinet Ministers, jealous of their juniors or unable to stop competing or just plain arrogant, could be unpleasant to work with. Not Nigel; the old man was steady and kind and thorough. His retirement in due course would diminish the government, however peacefully he moved over. Even if it created a vacancy.

'Because it is there,' Elaine had said. He had never worked out exactly why he wanted promotion. Her sharp brain had forged the link with the motivation of all ambitious people. Someone like Boswood, by contrast, had a sense of public obligation. Dickson tried whether such nobility fitted himself, but found it rang false. His best approximation to selfless service was knowing that his own occupation of high office might keep out nincompoops, or extremists or fixers or fools.

If he didn't make the grade, he would always feel dissatisfied. If he did not try, to his utmost, he could never forgive himself – as, in secret, he had not pardoned the people he grew up with who accepted their diminished lot, whose dreams so rapidly died.

Because he had to: because, in the end, he was made that way. As swallows head south in autumn twilight, it was his nature and he had no choice.

One of the black-uniformed messengers hovered at the end of the row, waving a fistful of the pink paper slips which recorded telephone messages for those Members not at their desks. At last he attracted Andrew Muncastle's attention. 'Two for you, sir,' he whispered, pressing the slips into Andrew's hand. For a moment Andrew was distracted by laughter at a particularly effective response from Roger. Then, head bent, he examined the slips.

Both were from Miranda. One was timed at 1.15, when he had been walking over from the department, the other at 2.15, by which time he was heading into the Chamber. He cursed the fact that he had come up the back stairs and not through Members' Lobby where he might have picked them up at once. Both had the same words: 'Please ring – urgent.'

The next half-hour seemed interminable, with Andrew growing more anxious by the minute. There must be trouble. His liaison with Miranda was over four months old. He had not tired of her, nor she of him, as far as he could tell. Quite the contrary. Their lovemaking had introduced him to a new world of simply enjoying oneself and pleasuring another in complete openness and delight. He had never realised that was possible. Now it happened repeatedly, indeed grew better each time as if their attraction were favoured by God, a latter-day Adam and Eve. That was how it felt: primeval, exotic. Not wicked, not at all. He was supposed to eat the fruit, not reject it, as he had been rejected. It had a feeling of destiny, of the inevitable. He had not hesitated for a moment.

Moral values had not been a consideration. Andrew's church attendances were a matter of form, not belief. Tessa's passionate faith brought her neither joy nor inner peace and he felt no compunction to share it, instead condemning it as a sign of an inability to think for herself. The propriety of his affair was a different matter – what other people would think of it if he were found out. Any abandonment of Tessa would meet with strong disapproval from his local supporters. Not all of them had pristine lives, not by a long chalk. None the less they felt instinctively that their MP should do better.

Of course some constituencies would accept a divorced or remarried Member, but all hated a current scandal. To gain any sympathy for himself he would have to complain discreetly about Tessa, or imply that she was ill. That would be ungentlemanly. His grandfather would shudder at the thought. And there would be the effect on Barney. It wasn't on: so Andrew would have to shoulder the blame, implying that the fault lay with his own nature. A philanderer was unacceptable as an MP for all sorts of reasons. He would have been caught telling lies. If he could deceive his wife, what was to stop him deceiving anybody? He would not be what he seemed when he and Tessa, hand in hand and smiling shyly, had presented themselves to the selection committee. Above all, his behaviour would be seen to attack marriage itself, the most cherished but abused institution of British society.

With Miranda's worrying messages nestled in his hand, Muncastle found his mind was working extraordinarily clearly. He looked around at colleagues and the whips and considered what effect discovery might have. A flurry of interest in the newspapers, but not much – Miranda would see to that. There was the equivalent of honour among thieves in the newspaper world. Nor was he important enough for more than a little sniggering. It might not be terminal. Several Cabinet Ministers had made discreet transfers from one spouse to another, at some point in their careers. It was not impossible.

Sir Nigel was on his feet again; Andrew composed his features into an expression of earnest support, but his mind was exploring unfamiliar paths elsewhere. He settled to examining that last novel consideration much more carefully.

It was not impossible to change spouses. Was he seriously planning to abandon Tessa and switch to Miranda? Almost immediately the idea sounded silly. Miranda was probably not the marrying kind. Miranda opening a church fête, Miranda clutching a yelling baby, did not ring true at all. Nor was there any need: Miranda in bed was available without a marriage ceremony. Or even a divorce certificate. Maybe she preferred men who had a home to go to, leaving plenty of space for her own professional life. He and she never talked about such matters. He did not want to take any risk of disapproving of her lifestyle and so perhaps losing his own place in it.

There was another option. Not remarrying, but allowing his marriage to slide quietly into oblivion, a no-fault separation, a quiet quickie divorce, so there was no longer any pretence.

Advantages leapt to mind. A single man could have girlfriends. He could then be seen escorting Miranda as his lady, perfectly safely. The gossip columnists would ogle. The unmarried girls of the constituency and their mothers might get excited. The local press would be forever marrying him off to this or that neighbourhood garage heiress. He might even have some fun taking one or two out down in Hampshire, warning Miranda first of course, momentarily raising their hopes, keeping everyone guessing. The start of a new image: a bit of a change for that dull stick Muncastle. As long as it helped his career in politics, and did not hinder it.

The clock ticked towards the moment when heading for the phone would be acceptable. Most likely, he would do nothing, but carry on as now, squeezing every last drop of excitement from his stolen hours with Miranda. Hoping Tessa would recover. Once she had been beautiful, with a delicate smile which touched his heart. She seldom smiled these days. He could accept for a long while yet his responsibility to her, to ensure she was not hurt. And the child mattered: his son was important to him. Though if fresh choices were on offer he had begun to think them through.

'Do you need me for a moment, Roger?' Andrew whispered in Dickson's ear. A quick exchange established that their next departmental meeting was at five. He hurried out with a sigh of relief, and headed for the phone cubicles nearest to Central Lobby.

Her voice sounded strange, not her usual friendly gurgle. 'Sorry, Andrew. We've got problems here. Can I see you tonight?'

Rapidly he checked his diary. 'We vote at seven, then we're free. Where?'

A pause. She was talking to somebody else at the same time, not paying him full attention. He was astonished and disturbed.

'I have to eat, then come back to the office. Can you find Il Portico in Vauxhall Bridge Road? Station end. Small place, good Italian food, not too public. See you there.'

She did not wait for him to respond, but rang off. No endearments, no nothing. He felt cold and a little angry.

Il Portico was easy to find. A friendly place, a family business, it was well accustomed to trysting couples. Andrew arrived first and chose a small table in the darkened extension, all false frosted ceiling and candles in wax-laden bottles. They could not be observed from outside. Should anyone ask, he would say Miranda was doing an interview.

With some surprise he realised that this was the first time he had been out with her. Sliding once more into musing about their relationship, he decided that if she was calling an end to their affair, and if he had the chance to do this again with somebody else, then going out for a meal was definitely on the agenda. With bed and sex as well, afterwards. That's how most people did it. And if Miranda was about to say goodbye he would keep his eyes open for a replacement. There would never be anyone like her, of course. But never again would he do without a little love and affection. It kept him sane; it made him human. There was more to life than just his job.

A touch of cold air announced her arrival. Normally Miranda bounced into a room, dominating it instantly, kissing everybody,

293

showing off her body, attracting envious whispers. Not this time. Almost at once she sat down and slipped her coat over the back of the chair, her face sombre and set.

It was obvious that Miranda was both hungry and in a hurry. She munched garlic bread in silence and gulped a glass of wine as Andrew sipped his drink and watched her. Only when half a veal escalope *alla pizzaiola* and a pile of potatoes had disappeared did she wipe her mouth with her napkin and put down her fork.

'That's much better. The food is OK here. First meal all day.'

'You'll get indigestion, eating too fast.' He was caring but wary.

A flicker of annoyance crossed her features, then she shook her head slowly. 'I'm lucky to get half an hour out of that place at all today. We let another twenty staff go including production this morning. The recession is knocking our industry sideways.' In a gesture of great weariness she rested her cheek in her hand.

He pushed bits of white sole around his plate, and waited.

She seemed to relent. 'I needed to talk to you, Andrew.' Her voice was low and urgent. 'The *Globe* is facing a real crisis. It may fold – or, at least, the owner may decide that the losses are too great. I've been asked to consider my future very carefully.'

He was not sure what she meant. Cautiously he asked, 'What's the time-scale?'

She shook her head vaguely. 'We don't know, though obviously it would all be neat and tidy if it closed on January the first. We're cutting costs sharply. If we survive through this winter things may pick up. All bloody depressing, I can tell you.'

The waiter discreetly poured more wine. An old man with a warm heart, he was concerned; he did not like his customers to be unhappy. Had he known them better he would have begged the beautiful *signorina* to cheer up, maybe presented her with a single flower. But these two were strangers to him. She might be offended. He retired to the warmth of the bar, defeated.

'Are they telling you you're sacked?' He kept his voice neutral.

She opened her eyes wide and seemed about to protest, as if he had said something foolish, then stopped. She continued: 'No: but it means I may have to move. In fact I may have to go back to Australia.'

It hit him, hard, somewhere in the solar plexus. So the end had come, just like that. He swallowed, then was ashamed of his own sarcastic tone. 'You surprise me, Miranda. I thought you were well in at the *Globe*. With the owner, I mean.'

Her look hardened. 'I am, in a manner of speaking.' So it was true: some of her grafting had been done on her back. 'That doesn't help the balance sheet. For the moment my job here hasn't finished: the editor

294

and I will turn the thing around if it kills us. If we don't succeed, then it's the *Globe* itself which will die. But I needed to talk to you tonight, before you MPs all slip away for the Christmas recess. If the thing collapses, I will probably be snoozing a few hours afterwards on board a Qantas plane. I might not be able to explain why, or say goodbye.'

He sat back, mouth open. The naked suddenness of it floored him.

Then good breeding told. His manner became stiffer, more controlled and formal. He leaned forward.

'I am so very sorry to hear all this, Miranda. I had no idea the business was in such trouble. Am I to take it that this could be the end for us?'

Her head was bent, hair almost black, falling around her face. In the candlelight her expression was hidden. She nodded her head. Then she raised her eyes, and he saw the tears rolling silently down her cheeks.

'Oh, Miranda, don't . . .'

Her distress matched his, moving him to the very quick. All his new-found resolutions about passing on from her without a qualm, about seeking a replacement as soon as possible, vanished in a trice. He pulled a clean folded handkerchief from his breast pocket and proffered it. She pressed it to her mouth and cheeks, a look of abject misery on her face.

There was nobody nearby. The waiter, wise in the ways of lovers, stayed hidden. Andrew placed his hand over hers and squeezed it.

'I think I'd better get to the point, and quick,' she muttered. 'Then I must get back, or it really will be the sack, special relationship with the owner or no.'

She tossed her hair in defiance; a little of the old fire flashed.

'If I have to go back to Australia, Andrew, I want you to consider coming with me.'

Once more his mouth opened and no sound came out. He took a deep breath, but she cut in.

'No: listen. I've had a lot of men in my time, Andrew, but no one ever like you. You're so formal, and British, and considerate, and kind. You're manly, but without all those miserable macho elements that bedevilled all my other blokes. You make me feel special, so womanly – oh! God.' For a moment she could not continue. 'I earn my living as a journalist but I can't find more than a few banal words to tell you what you have come to mean to me. It's as if I didn't really exist before I met you. I wasn't a whole person. Now I am. Am I making sense?'

Gently he refolded the handkerchief as she wept and wiped first one cheek, then the other. 'I know exactly what you mean. It's as if our . . . what we do together . . . is a spring of water falling on stony ground, bringing life, and joy in living. Now a flowering tree grows, and its fruit are perfect, invigorating. All you have to do is . . . reach out and eat. Am I getting close?'

She smiled at him through her tears, a look of sweet accord, as she did sometimes after lovemaking. 'You were going to say, our *love*; and you stopped, Andrew.'

She waited, but he said nothing.

'It's time for me to say I love you, Andrew. So very much. I guess I didn't realise until suddenly this morning it looked as if I might never see you again. That's why I panicked and phoned. So now I'm here to tell you, and hope with total conceit and vanity that you may feel the same way. You don't have to say a word, or decide now. That would be crazy, with a wife and child. I do recognise the difficulties.'

'Those,' whispered Andrew wryly, 'are not the only "difficulties", as you put it.'

Miranda pulled a face. 'Oh, your political career. Does it mean that much to you? Seems to me you're paid peanuts to be trodden all over, working insane hours, too much responsibility and no real power. And as you climb higher up the greasy pole you just increase your visibility for the tabloids to throw shit at you. There's a better life than that, Andrew, if you want it.'

'Where? With your owner's company?' He was incredulous, but a politician's wariness led him to find out as much as possible.

She shrugged. 'Don't knock it. It's a hell of a big corporation with interests all over the world, not only in Australia. You could earn big money, and have something worthwhile to do.'

He sat back with a faint laugh. In a curious way, despite all her bad news, life was looking up. 'Plus yourself. You make it all sound tremendously tempting.'

Her pain had eased, but she was still troubled. 'I have to go. Thanks for supper, sweetheart. Like I say, it may never happen. But I wanted you to know. If it does, think about coming with me, or coming later, at a suitable point. You'd never regret it.'

She had not asked, do you love me? She had not wanted to know whether he would come. Perhaps she had sensed by his muted, guarded reaction that her assessment of the alternatives was not the same as his. Neither was the idea wholly preposterous. Maybe she realised he could indeed be tempted by such an exotic proposition, but needed time. The bait had been cast. He would only be caught, her English gentleman, if he wanted to be.

They parted there and then, Miranda pulling on her coat without ceremony. He rose hesitantly in his place. With a quick movement she took hold of his face in her hand and kissed him, thoroughly, full on the mouth. The waiter, hovering, smiled: the lovers had made up their tiff.

After she had gone the place seemed suddenly empty. The bottle of wine was still half full, the cheese board available. He sat down again slowly and motioned to the waiter. Time for some deep thinking, alone.

Two angry men faced each other across a paper-strewn desk in the inner office of the North-West Warwickshire Conservative Association. The door was shut tight and the men were speaking in low, fierce voices. Anyone listening through the thin partition would have deduced that there was a row going on, but the plasterboard-muffled syllables ran together in an indistinguishable mumble and gave nothing away. Only the tone, of controlled anger on one side and fury on the other, told a tale. Not that anyone else was listening. The moment for the confrontation had been chosen with some care, long after the two staff and volunteers had closed desks and drawers, left notes out for the milkman and gone home.

Agents were known to be fiery people. A choleric temper was tolerated. To keep the show on the road, to ensure all committees, councillors and candidates did their duty required an unusual combination of talents. The party's professional agents, particularly those of long service and with a background in Her Majesty's armed forces, were allowed short fuses. Cherubic types would not have lasted five minutes.

The agent was permitted to shout at the MP. Indeed, the agent was often the only person permitted to bawl out a recalcitrant or erring Member. It was the chairman's job, really, but many chairmen and women were overawed by a famous or long-serving Member. A chairman's rebuke was more likely to start with a self-deprecating grunt and a 'Look here, old boy. The committee have been wanting me to have a word with you . . .' – which the Member had long seen coming. An angry agent was another kettle of fish entirely.

Tom Sparrow could smell trouble a mile off. Twenty-two years in the Royal Fusiliers all over the world, rising through the ranks to warrant officer, had stamped him with character, resolve and courage. He needed to face his Member of Parliament in the worst mood he had ever seen. Roger Dickson, normally so urbane, charming and considerate, was staring at him across the desk, his face contorted with fury, pounding his fist.

'What did you *say* to the buggers, Tom?'

'Now then, Roger. I gave nothing away. What do you expect? But when the *Globe* journalist comes on and asks for Mrs Stalker, and then says, all innocent-like, that this is the number she left if anyone was to contact her, I was a bit flummoxed. I thought it was a mistake. So I asked why Mrs Stalker should be leaving your number instead of her own. And that's when he told me.'

Dickson was breathing hard. He enunciated the words with precise care. 'Exactly what, please?'

'That you and Elaine Stalker were very friendly – gossip had it, too friendly – and that she was going round saying she had a special relationship with you.'

'*Bollocks!*' Dickson spat out the word.

Tom Sparrow was equally angry. He had trusted Roger. 'What exactly is bollocks, Roger? That you two may be having an affair, or that she might tell anyone?'

Dickson bit his lip, dragged the chair away from the desk and sat down heavily. He looked around, as if seeing the untidy room for the first time. Above the blocked-up fireplace a poster from the last election bid all and sundry to vote for him. A photo of himself, Caroline and the children, the original of the one on his successful election address, hung on the wall.

'She would not tell anyone. She would not say a word.'

The atmosphere shifted. Long accustomed to worming the truth out of men in his years as an NCO, Tom Sparrow perched slowly on the edge of the desk. 'Maybe you were seen.'

'But where? We're never together in public. I don't take her out to dinner, if that's what you mean. She has as much to lose as I have – more, in fact. Her seat is much less safe than this one. Her career is much less secure.'

'Do you need me to remind you that there is no such thing as a safe seat?' Sparrow was grim.

'I know. Or a secure job. Even if the Prime Minister detests the press hounding his Ministers.'

Sparrow had too much tact to mention any names. Roger's unsettled demeanour was telling him a great deal, but not yet enough.

'You're very attached to her, Roger, aren't you?'

The other man shifted uneasily and laughed, a sad, hollow sound. 'What makes you think that, Tom? Is it so terribly obvious?'

'Because I know you. I know how important your career is to you. You wouldn't be risking it just for a fling. She must be something special – she is, of course, I've seen her on TV, and been to her house. I've always felt the party ought to make much better use of her. You have taste, I'll say that.'

Dickson grunted, brooding. He ran his finger over the faded gold beading of the leather-topped desk, backwards and forwards. Sparrow had never seen him like this before, warring with himself. Sparrow's own feelings towards his MP were affectionate, paternalistic and anxious. For so long had he channelled his energies and regard into the party, into this younger man and his success, that his work was in effect his family. It was threatening to disintegrate in front of his eyes. His indignation and anger rose again.

'And what are you going to do, Roger? It has to stop, you know. Love or no love.'

'No.' Dickson passed a hand over his eyes as if trying to shut out a picture. He turned his back on the photograph on the wall.

Sparrow caught the movement and allowed his own glance to linger pointedly on Mrs Dickson's cheery face, Roger's children dressed and primed for the official photographer. Roger uncertain, irresolute, divided was a new phenomenon and deeply disturbing. Time to be brutal. He gestured at a newspaper on his desk.

'I wouldn't trust that bastard not to phone Caroline and ask her.'

Silence. The rules Roger Dickson set himself – not to think of his wife and his mistress in the same instant, not to get them mixed up – were in danger of breaking down under Sparrow's skilled onslaught.

'What are you going to do, Roger? You know perfectly well what could happen if this gets out, however discreet Mrs Stalker may be. You have your duty to the government, first of all. And we can't afford a by-election, here or anywhere else.'

It was hard to tell whether Roger's continued silence was the recalcitrance of a naughty child or agonies of guilt at wrongdoing, or simply that the man, usually so fluent, could not see the way ahead and did not know what to say. Sparrow considered for a moment, but the confused expression on Roger's face led him slowly to this last conclusion. He leaned over and placed a sympathetic hand on Dickson's shoulder.

'You don't need me to give you any advice, Roger, but if I were in your shoes I'd look for an opportunity to bring it to an end, soon as you can.'

A look of pain crossed Dickson's eyes. 'I need her, Tom. I *need* her. I never thought that would happen, but it has. I haven't told anyone else. I'm not sure even she knows. But I wait for the moments we can be together...' His voice tailed off. The words sounded silly, inadequate, foolish. Like most Englishmen he was no more used to articulating his emotions than he was to examining them with any honesty.

Sparrow spoke softly. 'You're not going to tell me that you can't live without her, are you? Because in that case you can give up politics, at least round here. The party workers are fond of Caroline and wouldn't forgive you. If you want Mrs Stalker that's two divorces and two ruined careers, not one. Is that what you're contemplating?'

Dickson sank lower into the chair. A clock in the corridor outside struck seven. Sparrow stood up with a sigh. 'Look, I have to go now. There's trouble with the women's committee and I promised I'd attend their meeting tonight. If I leave you here, will you lock up, and switch on the answerphone as you go?'

The agent reassumed his official demeanour, collected papers and files, slipped on coat and scarf, fussed over a handkerchief, car keys, gloves. The nights were chilly: it would soon be Christmas. Dickson was still sitting slumped in the chair, staring at the middle distance, fingers of one hand wavering, tremulous, slowly backwards and forwards on the desk edge.

Sparrow hesitated. A sudden fear surfaced, urgently. 'Goodnight, Roger. And think on. You won't do anything silly, will you?'

Dickson spoke almost to himself. 'What, sillier than I've done already? No, Tom, don't worry. I'll be all right. And thank you for the advice.'

Twenty minutes later, Sparrow used his car phone to call into the office. His own voice answered; the answerphone was reassuringly switched on. For the rest of the evening he tried to concentrate, and wondered sadly if there was anything he could do to help.

The meeting between Warmingshire county councillors and local MPs trotted quickly through matters of mutual importance, then drifted off into how many new car parking spaces were required for the council's ever-increasing, ever-better-paid staff. Elaine, bored, made her apologies and slid away.

An hour to spare. Too much time to waste, yet not enough to get home before attending South Warmingshire Ladies' Circle choir concert. She could murder a cup of tea. The map of the constituency, spread out on her lap, gave her an idea.

On an impulse she telephoned the Eventide Home. Mrs Swanson was not on duty, but her deputy was glad to report that Mrs Holmes was in good health and would be delighted to see her. They would go and tell her right away. A few moments for Dorothy to put herself in order would be appreciated. That means she's putting on her wig, thought Elaine. The old lady must be allowed her dignity.

On several occasions Elaine had taken up Dorothy Holmes's invitation to friendship and found her a lively, intelligent observer who, though frail, refused to give in. Whatever Elaine's own problems and disappointments, the old lady's vitality and continued mental energy were always a tonic. Talking about times past brought history to life, for the old lady remembered Queen Victoria clearly, had heard both Lloyd George and Churchill speak and had first attended a debate in the Commons during the First World War. She had been inspired to enter nursing by the death of Florence Nightingale in 1910, but had faced implacable opposition from her middle-class family. The war had given many well-bred women precious opportunities so long denied. She entertained her visitor with horror tales of primitive nursing at the front and later in field hospitals in Egypt where she fell in love with a dashing young officer, wounded in the leg.

'He turned out to be a big mistake, my Oliver,' Dorothy reminisced, gazing into the far distance. The man had been dead forty years, before Elaine was born.

The two women were drinking tea laced with a little whisky and tucking into a box of House of Commons chocolates left over from her last visit.

Dorothy's theatrical voice told the tale. 'He was a drunk, you see, a serious alcoholic. I didn't know that at the time; men always drank heavily then, unless they were TT or chapel. He had a lot of pain from that wound, that was his excuse, but really it was because he could never settle to a humdrum civilian life. I had to cover up for him. After the babies were born I got my old nanny in. I went back to work to pay the bills, nursing privately, just odd jobs, mostly sitting at night with the dying. Better than waiting for Oliver to come home, hitting out at all and sundry, including me.'

She looked curiously at Elaine. 'You don't talk about your husband much. Aren't you happy with him?'

'I don't know.'

It was the first time she had admitted to anyone her uneasy sense of a problem growing beyond her control. Normally all her remarks about her husband were pleasant and appreciative. Slowly, Elaine began to feel for new words. Talking in negative terms about her marriage felt strange and unpleasant.

'He's a good man – nothing like your Oliver! – and we've been married a long time: sixteen years. Our daughter was born a year after we married and we both dote on her. But he just doesn't share my life at all. I don't think he wants to. I've got used to that, but it's such a demanding existence I lead, and I need to talk it through with someone who knows me well. Not every night, only occasionally. I'd much rather it were my husband, but he's . . . well, not there, literally and in every other sense.'

The old woman looked at her shrewdly. 'He probably finds your new-found importance hard to take. Men, especially married men, have big egos, you know. They much prefer to be king in their own castles, not troubadours to a queen. How about somebody else? In my day it was quite accepted for a married woman in high places, once she had done her duty producing an heir, to find her own friend, as long as both were discreet.'

Elaine was silent. Dorothy leaned across, tapped her on the knee and forced her fine vowels into a conspiratorial whisper.

'You have got somebody else, haven't you? Is he nice? Handsome? Rich? No, no, that would not entice a clever woman like you. Things have changed since my day: you earn your own money. So he must be somebody interesting. Someone in the political world. Am I right?'

Despite herself Elaine was laughing. 'Dorothy! Don't be so nosy.'

'Oh, go on. I'm only an old woman. Your face lit up when I mentioned a friend. Is he one of the other MPs?' She caught Elaine's hesitation. Putting her gnarled hand on Elaine's arm, she said softly, 'I think the world of you, Elaine Stalker. I'm not about to tell tales out of school. If you have a lover, so much the better. You'll be an old hag like me one day. Enjoy your youth and health while you have them.'

Elaine swallowed hard, opened her mouth to answer and burst into tears. All the tension of the last few weeks came flooding out, inarticulate and confused. So planned, so ambitious a life had taken an unexpected turn in which instinct and emotion loomed large and dangerous. For so long she had lived and thought like a man in a man's world, and been supremely successful, as if camouflage gave an added advantage. Like the religious convert she was more zealous than those born to it; she could manipulate, cajole and intimidate as well as any man, and with the same goal in mind, namely to get her own way. Now she was trying to cope with an unfamiliar set of feelings arising from the most female side of her nature. Her inexperience showed, like flesh through a threadbare garment, and she was scared, and worn out from trying to understand.

Dorothy sat back, distressed, pulling a lacy handkerchief from her sleeve and waving it helplessly at her visitor. The perfume of old lavender filled the air.

'Oh, there. I am sorry. I didn't mean to upset you, my dear, not for the world. Oh, dear.' And she began crying noisily herself.

'Nonsense.'

The scene of two weeping women was so incongruous that Elaine gulped, half choked, and eventually laughed cheerlessly. Pulling herself together she scrabbled in her bag for a tissue.

'It's just that I'm in such a muddle, Dorothy. I don't want to lose my husband but I'm beginning to lose touch with him. I want to be close to him again, but I'm forgetting how. With Roger I have exactly the opposite problem. It all started as a bit of fun but I'm getting far too fond of him. There's not a chance of us ever getting together – married, I mean; and it wouldn't work, anyway. I couldn't be the kind of wife he needs and he has one already who suits him fine. But what am I to do if I fall in love with him? That wasn't in the game plan at all.'

'It sounds like you're in love with him already,' Dorothy observed.

Elaine sighed. 'You may well be right. I'm extremely reluctant to examine my feelings too closely, for fear of what I might find. If truth be told, Dorothy, I started the relationship in part for what I could get out of it. I thought it might assist my career – he's in a position to help. We were to be equals – comrades in arms. And it is like that most of the time. But it's hard to sleep with a man, over and over again, and not get – at the very least – extremely fond of him.'

'Some women can; but you're a good woman, Elaine, a loving person. Does he love you?'

A tear dropped slowly down Elaine's cheek. Surely that could not be the problem – that she, always so self-sufficient, was in love and wanted the man to fall in love in turn? But what for? What would it serve, if Roger were mooning about over her instead? That would have been inconvenient, and she would have brought the affair to a swift and probably tactless end.

'I have no idea. He doesn't say. He keeps coming to see me, but that's not the same thing.'

'Does he make life better or worse?'

'That's easy. Better, infinitely so. Without him I think Westminster would be a terrifying, empty place. It's so competitive, so macho, so aggressive. The politics are marvellous and that side I adore. I love having a ringside seat. But without Roger I should feel lost and unhappy. With him, to be honest, life is great. And he's wonderful in bed. I should feel guilty, but I don't. Do you condemn me?'

'Condemn you? Silly girl! Of course not. I envy you!' The old lady shifted painfully in her chair and smoothed her skirt down over tired legs. 'Damn this arthritis. Do you know I'm still shrinking – I am an inch shorter than I was this time last year.'

'I think that's enough confession for one day.' Elaine reached ruefully for her handbag and took out powder compact and lipstick to repair her blotched face.

'Ah! Do you feel absolved?' Dorothy had been brought up a Catholic. The theatrical voice was back and she spoke like a mad old priest.

Elaine ran her little finger over the lipstick, then turned to her friend. Dorothy was looking frailer than usual. 'Yes, I do. It's such a help even to talk to you. I suspect Roger, Mike and I will toddle along as we are for years, unless something happens to change things. I don't need to ask you not to say a word, do I?'

'I should be most offended if you thought I would breathe a dicky-bird.' Dorothy pretended to be cross. 'Just love them both, if you can. And your daughter. I shall take your secret to the grave, which probably won't be long now.'

Elaine knelt down by the old lady's chair. 'You're good for many years yet, and you know it. But don't go without saying good bye, will you?'

Dorothy reached out her skinny arms and placed her hands on each side of Elaine's face, in a curious imitation of Roger's own manner when bidding her farewell. It made Elaine feel like an innocent child, as if all the pain and frustrations were somebody else's. Elaine kissed her on the cheek and gave a gentle, careful hug.

Dorothy chuckled, and waved her away. 'Go in peace. Give your love freely: you will always receive love in return – maybe not from the same person, and perhaps when you least expect it. Don't forget; and come and see me again.'

'It isn't enough. I can earn that in an hour in Amsterdam.'

'For God's sake don't say that!'

Two half-dressed men glared at each other, like two stags in a test of strength, panting hard. One was slight, young and defiant, almost triumphant, crumpled shirt undone over boxer shorts. The other, noticeably overweight, in a velvet dressing gown tied loosely with a gold cord, was red-faced and angry, hand raised as if to strike. With a helpless gesture he let it fall.

Peter lay back on the basement bed, shapely legs crossed at the ankle, wiggling his toes cheekily. One hundred pounds in notes lay untouched on the pillow beside him. It had seemed wiser to ask Nigel to come into his pad rather than knocking on the door of the big master bedroom upstairs as a supplicant. Here everything was smaller in scale, poorer in quality, less sumptuous. Not that Nigel Boswood went in for lavish furnishings, but upstairs the polished tables and chests of drawers topped with blue vases on which dragons chased old men were antiques and kept spotless; the carpets old, expensive and discreetly faded. Down here was all wool-and-nylon fitted carpet and a few rugs, the furniture not grand at all. Habitat, at a guess. A servant's room. He was a servant. No problem about that; but the labourer is worthy of his hire.

'It's not enough, I tell you. A hundred quid here and there won't keep me in decent clothes. Can't you manage a little more?'

Nigel looked suspicious. In a sudden movement he grabbed the boy's arm and pushed up the shirtsleeve. 'Have you been acquiring any expensive habits, Peter?'

'No, of course not. I'm not stupid.'

Peter pulled his arm away crossly and rolled down the sleeve. Pity the old fool, so out of date. It wasn't necessary to inject it these days. Crack could be smoked, leaving no mark. Not as messy as cocaine. No danger from a dirty needle. Then there were uppers, which an American client had introduced him to. Amyl nitrate in tiny capsules. Slip one under the tongue, let it dissolve. Stank like a jockstrap, but had a powerful effect. Fabulous for group sex. Made two- and three-hour erections possible if you were careful, though it left you feeling groggy and crazy for days after a big humping session. And Peter was careful. Counteracting the debilitating effects required a good diet, lots of vitamins, fruit juice and the like, with a daily swim and occasional workout. Nothing too energetic; hefty musculature was not in his line. Nor had he dared offer anything to Nigel. The man was a real stuffed shirt these days. Getting to be a drag.

The boy waited, sighed, stretched. 'Well?' he demanded in his turn, but his tone was coquettish, not hostile.

'It's not as easy as it was, Peter.' Nigel seated himself gently on the other side of the bed, reached out a hesitant hand, and stroked the boy's exposed belly. The hair was golden and soft. The summer tan had faded but the skin still had a natural glow. 'I had to pay over a lot to Lloyd's and the payments will continue for some time. I was obliged to sell a pile of shares to pay the last lot. That means I lose the dividends as well.'

'But you're rich!'

'Not quite as rich as I was.' Nigel's voice, to a friend, might have revealed anxiety. He was in no danger of becoming a poor man overnight, but he needed his lover to understand that two or three hundred pounds every week on top of everything else was making a big hole in his finances.

If Boswood's intention was to elicit sympathy his ploy failed. Peter simply did not believe him: the old grouch was being mean. Alternatively, if it were true and the milch cow was drying up, it would soon be time to make a quick exit. Maybe that was a good idea anyway.

Nigel was crying. Oh, Lord. Peter heaved himself up on an elbow. He leaned across and stroked the old man's face. 'Don't. It won't make things any better. You knew that sooner or later I'd have to go on my way. I've been with you far longer than with anyone else, ever.' It was not true, but only he knew that.

'At least stay till after Christmas. You're coming with me to Davos, aren't you? That's all booked and paid for.'

The old man's eyes pleaded. Year by year the House of Commons challenged the Swiss Parliament to a friendly skiing match in the first week after New Year. Nigel had been attending intermittently for years, enjoying himself hugely, being pitched against ever older and creakier opponents. Younger members of the team were always welcome. In that liberated atmosphere where ski pants replaced business suits for a few days, no questions were asked. All Scout's honour not to say a word. Several others would be accompanied by secretaries or research assistants. There was no harm in it, being let off the leash for a while, then resuming normal service as soon as possible. Not that he intended to tell anyone exactly what his relationship with Peter might be; discretion was still the order of the day. But going without him now, after all the weeks of dreaming about it, would be a miserable business.

He looked helplessly at the boy. 'Please?'

Peter's creed included being nice to all his lovers. You never knew when you might need them again. He squeezed Nigel's hand and smiled up sweetly. 'All right. I won't let you down, Nigel.'

Time to make up the quarrel, to reassert the dominance of this relationship. Peter gestured down at himself, with a mischievous giggle. Under the cotton pants he was stirring. Easy to do, with a little concentration, and flattering to clients, especially when they were upset. Concentrated their minds wonderfully. He moved Nigel's hand to touch his crotch. A gasp, a muffled sob, broke from the old man's lips.

The tiff ended as it had begun, making love. If that was what one called it.

The card with the *Globe* phone number was still in his jacket pocket. This needed some thought.

'Yep?' Betts's voice was rasping, irritated. He had no idea where this sore throat had come from but it was making life difficult. And the weather was terrible. Getting soaked through in the line of duty wasn't his idea of fun.

'Who? Oh, yeah, I know. Yeah, I remember.' A pause as Peter carefully explained his business.

Betts listened hard, lit a cigarette, blew smoke straight into the air, coughed, banged his chest.

'In that case we had better meet, Mr ... er, Peter,' he suggested. 'Same place as before? Certainly.'

At the other end, cradling Nigel's telephone into the crook of his neck as he wrote down the details, Peter was feeling excited. 'About six. It gets crowded later,' he suggested. What he meant was that a potential client came in about eight. A tall, slim chap, well-dressed, velvet collar on his overcoat, usually alone, though once with a group of people. Civil Service type, at a guess. He had eyed Peter several times recently. With a little encouragement he might open up and start chatting tonight. Not for Nigel's eyes, and certainly not for a newspaper's.

'Good evening.'

Betts uttered the formal greeting as he half rose, quickly wiping the beer froth from his moustache with a grubby handkerchief. His mac on a nearby peg steamed in the warmth of the pub's open fire, sending an unpleasant odour of vinegar and ancient tobacco into the air. A tequila sunrise was already waiting on the other side of the circular table.

The boy was certainly fine-looking, with the kind of physique, manner and style likely to attract both women and men. Maybe he picked up wealthy women as well from time to time. There would be better money in faggots, though. Men had access to more spare cash; and, since it was a stigma where it wasn't illegal, they would pay readily. For a good lay, a lot, presumably, and keep coming back. Exposing themselves to further payments, not for services rendered but for silence.

Maybe there was a little black book of names and addresses which might be worth a bob or two. Even a biography. Madam Cyn's had been a very lucrative operation, leading even to a bitter-sweet film of her childhood, *Wish You Were Here*, which won its teenage star an Oscar. You could go a long way on the memoirs of goons like this. But Cyn's book was enlivened most of all by those strange sad photos of fat middle-aged women and half-naked tubby bald men, specs on nose, with besotted expressions. They cuddled the homely prostitutes for Cyn's camera as they might their wives, if only their wives would let them. The wickednesses of that generation were trivial and absurd. People laughed, then wondered, then pitied. A distinguished Cabinet Minister with his pretty boyfriend was a different matter.

'You mentioned a figure when I met you a few weeks ago.'

The skirmishing had started. Betts put his head on one side. He had checked his notes but wasn't letting on. 'Did I now?'

'You did. Twenty-five thousand, you said. That doesn't sound enough to me. I shall be risking prosecution. My name and face will be well known. I should expect more than that.'

Betts spread his hands self-deprecatingly. 'It would not be for me to decide. And it all depends how good the information is. We should need dates, times. And . . . methods.' He paused significantly.

'How he does it and how good he is?' Peter laughed, a cynical edge to his voice.

Hastily Betts gestured. 'Keep it quiet. You never know who's listening. We should want to know everything. It's your best protection against him claiming that it's all lies, see? We're a big company and if there's anything we can't use because of . . . er . . . newspaper policy, there may be another in the group. In Australia, perhaps, like the Prince Charles and Camilla tapes. A country which is, shall we say, a bit braver, prepared to stick its neck out. They all pay.'

Peter sipped his drink. 'Would we be stopped publishing anything?'

'What do you mean? Well, there are laws on pornography. Prosecution under that heading is pretty unlikely, however, given the naked bodies you can see flailing around these days on the telly. Tits and bums everywhere, nobody has standards any more.'

A bout of coughing seized him. Peter wrinkled his nose in disgust. Perhaps it would be wise to gargle before turning in tonight, just in case.

Betts wheezed a few times, then continued. 'Do you mean censorship? Privacy laws, that sort of thing? Nah, they can't get us. If one party goes to the press and invites us to infringe his privacy, then we're in the clear, see, even if the other party would rather all concerned kept their big mouths shut. You'd have to sign your willingness to co-operate in front of our lawyers as witnesses, of course, before money could change hands. That's normal practice.'

'Who's manipulating who?' Peter was speaking softly, almost to himself. 'The story of my life, that is.'

Betts misunderstood the remark. 'Yeah, that's exactly what we're after, the story of your life. Particularly since you met our famous friend. We would need to know all about him. You would come into our office, or to a secret location – a hotel, maybe. We'd take several days over it, taping all the time. All on the record, unless you wanted to stop. But it's best on the record: protects you.' The scene was moving nicely. If Peter, so wary, so clever, so arrogant, could be persuaded to see the paper as friend and protector, the job was half done.

'And the money?'

'One-third into your bank account the moment the contract is signed. One-third after the interviews, when we're satisfied, you know, that you've fulfilled your part of the contract. And one-third on publication.'

'Any currency I like? Abroad?'

Betts had no idea but was not about to prevaricate. 'Sure.'

'And I could clear off immediately after the interviews – I don't have to hang around till publication day?'

Betts scented danger. 'No . . . oh, but we'd need to know where you are. This would be an exclusive contract, Peter. That means you contract not to talk to anybody else. Otherwise no money.'

Peter was thinking hard. He changed tack. 'You mentioned photographs. What kind? You couldn't publish pictures of us naked. That would be going too far.'

or some such. Pictures like that would be worth a fortune. And you, get in there and give him a kiss. Just as the flash goes off. But don't bury yourself, see? Face the camera. We need always to know it's you.'

A profitable hour passed as Betts explained the potential arrangements. He shivered at the boy's calculating coolness. Most people in this situation, about to shop a lover to the press, were scared and uncertain, or alternatively vengeful and full of glee. All were nervous, but not this one. Few went into it in such detail, like a business transaction. The boy made not a note but listened and nodded as he put away two more expensive drinks.

The door opened and several new customers entered, shaking rain from coats, laughing and joking with the landlord. Outside was dark and miserable. The journalist sensed suddenly that the boy's attention had wandered. Betts stubbed out his cigarette and rose to his feet.

'I'd better be getting along. Now you said you'll be on holiday in

Betts's eyebrows rose in astonishment. 'You got any pictures with him naked?'

'No. Not yet. I doubt if I could get any either, so don't raise your hopes. Nigel's not a wanker like that. But we're on holiday soon and it would be quite natural to get some pictures of us together. Then he couldn't claim he didn't know me from Adam.'

'Certainly. Those sort of snaps are essential. No snaps, no story. Get him to hug you. For your personal album, your eyes only, that sort of thing. See if you can get him to dress up a bit at a party. The fairy queen, January. If you get any decent pics, ring me, will you? The *Globe* would be proud to print your story.'

'I'll bet,' said Peter quietly, with a crooked half-smile. He did not get up, but shook hands. The discussion was over.

Outside Betts turned up the collar of his coat. The boy left him distinctly on edge. This wouldn't be an easy catch, not like the average jilted lover. The problem would not be rival rags, but persuading him to do it at all. His trade depended on discretion.

Next time, if there was a next time, the two of them would delve nice and deep into motives. Being taken for granted by one of the country's richest men would be a good starter. He would let the lad think he was being really smart, outwitting everyone: his vanity would be his downfall. That was it. Betts looked forward to further progress.

CHAPTER NINETEEN

'My dear Nigel. Come on up.'

The Prime Minister pushed his spectacles back up his nose with a preoccupied gesture. He was in shirtsleeves. Whatever improvements may have been wrought on Number 10 over the years, the heating system was never quite right. As a result the little flat under the sloping eaves, used in the evenings for private work and more intimate conversations, was too hot. Fiddling with the controls made him exasperated: it reminded him too much of the impossibility of running the economy at a steady temperature. To visitors like Nigel Boswood he would murmur apologetically, then shrug and give up.

At least up here human scale predominated. Downstairs in the grandiose state rooms one always felt awkwardly on show. He was forever embarrassed at catching sight of himself in huge framed mirrors, and scared to turn around quickly for fear of clumsily knocking over some priceless piece of porcelain. He didn't care much for the Turners on the walls, either – murky and grim, with moody cattle on dark hills, discards from the painter's off days. The family liked living here now, especially not having to wash up; but it was hard to tick off a recalcitrant colleague while perched on a satin sofa, trying to avoid dirtying a fabulous old carpet, the price of which would buy any number of houses up north. At home he would wear slippers. That wasn't done here.

'What's your poison?' The Prime Minister motioned Nigel to the sofa. It was too soft and too low. Nigel found himself buried in upholstery. Puffing slightly, his legs splayed in an ungainly composition before him, he felt at a disadvantage. With an effort he heaved himself upright and asked for a gin and tonic.

The PM went to the door, opened it, called down the drinks order and returned to the chair.

'Don't you have an intercom?' Nigel asked, astonished.

The PM chuckled. 'That might work both ways. I prefer to have some private conversations.'

A tubby woman in a white apron brought up the tray which the PM took himself and put down on the desk. The conversation drifted in a desultory manner for a few minutes. The PM cradled a bitter lemon in his big hands, and examined his Secretary of State for the Environment carefully and without comment. The subject of the visit, requested by Nigel, had been whispered on the phone from Number 12 by the Chief Whip.

Sir Nigel Boswood was looking old. Even in their forties there was a noticeable difference between men who exercised modest self-discipline, such as the Prime Minister, and those who preferred self-indulgence, like Nigel. By the late fifties the gap was widening. And Nigel was approaching sixty.

'Roll on Christmas, what?' Nigel intended his voice to sound bright but the dark room invited intimacy, not brittle formality. He tried again. 'It's been a tough twelve months. Let's hope next year will be an improvement.'

'I'll drink to that.' The Prime Minister spoke with feeling and raised his glass. 'Mind you, we started the year at war in Bosnia and sending in the Tornadoes in Iraq. I confess I'm more worried about other areas of the Middle East. While we've all been distracted by Saddam, the power of fundamentalism is growing. The Iranians have been arming themselves heavily, and one wonders, for what? Makes me uneasy.'

Nigel looked into his glass, wishing it were a crystal ball. 'The electorate might prefer us to turn our attention closer to home, Prime Minister. Foreign policy bores them, mostly. But the money in their pockets: that matters. Do you know the unemployment rate in my constituency is eleven per cent and still rising? And it's party supporters as well who are out of work. The shops are full but nobody's spending any money. How long will this go on, do you think?'

'We have seen some growth this year, Nigel.' The tone was almost petulant. 'Don't they realise the recession is over?'

The Prime Minister rose and stood looking out of the small window. Down Whitehall street lights twinkled as office workers heading for home turned up collars against the chill wind. He envied them.

He continued, 'Much of what's happened since the election has been quite outside our control. Do you know what Macmillan said, when asked what as Prime Minister he feared most? "Events, dear boy, events." I know exactly what he meant.'

'I heard him. I was at the meeting,' Nigel reminded his leader with acerbity. To hell with it. 'You seem to be telling me that we can't anticipate or avoid or persuade or change things, but only react? After the event, never before? I don't accept that. Perhaps, Prime Minister, if you gave a stronger lead we might have greater influence over "events".'

The Prime Minister was frosty. 'Is this what you came to say to me, Nigel?'

Boswood was equally annoyed. 'In a minute. I'll get this off my chest first if you don't mind. Your trouble, Prime Minister, is you're too damned *nice*. You let everyone in Cabinet have their say in the hope that as reasonable men and women they'll agree. But they don't, on principle, because they're all fighting each other for the top job: your job. Ambitious people always do. You're kidding yourself. I'd have thought you'd have realised. *The only opinion that counts in the Cabinet is yours*. If you make your mind up and stick to it, the power of your office is such that you'll get much of what you want.' Nigel sighed. 'I apologise, Prime Minister. I think very highly of you, and I want the verdict of history on your administration to be as positive as possible, that's all.'

The older man stretched his limbs, rubbing one calf. His right leg was going to sleep. Time to get to the point.

'I am here to tell you I wish to resign, but at your calling. At once if you want, but if you prefer me to stay till a convenient dropping-off point I'll do that with pleasure. That would suit the department as we're in the middle of a big Bill. So my job is at your disposal.'

The Prime Minister refrained from pointing out that Nigel's job was always at his disposal, whether the incumbent liked it or not. 'Do you wish to go because you disagree with government policy – is that it?' If the man was going to be a troublemaker on the back benches, it would be better to persuade him to stay.

Nigel shook his head vigorously. 'No, no. I don't disagree with government policy. I would just like to know, sometimes, what it is. Enough of that. I've done thirty-one years in Parliament, Prime Minister. I've been a front-bencher since I became a whip in 1970 – that's a very long stretch indeed. In fact I believe I'm the longest-serving Minister.' That was true.

The Prime Minister was watching him gravely. Nigel's glass was empty but a refill had not been offered. The warmth of the little room made his jacket sit heavy on his shoulders. Nigel took a deep breath, conscious of great sadness, of a dying within himself. When he left this room it would be all over bar the shouting, and probably not much of that.

'This coming year I shall be sixty, and celebrating ten years in Cabinet. Far more than I ever thought possible. It has been an enormous privilege; I wouldn't have chosen it any other way. But it takes a toll of the human frame, too, though fortunately I haven't got a wife and family to worry about. I honestly don't know how you chaps manage. I want to get out while the going is good, while I still have my health and sanity. Give you enough time to appoint a successor.'

313

'You're a good man, one of my best Ministers. I shall be very sorry to lose you.' The Prime Minister's sincerity was genuine, but his mind was already moving ahead. Boswood's replacement would almost certainly be yet another person younger than himself. Baying at his heels, they were. When the time came Margaret hadn't wanted to go, not at all. He wondered uncomfortably if his own demise would be as messy. 'Will you stay on in Parliament?'

'No, I don't think so. I plan to stand down next time. Oh, Milton and Hambridge would have me, I'm sure. But it's not fair, an old man hogging a safe seat. It ought to go to some young bright spark who'll be a Cabinet Minister in his turn. I imagine you would send me to the Lords?'

The Prime Minister nodded his assent, smiling slightly.

'That will do me very well. Thank you. I should enjoy being active there, saying my piece. I have many interests, as you know. Might write something. Travel. Theatre, gardening, bit of shooting.'

Downstairs a clock was striking the hour. Nigel Boswood was acutely aware that he was now rabbiting on. Some imperceptible shift in the Prime Minister's demeanour suggested a whiff of impatience. On an invisible signal, both men rose. The Prime Minister offered his hand, shook Boswood's warmly, murmured a few words, showed him down the short flight of stairs and ushered him deftly into a tiny personal lift. In a few moments Sir Nigel Boswood was walking out into the rain, blinking slightly, with a leaden heart.

The Prime Minister was on the phone. 'As you suspected . . . Yes . . . At a time of our choosing, which is helpful . . . Oh, I would expect at the next reshuffle in the summer.'

He listened for a minute, doodling on a pad next to the phone. His wife would be back soon. Out tonight, black tie at the opera. Boxes afterwards, till two o'clock in the morning. He used to do them in bed till his wife complained.

'No, not a word. Whatever the state of his personal life he keeps it to himself.' A pause. 'I hope not – we can do without any more scandals. I know you're paid to think the worst, Chief, but on this occasion I think you're wrong. Just turn your mind to his replacement, will you? It would be easiest if we can simply slide Dickson up . . . Yes, I know he hasn't been a Minister long, but neither was I when Margaret took a chance on me. Keep an eye on him, and report back . . . What? . . . Oh, *Traviata*. Weeping and wailing and gnashing of teeth. Just like politics . . . Yes, I will. Bye.'

Elaine hung her check jacket neatly over the back of a chair, smiled at her daughter, seated herself expectantly at the kitchen table and opened the large brown envelope. A pile of Christmas cards still waited reproachfully to be addressed and posted; plastic holly and tinsel lay in a heap on the sideboard. Karen's finger rubbed absent-mindedly at a sticky mark on the table left by a bunch of fresh mistletoe. Both hoped the family would have a happier time than last year.

'Make me a coffee, will you, darling, while I read this?' Karen seemed pale and listless. Conscious that her own manner might have been a little offhand, Elaine added cheerily, 'What will I find? Is your school report good or bad this term?'

The girl shrugged and moved to the kettle. Since half-term it had been difficult to concentrate. Now holidays had arrived a blitz on homework was planned to catch up. Everyone claimed GCSEs were easy, and so they were – provided you had nothing else on your mind. She felt tired, dejected, distracted. Next year would be much harder, doing A levels. Assuming she got through this lot.

The kettle boiled. The girl spooned Nescafé into two mugs and added sweeteners.

Elaine looked up, nodded thanks. 'You never used to drink coffee, Karen.'

'I do now.' The coffee revived her low spirits. Not sleeping didn't help. 'You never used to take artificial sweeteners, Mum.'

'Touché.' Elaine patted her hips with a laugh. 'Have to now. Trying to compete with my beautiful young daughter.' Raising her eyes to Karen's face she looked for a girlish response but the pleasantry met with a stony stare.

Her mother subsided, reading steadily, flicking over the slips of paper on which different class teachers and tutors' remarks were penned. A frown slowly creased between her eyes. After several minutes she turned to her daughter.

'This report is really not good, Karen. Several teachers say you're not paying attention and are careless. One believes you are clearly working below your capacity. You usually get compliments. Should I be worried? Are you?'

'It'll be all right, Mum. I've had a hard term.'

'I know we don't spend as much time together as I would like. Is that what's bothering you? Or is it something else? Whatever it is, Karen, you can tell me. I am your mother.'

That was the whole trouble. The girl shook her head. She had thought long and hard about telling somebody at school. Her best friend, maybe, the one she always told everything, sworn to secrecy. Girls at school, in the dormitory at night, discussed sex constantly, shivering with anguish at the less pleasant side of sexual encounters. Mostly made

315

up, she now realised. Innocents, the lot of them, and the talkative ones knew least of all.

A gap had now opened up between herself and her schoolgirl pals. You couldn't really keep a secret with that lot. Even a friend sworn to silence might blurt out sooner or later that Karen Stalker knew more about sex than she was letting on.

And how on earth could she explain to anybody, best friend or no, about her mother's affair? It was impossible to believe that it wouldn't get out. Anybody in school would tell, at the drop of a hat. There was a mysterious umbilical cord which bound that school to the tabloid newspapers. Hadn't they found out somehow when she had been caught smoking behind the bike sheds? How much more interested they would be in a hot story involving her mother, vastly more titillating than a quick smoke. Their house would be dogged by cameramen for weeks, camping out on the lawn and trampling the flowerbeds, rifling the dustbins. Quizzing her pals, embroidering and exaggerating and lying. Not that the whole horrible story needed additional material.

Thus confiding in someone had been considered and dismissed. Yet she had to talk to somebody or she would burst. Should she tell her mother? If so, there was no time like the present. Karen felt her pulse quicken and took a deep breath.

Mum was looking cross. And impatient: glancing at the clock. More interested in the school results than in Karen herself. More concerned to get away to her next important appointment than to stay here and talk. A sob rose into Karen's throat, but with a defiant toss of her head she forced it back.

Let it be a test for her mother. Couldn't she see the turmoil in her only child? Wasn't misery writ large all over her face, or was she, Karen, already that good at hiding her feelings? Maybe it ran in the family. Politicians had to do it all the time. This business with Roger meant Mum must be playing a part every day, pretending to feel one thing when another powerful emotion was surging through her. Pretending to love Dad and miss him, when in reality she was hankering after another man entirely. Quite a performance.

It was awful, the notion that Mum had stopped loving Dad. She must have done, to start this game with Roger Dickson. Maybe Mum didn't love her either, not any more. Maybe it was her fault that her mother had somehow lost emotional contact with the family, got bored, looked for excitement elsewhere. Her parents had always loved Jake best, spent so much precious time with him, exulted at his tiniest gain, been broken when at last he slipped away. Her mother had cried inconsolably for days, a heart-breaking grief, a sound which Karen would never forget. She was only four then. Though the small girl had tried so hard to make it up to them, she had never been able to fill that gap. Karen lowered her head. She could not talk to her mother. Not yet.

'It's been a tough term, Mum. I wasn't too well at the end of it. They expect such a lot.'

Her mother was puzzled at the child's unhappy tone. What on earth was eating her? Maybe Roger would have some ideas. She would be seeing him this week, back at the flat for the last few days of term. A feeling of inadequacy nagged Elaine. Bringing up a teenager was tricky: at times like these, when the girl was so confusing, so impenetrable, being a mother was by far the hardest thing she had ever attempted. Other mothers had time to talk to each other and share tips and commiseration, but not she. Not knowing many other parents in the same boat sufficiently intimately to share her worries, Elaine did not realise how frequently others felt exactly the same bewilderment.

She pressed her daughter's hand. Once more the demands of her job were in conflict with her family. She and Karen had not sat side by side in the same room for ages. 'You having boy trouble?' she enquired gently. 'Is anyone at school getting at you?'

The hollowness of Karen's laugh startled her. 'Boy trouble? You must be joking. Not in that place.'

'I'm serious, Karen. Don't laugh at me. Are you being bullied or teased at all because of me?'

How like her mother to think of herself first. Karen felt bitter. She had not picked up her mother's more subtle concern, that her public life might be hurting her child.

Karen rose. She was so tall now. 'I am not being bullied, Mum. I'm going to work hard this holiday. That's why I can't come to your office this time. I will get my head down, I promise. Will you please stop worrying?'

'Naturally I worry. Are you sure you're happy at that school?'

'Well . . .' Karen hesitated.

'Go on.'

'You and Dad won't agree.'

'Try us.' Elaine was feeling impatient. Playing new games with her daughter left her at a distinct disadvantage. Only one person in the room knew the rules and it wasn't her.

Karen's voice took on a wheedling tone. 'Could I leave school after GCSEs and do my A levels at college?'

Her mother's reaction was hostile, as anticipated. 'And where would you live? You can't stay here on your own. I know you'll be sixteen by then, but that's much too young. That's the whole idea of boarding school, Karen, sweetheart. Somebody looks after you while we're away. It stops us worrying.'

'It'd be cheaper: college is free,' Karen offered hopefully.

'That's not the point and you know it, Karen.' Her mother allowed a touch of severity to enter her voice. 'If you want to convince me that school is not the right place for you next year, you'll have to come clean and tell me why. I'm not going to call you a liar, Karen. If you tell me nothing is going on, I must believe you. So why do you want to leave school? Poor reports are not enough, you know. You can't blackmail us into getting your own way like that. So I will ask you one more time – is this bad report due to something that has happened at school?'

The girl swallowed hard. The word 'blackmail' cut her to the quick. Karen knew all about blackmail. More than her mother did, by a long chalk. Wanting to leave school was simply an attempt to enter into the adult world, not be regarded any longer as a child. To hide her pain she swiftly turned away. Her tone hardened. 'No, Mum. It's nothing to do with school.'

Elaine reached out and held her arm. 'You sure?'

Karen almost shouted. 'I told you! Stop nagging, will you! It's nothing to do with school. I want to leave, that's all.'

'Tell me. I'm on your side.'

'Oh, yeah. And I'm on yours, Mum. More than you realise.'

The two women stared each other down in mutual incomprehension. The moment for intimacy had passed, yet Karen realised with shame that her mother had tried hard, had given her every opportunity. The girl relented, stepped back, bent her head, kissed her mother on the cheek. Then she stood up.

'I guess I'm just having to do some fast growing up. Not easy.'

'It never was. Just remember I've been through it all, sweetheart. Your mother's not a complete innocent.'

'I know that.' Under her breath, so that her mother could not hear.

Speedily Karen was out of the door. Her backward glance was full of sadness, but she gave her mother a half-wave.

The kitchen went quiet. Elaine sighed and wished Roger would phone, to cheer her up. She reached for her address book and the pile of Christmas cards.

For several days more, Karen Stalker brooded until her head ached. Her hurt was settling into depression; she was listless, tired, yet could not sleep. She had not yet developed an adult's capacity for reticence. Boarding school is not a place for secrets. The shared intimacy of sleeping in the same room, of bathtimes and showers, of girls learning about development and menstruation and sex all at the same time, precluded privacy. The group had a rhythm and synergy of its own. If one had flu, they all caught it. Only on home matters was silence acceptable. Many of the girls came from broken homes – nearly half, in Karen's class. Packed off to boarding school like so much baggage. Shuffled around at holiday time, meeting parents' new partners, weighing in the balance and being weighed, found wanting, in an atmosphere rigid with resentment. Most covered up, lying a bit, showing off expensive presents acquired instead of affection, and bitterly played off one parent against another.

Until now Karen had despised them, pretending like that. On her more reflective days she felt pity for these innocent victims of divorce. If the affair continued, if her mother was found out, there could be a divorce in her own family.

The person who would be most hurt would be her father. Maybe he would go and punch this Dickson. It would serve the man right. Karen's imagination, brutally enlarged by events of recent weeks, had no trouble following the scenario further. Supposing her father were arrested and ended in court charged with assault? The newspapers would have a field day. Her father would lose his job. Roger Dickson and her mother might both lie through their teeth about the whole sorry business, but nobody would ever quite believe them again. Least of all their own children.

It dawned on her slowly that she could do something, without hurting anybody's feelings, provided she were clever about how she went about it. The world she knew was becoming disjointed, joyless, its old reference points irrelevant. She had to talk with somebody. But not with her mother. One other person knew all about this: at least, not the part involving herself. The part involving Roger.

Roger Dickson did.

It was his fault. It must be. He must have seduced Mum, dazzled her with his clever talk and flattery, or entrapped her somehow. He had a hold over Mum which only he could break. Why else would a happily married woman take up with another man? On television he was charming, attractive and accomplished. Vaguely there stirred an appreciation of what her mother might see in him. But her father was like that too. The only difference, from what she could tell, was that one was totally devoted to politics and the other wasn't. A mark in her father's favour, in her view, as it used to be in her mother's. Dad was a real person.

That half-term week spent working in Mum's office, for all its terrible outcome, had been useful. Karen knew how to go to a library, look Roger up in *Who's Who* and find his constituency office in the phone book. Luckily, North-West Warwickshire wasn't far away. Should she ring first? She hesitated, thought hard for a moment. On the phone there could be an interrogation from a stranger, demanding to know why she wanted to see him. It might be easier simply to turn up. Late on a quiet afternoon before Christmas, Roger Dickson himself might just be there.

Tom Sparrow totalled the column again, compared it to the one on another page, and grimaced. It had not been a good year financially, despite the slow recovery in the economy. Subscriptions were modestly up but company donations were disastrous. There had been no compelling reasons to squeeze more money out of reluctant local donors – there would be no general election, thank goodness, only the Euro-elections. The overdraft from those would probably hang around for years.

The knock on his office door was a welcome distraction. A tall young woman – no, a girl; she could not have been more than seventeen – clad in funereal black from head to toe as was their wont these days, stood before him, hand on the door-knob, her manner hesitant and anxious.

'Er – I'm sorry. I was looking for Mr Dickson, the MP. I would like a word with him, if possible. Please.'

Sparrow frowned and pulled a newspaper over the accounts. 'How did you get in? Wasn't the front door locked? There's an intercom.'

Karen looked puzzled. 'I just opened it. Did I do wrong?'

'No, no.' Sparrow recovered himself and smiled. The clerical help was forever forgetting to lock the door on leaving. Of course there had never been an incident round here, not even a brick through the window at the height of the poll tax débâcle. But it was distressing that office staff were so casual about safety. He would tick them off in the morning.

'I'm afraid Mr Dickson is not here right now. My name is Tom Sparrow. I'm his agent. Could I help you perhaps?'

'No, no. But I would like to see him. Could I make an appointment?'

Tom reached for the diary, trying to sum the young woman up. Not old enough to vote, at a guess. Student? A grant problem? Parent trouble, maybe. People asked MPs about the oddest things. One chap wanted to discuss his son's divorce settlement. You never turned anyone away. Not a punter. A kindly word might be worth a vital vote or two in an election. Anyway, serving the public was all part of the job.

'Mr Dickson is not holding any advice bureaux now till after Christmas. Nobody comes – they're all too busy shopping. However, he is around, so if you wanted to I could slot in a time. Tomorrow morning, maybe? Perhaps I could have your name?'

'I'm . . .' Karen stopped. Her original plan was to give a false name. Yet she wanted to be certain that Dickson would see her, not fob her off. She looked Sparrow straight in the eye. 'I'm Karen Stalker.'

Sparrow began to write it down, then looked up quickly. 'Could you spell that please?'

She did so, slowly, as he wrote. Sparrow put his pen down, clasped his hands together, examined his fingernails and then looked at her quizzically.

'Would that be Stalker as in Mrs Stalker the MP?'

The atmosphere suddenly went very cold. Karen turned white. *This man knew*. She had made a terrible mistake.

There was no going back now. Insolently she stared back at Mr Sparrow, her face grim.

'Yes.'

'Are you by any chance a relation?'

'I am her daughter. And I need to see Mr Dickson, please, as soon as possible.'

'Does your mother know you are here, Miss Stalker?'

The girl laughed bitterly. 'No fear.'

Sparrow motioned her to a chair. Karen subsided into it unwillingly, knowing she was trapped. Calmly, precisely, the agent went into the outer office and put the latch up on the main door, switched the phone on to automatic answering, then returned to the inner office and closed the door. He sat down behind his desk, crossed one leg over the other and leaned back, watching the girl.

How like her mother she was. Dark-haired, but the same wide-awake eyes. Extraordinarily pretty. Not quite Elaine's sharp intelligence, at a guess. Or maybe she was only a bit young, yet. Like some of the young lads under his command in Kenya – not much more than children, but uppity if patronised. Must choose his words carefully. He spoke very slowly.

'If you have a problem, Miss Stalker, you really ought to talk to your mother. She is also your MP, which Mr Dickson isn't.'

The girl was silent, hostile. In normal circumstances Sparrow would have made excuses and turned her away. Not this time.

'Or is the problem something to do with your mother? Is that it?' His words hung in the air. He faced Karen squarely.

She tried to return his look but her gaze wobbled. Slowly tears welled up in her eyes. Defiance turned into dejection. Her young body sagged, a picture of abject misery.

Sparrow was not an unkind man. Devoted to politics and with firm views on loyalty, his main task was to get Roger re-elected. If not Roger, another MP from the party which paid his wages. Loose cannon like Miss Stalker had to be tied down as swiftly as possible. A candidate holed below the waterline would sink without trace, dragging all on board with him. How much did she know? How ready was she to tell?

'I think, Miss Stalker, you had better tell me all about it. Then if Roger can help at all I'll make sure he finds time to see you. How does that sound?'

Karen was well aware that she could have insisted on saying nothing, seeing Dickson in private. Yet it was clear, the moment she mentioned it, that this man knew the name was special. An agent would not breathe a word, certainly not one who had been around a long time, who would live and die for the party, as before in his life he had pledged to die for Queen and country. Her mother had been heard to envy this constituency its greatly respected central guardian. He was a man you could lean on for advice. You could rely on a trained professional like Mr Sparrow.

Karen took a deep breath and leaned forward. It all came in an anguished rush. 'I believe my mother and Mr Dickson are having an affair. They are both married and it's all wrong. I wanted to ask Mr Dickson to stop.'

There. It was out. She sniffed with relief, blew her nose and waited. Sparrow's eyes widened and his mouth twitched. Brave lass, well done. Nevertheless, there was a hint of menace in his voice now.

'Who told you this, Miss Stalker, may I ask? Was it your mother?'

'No, of course not.' Scornfully. 'I haven't talked to her about it. She doesn't realise I know.'

'Then we ought to explore how you did find out. The first problem, as I am sure you will realise, is to keep it a secret. So how do *you* know all about the alleged affair?'

Karen miserably scrunched the damp tissue between her hands. 'Oh, several things. He keeps phoning her. I don't hear the conversations, of course, but she looks so happy when he's been on. And he writes her little notes.'

'Does he, by Jove!' Tom Sparrow muttered under his breath. 'Do you have any of these notes, Miss Stalker?'

'I did have. I gave it to . . .' Karen's voice trailed off and she stopped dead.

'Who, pray?'

A stubborn expression like a mask came down over the girl's face. She said nothing.

'You had a letter from Mr Dickson to your mother, a letter which might have been interpreted as . . . ah, incriminating, shall we say? Who did you give it to? I think you had better tell me.'

Silence. That smelled bad.

'You haven't given it to somebody else, have you? Outside the family?'

A barely perceptible nod.

'Outside the party?'

Slowly, woebegone, another nod.

'It wasn't a journalist or anyone who could make trouble, was it, Karen?'

The air froze.

Karen closed her eyes. Her heart had stopped beating, she was suspended in space, disintegrating, whirling away from everything kind and familiar, a soundless scream coming from her lips, unheard, at the edge of the world.

'Karen? Miss Stalker?'

The room was still there, but different, as if all the old atoms had been smashed by an overwhelming force and rearranged. The nature of substance had changed. She was an alien.

Aliens fight, are aggressive, go on the attack.

She sat up straight. Her new voice sounded hard, uncompromising.

'Yeah, but he won't do anything with it. He can't, see?'

'Who was it? Why not?'

'It was a bloke from the *Globe*.' Karen heard the sharp intake of breath. 'Oh, don't worry. He can't hurt your precious Mr Dickson, or my mother. He can't do anything with it because he would have to explain how he got it off me. And that is not a very nice story, as I am under age.'

'Oh, Christ.' Sparrow put his head in his hands. Poor kid.

'I don't want any of that to get out. My mother doesn't know. I just want to see Mr Dickson and persuade him to leave her alone.'

'You're not the only one,' Sparrow remarked drily.

The two looked at each other, and briefly understood. But as their loyalties and objectives were different their methods must diverge. Sparrow considered. If he made this experience as unpleasant as possible the girl would not be tempted to tell her tale again in a hurry.

'Talking to a journalist, whatever the circumstances, which we won't go into, was not smart you know that?'

'Of course I do. I can't think of anything else.'

'And you must not – must *not* – tell anybody else, do you hear? If we're to sort it all out quietly, the fewer people who know the better. A journalist! A bloody journalist. Jesus, Karen, you of all people should have realised. What did he say to you – that he knew all about it anyway, and you might as well tell him?'

She nodded dumbly.

'And did he give you any evidence of that? Before you opened your big mouth, I mean?'

'He said they had been seen together at the Party Conference in Blackpool.'

'Oh, really? Mr Dickson was with his wife at Blackpool. Your journalist was probably making that up.'

Her mouth dropped open and the belligerence faded. An expression of fear and hopelessness slowly suffused the girl's features.

Sparrow leaned forward. 'You realise he probably knew very little?

323

Maybe nothing at all. Perhaps he was fishing – they do that, you know. Find some gullible soul and wheedle it all out of them. Then they've got their story – after, and not before. You probably told him everything he needed – you, little Miss Karen, all by yourself.'

He was striking home. Her head was up, face full of suffering. 'He won't tell. He can't. He would end up in jail. I'd give evidence. If he were to tell, or try any blackmail, I'd put him behind bars for ten years, I swear I would. And he knows it.' She rose suddenly. 'Look, Mr Sparrow, I would do anything on this earth to help my mother. Will Mr Dickson be here tomorrow? I need to talk to him.'

Sparrow spread his hands dismissively. 'I really think that would be most unwise, Karen. We have already agreed that we must keep all this as quiet as possible. But I will have a word with him. Another word. And I am afraid that will have to do.'

She was frightened. This man, who ought to be helping, had turned into a brick wall. 'But I must talk to him and persuade him. He's leading her on. He's more senior – she has to do what he wants. Don't you understand?'

'Karen, we do not know that. The adult world is still a closed book to you, that is plain. Now if you have any sense left in that pretty head of yours, young lady, you'll stop trying to interfere in things you know nothing whatever about. What you are trying to do is very stupid.'

Sparrow rose formally and moved from behind the desk. 'If you take my advice you will go home right now, and you will not say a word to anyone. Not even that you have been here – do you understand? We have not had this conversation, you and I. You will speak to nobody about this affair. And, in particular, no more journalists. You have done a lot of damage already. I suggest you now leave, and keep your mouth shut from here on. Leave it to other people to sort out.'

He showed her to the street door, pushed her outside and locked it, pulling down the blind. For a few moments she stood disorientated in the street, tears running slowly down her cheeks. The sheer cruelty of Sparrow's reaction cut her to the quick. She had not expected sympathy nor sought it, but her own pain was bad enough without having the salt of guilt rubbed into the wounds. Coming to this office was a disaster.

The agony came not merely from her own dejection and the way Sparrow had so curtly dismissed her. If this man knew, then the story was out, or nearly. The looming crash of her family, the tragedy of her parents' divorce, was now truly on the agenda. And it was her fault. Stupid, he called her. Stupid! What an understatement. What a silly, crass, idiotic little madam she had been.

It was dark, cold and windy. Shoppers pushed past unheeding, laden with carrier bags. Somehow she found herself at the right bus stop and waited for the bus home.

Roger seemed preoccupied. Unusually for him, he made love only once, satisfying an urgent need, but then lay back and pulled her close to him, nestling her head on his shoulder.

'You're miles away,' Elaine remarked.

His laugh was soft, confidential. 'Sorry. I do have things on my mind. Things are moving at the office. Nigel has been to see the boss and told him he wants to retire. I don't know when, but it means changes at the next reshuffle. Probably in the autumn.'

'Ooohh!' Her mouth a rounded, excited O, she sat up. 'Is it known? Will you be involved?'

'Heavens! Patience, my dear Patience! I've no idea, though Nigel told me he believes the PM wants to promote some younger blood, not shuffle the same old faces around. Bit of a tip-off, that, and not to be ignored. But no, it's not official yet.'

Conscious of the compliment he paid her in revealing these confidences, she fell back again and stroked his chest. Absent-mindedly he took hold of her hand, stilling its movement, and kissed her fingers.

'It could be that his announcement comes in the nick of time. For him, I mean, not for me. That remains to be seen.' Her silence encouraged him. 'Nigel says he is going because he is getting old. It's certainly true that he has been in Parliament over thirty years, quite a stint. But there are other rumours. Maybe he's getting demob-happy, but he is being careless.'

'Go on. I'm listening.'

'He has a boyfriend. A kid of some kind, not very discreet. Installed in his basement.'

'You're joking!' she breathed, eyes wide. Then: 'But maybe he doesn't know about his funny tenant.'

'Like the Lamonts? No. He knows. The young man in question has turned up at the Commons and made a fuss about not seeing him. Pretty boy. Hard eyes, very knowing. Came to the department once; I had to deal with him. He looked slightly high to me. Trouble writ large, if Nigel isn't more careful.'

'I wouldn't have thought it of him. He's such a respectable character, and so decent. You can't see Nigel like that, can you?'

'Why not? You women ought to be able to tell – the wrong vibes, perhaps – though Nigel is always so gracious with women that I can well see you might miss it. It's been known for a long time that he was that way inclined. The whips' job is to protect our people so we hear all sorts of things which go no further.'

'He's mad. He'll get caught. The press are sniffing for a scandal. Why on earth does he run a risk like that?'

Roger sighed. 'Who knows? Maybe under that jovial exterior he is lonely. Or in love: it happens, even to old men. Why do you and I do this, Elaine? You understand the pressures of office, of living endlessly in the public eye, better than most people. Being correct and proper all the time. Being nice to people you can't stand. Even experienced politicians need some haven in their lives where they don't have to pretend. Somewhere, or someone, to be totally honest with as you and I are. The paradox is that we have to lie through our teeth to preserve this secret garden. Maybe Nigel got fed up, pretending.'

'He's gone a daft way about it,' she mused. 'Better to choose one of your own kind. Not a stranger.'

'This chap's manner suggests he's no stranger to Nigel now. And if he carries on ... before too long he'll be public property. I hope I'm not the one to have to warn Nigel, though I guess that will be the Chief's job.'

The house was empty and she was alone. School was finished. Her father was God knows where working, for loads of people were flying away for the holiday. Her mother was still in London. Probably with Roger. It dawned on Karen how easy it must have been, with Dad away so much. Unwillingly her mind turned to her father's continued absences. His pilot's job required it; she had never heard her mother complain. The other way round, however, was a different matter. Dad seemed to resent the fact that Mum was not around when he came home. How odd.

Karen sat exhausted at the kitchen table, too tired even to take off her coat or put on the lights. It was a long time since she had eaten and her mouth was dry and furry. Her thoughts were an unhappy jumble. She had long since abandoned the effort to create order from the chaos in her brain. None of it was making any sense anyway. Why was it all right for Dad to be away, but not for her mother? Was that the way the world ran? It used to be so, in Victorian times. Men worked, women stayed home. That was ancient history. Not any more, surely?

The house was dark. That was comforting. Dark, quiet and warm: the heating had switched on automatically. Victorian women had had to rise with the dawn, blacklead grates, dump ashes and light fires so that husbands could shave and wash. Servants, those wives. Not much more than slaves. How amazed they would have been at timers and programmers and thermostats and gas boilers humming away and radiators all over the house, instant and effortless. How minuscule the changes in men's attitudes meanwhile. But if men were not all New Men it must be, in part, because women preferred them that way. Maybe women had trouble adjusting too. It was a muddle.

Dark, quiet, warm, empty. A house without much personality, a shell, smart and fairly new, resembling lots of others. It had not been part of the Stalker lives long enough to have accumulated history or memories. She should put the lights on. There was no need. She should take her coat off and hang it up. Later. She was alone in the house. It would be nicer with a cat or dog, some other living being, but a pet had never been a practical proposition.

Listlessly Karen wandered around the kitchen, picking things up, aimlessly opening cupboards, disorientated and troubled. There was a fresh bottle of milk in the fridge, which must have been left by the neighbour, Barbara. Karen dolefully considered writing herself a reminder to check how much money the milkman was owed, but the effort was too great. Barbara was nice but too talkative and brain-dead. It was a depressing duty sometimes to listen to her gushing on about how wonderful the Stalker family were. The lights were on in the house across the drive, a modern construction almost identical to their own. Barbara could be glimpsed behind her net curtains moving around in her kitchen. Karen decided against seeking her company. Silly chat seemed inappropriate after all she had been through. The misery in her heart demanded its price. She needed to be alone.

Warm, empty, quiet. She was thirsty. Greedily she drank milk straight from the bottle, and left it half full on the table. An overwhelming weariness seized her. A voice in her head warned that the most sensible thing to do was simply watch TV or go upstairs to bed, yet such mundane activity seemed an anticlimax. Tomorrow she would feel better: perhaps. Or perhaps not, with yet another night to get through wide awake and worrying.

A terrible sense of isolation and despair made her limbs leaden and her head spin. The house was all hers. She could do anything she liked, yet nobody would notice, nobody would care. Nobody ever did care: all the adults she knew were so preoccupied with their own lives that there was no room for her. She was useless, dispensable, discarded.

The little sensible voice telling her she was beat and should simply go to bed was growing fainter. Karen restlessly moved around the ground floor of the house, still in her coat. The milk had moistened her mouth but had not satisfied her thirst. She entered the living room and viewed the room's plain furnishings with a feeling of mounting resentment. Why couldn't her mother be like other women? Other people had lovely stylish homes, but not the Stalkers. Other mothers spent ages fiddling with decorative schemes and catalogues; in this house, Elaine's hurried choices were serviceable and simple, nothing dramatic, as if she did not care about her home any more than she bothered about her lonely young daughter.

Karen's eyes filled with tears of self-pity but she shook them away. It was about time she behaved as an adult – that was the advice being flung at her from all sides. An adult would head straight for the drinks cabinet. A whole cupboard full of whisky and wine and liqueurs. She walked over and picked up the bottles, examining them with mingled curiosity and defiance.

There was the Tia Maria, and ouzo, from Greek holidays. Or Drambuie – that was her favourite, when her parents allowed. She poured a little into a glass and took a swallow. It slid down remarkably easily, and a warm surge began to spread from her stomach. She began to relax; it was at least something to do. A feeling of well-being started to take hold, replacing the desolation she had brought home with her. A casual thought surfaced in her mind which suddenly felt like a great idea. Maybe she should get drunk: that's what adults did when they felt miserable.

She would have to find out sooner or later how much she could take without passing out. After all, she argued with herself grimly, she was discovering how much emotion she could handle: maybe it was time to establish her physical capacity as well. The still small voice packed up entirely and was replaced with a demonic whisper somewhere behind her right ear. It would be perfectly safe to get thoroughly drunk in the house on her own – far better than doing it inadvertently in public and making a fool of herself. The matter was decided forthwith.

Her legs began to feel a bit wobbly and for safety's sake she carried a couple of half-full bottles of liqueur and a glass to the sofa, flopping down with a giggle, her coat flapping around her. A pile of newspapers and magazines on the arm slipped haphazardly to the floor. It didn't matter. There was no serious problem: no Betts here tonight. No horrible man pushing his fingers, and worse, inside her. Her brain locked on disapprovingly. 'Worse'? That was not being very adult. It had a name: *penis*. Shocked, she said it out loud, and toasted it with another drink, then said it louder, and cackled at her own boldness. Other horrible words flitted through her brain like plankton under a microscope, wriggling and changing shape and swimming away out of reach. Each time she caught one she said it, then shouted it: *Court case! Rape! Jury!* The picture slithered into her mind of what would happen if she carried out her threat to report him. She would have to stand up in court, in the witness box, wearing her best clothes, and tell everybody exactly what he did. The horrible details. That moustache all wet and slavering, reeking of tobacco. His hard bony hands, and the triumphant look on his face. Not for herself alone could she stand up in court, not in a million years: not even to stop him ever trying it again on anyone else. She would rather die.

It wouldn't stop him, or other men either. Whatever happened men would try it on, and use their superior strength, pretending they had not heard the woman's protests. Some men even preferred it that way. It excited them more if the woman struggled. The whole business was sickening.

Karen could hear herself whimpering, but the demonic voice was ready with further hissed advice. She was not yet drunk enough: total obliteration was possible, but she had to get a lot more down first. Right to the point where she passed out. She poured another drink.

How good she had tried to be. Other kids faced with the same combination of parental neglect and adult indifference would have done something really stupid. That was the word both the school doctor and the agent had used: *stupid*. It was true, yet she bitterly resented Sparrow's lumping her in with all the nation's yobbos. Wildly she looked around. What would constitute doing something really stupid here? Breaking all the windows, maybe, or setting fire to the house. That would make them sit up and take notice. It would cause a lot of trouble. Experimentally she tossed a few cushions around, then stopped. That was all she was capable of, these days, causing trouble. Not only for herself. What would happen if that *Globe* freak let it out? Her mother and Roger would be all over the newspapers. And Sparrow knew. How did he know? Maybe Roger had told him. It would all be known about soon. It was all her fault; she should have been a better daughter. With a maudlin sob she told an almost empty bottle that she had done her best: without help, which seemed never to be forthcoming, she did not know how to do it any differently. It might be better to put a permanent end to all this misery. At least Jake, wherever he was, was no longer twisted and weeping in pain.

An overwhelming urge to explain before it was too late pushed her unsteadily towards her mother's desk. She would not be home tonight and that was fortunate: looking in the mirror Karen realised with a satisfied grimace that she was already in quite a state. Angrily she tossed off another glass of Drambuie, sat down and rooted around for paper and a biro, and began to write. Putting something on paper became a monumental necessity. Her hands would not obey without a struggle and the resulting scrawl was a mess. So what: no teacher would be writing a report on its legibility. Its content would be clear enough. Then they would all be sorry.

As she finished and stood up, the chair fell over. She gazed around the room and tried to focus. It was a bit of a tip now. She shrugged heavily. She was dreadfully weary. After all this miserable introspection sleep was still the best remedy and was calling her insistently. The little voice agreed and urged her stumbling up the stairs, the coat now trailing, half on and half off, one sleeve caught. At the top she stopped. In the bathroom cupboard there might be something to help. The evening had been a voyage of exploration: the drink had gone down nicely and left her feeling floaty and a bit silly, marginally less dismal, certainly less guilt-ridden. If she never woke up she no longer cared. That would teach them. A couple of her mother's Mogadons would round everything off perfectly. What a pity it was so difficult to see them in the gloom, or to remember how many she had taken already.

A sleepy glow began to suffuse her body as the burden of a fearful day slipped slowly from her shoulders. Leaving the conscious world would be a pleasure, and so easy.

At the entrance to her mother's bedroom Karen stumbled heavily and nearly fell. It seemed wisest to take the hint and not try to go any further to her own room. The swaying bed was wonderfully big, bigger than her own, with a vast inviting eiderdown. She half fell on to it, dragged off her coat and pulled the coverlet roughly over herself.

Her face was close to the edge of the bed and her bleary glance fell on the telephone. Maybe she had gone too far and she was going to die: perhaps she ought to ring Samaritans or something. At least they would listen. Yet what did it matter if she did die? That might solve a lot of problems, for everyone else as well as herself. She would no longer be around to get in everybody's way. In truth there wasn't much to look forward to. Perhaps giving up was the solution. To bow out was a much more attractive idea than living any longer in that crazy, unwholesome world beyond the four heaving walls of her mother's bedroom.

One more clever notion came into her addled brain. Groggily she reached for the telephone. Dredging up some remaining energy she fished clumsily in her coat pocket and after several false tries found a piece of paper. She dialled the number on it with a grim smile, slowly rubbing her eyes.

'Hello,' said a voice. 'This is the North-West Warwickshire Conservative Association, Tom Sparrow speaking . . .'

Now she would tell them: tell them all. Emboldened by drink and hopelessness Karen Stalker let loose exactly what she thought of Tom Sparrow, Roger Dickson and all their doings, dimly aware that her slurred words were emerging uncontrolled and distorted. The tablets seemed to be working. With a final lunge she managed to replace the handset. There was no more to be said, ever.

Then she tugged the soft warm eiderdown over her face, and at last let go, sliding rapidly down and down and down, where there was no more thought and no more pain and no more tears. Only oblivion, and peace.

Roger Dickson pulled on his shoes and heaved himself to his feet with a long sigh. 'I never want to leave, Elaine. I don't know about you, but you make me feel so special.'

'Then you'd better keep coming, hadn't you?' Elaine understood her hold on this man. Coquettish teasing and flirtation were still the order of the day. Soon it would be two years since Roger Dickson had entered her life. 'I shan't turn you away. Make the most of it while you can.'

It was always 'you' and 'I'. Two separate people. Never 'we'. 'We' was for couples, recognised and acknowledged as a single entity. Married people or partners, people seen together. She used 'we' when she meant herself and her husband, the Stalkers: 'we have a child', 'we have a house'. With Roger she was a single, independent person. So was he. And yet that made their deepest coupling, its physical joining of body and limbs, sliding into place as one, all the more powerful. Only then, in animal darkness, loving each other without words, was union possible.

He came to her and kissed her on the forehead, then held her so close, as if to absorb her into himself, into his very body. She put her hand inside his coat and jacket, searching for the warmth, and rested her fingers on his shirtfront near his heart. Everybody else she met had an appearance. Roger had a feel, too, and a taste. All five senses could be satisfied by him, sometimes all at once. As he spoke she could feel his heart pulsing under her fingers, rub her cheek against his five o'clock shadow, taste still his sweetness in her mouth, smell his skin, his soft odour which was subtly different when he left her, hear his breathing, sense the nearness of his body and pull the whole impression all together by standing back and looking, fixing her last picture of him each time in her mind.

That private view was precious. He was so successful now outside, was photographed more, and was changing slowly in response to the demands of his public image. His hair was a little shorter and always trim, and he had lost a bit of weight. He smiled a lot now, but a broad grin, not that gentle half-smile which revealed his struggling soul, only for her. He chose his clothes with more care and his suits fitted better. Spent more money on them, most like. Her private Roger was becoming less and less part of his persona. She was conscious of the danger of losing these secret images and fought all the more fiercely to retain them in her mind. She wondered with a twinge of jealousy whether Caroline had the same problem, or whether, seeing Roger daily, she noticed these changes at all. It was getting harder.

He started up. 'May I use your phone? I forgot to check the answerphone back at the office. I can leave a message on it for Tom, too. Save me a bit of hassle in the morning.'

'Certainly – go ahead.'

It was nothing unusual; she turned away politely. From his briefcase he took a touch-tone gadget which enabled him to listen to the tape at the other end. He rang once, listened, frowned. Made a note. Listened again. Pulled the handset away from his face, looked at it, puzzled. Looked up at her.

'Elaine, what's your daughter's name?'

'My daughter? Karen. Why?'

'She appears to have left a message on my answerphone. Very peculiar, I can't make it out. Why would she do that?'

'I've no idea. She's supposed to be at home swotting for her exams. Why on earth would she be leaving a call on your number?'

'Hang on, I'll wind it back and you can listen for yourself.' He pushed buttons and handed her the phone. 'I'm afraid she sounds drunk. I hope it's nothing serious.'

Dubiously, as if it might bite, Elaine took the phone. 'If I repeat what she says, will you write it down? When would this have been recorded?'

'Let's see – the office will have closed about six, and that's the fourth message on the tape. Seven? Eight? Not that long ago, anyway.'

Increasingly alarmed, Elaine listened to the tape. 'Something about drinking. Wanting to speak to you, Roger. Why should she want to do that? . . . Rude about your agent. But she's never met him, as far as I know. How peculiar. Being very rude indeed . . . Well, I didn't realise my little girl knew words like that!'

Silence. Elaine gasped, sank to her knees, eyes wide with horror. 'Play it again. The bit at the end, not all of it.' She listened once again, then scrambled to her feet. 'She says she has taken tablets. Mogadon. She must be at home. There were a few left in a bottle in my bathroom. Oh, Christ, Roger, she's trying to kill herself. God in heaven!'

Cradling the phone in the crook of her neck as if it were her lost child, Elaine turned beseechingly to her lover, tears streaming down her face. 'Oh, no, no. Not Karen. Not Karen as well. We lost Jake. Not Karen. No, no. Why? Why – what's going on?'

'Are you sure that's Karen – quite sure?'

'Yes. She sounds very strange, but that is her. I think I've got it, Roger. If she's phoned you, or has talked to your agent, then she must know there's a connection between us. Maybe that's what she is trying to tell us.'

Roger was rough. 'Never mind that.' He seized the phone from her. 'First we call the police and an ambulance. Will they have to break in? Let's hope to God she's at home, not somewhere else. Think where else she might be.'

Elaine's mind dissolved in a confusion of names, numbers, terror and panic as Roger spoke quietly to the police, gave Elaine's name and address, explained that she had had a phone call and feared that her teenage daughter might have done something foolish. All in a clear, sensible, authoritative voice. 'Who, me?' He hesitated. 'I'm just a friend. Mrs Stalker is here but she is very upset.'

Elaine seized the phone from him, gabbled, her voice all out of control, her fear sliding down the line. Confirmed. Yes. The MP. Please, at once. She would leave for home immediately. In the States. No need to contact him yet. Her daughter had sounded drowsy. Time? Oh, not sure. Not long ago. Yes, right away.

'Try phoning home,' Roger suggested. 'It may all have been a joke, though it didn't sound like one to me.'

Elaine tried, allowing the phone to ring a dozen times. No answer.

'If she's passed out, that's not surprising. Doesn't mean she's not there. Is there a neighbour?'

'Yes.' A rush of relief. 'She's not far away.'

It took several minutes of agonised explanation to get through to Barbara what was going on. Elaine's voice quavered in terror and irritation as the awful phrases were repeated. Drunk. Tablets. Seems to have passed out. At last the penny dropped.

'Don't worry, Mrs Stalker. The house is all in darkness, but I'll go over there right now. I thought I saw her coming in earlier. I'm sure it's nothing serious. You know what kids are like. You're coming? Right, see you shortly. Don't drive too fast. We don't want another casualty.'

Elaine's mind had not focused on the long drive. Her hands shook as she reached for her keys. Roger waited quietly.

'Do you want me to drive you?'

'Don't be silly. That would be the first thing everybody would notice. No one knows yet what Karen has done, if anything. And if there's trouble I shall need my car.'

Roger smiled softly. 'So we're not owning up just yet. In that case, we have one more quick phone call to make.'

Once more he dialled his office and used the touch-tone. This time the code was for 'Delete'. He waited, redialled, listened to the now silent tape. Nodded at Elaine, satisfied. 'All done,' he whispered.

Then Roger turned to her and gave her her marching orders, like an experienced officer to a terrified soldier about to go over the parapet. 'Listen to me. Take care, and drive carefully. You are to phone me and let me know what's happening, and if I can help in any way, ask. Don't worry too much, it's probably nothing. If she is upset you have the whole of the Christmas holidays to spend with her. Take as much time as you want. The whips are very understanding about things like this.'

They stepped out into the darkened hallway. In a trice the flat was locked and she ran down the stairs. He waited, hearing the car door slam, hearing her rev urgently away.

Footsteps on the pavement outside passed and died. When all was quiet once more he walked down the stairs and out into the night.

The next few hours passed in a blur. Afterwards Elaine could not remember it all, the jumble of noise, lights, stomach pumps, nurses, stethoscopes, drips, bleeps, trolleys, low voices, dark glances, white coats, questions, incomprehensible instructions.

Barbara had turned out to be the soul of efficiency. She found Karen before the ambulance arrived and shoved fingers down her throat, making her sick on the spot. A reporter from a local agency who made a habit of listening into police radios arrived as the ambulance left, and after a few quick photos of the house jumped back in his battered car and followed the vehicle to the hospital. At the entrance to Casualty he nearly became a casualty himself as two local thugs, bloody-headed after a minor battle, took exception to his flashbulbs and threatened to beat him up in the car park. By the time Elaine drove up, face ashen, press reinforcements had arrived. So had the hospital's press officer, who barred the way with cool competence. It would all be headline news tomorrow. Especially if the child died.

Elaine waved everyone away. Just a cup of tea. Sorry to be a nuisance. No idea what had happened. A phone call. Who knows, with today's kids? Bad school report seemed to upset her, but you wouldn't think . . . He'll be in New York in an hour or so. Phone number. Ask him to call here. Thank you. I'll stay with her.

The trolley with its immobile occupant was wheeled into a single room in intensive care. All around men and women were dying, denied the dignity of doing it in their own beds. In the end Elaine gave up the futile effort to remain sensible and controlled and huddled in a chair at the foot of the bed, away from prying eyes, helpless and alone. Wanting Mike. Wanting Roger. Willing her child to live. To wake up, and not be damaged.

Divine punishment. Revenge. She was being punished, for denying her family, for breaking her marriage vows. However rationalist Elaine's upbringing, however seldom she turned to God, *in extremis* her incoherent mind feared that those long coils of superstition might be true. Swear a vow before the vengeful deity and you must keep that promise. To break it, for whatever reason, however driven and necessary, meant retribution. Vengeance is mine, saith the Lord: I will repay. Maybe through the mechanism of a guilty conscience, maybe by being found out. Or through the tragic effects on other people like Karen, more vulnerable, less able to cope. Elaine could live with ambivalence; it had become her nature. Without it politics would have been an impossible world for her, with its constant deceptions. Lying about her lover was no problem, especially as his love brought such joy; that piece of double-talk made surviving easier, not harder. But that was not true of her family. Politics was a brutal world, depressingly and catastrophically destructive – not least of the lives of those not directly involved. Innocent victims. Like Karen, whose laboured breathing, hour on hour, now filled the sterile room as her soul struggled to leave it.

Even now Elaine felt horror at the pattern of her own thoughts. She had thought about herself, how she was being punished. Not about Karen's suffering, or why she had done it. Look what damage this political life had wreaked already. Once her children's needs would have come first, automatically. No longer.

Elaine gazed at the supine body, almost unrecognisable under curling tubes, straps and masks. The hissing of a ventilator, sinister and mechanical, was the only sound. Still she had not thought through what Karen had done or meant to do, or why. It was almost too painful to contemplate. Yet what made a healthy fifteen-year-old take tablets and make a phone call like that?

Her contacting Roger's office must mean that her daughter knew about the connection. That alone would be enough to throw a young life into turmoil. What did she know? And, if she knew, who else?

Elaine's mind twisted and turned, but she could recall no hint from anyone, no leer or nudge or wink. She was quite certain that neither she nor Roger had left a trail. Not that the newspapers needed evidence. Effective innuendo could be constructed on almost any juxtaposition of a famous man and an attractive woman. Proving the negative, eradicating doubt, was then almost impossible. Nobody need tell the truth to be hailed as an investigative journalist of the highest order.

Not that Elaine had any intention of telling the truth. Except perhaps to Karen, if she asked. When she woke up. If she . . .

There was no one around. She moaned softly, then put her head in her hands and begged, praying half openly, half silently, not just for her daughter's life, but forlornly, as for a lost cause, for strength for herself, for Roger, for Mike, for the bad times which almost certainly lay ahead.

Then towards dawn Karen stirred and sighed.

The monitor bleeped urgently and a red light flashed. Elaine woke from her doze with a start, but a doctor and nurse were already bending over the bed. Karen wriggled, shrugged them off, muttered. The doctor lifted her eyelid, felt her pulse again, checked a printout, turned to the nurse, prepared an injection.

'What is it? What's happening?' Elaine pleaded.

The doctor spoke cautiously. 'Her blood pressure appears to be almost back to normal. Pulse is still erratic, but stronger. Out of her coma, Mrs Stalker, I believe. It looks like we caught her in time. She seems to be sleeping now.'

Elaine's heart missed a beat. 'She looks so strange. You sure?'

He pointed at the girl. 'She's in one hell of a drunken stupor still, and will have the mother and father of all headaches when she wakes up. But she should recover from all that. We will keep her in a day or two. Alcohol poisoning's not funny even without nitrazepam on top, and you never know. However, she'll be all right with us now, if you want to go home.'

'Not yet. My husband should be ringing soon.'

'Fine. We will make her comfortable. You can tell him the scare's over. No need for him to worry.'

A great flood of relief washed over her. Standing for the first time in hours, she staggered and almost fell. The doctor caught her arm, and suddenly she was laughing hysterically, clinging to him and talking gibberish as he made soothing noises, until at last the tempest subsided.

A nurse entered to say that her husband was on the line. With an effort her public persona reasserted itself as she walked into the corridor to sympathetic smiles and glances from the departing night staff. A ray of weak sunlight suffused the waiting room. The conversation with Mike was disjointed, his stilted words failing to match the terror she had just lived through, the gushing relief of its end. For a moment she toyed with the notion of playing it all down, but then he would have wondered at the urgent message to phone. In the end she stuck to a simple description of what had happened and her official belief that it was a silly accident caused by experimenting illicitly with the contents of the drinks cabinet. The sleeping pills were not mentioned. There had been so few in the bottle that even if Karen had taken them deliberately it was reasonable to suppose she had only meant to scare them.

In all her explanations with both Mike and the police Elaine found she stuck rigidly to the claim that Karen had phoned her at the flat. It was much easier that way, especially as there was now no evidence to the contrary. In time she almost came to believe it herself.

Leaving Karen behind and brushing away pressmen, she returned to the house, intending to bathe and change before going back. She wanted to be at the bedside when eventually Karen woke up.

The house was a disaster area. Wearily Elaine walked around, picking up bottles, righting furniture. The neighbour had already been in and washed the vomit from the bedspread. Now it lay on the kitchen table drying out, garishly pink in the dawn light, the large darker wet patch leaving a tidemark. With a furious gesture of rejection, Elaine bundled it into a black plastic bag and dumped it by the bin. Something, even an inanimate object, had to bear the weight of her distress.

Her study was in total disorder. Papers and Hansards littered the floor and Drambuie was spilled all over the place. Mechanically she began tidying up, sorting into piles, throwing away. One piece of paper stopped her in her tracks. It was covered in scrawl, spidering across the page, up the edge, over the other side. Karen's handwriting, but disorderly. Puzzled, Elaine sat amongst the debris and tried to decipher it.

In the note Karen told her mother what she knew about the affair and begged her to end it: she did not want her parents to divorce, and she was sure it wasn't her mother's fault. Perhaps it was her own, in which case she was sorry for being so useless.

Elaine sat still for a long time, reading bits out loud. Then, crying quietly, she folded the paper and put it in her pocket.

Gerry Keown in ordinary clothes stood shyly clutching a bouquet of sweet-smelling flowers which must have taken a fair chunk out of that week's wages. The Ulster accent was noticeable. He looked sheepish and was blushing under his dark hair though his eyes were watchful. To get into the hospital had taken quite some effort, given the administrator's laudable determination to keep media and gawkers out. First he had telephoned security, who carefully checked his identity with the Commons office. On his arrival he had shown his Commons pass. His name had been given to the ward sister, who asked Karen whether it was familiar. The girl's immediate request for her hairbrush was answer enough.

'I do hope you don't mind.'

'No, of course not. It's really lovely of you to come, Gerry. I feel such a fool causing all this fuss.'

'That'll teach you to lay into the liquor.' He seated himself respectfully. Elaine had made a few remarks to satisfy the press.

The two chatted, both feeling uncomfortable in unfamiliar surroundings. Karen examined the tall slim man with his sea-green eyes with more appreciation, remembering ruefully that it was her rejection of his ordinariness which had led to her accepting Betts's invitation in the first place. She would have done much better to stick with Gerry. He might have greater potential for being boring and have far less cash to play with, but he was safe.

She put her head on one side. 'You a Catholic, Gerry?'

He swallowed. 'Yes, I am. Does it matter?'

Time to be bold. 'Do you believe in sex before marriage?'

His glance darted round the room, took in the white virginal bed in which she lay, propped up, his flowers nestled by her side, dark circles under her eyes. What was she getting at?

'I don't believe that sex should be the central factor in a relationship,' he answered slowly. 'That's how I was brought up. There are more important things.'

Whatever he had said, Karen appeared satisfied. 'Good,' she said. 'I think so too. When I'm back in London, could we go out again?'

The man's face broke into a smile of pleasure. 'I'd be delighted. You get yourself better now, then tell me when you're coming.'

The girl sniffed at the flowers. Colour was returning to her cheeks. 'I will indeed, and shall look forward to it.'

CHAPTER TWENTY

Nigel Boswood was well aware that he looked silly, perched on the big comfortable bed in his crimson velvet dressing gown, plump white-haired chest bared and a wilting bunch of daffodils in his hand, smiling for the camera.

'Hold still!' Peter admonished. 'How am I supposed to get a souvenir, to gaze on for the rest of my life in nostalgic adoration, if you keep fooling around?'

The boy seemed to have grown taller since that first night in Amsterdam. His jawline had put on more bone; the babyishness had gone. A charming light-brown moustache, grown after Davos to avoid shaving windbitten skin, now graced the upper lip. The hair was still wispily blond, though Nigel had grumbled about a bottle of hair-lightener left carelessly in the upstairs bathroom. The effect was, if anything, to make Peter's looks more striking, more masculine. The trim body on which Nigel feasted his eyes was a boy no longer, but a young man with hard eyes, firm buttocks and a knowing air.

'Haven't you finished yet? If I don't get a move on I shall be late for this dinner.'

'Oh, the dinner.' Peter airily waved it away. 'You're the most important person there; they won't start without you.'

He fiddled with the camera, squinting with the viewfinder, a sly look on his face. The daffodils were drooping. Peter pointed at them and crooked his middle finger with a lewd remark. Nigel grinned and tossed the bunch aside on the bedside table. The camera was then perched on top of the chest of drawers and propped up with a towel, pointing at the bed. In a trice Peter was seated next to Nigel and cuddling up. 'Now, don't move. Just one or two more. I've set the timer; we have about five seconds. Say cheese.'

Nigel had barely opened his mouth to protest when the shutter went off with a dull click. Peter fell off the bed laughing.

'No, that won't do! You looked like a fish out of water. Wait, I'll do it again. This time would you please smile? Just for me.'

'I don't think this is a good idea. What's it all for, anyway?'

'I told you. You've made me so happy, Nigel, that I want a teensy-weensy souvenir. Very private. To keep next to my heart. Ready?'

The timer hissed and the camera shutter clicked again. Boswood suddenly felt apprehensive. At Davos on the ski slopes Peter had been dancing around like this, a glint of determination in his eye, camera in hand. The camera was new, too. Automatic, didn't need flash. Surely a boy with his background would be ultra-cautious what 'souvenirs' he acquired on his travels?

But Nigel found it hard in his current mood to sustain any anxiety. In the months since Peter turned up at the House of Commons his life had been transformed. Now he understood why uxorious men return home nightly, eager to dine with their wives and to lie with them afterwards. Having Peter installed in the basement was like being married, even though the younger man sometimes played hard to get, or threatened to leave, to go back to his sister or to the Netherlands. It was designed to maintain Nigel's dependence, even he could see that: to retain his love. No harm in it. This coquettishness was all part of the delightful sexual game Peter played with his lover, like a young bride married to an older man.

His immaturity showed, naturally. Constantly asking for money; but then most young people seemed to go through it like water. Given the age difference, a generation gap was to be expected. After the little row about money before Christmas, Nigel increased the amount and ensured it was left regularly, in large-denomination notes, always cash, in a House of Commons plain envelope on Peter's pillow at the beginning of every week. It seemed to help, too, that Peter now visited that sister in Stoke Newington regularly. The complaints about penury had ceased. Maybe she helped him out as well.

It did not occur to Nigel that he was being had for a sucker. Or perhaps, in so far as he ever suspected the fact, his mind was firmly closed to the possibility. He knew little about the boy's background and did not enquire. That the incident in Amsterdam was a pick-up he did not doubt for a moment, but his romantic side wistfully concluded that Peter, an ordinary British boy seeking his fortune working abroad, had been hard up and that he, Nigel, had simply come along at the right time. Lucky for them both that he had. The bond between them was so powerful that anything sordid had now been effaced.

How quickly Peter had understood Nigel's self-loathing, how gently he had dealt with it, talking quietly, kissing and loving, so that gradually the old pain and desperation fell away. Never completely: its shadow remained, but it was such a joy to be relieved of its lifelong burden. Nigel was at last content.

'Did the snaps from Davos turn out at all?'

'Don't know yet,' Peter lied. 'I shall have to be careful where I leave them. Mr Ferriman won't want pictures of him and his girlfriend getting into the wrong hands.'

'They did make it rather obvious, didn't they?' Nigel chuckled.

'Can't see what she saw in him at all.'

'I hope the one of us coming downhill together turns out well. I hadn't realised you were such a good skier, Peter. Really made up for my clumsiness this time.' He gestured ruefully at purple bruises on his thigh. 'Lucky not to break anything. I may give it up, before I have an accident. Sixty now, you know.'

'You don't look it and you certainly don't act it.' Nigel demurred graciously as Peter wound the film back in the camera. The boy wagged a finger. 'Don't run yourself down. You're still nifty on a pair of skis, and good for many years yet. I enjoyed watching you. It was a marvellous holiday.'

'It was fun, wasn't it? The snow was as good as I've known it and the après-ski was excellent this year. Wasn't that Ancient Worlds party a scream? Of course there's always a last-night party, and they've been wilder even than that. I was a bit concerned at first but everyone joined in, and it was all so innocent, just a bit of larking about, really. I thought of going as a slave-driver, but in the end that would have been a bit dull. You were right about that. Your idea of an Egyptian queen was brilliant. You don't think I overdid it?'

Peter appeared to be struggling with the camera, which might have explained his grimace, or perhaps he was having trouble keeping a straight face. 'Well . . . everyone knew who you were, of course. Even with the make-up. Freddie Ferriman stole the show with his Dance of the Seven Veils, so although it might dent your ego I don't think you were really the centre of attention.'

'I hope not. Though it was only a party, and perfectly harmless. But I'm glad that you didn't take any photos there. Could be misconstrued.'

Peter nodded, inscrutable, then smiled.

He didn't take them, but they were taken.

'. . . and the government's commitment to ensuring that hazardous waste from other countries does not reach our shores remains as firm as ever.'

A faint scattering of 'Hear, hears' greeted the Minister's statement. Roger Dickson eased himself back into his chair and wrinkled his nose at the portrait of Joseph Chamberlain with his purple orchid on the wall opposite.

What would Chamberlain, arch-advocate of the empire, have made of all this? Wednesday mornings in European Standing Committee A of the House of Commons were tedious in the extreme. None of the histrionics downstairs occurred. No TV or even radio; the press were next door, watching Kelvin MacKenzie, editor of the *Sun*, explain with raucous pomposity how he understood the national interest better than those elected to do so. Meanwhile hardly anybody attended this weekly committee. Parliamentary democracy, wittered the Euro-sceptics, was at risk from the depredations of the faceless bureaucrats in Brussels. Not half as much, in Roger Dickson's informed opinion, as from the laziness of Members of this House.

Dickson looked around. He watched the flabby expanse of Labour MP Mrs Dunwoody in a floral tent as she sourly demonstrated her hostility to all things European, while David Harris on his own side courteously responded. They resembled Jack Sprat and his wife.

Dickson glanced behind and was reassured by Elaine's presence. She looked a bit despondent. The pressure of work had kept them apart for three weeks now. He would have to make an effort soon, for her sake as well as his own. A watery spring sun filtered into the room. The season demanded it; the sap was rising. In the royal park crocuses in yellow, purple and white unfolded across grassy banks in great swathes of colour, as if Her Majesty's velvet cloaks had been lovingly spread out to dry. The black swans and pelicans in St James's Park had been at it already – some pairs were being followed even now by anxious bobs of quacking brown fluff. He ventured a wink at Elaine.

Behind Roger, Andrew Muncastle was feeling glum. It was weeks since he had seen Miranda in Il Portico; there had not been a single phone call. That could be because she was working flat out to save the newspaper, which still stubbornly appeared nightly on the news-stand by Victoria station. On the other hand it might mean she had already left the country, and had changed her mind about inviting him to join her. Frankly it had been a strange suggestion. Of course haring off would have been impossible, with all the work overwhelming Ministers at the department, not to mention the government's desperate unpopularity. However much of a heel he might know himself capable of being, Andrew would not have walked out at such a tricky time. But what if Miranda was even half serious? Then the offer might remain open – assuming she had had the power to make it in the first place.

If this silence continued he would be faced with the risk of calling her himself – never wise, especially in view of the *Globe*'s reputation – or giving her up without a final word. He wished she would call.

Andrew shifted in his seat. Remembering Miranda he was suddenly too warm and took off his jacket. In the bored stillness of the room his action promptly drew all eyes. He blushed, for it was as if they could read his thoughts. He was unsure which would have embarrassed him more – that he daydreamed about a stunning woman with skin like amber and mocking eyes and a warm welcoming body; or that he had the chance to leave behind the dusty world of Westminster and fly to the sun and instant success.

Seated on the platform near the chairman, Marcus Carey was also failing to pay full attention. He did not need to: the Environment Department's expert on waste disposal, spectacles perched on his quivering nose, was at Marcus's side, only a few feet from the Minister, ready to pass scribbled notes should Mrs Dunwoody turn nasty. Not that it mattered. The discussion was for show and not much else. It would all be decided at the next session of the European Council of Ministers, and would then be a *fait accompli*.

Nestling in Marcus's pocket was something much more significant. It could make him as well known as the MPs before him. If he played his cards right, he, Marcus Carey, in the next Parliament, might well be sitting on those green benches himself.

For after careful consideration of his curriculum vitae, after glowing references from such luminaries as Sir Nigel Boswood, after an agonising weekend at a secret hotel with thirty others undergoing a battery of tests and explaining himself in repeated interviews, Marcus had that morning been informed that his name had been put on the the list of approved candidates at Conservative Central Office.

On the list: the first hurdle over. How amazing British democracy was. In most other countries in Europe, as the son of an immigrant he would not have even been a citizen, let alone permitted to stand for Parliament. Here, however, he could truly say he had received nothing but encouragement, at least officially, whatever the strange looks and whispered comments of others, including some of his fellow hopefuls.

Marcus gazed round the room. Everybody present had successfully cleared the next big hurdle: being selected for a winnable seat. Dickson had fought a bad one and earned his spurs before gaining his current constituency. Mrs Stalker had got in first time. Possibly it helped being a woman. Yet of all the dozens of spare good seats at the previous election only six had dared select women and only one, in West London, had been brave enough to pick a black man. The women faced odds of nearly ten to one. The odds facing Marcus Carey were far more adverse.

Marcus's gaze remained on Elaine. There might be a chance to emulate Mrs Stalker. Access to a good seat first time might not be impossible, given his close links with Nigel Boswood. Rumours were flying round the office about the old man's impending retirement. Almost certainly it would mean his leaving Parliament at the next election. That created one of the juiciest vacancies in the country. *And he, Marcus Carey, ought to try for it.*

Wasn't he special adviser to the Secretary of State? Speechwriter, amanuensis, colleague and friend? More or less, anyway, though most of his work was for Roger Dickson. If Sir Nigel could trust a black man – not any black man, this black man – at his side, the selection committee need have no worries. He would hint that having worked for Sir Nigel he now wanted to deliver the speeches as well as write them: a suggestion to be offered, naturally, with a modest dip of the head. Suitable phrases began to engage his mind. It was only a matter of time.

The old Rover drew to a halt in a layby opposite the school. Elaine switched off the lights and sat for a moment in the gathering gloom, watching other parents in flashier cars fussing over their offspring. She turned to the daughter sitting quietly beside her and appraised her frankly.

Karen's dark hair had grown; no longer did she affect a tomboyish, challenging style. The girl was pale and had lost a lot of weight, but seemed less listless. Her hands showed tendons and blue veins stark under white skin, but they were resting calmly in her lap. Whatever had been burning the girl up before Christmas appeared to have lost its intensity. Or perhaps the child was learning to cope better, was growing up. About time.

Elaine caught herself sharply. It was not wise, or right, to assess Karen in such negative terms. Maybe this was half the problem, her own tendency to treat activities such as returning the girl to boarding school after the weekend break as tedious chores, as a nuisance and intrusion into her own busy life. Her petulance could well have communicated itself to Karen. What a mistake not to see the regular half-hour journey as a precious opportunity for uninterrupted discourse. Maybe taking those pills had not been an accident; Karen had been trying to tell her something – perhaps most of all that it had become almost impossible to tell her anything.

The familiar car was warm and comfortable, a cocoon of intimacy. Elaine took one of Karen's hands in her own and stroked it. The girl half smiled back, her eyes soft and dark in the dusk.

'You sure you're well enough to go back to school, Karen?'

'Sure, Mum. I'm much better now.' The voice was low, but assured and steady, belying her wasted appearance. 'Anyway, I can't take much time off or I'll get too far behind.'

'You know your father and I love you very much, Karen.' It was an invitation. The girl smiled again and nodded. She was thinking how pretty her mother looked these days, slim and elegant, hair a lovely gold colour which suited her, bright-eyed and perfectly made up. Karen felt a twinge of both pride and regret, especially for her own gawkiness. The girl felt deeply uncertain what fashion style to adopt herself; while she rejected much of the appearance which had given all the wrong signals

344

to Betts, an alternative had not emerged. For the moment she reverted to schoolgirl non-chic. No wonder another man was passionately attracted to her mother. Dad was mad, leaving her to her own devices so much and taking her loyalty for granted. It was all becoming more understandable by the minute. If her mother were not entirely innocent in this affair then neither was she wholly guilty either.

'I know you do, Mum, and I love you too. When I woke up in that hospital bed and saw you there, all upset, I felt terrible, because I could see I'd hurt you so much. I'm very sorry for causing so much trouble.'

It was the first time she had mentioned the event. Elaine gave an encouraging look. Expecting further confidences, Karen's next words surprised her.

'Did you tell Dad not to come?'

'Dad? Yes, I did. There was no point in his traipsing back across the Atlantic. You were out of danger by then, and snoring like a pig in your alcoholic stupor. You put away nearly all my Drambuie, young lady, and what you didn't drink you spilled on my good carpet! Let me know next time and I'll find you something cheaper.'

The teasing brought a rueful giggle, but the girl had acquired a tougher skin and would not so easily be put off. 'Dad should have come. It was important.'

Elaine sighed. The child was right; she was not the only one to have felt abandoned at a time of great need. 'He has a busy and important job, Karen, as I have. You can't blame him for that. It's no use feeling resentful. It's harder for some men, especially when a daughter is involved. The first whiff of woman trouble and they run a mile. Your father was always like that, I'm afraid, and we won't change him now.'

'Are you and Dad going to get a divorce?'

With an effort Elaine kept her voice even and firm. 'No, I don't think so. We're going through a bad patch at the moment; it happens in the best of marriages. Not your fault at all, sweetheart. But – it might be best if you don't interfere, and leave us grown-ups to sort it out ourselves.'

The term 'grown-ups' carried an irony which was not lost on her daughter. Karen had heard words like this before, not long ago. Her mother was volunteering very little. For the third time Karen was obliged to reveal her own secret knowledge, fearful of its reception, dependent only on the kindness of the recipient.

'I know all about it, Mum – you and Roger Dickson.'

Silence. Jagged denials flickered through Elaine's brain – how can you know? How can you imagine what it feels like to lie with him, and to love him, you who have never loved anybody, yet? How can you guess the pain of loving a man belonging to someone else, unable to acknowledge you even in passing? But she kept her own counsel. It would be wrong to burden this youngster, struggling with all the miseries of adolescence.

Karen waited, then tried again. 'I know it's none of my business, and whatever happens, Mum, I will still love you. And I won't say anything, I promise.' She meant to add, 'It has caused enough chaos already, my distasteful knowledge', but thought better of it. She continued, 'But if you and Dad are going to split up, that does affect me, doesn't it?'

'We are not going to split up. I intend to stay married, Karen, you can rely on that. I love my husband, my home, my family. If Daddy and I have drifted a bit, that's probably my fault, and I can and will do something about it.'

Elaine was entirely sincere. She had taken her marriage vows with determination and conviction and had always intended to keep them. The liaison with Roger was unplanned but its existence did not change her views on the preferability, if it could be managed, of fidelity. Anything else was lesser, a failure.

Not that she had considered how the affair might end, though end it must, sooner or later, if she meant to stay married. It did not have to end, not for years yet, as long as exposure was avoided. She was newly forced to think about it since Karen's outburst on the answerphone had suggested the matter was leaking out. She turned to her daughter.

'Do you want to tell me how you found out about Roger and me?'

Karen swallowed and turned to look out of the window. She was thankful the darkness hid her face. 'It wasn't too difficult, Mum – you've been leaving a trail for months.' That was all she would permit herself.

Elaine was close to tears. Karen realised she was treading on unforgiving ground and stepped back from the brink. She twisted a lock of her hair around a finger and tried, childlike, to chew it but the strands were still too short. Her voice took on a wheedling tone.

'Mum, did you think any more about my leaving school and doing my A levels at college?'

Her mother slowly returned to the warm car and the darkening night. Karen would have to go inside shortly or be reprimanded for lateness.

'Explain to me why school is suddenly so unsuitable.'

Karen tweaked her school tie with an impatient gesture. 'Wearing uniform like this; make-up and jewellery banned, having to do games whether I like it or not, and loads of rules. We're treated like children when we're not. I know it's supposed to be one of the best private schools, but that's part of the problem: it's really peddling a very old-fashioned form of English education for the daughters of rich foreigners. I don't fit, which is daft, considering I'm the daughter of a Tory MP.'

Elaine pulled a face. 'I can see what you mean. Remember when we brought you for interview, and asked where we might eat, thinking there might be a McDonald's around the corner? We were directed to the best restaurant in town at thirty pounds a throw.'

With barely suppressed excitement Karen realised that she was winning.

Her mother continued, 'Look: we preferred you to stay at school partly because it has discipline. We don't want you running wild and forgetting your studies. Are you sure you could cope at college?'

Not trusting herself to speak, Karen nodded. Elaine hesitated. There was a hint of undue pressure being put on her by her own daughter. Chip off the old block when it came to getting her own way, Elaine noted in wry amusement.

'Then we'll do a deal. You work for your GCSEs and get yourself completely well, and I'll check out the colleges. How's that?'

The girl's eyes danced in triumph. 'Yes!'

'Fine, Miss Clever, but you have to keep your side. No more wearing yourself to a frazzle, and no more binges, do you hear? I can do without funny phone calls.' Both sensed with relief that the subject, having been aired, was closed. 'And I don't have to tell you not to gossip about your own family. If you want to talk on that, or anything else that might be bothering you, I'd rather you did me the courtesy of tackling me first. I am your mother. You can ask anything, though I can't always give you a simple answer; to some questions, there is none, not yet. You, on the other hand, can tell me anything. I wouldn't be shocked.'

Karen leaned into the back of the car and collected blazer, hockey stick, scarf, bag and a pile of fluorescent folders covered in pop star stickers. Keeping her expression light, she kissed her mother and headed off into the gloom.

'Oh yes, you would,' she whispered to herself.

Mrs Margaret Perkins shook the rain from her headscarf, put her key in the lock of the front door at Ebury Street, wiped her feet and trudged down the polished tiled hallway to the kitchen. Placing her bunches of scarlet and yellow tulips in the sink, she ran cold water first for the flowers and then for the kettle. A broad, dumpy woman, Mrs Perkins hung up her coat near the Aga to dry, patted her damp grey curls into place, turned on the radio, donned a pink apron and settled herself at the kitchen table. The sound of the *Jimmy Young Show* filled the air and she hummed along tunelessly. Time for a quick cuppa first.

Another week. Not that she was complaining. Being daily help to Sir Nigel Boswood for nearly twenty years, and to his absent-minded old aunt before that, must be one of the best cleaning jobs in London. Lovely man to work for, Sir Nigel. Easy-going about holidays and time off, like when her daughter was ill. The pay wasn't bad – considering how tidy he was in this beautiful house with its fine furniture, not bad at all, and always on time, left in a Commons envelope on the table here every Friday.

Mrs Perkins had no qualms or snobbery about being a cleaner. Her mother had been a skivvy all her life in grand houses like this. Two sisters worked for an agency servicing City office blocks, all pay slips and claim forms and tax and home on the bus exhausted before the pin-stripe brigade arrived, while her brother was shop steward for hundreds of cleaners over in Lambeth. He didn't approve of her eating out of the hands of the aristocracy; she didn't care for his left-wing ways. Mrs Perkins voted Tory and was proud of it.

She would have to do that basement; it couldn't be left any longer. Fervently she prayed that Mr Peter was out. Knowing and caring for every square inch for so long, she felt it was almost her own home. He was the intruder, not she. There was something about that peculiar young man which stuck in her craw. Sir Nigel's guests were none of her affair. She was the soul of discretion and never gossiped about her employer outside, loyalty and pride jointly keeping her mouth firmly shut. But that Sir Nigel's naivety and kindly nature were now being blatantly exploited she had no doubt whatever.

It was her choice to tackle the flat. Sir Nigel had said gently to leave Peter alone. After much brooding at the top of the basement stairs and sniffing unhappily until her high standards overcame her caution, she had had sharp words about it with Sir Nigel. You could not, in a house like this, ignore a whole floor. The boy was clean enough in himself, she would say that for him, always in a crisp shirt and fresh socks, but he never once changed the bed or pushed a duster over a surface or emptied a wastepaper basket. Not that you could expect boys to do for themselves. Sir Nigel was giving her extra money meanwhile. What really worried her was the thought of the monumental cleaning job facing her if and when the young man cleared off, as doubtless he would sooner or later.

Housework does not get done by contemplation. With a sigh she reached inside a cupboard and collected dusters, spray polish, window cleaner, plastic rubbish bags and the vacuum cleaner. Duly laden and with the radio tinkling from under her arm, she headed for the stairs down to the flat. At the door she paused and turned off the radio, listening for a moment. Not a sound, except for street noises outside. She tapped cautiously. 'Hallo? Anybody there?' No answer. Satisfied and relaxing a little she turned the door-knob and went in.

The place was a pigsty, with a dusty film over everything and the mixed odours of talcum powder and aftershave and something else less palatable. Methodically she set about emptying bins and picking up clothes strewn around the floor, clucking in disapproval. A full ashtray sat on the bedside table; its crumbled contents gave off an acrid sweetish smell. Mrs Perkins's stolid face set grim. He should not be doing that in this house, whatever he got up to outside. Her sense of the violation of a happy home was increasing by the minute.

On the radio Jimmy Young was immersed in a discussion on euthanasia. Mrs Perkins was not unintelligent. Working steadily, she listened and commented back. There were two sides to the argument, she could see that. She did not want to suffer nor be a burden to anyone, if she had cancer or a stroke. Better then to finish it all quickly. On the other hand it was unwise to give too much power to doctors, ever. With the wrong encouragement from greedy relatives they might get far too enthusiastic. She did not envy Sir Nigel and his ilk having to decide on tricky questions like that, and was glad her responsibility was confined merely to looking after him.

The bathroom was in a diabolical state. Not only were the best bath towels stained and strewn carelessly in the wet all over the floor, but the bath was still full of grey water, mirrors smeared with flecks of toothpaste, the washbasin plug-hole disgustingly blocked by shaved bits of fair hair. She pulled out the bath plug and watched the scummy liquid slushing down the hole. This would never do; Sir Nigel would have to hear about it.

The radio discussion shifted to the differing needs of young people nowadays. Lips pursed, Mrs Perkins sprayed the mirror and rubbed vigorously. This one here could teach all those do-gooding social workers a thing or two, the lying way he took advantage. Back in the bedroom she started collecting clothes, folding and putting away. The label on one sweater was Pringle. It was wool and cashmere, lovely and soft, not your usual Marks and Spencer. Puzzled, she counted eight sweaters and two leather jackets, tossed around as if of no value. And yet this little lot alone must have cost all of a thousand pounds. Not short of a bob or two. Mrs Perkins's mouth snapped shut. She would not permit herself to consider where the money might have come from. That was not her place.

The room took on a tidier aspect as the unmade bed slowly emerged from its disorganised coverings. Mrs Perkins collected several bags of laundry and headed upstairs. Returning with an armful of fresh-smelling clean linen, she began to strip the bed.

Picking up a pillow she began to shake it out of its slip. A small yellow and black envelope fell out with a plop. Ever conscientious, Mrs Perkins made to put it somewhere safe, but natural curiosity persuaded her to sit for a moment on the edge of the bed, cradling the packet in her hand. Nobody was watching, nobody would know. Furtively she tipped the photographs out and began to examine them.

As she told herself defensively afterwards, she was only hoping for evidence of good in Mr Peter. A nice photo of him cuddling his mother, perhaps, or walking a sweetheart bashfully in the park: that would have convinced her that though foolish and inconsiderate and a bit strange he was not a bad boy.

Peter was not hugging his mum. The pictures were dark and seemed to be of some sort of party, with people prancing around clutching wineglasses. Some of them looked drunk. All were got up in silly costumes, outlandish and bizarre. She screwed up her eyes, turning the first picture this way and that. That was certainly Mr Peter, rouged and sequinned, wearing some kind of short white toga pinned at the shoulders, a broad gold belt pulling in his waist like a girl's. Peter's partner was tall, grey-haired and tubby, ludicrously attired in Egyptian-style dress, silver pleated and off one shoulder with a long skirt out of which sandalled feet poked with red-varnished toenails. A silver and turquoise headdress, slightly askew, obscured the face. A pendulous breast was exposed, its nipple painted red. The breast was hairy, shaggy and grey. The tall man had one arm around Peter, who in turn seemed to have his hand touching his companion's genitals.

Mrs Perkins swallowed. The next photo showed the two in an embrace, faces in profile to the camera, lips together, pouting and wet. She shuddered, but could not stop now. A third had Peter roguishly lifting his little skirt while the friend pretended to cover his eyes with a fat white hand. The boy's long sleek legs were almost womanly. That would explain all those hairs in the sink. The man's headdress was slipping, tufts of grey hair peeping out.

Maggie Perkins was a Londoner, resident all her life in one of the world's most sophisticated cities. She had no strong feelings about homosexuals, if that was their preference, as long as they didn't do it in the street. That word 'gay' always seemed a bit silly to her as it didn't appear to make them very happy; still, we were all as God made us. There were lots so inclined, on telly and in the theatre. Look at Larry Grayson, and wonderful Frankie Howerd, and that lovely Colin from *EastEnders*: you couldn't think ill of them. Ballet was full of them, poofters all. Rock Hudson, they said. Artists too, like that chap who painted those swimming pool pictures her daughter liked so much – David Hockney, that was it – he was one. Even Julian Clary: at least he made her laugh. Pushed, she might have admitted that her brother was probably like that. But being queer was one thing; flaunting it and making fools of people was quite another. These photos were different. This was nasty stuff, crude and tasteless, like the pictures in the *Sunday Sport* which Mr Perkins sometimes bought and hid with an apologetic shrug from her disapproving gaze.

It was impossible to come this far and not complete the journey of unpleasant discovery. Heavily she rose, taking the photographs closer to the window. Outside it was still drizzling. The next photo was clearer because the figures were closer to the lens. The big man, Peter's companion, was not looking at the camera, but perhaps he had heard its whirr for there was a startled, almost frightened look on his face. The strange headdress was completely askew. The shape of that head was familiar. The nose, that chin-line. She squinted at the eyes under their make-up.

Then Maggie Perkins's mouth dropped open in horror.

There was no need to warn her employer. He already knew. The tubby man in the photograph was Sir Nigel himself.

'I'll have those, if you don't mind.'

The voice was cool and light but full of menace. Peter always walked quietly, which unnerved her, but he was so close she could feel his breath on her arm. She jumped in terror and the dreadful photos, relieved of her restricting grasp, tumbled in a mocking cascade on to the carpet at her feet. Mumbling apologies she went down on hands and knees to collect them up but Peter nimbly was there first. He stood before her, calm and sinister, and held out his hand.

'And the rest of them, please.'

Alien: that's what he was; evil and cruel and alien. Maggie Perkins reflected quickly what to do. Her family came from old British stock. Her dad had been killed at Dunkirk, an old uncle at Gallipoli. Courage had never been lacking. She folded stout arms across her ample bosom, took a deep breath, squared her shoulders and looked her enemy straight in the eye.

'Whatever you are doing, Mr Peter, it's not right and it's got to stop, do you hear? Sir Nigel is a good man, one of the best. You've got some sort of hold on him, haven't you?'

Peter leered at her. The new moustache drew attention to his soft girlish mouth and pink lips.

'None of your business, dear Mrs Perkins. You're just the cleaner.'

That did it. Mrs Perkins's eyes blazed. Her voice turned hard, almost hissing, as she spat out the words with all the contempt she could muster.

'You're dirt, you are. I know what you're up to. Leave him alone, do you hear? You've overstayed your welcome in this house. You had better leave, and quick. Out! I mean it – out!'

Peter glanced through the photographs, his nonchalance scary. 'Oh, yeah? And are you going to make me? What are you going to do, call the police?'

From the back of Mrs Perkins's mind came the phrases and tone used by her brother when talking about trade-union business. She gave not an inch.

'I come from a large cockney family, Mr Peter. If that is your name.

We don't like your sort. And if you were to be found a few days on in the gutter not far from here, beaten daft, well now: that'd be none of my business either, as you put it. Do I make myself clear? Somebody will pay for this, you mark my words.'

With considerable dignity and a pounding heart Mrs Perkins gathered up her dusters and polishes and swept towards the door, banging it behind her. Her heavy steps clumped steadily up the stairs and away.

Peter held his breath till she was gone and whistled softly through his teeth. He placed the photographs carefully back into their packet and reached in the wardrobe for a leather jacket.

'Right, Mrs P.: somebody will pay. But not me, at all. Your posh friend, perhaps. Or someone interested in him. We shall see.'

In a dusty upstairs room at Milton Conservative Club the Finance and General Purposes Committee of Milton and Hambridge Conservative Association had just been informed that their much-admired Member of Parliament would not be standing again. Since no one present could remember last time this had happened over thirty years earlier, none had the faintest idea how to react. It seemed wisest to keep one's eyes firmly glued to the floor examining old cigarette burns and wait for someone else to speak.

It fell to Mr Bulstrode as chairman to break the solemn silence. He was a retired bank manager, yet inside his discreet breast lurked a radical heart. Once, long ago, he had dreamed of standing for Parliament, but it was an impossibility for a lowly bank clerk, and now he was too old. The advent of a new Member might make life jolly interesting. Time to wake the area up.

Next to him the vice-chairman pushed rimless spectacles up his long nose. Mr Standish was senior partner in the small town's main solicitors and knew everybody's secrets. He had been on the committee nearly twenty years. The prospect of a selection committee excited him enormously. The choice must fall on a lawyer, of course. Making laws was much too important to be left to anybody else.

The chairman of the ladies' branches, Mrs Farebrother, sat up straight. She would miss Nigel; he was a good sort, genuine and kind. Once the wife of a rural dean and now his widow, Mrs Farebrother claimed aristocratic connections. A secret admirer of the Duchess of Devonshire, she adopted the same style of high-collared blouses fastened with a pretty pearl pin. How terrific, choosing a new MP. Mrs Farebrother's nimble mind ticked off the necessary qualifications. Willing to live in the area, as Sir Nigel had long done. Not too Thatcherite either; many of the voters here were elderly and not well off. Somebody rather special, even unusual, not the typical smooth lawyer up from London offering to do the locals a favour.

Mrs Farebrother glanced down to the end of the table where the Young Conservative chairman was whispering to the agent. Not paying attention again, young Fred. The association was lucky to have YCs, considering how many young people went away to college and came back with awful leftish ideas. From the wall opposite a large framed print of Churchill, cigar in mouth, was reassuring. He once said that if you were not a socialist at twenty you had no heart; if still a socialist at thirty, you had no head. Quite.

Fred Laidlaw was certainly no socialist; and he was ambitious. He wondered if he might try for the seat himself.

He turned to Mary Morgan, the agent. 'They want somebody to wake them all up here, Mary, don't you think?'

A terrified look came into her small watery eyes. She had never managed to qualify as a proper agent, which was useful in its way, for it meant the association did not have to pay her the going rate. Warm-hearted and unheeded, committed and agonising, Mary wished Sir Nigel could stay for ever.

Mr Bulstrode turned to her impatiently. 'Now then, Mary, we are all upset at Sir Nigel's announcement. Been 'ere a long time and we're all very grateful.'

Mrs Farebrother cleared her throat meaningfully. The chairman realised that this moment needed more than a quick vote of thanks suitable for an after-dinner speaker at Rotary. He straightened his shoulders and turned to Nigel, who sat forlornly at his side.

'You've served us very well, Sir Nigel. We don't all 'ave your eloquence to say what's what, but you will be an 'ard act to follow, mark my words. The passing of an age.'

All present nodded vigorously. Nigel felt a lump form in his own throat. Bulstrode was gaining confidence.

'Now, Sir Nigel, you've indicated we're to keep quiet for the moment, which we will all respect. The next election is a good way off, but we 'ad better be ready. Do we 'ave your agreement to proceed with choosing your replacement?'

Nigel had not thought seriously of this next step, in which he would be little involved. He nodded his assent sadly. The world would continue here after his demise. The committee were right to say: the king is dead; long live the king.

He faced lonely decisions of his own. If he continued living in the area it could make things awkward for his successor. How fortunate that other pleasurable matters filled his mind. He wondered a mite mischievously how these good people might take to his turning up at a future function with Peter in attendance.

The chairman smiled benignly at the committee. 'And now I think we cannot simply allow this 'istoric moment to pass, ladies and gentlemen. I suggest we all assemble in the bar downstairs in the club, and the drinks are on me. Remember, not a word to anyone.'

For some weeks Peter avoided Mrs Perkins's hostile stare by keeping out of the way when she was due. Eventually he tired of lurking in the park opposite and waiting till her plump figure could be seen clumping off down the front steps. He had overstayed his welcome; he'd never spent so long in one place before. The only question was where to go.

Back to his sister's cramped house in Stoke Newington, perhaps. She was her mother's daughter all right, with her scatty ways and erratic affections. An endless stream of disorderly children and stepchildren regarded him as an interloper and made life unbearable by stealing his clothes. And it was a nuisance having to contribute to the housekeeping: everywhere else he might stay, the cash flow was in the opposite direction.

Or there was the smart London flat of the new man, who seemed more discreet than Nigel Boswood. A fresh relationship was stimulating and this man had sophisticated tastes. That was hardly surprising since he also had a wife in the country. She did not come to London much if ever, being engrossed in her garden, her small children and the local Mothers' Union.

There was always Amsterdam. He had not neglected his contacts and had used Nigel's phone to keep in touch. Hermann had not been well: but since Peter shrank from sick-rooms he decided to wait until his old flame was fully recovered before his next visit.

On the way home at last in the comfortable leather seat of the ministerial Jaguar, Nigel felt jaded. He would go in late the following day. There was too much legislation, too much urge to reform, merely because they had the power to do so. Perhaps ministerial work, however trivial or unnecessary, expanded to fill the time available: Parkinson's law, true as ever. Nor had the parliamentary timetable eased. Recently the hours had been as ghastly as any under Mrs Thatcher, who once said that home was a place to go to when there was nothing better to do.

The Jaguar slid to a halt in front of the house in Ebury Street. The upper floors were in darkness. Tonight there was only one red box to attend to; an enquiring shake revealed it to be lighter than usual. Nigel stood briefly on the pavement looking down past the railings. From the basement flat came the sound of a radio, and a bedside light gleamed behind drawn curtains. He realised that he had not seen Peter for several days. A good reason, therefore, to put the box on one side for an hour or two and be soothed from his weariness by Peter's skilful hands.

For a moment Nigel paused in the hallway and recalled the image of Peter on the staircase the first night he had come here, with the light shining from behind making his naked body glow like a young god's. The memory caught his throat. It felt so right, as his parliamentary life approached its natural end, to be close to youth and love. Retirement with Peter would be a time of fulfilment and great happiness, before he got too old.

There and then, standing in the still darkened hall, Nigel made a momentous decision. He would tell people: he would come out. Not just yet. After leaving Parliament probably. It would need discussion with Peter himself first, of course. They would have to talk through the implications with great care and not do anything in a hurry. He would change his will, leave Peter this house perhaps, so he should not lose his home when eventually he, Nigel, died first, as was likely. The boy might demur, not wanting him hurt; yet Peter might be better equipped than Nigel to cope with the announcement, coming from a generation with more casual attitudes to sexual diversity. Peter would know what to do and say; he would rely on him.

For Nigel could not escape his own decency. All his life he had lived a lie, though he had never covered up as some do by joining loudly in critical remarks about homosexuals. His conscience now stung. Gay people were subjected to such awful prejudice, such dreadful things were said. Yet if a person like himself were to take the plunge, to stand up and be counted, to say, 'I am gay', it might make things easier for many others.

His mouth wrinkled in amusement. Perhaps the chance would come in a House of Lords debate. Lord Boswood would put his name on the list of those who wished to speak, but say not a word in advance. No leaks, no hints. That would render it all the more startling and effective. Peter would be up in the front row of the gallery, looking fondly down on him. Their Lordships were reasonable people, far more so than in the Commons. Although there might be a shocked silence at first and one or two would never speak to him again, the rest would murmur a few words of support in the bar afterwards and then change the subject. Matthew Parris had survived: so could he. And live openly afterwards, with pride if not glory, never needing to tell a lie again.

Nigel sighed softly. He felt as if a great lifelong burden had been lifted from his shoulders. The hated box was abandoned unopened in the hallway. He must tell Peter at once. He ran up the stairs as fast as his legs could carry him, pulling off his bow-tie on the way, feeling like a schoolboy on the first day of the holidays. In his bedroom he hung up his suit, setting aside his public persona like an unwanted skin, and donned the red dressing gown, folding its quilted collar panels over his middle and tying the cord firmly. As an afterthought he cleaned his teeth and rinsed.

He pushed open the basement flat door, calling softly. The radio, switched on, sat on the bedside table under the small light. The place looked unusually tidy, for Peter. Perhaps Mrs Perkins's complaints had struck home.

There was no sign of the boy. The darkened bathroom was empty, clean and unused. Nigel was nonplussed. Perhaps he had popped out to buy a takeaway: after all, the vote had been late. The bed looked as if it had not been slept in. Might as well wait. Nigel kicked off his slippers and settled himself on the bed feet up, leaning back, hands folded under his head, half listening to the radio discussion. What a relief it would be when he was no longer a Minister, to refuse all invitations to silly broadcasts, early morning or late. He would miss the constituency; somehow he did not feel the provinces would be quite so free of homophobia as London. It would be interesting to see whether requests to speak would still come from the Milton and Hambridge area after he came out. If so, he would accept gladly, to show he was still the same old Sir Nigel, not metamorphosed into a monster with horns and a forked tail.

The midnight news came on. Nigel surfaced from his doze with a start. Peter was awfully late. How strange.

He heaved himself off the bed, ambled into the bathroom and put on the light. Just as he was about to relieve himself, the message on the mirror caught his eye.

It was in red lipstick – the same colour as Peter used sometimes when they played very private dressing-up games. Nigel's eyes were not focusing properly and itched with tiredness. He rubbed them, leaned forward and peered at the garish capitals:

SORRY, NIGEL. GONE HOME. SEE YOU SOMETIME. LOVE, P. XXX.

Red lipstick. Unmistakable. With shaking finger he traced the dreadful words; that was Peter's writing, all right. Not his imagination. Not a joke.

What did Peter mean, 'Gone home'? This was his home, for as long as he wanted it. The future stretched ahead, the two of them together, like any other couple. Out and open and in public: respected, not reviled. Having dinner parties, holding at-homes, here. At home. In this house. Where else? This was home.

Not for Peter. He had once said in a revealing moment that he had no home, only the next bed, in whatever country he could earn a living. Nigel looked around wildly, opening cupboards and drawers. The boy's personal things had gone, along with his original holdall. Neither cheque book nor passport was in its usual place. The drawer which held clean underwear was empty.

Stumbling over the dressing-gown cord he returned to the bathroom and stood for a long time, staring with unseeing eyes at the terrible message, whispering the words over and over.

Then a great animal cry rose from Nigel Boswood's throat, a cry that tore his heart from its cavity, that set dogs barking and cats running out in the night-black square, a cry of anguish and longing and desperation, as he crashed his own head into the mirror, once, twice, again and again, destroying the fateful image, and smashing it to a thousand shivering pieces.

He was still sobbing hysterically in the morning when Mrs Perkins found him, flung across Peter's bed, clutching one of the boy's many sweaters. There was blood everywhere, in sticky rivulets down the remains of the mirror, all over the pillow in which Sir Nigel had buried his head, weeping fit to die, and worst of all in a horrible black caked mask, eyelids gummed tightly together, on his wild and tragic face.

She understood at once without words, picked him up and cradled him in her ample lap, as she would a hurt child, crooning gently, easing his pain as well as she could. As his agonies slowly subsided she fetched towels from the bathroom soaked in cool water and bathed the cuts, taking out small shards of silvered glass and pressing a dry towel to stop fresh oozing. Most of them were superficial, fortunately, and would be best left uncovered, though a purple bruise and swelling disfigured the fine brow.

At last he sat still and helpless, head bowed, in an armchair.

'Well, sir! You look a mess, and that's a fact,' Mrs Perkins began formally.

Nigel looked at her mournfully. 'He's gone.'

'Yes, sir, he's gone. I'm not surprised.' She bit her lip. The man was in enough misery. No need to rub salt in the wounds.

Boswood's fingers touched one of the cuts, making it bleed again. He looked in puzzlement at the wet smear of blood on his fingers.

Mrs Perkins decided to take charge. 'If I might suggest it, Sir Nigel, you really ought to take a couple of aspirins and go to bed. Upstairs, if you don't mind; that will give me a chance to clean up down here. I will phone your office and tell them you're not too well and need a couple of days off.'

He stared at her dumbly. 'I will kill myself,' he whispered.

Mrs Perkins swallowed hard and kept her voice even. 'No, sir, we won't talk like that. I'll stay tonight in the spare room; if we need to, we can call the doctor tomorrow. That'll give us time to concoct a story to explain all those cuts – you slipped and fell against the mirror, perhaps. It was an accident.'

Like a baby, he was, leaning on her, one hand clutching a clean towel as they stumbled upstairs. In his bedroom Mrs Perkins did not hesitate but stripped off the blood-caked dressing gown, averting her eyes respectfully, and dressed him afresh in clean cotton pyjamas. Meekly he sipped water and swallowed tablets, then slipped into troubled sleep.

'Right, ladies and gentlemen! Are we all done?'

Pushing away a well-cleared plate, Mr Bulstrode assumed once more the manner of a man about significant business. Around him the selection committee, now grown to around a dozen earnest members, rose hastily to its feet. Stickler for punctuality, the chairman.

Upstairs the committee room had been transformed. It would not do to lose a worthy candidate simply because a bad impression had been gained from the room's usual air of neglect. Mary and Mrs Farebrother had slaved all the previous day removing layers of accumulated grime, leaving Mary allergic and sneezing and revealing far too much peeling paint for Mrs Farebrother's punctilious taste. The result was patchy but effective. Mr Standish had brought in a blue-patterned rug to hide the stains on the old floorboards, which gave the room a jaunty, almost festive air. On the baize tables, now arranged in a large U, they had laid a blue cloth and placed on it jugs of water, glasses, ashtrays and bowls of mint imperials. It would be a long day. Lastly they added a small pot carrying Margaret Thatcher's younger image with an assorted bunch of early roses from Mrs Farebrother's garden. When the chairman protested she reminded him pointedly that the English rose did not belong to the Labour Party. As the day wore on rose petals fell on the table one by one, to be swept away between interviews; when one lady candidate stopped in mid-sentence, eyes wide with horror as a hairy caterpillar emerged from the biggest rose, even their provider admitted that the chairman had probably been right.

Mr Bulstrode sipped from the remains of his pint, then hid the empty glass on the floor behind him. The committee was not looking happy.

'Would I be right in thinking, ladies and gentlemen, that we've not been much impressed by what we've seen so far?'

There were gloomy nods all round. The vice-chairman, Mr Standish, fiddled with his pencil, searching for words. 'It's not that there's anything wrong with them. All very good, very clever. But I haven't yet seen the one who's right for us.'

Mrs Farebrother turned to the chairman. 'Why do you think we've not had a brilliant selection?'

'No idea.' He shook his head. 'Mary, do you hear anything on the agents' grapevine?'

Mary hesitated. Ever loyal, she was torn between anxiety not to upset anybody and her professional position, however tenuous. 'I think the worry is, chairman, that with such as well-known figure as Sir Nigel his personal vote might be very strong, and would disappear. We might have been relying on him too much, and not be as well organised or as well off as we should be.'

'They think we're a disorganised shower, do they?' Mr Bulstrode was clearly offended. Still, if Mary's observation was true, there would be plenty of time to put matters to rights before the next general election. A more competent, properly trained agent might be a start. And a stronger committee.

'We haven't done much canvassing here for some time, either.' Mary felt emboldened. 'We keep going to help weaker seats nearby and trusting to luck for ourselves. Candidates don't want to feel they'll have an uphill struggle.'

'Well: we 'ave another batch to see this afternoon. A lawyer, a university teacher, two businessmen – no, one's a woman; and, if the committee will allow, young Fred Laidlaw's asked to be considered. It's my view we should give 'im the chance.'

'He's not on the approved list,' Mary objected timidly.

'Correct, but we 'ave the right to adopt a local candidate. 'E can go on the list afterwards,' the chairman reminded her testily.

It was agreed that Fred should have his turn. Mary went to phone him and to bring in the next victim.

The day wore on as each interviewee, nervous or laid back, well informed about the constituency or totally baffled, mouthing platitudes or (less often) profundities, made a short speech and fielded questions. Each was asked the same points and was secretly marked by each panellist as objectively as possible. All present regarded the process with the utmost gravity. On these deliberations rested far more than the replacement for their retiring MP, but the style of politics in their neighbourhood for decades to come. That it was a fascinating exercise, spotting winners, a bit like Miss World, added to the fun.

It was a weary group, rubbing eyes and cracking finger joints, which girded up their loins in late afternoon for the last stretch. Tea was brought in. The chairman took off his jacket, thought better of it, and put it back on again.

'Two more, and the last one's Fred. Right: let's 'ave the next chicken for the slaughter in, shall we? Thank you, Mary.'

Twelve faces looked up with various degrees of expectation, curiosity and welcome as Marcus Carey walked in.

Twelve mouths dropped open; or rather eleven, for it took Mr Bulstrode a few seconds to catch up with the stunned silence of his companions. Then he saw and his jaw fell also. There was a sharp hiss from Mr Standish as he pursed his thin lips. Mrs Farebrother felt herself going pink, then, furious with herself, dropped her eyes. Was she not the former wife of a clergyman, a man of the church? Were not all men created equal in the sight of God and made in His image? Deeply embarrassed at her own confusion, she scrabbled around among her papers to find Marcus's details. Good degree, relevant experience, special adviser to the Department of the Environment. Excellent on paper. Right age, married. Born in Britain. Already ahead on points. Yet the most significant fact of all about Mr Carey was omitted. There was no mention here that he was black.

Marcus was accustomed to the barely suppressed gasp of surprise as he walked into certain rooms. Although over three million British were black in varying shades, their presence in company like this was extremely rare. Not that the Labour Party found coping with the transition to a multiracial society any easier. Blacks were still banned from many working men's clubs, were still heavily underrepresented in the union hierarchy, and most infuriating of all were patronised by left-wing councils as always in need of white help, and thus not yet fully qualified to become citizens.

In his best grey suit, sober tie and highly polished leather shoes, Marcus looked more self-assured than he felt. His palms were sweaty and seemed too big. His mouth was dry, making his voice almost falsetto.

'Now then, Mr Carey!' Mr Bulstrode was overdoing the gruffness. The whole committee was twitching, moving hands, touching ears, looking distractedly out of windows. Only elegant Mrs Farebrother, still flushed but back under control, gazed at Marcus directly. She gave him a small encouraging smile.

'We'd like you to tell us in your own words why you should be the next MP for this division.'

Marcus stood, feet slightly apart, trying to stay calm.

'Mr Chairman: thank you for asking me here today. You have in Sir Nigel Boswood one of the most greatly admired and loved members of the government who will be sadly missed. I can say that, perhaps, with more authority than most, for I see Sir Nigel every day at the Department of the Environment. He is a marvellous man to work for – thorough, responsible, helpful, knowledgeable about his own subject but never losing touch with ordinary people. I know him; he appointed me to this job: and I believe that I may lay claim to follow in his footsteps.'

But Marcus was not trusting to luck. A week earlier he had prevailed on Nigel to write a short private note, somewhat against the older man's better judgement, to the chairman, setting out the special qualities Marcus would bring to the post. As it ended with the standard phrase widely used in references, 'I would recommend this candidate without reserve', the letter could easily be taken for vigorous support. That was good enough, at least for Mr Bulstrode. He watched Marcus carefully.

Questions flew around the table, like cricket balls from bowlers of varying degrees of skill. Marcus dealt with them all as an experienced batsman, scoring each time. The committee relaxed a little; this was more like it. They could understand why Cheltenham decided to take a risk with John Taylor – but this was a much safer seat, with a rock-solid majority.

Standish, still with an expression of undisguised horror, was signalling a frantic desire to ask a question. Bulstrode decided to ignore him and turned instead to Mrs Farebrother. She took a deep breath. She owed it to Marcus to warn him. Or at least to see if he was well prepared.

'Mr Carey: if you don't mind my asking, how will you cope with remarks about your colour?'

She watched for any weakness, a flash of annoyance, but there was none. Marcus pulled his shoulders back. Apart from Mr Standish, whose face was now rigid and furious, the whole committee was leaning forward attentively.

Marcus's voice was sincere. 'I am glad you asked me that. It is far better to face these . . . ah . . . more difficult matters than pretend they don't exist. My father came here forty years ago, following the advertisements placed in West Indian magazines by the then Tory government. He was and still is proud to be British and regards most of us as nowhere near patriotic enough. He was employed in the dockyards in Southampton and studied at night school, working his way up to deputy works manager. I am proud to be that man's son.'

Mrs Farebrother could picture it. How disappointing the man must have found this damp, inhospitable country. What determination must have been required to stick it out, and more, to slave away at midnight books, to be ambitious, never to give in.

'Let me say this, though,' he continued with a smile. 'I have one enormous advantage. Within a week of my photo appearing in the local press, I'll be instantly recognised all over the constituency. It takes most prospective candidates years to do that. I think that's half the battle, don't you?'

The committee tittered discreetly. Mrs Farebrother was thrilled. She hoped he meant what he said, and could cope.

There was an appreciative light in the chairman's eye also. He drew the interview to a graceful close, then rose and showed Marcus to the door, shaking his hand, a gesture he had not offered to any other candidate. When Bulstrode resumed his seat without comment, a more satisfied expression had settled on his features.

'And the last one, ladies and gentlemen! Mary, we'll have young Fred Laidlaw in, if you don't mind.'

By comparison with Carey's experienced smoothness Fred was very green and hesitant. Stumbling to his seat, he slouched, one hand in pocket, till Mrs Farebrother's raised eyebrows showed his mistake. With a muttered apology he sat up straight.

Mr Standish was by now in a foul mood. Invited by the chairman to lead off, he almost spat out his question: 'What is your answer, Mr Laidlaw, to the rising crime wave?'

Fred's mouth opened, but no sound came out. He cudgelled his brain for a response and decided to make a virtue of ignorance.

'I am not sure anybody knows, Mr Standish,' he ventured.

Mrs Farebrother covered her mouth to smile unseen. That was the first honest answer to that question they had had all day.

As no more seemed to be forthcoming, Mr Standish tried again. Asking this puppy to come before the committee had been a big mistake. 'Well, then, are you in favour of capital punishment?'

That was easier. Even if it sent steam through the ears of such as Mr Standish. 'No, I'm not. Too easy to top the wrong person.'

Perhaps Marcus was fortunate that Fred's gawkiness stood in such sharp contrast to his own courteous manner. Or perhaps Fred was more than unusually unlucky, for Marcus would have been a hard act for anyone to follow. Walking out head bowed, Fred reflected ruefully that simply wanting to be an MP was nowhere near enough and that considerable homework would be required before he dare try again. He resolved to put the whole matter down to experience.

Outside it was almost dusk. Street lights glowed first a dull orange, then burst one by one into garish light. Flocks of black starlings screamed and scrabbled for roosting positions, clattering against the windows as if demanding admission. Mr Standish winced. *There would be no black candidate here*. Should never have been allowed to enter the country in the first place, stealing jobs. A Tory candidate? Absolutely not. Over his dead body. He'd see to it.

Mr Bulstrode knew who was top of his personal list and wondered how the others had voted. 'Now you know the rules. We can choose three or four to go into a second round, if you want. Or we can skip that. The winner goes to a full meeting, makes a proper speech and answers questions.' He glanced with interest at the summary sheet handed to him by Mary. 'Well now – it might 'elp if I tell you that one person came out 'ead and shoulders above all the others.'

The chairman was enjoying himself, keeping them all in suspense.

'Go on, then!' Mr Standish remonstrated. 'Who is it? Who's our man?' It had not occurred to him that it mightn't be a man. The women candidates had been uniformly terrible, in his view.

'Of the twelve here, eight scored the same name first, several having him way ahead. Three put him second, with this morning's estate agent first.' Mary shuddered; he had not been her type at all. 'One did not give our winner any marks at all, which I can only presume was a mistake.' Mr Bulstrode glared at Mr Standish, whose narrow face slowly turned colour from pasty through scarlet to puce. Mrs Farebrother's eyes widened in delight. It couldn't be, surely, that most of these good people here had done as she had obliged herself to do, forced back her instinctive antagonisms and insisted on evaluation on merit? Under the table she crossed her fingers.

'Our winner, ladies and gentlemen, by a long chalk, was Mr Marcus Carey, whom we saw this afternoon. I must say that I agree with that entirely. He was excellent and dealt with all the questions nicely, even the – shall we say – most delicate. I think he will do us 'ere in Milton and 'Ambridge very well.'

Most of the occupants of the room, unknown to Mrs Farebrother, had followed a similar odyssey to her own. Now several faces beamed, looking at each other as if sharing a happy conspiracy. Mary clapped her hands with delight. To surprised stares she twittered, 'I thought he was lovely, just like Sir Nigel when he was young. I'm so glad it's him. Much nicer than the others.'

'I move we accept him now, and I suggest we ask if he will be kind enough to bring Mrs Carey to the open meeting,' offered Mrs Farebrother helpfully.

The chairman checked his notes. '*Dr* Carey, it is, not Mrs. Good idea, we'll see to that. That's it, then. Thank you all—'

'*Wait a minute!*' Standish was on his feet, his chair clattering away behind him. Committee members in various states of collecting papers froze. Trouble, had there been any trouble, was not anticipated from Standish, always the soul of propriety. The meeting was finished, the decision taken.

'You can't have him.' Standish was quite definite. 'You can't. He is totally unsuitable. The idea is quite unthinkable!'

Proud and rigid he held his position. Behind him he could feel fingers pointing. Bulstrode was also on his feet, leaning on the table on his fingers in an aggressive pose. He was not about to have his authority challenged.

'And why not, pray? Mr Carey was on the list good and proper, which is more than we could say for young Fred. He 'as a brilliant CV. He's exceptionally well thought of by Sir Nigel; I 'appen to know that. He dealt with everything we threw at 'im with great distinction and . . . and dignity: yes, that's the word, dignity. I should be proud to go canvassing with that young man. Do I 'ave the feeling of this meeting, or not?'

Rapidly all present made a choice between the belligerent figure of Bulstrode the retired banker, kindly, decent, occasionally silly, but as honourable a man as any in Milton and Hambridge, and his arch-rival with the long nose and thin smile who knew too much about them all and had never managed a kind word in his life. An affirmative chorus flitted around the room.

'Mary is right, as you are, chairman. Mr Carey it is,' Mrs Farebrother firmly summed up.

Standish was left protesting and spluttering, mouth agape, alone in the disorderly remains of the room as his erstwhile friends and neighbours crept past and avoided looking at him. It was impossible! They were all mad, even thinking of having a black man as a Tory candidate. No more pussy-footing around. What was he? Not a proper man at all, still swinging from the trees in Africa. Fit only for manual work, scrubbing toilets in hospitals. Most of them could barely read or write. Drugs – weren't most of the drug problems of this country due to them, bringing in cannabis and getting high all the time? The whole idea was preposterous, ludicrous, horrible. A black man here? Never!

He would appeal to the Prime Minister. The selection had not been properly conducted. It would have to be done again, this time with himself in the chair. He would vet the applicants first, insist on photographs with the forms. He would write to the Party Chairman in protest. He would mobilise local supporters. He would say his piece in the press, though it would have to be tactful – the chap didn't have enough experience, or was unsuited to the area. Not a matter of colour, not at all.

Even as his fevered mind ran through the options, Mr Standish grimly realised how limited was his scope for action. For almost fifteen minutes he stood in the empty room, muttering to himself and banging the unprotesting table with his fist, until at last its rickety legs gave way. It collapsed to the floor with a sudden crash, sending the few remaining mint imperials rolling over the floorboards. The vase of flowers fell and broke right across Mrs Thatcher's profile, limp petals and stems lying in a spreading stain on Mr Standish's own carpet. Cursing he pushed the furniture roughly out of the way, bent down to brush the wet leaves off and started to roll it up. Then his foot caught on a sweet and went from under him with a sharp crack.

When Mary and Mr Bulstrode entered the room to find the cause of the commotion, they found their erstwhile colleague prostrate on the floor, clutching his thigh and whimpering in pain. Mrs Farebrother permitted herself a moment's satisfaction as Mr Standish writhed and moaned, before reverting to her Christian duty and summoning an ambulance. Mary, ever superstitious, was deeply thankful she had openly approved of the new dark arrival in their midst. Mr Standish had taken against him so virulently, and that wasn't right. It was God's law that we are equal. Somehow Mr Standish's accident seemed, in a way, a warning.

Part Three

CHAPTER TWENTY-ONE

There was, predictably, a row about Marcus Carey's selection but the tone was curiously muted, perhaps because the result was such a surprise. For a complete unknown to be chosen to succeed the much admired Sir Nigel Boswood, and one who was black, must imply that this person is in possession of remarkable qualities. Four people resigned ostentatiously from Milton and Hambridge Conservative Association and looked around to find no one else following their lead. The chairman gamely stood his ground and explained bluntly that Marcus was much the best of an excellent bunch. Mr Standish was left fuming helplessly, flat on his back for six weeks in hospital with his plastered leg in traction.

Nigel, the Dicksons, the Muncastles and Elaine, among others, sent supportive messages, while a shower of national and international congratulations of varying degrees of hypocrisy cascaded around Marcus's bemused head. The hate mail came too, usually without stamps, misspelled little missives in capital letters on lined paper torn from cheap exercise books. The Prime Minister, challenged at a fund-raising dinner about the new black Tory, smiled vaguely, said he knew the man and he was very good, and that this proved the Tory Party were well ahead of Labour. Right-wingers meticulously cultivated by Marcus in the days when his potential for candidacy was a joke were nonplussed, but broadly welcomed another supporter to their wing of the party. Even Baroness Thatcher, who had long represented an ethnically mixed constituency in North London, when asked her view in the transit lounge at Taipei airport, expressed pleasure at his adoption as representative of those newly enriched families she was so proud to have had a hand in creating. Carey himself, though pursued for weeks by a frenzied press, wisely refused any comment. It was a highly successful tactic: every time he appeared on television surrounded by screaming pressmen shoving mikes up his nostrils, another batch of admirers was gained.

Sir Nigel Boswood weighed in immediately to welcome the choice of a 'distinguished, loyal member of our party' with a 'fine track record' who would 'offer many years of conscientious service to Milton and Hambridge', which he himself had been so proud to serve. Under these circumstances it was impossible to keep his impending retirement quiet, but the bold choice of Marcus moved debate so much further on that his own sadness seemed trivial by comparison.

Several people remarked that Sir Nigel seemed to have aged a lot recently. The scars on his face, mainly superficial, healed quickly into unaccustomed fine wrinkles on his previous smooth features. With some juggling of timetables he had remained in seclusion until no further excuses about his face were required. As attention switched to Marcus, Nigel found himself bowing quietly and without ceremony out of the local limelight. It left him feeling utterly bereft, with a terrible sense of anguish and loss. The thought of suicide recurred briefly, but putting an end to it all suddenly seemed not noble but foolish, an admission of defeat. Instead he counteracted his misery the only way he knew how, by throwing himself into his work. He stayed late at the department and in his large dismal room in the Commons basement, ignoring Chadwick's ostentatious yawns from the outer office. He thrust himself once more into detailed papers which had been somewhat skimped and neglected, he now admitted dolefully, during the disastrous dalliance with Peter. Thereafter the demands on his time inexorably increased, for, as all Ministers discover, completing the homework night after night promptly creates more of the same; the Minister who impresses civil servants with enthusiastic assiduity has only himself to blame for much fuller boxes the subsequent week. The overriding task of officials is to keep their Minister so busy he has no time for reflection, or he may end up that dreaded nuisance, a Minister with original ideas.

Retirement from the front bench loomed as a much less attractive prospect than when Peter was on the scene. In tearful moments late at night, whisky in hand, Nigel realised with an emotion approaching utter despair just how much of his own future he had invested in the boy, and wondered how he would cope when the red boxes no longer appeared.

Back in the constituency Marcus Carey made headway. Most of those who interested themselves locally in political life wisely waited for the chance to meet the man and make up their own minds. Alison joined him for the main adoption meeting and smiled loyally at everyone. Startled once more, this time to find their candidate married to a white woman, pretty and slim with neat brown hair and intelligent eyes, those present were embarrassed at their own tolerance. In the shifting world of the 1990s the old certainties about what was and wasn't acceptable were vanishing. The stage looked set for an easy ride for the new man.

Peter rolled over on his back and rested his head in the crook of his white underarm, aware that cradling his blond hair softly in this fashion made him look adorably feminine. With his other hand he caressed the lanky body of his new lover and slithered his fingers over sleek body hair, massaging taut tendons in the shoulders. His voice had a practised tinge of genuine regret.

'I may not be able to visit you very often. The press are chasing me over an old relationship. You wouldn't want to be seen in my company while that was going on.'

The man twisted half around so that he could rest his head on Peter's abdomen. 'Might it be anybody I know? Perhaps I can warn you,' he suggested conspiratorially.

Peter ruminated. 'It could be, I suppose. Big cheese in the Department of the Environment.'

The man kept his surprise under control, but the well-educated voice elongated into a drawl. 'Ah, I see. Civil servant? Or politician?'

Peter's amused silence at the first suggestion and knowledgeable shrug at the second told him all he needed to know. 'An older man, shall we say, then? Unmarried?'

A giggle. 'You can say what you like. I'm saying nothing.'

Then Peter halted the conversation by leaning over and kissing him on the mouth, making the kiss rich and irresistible, until the man's eyes began to glaze over.

The younger man spoke so softly the sibilance hung in the air. 'No more questions. I don't talk about you, and I don't talk about any others, savvy? We'll have to be careful until it all blows over. That's all.'

Andrew was preoccupied as he headed out of the Chamber towards the whips' office. A reshuffle was due in the summer, everyone now agreed. Naturally he wondered if his name was on any lists, even though he had been a PPS for less than a year. The next few weeks might be crucial. Men in his position were often sent to the whips' office, not as now with a message demanding the prompt appearance on the front bench of the next whip on duty, who was late, but as an appointee. The thought had its appeal. Both Boswood and Dickson had served their time there, and both spoke of it with relish as the finest place to learn all the doings of parliamentary politics. Yet he was unsure how effective he might be in this difficult Parliament at twisting the arms of recalcitrants to persuade them to vote. Faced with belligerence or superior intellect he feared he would give up without a fight.

Look how easily he had given up on Miranda, for example. Four months had passed and he had not seen her, not dared. He recognised his own inertia for what it was: fear that she would simply tell him it was all over. Outright rejection was to be avoided at all costs. He had left plaintive telephone messages on her answerphone but she had not replied. Perhaps she had taken his coolness, at their last meeting, as unwillingness to become further involved; but he had only been startled, and unprepared for her offer. She came into his mind in the first moments of waking, the instant he realised that he was in his own bed and not hers; the memory of her body lulled him to forgetfulness as he turned out the light. Yet he yearned for her, more than he could have believed possible.

Damn Parliament for keeping him so busy. Although it was spring he felt sleepy, as if in hibernation. The timetable was a stinker, despite all the promises of an easier session after the Maastricht marathon. The result of voting late night after night was an enervating exhaustion. If he had failed to pursue Miranda with any urgency since their strange discussion in the Italian restaurant, it was in part because he needed every ounce of energy for his job.

Then it happened. He saw her, standing self-consciously in the lobby, her ID card displayed prominently on her bosom. She was dressed more modestly than usual, her skirt still tight but almost reaching her knees and the stance less confrontational. She was talking to Brian Gould and had not seen him. Andrew hesitated, then delivered his message quickly and returned to the lobby.

Gould was expounding his theories of the collapse of Europe. Born in New Zealand and like many former colonials in love with the motherland, he failed to understand how any true Brits could be attracted to the high-flown nonsense of the European idea. Miranda's own accent could be heard as she commiserated.

Andrew approached quietly from behind so that he was almost at her side without her becoming aware of him. Her perfume was different, more suited to the modest surroundings, but still delicious. She looked well if a little thinner.

'I wouldn't believe a word this renegade is saying, Miss Jamieson,' Andrew said with mock gravity.

At his voice Miranda jumped and a flush spread over her skin. Gould stopped in mid-sentence. The attention of his audience had obviously wandered, or rather galloped off in another direction. It was clear this new lobby journalist was more interested in dim Tories on the make than in intelligent socialists. Resentfully he walked away.

Andrew watched his retreating back briefly. 'It's good to see you here, Miranda, but it's not your usual beat, is it?'

'Correct, but we're so short-staffed that someone has to do it while our political correspondent takes time off for a nervous breakdown.'

'I was wondering . . .' He stopped. She waited, but a grin slowly spread over her features. To Andrew it was as if sunshine had burst into the gloomy interior of the Commons. He took a deep breath and tried a different tack. 'Would you, by any chance, be working too hard? If I can assist you in any way, you know I'd be happy to oblige. Tell you the gossip, that sort of thing.'

There it was: she laughed out loud, the old gurgle that set his hormones racing. Lightly she touched his arm. 'You're right, I have been neglecting my other duties. Very remiss of me, and quite foolish. I couldn't return you calls because I've been working half the night. First things first.'

A whip had spotted the PPS talking to a journalist, had sidled up and was trying to eavesdrop. Andrew gave her a warning look and Miranda dropped her voice.

'Forgive me. I'd love an informed, *active* discussion of some of the points raised with me today. I was hoping I would see you. Let me get some copy filed, and I could see you later. How does that sound?'

A great surge of relief rolled over Andrew. It was all he could do to prevent himself picking the lovely woman up there and then and hugging her for all to see.

By spring many of the troubles at the *Globe* were being resolved. The new computers had begun to show their capabilities. Fresh editions could be churned out at the push of a button, displaying superb high-definition colour photographs beamed by satellite with never so much as a smudge. Redundancy bit deeply but costs fell sharply along with the time taken to produce each edition. Slowly the newspaper gained a small edge over its main tabloid rivals. Companies desperate to spend their way out of recession gratefully accepted the lowest advertising rates in what remained of Fleet Street. Debts and gearing which had reached astronomical levels started to subside. The economic recovery helped too, though it was still sluggish. Other papers in the same group, on the owner's orders, pitched in to assist, quoting *Globe* stories with approbation. The paper's remaining journalists, unaccustomed to positive attention deserved or otherwise, began to feel less like mangy dogs. By the summer a few new faces had appeared to fill gaps and even its own staff were speaking hopefully of the paper's future.

Deputy editor Miranda Jamieson's intensive efforts were credited with much of the success of the rescue operation. She stopped checking flights to Melbourne and recovered much of her normal aggressively flirtatious manner as the frown mark eased from between her brows. Officially she was still dating Matthew Frank, who claimed to know a good woman when he saw one. That she was also involved seriously with someone else, who was, she hinted, in Australia, suited him fine; too many women wanted to drag a chap to the altar even in these laid-back days. Their photos together at the first night of Andrew Lloyd Webber's latest hit, Frank with a self-satisfied grin on his rubbery features, Miranda hanging on Frank's arm with her cleavage thrust towards the paparazzi lenses, appeared on all the diary pages, keeping everyone agog. It was all a thoroughly professional business, supporting both their newspapers. Her spare time was, however, still spent with Andrew Muncastle.

Andrew never ceased to marvel at her. Knowing she chose him above all others his self-confidence increased, with diffidence and coldness replaced by more warmth, albeit still reserved, for he still found it difficult to be the first to unbend. When Marcus turned to him and Roger for advice on matters arising from his candidacy, both were happy to give it, with the three of them becoming regular diners at the Gran Paradiso restaurant in Wilton Road, tucked away behind Victoria Station. At home, as it became clear that he no longer needed Tessa for sexual activity, she became less fearful and thus more welcoming. There were no more anguished rows. Barney became aware that his parents were getting on better and in turn lost some of his awesome solemnity, so they could enjoy his earnest presence more together and at last had some family pleasure to share. Even Miranda had stopped talking about choices and Australia, though he caught a romantic glow on her face sometimes as they made love.

All in all, it was turning out not so bad a year, despite all the pressures. More than that. As late spring turned to summer and he sipped a Pimms once more on the Terrace with Miranda in celebration of the day they had met there two years earlier, Andrew wished it could all go on for ever.

Jim Betts blew a large smoke ring experimentally into the air and watched as it disintegrated around the fair head of his latest catch. The editor's room was filling with a blue fug which made eyes water, and produced occasional furious looks from Nick Thwaite, who was again trying to give up cigarettes. With what he hoped was a sardonic smile playing at the corners of his mouth, Betts observed the proceedings and made occasional notes. He was mightily pleased with himself.

The boy sat impassively, blue eyes darting with amused disdain from one to another. He looked well, with a fine tan remaining from a recent visit to Mustique in the company of a continental prince who had conveniently paid in Deutschmarks. On the table, spread out, were several packets of photographs, some apparently ordinary, of friends laughing together on ski slopes, some bizarre or pathetic, posed in a bedroom somewhere, of a paunchy old man clutching daffodils and wearing nothing but a red dressing gown and a besotted smile, cuddling an apparently naked version of the young man now seated opposite.

Editor Steve McSharry pushed the photographs around with a paper-knife and fought down a feeling of distaste. It was not his job to judge but to sell newspapers. Once, when young, McSharry had dreamed of unmasking corruption in the halls of state through superb, unadulterated journalism. Exposing poor old Nigel Boswood as a raving queer with a knowing hard-faced rent boy had not quite the same nobility of purpose. Some day, he vowed, he would write a powerful bestseller exposing the whole sleazy business of tabloid journalism – and thus regain a huge measure of professional respectability, without changing the system one jot.

'Right. I think we have ourselves a magnificent and very moving story. Evil Cabinet Minister seduces under-age teenager. Very timely, with all that talk of changing the age of consent. Oh, Sir Nigel, do not touch me. How my life was ruined, by tragic unemployed youngster. Well done, Jim. Now the next step is to talk to our lawyers and get contracts signed so we can start paying you. I have our chaps lined up. Once contracts are in order, I'm sure you understand what "exclusive" means, Peter: it means not talking to anybody else, no hints, no nothing. You won't get better money than from the *Globe* anyway.'

The boy nodded. It was like dealing with any other client: ask more than you think you'll get and watch for the blink. The *Globe* had not blinked. No point in blowing the chance by checking elsewhere. Wise, however, to appear knowledgeable.

'I'd like a copy of the contract to check over lunch, please.'

'Sure. It's all standard. Then there's a lot of work to do, taking down the whole story. Every gory detail, please. Spare me nothing. I have no sensitivity and neither have our readers. Jim, you and Peter here are going to get to know each other a lot better. A quiet country hotel somewhere. Full drinks cabinet, room service meals, charge the lot. Can you handle it?'

Betts averted his gaze from the too handsome boy. 'Can we have two rooms, boss?'

The editor turned, puzzled at first, then laughed at Betts's discomfiture. 'If it will help you, take a typist, or that long-legged young lady from reception you've been ogling. She'll keep your reputation intact, if that's what's bothering you. She can charge overtime – no questions asked. Anything else?'

Peter stirred himself. 'Do you have any idea when you might publish?'

McSharry considered. 'We may be pushed to run it in the next week or two; it's too close to the summer recess and there's still a lot of sport around. We need plenty of space for this, with all those great photos. I think we'll get that Nefertiti one enlarged and splash it all over the front page. Maybe run it a week earlier as a teaser – "Who is this?" I'd like as many pages as possible – four or six at least, for two or three days on the trot. And we want a big impact. D'you know, it might be best during the conference season. Much more interesting than all those speeches. On the other hand we're expecting a reshuffle: about time too, given how useless they are. Your man is likely to be involved, in which case we can announce he's been sacked, and why. He can't sue, as the substance of the copy will be true. I'd like to get a couple of interviews done with him right away too, Jim, blind – get his views on homosexuality and the age of consent, you know the sort of thing. If he isn't ditched so much the better. He will be by the time we've finished with him.'

It suited Peter also to stay out of the limelight for a while. The new British client had volunteered to hold the office fort in London while his family spent a month sunning themselves in a Spanish villa north of Malaga. Knowing he would have to clear off once the story broke gave an added piquancy to the latest liaison. He too had learned from the dying weeks of the Boswood business. His original instincts were correct: no long affairs, no suffocating love and adoration, no promises to stay for ever. Stuff all that. All that affection and romantic talk had begun to get through to him. It had made him almost wistful at times and took the edge off his protective armour. He almost felt sorry for the old fool. Had he stayed any longer, he might have stayed for ever. Like being caged, or buried alive.

Martin Chadwick poked his head round the door, his expression studiously neutral – an essential skill in a civil servant. He had practised many times in a mirror and knew he could trust his features not to betray him. The tie chosen that morning was relatively dignified, for the ministerial reshuffle was due and by the evening he would be introducing himself to a fresh face. He wondered who his new boss might be. He himself was also overdue a promotion. If Sir Nigel's replacement were interesting, he could arrange to stay another year to bed the new man in. If not he would graciously make way for a new private secretary of the incumbent's choice.

'Number Ten on the phone, Secretary of State. Shall I put them through in here?'

It was a silly question, for Nigel was not about to leave his inner office and take an important call from the Prime Minister in full hearing of his staff. He waved the official away with a nod and waited for the phone to ring once.

This was it, then. The end of his long career, the beginning of the twilight which led downhill into old age and death. How unkind of the Prime Minister to do it by means of a telephone call without the courtesy of a face-to-face meeting. There would be effusive thanks, of course. A pleasant letter on Number 10 notepaper would arrive, the text cleared with him before publication in tomorrow's *Times*. He could even write chunks of it himself, provided it wasn't too long. Whatever he wanted. It didn't matter, now. From the moment the phone handset returned to its cradle he would be an ex-Minister and, like Lucifer expelled from Elysium, would be wiped from the face of the earth. He postponed the moment as long as he could. The phone trilled at him urgently. His dismissal might be inevitable but it did not have to be welcome; he did not have to rush it.

Not a dismissal. What could he have been thinking? This was a resignation, at his own request. Nearly all ministerial careers end in tears, most at a time and date emphatically not of the Minister's choosing. The spectacular cases resulting from ministerial mis-behaviour are a minority. Most are dropped, shaking their heads in puzzled resentment, because of failure to make the grade. Thus Boswood was lucky and knew it. His longevity on the front bench made him a rare bird indeed; his gracious decommissioning rarer still. It was unmanly to gripe if the Prime Minister didn't want to see him in person.

'Nigel?' The voice in his hand squeaked impatiently. With a start his reverie ended and he put the phone to his ear, trying gruffly to clear the lump in his throat.

'Prime Minister. Good morning.'

'Ah, I'm glad I've got you. How are you, Nigel?'

The Prime Minister never was very good at getting to the point quickly. Still, he must be finding this interview as difficult as his listener.

'Fine. How can I be of service, Prime Minister?'

Now he would say it. Boswood braced himself, biting his lip.

'Ah, Nigel. Do you remember our conversation just before Christmas, about your wanting to leave? I've kept it in mind, obviously. But I wanted to ask if you would mind staying on a bit longer. The reshuffle is much more extensive than I'd imagined and if you go too it will look rather like Macmillan's night of the long knives – like a panic move. Do you get my drift? Also there's a bit of a shortage of obvious candidates for the job. Dickson really hasn't been a Minister long enough to risk, and putting Virginia there, who could do it, will look like criticism of her work at Health. So would you mind staying?'

Nigel's eyebrows shot up. He wondered if Chadwick was listening on the extension. Mind staying? He examined his reactions quickly. The emotions he expected and sought, pleasure and relief, stubbornly refused to come. He felt instead chagrined by the Prime Minister's cool approach. Everybody likes a little flattery. To be told you are wanted because you are by far the best for this particular job is delicious and (naturally) undeniable. To be asked to do a job as a bit of a favour was faintly patronising and deflating. To have it implied that you are an afterthought, that the PM is in some small way not sure if the favour is worth doing, was deeply hurtful.

Perhaps the Prime Minister, usually so punctilious, had simply forgotten Nigel's own sensitivities. He decided to give him the chance to put matters right.

'Are you sure you want me to carry on, Prime Minister?' The emphasis, not so subtle, was on the *me*.

'Well, yes, please. Is that all right? The press release has been prepared and it'll be a terrible nuisance if we have to change it.'

The PM paused and a silence ensued. Clearly the conversation was at an end. Boswood's lip trembled briefly, then his jaw jutted forward. His voice sounded huffy and he made no attempt to hide it.

'If it helps, Prime Minister. But I still wish to make way for a younger man in due course. I leave it in your capable hands.'

No sooner had the phone pinged softly back on its rest than Chadwick was at the door again, hands clasped before him, a smug expression on his face. Quite suddenly Boswood, who seldom thought ill of anyone, disliked this man – not just his secure and comfortable existence, his well-pensioned safe-for-life job, his docile wife and pretty children and the rose-strewn house in Sittingbourne. No, he disliked and detested his ruthless detachment, his ability not to care, merely to administer, to shelve difficult problems until the fickle press and twitchy Ministers found something else to chew on. Chadwick's was a charmed, protected life, as devoid of passion or commitment as it was possible to be. How Peter had opened his eyes! The cruelty and amorality behind such bland mannerisms were now visible as never before. Stung to the quick by the Prime Minister's casual ingratitude, Nigel reached for a pile of files with a deliberately possessive gesture.

'I'm staying on,' he averred brusquely. To his grim satisfaction, Chadwick's mouth dropped open. The man gabbled a few words of congratulation as Boswood waved him away. Here was one character he would not miss, not at all, when the time came.

At the other end of the phone a nasal Betty Horrocks sniffled her deepest apologies. Her duties as chairman of Whittington Conservative branch were enjoyable, occasionally arduous but seldom hazardous, until now. Taking old ladies home in the pouring rain the previous week had given her a filthy head cold. It had been so wet this summer, a real disappointment; all the gardens in Whittington were doleful and soggy and the church fête had been a washout. Even more calamitous results for the Whittington ladies now had to be reported to their Member.

'I don't know how to tell you this, Elaine, but we've had to cancel tonight's meeting in Whittington village hall. There's summer flu going around and a lot of our supporters have phoned in to say they can't make it. To tell the truth I'm not feeling too bright myself. So would you mind very much if we postponed it till another time?'

Mrs Horrocks blew her nose.

Mind? *Mind?* No, Elaine didn't mind. The ladies at Whittington would have offered a friendly audience and tittered at every anecdote however trivial. But to learn at midday that a busy weekday evening had suddenly become free, even during recess, was like experiencing divine intervention.

Elaine sympathised: 'I'm sorry to hear about the coughs and colds. It sounds as if you should take care of yourself as well. Thank you for phoning to let me know and saving me a journey. I'll agree to come again on another night, on one condition.'

Mrs Horrocks was unsure what was coming. Torn between respect and affection for Elaine and her usual bustling no-nonsense approach she hesitated. 'And what might that be, may I ask?'

'That you don't let on to *anyone* else in the constituency that the event has been cancelled, not yet, so that I can have an evening off and go home. If it gets out that I've nothing to do the phone will start and my precious time to myself will evaporate. Is that a deal?'

Mrs Horrocks laughed uproariously if croakily. 'Of course, my dear.'

With one bound she was free, thought Elaine with almost childish glee as she stuffed papers hurriedly into an old briefcase and headed down the stairs into the car park. She was wilting under the demands of the long summer recess, the only time in the year when she could join her constituents at work and school in a constant round of duty visits. Going home would be wonderful, especially as the weather seemed set fair for the evening.

The Rover was feeling its age and protested noisily as she put her foot down and slid away from London traffic. She munched a chocolate bar instead of lunch and luxuriated in feeling guilty. It would be nice, she mused wistfully, to go out and buy a new car. One with air-conditioning, so that on days like this she could arrive at a function fresh, not like a limp rag in desperate need of a shower. Then she could be with less hassle and effort what her public wanted her to be: icon and servant, inspiration and entertainment, thinker, campaigner, and on top of all this a successful mother and wife.

Wife – and lover. Surely this could not go on for ever, this state of double pleasure. It must end, but how? How, without hurting anyone? It would not even be true to say she felt herself being torn apart. Her reactions to the dilemma were curiously quiescent, perhaps because for the moment there was virtually no problem. With Mike away such a lot it was easy to deceive him, without even considering it disloyal, so routine was it. There was plenty of time to see Roger in . . .

With a jolt she realised how casually she accepted that two men shared her life. That made her immoral, surely; or amoral, perhaps, devoid of morality. Cautiously she prodded her battered conscience. Karen's illness had shaken her complacency, but now that the girl was much better and expecting her GCSE results any moment the impact of that night of terror had diminished. How strange that she, who blithely entered Parliament with such strong views on the importance of traditional marriage and family, should find herself in this position. Circumstances change things. Or maybe those principles were only codes of practice, to be modified and discarded at whim. How frightful if barely two years as an MP had made her as cynical as the rest of them already.

Troubled, she considered what her double life was doing to her, then perked up, reassured. If she were really such a calculating bitch it would show, and neither Mike nor Roger would have anything more to do with her. Two fine men, both loving and lovable; charming and attractive in their different ways, professional men, wrapped up in their work, both apparently needing her, but excluding her also from much of their lives, so that both her partnerships gave plenty of space, to herself and to the men. Perhaps that explained their durability. Seeing neither man for very long, with long periods between contacts, diluted their emotional demands on her. With Roger, even with Mike had he wanted, she could concentrate and summon up all the intensity needed, not cold-bloodedly, but with a rush of joy and exhilaration. An intense continuing affair which never let up with sex every night of the week would have exhausted her *mental* capacity in no time; that might be a fairy-tale relationship but it would never have suited her. Her first and last love was always politics. For Mike it was flying: he was bewitched by the wide soaring skies above the cloud cover, reaching out to touch the face of God, as all pilots do. Roger was the same in his world, which was also hers. This was the reason they understood each other so well: there was always tomorrow's debate, next week's vigorous row, this month's hot issue, in a political life which was carried forward on its own thrilling momentum. Everything else came unavoidably second: family, children, home, lover, spouse.

Husband. Hadn't seen him, it seemed, for ages. Freed of the constraints of motorway driving, Elaine wound down a window, slipped the Brandenburg Concertos into the cassette player and headed along the pretty back lanes leading home. The familiar music restored a soothing touch of orderliness. Rain-spattered hedgerows were still full of wild flowers, bright and undisciplined, the trees showing a hint of shorter days as their lush green foliage, welcome product of the wet summer, slowly dried out and began to rustle. In cottage gardens gnarled mossy trees were laden with apples and plums. Flower baskets hung on village lamp-posts were starting to straggle but red and pink geraniums kept up their summer-long extravaganza. She hoped Barbara next door had remembered to keep an eye on hers.

On the familiar journey between office and home, her thoughts oscillated without rhythm or conclusion between her lover, her husband and her job. Elaine knew she was not really happy unless she had something demanding to get on with, preferably with a deadline to meet that others would have found punishing. Like those years on Barham council, starting so young the year Jake died, when she needed to assuage her grief with busy days and over-full timetables. Exactly ten years ago she had been at the same time vice-chairman of social services, a senior member of the health authority, teaching twenty hours a week at the local prep school and with Karen still a small child. Mike was away most of the week, so she coped mainly by herself. *And loved it.* It had been a surprisingly good period as the pain of Jake's loss slid to an ache, a time full of achievement, increasing ambition and hope for the future. The council's busy agenda gave its part-time politicians more than enough to do. She had relished it: had pushed hard and made things happen. It had given her a real buzz. At Westminster there was no such power. No one told you when you left local government and headed for national platforms that as an MP you would exchange power for obligation, importance for impotence. It was partly that the time-scale was different. It could take weeks to see a Minister, and months after that for a decision, as often as not a refusal however effusively worded. The newest member of the smallest local council's majority party had more power than any MP.

Nor had she control of her timetable now. She had not realised how many hours would be required in the patch. Mike had not changed his rotas, yet they were lucky to see each other more than once a month. She was only home at weekends while he could not easily guarantee being there at the same time. Even weekends could be difficult for her.

She shook herself, as a dog might after getting wet, and changed the tape. The extent of her negative thoughts surprised her. Next year it should get easier to manipulate the timetable, and leave more time for herself. And for Karen.

And for Mike.

Now when did he say he would next be home? The carefully arranged conjunction, as of two planets spinning in unconnected orbits, had completely slipped her mind. Mike's diminution in her life was entirely understandable; and avoidable, if she made the effort. That would be necessary if the relationship with Roger went into decline, or if she were ever to attempt to break with him and return to normality. She pulled a wry face. Normality seemed so unattractively dull. How fortunate that Mike never complained if she were not there; just left loyal messages stuck to the fridge door: 'Kilroy was here. Hope the speech went well.' Almost a lodger. There were only 108 waking hours each week and around 80 were spoken for, week in and week out. Next year she would get it organised.

The house was in sight now; it was almost five, a beautiful evening. Pleasant enough to sit out for a drink, then shove in some laundry, open a bottle of decent wine, make an omelette and a salad, watch TV by herself – *Some Like It Hot* was on again – or feet up on the sofa with a John Mortimer or David Lodge novel. How thoroughly nice: no need to pretend, no need for a conversation with *anybody*.

Mike's silver BMW was in the garage. She was nonplussed for a moment, her first reaction a start of annoyance that her solitary evening would be up the spout. Surely he wasn't supposed to be home today? But then neither was she. Better make the best of it. She squared her shoulders, emptied her car and laden with files, bags and briefcase went round the back of the house to the kitchen door.

Mike's uniform jacket was slung over a chair, his papers and *The Times* on the kitchen table. The house was extremely quiet. The kitchen clock seemed to tick very loudly; afterwards, it would be that clock and its insistent reminder of irrecoverable time lost that she would remember. She was to give it away for Mrs Horrocks's next Bring and Buy sale.

She deposited her own things in her study, listening for sounds of life. He must be upstairs, asleep. In the hallway were his shoes, tossed carelessly near the front door. Nothing unusual in that. A pile of post lay on the hall table, some opened, the rest awaiting her attention. Two letters had fallen on to the floor and she bent to pick them up. Then she saw them.

Another pair of shoes. Woman's shoes. White, high-heeled.

Not her own.

Upstairs there was a sound. Elaine felt her mouth go dry. A tight knot formed in the pit of her stomach. The breeze from the open kitchen door wafted through the hall; somewhere a door slammed.

She looked up the stairs as Mike came out of their bedroom.

Eye to eye they met, man and wife. He was completely naked. And so was Barbara, the friendly, overweight, unloved neighbour, who was standing behind him.

Barbara gasped, covered her breasts in a curiously virginal gesture and ran back into the bedroom. Elaine could hear her yelping: 'Oh, my God! You said she wouldn't be here! Oh, God! Oh, my God! Mike, you are a pig. How could you?'

There was the sound of furniture being knocked over. Mike stood helplessly, impassively, at the top of the stairs, hands opened in an apologetic gesture, eyes unblinking. Even as she stood there, Elaine found herself coldly examining him. He was developing a bit of a paunch; the belly overhung a bit, making his private parts look smaller. Maybe it was true they shrank with age. That they had been in recent use was evident.

Barbara reappeared, crying and sobbing. She had managed to pull on a skirt and blouse, half buttoned, but not much else. Clutching crumpled beige underwear, tights and a string of pearls, she came stumbling down the stairs and went to push past Elaine. The powerful odour of sex and sweat came with her. Elaine wrinkled her nose and made herself stare. Mike did not move.

'It's your own fault!' Barbara paused, snuffling on the bottom step, her way barred. Barbara the interloper, Barbara it was who felt wronged, betrayed. 'You're never bloody well here! What's a man supposed to do – play with himself? He needs a woman, not a . . . a poster on the wall. He can't make love to you when you're on the telly. Fat lot of good you are to him .'

The woman's flesh was white, pudgy, excessive. A substantial veined breast was escaping loosely from the blouse. Coldly Elaine handed Barbara her shoes. 'I should tidy yourself up before you go outside,' she suggested in an icy, level voice.

It was an eternity while the weeping woman shuffled into more clothes in the kitchen, knocking papers wildly off the table in her haste. At last the back door banged shut. Elaine turned her attention once more to her husband.

Mike. Mike was *hers*. No one else's. Certainly not that stupid cow's from next door. Maybe what she said was true: that her husband had been neglected. But they were a couple, they had been through so much together, had made each other promises, had conceived and birthed children and watched one die, had shared their bodies, their ideas and joy and laughter. And sex. And *sex*.

Her body moved. Feet apart, lips now parted, she swayed slightly from side to side, willing her husband to compare, to continue if he wished. But not with that bitch, not with an outsider.

She kicked off her own shoes and began to climb the stairs, slowly, forcing her stockinged feet down into each tread, feeling the stubby carpet with her toes, as the wood sighed and creaked with her weight. She was breathing hard, her mouth slightly open, her own nipples hardening against her blouse. The sight of her familiar man unfamiliarly naked and the naked gross intruder woman, the powerful smell of the sex, the warm house on the soft summer evening, all combined as an extraordinarily heady aphrodisiac as she climbed the stairs towards her husband. She kept her eyes firmly fixed on his bewildered face. By the time she was halfway to the top her own blouse and bra were discarded and the trim office skirt followed. Hers was much the better figure, with its narrow waist, the black suspender belt curved tightly over firm buttocks, the dark stockings shining over well-shaped thighs: hours in the gym had seen to that. She felt supremely inviting, powerful, dominant.

She put her hand flat on to Mike's chest. From his expression she could tell he knew what she was doing, what she was asking. His eyes lost their dullness and lit with horror, but also with something altogether more animal, more primeval. His toes curled around the edge of the top step. His breath was rasping and fast, his skin clammy to her touch.

Had she known his thoughts or the history of the day Elaine might have forgiven him. Barbara hadn't been a long-term thing. She had been there, inconsidered and ignored, popping in as he came home when Elaine was busy, making him coffee, settling herself unasked at the table, chattering inconsequentially with such pleading eyes. It was all an accident. *No, that was a lie.* He had seen her several times during the summer and found himself watching the large buttocks moving almost independently, wobbling unattractively in their cotton slacks. He had been tired and not quite quick enough to turn his glance away as she busied herself at the cooker for him, so she had caught him at it, and had blushed furiously and with great longing, like a big soft dog needing to be patted. It was such a while since he had had a woman, Elaine or anyone else, and celibacy was certainly not part of his natural make-up. As Barbara turned to face him, his eyes had wandered of their own accord to the curving V between her thighs. She was close enough to touch, standing there, hands clasped, feminine and available, wanting it as much, as simply, as he did. He had leaned across and stroked her thigh as she quivered under his hand, and moved closer until his fingers slipped firmly inside the V. The bargain was made. And so it had happened, then and again on one other occasion, and by arrangement today when he was sure Elaine would be absent. And interrupted before he was finished; indeed, just as he was getting started. The memory of the woman's thighs reminded him. Not bloody finished yet.

Elaine could sense it, and she gestured at the open door behind him.

'This is my bedroom,' she said, with a hint of menace in the allure of her voice.

As his wife breathed to speak, her shoulders moved so that Mike saw as if for the first time her clear firm living flesh, and her breath was soft on his own body. His look took in her breasts, the curve of her belly, the thighs, clean and straight. The erection which had died a few moments ago began to resurface as if to salute this lovely, angry female. As she had guessed might happen, there arose in her husband the same undiluted lust for her as when first he had seen her at university and had wanted badly to bed her long before he even knew her name.

Her low voice set his nerves tingling. 'Mine. And yours. We haven't employed it properly together for a long time. Perhaps you'd better show me what you've been using it for.'

He moved backwards unprotestingly, only needing her to make the move. So she made him make love to her: for the first time in their lives without affection or kissing on the mouth, but kissing and sucking and biting everywhere else, as animals might, crying and hurting, until she cried out with it: 'Show me what you did to her! Show me! Show me!'

And he did, with fierce passion and force, expressing all the pent-up frustration, not merely the months of empty asexuality, not only the denial and exclusion from her life, but the slow ebb of sovereignty in his own home as his wife had become seduced by life beyond it. And she, in an exact matching, knew precisely what hurt him as he pounded into her, and both struggled with it and grew wilder, needing the appalling reminder that she was a woman first, last and always, and that this was her wedded man whom she had betrayed, long before his betrayal.

On the bedclothes she could detect Barbara, and with a yell hurled the pillow over to the other side of the room, knocking over ornaments with a crash. Love, they call it. This was not love, this furious coupling. His shame turned to anger and to brutality, but it was she who forced him and he could not prevent her or stop himself, as if she were the stronger partner and he an errant wife for whom forced sexual congress was the punishment.

And then as he climaxed she hit him, hard across the face, again and again, crashing her forearm into his mouth until he bled. He screamed out like a wounded beast and collapsed down on top of her, wiping his bloodied cheek on her breast, whimpering, as a terrified infant might nuzzle its mother. And he wept, as if his heart would break, as he never wept when their baby died; and he said terrible things about her absences, and her turning away, and her leaving a black hole in space without gravity or life-forms, where once there had been love and sharing and hope and fulfilment.

He did not fight back. She swore at him, obscenities rising in her mouth like bile. She hit him again, kneeling over him as he raised his arms to protect himself, turning his wounded face away. She howled out all her own misery and agony, not knowing or caring, aware only that everything must unavoidably change. But that it should change in such a fashion was a terrifying blow. The world she took so much for granted had vanished, the moment Barbara's white shoes had fallen to the hall floor.

Eventually her passion was spent. The two lay still, tumbled together but not touching. Now, having fought what had come between them, they might once more have come together; but it did not happen and the moment passed. She pulled the duvet around her and stumbled towards the door. She left her husband sobbing quietly on their bed, curled up like a child brutalised by a drunken parent.

She was a mess, besmirched with bloodstains, fouled with disgust and horror and sex. For the second time in less than a year her home had been invaded by invisible demons. What was happening to her? In a daze she showered, the green shower gel incongruous, stinging and crude. She searched dully in the airing cupboard and found and pulled on underwear, clean cotton trousers and a sweater. Absolutely drained of emotion she towelled her hair and tied it back. Habit, healing habit, was slowly returning. She put out fresh towels, even tapped on the bedroom door and spoke in a low voice: 'Bathroom's free.'

Devoid still of conscious sense she went downstairs and wandered around for a long time, touching everyday objects as if they were unreal. After a while she found herself in her study, where she first reached for the Glenfiddich, then decided against. Her daytime mind with its natural defences was slowly returning. There was no point in getting drunk; she would be tempted into a parallel confession, if only to make Mike feel better, and that would not do. Only one person in this house had any explaining to do and it wasn't her.

In the kitchen she sat down at the table and tried to think. The loud ticking of the kitchen clock got on her nerves. Irritated at yet another intrusion she put the clock in a drawer, where it ticked softly on in protest. With a start she realised it was nearly seven. Suddenly she felt totally exhausted, put her head down on her arms on the kitchen table, and fell asleep.

'Would you like some coffee?' Mike was dressed, smelling of soap and standing sheepishly at the door.

She nodded wordlessly. He busied himself in silence for a few moments, then put the mug in front of her, found her sweeteners and set them like a peace offering on the table. After a moment's hesitation he sat down opposite her.

Married people do not sit opposite. You can tell them in restaurants, seated side by side, those who know each other very well, who no longer need to gaze into the loved one's eyes; who have no compulsion to touch toes or legs under a table, or to feign lovemaking, for they have somewhere to go to make love, all night if they want. You can tell married people in a bar: they are the ones who do not chat animatedly to each other, who do not ask if the drink is OK, who are no longer endlessly solicitous of the other's welfare. With married people a *modus vivendi* has long since been established, discarding the bits that don't suit, like throwing away the peel of an orange or a banana or not eating the marzipan off a cake. Married people do not sit opposite in their own kitchen to talk quietly to each other. This marriage had ended. Elaine felt real foreboding and fear.

Mike took a deep breath and started. The side of his face where she hit him was swollen red. Tomorrow his flesh would be dark and livid, a mark of Cain.

'If it will help, Elaine, I'm sorry.'

She waited.

'It's not a longstanding ... er ... affair. I don't expect you to believe that, but it's true. Only for the last few weeks.'

He needed to explain, but part of the revenge was to deny him the chance. She waved him away.

'I don't want to know the sordid details, Mike. Just tell me what you want to do.'

He took a long swallow of his coffee and examined the remaining contents carefully, as if the answer lay at the bottom of the mug. His sigh of resigned despair touched her to the quick.

'I don't know; only that I don't want to carry on as we have been doing. I love you very much – well, I did. You've not been around much for me to love since you got elected. Don't get me wrong, I am very proud of you, and Karen is too. But you're never here. And when you are you never have time for us, only for your bloody voters. They get the best of you – the only time we see you with your hair done and make-up is when you're going out, never for me or Karen.'

'But I have to get dressed up for my job!' she protested. 'The last thing I want when I have any time off is to wear a flipping suit! Have a heart – you take off your uniform the moment you get home.' The gold-braided jacket was still on the back of the chair, mute testimony to the last moment when their marriage was still intact. She allowed resentment to well up. 'Looks as if you take off everything else too.'

He swallowed hard. 'We cannot carry on like this. We don't have a marriage any more. We'd have had to talk about it sooner or later – had to make an appointment in our diaries to do so, probably.'

'That's as much your fault as mine,' she flashed, but she was tiring of the argument. She knew what she ought to say was that she loved him too, liked being married to him, wanted him to stay, would make amends, spend more time at home. It would have been extremely difficult to extricate herself from her current obligations, perhaps even finish with Roger, but not impossible. Coolly, shocked, she realised that she did not want to. The last occasion when she had consulted her diary, apart from crossing off tonight's meeting, had been when Roger had phoned her at the flat to ask her if she could keep Tuesday free. Her happy affirmative, in contrast with her profound reluctance now, told her all she needed to know. To keep Mike happy would require dramatic alterations in her life, options she was not willing to put on the table. Especially not giving up Roger. Of course there were sacrifices in having a secret affair like that, but in one sense each loss was a comparative gain. No public appearances with him meant no pretence, no obligations of any kind. No birthday cards, no cufflinks, no agonising over gifts at all – they were *verboten*. Yet the risks added spice and made each moment precious – exactly the opposite to taking it all for granted and becoming jaded as with Mike. Tonight's extraordinary performance could not be repeated; it had been a dangerous row of monumental proportions which ripped apart her perception of sex with her husband. She and Mike would not have intercourse again.

He was right, it wasn't much of a marriage.

'I am not going to fight you,' she whispered. 'Do what you want.'

He looked at her as if to say more, then his mouth tightened and he shrugged just slightly. Instead he gathered up his papers and jacket and went out. She heard his car revving throatily as it scrunched away over the gravel.

CHAPTER TWENTY-TWO

Softly, imperceptibly, summer days turned cooler and shorter. Karen Stalker collected a clutch of respectable GCSEs with five A grades, which enabled her to move on to a college of further education in the nearby town. Out went the hated stained school uniform, striped tie and masculine blazer with its tattered inked-over badge, yet the sexy black fashions of a year earlier did not reappear, even though her figure would have suited them. Too many lessons had been learned to forget in a hurry.

Her own resilience surprised her, but then she was her mother's daughter, tough and practical and not much given to introspection. Perhaps a blessed mechanism of self-protection was at work. As time went by the number of nights diminished when she lay awake grieving either for herself or for her parents. It helped not to hide matters away but to allow her thoughts to flow freely, to try re-arranging them in a more orderly sequence, like cutting up meat into small chunks and chewing thoroughly before attempting to swallow. Gradually the pile of worries heaped on her plate seemed to come under control. It also helped to be working hard at her studies, keeping her sights firmly set on A levels and university in two years' time.

At any rate she could ensure that her own life was not wrecked by all the strange goings-on at home. Those she loved seemed so preoccupied. Thus she learned by example how to be self-absorbed in a self-centred world, to become more self-sufficient and not to cry for help. Her mother noticed the change and approved. She put the girl's disciplined calmness down to increasing maturity and the college atmosphere, and congratulated herself on successfully shielding the child from the most recent trouble.

For Karen knew nothing about the incident involving the white shoes. However furious and bereft her mother might be there was no point in dragging Karen in as well. The matter was entirely between two adults, or rather three. It had caused enough misery and was better kept contained. That also seemed to be Barbara's attitude, for after a few days moping around her house weeping and hiding from Elaine she had packed her bags and disappeared. A 'For Sale' sign soon appeared in her driveway.

Elaine's instinct dictated that it would not be right to turn Karen's mind against her own father, who might have been foolish but in a bleakly endearing way had shown that he was only human. Indeed many of the events of that miserable afternoon reminded Elaine of what had drawn her most to her husband when he was younger: his sexiness, his willingness to take risks, his disregard of convention. In challenging him to lovemaking, she had queried whether he too remembered those early days; and he had.

Mike had left the house and not returned, staying the night in an airport hotel. His office let her know his whereabouts at his request from then on, precisely, impersonally. How ironic that she knew more about his movements now than before, when they had been ostensibly happily married. Elaine felt no urge to chase or plead with him. He was the one who had misbehaved and been caught; he the one who had left that night. It was for Mike to make the next move, as she continued living in the same house, paying the bills and acting as if nothing had happened. It was as if she were scarcely breathing, in the hope that nothing would change, that no awful decisions would be required from her. She reasoned that making any contact with him would have been unwise, would have raised the emotional temperature once again. If this marriage were to fall apart it would do so gently and without further recrimination. Old love and shared tenderness in the past meant not wanting to hurt or damage each other any more. So, for the time being, there would be no lawyers, no signed papers, no divorce. Perhaps if everything were handled with kid gloves now, some day the two could be friends again in a wary fashion; or at least not enemies.

It could not be kept a secret for ever. Eventually one quiet Friday afternoon on the way home from college, in answer to a simple question, Elaine told Karen that her father had left, that it was nothing to do with Roger, that the two had simply decided to live apart for a while, that it was not even formalised, they were not legally separated and as far as she was concerned did not want to be. The girl wept a little, but her mother seemed resigned rather than actively unhappy. Her father's leaving was no surprise, given the decoupling which had been under way for some time, on which Karen herself had commented after his non-appearance at her hospital bedside. Elaine repeated without much conviction the formula that all marriages go through bad patches, as Karen remarked how common was this pattern among her friends. Making marriage work must be fiendishly difficult.

There were changes afoot elsewhere. Gerry Keown was promoted, after two and a half years in the job. Martin Chadwick arranged for his own rapid elevation out of Nigel's glowering clutches and was put in charge of the forthcoming environment summit in London; Fiona Murray from Roger Dickson's office, red-haired, sleek and self-controlled, took his place. The housing market was moving at last, though sluggishly. Finland and Austria completed their negotiations and prepared to join the European Community, with two more countries close behind. The British economy returned to modest growth after three years of decline, indeed had the highest growth rate in Europe, though since all the other countries were in trouble that was nothing much to boast about. Over 200,000 UK companies had gone out of business in the longest recession since the 1930s. There were race riots in Potsdam and Leipzig against Turks and Romanians, in Marseilles against black migrants from the Magreb, in Los Angeles by black Americans against Koreans. The north of Italy plotted secession from the rest, fed up with paying for corrupt national politicians and the Mafia. The Channel Tunnel project was put back another year. Latvia joined Lithuania in returning a new communist government, while the Russians became the world's biggest suppliers of arms for hard currency. President Clinton cut the American defence budget by $76 billion and survived an assassination attempt by a disgruntled ex-soldier, while Jacques Delors prepared to rescue France. The dismal, debt-ridden nineties, breaker of promises, graveyard of hope and harbinger of despair, rolled on. Only the currency speculators were smiling.

By autumn, the political atmosphere in Britain had shifted, as if a vast iced-over lake was beginning to experience the first hints of a thaw. Under the feet came rumbling tremors as if great ice-floes were breaking off and starting imperceptibly to move. From this point the time to the next great contest was shorter than the distance from the last. In a Parliament lasting a maximum of five years the halfway mark had been passed. All thoughts began to turn towards the next general election.

'Roger! You there? Do you want your white tie as well as black?'

Caroline Dickson waited for an answer, her arms full of clean shirts and underwear. It was already dark and the lights in the bedroom were switched on, reflecting off gold and green House of Commons cufflinks and the pearl buttons on his dress shirt. Packing for Party Conference was a tedious but essential chore yet never quite routine. The Dicksons had chosen to go the following day, Monday, ready for an early attendance on Tuesday morning, and to stay till Friday and the Prime Minister's hopefully rousing closing speech to the party faithful. Caroline was proud that Roger was now a recognised figure, called on to speak at fringe meetings and to do the rounds of receptions and balls. There had been so much uncertainty about the summer reshuffle that the Department of the Environment would be taking a back seat, though a junior Minister from the Lords would be addressing a question-and-answer session on the council tax, which came to much the same thing.

The conference location this year was Bournemouth. A great improvement over horrible old Blackpool, Caroline reflected, Blackpool with its ghastly boarding houses and miles of boring windy promenade going nowhere. Bournemouth, blameless Bournemouth, with its neat flower-beds, studiously snobbish, had survived the recession reasonably well, though its genteel elderly grumbled over low interest rates all the way to the bank.

There was no answer from downstairs. Caroline placed the garments carefully in the suitcases and went to lean over the banister.

Roger was in the darkened hallway, phone pressed to his ear with one hand, banging the other fist hard in a gesture of impotent fury into the wainscoting. One look at his grim face made Caroline retreat quickly. She sat on the top step, head cocked.

'They've done *what*? Oh, Christ . . . Yes, I see . . . Yes, of course, Chief. My God, we could have done without this.' A pause, a nod. He reached for a pencil. 'Where is he, may I ask? . . . Right. Is he OK? . . . No, I'm serious. He'll be horribly upset.'

The call continued for a few minutes more, with the other voice agitated and rapid. Then Roger put the handset back on its cradle and stood, hands thrust in trouser pockets, head bowed.

'Sounds like trouble.' Caroline was matter-of-fact.

'Too right. That was the Chief Whip. Remember the Parkinson business at the Party Conference in 1984? Dreadful for everyone concerned, except the press, who had a field day. Well, we're about to have a rerun. With a modern twist.'

Caroline raised an eyebrow. Her husband looked worried, not amused or detached. That meant they would be close to the matter. She decided to tease a little, to try to lift that black mask.

'Really? Roger, what have you been up to?'

He looked up quickly, then passed a hand over his brow, as if trying to read a hidden message. Immediately Caroline regretted her levity, and went downstairs to stand beside her husband. He turned to her and slipped an arm around her waist.

'Not me, sweetheart. Not this time, anyway. It's Nigel Boswood. It appears he's been harbouring a prostitute in his London house who has been singing to the press. It's all over the first editions. The *Globe* has some lurid photos, which clearly show poor Nigel compromised. Not pleasant, especially not for him.'

Caroline sensed that there was more to come and teased again, gently. 'Nigel is a lovely person. Maybe being seen with an attractive woman might do his reputation some good.'

With a start Roger realised how little he talked to his wife about his job and the people with whom he shared every waking hour. Caroline was not the sort to indulge in political gossip. Her guileless remark revealed her ignorance of the long-standing rumours about his boss.

'I know what you mean, Caroline, but this is different. For a start, the tart is one-third Nigel's age, young enough to be not just a child but a grandchild. Secondly the photos are, I hear, absolutely diabolical, with Nigel dressed up as some wild-eyed Egyptian queen, which is almost appropriate – because thirdly it isn't some busty madam, it's a boy, and under age at that.'

'Oh, my God.' Caroline sat down again on the bottom step, her eyes wide with horror. 'I never realised Nigel was . . .' Her voice tailed off. 'You know . . . like that. What has he been up to, Roger? What did the Chief say?'

Her husband gave a helpless shrug. 'Not much more than I've told you. Apparently the press are besieging the hotel in Bournemouth, as you'd expect. Nigel went up there all innocent this afternoon. I'm asked to go and help all I can. The lawyers are on their way. We'll have to decide tonight whether we can sue.'

'How awful.' Caroline began to think through the implications. Her husband was very close to Nigel Boswood and would want to be sympathetic and helpful. If Nigel were unable to do his work it would naturally fall on Roger's shoulders. On the other hand, if there was nastiness it did not do to be too close to it. Dirt has a habit of being contagious.

Roger continued in a sombre tone, 'They've tried for an injunction against the paper but got nowhere. We never got around to tightening the law on privacy; we argued about it, messed about but never made any effective changes. Not that it would do any good, anyway. We never got round to fulfilling those election promises we made so blithely to homosexuals either, about changing the law. This little squirt who's about to ruin Nigel's life is held legally incapable of making up his own mind who he wants to sleep with. So the police and the Vice Squad are likely to be involved, gross indecency or something of that ilk.'

He paused for breath, his voice bitter. Caroline put out a hand to him, beseeching him not to take the pain into himself. It was nothing to do with him. Angrily Roger scowled at his wife. He wanted Elaine, quickly, suddenly. She would understand the appalling guilt and fury welling up in his own breast. He had known about this for – what? – ages, since the boy had appeared draped provocatively on Nigel's bed at Blackpool. A year ago. He could kick himself for having fastidiously said nothing whatever to Nigel, not asked any pointed questions, not faced the man with the danger and wholesale foolishness of his actions, as a former whip should. He should have discussed the matter in confidence with the Chief Whip, dreadfully disloyal as it would have seemed at the time. Then Nigel would have been released promptly as he had requested last summer, instead of trailing on. Dickson struck his forehead with the palm of his left hand in a gesture of despair, trying to get his own brain into gear. Worst of all, the party was responsible, for the reasons he had blurted out to his wife, and which he would elaborate for weeks to come to Elaine: because, in the confusion and muddle over the Exchange Rate Mechanism and Maastricht and the Euro-elections, all the rows over the loss of sovereignty to Brussels, no one had thought to make good use of the meagre powers which still remained to the Westminster Parliament, to abolish outmoded laws affecting millions of ordinary people. All it would have taken was a bit of courage, a little finesse, a willingness to create a result instead of this pathetic waiting for events to overwhelm them.

Now one smart boy had pocketed a fat cheque and talked. Sold his photos for a mess of money, and sold Nigel down the river at the same time. Poor Nigel. Poor tragic bastard. The thought of his mentor galvanised Dickson into action.

'We have to go tonight, Caroline. The car's ready. How long will it take you to finish packing? Twenty minutes? Fine. We'll leave as soon as you're done. Take everything I might need. I have to make some phone calls. God almighty, what a business.'

As she ran back up the stairs, Dickson hesitated, waiting till the bedroom door banged shut and Caroline could be heard muttering to herself. Quickly he dialled Elaine, spoke low and urgently, told her the gist of the story. 'There will be press everywhere. Keep your head down.' He spoke next to Fiona, who already knew, warning her to be ready for a huge media onslaught. Then he rang Andrew and arranged to meet. He called the hotel twice but Nigel's line was engaged. He paused, phone in hand, his eye running down the yellow departmental card with personal numbers which he kept in the inner pocket of his wallet.

His heart sank and he put the phone down quietly. It was all worse, far worse than he had first thought.

Below his own name, below the other Ministers and their private secretaries and drivers and car phone numbers, below Andrew

Muncastle the PPS, one name jumped out. One name whose significance he had not appreciated till now. One person who would, even more than Nigel Boswood himself, bear the brunt of the terrible fear and hatred which would pour forth as a result of tonight's revelations: Marcus Carey, special adviser to the Department of the Environment, and Nigel's chosen successor at Milton and Hambridge.

Caroline drove quickly through the darkness as Roger brooded and answered her scattered questions. 'We have to do everything we can to avoid a by-election,' he explained grimly. 'Partly for the obvious reason that we can't afford to lose with a tiny parliamentary majority. Look at Newbury and Christchurch. And I'm not so sure that we'll win them all back at the general election. Do you realise we haven't won a by-election for five years? Not even with 20,000 majorities. Nigel's is of that order, I think.'

BBC radio news crackled as the announcer read pallid lines about Boswood's refusal to comment on stories about his private life, being closeted with his lawyers, yet the excitement in his voice alerted his audience. Roger turned the volume up for a moment and listened, then continued.

'Worst, he has the Liberals second. About the only thing they're good at is winning by-elections. They'll use whatever methods they can. Thoroughly nasty lot. God, I hate them.'

'I thought you hated socialists.' Caroline was not really interested, but if Roger needed to talk her duty was to encourage him. She did not realise he was not muttering to her. In the car with him, warm, understanding and entirely on his wavelength, was a woman slightly younger than herself with a mass of blonde hair and gleaming pearl earrings, a woman who understood the complex subterfuges of politics and where the invisible shifting line was to be drawn between cynicism and decency. With her he could voice his real feelings and soothe his conscience, which insisted that he was in part responsible both as a member of a government which had failed to deliver and as friend, colleague and ally of the hapless target.

'I don't like what the socialists stand for,' he began to explain slowly. 'But on the whole, when we fight Labour, we fight nose to nose and can recognise what we're fighting about. There's a clear and consistent philosophy there, however much their theoreticians and image-makers dress up the rhetoric. If you want greater equality, you tend to vote Labour. If you want greater opportunity, you tend to vote Tory. At least with Labour I understand my opponents' beliefs and I respect them. The Liberals are a different kettle of fish altogether. You never know what they stand for, from one election to another, even from one by-election to another. One minute they're demanding a carbon tax to stop global warming, the next they're campaigning against VAT on fuel. In by-elections they can sneer and criticise and moralise and be holier than thou to their heart's content. I hate them. I really do, far more than Labour.'

'You think they would be strong in Milton and Hambridge?'

'Strong? My God, they would make mincemeat out of Carey. It doesn't bear thinking about. He's a nice bloke, but – I mean! Alison's a good girl. Perhaps he should pull out graciously and refuse the nomination: but that'd cause a hell of a row as well. And to be truthful, if I'm right, it wouldn't make much difference. We simply have to persuade Nigel not to resign his seat, not under any circumstances.'

Dutifully Caroline followed his points but was aware he was assuming more knowledge than she possessed. 'Will he resign as Secretary of State, do you think?'

Dickson realised his lack of awareness of Boswood's state of mind. 'I've no idea till I talk to him. He was wanting to resign earlier this year but the PM wouldn't let him. Now the PM will be the prime mover. He loathes having his Cabinet chosen for him by the press. That's why he let Mellor drag on for months and why he didn't make the Chancellor resign after Black Wednesday. It's a big personal mark in the Prime Minister's favour – Margaret used to slip the leash at the first sign of trouble – but it can prolong the uncertainty and make things worse. I can't see that Nigel can stay, frankly. The best might be if he quits the department but not the Commons.'

He stopped suddenly, not wanting to embroil his wife; but Elaine would have leapt at once to the conclusions that were already dancing in his own brain.

Caroline was not stupid. She drove quietly for a few minutes, clearing traffic on the M3, then settled into the middle lane of the motorway, turned down the radio and slowed slightly. Her head half turned to her husband.

'If that happens, what then, darling? How does it affect you?'

He decided to be flippant. No point in raising her hopes. 'Oh, nothing much, probably. If the PM thought I was ready for a leg-up he could have done it in July. I haven't been a Minister of State all that long and it's usual to do a fair stretch before getting into Cabinet.'

'Huh!' His wife's loyalty leapt to the fore. 'How long was Virginia a Minister of State before getting into Cabinet? Or Portillo? Or Mrs Shephard? Or Peter Lilley, come to that? One moment Lilley was stumbling around in the Budget debate as the Chancellor's PPS, and two years later he was Secretary of State for Trade and Industry. You've spent three years as a whip, too, don't forget. If the chance comes, leap at it. I'll back you all the way. After all, you are my husband.'

Roger did not answer. Being in the right place at the right time could be all that really mattered.

Two groups of men in two rooms, late that night, a hundred miles apart. Both with lawyers and briefcases and papers.

In the *Globe*'s penthouse suite the owner was on a fleeting visit. He was making Australian wisecracks as he sipped champagne and fingered enlargements of Peter's photographs scattered around the leather-topped desk. Behind him in a dark shiny suit the paper's senior legal adviser hovered on tiptoe, wary and self-congratulatory. There would be no libel case, not with these photographs. A picture was worth a thousand words. And a few thousands pounds; cheap at the price. He hoped his junior partner was enjoying the boy's company in that secluded hotel in Guernsey, well out of sight at least till Thursday. It didn't matter much after that: the whole story would be known by then.

With the owner sat McSharry, the editor, smiling quietly to himself, a glass of orange juice untouched at his side. There would be more work to do this night before he could relax. By contrast, the news editor Nick Thwaite had spread himself expansively in a large leather armchair and cradled a treble whisky, proud that he had created this jewel in the crown. But the editor and the owner between them knew better to whom to give the credit: each naturally to the other, at least in public.

Jim Betts sat a little way from the stars, nibbling a hangnail watchfully. It was said that the editor had once been a lowly reporter on the very same newspaper, and had walked out in a blaze of glory after a spectacular row, vowing to return some day, in charge. It had taken him just ten years to do it. His elevation meant there was hope for anyone, though Betts preferred to avoid trouble if possible on his way to an editor's chair.

Of the men in the penthouse none was driven by an overpowering interest in money. Motivations varied, but the excitement of the chase, of scenting a quarry, particularly a Cabinet Minister, of forcing a resignation and thus making a dent in history, ultimately demonstrating that there was still a place for newspapers in an increasingly electronic world – and that it was still newspapers, especially the tabloids, which set the agenda of popular culture in the United Kingdom – these noble notions grabbed such men, raising their blood pressure, morale and glasses all at once.

McSharry turned over suggested layouts and enlargements, emphasising his words with swift strokes of a blue pencil.

'Last Thursday, Friday and Saturday we led on the front page with the blown-up photograph of Boswood as Queen Nefertiti with a thousand-pound prize for guessing who it was. We had several correct answers including one from Switzerland faxed in this morning – could have been a waiter at the party, I suppose. Tonight's edition has six pages devoted to the story, and the next day's the same. Not quite as good as a topless royal, but almost.'

Thwaite leaned over and picked up a proof sheet. 'You'll love this.' He winked at the owner, and began to read out loud:

NAUGHTY NIGEL NOBBLED

Naughty Nigel Boswood, boss at the Department of the Environment, shocked Tory faithful arriving in Bournemouth with amazing revelations of his secret sex life. Sir Nigel, 61 in January and 30 years an MP, tenth Baronet and cousin to the Earl of Cambridge, moves in the highest circles and had an impeccable reputation – until now.

A lifelong bachelor, for the last two years Sir Nigel has had a love nest in the basement of his £300,000 Mayfair house, where he set up a boy then aged only 18. Victim Peter Manley was taken penniless from the streets and obliged repeatedly to perform perverted sexual acts in return for a roof over his head.

Even now Sir Nigel Boswood, caught with his pants down, is denying our allegations and threatening to sue the *Globe*. We say, *Go ahead, Sir Nigel* ... Talk to your fancy Mayfair lawyers: you'll need them. It isn't a writ you should be serving. It's a stretch in jail.

Betts wriggled and smirked. His deathless prose sounded rather fine. Thwaite put down the newspaper, chortling.

The owner was intrigued. 'You're going to take him over two things – hiding his love life and exploiting this kid? What about the police?'

'The police can't act without a complaint, and right now we have the complainant,' Thwaite replied. 'We plan to bring the boy back mid-week. He still won't say if he'll press charges, and without him there's not much of a case; the photos may be enough to convince the general public and sell a few more newspapers, but they might not stand up in a court of law. I mean, none of the pics shows them actually doing it, do they? If the boy says he was just posing, with a good brief the jury might throw it out. The Director of Public Prosecutions has suffered enough setbacks recently without risking any more. It doesn't matter much to us, anyway. The contract is exclusive with or without the police.'

'I know him best and I don't think he will press charges,' Betts averred. The four looked at him; they had almost forgotten his existence. 'I mean, it stands to reason. He's a tart, isn't he? Had a few more lovers than old Nigel, I'll bet. If there's enough money flying around from the other papers, some bright spark will come forward to tell the true tale of Blue Peter, whoever he is.'

'Murky waters,' said the owner, and chuckled again. Tomorrow he would be off to Los Angeles and then to Beijing, where lucrative contracts for cable television were being dangled by the Chinese government. The Americans were also interested in a new satellite Voice of America operation, now that so many Chinese owned TVs. With a bit of luck and hard bargaining he might land both.

In another penthouse suite on the coast a group of deeply worried men sat in high-backed chairs arranged in an awkward semicircle. Their conversation would be exceedingly tricky, every word chosen with the utmost care. There was no champagne. The floor was littered with newspapers, turned face down in a tactful gesture.

Nigel Boswood slumped forward wretchedly, head in his hands. Dickson and Muncastle, both troubled and anxious, sat at a respectful distance almost opposite. In the background, trying to be invisible, was the special adviser, torn between shock at the night's revelations and excitement at their possible effect on his own life, his features composed into non-judgemental sympathy. The suite belonged to the Chief Whip, who stood near Nigel, a hand briefly on the man's shoulder. His considerable negotiating skills had helped the government survive in this ghastly, difficult Parliament, so far. On one occasion he threatened refusniks with being shopped to their wives. There was no such scenario now. Nigel may have landed the government in a pile of ordure, but he needed help, not condemnation.

Two lawyers conferred in hushed tones. One, the Attorney-General, was charged with giving the government legal advice. He was often in attendance at Cabinet though not a member of the Cabinet himself. He was tall, burly and good-natured. The other was better known, often pictured in the tabloids during lurid Old Bailey cases: a spare, bloodless man in a dusty black suit and a shirt with a frayed cuff, well into his sixties but not looking it. Since the Attorney's responsibilities were restricted to advising the government, a distinction adhered to scrupulously, Mr Wharton had been hurriedly retained on Nigel's behalf. As a successful practitioner in the esoteric world of libel law, he would charge his client over £250 for each hour's service. The clock had been ticking since the first phone call.

Earlier that evening Andrew had cautiously phoned Miranda, who had been willing to volunteer information, which now he shared, without revealing its source. 'The *Globe* intends, I understand, to run next a complete interview with the boy who calls himself Peter, complete with more photographs. Skiing in Switzerland last winter, all very ordinary, the idea being to show it was a long-standing relationship, not a one-night stand.'

The picture of Nigel in a dressing gown was best not mentioned; everyone would see it in due course. Nor did it matter that the *Globe* were being wildly inconsistent, claiming both that the boy was forced into an unhappy relationship and that it had lasted a long time and involved cheery holidays. Consistency and reliability are not required of such newspapers.

Andrew had the attention of the room. 'That's day two. Day three is Wednesday, when party night will be described in vivid detail. Some of those pictures have already been published but I gather they're having difficulties with their own lawyers as one or two are a bit risqué.'

The Chief Whip kept his face impassive but raised a condemnatory eyebrow. 'No doubt they'll appear sooner or later. The *Sport* would be thrilled to have them,' he remarked drily. 'Go on, Andrew. What else does your mole say?'

'Day four is Thursday. A lot of tear-jerking stuff is planned, all about this tragic boy's early life in care, and how he was exploited by Sir Nigel here—'

The object of the exercise gave a great racking sob which hung on the air as a reproach to them all.

Andrew swallowed. 'Sorry, Nigel. You gave them an interview during the summer, didn't you? One of many, I know, but they've picked up particular questions about young people, homelessness and so on. You said you were worried about youngsters sleeping rough and wanted to do more for them. It's going to be twisted and used against you, I'm afraid.'

He turned to the Chief Whip. 'I couldn't find out any more than that. Sorry. My contact dried up at that point.'

The Chief was quietly impressed. Muncastle had made enquiries off his own bat; a little initiative was most welcome.

'Andrew, thank you. My guess is that they'll produce the rabbit from the hat at some stage, probably Thursday. That makes sense. It would grab all the headlines on Friday and Saturday and obliterate even the Prime Minister's pep-talk to the nation. Talk about wrecking the conference! I'm afraid all our efforts at news management this glorious week are looking distinctly bleak.'

Wharton coughed discreetly. The best cases were those where everyone concerned was determined to see the other side in court and both parties could afford to lose a packet. This case was sliding quietly through his fingers. He leaned forward unctuously. 'I know this may seem unnecessary, but I do have to ask, Sir Nigel: are all these stories true?'

The room's occupants held their breath. If Nigel denied it his word must be accepted and acted upon. Either way meant trouble.

Nigel nodded and accepted his fate wordlessly, tears running down his cheeks. He looked old and broken. The famous face was wrinkled, hang-dog, with none of the puffed-up bonhomie that had been his trademark. His companions sat sadly for a moment, moved to pity.

Roger broke the silence, as gently as possible. 'Nigel, we may not get another chance to talk much. Do you want to tell us what happened?'

Boswood shook his head. Yet he owed it to these people, who would defend and shield him for a while, to put the record straight. He spoke as none of them had heard him before, slowly, agonised, as if addressing a faraway shadow only he could see.

'I'm not sure I know myself. I thought he was the best thing that had ever happened to me. I was going to retire and live a normal life with him. Going to tell everybody – "come out". Stop lying. Live like everyone else. At least, that was the plan.'

Andrew examined his shoes in embarrassment; Marcus caught his breath.

The Chief was brusque. This was no time to be sentimental. From the sound of it, hurting Nigel's feelings was not at issue; the boy had done that with a vengeance, and utterly destroyed a good man. It was tragic but one had to be practical. 'Well, the truth is out now. Do we need to detail Mr Wharton any longer? If we can't sue he might as well go back to London.'

The lawyer rose. Quite right; no point in wasting precious time. Three other big cases lay on his desk in Fetter Lane – the washed-up actress who had never slept with the South African politician, the Essex builder with more money than sense who wouldn't dream of passing wads of cash under the table, the Sunday newspaper which had sacked its finance director after finding his fingers in the till. A busy few months loomed, win or lose. He gathered his papers with an air of anxious neutrality, shook hands rapidly and left.

Nigel rose and lumbered heavily to the desk where he rummaged through files. 'I've written a letter of resignation.'

The Chief held up his hand. 'Not yet, Nigel. The PM wants to talk to you when he gets here tomorrow. He'd like to test the water, find out what the party thinks. You're to say nothing, talk to no one. It mightn't be as bad as all that. These are the 1990s; maybe attitudes have changed.'

The Prime Minister had refused to make a curt dismissal, or a sacking of any kind. If Boswood were to go it was to be in his own time and of his own volition. The PM had stopped short of indicating that, for himself, he would be willing to have a gay man in the Cabinet. After all, gays could be senior civil servants – the law excluding them from sensitive posts had been quietly changed some time before. They could be generals as long as they kept quiet and slept alone. They could be bishops, and several were, provided they kept their hands off choirboys. They could serve in the police and write leaders for *The Times* and win prizes as top columnists. A fair number were MPs, it stood to reason. Surely the day would come when, just as divorced men could serve in the nation's highest offices, homosexuals could too. Thus the Prime Minister decided to wait a couple of days to assess public reaction. How seriously would the *hoi polloi* view Sir Nigel's tastes, and would they regard him as unfit for public office?

The public fell about laughing. That was the trouble. The question of fitness or otherwise simply didn't arise. The spectacle of a Cabinet Minister making a fool of himself convulsed the nation as they read their newspapers, eyes rounded and popping in every corner of the land. In a dismal world it was wonderful to have something ridiculous to laugh at. Press from other countries piled in, taking advantage of the opportunity to publish lurid details kept secret about their own politicians. Cameramen camped in the rain for days outside the house in Ebury Street, hung precariously like black crows from trees nearby, perched long ladders against the back wall and photographed the kitchen, the bedroom – anywhere – bribed neighbours for the rental of upper rooms and trampled over the last flowers in the park opposite the house. They laid siege to every property where Sir Nigel might be hiding. A nationwide search for Peter also took place, the hue and cry for Boswood's exploited victim, who sat tight in his hotel room in Guernsey behind drawn blinds with a muscular bodyguard and a thin-lipped lawyer watching his every move, until at last the press agencies were tipped off about his return to London on a scheduled flight into Heathrow.

Peter knew the press would be waiting but he had never expected anything like the howling mob which greeted him. The British rat-pack in full cry has to be experienced to be believed. Bewildered and scared, his dark spectacles knocked unceremoniously away from his face, Peter turned from one to another as the crazy scenes were relayed live on television, the flight arrival having been timed to coincide with the lunchtime news. As the *Globe*'s professionals had anticipated, the resulting front-page photographs showed their boy beautiful, vulnerable and tragic, the hungry leering faces of pressmen substituting nicely for his seducer. Even his travelling companions had been chosen with visuals in mind. Beside the burly bodyguards and the grim-faced lawyer he appeared younger, more frail. The editor looked through the latest batch of pictures from the airport and congratulated himself on such immaculate attention to detail.

Knowing the combatants apart from Peter and guessing who was the real offender, Elaine decided to test opinion. Mrs Horrocks and her ladies were invited to join her for breakfast in her hotel.

'What do you think of all this?' Elaine asked, gesturing at the reams of lurid newsprint. 'Is the Prime Minister right to turn down his resignation?'

The good women each hurriedly took a mouthful before answering. The food was splendid, much better than in their own more modest establishments. Conversation was intended as an accompaniment to such a good meal, certainly not an alternative.

'He was always a very good Minister, I'll say that for him,' Mrs Horrocks stated judiciously. 'I remember when he came to speak at our annual dinner – before your time, Mrs Stalker. I presented him with a cake. He was excellent; we all loved him.'

The conversation turned around the similarities with other notable dismissals involving morality. On each occasion it was not, officially, sexual misbehaviour which brought downfall; it was the lies, or the cover-up, or a side issue such as security breaches or corruption.

'You haven't answered my question,' Elaine pushed them. 'Can Nigel stay in the government, or not?'

In judgement the women turned their eyes to the next table where a respectable white-haired couple were deep into the *Globe*, mouths open and chortling, then back to Elaine. A politician pursued relentlessly by the press is damaged goods, not to be taken seriously ever again. Eyebrows were raised, lips pursed, shoulders shrugged. The party believed in winning battles. It chose with care almost by instinct the battles it would take on.

'No,' they said.

The conference was disintegrating into chaos. All the fine speeches on foreign affairs and policy towards the Third World, the valiant efforts to help the unemployed, were lost in the maelstrom surrounding Nigel Boswood. Pressmen who had waited two days caught him in the hotel lobby stretching his legs at what he thought was a quiet moment, and in an instant the hapless Cabinet Minister was surrounded by flashing bulbs and a blaze of spotlights. The resulting film showed the unfortunate man, mouth open in protest and face creased with misery, stumbling upstairs two at a time pursued by the camera-toting pack who were stopped by police at the first landing. The official line was still that he was not required to resign for a misdemeanour for which there was to be no prosecution. That he was running away from responsibility was nevertheless painfully apparent, and more damaging.

It would have been kinder to have let Nigel Boswood leave the government when he had tendered his resignation amid the sleaze of the first editions of Monday's papers. The pretence that a man in his position could continue as if nothing had happened was absurd and cruel. Had he quit then, the story would have continued to convulse the nation but would have faded relatively quickly; the Sunday papers would have tried to revive it, but the spice would have gone, for part of the point of such a story was to change history. Forcing a resignation was exactly that. Once that objective had been achieved, commentators would have moved on. Nigel might have kept his head down for several weeks, then surfaced gingerly in Parliament raising local issues. Preferably without any maudlin personal statements, of course. His leaving the Cabinet promptly but then remaining as a backbencher would have been regarded as positively helpful. The whips would have been distant but kind.

But by postponing the decision the Prime Minister unwittingly played into the hands of the *Globe*. By Friday Nigel's position was untenable. As a Cabinet Minister he could say and do nothing to defend himself. A denial would require him to sue. Failure to deny meant the tales were true. He had no room left to manoeuvre.

Boswood was completely unprepared for what was happening. Not that it had never occurred to him that the story might get out; he had planned for that, when Peter was part of his life, expecting to go public, proudly, shyly, almost at any time. When Peter vanished instead he assumed that the boy had walked out of his life for ever. Knowing very little about him and besotted with the boy, Nigel still found it impossible to accept his lover's true nature. Thus he had failed to arm or protect himself in any way.

The misery of losing Peter had been frightful enough, but somehow he had survived. He had believed that nothing so ghastly could ever happen to him again, but he had been wrong. Dully, moving about the hotel suite in Bournemouth like an automaton, Nigel rehearsed the horrible charges made against himself. In so far as he understood them, he knew them all to be lies. It was not true that he was sexually promiscuous and dangerous; most of the time he was celibate, far more than many bachelors. Peter was his first love affair, at least since university days. It was not true that he had persuaded the boy against his will: Nigel was incapable of such pressure. He was certain the boy had been willing and known exactly what he was doing. It was not true that the relationship had been one of domination by himself, dependence by the boy – much the other way round. Still something in Nigel's battered heart refused to accept that he had been had for a complete sucker. He could see how the media took the affair, but surely Peter had been decent deep down and somewhere along the line had loved him a little? Was he such a monster, he, Nigel Boswood, that a young man could not love him at all, only despise him, sufficiently to expose their most magic moments, to make him a complete laughing stock?

So the Prime Minister's misplaced kindness inadvertently caused his Cabinet colleague far more agony. The other loser was the government itself. The Prime Minister's closing speech to Party Conference was wiped off both front and inside pages. Journalists delved into files on paedophiles, mass murderers, rapists and other genuine criminals and made odious comparisons. Peter's mother reappeared and told her tale for a substantial sum. His sister decided to keep her head down for the sake of her own children. Two senior police officers who knew Peter too well decided to do the same. The Opposition, despite their stated support for gay equality, demanded Nigel's head and an emergency debate. The Liberal Democrats insisted on his leaving Westminster altogether; their eyes gleamed.

By Sunday night the Prime Minister knew he was completely boxed in. With a sigh, for he had tried, he reached for the phone.

'Who was it, Mum? Was it Roger?'

There was no need to pretend any more. Karen had not been trying unduly to listen in to Elaine's phone conversations, but increasingly she took an informed interest in her mother's life.

Elaine came into the kitchen looking thoughtful. 'Yes, it was. Boswood has resigned from the government. He stays in Parliament for the moment. Roger is made up to take his place. That leaves a vacancy, but the work is tailing off, so they're making another junior Minister instead, and that is to be Andrew Muncastle.'

'Phew! Do I congratulate you on being the girlfriend of a Cabinet Minister, then, Mum?' Karen was intrigued. Never having met Roger, having seen him only through her mother's eyes, it was automatic to feel pleased for him, for them both.

Elaine shook her head. 'No, don't be silly. I shall probably see even less of him now. Have to be even more careful. Not a word, miss, do you hear?'

Karen scowled. 'Now would I, Mum? After everything that has happened?' She stopped; that was the first reminder for some time. She coloured and dropped her eyes. Bravado still did not come easy. 'Sorry. What's the matter? Will you have to finish with Roger Dickson now?'

'I don't know. We'll have to see how it goes, I suppose. I have no claim on him, and I'm too fond of him to cause him any trouble. Yet with your father gone . . .' Elaine's voice tailed off sadly.

'Well, the government can sure do without any more scandals.'

Her mother winced. Karen was still too naive to know what was delicate and what wasn't. She had in any case inherited Elaine's natural bluntness. Catching her mother's troubled face, the girl moved rapidly to shift the subject.

'What about this new bloke – Andrew something? Do you know him?'

'Yes, I know him. We came into Parliament at the same time. He has done well, and he's a Minister already. Good luck to him.'

'Is he any good?'

'So-so. Competent. Nothing brilliant. Bit dull, really, at least in public. It hasn't stopped him being the first of our intake to make it to the front bench.'

'Why him and not you?'

Elaine laughed, but there was bitterness. She wondered how to avoid sounding jealous, and gave up. 'I ask myself the same question. Surely not because I'm a woman. Not these days, the years of equality and all that. Maybe because I'm a bundle of trouble masquerading as an MP and being a woman as well is just too much. By contrast Andrew hasn't put a foot wrong since he arrived. He has an impeccable pedigree. He has lots of useful friends and gets on pleasantly enough with everyone. He offers no risks at all. The fact that he's never done any TV or radio, ever, that he has no skill at putting a case over, no charisma, no imagination, or originality and about as much personality as my little finger seems to count for nothing. I'm not sure he is even particularly well endowed with brains, but that's no disqualification either. He'll make a first-class Minister.'

'You don't like him much.'

'There's nothing much to like. I should think better of him if he wasn't so bland. He's an example of what has gone wrong with this country. We seem to be ruled by civil servants – or people who wouldn't be out of place managing supermarkets. I don't fit.'

'You'll make it, Mum.' Karen came close and put an arm round her mother. 'If you really want to, that is.'

'Oh, stuff.' Elaine's mood lifted marginally. 'You sound like Roger. At least I'm sure the department is in good hands – he will be excellent. Do you know his nickname for me is "Patience"? All I have to do, he says, is carry on as now, making my speeches to an empty House, putting down boring planted questions, coaxing our ladies at fund-raising events, doing my bit on the telly. Be patient; it will bear fruit and I will make it. I think there's more to it than that. But I don't know what.'

'And even if you don't I shall still think you're marvellous.'

Elaine hugged her daughter with renewed affection. Thank God Mike had delayed his extramarital escapade till Karen was almost

404

grown-up. 'Now, young lady. You ready for an early start in the morning?'

Karen untwined herself from her mother. 'Yeah, and it's political history tomorrow, double period. All this stuff about charisma, Mum – sometimes it can go too far. I have to write an essay about Hitler and Mussolini. Do you think they had it?'

Elaine smiled. 'In abundance. You're right. Maybe dull Ministers are a better idea.'

It was not until the early hours of Monday morning that Nigel Boswood climbed out of a taxi and crept in the back way of his house, his face shrouded in a scarf. He had let it be known that he was headed for Scotland, so the place was deserted apart from a young policeman on the gate who uttered a soft, curt goodnight.

Without turning on the lights Nigel went all round the house, drawing curtains tight. For a while he would live in gloom, hiding from the daylight, until the rat-pack went off to chase another hapless victim.

He was dead, empty. All these events were so crushing that his mind refused to accept them. He felt slovenly, dirty, unshaven. Pulses in his temple pounded and his mouth was dry. He had not slept for days, nor eaten properly, but exhaustion was taking over. Tonight in his own bed he would try to sleep, and sleep on restlessly but deeply in the darkened room past midday, eyes shut tight, breathing slow and laboured as if he might never wake. Would that it would happen like that, a heart attack during the night perhaps. No more trouble to anyone. He took the phone off the hook and on an afterthought unplugged it from the wall.

A pile of unopened mail looked ominous and he ignored it. In the quiet living room he mixed a stiff drink, and then another. Moving dully, methodically, allowing habit to take over, he chose a favourite book to read and made his way slowly upstairs. Every step was redolent of Peter. The whole house would have to be redecorated, furniture changed around. He must fill the basement with jumble and rubbish, obliterate the memories entirely. Start tomorrow, give himself something to do.

A new blue dressing gown was draped on the bed. The old one had been too stained to save, after that incident with the mirror. He turned on the bedside light, put down the book and drink. Woodenly, devoid of all purpose except the simple objective of getting into bed, he pulled back the bedclothes.

On the pillow was a note written in a simple, careful hand. For a brief second his heart leapt. Maybe Peter was about to apologise, explain that the terrible newspaper stories were not his fault, that he was sorry for all the misery he had caused?

Then in the gloom Nigel looked closer and recognised the writing.

> Dear Sir Nigel, I don't know what you have done, I only know I
> don't believe what I read in newspapers. I am sorry about any
> trouble. It don't make no difference to me. I will be in as
> usual.   M. Perkins (Mrs).

At the bottom a PS had been added, a hasty afterthought:

> PS. Your a gentleman, Sir Nigel, one of the best. I will say that to
> anybody who asks me. If you want any help me and my family will
> stand by you.   M.P.

Nigel stood still for a long time. Only increasing stiffness eventually
made him move. He blew his nose, finished undressing and climbed into
bed, the note clutched in his hand.

CHAPTER TWENTY-THREE

Most Sundays Elaine Stalker refused engagements. There had to be a day in the week when she did not wear make-up or tights or smart skirts, but could slop around at home in jeans and a sweater, a day when she could revert to an ordinary human being. Not that this was time off. Sunday was the only day necessary chores could be attended to: tidying the garden, changing light bulbs, fiddling with the video, polishing shoes, sewing buttons back on jackets and blouses. She wondered if male MPs had similar problems, but concluded that on the whole their wives performed such tasks. No wonder divorced men look so harassed.

It was also the chance to keep the paperwork in check. Despite Diane's best efforts work could not be confined to weekdays and the office. Every weekend Elaine's briefcase bulged with reports she had meant to read, or preparation for next week's debate, or letters to sign which could not wait. All this invaded her home and spread itself over the kitchen table after Sunday lunch, as Karen watched the omnibus edition of *EastEnders*.

Sunday outings became restricted to unavoidable church parades. The cathedral had developed a nice line in commemorative services broadcast on local radio which brought in the crowds and filled the offertory plates. The Farmers' Service each autumn saw the place filled to the rafters with sheaves and stooks, loaves of decorated bread, baskets of fruit (mostly imported), an old farm cart, trays of hen and goose eggs and the stuffed head of a favourite champion Hereford bull, the whole set off with flowers and foliage in glorious harvest colours of red and gold and dark glossy green. Local farmers and their families in heavy tweeds, nails and necks scrubbed, arrived respectful and uncertain and were reminded firmly of their place in the rural social order by dean and chapter assembled in embroidered silk.

Last Farmers' Service had been a bit of a disaster. A visiting bishop had been invited to preach. He launched into a Green manifesto, lambasting those who ruined the land with too much fertiliser, who blocked up footpaths and set dogs on innocent ramblers, who

407

overproduced and then demanded subsidies, and whose subsidised exports were a main cause of the collapse of Third World agriculture. Seated in the second row beside the Lord-Lieutenant, Elaine could not see the frozen expressions behind her. She could, however, sense hundreds of backs stiffen grimly. They had their silent revenge as the plates came round, dropping derisory pennies from work-roughened hands. The collection raised only £15, and the visiting bishop was never invited again.

One service all year stood out, for Elaine as for many MPs: Remembrance Day. Her constituency was recruiting territory for several regiments. Each year there seemed to be a new smattering of young soldiers on parade, war-weary from the Gulf or Bosnia, or with the watchful air of those who have served in Ulster.

The grand old organ boomed out powerful rumbling notes as the congregation rose solemnly to its feet amid wholesale clearing of throats. The weather had been damp and the cathedral was not yet warm; the standard-bearers were blue with cold and the Brownies were shivering. Lusty hymn-singing would make everyone feel better.

After the hymn, a young woman infantry officer, top cadet in her year at Sandhurst, stepped forward to the lectern. In the front row her parents swelled with pride. Necks craned as the girl stood calmly in her smart green uniform, blood-red poppy at her breast. There was something about a woman dressed like that, incongruous but enormously sexy. Men, confused, lowered their eyes.

> I heard a voice from heaven, saying unto me, Write, from henceforth blessed are the dead which die in the Lord: Even so, saith the Spirit, for they rest from their labours.

Elaine looked around her. Of course she should be concentrating on the service but her constituents were much more interesting. Mostly over middle age, comfortable and well upholstered, peaceable and kindly. Once a year they chose to remember the cost of war without mawkishness or embarrassment.

The president of the British Legion, now nearly eighty, headed for the microphone. As a young man he had served with Montgomery in North Africa, losing an eye when the tank was blown from under him and all his mates killed. Medals clanked on his chest and his long lower lip was not quite under control as he started reading the Memorial of the Dead, his voice shaking with emotion.

> Remember, O Lord, all those brave and true, who have died the death of honour . . . to whom it was given to lay down their lives in the cause of Freedom and Justice . . .

Elaine felt suddenly very moved. Had she been required at that moment to make a comment out loud she could not have done it. That Europe was free at all was thanks to the sacrifices of such people and their comrades.

The cathedral waited. It was eleven o'clock. High in the medieval belltower Great Tom tolled as everyone silently counted. As the last reverberations died away the president drew himself up to his full height and spoke very slowly:

> Age shall not weary them, nor the years condemn.
> At the going down of the sun and in the morning,
> We will remember them.

Nigel Boswood had decided to attend the televised service at the Cenotaph in Whitehall. Why not? As a Cabinet Minister he would have been in the second row behind the Prime Minister and Leader of the Opposition, near the Queen in her regulation black. Now he was at the back. He was well wrapped up against the bitter wind, an extra-large poppy firmly pinned to his coat, neck muffled in the black scarf kept for this event year by year. Proper dress was *de rigueur*.

There was a streak of sheer defiance in Nigel's determination to come, but in any case the reasons for keeping his head down were diminishing. The Metropolitan Police had come to Ebury Street for a chat, but had been deferential and almost kind. Without a complaint from Peter, who seemed to have disappeared, there was to be neither prosecution nor libel case. Nigel refused to make any public statement and gradually the fuss died down. The press were off pursuing a bishop who had been molesting young monks. There was no longer any need to hide.

The war itself did not mean much to Nigel. Only six years old when it broke out, he had promptly been shipped off to relatives in Canada with his sister. He remembered the outward journey on board the great cruise liner, with deck tennis, a swimming pool ad children's shows, with the greatest enjoyment, which coloured his whole recollection of the following innocent years, until his return to a cheerless English prep school after VE Day. From the train, then, he was shocked at the devastation of Liverpool: a three-legged dog limping across bomb sites near the flattened Edge Hill goods depot, the yawning gaps in street after street in Wavertree where houses had received a direct hit, their inhabitants pulled out in pieces. The images stayed with him. The desire to do his bit became a driving force in his politics.

Behind him the Regimental Band of the Blues and Royals tinkled and hissed as stops were flexed, spittle discreetly emptied from trombones and bright brass raised to stiff lips. A gentle drum roll led the congregation into a very British hymn. Nigel joined in proudly. So what if God was an internationalist?

> Of every clime and coast,
> O hear us for our native land
> The land we love the most . . .

Tessa Muncastle tried to stop herself shivering and wondered if putting her gloved hands in her pockets would be too disrespectful. Hampshire might be in the lush south but half an hour in a November wind had penetrated all her defences. Next to her stood the standard-bearer of the Women's Royal British Legion, a stout lady in a navy-blue uniform, big feet in sensible lace-up shoes planted wide apart, huge white leather gloves like catcher's mitts on both hands, the Legion hat jammed unbudgeably on her head with several hatpins. The standard itself, having been paraded around the town, was propped up beside her.

'Terrible, isn't it?'

Tessa realised the standard-bearer was commiserating with her. She smiled ruefully. 'It is a bit chilly. Wish I'd worn something warmer.'

The woman leaned forward with a cheery grin. 'Long johns, that's what I wear,' she hissed. 'Borrowed me old man's, the short-leg ones. Look.'

To Tessa's consternation she lifted her skirt and showed the tell-tale white ribbing covering her ample thighs, like prepared hams in a butcher's. Tessa coloured in embarrassment.

The woman returned to attention. The MP's wife was nice but a bit po-faced. This was a solemn occasion, but there was always room for a giggle. Do her good to enjoy herself occasionally. Him too – took himself so seriously these days now he was a Minister.

Andrew held himself rigidly straight on the podium as the rest of the parade drew near, a large poppy prominently displayed in his buttonhole. Next to him stood the rural dean in flowing voluminous red, his unaccustomed portliness suggesting layers of fortification underneath.

Andrew was conscious that many eyes were on him. He worked steadily in the constituency; his photograph appeared on many a worthy occasion in local newspapers but his very blandness made him less than memorable. On this occasion he was available for everyone to gaze at for nearly an hour, when they were not scrutinising the parade for a favourite child or commenting rudely on the musical offerings. He realised with a start that he had first come to the area nearly four years ago after his selection as candidate. If his constituents were under-whelmed by him the compliment was returned. They were polite, but casework and local planning spats consistently failed to inspire. This area of Hampshire had relatively few problems; had he nothing else to do other than look after them and turn out on occasions such as Remembrance Day he would have become terribly bored.

The ministerial job was a different matter. Working for Roger, a new and inexperienced Secretary of State but with a friendly natural style, he was obliged to abandon his usual reserve and make every effort; they would be judged as a team. It was the internal unsung work at the department which unexpectedly he found he liked. He turned out to be capable in its low-key negotiations, where experts and pressure groups appreciated his attention to detail. Good thing too, on the whole. For rather too long his only thrills had come from seeing Miranda. As his career burgeoned there were fresh thoughts in his mind, their origins a document in his box, a briefing with civil servants. Life was busy and full. He was more content by the minute.

Out of the corner of his eye he could see Tessa looking frozen and miserable. A moment of unreasoning anger welled in his heart: could she not dress properly for an outdoor event in winter, or was even this to be a source of discord?

The lady standard-bearer gave Tessa a quick nudge. 'Look down there!' she pointed. 'The TA have brought their mascot. Well I never! Now we'll have some fun.'

Frowning slightly, Tessa peered down the wide street in the direction of the martial music. In the absence of the county's regiments in Bosnia the local Territorials, the reserves, had volunteered to put on a good show, especially as the MP would be present. First the Scout band came into view, boys of different ages and sizes, struggling to keep step, supported by Guides and Cubs. Behind the band came the Terriers in khaki. That this mixed troop, a quarter female, were not soldiers was immediately evident by the casual originality of their marching. In real life they were building society clerks and solicitors, garage mechanics and secretaries, relieving the boredom of their daily lives. Amused neighbours pointed to each familiar face in its unaccustomed cap, while the blushing objects of their attention tried to keep eyes front and stop themselves waving.

It was then that Tessa caught sight of the mascot and her heart sank. It was a large white billy-goat with an evil face, its horns waving dangerously. The troop secretary had shampooed it for the occasion and caparisoned the creature sumptuously in TA colours. Pulling hard, it was leering and skittering out of step in the front row under the partial control of the commandant, Mr Bulstrode the retired banker, who was red-faced from the effort of holding the brute back. Mr Bulstrode was both out of his area and a little out of his depth. There was no point in hassling people to attend a parade in nearby Milton if its MP was missing, as well he might be after all that fuss. A proper march-past needed a distinguished character to take the salute. Muncastle was nothing much, but as one of Her Majesty's new Ministers he would have to do. As long as this ghastly beast behaved.

As the groups approached the podium the goat began to scent people. That meant food: sweets, crisps, chips. Getting away would be difficult, for the man was holding tight. The parade stopped and the band rested, at ease. The animal stood balefully eyeing the crowd, head up, as all fell silent.

The goat felt Mr Bulstrode's grip slacken minutely.

Just at that moment the Scouts put cornets to lips and in undignified mistune blasted out the Last Post. The goat, startled, jumped off all fours, jerked its head back, found itself free, looked around wildly and then made a bee-line for a half-eaten chocolate bar sticking out of the drum major's pocket. The crowd scattered from its path with yelps and squeals as all semblance of dignity collapsed. Moving remarkably fast, the billy clattered towards its objective. Grasping the chocolate in protruding yellow teeth it began to gobble quickly, but had not counted on the angry youngster. In furious retaliation he lifted the drum with a yell and crashed it down on the goat's head, splitting the drumskin with a loud twang and leaving the rim and remains encircling the animal's neck. The beast's amber eyes rolled unfocused; then, as instinct took over, it put its splendid horned head down and charged the boy full tilt.

In an instant there was uproar as the big goat, somewhat hampered by its unusual collar, careered on into the crowd, which scattered in all directions, screaming and laughing. Bulstrode waded in, scrabbling in the road for the leather lead, but the animal was not about to relinquish its new-found freedom. With a skip it dodged neatly out of the way. Mothers snatched babies from prams and clutched them to their breasts, old ladies in terror pressed themselves flat against shop windows, young men came out of pubs and ran around whooping. The hefty goat, no mean beast, chocolate wrapper still hanging from its lips, charged aimlessly and vengefully about. The lady standard-bearer, a broad grin on her weatherbeaten face, deftly moved Tessa out of the way. On the podium Andrew and the rural dean watched helplessly; once it was apparent that normal service was not to be restored, the two relaxed and joined in the general merriment.

At last the tiring goat was headed off by a group of Scouts and Terriers and was cornered down by the tandoori restaurant. Mr Ali was standing in the doorway, wiping his hands on a tea-towel, called from his labours in the kitchen by all the commotion. A panting heap of humanity and smelly long-haired goat greeted him as Bulstrode, face livid, strode up and took the leash again.

'I could make use of the animal, sir, should you wish to dispose of it,' Mr Ali said helpfully.

'I'll be in touch tomorrow,' responded the goat's minder grimly.

> Send her victorious,
> Happy and glorious . . .

A hand touched Nigel Boswood's shoulder. Not wanting to talk to anyone much, still full of tension at his first appearance at a public event, and brooding deeply on all that had happened to him, Nigel shook it off gently but not rudely, refusing to turn around or take notice.

The Queen was leaving, accompanied by grave bows and salutes from those she passed. Around him men in dark-grey and black overcoats pulled mufflers tighter, shook hands and dispersed. A group hovered protectively near the Prime Minister and those Cabinet Ministers who were present. For a few polite moments hostilities were lifted and the Prime Minister and the Leader of the Opposition chatted affably.

With a poignant twinge Nigel watched as Roger Dickson, smiling pleasantly, pulled on black gloves, detached himself with practised ease and moved to his Jaguar. He seemed to have grown into the job very quickly. Nigel reflected sadly that Dickson looked the part entirely – more than himself perhaps, for in the last year or two he had been increasingly conscious of being from the wrong generation. Yet it was his own attempt to change, to adapt to a way of life that would have been illegal in his own younger days, which had led directly to his downfall. It all seemed so unfair.

For a brief moment, the unnoticed centre of a slow-moving crowd, Nigel allowed himself the indulgence of a moderate dose of self-pity. If he was not to be famous and central any more he might as well have stayed at home and watched it all from the comfort of his armchair. He gazed around with sadness. He was there not only without purpose but deprived almost of identity. Most of those who should have recognised him pretended he wasn't there, while many others simply failed to place him at all.

A man moved from in front of Nigel, leaving him suddenly exposed and visible, silhouetted against the white stone, standing alone in the middle of the road. Dickson, hand on open car door, saw him, hesitated, then smiled and waved, and climbed in. His driver in the grey peaked cap stared impassively. Nigel noted it was Alec, who had been Dickson's driver before; the drivers must have swapped around to accommodate the new Secretary of State's preference. There was no further acknowledgement of him.

A hand tapped his shoulder a second time. Nigel shrugged resignedly; no one else seemed willing to talk to him. Opposite the Cenotaph at the corner of Derby Gate the Red Lion was open. Perhaps if this were a friend, or even an old acquaintance, it would be pleasant to invite him to the pub for a quick drink. That was what normal people would do. He would have to relearn normal behaviour, the little niceties that everyone else took for granted but which he had entirely misplaced in the years of ministerial grandeur. It might even be an interesting experience. Feeling more optimistic, he squared his shoulders and turned around.

Charles Edward Longhurst was an inch or so taller than Nigel and in his early fifties. Physically there was a resemblance, for the clean-shaven Mr Longhurst was a regular attender at professional dinners around the country, being a fine raconteur especially if the press were not present. As a result he was carrying only slightly less weight than Nigel, but, given the time spent exercising and lifting weights in the seclusion of his bedroom, the flush on his cheek was healthier.

Mr Longhurst looked into the eyes of the gentleman whose name was on the order sheet in his hand. The man's appearance had changed since he used to be a Minister; he was older, more bowed. Tiny lines criss-crossed the face and fell, reddened by the cold, into deep furrows by the side of his mouth and eyes. If he didn't know better he would have sworn some looked like scars.

There was no point in drawing attention to what had to be done. Mr Longhurst had dealt with some villains in his time and on occasion would have welcomed the glare of publicity, especially when a public figure got stroppy. But this fellow already had a beaten look about him, despite the enquiring, friendly expression. Longhurst spoke softly but directly so that Nigel was almost reading his lips.

'Sir Nigel Boswood?'

Boswood nodded and held out his hand formally. Longhurst was startled for a second, then took it in his own. Most people in his business did not shake hands.

'My name is Charles Longhurst. Superintendent Longhurst of the Metropolitan Police. Would you be so kind as to spare me a moment? We could go to Charing Cross station, sir. It's just across the way.'

Nigel's mind completely refused to grasp the enormity of what was happening and clung instead to trivialities.

'Charing Cross? Isn't there one nearer?'

The policeman nodded across the road. 'It is the nearest one. Used to be called Cannon Row, but you took over that part of the building for MPs and secretaries. It's at the back, same building, on the Embankment side. We walk through Derby Gate.'

It would look as if they were going into a parliamentary building; all so normal. Almost automatically the two turned and moved away, as the Marines began to erect crash barriers around the Cenotaph to deter vandals from destroying the wreaths.

'I'd rather take you for a drink,' Nigel offered bravely, gesturing to the pub. It looked suddenly inviting.

'Thank you, sir, but this has to be done in a police station.'

Nigel was puzzled. Was he being arrested? He decided to maintain the joviality. A little practice would do no harm. 'Afterwards, then?'

There was no answer.

At the gate which also leads to parliamentary offices the two men paused briefly and showed their IDs. Gerry Keown knew perfectly well who both men were, but there was a security alert on, what with all the bigwigs at the ceremony a few yards away. The supervisor had reminded gate staff to take no one for granted.

Possibilities, most of them irritating but not devastating, were surfacing in Nigel's brain. Perhaps his house had been burgled. Maybe his car, the second-hand but stolid Mercedes he had bought after his resignation, would turn out to be stolen; it had seemed an extraordinary bargain. Maybe, more worryingly, he was on a hit list for the IRA – or being warned he could no longer expect the daily protection of plain-clothes detectives with bulges in their armpits. So many times had Nigel been wounded that his system knew when to shut down, to shroud him in an invisible protection.

His eyes told him that he was being nodded through a large modern police station; that the uniformed men and women and the grubby bejeaned characters to whom they were talking were locked in combat, though perhaps some of the latter were undercover detectives or Special Branch, policemen too under the stubble. Somewhere a typewriter clattered away and a door clanged.

A moment later he was ushered into what was evidently the superintendent's office. It was furnished elegantly enough with modern reproduction pieces made from the kind of dark solid wood that had environmentalists demonstrating at the dockside. On the wall, in odd juxtaposition, hung a couple of Bernard Buffet prints of Paris, and a line drawing of Hendon Police College. The window-ledge sported a colour photograph of a smiling wife and two grown-up children. The room was well maintained and tidy but with a businesslike air. Charles Longhurst had his sights set on becoming Assistant Chief Constable before he retired, if not with the Met, then in a civilised spot in the Home Counties.

'You might want your solicitor,' the superintendent said helpfully and pushed the phone forward.

Nigel had not taken off his coat, but now he undid its buttons and seated himself with a feeling almost of curiosity.

'What? It depends. Perhaps you had better tell me first how I can help you, Mr . . . er, Longhurst.'

The policeman realised that the man had no idea why he was here. He sighed. A walking innocent.

'All right. Perhaps when I have explained you will want to call him. A complaint has been laid against you, Sir Nigel, under section 13 of the Sexual Offences Act of 1956, and section 1 of the Sexual Offences Act 1967.'

He paused. Nigel Boswood had a vacant look on his face as if his thoughts were not entirely engaged.

'That means gross indecency with a man under the age of twenty-one,' Longhurst continued carefully.

'Who would say that?' Nigel was suddenly indignant. Peter had gone: it couldn't be him. Any other would be from years ago, and could possibly be denied. Or it might simply be somebody lying.

Longhurst opened a large folder on the desk and flicked through the top pages. 'I think you would know him as Peter Manley, but we have half a dozen names and aliases for him in several countries. Sir,' he added as an afterthought.

A cold feeling started in the pit of Nigel's stomach and began to spread down his thighs. Still it seemed best to maintain the bravado. A man without friends must shift for himself.

'Peter? He's made a complaint? But I thought – that is, the police told me – he was refusing to make a complaint.'

'That's right, sir, he was. I interviewed him myself. But I think he's been put up to it by one of the newspapers. Wanting to keep the story going, I guess. Anyway he has made a sworn statement. That means I have no choice about acting. I am sorry.'

Longhurst sat squarely opposite, hands placed palm down on the table, as if he preferred to see people sit like that, to be sure of what their hands were doing. His apology was meant to anticipate and soften the impact of the message.

Boswood moved only imperceptibly, but all the thin cheerfulness had gone. His voice was gruff, deeper. 'Are you arresting me, then? Will I be charged?'

Longhurst lowered his eyes. There was something poignant about the man's simple courage and dignity. He had been through so much already. The officer had no desire to punish the man any further. The briefest acquaintance with the voluminous file on Peter, with reports from police forces in Belgium, Germany, Holland, France and Ireland as well as complaints from Malta and Madeira, told him all he needed to know about who was to blame and who likely to reoffend in future. Moreover, the names of two senior police colleagues appeared, buried in a sealed envelope marked 'Secret'. He had wondered if Peter even

416

knew who they were and decided it was best not to find out. There was nothing whatever to gain by making this nasty little prostitute and minor drug-smuggler answer in the full glare of publicity in a witness box. The newspaper must have offered a lot of money to make it worth his while trying again.

It was Longhurst's turn to say softly, 'That depends. If I charge you with a serious offence I have to be reasonably sure there is evidence, and that the case would stand up in court. There are photographs, of course. However, your Peter is a thoroughly unreliable witness, as I am sure you realise. We have an address for him at the moment, his sister's house in Stoke Newington. I am reluctant to go through all the motions only to have him vanish the day before the hearing. Yet he has placed a complaint against you, and I do have to take it seriously.'

There was silence. Both men waited, as if somebody else would provide an answer. Caution and puzzlement obliged Nigel to say nothing. The revelation of Peter's betrayal did not hurt him emotionally as much as once it might. As he had not seen the boy since spring, the powerful image, much of which had in any case been created in his own mind, was fading. That at least was a blessing.

The policeman continued, slowly, 'I am thus very reluctant to go to court, and I have sought the opinion of the Director of Public Prosecutions, who agrees with me. There is another option, in cases where a serious offence has been committed, where in view of the age or infirmity of the accused a formal caution is more appropriate.'

'What does that entail?'

'It's not at all the same as an informal caution. There is one essential element: an admission of guilt. If you deny the matter then I am obliged to put the matter in the DPP's hands. If you admit it we could proceed to a formal caution. It is up to you. That's why I thought you might prefer your solicitor here.'

The mental image of Mr Wharton's thin dry face, skin scraped and scrawny as if he shaved without soap, swam before Nigel's mind. Those piggy eyes would glitter at the suggestion of a big court hearing; he would rub together his long fingers and imply that only a fool would do other than plead not guilty, then allow the brilliance of his counsel, charging – what? – ten thousand for a two-day case, perhaps, to overwhelm the jury.

A jury. Men and women like Mrs Perkins – but in public she might purse her lips and condemn him for being so stupid. Or her brother, the one she told him about, whose left-wing sympathies would place him firmly against an aristo like himself. Civil servants like Chadwick, fretting at being kept from their work, wanting it all over and done, not prepared to make allowances. They would sit there, comparing him with the unmarked young boy he had allegedly debauched. Peter had steel inside; he would stand up to cross-examination very well, up to the point when he would burst prettily into tears. Any attempt to browbeat him or put awkward questions about his past would be parried by the cry that he was the subject of constant harassment by men, legally adults, who should know better, or by accusations that the defence counsel was trying to divert attention from the monster who was actually in the dock. And Nigel needed no reminder that the media would have a field day, whatever was said in court, and make up much of what wasn't, even before the verdict.

Nigel felt a flicker of anger. 'It sounds as if my former friend is blackmailing us both – pressuring you and me to get what he wants – and laughing all the way to the bank.'

Longhurst grinned ruefully. He was not about to tell Nigel that he played darts occasionally in a pub over the river, where one of the regulars was a Mr Perkins who had stoically absorbed at home the full force of his wife's indignation. The whole pub had had heated arguments peppered with much mirth about who was in the wrong in this case, but Perkins had stuck doggedly to his improbable tale that Nigel Boswood was a good man. It pleased Longhurst to find he was right.

'I think that about sums it up, sir.' He gestured to the file. 'I am afraid he was a thoroughly bad lot. I am sorry you had to get mixed up with him.'

Part of Nigel's brain told him he had no right to expect such a generous response. It would not be repeated, of course, if this business were removed to a courtroom. He frowned. 'What exactly do you want me to do?'

'If you tell me that you were guilty of this offence then I can formally caution you. It is not a light matter; it must be recorded and will form part of your police record. If you commit another offence it will be cited in any subsequent court proceedings. That means next time you could face a prison sentence, you do realise that?'

Nigel brooded. 'That means I plead guilty, to all intents and purposes. The party takes a dim view of people who break the law. Some of the party take a very dim view indeed of these kinds of offences – most of them, in fact. I used to myself, come to that.' He was quiet again, uncomfortable, reflective.

Then it hit him, what it all meant. With eyes full of misery he said quietly, 'If I plead not guilty you haul me through the courts. It will take months, and I might not get off, and I could have a homophobic judge of the worst kind and get sent down. Even if the case collapses or I am found not guilty I face a public trial, and it never stops – it never stops. God in heaven! If I plead guilty you caution me – what? Here and now? And if I do that, I *am* guilty. Marked, branded, packaged up and delivered to every bigot in the country. The press will have their pound of flesh whatever I do. And I could not remain as a Member of Parliament, not under those circumstances, not for a moment. It just wouldn't be on. How could I make speeches about the moral decline of the nation with that millstone hanging around my neck? I'd be a permanent laughing-stock. D'you know, they all ignored me out there? Paid their respects to the dead, but not even a "Good morning" to the living. And that's before what you're suggesting. Afterwards they would all . . . Oh, my God.'

Great uncontrollable sobs came from his throat, piteous and tragic. He had tried so hard to keep going, to rebuild his life, not only without Peter, but without position or influence or allies. He had determined, nevertheless, to retain some essential elements of self-respect. Within that tentative plan, to continue as an MP till the end of his term in a couple of years' time had become a necessity, an object of faith. The wounds would take that long to heal; then he could manage. 'Retired' was better than 'resigned'. One implied choice, the other denied it. Now he had abruptly come to the end of the line. Sir Nigel Boswood bowed his head, let his shoulders sag and wept noisily and heartbreakingly, like a woman.

Longhurst found a clean handkerchief and passed it mutely over the table. Boswood shook his head, for he neither wanted nor expected sympathy, instead reaching inside his pocket for his own. The white cotton stayed on the table, neither man wishing to retrieve it.

The officer waited politely for a moment, then cleared his throat. He would not be telling any funny stories at Police Federation dinners about this one. 'When you feel ready, sir, we should bring the discussion to a close and commence the formal part of the proceedings. I will call in my people. The interview will then be taped in accordance with the Police and Criminal Evidence Act. If you want me to postpone it for half an hour while you get your solicitor, or even a friend, I should be willing to wait, and I do strongly recommend it.'

Nigel wiped his eyes and blew his nose in the complicated, nostril-clearing way he had been taught as a child, as if germs could be kept at bay by physical force.

Longhurst had a final duty first. His solid paw rested briefly on the folder. 'One more matter, sir, while we are talking privately, man to man. I have read this file very carefully and I won't trouble you with the details, but you would be wise to have an HIV test, if you haven't already done so.'

It was the cruellest blow to deliver. Not that there was any information on Peter, nothing at all either way, but one or two of his friends were a different matter and the old man had to be warned. For a moment Longhurst felt it might have been easier to brush it all aside as none of his business. He watched Boswood warily. The older man was having difficulty controlling his features.

At last Nigel drew himself up. There would be no questions. The policeman was trying to be kind, dammit.

'We always practised safe sex, Mr Longhurst. There should be no problem. But I will do as you suggest. And' – he hesitated – 'thank you.'

His eyes met his persecutor's and understood, as the man about to be hanged understands the hangman, and forgives. With a slow, deliberate movement he reached for the phone.

Miranda Jamieson did not start out that morning with the intention of picking a fight with Jim Betts. After all, he had played a major role in putting the newspaper back on its feet.

Her own position at the *Globe* had changed in subtle ways. Her reputation rested on her struggles to save the paper during the terrible days a year earlier when circulation spiralled downwards and the new computer failed. By bullying, charm, energy, and sheer bloody-minded courage she had kept the whole thing going, surviving without sleep for days on end, still looking fresh at three in the morning. Her supposed link with the proprietor gave her instant authority but was never mentioned to her face. Thus she became involved more than she had planned in the business and management side of the paper, wrote for it rather less, yet (since she was neither editor nor news or features editor) had relatively little say in its overall policy and approach. There were times when she did not like what the *Globe* had become. She had made herself at the same time both indispensable and invisible.

Betts was walking down a corridor in shirtsleeves, hands in pockets, acknowledging greetings of fellow workers on all sides, the latest *Globe* edition with Boswood's resignation tucked ostentatiously under his arm. Had she seen him coming Miranda would have avoided him. In her current mood the paper itself seemed as much his victim. They cannoned into each other at a corner.

'Hello, beautiful!' Betts grinned roguishly at her. Maybe now he was the paper's star reporter she would look on him with more favour.

Miranda eyed Betts with distaste and brushed her skirt down as if something unpleasant had rubbed off from him. He had unsightly sores around his mouth – there was always something wrong with him, some minor illness implying casual disregard for his own health or cleanliness. She shuddered inwardly.

'Good morning. I gather congratulations are in order.' She gestured at the newspaper under his arm.

Betts preened. 'Sure, once we persuaded Honey Bun to make a formal complaint to the police. He wasn't keen, I can tell you. Seemed to think he was being compromised. I ask you! Somebody like that!'

'No doubt your persuasive powers were to the fore, Jim.' Miranda kept any hint of sarcasm out of her voice.

'Money, more like. Cost almost as much as the original story, but now the *Globe* will always have Boswood's complete scalp to its credit. You know that boy was the toughest negotiator I've ever seen. They could use him in the Cabinet.'

'They did,' Miranda commented wryly, sending Betts off into raucous laughter. 'Or at least one of them did. But I don't know; this paper used to have a serious content. I hope we can turn our attention to the genuine issues of the day occasionally as well.'

Betts's face darkened. Miranda was half smiling and apparently friendly but you never knew with her. He had the distinct sense that she was taking the mickey.

'This *was* serious,' he insisted. 'What they all get up to in private isn't separate, it's part of what they do and say in public. You can't divide them.'

'Why not? We all keep our lives separate here. Just because the features editor is having it off with the print room supervisor doesn't mean she can't do her job or that he can't push his buttons. Provided they're not screwing when they should be working. I mean, look at you, Jim: nobody is going to criticise you just because you're inside the knickers of Sheena on reception. It doesn't stop you being our star reporter. Incidentally you do know her husband is a karate champion, don't you? She showed me a photo of him, muscles everywhere. He'll tear you limb from limb if he finds out.'

The information was news to Betts. Perhaps Miranda was lying, though it accorded with the receptionist's tastes. He looked at her hard: there was only a wisp of mockery in the wide-open eyes. Perhaps she was hinting that he should choose someone else. It was time to call the bitch's bluff.

'I've always preferred classier women than that, Miranda, as you know. In fact you're my ideal. No, I'm not kidding. Now that I'm no longer bottom of the heap, maybe the lovely Ms Jamieson would deign to notice me? In fact I'm free tonight and I feel like celebrating. How about it?'

His boldness was offensive and unexpected. Now it was her turn to laugh. Pushing past him she delivered what she hoped was a telling parting shot.

'You've got balls, Jim, I'll say that for you. But right now the pimples on your face are bigger, did you know that? When you have grown up I may be interested. But not tonight, sweetheart.'

Miranda swept away, her tight skirt outlining a full bottom which sneered at him as she walked off. She would have been uneasy had she seen his frozen expression and recognised in it·a hatred born of humiliation. He caught the stare of a junior reporter in a nearby office. From the boy's smirk it was clear the tale would be all over the canteen before the hour was out.

It was a strange Christmas, the first Elaine had ever spent alone. After much discussion Karen decided to accept her father's invitation to spend part of the holiday with him in Florida. Visiting Disneyworld was a suitably adolescent thing to do and it seemed a shame to have an airline pilot father and not take advantage of him. There would be other people present, so the occasion could not get too fraught. It would also help her assess the chances of her parents ever coming together again.

Elaine could have passed the time with friends, and toyed with the idea of going skiing or on a package tour. Yet she was also becoming accustomed to being solitary, and secretly welcomed the opportunity. That she did *not* have to eat turkey or chipolatas or Christmas pudding was a terrific bonus.

Was she becoming completely selfish? The thought caused her some anxiety. She already knew her capacity for extremes of both altruism and self-centredness. Her job required her to listen to dozens of ordinary people week by week, then exert herself without stint or measure to help them. Had she not liked people in a genuinely unselfish way – and responded to them with natural warmth – she would have found that aspect of the MP's job impossibly frustrating. Instead it was the part where she felt most fulfilled.

Yet to have got even this far required real ambition. Even she had no idea where this drive came from or why she felt so single-minded. Some of it she could rationalise. If she became cross on behalf of a widow on income support, she might solve the problem more quickly, for the old lady and everyone else, were she a Minister in the Department of Social Security. Since the answers always had financial considerations, she daydreamed of promotion to the Treasury. She could even wriggle inside Roger's head as he took his seat at the Cabinet table. There must be moments when, having lost an argument or failed to persuade the Prime Minister, he must look across and reflect that there was always room at the top. Ambition, she was sure, was not lacking in the man she loved. That was one of the deepest springs of her love for him.

As Boxing Day slid peacefully by, one article in *The Economist* caught her eye. To amuse its readers over the holiday an opinion poll had been commissioned, inviting respondents to put names to famous faces. Predictably pop stars such as Madonna and Michael Jackson came top – their appearance was almost a trademark. The Prime Minister was only a little behind. Sir Nigel Boswood scored high but then the poll was taken soon after the fuss. By contrast Roger was known to fewer than one person in five. That would irritate him, even if it did mean he ranked ahead of most of the Cabinet. Then, to her surprise, she saw her own name. It appeared she was better known than anyone in government with the sole exception of the Prime Minister himself.

Elaine reached for another glass of sparkling Saumur and hugged herself, for there was no one else to do it for her. Then she fell into a slightly tipsy reverie. The finding did not mean a lot, and would only cause jealousy. Nor did it make her personal life any easier.

As it grew dark Elaine dozed on the sofa, the magazine fallen from her lap. A Marks and Spencer stuffed lobster had made a moderately satisfying Boxing Day lunch. Half a bottle of wine remained, slowly getting warm and losing its fizz. Karen had phoned to wish her Happy Christmas. There really was no reason to do anything more than choose a movie or good book and then retire to bed. The plan was to get up early and clear out the garage and prepare the spare room for painting. At least when Karen returned, she would see her mother had not wasted her time.

Slowly Elaine emerged from her slumber to hear the phone in the hall. How long had it been ringing? She woke with a start.

'Hello, sweetheart. Happy Christmas.'

It was Roger. Her heart leapt, and her voice despite her self-control fluttered with delight.

'And to you. I wasn't expecting to hear from you. Are you well? Is everything all right?'

'Of course. Why shouldn't it be? Caroline is off hunting and won't be back till much later. I've been shifting paper all day and am now done. I'm in desperate need of friendly company. What are the odds on your inviting me for a holiday drink?'

'Terrific!' she breathed. 'Come on over. The house is all yours.'

She half expected him to appear in a chauffeur-driven car, though that would have been ridiculous. At times his public image was more familiar to her than his private self. It was nevertheless wonderful to peep out of the upstairs curtains and watch him drive up in his own car, alone, dressed in a casual jacket and flannel trousers.

Deliberately she left the house lights off, except for a bedside lamp. Without ceremony both headed straight for her bedroom, where two years earlier Roger had comforted her after her terrible first Christmas as an MP. Drinks and niceties could wait, for what both needed and wanted was each other, a powerful meeting of minds and bodies, of skin and hair and eyes, making love as they always did, two people deeply attached to each other yet without ties or claims or rights, re-creating their passion with concentrated fervour. Only *now* mattered, for as long as *now* could be stretched into long loving moments together.

Since the flurry of activity surrounding Roger's promotion Elaine had kept discreetly out of the way, so for both there was an element of making up for lost time. He was persistent and vigorous, using her, pushing hard, saying little. It was as if the longings within himself were not to be articulated, for fear they were too carnal, too deeply separate from his other life.

Only when he was spent did he pat her rump gently in mute thanks. Then she fetched glasses, wine and a bowl of fruit and brought these offerings to him like a latter-day Cleopatra to her Antony. She slid in beside him in the warm bed, her golden hair tangled and gleaming in the soft light, poured a glass from a freshly chilled bottle and fed him sticky dates, one by one.

'I was a bit surprised to find you all alone,' he told her. He had heard from her whip that there were problems at home.

Elaine shrugged sadly. It would be unwise to spend precious minutes with her lover moaning; that way, he would soon stop visiting too.

'It happens. I'm not sure if Mike will be back. Wait and see, I suppose.'

'I'm sorry if things are not working out,' he added judiciously.

'Not your fault, Roger, honestly, and I think you're better out of it. I don't want you feeling any responsibility – if Mike and I do break up it's nothing to do with you and your name couldn't possibly be mentioned.'

That was the rule: their own liaison still had its strict limits.

It would not do to make the occasion too serious. Plumping the pillows up, she leaned back, hand behind head, raising her breasts, allowing the duvet to slip down, so that she was again uncovered and tempting. In due course she would take him again, when both were rested. There were questions on her mind but first she wanted to flatter him a little. A mistress has to work harder than a wife.

'I haven't really talked to you since you became a great man,' she teased. 'You enjoying it? Really, I mean?'

'God, yes. You bet. Cabinet is the only place to be. It's a much easier job than Minister of State, and much more interesting.'

Roger had been evaluating the matter himself and was eager to share his thoughts. He bent his legs up and relaxed, each arm resting on a knee, mouth full of fruit and a wineglass slopping in one hand.

'Easier?' she laughed. 'Aren't you overwhelmed with work?'

'No, that's the junior Ministers' job, poor blighters. All the slog and none of the fun. What I have to do is *think*.' He gave her a sly grin. 'And climb on the gravy train, arguing our case in Europe in mirrored halls over fine meals and wine. That bit I do enjoy, I must say.'

Elaine reached for a banana and peeled it slowly, eyeing him over the tip as she gently bit off the end, rolling the flesh around inside her mouth. The light in Roger's eyes was a request. Not just yet. Let him wait a bit.

'Well, now, Secretary of State. Which way do you think it'll all go? Will the European dream fall apart, or are the sceptics right to fear a United States of Europe eventually?'

'Who knows? I'm not a clairvoyant. Either way, I guess. The Community could disintegrate, and our curmudgeonly attitude could speed that disintegration. Not that western Europe will become another Yugoslavia, I don't expect that; we've spilled enough blood between us this century. But most people in this country underestimate the fervour elsewhere to get closer together. There's too much at stake, too much water under the bridge, for the "closer union" supporters to give up now.'

'You do express things differently, now, Roger,' she mused.

'More cynical, you mean?'

Talking with Elaine cleared his mind. He glanced at her appreciatively. He would never tell her, not exactly, what she meant to him. Especially not now that she was on her own. With Caroline there was always the faint feeling that sex was a bit puerile, the sort of thing horses got up to. Elaine took it all much more seriously, was by her very nature sexier, tried harder and made every coupling memorable. The way she was playing with that banana . . .

'Not exactly. You were pretty cynical when you were a whip, remember? Maybe it's me. These days, you're a statesman and I'm just a humble backbencher. There is nothing much I can teach you, and you've to be guarded in what you say. You can trust me, you know: if you want to try out ideas on me, they'll stay secrets.'

She finished lamely. It would be no fun if she got the same official views from Roger as did everybody else; she longed to help shape his thinking. That was an illegitimate aim. If the Prime Minister wanted her as an influential Minister he could appoint her any time. That it might never happen drove her to redefine her role with her Cabinet Minister lover, but it was a dangerous and perhaps forlorn game, and she knew it.

'Humble backbencher? I like that. Who came top in *The Economist*'s poll, then? Who beat me hollow? If that's humble, beautiful Mrs Stalker, then I'm as dust under *your* feet.'

He was in no mood for prolonged introspection. Leaning across her he opened his mouth and she put the last piece of banana in. He munched, then bent and kissed her breast, watching with satisfaction the nipple wrinkle and rise. She put down her glass, licked her parted lips once, then slid herself completely under the bedclothes to find him.

This time their lovemaking was lingering and thorough. She extended it as long as possible, knowing it might be weeks, even months, before another opportunity occurred. Outside a car drove past, but otherwise the night was quiet and frosty. A faint burst of music came from the pub down in the village, carried on the crisp still air. Only his cry, and their breathing together, panting and laboured, disturbed the silence.

Elaine rose and went into the bathroom to clean her teeth, then returned, drank a little wine to clear the taste of toothpaste, and lay beside him once more, caressing his resting body. The bed was warm and sticky, the atmosphere in the closed room almost fetid. Slowly then began the business of disengagement.

'That opinion poll won't help me, you know', she ventured. 'Just makes people cross.'

He pulled her towards him, settling her head on his shoulder. 'Right, but it should help you in the constituency,' he suggested. 'The voters like a celebrity.'

'I'm not sure about that. The election is getting a bit close for comfort. Do you really think we will win again?'

Roger switched into official mode. 'I don't see why not. Keating did, in Australia, won five in a row. Why shouldn't we? And it's our job to ensure that the electors don't get bored with us. So far in the UK they have proved more sophisticated than that.' He sensed her unease. He continued, 'You'll be all right here, Elaine, won't you? Your seat should be OK.'

She nodded with a show of bravado. It was almost impossible for an MP with a substantial majority like Roger to imagine the pressure on a Member for a marginal seat. South Warmingshire could go either way. In a landslide it would vanish and Elaine with it. Roger could be certain of getting back; she could not.

This two gaps, not one, were opening up between them – his elevation and natural reticence at sharing official secrets with her, and their differing expectations as the election drew nearer. At the beginning of the Parliament she and Roger had had much in common. Now an icy touch on her heart suggested that it would not take much for them to drift apart.

She stood by the shower and passed him soap and shampoo, standing naked, back to the steaming tiles, enjoying the way he rubbed himself down, soaping all over thoroughly. He owed her nothing, in reality; his failure to be grateful to her could not be altered and she would not have wished to press it. Since he never spoke of his need for her, never professed his love, she had no idea of it. She would have been astonished had Tom Sparrow told her of the argument in his office. All she knew was that Roger made a virtue of keeping his feelings to himself.

'I was just wondering . . .' she mused as she handed him a towel. He rubbed his face and hair, like a little boy under the watchful eye of his mother. She was startled to see how much more silver now streaked the brown, and stroked it, pushing it up off his face with her fingers.

'Go on.' He was in no hurry.

She plucked up courage. 'What happens to us now, Roger? I won't harp on about it, but the Boswood business scared me. Being found out, I mean.'

'Nothing new about that,' he said briskly. He reached for his clothes, the check shirt, an old sweater.

'Sure, but being with me puts you in far greater danger now you're in Cabinet. The press will be watching your every move. We have to be very careful.'

She wanted him to say wonderful things, that his love for her was greater than any fear and that he would never give her up. That was impossible; but it did not stop her wishing. She reached behind the bathroom door and pulled on a white towelling robe, tying it tight about her, a brooding expression on her face. Roger saw it and knew it meant trouble.

'You think too much at times, Elaine. If there's nothing you can do about it, don't let it bother you.' He ignored her 'we'. In this they were separate, not united.

She could stand it no longer, almost shouting at him, desperation making her voice hoarse. 'Don't you see? We must be *mad*. You're a Cabinet Minister, married with a family, a marvellous future ahead. The country needs men like you, honest and honourable and decent. You could rise right to the top, if you want – I've told you before. *What do we think we are doing?* How long can we carry on like this? I'm terrified, I tell you the truth, Roger.'

A grim shrug greeted her. *He doesn't want to talk about it.*

She continued, 'I don't want to be the cause of the end of your career. We will have to stop. We will have to start thinking about stopping, at least.'

He turned to face her at last, solemn and gentle, and placed his hands to her face as always when he left her, cupping her cheeks in his great palms. 'Do you want to finish? Is that what you're trying to tell me?'

'No, no. But we're running such a risk! *You* are running the risk, really, not I. I don't have that much left to lose; Mike has gone, Karen is growing up, and the seat is very rocky even if I bust a gut working it between now and the election. You have everything before you and I pose such a danger to you.'

'No one knows that better than I. But have I done something to upset you? I wouldn't hurt you for the world, Elaine. Do *you* want to give me up? Why should you think of stopping now?'

'Because I love you, you great clown.' Now she broke down and wept, covering her face with the white towelling sleeves, shaking his hands away, her hair tumbling around her hidden face.

He took her wrists firmly in his hands and prised them away from her face. He was not hurting her, but she was obliged to look up at him.

'Elaine, don't be part of the problem. You have always been special to me, because you are part of the solution.'

That was as far as he could go. Even so he had to bite his lip to say no more. In what must, he realised, have seemed a brusque silence, he pulled on his jacket and headed for the hallway.

It had not, in the end, been a satisfactory evening.

CHAPTER TWENTY-FOUR

The parliamentary day at Westminster was not the only event to start with prayers. On Monday mornings most departmental Ministers convene a meeting attended by all the team. A post-mortem is held on the previous week's events, congratulations or commiserations are offered for performances in the House or on weekend television, the day's press comment is dissected and deplored, an agenda for the subsequent few days is settled and, should enough energy remain from such short-term considerations, a little advance planning may be attempted. These gatherings are dubbed 'Prayers' from the era when Ministers were Christian gentlemen and no such discussion would have been thinkable without first calling on the Almighty to confer wisdom. These days Ministers preferred to manage on their own.

'Prayers' one grey January morning at the Department of the Environment had been convened as usual by the new Secretary of State. Everyone present was familiar with the long list of issues which bedevilled the department. The problem of the cost of coal no longer existed, as neither did the pits concerned, but the political bitterness lived on. The profound wish in all ministerial minds was that the recession too would soon be forgotten. Otherwise the next contest after years of continuous control could be distinctly tricky.

One person present would be unaffected by the result of a general election, assuming he was professional enough to leave no trace of previously expressed views. Since tradition dictates that new administrations are not permitted to see any of the papers of outgoing governments of a different colour (though civil servants may), that problem was not insurmountable. Martin Chadwick, fresh from success in arranging the latest environment summit, had been moved back closer to Ministers who found his laconic manner trustworthy and congenial. Discreetly Chadwick considered what changes the new Secretary of State had made. Matters of style, mostly, rather than substance, for Boswood and Dickson had been quite close, in temperament and in outlook. Roger Dickson preferred meetings held around a table rather than sitting casually in easy chairs, as Boswood had done – a trivial difference which, however, helped emphasise that a new man was in the driving seat. Dickson had gone further. He had ordered chocolate biscuits, though today no one was in a mood to enjoy them. One change he had so far failed to make: the tea, when it came, was execrable as always.

The junior Minister, Muncastle, was looking moderately pleased with himself, as indeed he should. His progress had been remarkably rapid for a man with neither a power base nor a forceful personality. Yet that greyness, Chadwick reflected, was regarded by officials as a point in his favour. With Muncastle there were no outbursts, no rages, no pointless stubbornness. He was always polite. He was acknowledged as hard-working and thoroughly competent. He was skilful at drawing out from a group their viewpoints and fallback positions, and would keep gently asking questions until at last someone present would come up with answers. This technique gave Andrew the reputation of being a superb listener and a subtle accepter of good advice, yet nearly always he got his own way. It would have been quicker to announce his own viewpoint right at the start, as many young Ministers did. That would have raised hackles and, in this rarefied atmosphere, made enemies. But Andrew made no enemies and collected quiet plaudits week by week. His adroitness at staying out of trouble, which frustrated colleagues like Elaine translated as lack of substance, stood him in good stead. Whether it helped him in the democratic necessity of explaining to the public what the Department of the Environment was up to and why was another matter. But then Dickson himself had been awkward with the media when he started and now was an accomplished performer. No doubt Muncastle, if sufficiently ambitious, could do likewise.

Chadwick switched his attention to the others present. Fiona Murray was settling nicely into her new role as private secretary to the Secretary of State and now sat primly in a nondescript grey suit ready to take notes. Power dressing had not yet hit female civil servants; most dressed so discreetly as almost to disappear. Opposite, the Lords Minister chatted amicably with Johnson the Commons whip and the PPSs. There was already one new face replacing Andrew Muncastle. Elaine had been on the list but passed over once again.

The future of the remaining person present also hung in the balance. Marcus Carey sat quietly, his eyes unnaturally bright, certain everyone could hear the rapid beating of his heart which had started the moment he realised Sir Nigel was going to resign.

It had proved impossible to persuade Boswood to stay at Westminster.

He had been, he felt, weak before, and that had led to all his troubles. Now he was adamant. He deeply regretted all the difficulties that would result but he'd simply had enough; there was no more fight left in him.

Marcus hugged himself. A by-election with all its attendant publicity might be brilliant for him if he acquitted himself well. Certainly he had no intention of funking it. Backing out did not occur to him. In his pocket nestled an envelope addressed to Roger tendering his resignation from the post of special adviser, as from midnight. He had no choice, even though it left him without job or income, for it was an office of profit under the Crown and would disqualify him from candidacy unless disposed of at once. The adoption meeting at Milton and Hambridge was planned for the following night. The election itself was set for Thursday 16 February, almost three months since Nigel resigned the seat. Next time Marcus set foot in Whitehall, all being well, it would be as a fully fledged MP.

Dickson ticked off the last item on his list, then banged the table for attention. 'Ladies and gentlemen! Today we are saying goodbye to our special adviser, Marcus Carey, for reasons you all know about. Marcus has been in the department sixteen months and in that time he has been an invaluable colleague. His contributions to our discussions, and his talents with speech-writing, parliamentary questions and preparation for media interviews have been first-class. We shall miss you, Marcus. I mean that.'

How Carey loved it. So much of his life he had hovered on the fringes; now all faces were turned towards him – Andrew nodding gravely, Fiona suitably acquiescent, Chadwick half smiling. Marcus could not trust himself to speak.

'So I've arranged to embarrass you a little further, Marcus, before you set off. Will you now please join us for a modest glass of champagne and a rather better buffet lunch that usual in the room next door, as we wish you God speed and good luck?'

Marcus felt the adrenalin begin to surge and grinned broadly. He pushed away the possibility that the champagne was premature.

There is something about Claridge's. The name evokes London at its sophisticated best, where style, comfort, wonderful cuisine and an overpowering sense of being totally pampered are available at the silent drop of a charge card.

Betts had been in some fine and expensive places but never anything like this. His journalist's urge was to pull out a notepad and jot down all the exotic details, perfect for an article on how the super-rich live. It certainly felt different, being on the inside with the *Globe*'s owner.

Black-coated staff in the high-ceilinged dining room welcomed his host as an old friend, greeted him by name and showed his party to what was obviously a familiar table in the window. Of course Murdoch, Packer and Conrad Black all got the same treatment, as did Maxwell in his day. And he, Betts, was here as a guest: a Rubicon had been crossed.

Betts took his time, as he trotted between Nick Thwaite and Miranda, and tried not to stare. As he sat down he wondered if it would be acceptable to remove the jacket of his dark new suit, but decided against it. The waiter handed him the menu. On its silky cover a group of elegant Victorians in evening dress paused on the threshold of this famous room. Above their glossy heads great chandeliers glowed as bewigged waiters danced attendance before huge displays of flowers. These days the waiters were mostly foreigners, Betts noted – even the head cook, Marjan Lesnik, whose name appeared immodestly at the bottom of the menu, was surely not born within the sound of Bow Bells.

Not that Betts was complaining. Of the five people now accepting large pink linen napkins two were foreigners, one of whom was picking up the tab, and McSharry the editor was not exactly English either. Betts quickly priced the courses: McSharry wanted goose liver with truffles at £14.50, followed by pot-roasted duck with apricots at £17.50. The owner was watching his cholesterol and jokingly ordered an even more expensive combination, a 'truffled celeriac remoulade' which turned out to be cold cooked vegetables at £14, and lobster at £28. There seemed to be a lot of truffles around, an excuse if ever there was one for lifting cash from unsuspecting customers. Betts did not fancy anything he did not recognise, so settled for a smoked salmon and caviar starter at £11.00 and a steak at £22.00. That would be followed by Monte Carlo strawberries at another tenner, and cheese, coffee, petits fours and liqueurs. At a guess, the bill for the five of them would come to at least £500, particularly now they were knocking back the Krug.

The lunch was in the nature of a celebration, for the *Globe* had just topped the half-million circulation mark. It was not entirely out of the wood, but the gloomy forest was receding. Betts settled down to enjoy himself.

The owner leaned forward. 'The question is, Nick, what are you going to do next? Toppling a Cabinet Minister is all very well, but that's yesterday's story. Who's on the menu now?'

He spoke without malice. This was purely business. If there were a better, surer, way to make money than by owning chunks of popular media he didn't know it. The issue in his mind was how to keep the *Globe* in profit, and that meant in the public eye.

'I wouldn't write Boswood off just yet,' mused Nick Thwaite. 'I've got somebody watching him up in Scotland. If he takes any young boys to his hideaway, we'll report him. The Scottish police take a dim view of chaps like him; very puritan country. Then we can run him ragged all over again.'

McSharry was dismissive. 'No, I agree with the boss. There's a limit to the amount of time you can persecute one poor bastard.'

Thwaite looked up in surprise. The editor, in using 'you', was absolving himself from responsibility.

'Are you saying he's only important as long as he's a Cabinet Minister?' Betts wanted to be clear.

The proprietor nodded. 'Get the guys at the top,' he urged forking slivers of truffle into his mouth. 'Ministers, bishops, princes. Not has-beens. Nobody else counts.' He raised his glass. 'Here's to big fools, the bigger the better. May we always finger them before anyone else.' Glasses were raised and clinked with glee.

'There are rumours about Boswood's replacement, aren't there?' Thwaite asked, turning to Betts. 'Haven't I heard he has a roving eye and one or two girlfriends? Didn't you check him out when he was a junior Minister?'

Jim Betts had a mouth full of the most succulent beef he had ever tasted and thanked his lucky stars he was unable to answer for a moment. At last he swallowed, helped by gulping down half a glass of bubbly. Miranda watched in distaste as the wine dribbled from the corner of his lips. Hastily he wiped his mouth.

'I checked but there wasn't much in it. He got drunk at a do at the Tory Party Conference in Blackpool and was fooling around. I think Miranda was there, weren't you? But there's not enough to go on.'

There was no reason why anyone present should be suspicious of his motives or information. Eyes turned enquiringly at Miranda, who flushed. Despite her giggle all her defences were up.

'It wasn't me! I went with Matthew Frank that night, if my memory serves. I often do. That's public knowledge.'

Betts decided to chance it. At the very least, putting pressure on Miranda might warn the lady to be less unfriendly towards him.

'You didn't leave with Frank, though. I thought I saw you with somebody who is now a government Minister, though he wasn't then.' There was the hint, just a hint, of menace in his voice.

'Ho ho, Miranda! What've you been up to?' Thwaite did not take Betts's insinuations very seriously. That there was sexual tension between Betts and Miranda was obvious, but he could easily understand her regarding the sandy-haired chap with the grubby moustache as beneath her, particularly if her choice instead rested on the older man at her side. The paper's owner and Betts came from different planets. The calm Australian radiated real power and was watching Miranda in sly amusement.

Betts began to bait softly, his eyes malicious. 'Come on, Miranda, tell us. He's married, isn't he? Andrew Muncastle. Got a nice wife, a little boy and a big future. So what's the great attraction? Is he good in bed, then?'

Miranda froze, her face livid as the others laughed at Betts's effrontery and her discomfort. She pushed away her plate.

'God, Betts, you are foul,' she muttered.

The unanswered question hung in the air. The whole table was looking at her, men of the world examining a beautiful woman. Even as she aroused them, in that instant she was isolated, the sole female. Her private life was a source of constant speculation at the *Globe* office. Betts was not the only man present to regard her as occasionally too choosy for her own good.

The sweet trolley arrived to general appreciation and for several minutes conversation languished as samples of cheesecake, soufflés, delicate fruit puddings and tarts were handed around. Claridge's did not stint their customers, though the management would be disappointed if anyone was still hungry by that stage.

For a moment the table was distracted. Betts was aware that Miranda was trembling. She caught his eye, tossed her hair and brought herself under control, then turned and faced him directly. Her voice was so low that, although the others were aware she had spoken to him, they could not hear what she said.

'Don't even think about publishing anything about Andrew, Mr Betts, or I'll make sure you never work in newspapers again.' She bared her white teeth at him. 'Do we understand each other?'

Betts nodded dumbly. He had no doubt she meant it, as she glanced over her shoulder at her distinguished companion, who was saying nothing but smiling to himself.

The gossip switched to other well-known names who were working hard to make themselves targets for the *Globe*: the archbishop said to have made two parishioners pregnant – one might be carelessness, but the second suggested a divine plan to help newspapers. Divorcing royals would keep the *Globe* and its rivals happy for a while, with fun to follow in identifying the latest paramours. Now that nearly all the House of Windsor were funded by the Queen herself instead of the state, most had quietly scaled down their public activities. No pay, no show. Only Diana, busy building herself an independent court, though resourced goodness knew how, was frequently seen smiling at cameras, shaking what remained of the hands of lepers and AIDS victims. The road to heaven is paved with bad intentions.

Betts resigned himself to chasing royals for a while. Yet Miranda's reaction to the Muncastle name made her instantly vulnerable and offered the opportunity for revenge, without anyone pointing a finger at him. If the *Globe* couldn't use the information, perhaps a friend elsewhere could. Serve the bitch right.

The stuffy atmosphere of the committee room above Milton Conservative Club was not helped by the persistent blue haze of Keith Freemantle's cigar. Senior party agents come in all shapes and sizes. Mr Freemantle, recently retired from active service but brought back into the fray to supervise the by-election, was short, stocky and energetic. A Midlands accent which raised eyebrows in Milton if not in Hambridge betrayed origins and long years of devoted service in the nation's second city. Freemantle favoured striped shirts and non-matching silk bow-ties intended to cause comment, thus making a statement about the unconventional means frequently necessary to do his job.

Outside the night was gloomy and wet. Crowded with Freemantle round the rickety baize table were the candidate and his wife, nervous and strained; the official MP 'friend', the ebullient Freddie Ferriman, thumbs hooked behind braces; Mary, the part-time agent, already exhausted; Mrs Farebrother, the ladies' chairman, and Mr Bulstrode, the chairman; Fred Laidlaw, the Young Conservative chairman, enthusiastic at his first-ever election; next to him Ferriman's tall American girlfriend Marlene; and an earnest young man from HQ's research department by the name of Dominic Quincy d'Abo.

Freemantle looked around, sighed and decided to brief all present in the simplest possible terms.

'First, timing. Polling day is Thursday, February the sixteenth. That's thirteen working days from today, not counting Saturdays and Sundays. Nominations are due in tomorrow, so it's on parade at nine sharp at the council chambers in the morning, Marcus and Alison, please. The press will be outside for a photocall. Our returning officer is the council's chief executive, Mr Day. Seems a reasonable bloke. We get the full list of nominations before five o'clock. We expect lots of hangers-on.'

'The National Front are thinking of standing,' Fred murmured. He harboured no resentment at Marcus's nomination but could not help reflecting that there was a lot of avoidable trouble ahead.

'Creeps,' said Freemantle crisply, implying that anyone worried by the Front deserved the same epithet.

'What about postal votes?' Mary piped up. It was not that she wanted an answer, but it seemed an intelligent question.

Freemantle gave her a withering glance and puffed smoke at her. 'I'm afraid today was also the last day for applications for postal votes. It's too late, dear. If they're not actually dead and want to vote we can take them to the polls. Shouldn't be a problem: we'll have lots of cars on polling day.'

'It's winter,' said Mary faintly.

'Certainly, but we're also still working on the old register so most will be dead anyway.' There had been a choice about waiting for the fresh register at the end of February, but traditionally no more than three months should elapse before a vacancy was filled. Any longer risked the Liberal Democrats seizing the initiative and moving the writ themselves.

Bulstrode intervened. 'We 'ave all the appeals letters ready to go out. The kitty is pretty empty 'ere, but we're 'oping we can do well enough to 'old some over for the general election.'

'That may be a bit ambitions,' Freemantle told him. 'There are nearly sixty-three thousand electors in this seat so your permitted expenses are just over twenty-eight thousand pounds and you'll need every penny.'

'You sure?' Fred asked doubtfully.

'Of course. You're allowed over sixteen thousand pounds for a county seat plus eighteen point six pence per elector. It isn't like a normal election at all when the limit here would be – let me see – around seven thousand pounds. How much did you spend last time?'

'Bit less than that. Around five thousand.' Bulstrode was embarrassed. He and the wealthier committee members had provided most of it. The appeals list, desperately cobbled together at the last minute, owed more to hope than to history. It was increasingly clear that the by-election would be a frightening new experience.

Freemantle responded testily, 'Even with that increased limit, it's easy to go over. Nobody, but nobody, spends or authorises any money without my express permission. I'm not having a lifetime's career ruined by a successful court challenge over expenses. Is that clear?'

Everyone present nodded gloomily. Freemantle gestured to Dominic. 'Your turn. Give us your political assessment.'

The young man glanced at his notes. 'We currently hold the seat by a large margin – Sir Nigel had three times the vote of the loser at the general election. Really, we have every chance. It would in fact take a huge swing to topple us.'

Mrs Farebrother raised an eyebrow. 'The Liberals have changed their candidate. The chap who did it last time was a bumbling old idiot. They've picked a thirty-year-old computer whizzkid by the name of . . .' – she consulted a press cutting – 'Nicholas Spencer. Oxford and Harvard, no less. Got a house in the middle of our best ward. Sounds very smooth to me. He'll go down well with our traditional voters, especially around Milton.'

Dominic raised his head. 'Nicholas Spencer? If it's the same chap, then I know him. We were up at Trinity together.'

'Well, I hope you're not planning to go and help him,' Freemantle commented tersely. These wet-behind-the-ears types who thought everything could be done on the old-boy network drove him up the wall.

'However, you're right, we can expect some tactical voting. Our task will be to encourage the *Labour* vote as far as possible, so we'll constantly attack Labour and ignore the Liberal. Pretend he doesn't exist, see. No mentioning him in leaflets or on the doorsteps. If anybody asks the Liberal candidate's name, look vague and say you've no idea, OK? We don't want them riding to victory on our coat-tails.'

The discussion continued for another hour as poster sites were booked, literature approved, canvassing allocated, timetables and transport arranged. Eventually Freemantle stubbed out the remainder of his cigar. Another by-election; another test of stamina, courage and wiliness. Another occasion when the electorate, freed of the burden-some obligation of choosing a whole government, might feel free to blow raspberries.

'One more thing,' he said sternly. Those whose attention had been wavering sat up. 'We're going to win this seat. I don't want to hear any talk to the contrary. We win all the seats I fight, always. Marcus is the next MP for Milton and Hambridge and that's how we're going to talk about him. No moaning minnies. Is that clear?'

His audience exchanged encouraging half-smiles. All set: candidate chosen, first-class organisation, a safe seat. It was hard to understand why everyone present felt uneasy.

In a room over a shop in downtown Hambridge, not far from the aircraft factory, another meeting was taking place. Mr Standish was by now fully recovered from his accident, though arthritic twinges on damp days were an uncomfortable reminder. He had had plenty of time to think through his opposition to Marcus Carey. Whichever way he looked at it in those long weeks out of action, he had come to the conclusion that he could not and would not accept an intruder as his future MP. The country was already going to the dogs. The socialists had always cultivated the black and minority vote, and were welcome to it. He was a patriot.

His views as reported in the local newspaper had drawn quite a response. Briefly he toyed with the idea of helping the Liberals but they seemed much too eager. Nor did he wish to stay in the wilderness for ever. Better to make a temporary protest, until local sanity was restored and his good sense would be the better appreciated. Then he would be invited to return in triumph to the local Conservatives, preferably to replace that fool Bulstrode as chairman.

Tonight's campaign meeting of 'Independent Conservatives' to choose a candidate to stand against Marcus Carey was the outcome of his cogitations. As for the candidate, Standish naturally expected it to be himself.

The little-used room was half full of damp people shaking out umbrellas and hanging sodden jackets on the back of their seats. In the front row sat an assortment of old ladies in motheaten coats, one carrying three torn plastic bags stuffed full of personal belongings, a hopeful look on her face. Nearby a couple of nondescript men in stained raincoats gave off a faint tired smell. Further back two ex-forces veterans, one with a stick, sported proud campaign medals on their chests. Beside sat a teacher who was telling them to nods of agreement that discipline in schools could only be kept by beating children, and that the party for which he had voted all his life had gone soft on crime. An elderly couple who had lived in South Africa and thus knew all about blacks sat close together, holding hands. The young girl journalist from the local paper kept quiet, wondering if she was the only press representative present and whether she would be brave if anyone got nasty. She need not have worried. The sour-faced man in the donkey jacket sitting slumped and morose at the back was, unknown to everyone else, from Special Branch; all those attending had been secretly photographed as they entered.

Standish counted: about thirty people. Not enough to win the seat, maybe, but enough, if they were willing to do the legwork, to get leaflets delivered and dent the majority sufficiently to ensure the other side got in.

The teacher was asking irritably if it wasn't time to start. Standish checked his watch, but as he gathered his papers there was a loud commotion caused by a group of late arrivals. It appeared that a band of local skinheads had decided to join the fun. The hint in Mr Standish's remarks as reported in the *Hambridge Gazette* was that the black was to be stopped at any cost. That suited them fine. Shaven heads agleam and chains a-jingle they clumped in and settled noisily at the back, swigging from a bottle of cheap whisky.

The lawyer rose, pushed his spectacles up his nose and cleared his throat. He felt suddenly very nervous. No time for second thoughts. Given the motley crew now present with their likely short attention span, it was best to get cracking.

'Ladies and gentlemen: we are here tonight to consider putting forward a candidate for the by-election. I don't know about you, but as a lifelong local resident and . . . ah . . . right-wing voter I really do not feel I can support the official candidate.'

'Hear, hear!' piped up an old soldier. His companion banged his stick on the floor in approval.

'I am not a racialist . . .' Standish made to continue.

'But I am!' yelled one of the skinheads. His companions hooted and nudged each other viciously. One fell off his chair with a crash and was hauled back with a friendly cuff by his pals.

438

Standish swallowed hard. 'As I was saying: I do not consider the official candidate at all suitable for this area, and I propose we put up our own choice, to go under the Independent Conservative banner.'

'Good idea! Quite right!' The old lady in the front was on her feet, brandishing her umbrella.

'Er . . . thank you, madam.' Standish frowned and motioned her to sit down. 'As I was saying . . .'

A stick was raised. 'Might it not be a good idea, sir,' enquired the old soldier gruffly, 'to support the National Front?'

'I've thought about that,' said Standish, briskly. In fact he had dismissed the idea very quickly. The Front was a recognised bunch of nutters. He wanted to make a serious point. 'We'll get far more votes if we call ourselves Independent Conservatives. That's what we are, after all.'

'King and country!' shouted the old lady at the front, jumping to her feet again. 'That's what we should be fighting for! Rule, Britannia . . .' And she was off, singing in a high, wavering voice.

Standish tried to wave her down, but the rest of the audience, thinking this was part of the agenda, struggled to its feet, and with the skinheads bawling loudest joined in with varying degrees of tunefulness but total sincerity: 'Britons never never never shall be slaaaa-aaaves!'

Standish noted with a sickening feeling that the menacing young men at the back thought it appropriate to accompany the anthem with Nazi salutes. It was fortunate that the old soldiers, standing to attention at the front, did not see them.

Before the audience launched into a reprise, Standish shushed earnestly, and as they subsided into their seats he continued quickly, 'I take it that's agreed. Thank you, ladies and gentlemen. Now, who do you want as your candidate?'

'Not you!' yelled a skinhead. He was huge, as wide as he was tall, with a wild black moustache and two days' growth of stubble. 'Too bloody high and mighty!'

'Yeah, Big Dave's right,' agreed his colleague, a tall, gaunt youth in leather with an amateurish tattoo of a bloodstained knife on one cheek and 'Terry' on the other. He stepped out into the aisle and walked forwards, boots clanging menacingly, examining everyone present with a practised hypnotic stare. At last he found what he wanted and stopped before a nondescript little man in a mackintosh. Leaning forward he grabbed the man's lapels in one hand and hauled him out, propelling him threateningly towards the front.

'He'll do: we'll have him.'

The lawyer was taken aback. 'Him? Ah . . . who is he?'

'No idea. Dun matter. We want 'im, don't we, lads?' The skinhead leered at the little man, who nodded quickly. At the back there was whooping and cheering. 'Yeah! Vote fer 'im!'

'I see. Well now, Mr er . . . What do you do for a living?'

Standish's effort to regain control of events brought forth more unaccountable merriment from the skinheads. The old soldiers turned around, irritated and prim.

'I . . . I work for the council,' the man gasped at last. He pulled himself together and pushed the skinhead away. 'I should be glad to stand. Name's Parrot. I agree with everything you said.'

'Put it to the meeting!' suggested the more belligerent of the old soldiers. Standish stood stock still with his mouth open. The old man rose and brandished his stick. 'Here, I'll do it if you won't. I move that Mr Parrot be our candidate. All in favour?'

A forest of hands went up. To most it did not matter who was to be the candidate: having a name on the ballot paper, any name, with all the publicity that would generate, would be enough. If Parrot wanted it, let him have it.

'We'll need five hundred pounds for the deposit,' Standish said glumly. 'And some money for printing.' He would have dipped in his own pocket had it been himself. Now he felt honour bound to make a contribution, but not quite so much.

'Five hundred nicker? Don't worry about that,' the skinhead leader Terry winked.

'Really? Where will you get a sum like that?' Standish was cold.

'Don't you cast aspersions. We earn that kind of money in a good week, mate.' Terry grinned. 'An' if we don't, we'll nick it for Mr Parrot, won't we, boys? When d'you want it?'

Standish knew when he was defeated and this time accepted the fact with the best grace he could muster. He had spent far too long in hospital recently to risk a recurrence at the hands of Terry, Big Dave and their mates. Moreover, there was a job to be done. Whoever this Parrot was, it would fall to himself to ensure some dignity and legality to the proceedings. 'Tomorrow. At the council offices. Can you make two o'clock? No later – the deadline's four.'

'No sweat!' The skinhead leaned across and gave the wilting Parrot a bear hug which made his bones creak. 'See ya there, Parrot!'

'Wait! I need at least eight signatures as assenters to the nomination. All those of you who live in the constituency and are on the electoral register.'

As the leather-jacketed youths and others queued to sign the nomination papers, Mr Standish had a queasy feeling that he had been stitched up. He had once heard Mrs Farebrother mutter obscurely after one of his own interventions that in politics you cannot always choose your companions. Her meaning was somewhat clearer than half an hour ago.

'Tip for you.' Betts took a drag from his cigarette in true Humphrey Bogart style, keeping his mouth close to the earpiece.

'Yeah? What's that?'

'An MP – a Minister, just appointed – plain, dull, married, one child, very identikit, but seems to be moving fast. Got a girlfriend. Lovely bit of skirt. Make a good spread.'

'Oh aye. Who'd be interested in him, then?'

'We would, except that the dame in question is also having it off with our owner, though he'll take you to the cleaners if you hint as much. So we have a Minister in the owner's pocket as well.'

'Well now, that's more interesting. What's he Minister of?'

'Come *on*. You interested in the story or not? What's in it for me?'

The voice at the other end chuckled knowingly. An amount was suggested and haggled over briefly. The transaction gave the betrayal a vicarious authenticity, as if money were the sole motive, but Betts was not really interested in any sideline funding. It would suit his purpose simply to have Miranda's name dragged in the mud, and her toffee-nosed boyfriend with her.

'It's in the post, Jim. Consider it done,' the disembodied voice confirmed. 'Now spill.'

The easiest way to help in the by-election, Elaine decided, was to drive down early on a Monday morning, spend all day, then carry on to London in time for the ten o'clock vote. To her pleasure Karen expressed an interest for the first time. A day on the hustings could be justified as educational. Not that the college worried about attendance; it was all so different to school.

'I've no idea what we'll find when we get there, but basically we do as we're asked, darling.'

The old Rover, bought in the first flush after the election, was sounding creaky. Maybe it was time to check out a Toyota, newly built in Britain. Elaine reflected how complicated the world had become since her childhood. She glanced at Karen, who seemed relaxed and happy, twisting to make the seat belt comfortable.

'Yeah, I don't mind. What d'you have to say on the doorstep, Mum? I don't really know enough to argue politics with people.'

'That's true for most of the canvassers, so don't worry about it – arguing is my job, not yours. Look, what we want is to get the maximum number of our voters out on the day. To do that, we have to identify them first. You can't rely on the canvass for the previous general election – people go all peculiar in by-elections. What you do is smile sweetly, flash your blue rosette, say clearly who you're representing and ask if they're supporting us this time. If the answer is "yes", ask them if they'll take a poster, and make a note. If it's "no", skedaddle quickly. You don't have time to hassle. It's usually a waste of time, anyway.'

'What if they say they don't know?'

'A lot of those don't vote – probably as many as a quarter or a third of the register this time. If the most recent canvass was properly done we can judge if they've been ours. And that's when you call me in, or another old-stager, while you buzz off to the next house.'

Karen was intrigued. 'Are you good at converting them, Mum?'

Elaine chuckled. 'I try! Sometimes the very fact that someone has called is enough to jog them out of their apathy, especially if it's a face from the telly. But if I seem to be getting stuck, come and fetch me. The dirtiest trick in the book is the confirmed opposition supporter who'll say he's "not sure", solely to keep the canvasser talking. I used to do it myself in Barham when you were little – kept a Labour chap going for half an hour one night, then told him he'd failed to convince me and I'd be voting Green. He was so upset I thought he was going to cry. Rotten thing to do.'

Karen giggled. 'Cruel world, isn't it?'

Her mother shrugged. 'Isn't it just. If today puts you off, I'd be half sad, and half happy. But it's good to have you with me.'

Campaign headquarters had moved to a vacant shop in Hambridge High Street following complaints from Milton Conservative Club members that their car park was always full and that a man could not sup a quiet pint on a Friday night without having every unguarded remark plastered over the Sunday papers. The shop was easy to find, its windows festooned with posters. A large bunch of blue and white balloons left over from a ministerial walkabout in the town centre had been tied above the door; blown about, several had burst and remnants flapped limply in the wind. One of the posters had been defaced with an obscene remark over Marcus's name. A Land-Rover was parked in front, also decorated: this must be the battle-bus, laden with handouts. Elaine wondered why it wasn't out and about, in use, at eleven o'clock on a Monday morning.

It was a cold, windy day, not the best weather for doorstepping. The two women fastened coat and jacket, checked gloves, pens, rosettes, handkerchiefs and clipboards, and headed into the shop.

Mary Morgan was ready to weep. It was not her fault that the canvass cards for the best ward had disappeared, though since the ward chairman had defected to the Liberals he had probably taken them with him. It was not her fault, either, that the local party was not properly computerised so that printing out a fresh set of cards was proving beyond her, nor that the photocopier kept breaking down – there had never been the money to replace it. If the powers that be, these exasperating types from Smith Square, wanted a posh modern office they should provide the money. But if they were so darned clever, she thought savagely as she kicked the reluctant machines, how come they ran up an overdraft of nineteen million pounds? At least Milton and Hambridge was solvent. The comparison comforted her and she calmed down momentarily, as Elaine and Karen entered.

'Hello, I'm Elaine Stalker.' Elaine held out her hand.

'Yes – yes, I know who you are.' Mary was puzzled.

'Weren't you expecting me? Central Office asked for volunteers and I told them I'd be coming today. This is my daughter.' The office appeared to be empty except for Mary. The only sound came from a rackety printer. Piles of dusty paper lay on chairs, in corners, on tables. Full ashtrays left over from Saturday had not been cleared. Dirty coffee-mugs filled a sink, empty drink-cans overflowed from a plastic-lined bin. The air was stale.

'Yes, they did send us a list. It's here somewhere.' Mary gestured vaguely behind her. 'Mr Carey's gone with Mr Freemantle to the station to meet Mr Dickson, the Cabinet Minister, who's speaking at a lunchtime rally.' She added accusingly, 'It's a bit early.'

It was news to Elaine that Roger was in the area. When she had seen him the previous week he had not mentioned the fact, but such visits were often arranged at only a few days' notice.

'Well, since I am here, what would you like me to do? Have you finished all your canvassing? Perhaps I could call on some doubtfuls. I could catch the rest of the team up at lunchtime.'

'Canvassing – no, we're nowhere near finished. I think we're about halfway.'

Elaine was astonished. 'Ten days to go, all those extra helpers, and still loads to do? Never mind. Perhaps you could give me a map and some cards. How about a guide, somebody who knows the area and the issues likely to crop up?' She waited expectantly.

Mary sighed and looked helpless. 'I'm afraid . . . there's only me here at the moment and I can't leave.'

Elaine was getting cross. 'Isn't there somebody you could phone?' She pointed and left unspoken the question whether this singularly useless person could use one correctly.

Mary picked up the flavour of annoyance and did as she was bid. A moment later she reported happily that Mr d'Abo was on his way, and offered a cup of coffee, apologising that there was no milk.

It was another twenty minutes before the warrior band was ready. With Karen in the back Elaine settled behind the wheel of the Rover. She turned to Dominic. 'Now, do you want to direct me?' she asked politely.

'Me? I haven't the faintest idea. I'm as new to the area as you are.' Dominic was very grumpy indeed at being pulled away. Marcus wanted a press release for lunchtime and it would be late, all because this jumped-up backbencher was insisting on an escort. He couldn't be expected to be everywhere at once.

After several false turns they found the area allocated to them, parked the car and started. The smart half of the ward proved barren ground; almost everybody was out except for a Swedish au pair and a forgetful old lady who assured her she would be voting for Sir Nigel Boswood as usual. Somewhat discouraged Elaine turned her attention to the lower end of the ward, where tight clumps of terraced council housing looked more promising territory. In her own patch she attracted much support from workaday voters in streets like this. Karen was blue with cold and Dominic was snuffling. Nevertheless there didn't seem to be much else to do for the next half-hour except plod on, turning coat collars up against the drizzle.

A corner house had an inner light on and a new BMW parked in its carport. Its smart front door indicated a purchased council house, a likely source of support. Dominic was pushed up the path while Elaine and Karen carried on. The next four houses produced five 'Don't knows' and two antis, though to Elaine's relief their preference was Labour. The morning was proving unduly depressing.

It was not for several minutes that the women realised that Dominic had disappeared. As they retraced their steps, it became apparent that he had got no further than the first house, and must have made the cardinal mistake of accepting an invitation to enter.

The doorbell chimed a version of *Eine Kleine Nachtmusik* as Karen and Elaine shivered on the doorstep. Over their heads a red lamp was switched on, casting a warm glow in the gloomy day. The door swung open. On the threshold stood a tall blonde in tight black leather, a short skirt revealing tanned thighs, the top in the form of a buttoned sleeveless waistcoat emphasising a size 44 *embonpoint* billowing over the top. Behind her the hall was cream and plush with a pink shag-pile carpet. A Russell Flint print of half-naked girls adorned a space at the bottom of the stairs.

'More of them! Come in, come in,' warbled the blonde, and stood to one side. Elaine hesitated as Karen stared goggle-eyed. 'You're Mrs Stalker, aren't you? Come on in, just for a minute. We're voters too, you know.'

That being undeniable, Elaine took a deep breath and followed her down the hallway. The sound of merriment assailed her. She turned into the living room with red walls and a black ceiling, its curtains drawn against the light. And there the luckless Dominic was splayed out on a red velvet sofa, a look of terror on his face. Beside him perched on the arm was a black girl wearing thigh-length shiny boots, a red lace G-string and a diminutive red bra, who sipped a cocktail and stroked his hair. The room was viciously hot. A sallow man with a proprietorial air and a thin moustache was smoking from a long cigarette holder. In the corner stood a television and a stack of videos. Dominic, brow beaded with sweat, was clinging to his clipboard as if to his virtue.

Elaine blinked, then took brisk charge. 'Good morning, ladies, sir. We are canvassing for Marcus Carey, the Conservative candidate. Now there are, let me see' – she examined the clipboard in Dominic's stiff fingers – 'five voters here, four ladies, one man. We'd like to know if you'll be voting for us?'

'He don't live here – lives off us and on us, but not in the chicken run.' The black girl gestured to the man, who wagged an admonitory finger. 'You can't talk to the other girls – they're resting. Good business last night. We all take an interest, though. Pity about that poor man, Nigel Boswood. He should've come to us. We'd have sorted him out, wouldn't we?'

Elaine hauled Dominic to his feet, smiling despite herself. 'I simply need to tick you off and not bother you any more. Polling day is a week on Thursday. Will you support us?'

'Oh, yeah,' grinned the blonde. 'You can put us girls down. We're in favour of free enterprise, we are. Citizens' Charter and all that: looking after the customer, innit? The Prime Minister is lovely. Why didn't you bring him? If he came here we'd . . .'

The party fled before the graphic details of the potential Prime Ministerial entertainment could be enunciated. Four precious ticks could be entered on the computer. It seemed wisest to head back to headquarters.

Marcus, Keith Freemantle and Roger had arrived. Elaine was greeted with hugs and kisses by all three. Two more volunteers were clearing space on tables and the place had begun to hum. Coffee was offered again, this time suitably accompanied; Mary was looking happier.

In public Roger and Elaine were awkward, almost gruff with each other. The danger of discovery was so real that even an undue friendliness might have produced gossip. Both were aware that Karen was observing them with undisguised curiosity. Elaine sighed inwardly. A strange melancholy romance it was, only enacted in bed; however deep and close after making love, the warmth did not, could not, exist at any other times. Roger might joke with another woman colleague; she might tease a man, and certainly had no compunction about describing, out of his hearing, Dominic's introduction to Hambridge tarts. Together under watchful eyes they had no choice but to be cool and formal. Yet after a while all love affairs, legitimate or otherwise, need something more than sex and pillow talk. Most relationships mature, as tastes in common are explored, other experiences shared. With Mike she had learned over the years to walk down the street with longer paces than usual so as to fall into step with him. She used to know how high to wear her shoes in order to be exactly the right height to put her head on her husband's shoulder. With Roger she knew none of these things, for they had never walked down the street together, only once in the dark at Blackpool. It was all encapsulated, limited, the boundaries immovable. It was beginning to feel like a straitjacket, not a release. And yet he was still by far the best thing that had ever happened to her.

Karen was not tempted to compare her father and Roger. Her father had been away a great deal during her years of growing up. She wondered if it might have been something to do with the dead baby; he had become withdrawn, as if reluctant to entrust his soul to any living being. At least her mother had made the effort, becoming stronger and more diverse in her life afterwards, and closer to her remaining child. The way Elaine handled the shambles of the morning made Karen proud and certainly showed her mother in a more human light. The girl looked candidly from mother to lover and back again. They made a handsome couple, real politicians, capable and wise and powerful. Her mother's face was flushed and pretty, her hair tumbled with the wind. In an ideal world, great prince and beautiful princess, they would be acknowledged as equal partners, like the Queen of Sheba and Solomon. How much duller today that people who adored each other could not show their affection, that formalities had to be observed. It couldn't be making them happy.

Monday is often a lean news day when reporters are glad of an opportunity to get out of the office, where hangovers and boasting of weekend conquests predominate. Jim Betts had done his share of the boasting, naturally, but then he had always been an accomplished liar. A kidney infection had left him feeling a bit under the weather, not helped by a ban on mixing alcohol with medication. Thus his mood was not of the brightest on this dismal February morning as he lounged on a squeaky chair in the town hall in Hambridge, not too far from the gents' toilet just in case, waiting for Dickson and the entourage to arrive.

The place filled slowly with party faithful bussed in from all over the region who were now shaking coats and plastic rainhoods and commiserating with each other. It was generally agreed that this must be the wettest by-election ever. With a higher proportion of women working of any major country, the availability of people of middle age during daylight was somewhat limited: thus most of the audience were aged over seventy, many of whom had already found the excursion tiring. Security considerations made it a ticket-only affair. In fact there were no ordinary unconverted present waiting to be suffused with amazement at the pearls of wisdom about to drop from Roger's or Marcus's lips. The event was directed solely at Betts and his press companions, including the photographers sprawled out on the front row and prowling up and down the side aisles looking for character shots.

Betts had every intention of ignoring the speech. Most of the article for the following day's sketch was already written, gleaned from remarks made by harassed party workers scurrying in and out of campaign headquarters, including Mary, ever honest, who confessed to being 'not optimistic'. That was his headline. Labour were hardly bothering. At Liberal HQ morale was high.

Carey seemed to know it too. His manner lacked the eager confidence of the successful. Instead his posture was stooped as if carrying a heavy weight. The murky light inside the town hall made him look blacker; had he been European there would have been tell-tale circles under his eyes. Betts liked that line and made a note of it. The wife was not there either. She had the excuse, as a doctor, of having patients to see, but, whereas Carey with his white wife appeared modern and competent, without her he looked vulnerable and ill placed, like a little boy at a grown-ups' soirée, or a slave at an auction.

As the platform group entered, Betts sat up and took more notice. So Mrs Stalker was here too! That couldn't be a coincidence. Rapidly energised he began to scribble notes on her appearance – the blue suit, tousled blonde hair a little longer than it used to be, slim and fit. She must be – what? – thirty-eight. Dickson was a bit older but not much. She looked ten years younger and very fetching except for that controlled expression around the mouth. Betts could almost fancy her himself.

From the high point of the platform, seated behind the long table with its blue tablecloth adorned with posters acclaiming his name, watching as the supporters lifted their faces in anticipation, Marcus Carey for the first time wondered quite what he was doing there. Alison was right: this had all been a terrible mistake. Instead of being so ambitious he should have tried his hand first as a no-hoper in some horrible inner-city seat, to win his spurs, and to grow some scar tissue. As it was, what should have been the greatest opportunity of his life was becoming a nightmare, not because any one small correctable thing was going wrong but because the whole mixture was sour and curdling. By-elections were bad news for everyone, particularly the defending candidates, sacrificial lambs put up for the slaughter: their greatest burden was the government's failures, and the longer a government had been in power the higher the heap of errors to plague them. The British believe in devilry and spells.

A favourite British Victorian painting, *The Scapegoat*, shows the animal haunted, desperate and mad, left in the wilderness by the self-righteous Hebrews to die in expiation. It was but a small step to transform that pitiable creature into human form. The key feature was a slow death, in public. Marcus knew all about it.

Karen was learning fast. She had no desire to join the platform group and had hung back as the greats including her mother headed up the main stairs, had taken a different entrance and come in from behind the audience. It would be interesting to watch Roger and Elaine in action. And Marcus too, but he seemed dwarfed by the grandees. Thus she became aware of the scruffy man in a raincoat several rows in front writing in a notepad.

It was him. *Him again*. The smell of alcohol and cigarettes and coffee mingled with sex and violation and pain powered through her. The room went cold. She felt sick and began to tremble. In the pit of her belly a throbbing pain, physical reminder of that appalling night, gripped her. Her head went up and for a moment she nearly cried out, but then slunk back into the shadows at the back of the hall and fought to regain control. The bastard was not going to haunt her, nor try it on again. He could not get at her. She would not make the same mistake. An opportunity to punish him, however, would not go amiss. From then on she was watching Betts and no one else.

'The government are keen to ensure that the environment is maintained and preserved, of course we are,' Dickson smoothly assured an elderly questioner. 'The problem, as always, is to reconcile conflicting priorities. This year the government have put an extra twenty million pounds towards the cost of insulating homes. You should ask your council about it.'

'It's Liberal-controlled,' Elaine hissed.

Without a break Dickson continued, 'And if you're not satisfied with the response you should demand some action from this Liberal-controlled council. I'm afraid they're not known for their competence.'

'Hear, hear!' came from the audience. Experienced hands, they knew when to applaud. Several old gentlemen, previously fast asleep, awoke with startled expressions, checked that the meeting still had some while to run, and discreetly dozed off again.

Even Dickson was not trying very hard, Betts noted. There was no point. Journalists including Betts himself, shifting, uncomfortable and bored on the hard chairs, were taken care of by a press handout containing the quotable bits of both Dickson's and Carey's speeches.

A chair creaked quietly behind him. Betts decided to check out the audience and half turned in his seat. To his considerable shock he found himself staring straight into the eyes of a bitter young face from the recent past.

'Hello, James,' Karen said in a hoarse whisper.

Before he could stop her she leaned forward and snatched his notebook out of his hand. He opened his mouth to protest but shut it again quickly. The last thing he needed was anyone noticing that he knew Miss Karen Stalker. With baleful eyes and a twisted smile the girl flicked over the pages. The notes were in bad shorthand which even he could barely read, but proper names were written in capitals. Most of the girls he knew in the office were clericals who could do Pitman's with far greater skill. Karen glanced up and took in his fearful expression. It clearly panicked Betts to think she could follow the squiggles. Hiding her ignorance, she raised eyebrows on page after page as if reading, then paused at last at her mother's name. Deliberately she tore out the page and the ones following and preceding it, then handed the mangled notebook back to its dumbfounded owner.

'You won't be needing these, James, dear,' she said quietly, and stuffed them in her pocket before rising elegantly and moving to the far side of the hall, where she leaned against the wall, arms crossed, and stood watching him like a warder in a prison.

Her action rang a bell. If only those antibiotics did not make him feel so spaced out. Then he remembered the letter torn in quarters and secreted in his raincoat. After that chaotic evening he had emptied his pockets and, never the tidiest of souls, put the bits somewhere safe in the flat. Worth retrieving, surely, if that big affair was still on. Then he caught Karen's unforgiving eyes. She could not be seventeen even now, yet she had a toughness which belied her years. He felt deeply apprehensive. He had never forgotten her threat to scream to the police if he linked her mother's name with Dickson. Sixteen months ago he had been unsure whether she was capable, but after today, looking at that young face so suffused with hatred, he understood that she would not hesitate. Indeed her manner suggested she would relish the prospect of rubbing his face in it. Betts slumped back in his seat and let his mind wander. He needed a drink.

Keith Freemantle considered starting a new cigar and decided against it. No point in wasting any more of his precious Davidoffs on this lot.

In a corner of the committee room a heater puffed steamy vapour into the air. Unused posters wilted on an empty chair; the printer stood silent at last. With a sigh Freemantle surveyed the collection of grey faces around the table.

Mrs Farebrother had worked like a Trojan and now had a bad cold. She sat sniffing and muffled in a scarf. Bulstrode, his expression set in gloom, had placed himself as far as possible from Freemantle, as if party HQ were the enemy. Marcus Carey sat beside his chairman, trying to draw comfort from his stolid Englishness. Freddie Ferriman was still cracking jokes but no one was laughing: he would sleep alone in Hambridge's only hotel that night, for a bored Marlene had returned to London. Dominic, whose morose face had marred (or symbolised) the entire campaign, was pottering around in the back room. Fred Laidlaw was out doggedly delivering last-minute leaflets in the rain, and Mary had been sent home to bed. All their diminishing stores of energy would be needed the following day as the polling stations opened.

Freemantle took a deep breath. 'Well, now, lady and gentlemen, we're on the last lap. We've put up a good fight, and whatever the result tomorrow Milton and Hambridge can be proud of the way it has handled itself. And proud of its candidate.'

'It's been a bloody shambles,' muttered Bulstrode. Faces turned towards him; certain things needed to be said, and now was the time to say them. He folded his arms aggressively. 'All right, we weren't the best-prepared constituency. Never needed to be. We always won easily with Sir Nigel; we made it our business to 'elp others nearby. But I must say that if Central Office think they know 'ow to win by-elections then I beg to differ.'

His audience waited.

'You over-estimated 'ow many 'elpers we could provide with two good legs and an 'ead on their shoulders. It's no use producing thousands of leaflets if no one can deliver them. By asking people to do too much you annoyed them – not that some needed much excuse for clearing off, I grant you.'

'It's not as bad as that. We've had a thousand volunteers from all over the country,' Freddie protested. What a dismal bunch. He would be heartily glad to leave this God-forsaken hole for ever.

Bulstrode was warming to his theme. 'Aye, and many of them altogether too posh for us. It may be a safe seat – or was – but a lot of the residents are ordinary working people. Toffee-nosed accents on council doorsteps 'ave gone down very badly. And ordering our local 'elpers around. Bloody arrogant, I call it.'

'I will make a note of that in my report,' Freemantle offered weakly. Ingratitude, he called it.

Mrs Farebrother cleared her sore throat and tried to pour oil. 'Please understand that we appreciate all the assistance. We have felt overwhelmed, that's all. Swept aside. The little local sensitivities ignored. Not me, but that's what my ladies say.'

There was a pause. Nobody had mentioned the candidate, who sat sombre and silent. The heater hissed dolefully. Mrs Farebrother blew her nose.

Bulstrode heaved a sigh. 'We've been lumbered in my view with a double burden: crass incompetence at Central Office and the effects of the recession. I accept that perhaps we're being too critical. 'Owever good the campaign, we would 'ave been up against it. Too many people round 'ere 'ave been made redundant. Too many businesses crashed. People lost their 'omes, or even those who 'aven't worried about it. 'Ere we are, asking for a vote of confidence and it's no surprise if we don't get it.'

He gestured at Carey. 'What upsets me is the thought that Marcus 'ere is going to get all the blame. 'E doesn't deserve it, Freemantle, and I 'ope you put that in your report, too. In current conditions if we'd put God Almighty up 'e'd 'ave got 'ammered.'

Freemantle leaned back in his chair and put his fingertips together. 'We are not defeated yet,' he pointed out firmly. 'Remember the last general election? The voters showed more sense than all the opinion pollsters put together.'

Nobody believed him. The evidence of the doorsteps was against him. The meeting settled a few necessary arrangements for the following day and broke up.

Almost by instinct Bulstrode and Mrs Farebrother came together and approached Marcus, facing him. Bulstrode spoke for them both.

'Marcus, you've done us very well. I accept that your colour 'as been an 'andicap, but that can't be 'elped. It's a wicked world at times. You conducted yourself as we would 'ave wished. Thank you, and don't blame yourself.'

What were intended to be kind words came out curtly, like a dismissal. Any invitation to carry on, to continue as candidate for the general election, was entirely missing.

Mr Day would be heartily glad when it was all over and his fiefdom returned to slumber. Of middle height, middle age and middle-of-the-road opinions, Trevor Day was happy that his ambitions in life – to be chief executive of a charming middle-sized borough somewhere in southern England – had long since been realised. Necessarily and scrupulously non-partisan, he enjoyed his local status, serving as chairman of Rotary, attending Chamber of Trade meetings, hovering and organising and staying humbly in the background, while others disported on platforms and exposed themselves to public ridicule. No unpredictable electorate was going to turf him out. Provided he kept a clean show on the road in the best tradition of English local government, he could expect to stay in this job for life, and retire contented and appreciated in due course.

There was just time to give last-minute instructions to his counting staff, mainly bank clerks and clerical workers who had done it before. It was approaching ten: the polls would be closing any minute. Policemen were arriving, television reporters were getting ready for a live trail on the evening news, and the school hall was filling up. In one classroom tea urns were bubbling gently, in another a bar with an occasional licence was under the firm control of the school's governing body. Crisps and hotdogs were already on sale. It was, after all, a grant-maintained school which never missed a chance to turn a handy dollar.

'Now you all understand what we're doing. Bit different from usual with nine candidates, though we expect most of them to lose their deposits if they get less than five per cent of the turnout. That means watching for every vote, though.'

'Nine! Merciful heavens!' a woman counter whispered to her neighbour. 'Still, it's been a real treat. I like that Screaming Lord Sutch. Brings a bit of life into the place. When it's over I shall try to get his autograph.'

'My Bernie fancies Miss Whiplash. I think he's voted for her.'

'No kidding! You'll have to get yourself all kitted out with the gear, then, if that's what he likes.'

'Been a bit of trouble, though. I suppose you'd expect it with a black candidate. The National Front ought to be banned.'

'Yeah, you're right. My grandad fought people like that in the war. He says if they got half a chance they'd put us all up against the wall and shoot us.'

'Well, we're doing our bit for democracy tonight, and that's for sure. What's Mr Day saying?'

'. . . and when we've done the first count, which ensures that all the papers are there and the totals agree, we put them all back in the ballot boxes, shake them up a bit, then count again. So the first time we don't sort into candidates, the second time we do. Is that clear?'

On cue on the dot of ten the Liberal Democrat Party made its entry, jackets adorned with outsize rosettes like huge orange cartwheels. Nicholas Spencer was taller than most of his supporters, eyes bright with anticipation, his acceptance speech ready in his pocket but already off by heart. His wife hovered beside him, her face rosy with pride.

At the door a gaggle of wildly dressed supporters of the Monster Raving Loony Party, leopard-skin tights, pink feather boas, silver top-hats and all, pushed their way inside to the genial amusement of the police. This lot were not the problem. They had put up two candidates in order to get double the number of tickets to attend the count, and were clearly intending to have a ball. Their merriment was infectious, provided they did not get too drunk. Trailing after them came Lindi St Clair, Miss Whiplash, leaning on the arms of a sullen boyfriend, posing for photographers and exposing acres of goose-pimpled flesh. She made a fuss about being made to leave her whip at the door, but was mollified when a handsome police inspector informed her that everyone would recognise her magnificent features without it.

A bedraggled group in one corner were munching wholegrain sandwiches and drinking homemade lemonade. The Greens knew their day had come and gone, in Britain, in Germany, in Europe. All the main parties made green noises. Still, they had done their best.

The inspector wandered over to Day. 'I don't suppose our fascist friends will arrive till the pubs close,' he commented.

The two were old friends from Rotary. Day grinned ruefully: 'Which candidate did you have in mind – the National Front or Mr Parrot and his cronies?'

'Parrot!' The policeman nearly spat out the word. 'I wish fools like him were disqualified from standing, but they're not. Only peers and idiots – and he's none of those. He works for you, doesn't he? What possessed him to get involved?'

Parrot had attracted more attention in the last three weeks than in the thirty years he had worked in a dusty office at the town hall. 'Search me,' Day shrugged. 'He took us all by surprise.'

The ballot boxes began to appear as the Conservatives, ragged but cheering each other up, came into the hall to quick glances and whispers from the counters. Marcus and Alison, quiet and dignified, walked hand in hand. You had to admire that Carey bloke. Courage, if nothing else. Take a good look, we'll not see him again round here.

For the next forty minutes the black boxes arrived thick and fast, banging and clattering their contents on to the long wooden tables. Trevor Day took his jacket off and set to. The swish of paper filled the air as the old-fashioned system swung into action, watched by apprehensive activists. No button-pressing here, simply small white slips of paper marked with that single X against the voter's choice, in slowly rising heaps.

Marcus Carey approached his Labour opponent and shook hands. Together they stood, notepads in hand, peering over the shoulders of the counters, disconsolately checking their support. Each batch of twenty-five votes contained some nine or ten for Marcus and two or three for the Labour candidate, who laughed hollowly and shoved his pad back in his pocket. For both the numbers brought the same message. The Liberal Democrats were collecting nearly half the vote and that would put their man well ahead, on track for a famous victory.

'Awful campaign, wasn't it?' The Labour man was friendly. Now the contest was over there was no point in being otherwise.

Marcus was staring at the piles of votes. 'Makes you feel very strange, don't you think, looking at all those crosses? People voted for me whom I've never met, yet they know all there is to know about me, or think they do.'

His opponent shrugged. 'I've never looked at it quite like that.

Perhaps I will if I'm ever selected for a winnable seat.'

That hurt, though it was not intended to. Marcus continued, struggling to put into words the sense of a sacrament that comes at the count to many candidates. 'I feel I owe them all a huge obligation, especially the ones I don't know personally. They put their faith in me. And I've let them down.'

'Don't talk like that.' The other man spoke sharply. There was no need for party banter; that Marcus was exhausted was all too apparent. 'You've been the victim of prejudice, and people like you and me are both in business to fight it. Don't let the bastards get you.' He dropped his voice. 'If you ever feel like joining us, let me know. You put up a good fight. Though I can't guarantee you'd have an easier time on our side, to be honest.'

Before Marcus could reply there was a shout from the main door and a crashing sound outside. The socialist jerked his head in the direction of the noise. 'Here come the real enemy.'

In the doorway Big Dave was arguing loudly with a policewoman half his size, baiting her. In his pocket was a ticket which he would produce eventually, but for the moment belligerence was much more fun. Behind him menacing grunts egged him on. The inspector strolled over, a cold glint in his eye.

'Can I help you gentlemen?'

'Yeah. We wanna come in and the bitch won't let us.'

'WPC Collins is only doing her duty. Official tickets only while the count is on.'

With a yell, five yobs pulled out their tickets with a flourish. The policewoman looked relieved and the inspector frowned.

'Right, but any sign of trouble and you're out, do you hear?'

The skinheads swaggered inside, followed by Standish and the diminutive Parrot sporting Union Jacks in their buttonholes. The inspector eyed them both with disgust.

Parrot took one look at the crowded hall and scuttled into a corner. There he sat for the remainder of the count and would not budge. Standish stood hesitantly on the threshold. He did not look forward to facing Bulstrode and his erstwhile friends. The whole election campaign had been truly dreadful. He wished he had applied for a postal vote and gone on holiday instead.

'Keeping funny company these days, aren't we, Mr Standish?' enquired the inspector coolly. The solicitor would probably be wise to keep away from Rotary dinners for a while.

The evening seemed to last for ever, yet it was all over too quickly. At last Trevor Day buttoned up his jacket once more and climbed on to the platform, to announce that Nicholas Spencer had come top of the poll as expected, more than doubling the Liberal Democrat vote, ahead of

Marcus, who was 12,000 down on Nigel's last result. Most of the lost Tories seemed to have transferred straight to the Old Etonian. Labour was philosophical about the halving of their own vote, accepting that they had been out of the frame from the start. Then the fun began. Mr Parrot was next with 611, then the Greens with 466 and the better-known Loony, Lord David Sutch, collected 278. The official National Front candidate took 133, Lindi St Clair 72, ahead of the other Raving Loony at 60. The latter four had taken slightly over 1 per cent of the vote between them. The Liberal majority represented a swing from Marcus Carey to his opponents of just under 25 per cent. Compared with Christchurch, it was not bad: except that the seat was lost, and possibly for ever.

Nobody except Freddie and his girlfriend retained sufficient energy for a last drink.

Alison Carey handed Marcus his coat, 'Come on, let's go.'

He shrugged her off. 'I'm going to walk back. I need some fresh air – be on my own for a bit. I won't be long.'

Outside the cold air assailed him, but at least it had stopped raining. God, what a mess the whole business had been. His face stung from the humiliation, from the names he had been called, from the furious aggression his colour had brought out in so many people. Now he knew what it meant to be on the receiving end of racial hatred. It was inexplicable; he had given them no reason; he had conformed intimately to all their norms. What more did they want of him?

The skinheads caught up with him at the corner of the darkened High Street and dragged him without a word into a deserted alley. First they pulled off his coat and played Sir Walter Raleigh with it, forcing Marcus to tread it repeatedly into a puddle. Then they taunted him to put up his fists against the smallest of their number, and, when he shook his head and wearily refused, stood behind him breathing foully down his ear and did it for him, holding his body upright as blows slugged into his face and chest. He gasped as ribs crunched and gave way, and sagged in their arms and tried to cry out; a huge paw covered his mouth. As the stars sizzled and rushed towards him he prayed they would get bored quickly. Then they let him fall into the wet gutter, and kicked him with cries and whoops of laughter, dancing around until lights were turned on in neighbouring houses. At last they ran off into the night and he was silent and lay still.

CHAPTER TWENTY-FIVE

'Could I speak to Andrew, please?'

The Australian accent made Tessa go cold. She had always known the moment would come when Andrew's mysterious girlfriend, whoever she was, would simply turn up. That he had a girlfriend she had suspected for some time. The contrast was too strong between his vigorous appetites in the first years of their marriage and his complete acquiescence more recently in her celibacy. These days he did not touch her, nor bother her in any way, nor beg or plead, nor even criticise. Their public embraces were no more than the brushing of lips on cheeks, though done with courteous regard. Different bedrooms suited Andrew's strange working hours and excited no comment; for so long had separation been part of their lives that she had stopped agonising about it and it appeared that Andrew no longer noticed.

Tessa had prayed, but it was hope against hope that Andrew had simply forgotten the pleasure of sleeping with a woman. His job was all-absorbing, yet parts of his deepest soul must be left untouched by red boxes and folders marked 'Secret'. That was a consolation, oddly enough, for she could admire her husband the better for not being entirely absorbed by his career. She knew Andrew too well after nine years of living with him and was certain that quietude had not replaced longing. A lover, however low-key, would have satisfied his animal hunger. That he had someone, somewhere, who was the regular object of his affections and servant of his needs, she had no doubt. One person, not several, not one-night stands, for he was not the sort to take stupid risks; someone who left him content and better able to meet life's other challenges. Otherwise he would have turned on her; their neutered marriage would years ago have broken up in bitter acrimony.

Tessa could hear her own breathing, rapid and shallow. The voice at the other end of the phone gave nothing away, yet within an instant Tessa knew this was the woman. The tone was strong and self-confident, as if the owner were used to getting what she wanted. Andrew would be drawn to a woman like that – indeed, one element in her own attraction a decade ago was that he could *not* have his way with her, that she was strong enough to refuse him. Inside him was still the hesitant little boy who liked to be told by women what to do. Her heart skipped a beat as she wondered if the woman were married, but suspected not: Andrew would shy away from too many complications.

Tessa listened carefully, aware that she was gripping the phone too tight, as the request for Andrew was repeated. A foreigner: that would fit. Andrew would be enticed by somebody different from his cool English wife. A foreigner would hold an MP in some higher awe, which would suit Andrew's ego perfectly. He might even kid himself that a foreigner didn't count. In his traditional world strangers and women were not on the same plane as chaps he knew well, and did not deserve or receive quite the same consideration.

A spasm of irritation seized Tessa. The woman had made no attempt to ingratiate herself. It was as if Tessa herself didn't count, even to a rival. That, too, fitted. Andrew's lover would long since have picked up his offhand attitudes to his official partner. The person on the other end knew Andrew, wanted Andrew, thought like Andrew and would have no truck with anybody lesser like herself.

'It's a bit late,' Tessa played for time. Her voice sounded high and unreal. This was not really happening. 'I'm not sure if he's still up. Who shall I say wants him?'

'Just tell him Miranda, will you? I'm sorry to bother you, but it's urgent.'

So that was it. Miranda who? Tessa racked her brain for a name from the Commons, a research assistant perhaps, but drew a blank.

'Miranda? Will he know who is calling? Is it business?'

The voice was testy. 'Yes, he'll know. And it's personal, if you don't mind.'

This must be serious, to be phoning at eleven on a Sunday night, to share nothing, to insist on speaking to him and to ignore her presence. Suddenly Tessa felt anxious. Whatever was going on, she was in it too. As the wife. That meant that her first duty was to protect Andrew. Her own needs were secondary.

'Just a minute. I'll go and get him.'

Her husband was in an armchair. In his lap fluttered a draft of the latest White Paper, annotated in biro and fluorescent marker. He had fallen asleep and was leaning awkwardly to one side, his pen on the floor. Tessa looked at him for a few seconds, her heart fast and shallow, a salty taste in her mouth. This was the last moment the fragile edifice of their marriage would be intact. She bent over him and shook his shoulder.

'Andrew, phone call. Says it's urgent.'

458

He was awake in an instant and half out of the chair, papers scattering. 'Who is it?'

She knelt on the floor at his feet like a supplicant, gathering up paper. Straightening to hand him the folder, she looked him in the eye and took a deep breath. 'Miranda. She sounded worried.'

There! It was done. In four words Tessa had admitted she was aware of Miranda's existence, knew all she needed to know of the relationship with her husband, and declared that she for one was prepared to stand by him.

His face turned to stone. Without a word he went out of the room and to the phone, closing the door after him. Tessa stood motionless and pondered, listening to the indecipherable murmur of his voice. Then quietly, deliberately, she opened the door and stood waiting, back to the wall, watching her husband.

'I don't believe it,' he was saying flatly.

Miranda was exasperated. It had been tough enough getting through the wife's head that she needed to speak to him; now it was plain that Andrew was failing to put two and two together at his usual speed. 'You go and get the first editions then, Andrew. We're all over the place, you and me. Photos from that do in Blackpool – I guess that's the only time we've been seen together, though I can't be sure. Somebody's shopped us.'

'But why?'

'Oh, don't be so *dumb*. Because you're an important personage these days, Minister. You're worth exposing. And somebody may have it in for me, too. I haven't done my job without treading on a few toes. The question is, what do we do now?'

'I need time to think. Wait – I'll see you in half an hour. Not your place – oh, the middle of Westminster Bridge, Parliament side, that will do. Will you be there?'

He glanced over his shoulder. Tessa was listening impassively. Not that it mattered now, keeping things from her. She would know when she saw the papers. He jerked out 'Goodbye' and put the phone down.

'I have to go out,' he said brusquely. 'I'll explain later – in the morning. There may be a lot of phone calls. If they bother you, Tessa, take the phone off the hook. The only ones of importance are from the department. All the rest are "No comment" – understood?'

She nodded. She understood all too well. It was better that *she* rather than *he* answer the phone, or take the decision to disconnect it. Already Andrew was treating her as if he were a general briefing his troops before a battle. It was a compliment in a way, knowing he could rely on her. Tessa turned her mind to what might happen in the next few days, and what she might hope to salvage – for herself, for Barney and for Andrew.

Very slowly, hearing it click and burr, Miranda put the phone down. On her lap the first edition of the *Herald* blared the headline 'POLITICIAN IN LOVE TANGLE WITH JOURNALIST!' with fuzzy photographs of herself and Andrew, side by side at that party, not looking at each other, but clearly joined by the smiling ease with which they occupied the same space. They must have been spotted in the background of a picture whose original subject was somebody else. The story was lively enough. Allegations that Andrew Muncastle, Minister for Housing at the Department of the Environment, was having an affair with the deputy editor of the *Herald*'s arch-rival the *Globe* were padded out with tittle-tattle. Tessa was pictured doing the meals-on-wheels rounds in Hampshire villages, the photograph Andrew had insisted should appear on his election address. His grandfather Sir Edward Muncastle stared from the page in a picture dredged from obituary files. The old man was facially similar to Andrew with the same patrician glare. Miranda was also shown more prominently, on the arms of Matthew Frank and in earlier pictures with several other well-known men, suggesting that she cast her favours both widely and indiscriminately. Extracts from a candid interview she had given to Lynn Barber of the *Independent on Sunday* three years ago were widely quoted. Over a Rabelaisian lunch at Simply Nico, Miranda had confessed to frank amazement at British male manners, remarks which now sat bleakly next to the revelations of her association with one of Her Majesty's most po-faced Ministers. The implications were clear; she was either a liar or a fool. This led to lively speculation about her boyfriend's tastes fuelled by concentration in all the photographs on Miranda's munificent cleavage.

'You can't expect me to be impressed, sweetheart,' said the other person in the room with her.

She turned and faced him, hands on hips. 'There are times when you think I live for work alone. I don't. He's a fine chap in his own way. I've become more than keen on him, if you must know.'

The *Globe*'s proprietor chuckled. 'There's not much I don't know, Miranda. You and your British boyfriend are in a mess. But then, when I look at you, my beauty, I too am besotted. You just tell me what you want and your sugar daddy will assist. My offer is still open, though not for ever.'

She was wary. 'He doesn't know about you. I don't want to tell him.'

The owner shrugged. 'That's up to you, baby. I guess you're about to find out what your playmate is made of, aren't you?'

'Yeah.' She was pensive. Then she bent over the owner, and kissed the top of his head. 'You've been good to me. I'll give you an answer. Soon.'

With a touch of annoyance Andrew realised that he had chosen the wrong side of Westminster Bridge for his tryst. The taxi would have to trail all round the roundabout and come back. He searched in the gloom; several figures had chosen a late stroll on the bridge on a fine moonlit spring evening as a way of blowing away the blues, or bowing to them. None was obviously Miranda.

The magnificent river front of Sir Charles Barry's Westminster masterpiece was lit up all along its length. Its image floated like a fairytale castle on the shimmering waters of the Thames. On a Sunday hardly anyone was active inside, though the lights were on in the Speaker's apartments under Big Ben. Somebody else working late.

'Hi.'

She was at his elbow, and linked her arm in his. Together and silent they leaned over the bridge, arms resting on the parapet, and stared into the water below. Green lights under the arches to warn shipping turned the heaving swell a lurid yellow. On the far side the lights of St Thomas's Hospital, white and clinical, lit up the sky. Behind stood the former Greater London Council building, home to London government for a century until Margaret Thatcher, despairing of its powerful opposition to her, abolished it. Now hidden under scaffolding it had become a lifeless chrysalis, awaiting its metamorphosis into a Japanese hotel.

For several minutes Andrew and his lover huddled together, each trying to draw warmth from the closeness of the other. At last she spoke.

'You seen the papers?'

He had gone via Victoria station, his coat collar up high, and bought a fresh inky copy of the *Herald*. He nodded. 'I imagine it'll be in all of them tomorrow.'

'Not in ours. The owner won't have it. Not that it matters; our story's now public property.'

He was deeply troubled. 'I really don't know what to do, Miranda. I suppose we have been lucky this past – what? – two and a half years. Not lucky – careful. But I always thought, with you in the business, that we'd be left alone.'

'Think again, lover; no one is immune.' She was less upset than he was. To his puzzlement in the moonlight she looked almost serene.

'It's all very well for you to be so casual about it. You don't have a family and a career to worry about.'

461

Miranda turned, leaning back across the parapet, letting her coat fall open. At the same time she half raised one leg. He gasped as she rubbed her toe slowly and provocatively against the other shin in open invitation. She was laughing quietly, and as he watched incredulous she moved a moist tongue over her lips, her teeth gleaming in the gloom. He could feel himself becoming aroused – here, in public, as if she were a cockney tart charging a tenner a trick, and he ready to accept.

'For God's sake, Miranda, what do you think you are doing?' He tried to pull her coat closed.

'Reminding you.'

'Jesus, not here. And we can't exactly go back to your place, can we? It'll be crawling with photographers.'

'We could, if you wanted.' She rubbed the leg again.

He bent down with a swift movement to push her leg down, but she was quicker, and closed her thighs, trapping his hand inside the muscular warmth. He knew from the triumphant grin on her face that she was wearing no pants, as he would find if he moved his fingers only a fraction upwards. Then she pulled his head down to hers and kissed him hard and full on the mouth, lingering for several moments till he gave in, and held her close, pushing himself against her. Helplessly he knew he could not simply go home that night; he would have to have her.

'That's better,' she murmured, stroking his hair. 'You could come back with me, and it wouldn't matter. Remember my previous proposition. I've been offered a top job in Australia, editing the top women's magazine. My first editorship, and I'm going to take it. If I make a success of it, and I will, the next step would be something similar in New York – *Vanity Fair* or *Tatler*, perhaps. Big money, big job. But I can't do it alone. I need you, Andrew. You can be executive editor or whatever you want to call yourself. Your salary would be five times what you get here, and never mind the chauffeur-driven ministerial car, you can have three – a Mercedes, a Cadillac, a Bentley – you name it. And staff at your beck and call. You need to prove yourself a bit of course, the owner won't promote duds, but if you fancy a particular niche for yourself you say so. That's my offer and it's better than anything else you'll get this side of the next century.'

She moved his hand deeper inside her thighs, holding him there, where he could feel the welcoming moistness. He groaned desperately and leaned his head on her shoulder.

She nibbled his ear, and whispered to him. 'You get me too, of course. Marriage if you want it, even kids. Or not: I am at your command.'

In a moment she had unzipped him and, draping his overcoat around them both, hitched herself up on to the parapet and opened herself to him. A car went past and hooted, but they took no notice. His arms held her tight to prevent her from falling as he pushed and emptied himself into her; so great was his need, and so crass the occasion, that it did not take long, with Miranda giggling and panting in his ear.

At last he eased away an inch and tidied himself, but her legs were still around him, her sex hidden in the darkness of his coat. Holding her firmly with one arm, he caressed her clitoris to ensure she was satisfied; he heard the sharp intake of breath and felt the jerking as she responded. For several more moments they clung together, her head resting on him. Then by mutual consent she slid back on to her feet, wriggled her skirt down and kissed him gently on the lips.

'You never cease to amaze me, Andrew,' she said shakily. 'I love you very much, do you realise that? That's why I want you to go with me. Please.'

'I love you too, more than I can begin to tell you.' It was true. Every fibre of his being screamed out for her, to head for the nearest bed and have her again, properly, slowly, for hours, until neither could imagine needing more. All that this extraordinary wild episode had achieved was to rekindle his need for her, just as Miranda knew it would. She understood him all too well. He suspected Tessa did too, though she would avert her thoughts from any consideration of his sexuality, as if a whole person could exist without it.

He was faced with a conundrum. Life with Tessa was bearable only because Miranda was there. Without Miranda, he could not imagine that his carefully constructed façade with Tessa would survive for five minutes. Now he had discovered how wonderful and vivid sexual congress could be, how much meaning love gave, he could never again live without it. Without Miranda, with Tessa alone, life would be impossible.

But life with Miranda and without Tessa...? Suppose he chose Miranda? Divorce, from Tessa, would surely follow. A divorce would be damaging if he continued in the political world, but would not matter at all if he was off to Australia.

Then there was the child. Of course he would apply for custody, and make out a strong case. Barney would love the Antipodes; it was a younger, more open-air life, with swimming and sailing, no uniforms, fewer rules all round, less ingrained unnaturalness. Perhaps his grandfather would come out to join them, and enjoy sunning himself by a pool, wearing a broad straw hat and a sun-wizened expression like all the other ex-pat Brits who had found paradise near Sydney. The memory of Tessa would fade, quite quickly. He was certain of that for himself, feeling almost guilty at how little impact she had made on him, other than the negative. The boy was eight – old enough to remember;

but he too would soon forget, especially if he settled quickly into a new school. In fact Barney was the right age to go, before he was sucked into a cold boarding school on the Devon moors next year and became tied to the British way of life. Of one thing Andrew was miserably certain – that if the boy had the same upbringing he had himself suffered, his adulthood would contain all the same seeds for unhappiness. Miranda was offering them both a way out.

'Could I bring my son?' he whispered. 'He would love it. I might even get to know him better in Australia. I would like that.'

Miranda laughed, not at him but with him, sharing his pleasure. 'As long as he doesn't start calling me "Ma". I'm not into instant motherhood. But sure. I have nephews back home, they'd be delighted to introduce him around. And if he grows up as gorgeous as his dad he'll be a wow with the ladies in due course.'

Above them the great clock began to whirr and reverberate. Both looked up at the huge disks which marked the time for a hundred nations around the world. It was midnight. The tower seemed to draw breath before sounding, like a living thing. As the great notes boomed out on the night air, Miranda's laugh became uneasy.

'I feel like I'm about to turn into a pumpkin. Do I take it that the answer is yes, then? If I kiss my prince, does he stay a prince, or does he turn into a turkey?'

'He feels like a king,' Andrew answered, and kissed her once more. Then he broke away. 'Look, I have some talking to do back home. I won't come back with you now, but I'll contact you tomorrow. Now go, and sleep tight.'

Tessa heard him come in, hang up his coat, head for the bathroom. She waited, her eyes bright in the darkness, but he did not knock on her door; the power of habit was strong in her husband. If there was to be a confrontation it would be in daylight, under control.

She heard his bed creak and then he was still, though she could almost sense the intensity of the thinking going on on the other side of the wall. Quietly she slipped from under her own bedcovers and knelt barefoot at the side of the bed on the rug, hands clasped in prayer. If she was to carry out successfully tomorrow what she was minded to do, she would need strength from somewhere far beyond herself. If she failed, she would lose Andrew for ever.

Karen looked up. 'What's the matter, Mum?' she asked gently.

Her mother slowly placed the spoon on the table and pushed away the bowl of cereal. In her other hand the two-page neatly typed letter shook visibly. The shaking was picked up and magnified by a vase of early tulips in faintest blush pink, which nodded and sighed like sympathetic friends. On the wooden dresser a new clock hummed, its second hand sweeping inexorably.

Elaine spoke dully. 'Nothing. It's time for you to get ready for college. You'll miss the bus.'

In which case I would cadge a lift, as you well know, Karen thought, but kept it to herself.

'Is it from Dad?'

The question hung in the air. That it was not immediately answered was answer enough. Her mother's face bore an expression of utter misery. Karen rose and stood behind her chair, leaning down, arms across her mother's breast, dark head to fair, reading over her shoulder. Elaine did not stop her.

There were two letters, the first from a solicitor which formed a covering letter to another from Mike. Both had been typed on the same official typewriter, which suggested Mike must have dictated his letter to his lawyer's secretary, and had it checked before signing it. The realisation that this was only a semi-private communication brought a stab to Elaine's heart, even though he had been gone for over six months.

'He might have written a personal note in his own hand,' she whispered. 'Was that too much to expect?'

Together they read the letter from Mike.

Dear Elaine,

How are you? It has been a long time since we were in touch. I am sorry this has to be so formal.

I have met a very nice girl, an air stewardess called Linda. She is 36 and is on the New York run with me. We would like to get married. Actually we've known each other some time, but only got together recently. So I am writing to ask if you would agree to a quick divorce, which would save everybody a lot of trouble. If you like, it can be on the grounds of my adultery with Linda, who doesn't mind at all. You can take this letter to your own solicitors and I will sign a full confession at this end.

We hope to live in Linda's house in Surrey not far from Heathrow. Karen is welcome to come and stay either occasionally or permanently – I won't fight you over her, but she is old enough to make up her own mind. She will always have a home with us, if she wants it, and then she and Linda will get to know each other. I am sure they will get on fine. We would like her to come to the wedding, though it will be a quiet affair. It might sound strange to say it, Elaine, but I hope you will agree to meet my new wife eventually too – I am sure you will like her.

465

We had many good years together, Elaine, and I hope you will understand and forgive me eventually. I could never join in your political life and I felt very left out – not your fault, I guess, and I do not reproach you for that. I promised I would support you in your ambitions and it was me who failed. But we can't throw away those years and pretend they did not happen. It would make me and Linda very happy if we could all be friends, though I realise that is a tall order at this moment.

There are financial considerations, of course. My lawyer says he will thrash all that out with your side, but I don't want any disputes. The house is yours. I will pay off the mortgage for you, and I will support Karen till she finishes college or university. I can't do much more than that, but you have your own money.

One more thing – Linda and I would like to get this over and done quickly and I'm sure you don't want a long-drawn-out business. She is expecting our child in August and the tests suggest it will be a boy, so I am anxious to make an honest woman of her. I am sure you will understand.

The letters trembled and fell to the table. Elaine could not explain why she crumpled in sobs, great retching yelps that shook her for several minutes, as she scrabbled for tissues and was held closely, from behind, by her daughter.

The callousness of the letters destroyed all her equanimity at a stroke. Mike was not suffering, not he. Not at all. Within a few weeks of his leaving this house, cheek swollen and aflame, he had taken another complaisant woman to bed, a little younger than herself, and had got her with child. That latter bit had to be almost deliberate, if not on his part then the woman's. A thirty-six-year-old could not hang around if she wanted a family.

And Mike would get the best reward of all: a son, a replacement for Jake. She, Elaine, could never turn the clock back in the same way; she could not, or would not now, have any more children. She would be forty next year. Even had there been a suitable father in the offing, which Roger most definitely was not, the whole idea was unthinkable. Mike had never spoken of the dead child, yet he had grieved as much as she. Now he had taken the first opportunity of putting that part of his life to rights. He was to have a son, another son, and the baby and his mother would make him a very happy man indeed.

Elaine could see that all too clearly. She realised in the same instant that she did not have it in her to deny her husband his contentment, his consolation prize, after so many difficult years married to her. Some consolation prize! This second marriage of his had every chance of turning out well. An air stewardess, geared to customer satisfaction, was unlikely to put her own needs above those of the supreme customer, her husband. Anybody who could choose that as a job would probably slip into marriage with great deftness, especially if after years of the high life she was ready to settle to domesticity. If Mike could give her a good standard of living, Linda would return it with warmth and competent orderliness. The icing on the cake was that he would be living closer to his work. In that household it would be his job which counted, not his wife's. How very ironic; how neat, how obvious, how cruel.

Mike would not have realised it but his new-found joy with Linda hurt more than Elaine could say, for it was a pointed and detailed commentary on her own failure, as a wife and as a woman. Had there been some political success, her own priorities satisfied, to set against that omission, she might have minded less. But there was none.

Karen continued to hug her mother, gently, as if she were fine china and might break. 'Don't cry, Mum. It's better this way. You knew it was coming, sooner or later.'

The weeping subsided at last. Elaine patted her daughter's arm in mute thanks. Then a thought occurred to her and she twisted around until she could see Karen's face.

'Did you? Know it was coming, I mean?'

The girl returned to her seat and fiddled with her coffee-mug. 'Yes, in a way. Dad phoned last weekend when you were out and told me he wanted to get married again, and asked if I wanted to go and live with them. He tried to persuade me to meet Linda before making up my mind. He's very keen on her – I don't think you'll talk him out of it, Mum.'

'I wouldn't want to. He left, not me. If he's found someone else I can only wish them every happiness. May I ask what answer you gave him?'

The formality of the question reminded Karen that her position was not the same as her mother's. Her response was guarded and tactful.

'I'm in college here and I like it. If I move anywhere, it would be to London if you'd let me – it can be a bit of a drag up here on my own a lot. But it'd be taking a chance, uprooting myself and going to stay with a stepmother all dotty about her new baby. We might get on like a house on fire, or we might fight. I could easily make things hard for them, and for myself. There are lots of articles about step-parents in my magazines, you know. It didn't seem like a brilliant idea, to be honest.'

To her father, Karen had offered congratulations and thanks, and a promise to attend the wedding, but no more. She had pointed out the expenses of a new baby and hinted that the additional and unpredictable costs of a teenager might be better borne by her mother. Mike's written offer to support her, should she stay with her mother, was no more than a court would insist on, but nevertheless showed a willingness to accept that responsibility, and perhaps also to purchase her continued contact and fend off a guilty conscience. He need not have worried about that; Karen would take it upon herself to keep in touch. She was fond of her father but he had become a distant figure who, she suspected, would not have realised how much she had grown up in the last couple of years. Fathers never did.

'Mum, what are you going to do?'

Elaine was slowly recovering. She stood at the sink and splashed her face with cold water, patting it dry on the kitchen towel. The result was streaky black eye make-up on both her cheeks and the towel, causing Karen to laugh and point. 'You can't go out like that!'

Elaine peered in the little kitchen mirror on the window-ledge and dabbed at the mess. She grinned ruefully at her daughter. 'I guess I shall have to start all over again, sweetheart, and I don't just mean my face.'

Eight hours after bidding Miranda good night Andrew Muncastle sat at the kitchen table with his wife nibbling at toast and sipping coffee, half listening to the radio and pretending to read *The Times* and the *Daily Mail*, as the au pair fidgeted with Barney. The child instantly sensed something was amiss. He was awkward and clumsy, spilling a cup of milk on his shirt so that it needed changing and crying in frustration at his own inability to articulate his feelings. Outside the kitchen door loomed the figure of a uniformed policeman.

The au pair understood she had to remove the child to school as quickly as possible and was impatient with him. At last the door banged shut behind them as light bulbs flashed, and the kitchen went quiet. Tessa leaned across and turned off the radio.

'Don't you have an early meeting, dear?' she asked quietly.

Andrew folded *The Times* with an impatient movement. 'It's Monday. Prayers aren't till eleven. Gives the most distant chaps time to get in from Tavistock or wherever.' Gloomily he stared at the agency photograph of Yeltsin on the front page. In due course The *Daily Mail* and *The Times* would have a graphic account of his own doings; neither Murdoch nor Conrad Black were under orders from Miranda's owner.

Tessa was waiting, like a plaster saint. God. Her style was effective. Catholics learned a lot from the disciplines of their childhood; they could wear you down with that pained reproachful silence. He glowered at her resentfully, but she sat prim and correct, in a patterned blouse buttoned up to the neck and a dull long skirt. And three sets of knickers, for all he knew.

'There were quite a lot of calls for you last night, as you predicted,' she started again. If he would not volunteer information she would have to drag it out of him. 'The phone has been off all night, and as you can see we have some visible protection. It might help, before going out there to face the rat-pack, if we were to agree a line.'

He was silent, head in hands, staring at the table. Outside there was a rumpus and a bulb flashed at the window. With a grimace Tessa rose, pulled down the blinds, and poured herself more coffee. The two sat in the half-gloom.

'You owe me an explanation, Andrew. It's no use wishing you were halfway round the world; you're here with me in London and in a minute you have to leave. What do you wish me to say to them?'

Andrew looked at her; she was startled at the dislike in his red-rimmed eyes. He had clearly been awake most of the night.

'My God, Tessa, but you have summed it all up very neatly. I do wish I were halfway round the world. In fact Barney and I have the chance to be exactly that.'

He turned to her at last, and explained Miranda's offer, as she turned white and gripped the edge of the kitchen table to steady herself, and forced herself to breathe.

Not far away in the River Room of the Savoy, Miranda was also at breakfast, with Lynn Barber once again, and Valerie Grove and Lesley White of the *Sunday Times*. The smartly dressed women journalists, hastily summoned by phone call, were drinking champagne, tucking into fresh lobster and laughing uproariously.

'Honest! He's coming with me to Australia.' Miranda reached for the steel claw-crushers. The dismembered bodies of two large lobsters lay scattered on a platter before the women.

'But how did you persuade him?' Barber had an envious gleam in her eye. Miranda picked up another claw and placed it at right angles in the crusher, then slowly forced the steel closed. Pink flesh oozed out of the cracks in the shell. She placed the claw in her mouth and sucked. The obscenity was unmistakable and had her audience clutching themselves in merriment. 'Might have guessed! Miranda, you are a case!'

Barber, ever the journalist, wanted facts. 'You're going to marry him – is that it? Is he going to divorce his wife?'

'Dunno about the former yet, but definitely yes to the latter. There's no love lost as far as I know. Not been a proper marriage for years.'

Had she been pressed Miranda would have been hard put to find evidence for her certainty. She was sure in her own mind that Andrew had agreed to marry, but in the absence of a date for the event it seemed wisest to demur. At any rate, he was leaving with her, and that would be enough commitment for the moment.

'And he's going to give up politics for you?'

'Uh-huh. That didn't need much persuading. They get paid peanuts, you know. Not enough to keep body and soul together. He's keen on the idea of a more interesting job in the sunshine, as well as having me for breakfast, lunch, dinner and tea.'

'What more interesting job? Being your lapdog? You must be joking, Miranda. Are you sure that "We are in love and we're going to get married" story's going to stand up in the cold light of day? He wouldn't be the first politician to say one thing in bed and another on the doorstep the following morning, you know.'

Had Miranda been sober she would have been furious. As it was, liberally tanked with champagne since the early hours, everything said to her sounded incredibly funny, and added to the delight with which she greeted the wonderful new day. She waved the remains of the lobster claw at her friends.

'You'll see! Got myself an Englishman. Going to be a respectable married lady. Got to show me some respect!'

Lesley White raised her glass. 'I wish you both well, Miranda,' she said sincerely. 'The question is, when are we going to get a photo of you two lovers together? And is he going to resign his seat and cause another by-election?'

'No idea. Details not worked out yet. Don't know.' Miranda giggled. She reached for the bottle. 'Have 'nother one. Sugar daddy's paying for this lot. Bless his cotton socks.'

Once as a child Tessa had been taken to a bullfight in Spain. Although she had been dragged out screaming in the last few minutes, as the black bull, flanks heaving and wet with blood, had crashed in the sand, in her darkest moments she would confess that the hour leading up to that climax, the feinting and parrying, the teasing and testing, had forced its way into her imagination. There was something sacrificial about it, like the agony of Christ, though on Golgotha there was a higher purpose in all that suffering, and death conferred eternal life: at Easter the occupant of the dying earthly body was the winner. Not so in the *corrida*. In that battle of wills and strength the bull was bound to be the loser. If a person locked in a similar battle of wills had prepared properly and was guided by higher instincts, then the unthinking animal would again be bound to lose. This Monday morning she felt herself, if not the matador, at least his assistant, prodding and goading, looking for an opening beneath the withers to slide in a disabling *pic*, then another, jumping out of range, weakening the beast until it slid to its knees and acknowledged her superior will. At that point she would stop.

There was no matador here, but a growing mob of press now gathered outside their house baying for blood. The moment Andrew left he would be set upon and destroyed. Unless, of course, he followed the plan of action she would set out for him.

'There will be no divorce, Andrew. You have to understand that.'

'But why not? We could be free of each other by Christmas, and you could do what you want. No more politics, no more living in the public eye. You've always said how much you dislike it.'

'I promised to marry you till death do us part. Promised before God, and I meant it. I thought you did too. If you want to divorce me, Andrew, you will find it very difficult. I will fight you every step of the way, I swear it.'

She waited. It clearly had not occurred to Andrew that she was going to be uncooperative; he had planned for no such eventuality. In his arrogant world, most women did what men told them. At a guess he had done little planning of any kind. How slightly he knew his wife, her strengths. She felt emboldened.

'And this idea of giving up politics, Andrew. You're not serious, surely? It's been your life, your ambition. You're well thought of and making rapid progress. Your family are immensely proud of you. Would you seriously give all that up – a career which you have built up with such effort yourself?'

'I will have a better job down under. More money for a start.'

Tessa pressed home her advantage. 'At the beck and call of your girlfriend, no doubt. I bet you haven't seen a contract, have you? All on her say-so. That's fine, but how long d'you think it will last? What happens when she gets fed up with you? Where will you be then, after throwing up your career for her? Your sacrifice won't make her respect you – on the contrary. Strong women get cheesed off pretty quickly with men who're too easy to dominate. The thing that made you so attractive to her, Andrew, is first of all you're somebody else's husband, and secondly that you're tied to your job and needed here. Doubly unavailable, see. If once she won that battle to take you over, she would lose interest sharpish. When her ardour cools, where will you be then – in the Cabinet with the high regard of all your colleagues, or a beach hum somewhere on the other side of the world?'

Under the onslaught Andrew struggled to recapture the vivid imagery of the previous night. 'It isn't like that, Tessa,' he said weakly. 'She wants to make a home for me and Barney. New life together. I think I deserve it.'

Tessa sat up straight and prayed for strength. How typical that he should assume possession of his son. Never before had she used the child, and for the rest of her life she would confess the next few moments as a gross and venal sin. But if her husband was to be saved from himself, if his feeble nature was not to destroy their home, his career, their future, she had no choice.

'You will not get Barney,' she said. There was a steely edge to her voice. 'Don't even think about it. I will fight you for my marriage and my good name – indeed for your good name, come to that – but as God and all His angels are my witness I will fight you for my child. I swear it. You'll not get Barney. No, not ever. My God – you just took it for granted that I'd hand him over, didn't you? At least it means you care about him – that's something. But if you persist in your crazy idea of giving up politics and getting a divorce I will ensure that you never see our child again. I'm sure I will have the backing of your family on that. Do you understand?'

Her husband was totally taken aback by the ferocity in her voice. His son was his continuity, his guarantee of posterity, as he was his father's and grandfather's. His son carried his name, was part of him, of his future. Surely she could not fight him over Barney? He was not a baby and a court would often agree that a boy could be with his father, especially if a well-provided home was in the offing. But Tessa ought to see that he needed his son.

She did. It was dawning on Andrew that his wife had thought all this through with far more care than he had. Her advice on many local political issues had always been shrewd. Perhaps she understood the lie of the land; maybe her perspective, devoid of sexual passion but deeply rooted in all the values he had believed they shared, was sounder than his own. Maybe she knew how to stop him in his tracks better than he did himself.

He could not imagine getting bored with Miranda, ever. Yet Tessa probably had a point about Miranda growing bored with him. Habits do not change; Miranda would continue to have her pick of men. Winding up as Miranda's whining cast-off a million miles from home was a picture both ugly and depressingly plausible.

He glanced at his wife with guarded admiration, but he was not yet ready to give in, not by a long chalk. A warning bell sounded in his head. He decided not to attempt to browbeat her.

'The law is not so simple these days, Tessa,' he remonstrated mildly. 'The courts will take Barney's best interests into account. I think I'd put up a good case for taking him with me.'

She picked up the faint change in tone and responded in kind. 'Not if I put up a fight, Andrew. With a child that young it is usual to give control to the mother. I could hardly be called a bad mother, whereas your liaison with Miranda could be placed by a clever lawyer in a most unsuitable light. You can see that.'

'And you would have a clever lawyer.'

She nodded. There was no point in arguing about that.

'Look, this isn't a sudden thing,' he attempted to explain. 'Miranda and I have been talking about my going to Australia for some time. I can only apologise for deceiving you. But she's a grand girl, we are very close, and I'm sure our love will last.'

'That's what you said when you married me,' Tessa said softly.

The barb struck home. It was his inconstancy, not Miranda's, that was now called into question: his weakness, his pursuit of pleasure, his ability to be easily distracted from long-term goals. Yet of all the qualities he most admired single-mindedness was the most significant. That gave rise to the ambition and self-discipline which had resulted in his apparently effortless rise in the Commons. It marked him out from other men.

He passed a hand wearily over his eyes. 'I'm sorry,' he said quietly. 'I seem to have promised myself to two women at the same time. I don't quite know what to do. It's going to take a while to sort out. Can you be patient?'

'To the grave,' she said simply, but it was an offer, not a threat, a restatement of belief that the future could be better than today. On the table was a clear choice between honour and dishonour, between promises kept and broken, between duty and pleasure. He felt almost grateful.

Tessa's expression was sympathetic. It crossed Andrew's mind that she must be a good actress, so much under psychological control, when underneath she must feel like tearing his eyes out. What a pity these conspicuous talents were not on display in the bedroom. Some women pretended to enjoy sex even when they hated it, just to keep their partners happy. Had Tessa managed at least that, he would never have linked arms with Miranda that fateful night after the ambassador's party, never known how other people loved, how he could love.

'Tessa,' he started slowly, then tentatively reached out and put his hand on hers. She trembled, but did not withdraw it. 'Tessa: if we stay together, we have to do it on a different basis. We have to work at being friends again. I would like more children. I would like a normal home life. I can't be a monk, not after . . . well, you know. I can accept your not wanting to be more involved in my political work; that's not really a problem. But at home? If there's no real love here, then it won't work.'

She sat quite still but the struggle not to weep played out on her face. Then, a victory, drawing on strength coming from God knew where. She half smiled and squeezed his hand.

He persisted. 'Tessa, it must have taken great courage and determination to stand up to me as you have just done. Will you give up now, or will you take on board the next step, of standing up to yourself? Do you think you could try?'

'It will take some time. You would have to be patient too.' Her voice was so quiet he had to strain to hear. Then, suddenly, a soft chuckle.

'Maybe you've learned a thing or two from that girlfriend. Some of the gentle arts. Perhaps you could teach me.'

Andrew was startled. His acquaintance with Catholic teaching on sex was sketchy but he was pretty certain that some of Miranda's favourite activities were seriously proscribed. Nevertheless a window was opening, however small the chink. If the new life with Tessa were not a raving success he could always sublimate any excess energy into his work, tackling the consultation process for the White Paper, undertaking speaking tours of Scotland, and ensure he was always dog-tired at night. Or there might be other possibilities – discreet, careful women, less visible than Miranda, less draining, less vivid. For a moment her face swam before his eyes. With an impatient gesture he swept it aside and smiled at his wife.

'I suggest we say for the moment that we are facing marital difficulties but that we intend to sort them out. I have to talk to Miranda – have to. I'm sorry, I can't just leave her in the lurch. She thinks she's getting married.'

'I feel sorry for her,' Tessa said. There was no triumphalism in her voice. Her prey was on his knees before her; now was the moment for compassion.

Andrew rose to go.

'Wait!' she commanded. 'I will tidy my hair, and we will go out together. If they're going to take photos let them be of the two of us side by side. A picture is worth a thousand words. Isn't that right?'

After dropping Karen off at the college Elaine drove to Carvers' Rocks, a local beauty spot overlooking one of the network of Midlands reservoirs. On a weekday morning it was deserted, the view over the lake empty of all human presence except for a lone fisherman crouched in green waterproofs in the distance. A flight of black and cream Canada geese flew overhead, honking loudly, like bombers on their way to devastate some unlucky city.

Elaine pulled on wellingtons and a jacket and locked the car. A walk would do her good, or at least no harm. Here she was at the heart of her constituency, in one of its prettiest spots. On summer weekends the green slopes were crowded with city picnickers and covered in litter; during a damp spring, it appeared, more devoted and intrepid country-lovers took their litter home. She trudged down to the waterline half looking for ducklings. Waterhens hooted at her approach and fluttered away, leaving their offspring stranded on the bank. A swan was a better parent, standing its ground and hissing at her. An angry bluetit chattered at her, an insistent repetition which sounded like 'He did it! He did it! He did it!' She wished she had brought some bread or barley, or a camera, anything to distract her from the unpleasant thoughts crowding her mind.

Until Mike's letter no decisions were in the offing. It was vaguely known that her husband had faded away as one of her official appurtenances, but there had been no announcements that he had also disappeared entirely from her household. The intention, in part, was to enable Mike to return without a fuss, had that been his choice, but it also suited Elaine to pretend that nothing untoward had happened. She had no other male escort and politely refused invitations from divorced or widowed men, however well meaning or charming. Being seen out with anyone else even innocently would have forced the issue. She was content for the time being to leave matters as vague as possible. Since her own needs were met, by and large, by Roger Dickson, it did not matter much if otherwise she slept alone.

For so long had she been the central link in a threesome that it had begun to feel as if it could go on for ever. Elaine with Mike: married, public, easy-going, not very visible. His disappearance or, rather, non-appearance at public events aroused no curiosity. MPs who always turned up with a dutiful spouse in tow were less common these days.

But a divorce would unquestionably be a public matter, even if Mike took all the blame. With a pregnant girlfriend he could hardly do otherwise, though he might hint in court that Elaine had driven him to it. The apologetic tone of the letter suggested, however, that he was keen to avoid such nastiness. He always was squeamish, Elaine reflected bitterly. A quickie divorce was his request and she did not entertain for a moment any thought of refusing him. The baby would be Karen's half-brother and deserved the best possible. It was the least she could do.

But it was as if she had been seated for years in a familiar armchair, balanced and at ease, and then one of the arms had suddenly broken away. Marriage had been an undemanding prop. Taking it for granted had led to its destruction, she now realised; marriage needs as much effort as any affair, and with more subtlety, and for longer. Yet while it was there the construction had been a crucial part of her life. As a married woman she had certain roles and status and was treated with respect, particularly by her constituents. Given the parlous state of many of their own liaisons, the fact that their lady MP had managed to combine home, family and career was a definite mark in her favour. How competent she seemed to harassed women on their second divorce, or puzzled second wives struggling with stepchildren and three mortgages. How stable, how genuine, to old men wed for fifty years to the same loving wife. Elaine did not flaunt her married state, but she instinctively shared these values. There were times when she could not remember what had possessed her to start her affair in the first place.

But Mike had gone of his own accord: the affair had nothing to do with his leaving. At this point the old armchair creaked and sagged, revealing its fragile inner framework, the part she might have preferred not to see. Perhaps the affair had played a significant part, without her husband ever realising. Maybe, without noticing, she had stopped trying with him. If Mike had been all she had, she might have done her best to persuade him to stay that awful night; might have changed her ways, made the effort to meet his own needs rather better. Maybe some intensity had been transferred to Roger, as her husband inexorably lost his place at the centre of her emotional universe. Mike would have believed it was simply that she was enjoying her job at Westminster; his letter revealed no inkling that she might have someone else. But then Mike's male ego would have found that difficult to credit. It was better that he did not know. Let the guilty feelings remain on his side. She could get used to a one-armed armchair; or at least would try.

She would have to tell Roger. And he would show, in his eyes, or in a slight withdrawal of manner, that it worried him. Playing around with a married woman who had no intention of endangering her marriage and, by implication, his was one thing. She was not likely to push the affair too far, or demand too much. Like him, she would insist on secrecy and be prepared to accept all the unhappy sacrifices that entailed: no dinners under candlelight in bijou restaurants, no touching in public, no sweet looks, no gentle acknowledgement. On the other hand, playing round with a free woman, who might be on the lookout for a suitable catch, would be an entirely different matter. As Roger would see it, the risks then became enormous. A strong-minded woman like Elaine Stalker might well set her sights on pulling her man away from his loving wife and capturing him for herself. Her naturally competitive nature made that a genuine possibility. For a brief moment Elaine allowed herself to consider it, but Roger's family life had never shown the least sign of flakiness. It had always flattered her own ego that she and no one else had managed to entice this marvellous man into an illicit bed. It said something about her, not him. And if she regretted the loss of her own once happy wedded state she was not about to compensate for it by destroying his.

Yet her aloneness, more than anything else, spelled danger for her affair as well. All too clearly Elaine could see that Roger would wish to start pulling back, disentangling himself. Mike's letter was thus more than the end of her marriage. It must, sooner or later, herald the end of Roger too.

Elaine leaned against the wet bark of a tree. She had walked a long way sunk in thought, and was now close to the lone fisherman. He was in a world of his own, still, almost lifeless. Discoloured dark-green waterproofs were draped around a stolid body perched on a little folding stool, and he stared at the bobbing end of his line. He resembled nothing so much as a large, old toad. To Elaine the habits of the fisherman were incomprehensible. How could anyone just sit there all day? Without even a good novel to read, or a radio to listen to? Then it occurred to her that possibly the fisherman, like her, was lost in his thoughts and neither needed nor welcomed interruption. She began to retrace her steps towards the car.

It was deeply unpleasant, opening the front door to let Barney and the au pair in and forcing herself to nod to the policeman and smile at the eager cameras. Tessa drew the line at posing with Barney, but pictures of the three of them, two protective women and a wide-eyed child, were all over the front pages next day.

Yet she found in herself a newly forgiving nature; the press were only doing their job, as demanded by a voracious public. It was news because it sold newspapers. If as in France it was generally held that the private lives of politicians were nobody's business but their own, then the Muncastle home would not be such a target. The result, in Mitterrand's France, had been that hidden sins went further than mistresses, into slush funds and corruption. The Italians too had turned blind eyes for years but the uncovering of their political scandals had shaken their republic to its very foundations. Tessa reflected that the fear of discovery kept many politicians on the straight and narrow. Had Andrew believed he would be found out, he might have sighed but said, 'Thank you, but no thank you', to Miranda Jamieson on day one. Whenever that was.

With a sickening feeling Tessa realised she knew nothing whatever about the origin, duration or intensity of the relationship, and now, unless she asked Andrew – which was unthinkable – she would never know. A great chunk of her husband's inner life was lost to her for ever. On the other hand, if he had never started the affair, or even ended it quickly before discovery, their cold marriage might have foundered entirely, and sooner. Andrew would have found somebody friendlier to take his name, bear his children, support him in the constituency and bring him his morning tea. Divorced and remarried, promptly, before his climb up the ladder really started. She would have been left with no husband, no status, and no explanation she could legitimately offer. Only the child, had she been granted him by a court, to bring up alone. Tessa shivered and closed the door.

As she passed down the hallway she rubbed her palm almost by habit, but the usual comforting itchiness did not respond. Puzzled, she moved into the light and examined her hands. The appalling events of the last few hours must have intensified the eczema, surely. Yet her skin, though red and reamed with scar tissue, was free of blemish. She rolled up her sleeves; the sensitive patches inside her elbows were similarly smooth. For a moment she scratched with a fingernail until the skin broke down and she drew blood, but the fiery irritation was absent. There had been a happy time long ago when her skin was clear; Tessa struggled to remember what had occupied her then. She drew a blank, except for a vague remembrance that she had been rested and content and capable of doing what was expected of her. Maybe her body's new quiescence was telling her the same thing. Whatever demands Andrew sought to place on her, she could face them. He needed her, not simply as a public face and witness to his eminent respectability; he needed her to guarantee that respectability, by *being* the wife, not just pretending. Once that would have seemed worse than martyrdom. Now it felt like a role for life. She wriggled her shoulders experimentally and made herself think of the soreness between her legs. There was no pain, no flare-up. She looked at herself anew in the hall mirror, pushed back her dull hair from her face, trying different styles. Then she shrugged and half smiled, and went into the kitchen.

Barney was seated at the kitchen table, toying with a piece of bread and jam. Eight years old, he still had the earnest solemnity that had so enchanted Elaine Stalker in the Strangers' Cafeteria.

'May I ask you something, Mummy?'

Tessa turned around, surprised. 'Certainly, darling.'

'What are all those people doing outside? Is it because Daddy has a girlfriend?'

The child was looking at her steadily, but his eyes were brimming with tears. The au pair tactfully made herself scarce, leaving mother and son together. Tessa noted that he was not as tidy and clean as usual, as if he had been fighting in the playground. She considered denial, but the child's fearful expression demanded the truth.

'Wh . . . what do you know about that, Barney?'

'Simpson brought a newspaper into school. I tore it up, but it was all pictures of Daddy, wasn't it? Are you and Daddy going to get divorced?'

'No.' She brought to it all the firmness at her command, but the child was still waiting.

So many children at that private school came from divorced families: there must be times when Barney felt the odd one out. Tessa sighed, and sat down next to the boy, her arm around his shoulders, stroking his hair. For her it was an unusually affectionate gesture: the pain of the eczema and an innate fear that it might be contagious had long limited her physical contact with her son.

'Look, Barney. It's true that Daddy has had a girlfriend but it's over. He's going to stay with us, and we're going to stay together as a family.

We've had a bad time, but it's all right now. There's nothing to worry about.'

A big tear detached itself and rolled down his cheek. Tessa fished in his pocket and found a grubby tissue wrapped around a half-eaten sweet.

'Oh, Barney!' She laughed, and hugged him.

The child despite his tears was comforted. He pointed out of the window. 'Why are the pho . . . phut . . . photographers still there, then, Mummy?' Barney stumbled over the long word, but persevered and got it correct at last.

Tessa noted with admiration his courage and his determination to do things correctly. With surprised recognition she realised he probably got those qualities more from her than from his father. She was beginning to understand herself, as if a healing light were illuminating every corner of her own soul. Maybe prayers are answered.

'They don't believe us when we say there's no story. And Daddy's girlfriend is a very pretty lady – was, I should say – so the newspapers are being nosy.'

She was amazed at her own willingness to acknowledge Miranda's beauty. Why not? Andrew had decided to stay put. There were more important things than superb bodies. And she was not an ugly old woman herself, yet.

Barney gazed at her, sniffing. 'I think *you're* a pretty lady, Mummy,' he offered loyally.

Once Tessa would have coloured and felt embarrassed at any reference to her physical self. Now, fleetingly, she considered how Miranda might have responded.

'Why, thank you, Barney. That's the nicest thing anyone has said to me in a long time.'

The child grinned happily. 'Especially when you smile, Mummy.'

'What do you mean, it's all off?'

Miranda stared at him in anguished rage. When Andrew had called her office that morning, before the first editions of the *Evening Standard* hit the news-stands, he had been politely and cheerfully advised that Miss Jamieson was in conference, but would be happy to meet him later that day in the penthouse suite at Wapping, which could be reached by using the private lift in the foyer. For a moment Andrew debated telling Miranda's secretary to pass on his bleak message and not turn up at all. It would have been an ungentlemanly but effective way of getting rid of her. Yet in the end he owed her an explanation. To the intense curiosity of the secretary he made it clear that he would only attend if the discussion, even its very existence, was entirely private. In any case, the job was half done. By the time they met Miranda would know that, from her point of view, things had gone badly awry; the bunting would have been hidden, the champagne returned to its cellar, the party over.

He was not, however, prepared for the savagery of her response. It was immediately evident that she was not sober, and that she had been crying. Her face was red and streaked, mascara running down one cheek, lipstick smudged and blotchy. On the floor were two copies of the *Standard*, the later edition emblazoned with a full-length photograph of Andrew and Tessa, linking arms and tentative, on the doorstep of their home that morning, with the headline 'WE'RE STAYING TOGETHER', and 'Minister in sex scandal confesses all to wife' underneath.

Andrew had not accepted an invitation to sit; this was no time for niceties. Miranda waved the page menacingly under his nose.

'What the bloody hell's going on, Andrew? Twelve hours ago you're fucking me on Westminster Bridge like there's no tomorrow and promising to love me for ever. I came home and started planning a wedding, for God's sake! I even summoned my girlfriends and we went out for a hen party this morning to celebrate. Then I come back to the office and I am faced with – this!'

She shook the headlines at him in impotent fury, then tossed the offending paper over to the far corner of the room, sending a vase of flowers tumbling wetly to the floor.

His pulse was racing and he pursed his lips. To give himself time to think, he looked around. The penthouse flat was large and glamorous; through one open door he glimpsed a huge bed covered in pink satin, while another door opened on to a windy terrace with a magnificent view. The main room was carpeted in pink and white, with cream leather sofas and armchairs, all oversized and covered in bright silk scatter cushions. Fresh spring flowers filled the room with heady sweetness. A large painting on the far wall showed a helmeted man in an Australian desert landscape. There were no photographs or portraits to give him a clue, but this was surely the newspaper owner's pad. A substantial bar occupied one corner with more drinks bottles than Andrew had ever seen. On its polished wood surface an empty glass stood inside a wet ring by a frosted silver ice-bucket. Miranda must have been hitting the bottle hard.

Andrew Muncastle reverted to his most correct manner. 'I owe you an apology, Miranda. I was simply carried away last night. I cannot give up my job and my home, in the way I let you think. I never intended to, not at any point. I am deeply sorry for any upset I may have caused you.'

'You're upset! You! What about me? Anyway I don't believe you. I just don't believe you're that accomplished a liar. If you were I'd have spotted it long before now and never have dreamed of sharing my life

480

with you. Last night you were on cloud nine. You were all ready to drop everything and come with me. Now you're all lovey-dovey with that mouse of a wife. What happened?'

He examined his shoes, like a naughty boy carpeted by the headmaster. He wondered if the memory of what she had meant to him for nearly two years, the glory he had learned from her, would fade and be lost, or whether her vivacity, joy and excitement would linger. It would be best to put it all firmly out of his mind, of course. If he were to renew his efforts with Tessa and guide her to something approximating a normal sexual relationship he could not have the vivid presence of Miranda in bed with them. Remembering her as she was now, distressed and ugly, might help. He raised his eyes and stared at her stonily, taking in every unhappy detail.

'My God, Andrew, but you led me up the garden path,' she spat out bitterly. 'All these years, and I never fell for anybody. Played the field, lots of men, always had a good time: no kiss and tell either way, and most of them are still friends. No shortage of offers either – I've turned down better men than you, Mr Muncastle, more than once. Millionaires, media tycoons, men of real substance, not jumped-up squirts of MPs like you.'

She sounded as if she were trying to convince herself of his lack of worth. If blaming herself for making a mistake was going to help her Andrew was not about to interfere. He accepted the humiliation of the comparison. After this he would not see her again, and in his world money and media power did not confer status or respect. He felt no compunction to explain the difference to her. There were some things Miranda would never be able to grasp, of which the most significant was that he did not share her hierarchy of values. He dipped his head as if accepting a punishment but said nothing.

Miranda was infuriated by his silence. She came close and stood under his nose so that he could not help looking down at her and thus at her body. His self-control slipped and he swallowed visibly. Her lip curled in a sneer and she pulled off her jacket, slinging it behind her, then reached up and pulled down her low-necked sweater, revealing her breasts. Cupping them in her hands, she jiggled them up and down, running her fingertips up and over the nipples to make them stand up, and threw back her head, as if to invite him to sink his mouth on her neck.

'That's all you were ever interested in, wasn't it? A little bit of humpy-pumpy, that you couldn't get at home. What's happened – little wifey opened her legs to you at last, has she?'

'Stop it, Miranda,' he said quietly. 'I can't be with you, that is all.'

The finality hit her suddenly, and pulling her sweater back into place she flung herself sobbing on to the nearest sofa. Andrew stood helpless, a great ache of guilt numbing him. This was the downside, the price to pay, for the pleasure of her love; her heartbreaking wailing cut him to the quick. He had never, never in his life, aroused such passion in anyone. Nor caused anyone else such pain. And never wanted to again.

At last the weeping subsided and she peered at him from under wet lashes. Her voice was soft and distant.

'I am thirty years old, and I have made a good life for myself. I have a career and a reputation which I have earned: nobody did it for me. I thought I needed nothing more until I met you, Andrew. Then I realised I needed – oh, I don't know: something solid, and dependable, and real, and permanent, and not easily deployed or bent to my will. It had all been too easy. I wanted you because you were different. Can you realise how terrible it is to find out you're just like all the rest? You have ruined my life, Andrew. You must understand that.'

Time was passing and he felt a twitch of impatience. Back at the office there was work waiting.

'Oh, come now, Miranda, it can't be as bad as all that. I mean, after all' – and he gestured around at the sofas and the pictures – 'you've still got all this, haven't you?'

'What do you mean by that?'

'Well, it stands to reason. You were never short of men friends before, and despite your protestations of love for me at a guess you're not short now, are you? This flat must have cost a bob or two. What do you have to do to pay for its use, Miranda?'

'You bastard.'

He pushed home his advantage, hating himself. 'How does a nice Australian girl achieve all this, hey, Miranda? Isn't he a bit old for you?'

He expected her to fly at him and in readiness raised his arms to protect himself. For several seconds she sat stock still, staring at him. Them with cold dignity she rose and went to the door to the hall, opening it and standing with her hand on the handle.

'If you seriously think I am sleeping with the owner, Andrew, you are wrong.'

It was his turn to throw back his head and laugh – a raucous, unpleasant sound. It did not dislodge her.

'Everybody knows you do, Miranda. Don't kid me. I turned a blind eye when you and I were . . . you know. But not now.'

Her voice was low and cool. 'My God, Andrew, but you are a fool. More than I could ever have guessed. I was not going to tell you this: hardly anybody knows, because I always wanted to make my own way, and I have. And I would prefer that you keep it to yourself, please. The owner is not my lover; he's my father.'

Muncastle stood dumbstruck. 'What? But your name is—'

'Different from his. Certainly. He and my mother split up when I was small and I was adopted by my mother's new husband. But I'm his daughter all right. You can tell if you see us together, which is why you don't. When I started in journalism in Australia I did it entirely on my own; only when I wanted to come to England did I ask him for a job. And the Australian editorship is in his gift too, though I didn't accept until I was sure I could have it on merit alone. He'd make me executive vice-president tomorrow if I wanted it, but I don't. Not yet.'

'You never said a word!'

'Makes a difference, does it? You could have been his son-in-law, Andrew, in line to run the business with my brother, if you had wanted.'

Andrew gasped. The room felt hot and began to swirl in muddled colours around him, as if he were caught up in a kaleidoscope and would be shaken to pieces if it didn't stop. His mouth opened but nothing came out. Miranda watched him, a mocking look in her eyes. Only now did she know what Andrew Muncastle was made of. It began to feel like a lucky escape.

Miranda Jamieson was a warm and kind woman underneath all her flaunted sexuality. Observing her erstwhile lover gaping and swaying she felt a sliver of sorrow for him. He had been made a fool of, not her. Her integrity was intact: his *amour propre* damaged for ever.

'Andrew, why do you think I keep quiet about it? If I'm going to marry somebody it has to be for myself, not for who my father is, and not for my money, Goddammit. I thought it was you. I was wrong. And I am sorry I was wrong.'

He moved grey-faced towards the door she was holding open for him. Not the door to a new life, but the confirmation that he was only fit for the old one. At the door he was very close to her and paused.

'Miranda—' He had no idea what he wanted to say.

She pulled a wry face. 'Good afternoon, Mr Muncastle. That's the way out.'

The door closed with a soft, expensive click behind him.

CHAPTER TWENTY-SIX

By the middle of that momentous week Elaine was steeled for coolness in Roger. The Muncastle business must have affected the department and would naturally have made him extremely cautious, though he made no move to break a date with her pencilled in for Wednesday evening. Once Andrew and Tessa Muncastle had faced down the press and the Prime Minister had made it clear no resignation was in the offing the story went off the boil, though no doubt the riper Sunday press would make much of it at the weekend.

It was late, after the ten o'clock vote; as so many times before, Roger came to her flat, though he would not be sleeping over. Two red boxes, oppressive as ever, stood waiting in the hallway. Elaine made him a toasted bacon sandwich then, nose wrinkling at the tempting smell, another for herself.

'It's a curious business,' she reflected, pointing at a collection of well-thumbed newspapers. 'Some of the papers ignore the Muncastle business entirely, even the tabloids.'

'Depends who owns them,' Dickson pointed out. 'Muncastle's inamorata is deputy editor of one of the Australian group and a pet of the owner, so my spies tell me. They won't carry anything on it unless it blows up bigger. And it won't.'

'Can you be sure?'

'She left on the Qantas flight back to Australia this morning. He's back at work, tail between legs, suitably chastened and refusing to say a dicky-bird. No talk, no story. Finished. We hope,' he added darkly.

Elaine could not help satisfying her own curiosity, though she had long ceased to consider Muncastle a political rival.

'Will it affect his career?'

'Shouldn't think so, as long as he doesn't make a habit of it. He's competent, with all the right connections, and usually steers well clear of trouble. Most of the chaps will regard him as a bit of a lucky dog, given the beauty of the lady in question. We didn't know he had it in him – it might even help, raising his profile. Sorry, Elaine, you won't like

485

that, but it's still a man's world, I'm afraid.'

Roger finished his sandwich and wiped his fingers on a paper napkin. 'Thank you! The inner man is well fed. Now then, young lady, what about the rest of me? I can't stay late tonight, but I have a good hour yet. Come and give your old beast a cuddle.'

He held out his arms to her in a generous, affectionate gesture. To his disappointment the corners of Elaine's mouth turned down. She settled herself beside him, curling around, fingers playing with his shirt buttons but making no attempt to undo them, resting her head on his shoulder, tucked in, seeking comfort, not sex.

'What's the matter?'

'Mike wants a divorce.'

'Oh, no. Elaine, I am so sorry. On what grounds?'

Head bowed, she explained briefly. Roger sensed her distress. Even if the marriage had long since cooled, its loss was like a bereavement. He pulled her head down on to his shoulder again and kissed the blonde tangle, whispering endearments to her as she wept. There was no question of making love that night. The years they had already shared, and his immediate appreciation of the terrible effect on her, created an obligation to comfort each other, as friends, instead.

At last she was quiet. He shifted his position, holding her hand gently. More needed to be said. 'Tell me.'

'I'm afraid, Roger, that you won't want me now.'

'Hush, don't talk like that. Of course I do. And will.'

'I'm not a risk to you, you know that. But you might think so now that I'm . . . on my own.'

'You don't need to spell it out, Elaine. What we have always had has been over and above our other pre-existing arrangements.'

The words sounded awkward. Elaine wished she could quote poetry which would fit the moment, Browning or Rossetti, sweet and deep and full of love and sacrifice, but nothing came.

'It's not your fault, either, but I feel such a failure. I've lost Mike. I've lost all chance of promotion. I might even lose my seat – it never was very safe and the rumblings are ominous. I don't want to lose you too.'

'You won't. I promise.'

A silence. Then she spoke again, low and sad.

'What will happen to us, Roger? Will we be found out, like Andrew and his girlfriend? Will it all end in tears?'

'Why should it? He had an affair with a journalist, which is not smart. Once a teller of tales always a teller of tales. You and I, on the other hand, have identical motives for staying quiet.'

'We had. Not any more,' she reminded him.

'It makes no difference to me, and it shouldn't to you.' His tone was almost brusque. 'Plan A is to carry on as we are now. And if there is the least hint, Elaine, remember Plan B: deny it and deny it and deny it. If you and I both stick to the same story the press can pin nothing on us.'

She nodded. 'Any time you want to stop, Roger—'

'I don't.'

It sounded almost arrogant the way he said it, as if he were refusing all consideration of change. That was a surprise. Given the horrendous reminder that the Muncastle business had slapped before them it would have been understandable had he suggested lying low for a bit, or made the first moves to end the affair.

A surprise, and risky. 'You have much more to lose than Muncastle,' she warned him.

A soft light came into his eyes and he put her hand to his lips, caressing her fingers gently. 'I know that, Elaine. I have you to lose, and I don't intend to.'

Now was the moment to tell her he loved her, if ever there was a moment. He waited, and the moment passed, as he knew it would.

'We are neither of us about to be careless. So can we have less morbid talk, please? Wish me luck for tomorrow night. I have to do *Question Time* and no doubt will have to bat for Britain against the Aussie onslaught on prime-time television, not to mention explaining how the government fully expects to win the next election while ten points adrift in the opinion polls.'

'If it stays like that I shall definitely lose my seat.' Elaine had spent the previous weekend on doorsteps in her constituency and had not liked what she heard there.

'Not only you. As I reminded the Prime Minister, we really must switch into general election mode. Strictly speaking we have a while yet, but next year is quite likely. That means we could be electioneering barely twelve months from now – not long. Leaving everything till the autumn Budget is taking a hell of a risk.'

'Do you think he knows what he is doing?'

'The Prime Minister? As well as anyone, I guess. Knowing what to do and doing it are not the same, of course. Still, he has one successful victory under his belt and is keen to add another. I suggested to him the other day after Cabinet that we should be engineering a mini-boom in time for a snap election next spring and he looked quite shocked at the suggestion. There's a bit of a gap, you know, between being the magisterial all-wise leader of the nation and the tough boss of a fighting party. I don't envy him trying to be both.'

She eyed him archly. 'You'd still like to have a crack, though, wouldn't you? You're easily the best of the younger Cabinet Ministers. You can't, surely, be satisfied with playing second fiddle – or third, or fourth – to people only on the same level.'

He curled a lock of her hair around a finger and pondered. 'There's such a cost, Elaine. To the family, to me personally. Look: part is obvious – I would put Caroline and the children and everyone near me in such danger, in the firing line for terrorists and every crank going. I'm not sure I should blithely do that without thinking it through very carefully. The Prime Minister's wife had a miserable time when the security bungalow was erected down the garden and the bullet-proof glass went in behind the lace curtains. To some extent that's already happened. Even you're a target because of me. I bet the IRA already have this address and have a shrewd idea what I get up to while I'm here.'

She shrugged. 'You forget I'm still secretary of the backbench Northern Ireland committee. I'm in the firing line in my own right. All MPs are, anyway. The moment you start to think about it, the job becomes impossible.'

Unspoken knowledge hung between them. The Muncastle business was not an exact parallel. Having made a fool of himself with a lover might not affect Andrew's elevation to the rank of Minister of State in due course, if he were still judged right for the team; but any revelations about Cabinet Minister Roger Dickson's private life would destroy his chances of moving smoothly towards the highest job in the land. Such evil lies would be said about them both, and despite 'Plan B' neither would be able to sue. The outcome was inevitable. Roger would be forced to resign from the Cabinet.

'We're running too many risks, my darling,' Elaine whispered. 'I just can't see you as a backbencher, that's all. Sitting there in prim misery, rushing to do five seconds on early-morning television, dreaming up issues on which to get agitated, writing pompous pieces for the *Evening Standard* for three hundred and fifty pounds a time.'

With a dismissive gesture she indicated a Mellor article on the leader page adorned with a large photograph of the author.

'I should charge more than that.' He was trying to cheer her up, but her mood refused to lift. His voice became mock-stern. 'Don't let me down, little lady. I come to you for enjoyment, not for grief. I have more than enough serious matters on my plate without wearying myself with what I would write about if reduced to the back benches. What the hell! That's almost certain to happen, sooner or later. It all ends in tears, don't you know that? My job right now is to ensure that we don't all end up on the Opposition side, and your job is to help me.'

He disentangled himself from her with a suppressed sigh and went to collect his coat. Women who thought too much had their disadvantages. It sounded as if Elaine was beginning to back off. He hoped to God she was not serious.

He knew his own mind. Muncastle's priggishness had sickened him. The man was an amoral creep whose carelessness had let two women down. He, Roger Dickson, had no intention of getting caught in the same trap. Elaine was part of his whole mental make-up now – part of his inner world, his soul, though he could not willingly articulate that realisation to anyone, least of all to her. He would not give her up without a fight.

He would not give her up at all.

The whips deemed it wisest to let everybody go home early, so Thursday evening's business was quietly downgraded to a one-line whip. Elaine was feeling battered and groggy and headed gratefully for the empty flat, a microwaved dinner, a warming glass of Glenfiddich for company and the television.

Andrew Muncastle, foolish man, was still on the evening news, though he had slipped from first item to fourth behind the discharge from hospital of poor Marcus Carey. The occasion was an impromptu press conference given by Miranda Jamieson at Sydney airport in which she denounced all British men as half-baked homos. Elaine wondered defensively how much experience the lady had acquired. Judging from Miranda's demeanour her comment, at least in part, was to inform Andrew what she thought of him in the most humiliating way possible. You had to admire her nerve.

The commentary was accompanied by more pictures of the Muncastles smiling tentatively at the doorway of their London home. Elaine examined Andrew's martyred face intently. Beside him, hand clasped in his, his wife looked up at him. Talk of the Minister's resigning had died; the BBC presentation was clearly sympathetic.

Andrew had arrived in Westminster on the same day three years ago as herself. He had met his whip – Roger Dickson, same man – standing beside her in Members' Lobby. Their backgrounds were different, with Andrew already part of the system through his grandfather, but surely that did not count for much. It was balanced by the fact that as a woman MP she had more to offer, if the party were interested in making itself truly representative of the people who sent them both to Westminster. Yet he had placed his foot firmly on the next rung of promotion each time and was now a settled and, it appeared, indispensable member of the government. How was it done?

She fetched her copy of *Vacher's* and looked up his entry. He had gained early that precious place on the Select Committee on the Environment which had given him such insight into the department. Elaine had no clear idea how that was done, but the whips must have been involved somehow. Andrew had ruffled no feathers on that committee but had distinguished himself in sharp, ultra-polite inter-rogation of awkward witnesses. His membership guaranteed that he would be called to speak in tricky debates when he was frequently the only knowledgeable person supporting the government. When at the summer reshuffle a new PPS was required in that department, Andrew slipped easily into the gap. Appointed, in fact, to look after Roger. She had been surprised that her name had not come up. That was odd. Surely it didn't mean that, given the choice, Roger had chosen this colourless time-server instead of herself?

It took a long swallow of the whisky to steady her. Of course it meant just that, and for the most obvious of reasons. By the time Roger himself was promoted their affair was in full swing. He would not have contemplated her appointment so close to him: it would have been too risky. And he did not know her well then. Perhaps it had flitted through his mind that, were she unscrupulous, it was too open to abuse.

He might at the least have recommended her name elsewhere; but once he was out of the whips' office there was no way to do it. It would have sounded highly suspicious had a Minister touted around a name, and of an attractive female at that, if he were refusing to appoint her himself.

What about following in Muncastle's warm footsteps? Andrew's office on the backbenchers' committee was of interest to the Snakes and Ladders dining club of which she was not a member; their discreet canvassing, circulated lists of names and organised voting kept out people like herself very effectively. As for the coveted position on the select committee and other appointments: Roger's replacement as Environment whip was Johnson, who had leered at her once and then lost interest. She was clearly not in favour there, though, since she had never had a conversation with the man, it was difficult to comprehend how she might have upset him. Weren't the whips' assessments based on fact rather than fiction? Then she remembered that three people from her own region, including Roger, were by then already in the government. There was a crude rationing system to ensure that no area dominated too strongly. On any such calculation Stalker would have been pushed down the list, especially as the most distinguished Member nearby, who just happened to be Roger, probably never mentioned her.

It kept coming back to Roger, and to the fact that their affair seemed to have been getting in the way at all the crucial points. The most obvious contrast between her and Andrew Muncastle was this: that one of them was sleeping with Roger Dickson and the other wasn't.

The television screen filled with the credits and bouncy music of the current affairs programme, *Question Time*, recorded an hour or so earlier. One figure from each of the three main parties appeared, the fourth place taken by a commentator or industrialist or otherwise supposedly neutral figure, plus a chairman. The whole style was a throwback to days when discussion between intelligent beings was the bedrock of British debate.

This week's team was high-powered. The Secretary of State for the Environment was matched with the Labour spokesman on Trade and Industry, while Lord Blackthorn represented the Liberal Democrats. The Director-General of the Confederation of British Industry made up the foursome. All male, though nobody seemed in the least apologetic. When the team was all female, as on one occasion when Elaine herself was a panellist, it excited heated comment in the national press.

Roger would also be tuned in, back in the Great Peter Street house, probably with Caroline. He had conquered his fear of watching his performances on television and would be checking with a critical eye, chewing through the remarks made by the other side, debating how he might have demolished them better.

The first question from a member of the audience was about the qualities required by politicians. The panel had a choice. They could by mutual consent avoid the Muncastle issue, in which case the chairman was briefed to make a sarcastic remark before moving on to the next question. He needn't have worried. The Liberal Democrat peer, married for forty years to an extremely dull woman, licked his lips and sallied forth.

'I would have said,' he remarked unctuously, 'that if we are going to trust our politicians we do need to know they are honourable people. Not like the junior Minister in your department, Roger.'

Dickson folded his arms belligerently and glared, knowing the camera would pick up his angry face, more expressive than any riposte.

'Steady on!' the industrialist intervened. 'Your own Leader hasn't exactly got an unblemished history, has he?'

'Ah, but he confessed at once,' smoothed the Liberal (which was not true). 'The public appreciate that sort of honesty.'

The chairman was aware from his hidden monitor that Dickson's silent disapproval had dominated the screen for several moments. 'Would you like to add anything, Mr Dickson?'

'Certainly.' Roger leaned forward and ignored the camera, knowing that would increase the sincerity of his pronouncement. He allowed a steely edge to enter his voice. 'Andrew and Tessa Muncastle are good friends of mine. Andrew is an outstanding young MP and member of my team. I think they should be allowed to work out for themselves whatever personal problems they may have, and the rest of us should *mind our own business.*'

His mouth clamped firmly shut as it there were no more to be said. Elaine felt like applauding.

Supposing Roger had said, just once, with that same firm jaw, even while still in the whips' office: 'Elaine Stalker is an outstanding young

MP. It really is about time we stopped talking about women politicians as if they were freaks – she in particular is a remarkable person. I recommend she be appointed to high office without delay.'

He had never said that. The political atmosphere brought it back to her: she had seduced him in the first place, partly because he was so very special, partly because he was an irresistible challenge – and partly to help her career. She had made no secret of it: he would have expected it a bit. It had been natural to assume he would push her case. On that she had made a big mistake, it now appeared. The very qualities which made her love him precluded any such underhand activity. He was too decent, too cautious, to do any such thing. But the assumption that Roger would look after trivial details – like speaking well of her – had led her to a dead end, and to neglect fatally the necessity of promoting herself elsewhere.

There had been other ways, apparently insignificant, in which the affair had been destructive. More than once, knowing Roger was expected that evening, she had given up the chance to speak in a debate in order to rush home and wait for him. Wanting to watch him at every opportunity she had written the future dates of Environment Questions in her diary and refused invitations which would clash, including several emanating from Freddie Ferriman, who, given his reputation as a kingmaker, might have been useful. She had hardly noticed other tentative approaches from colleagues, whips or PPSs, so wrapped up in Roger was she. Believing Roger's kind-hearted assertion that all she needed was patience and that her promotion was only a matter of time, she had refused to join in cross-party agitation over women's issues or transport of industrial waste or excessive cuts in the armed forces or the size of the European budget, and thus failed to make other valuable friends. No wonder she quickly found the Commons a cool place; she had put all her eggs in one basket, and placed it at the back of the fridge.

Elaine watched the television, fascinated. Had Roger rehearsed he could not have done better. He was a fine performer these days, fearless, well informed, adroit and honest in his delivery. He was nowhere near the summit of his career but was capable of going much further. More than capable, in fact, of a fair showing in a leadership election.

Which possibly he would win.

This was important. She followed the thought through carefully. The current Prime Minister had promised himself and any friends who would listen, back at the time of his own elevation, that in his view there were other things besides politics, and that he would himself do the job no longer than the age of fifty-five. Elaine lay back and chewed her thumb, feeling guilty and disloyal. He wouldn't last that long. His predecessor had gone on too long too. The most likely challenge would come after a general election, if it did not go well. The opinion polls showed that none of the possible current contenders scored better than the Prime Minister, while the Foreign Secretary, a man in his sixties, was already planning his memoirs. But a new contender – Roger Dickson? – might change the political landscape entirely.

He would make a good Prime Minister. Even if, were they in Opposition, he would have to serve a term as Leader on the wrong bench first. Maybe that would be no bad thing. Margaret Thatcher had used her four years facing Labour Prime Ministers brilliantly, generating enough fresh ideas to carry the party through a string of election successes. Roger Dickson was perfectly capable of doing the same.

But not with her in tow.

Her reverie stopped suddenly. The final credits were rolling. Roger was obviously well pleased with himself, and so he might be. Smart, positive, friendly and believable, he looked every inch a potential future Prime Minister. But not with any skeletons in his cupboard. He must realise that. It puzzled her that he had not accepted her hint that the time was near to end the affair. It did not fit her picture of him, garnered over a long period, that he might be so arrogant as to imagine it did not matter.

Yet it must end. And if he would not come to his senses she would have to force the issue. Soon.

But oh, merciful God, not just yet. Not while the pain of losing Mike was still so real. Not until she had adjusted to the idea of being alone. There was a limit to what she could take. The break-up of her marriage and the uncomfortable adjustment to her public image and status – with the unpleasant publicity which was bound to follow even a quiet split – would take some time to absorb. The wounds needed a while to heal. She needed Roger now more than ever.

Dorothy Holmes was dying. To her helpless fury she could no longer dress or feed herself. Elaine sat by her bed in Eventide holding her limp hand. For the first time Dorothy was wigless. Instead of her usual formidable and startling appearance she seemed tiny and non-viable, like the dead chicks which fall out of trees in spring, scrawny, awkward, hairless.

'Bloody awful, this.' The old lady still managed a hoarse whisper. 'Can't do anything for myself any more. Have to have a bedpan. You'd think an old nurse wouldn't mind, but I do. So darned undignified.'

Elaine had brought chocolates as usual, but this time Dorothy showed no interest. Matron Swanson had been very matter of fact: 'It won't be long now, Mrs Stalker. It's good of you to come. She's had a series of small strokes and the next one will probably finish her. No point in sending her into hospital – she would never come out alive. At least here she has all her own things.' Elaine looked around Dorothy's bedroom. She could not imagine that the once vigorous and intelligent woman would have chosen the insipid landscape on the wall or the peony wallpaper with its matching frilly curtains. Dorothy's character was hidden in the cupboard along with Marie Lloyd sheet music and the oversized sherry bottle and the dusty pages of the unpublished novel she had written in dark nights nursing, waiting for someone to die, so long ago.

'Saw your Roger on TV the other night,' Dorothy was saying. 'It was your Roger, wasn't it? On *Question Time*? . . . I thought so. Defending that young Minister who went off the rails a bit. They give me morphine to dull the pain but it makes me dopey, so I sometimes don't let on when it's wearing off. That way the brain still functions a bit. I thought he was splendid. I can see why you're so fond of him.'

Exhausted, she let her naked head with its few sparse silvery hairs fall back on the pillows. The false teeth no longer fitted her skeletal gums and she could only articulate with effort; she had, however, refused point blank to see her visitor without her teeth in. The smell in the room was of disinfectant and talc.

'He is doing very well, "my" Roger. My real worry is that somebody may find out. It would do my career no good at all, but it would wreck his. The press are always looking for an excuse to hound a person, and this – having an affair with a fellow MP – would be a real cracker. So, Dorothy: just as I admit to myself, and to him, that I am very much in love with the bloke – and that he's worth loving and admiring, something special – it's all becoming much too dangerous.'

Dorothy said nothing. Her eyes rested on Elaine's troubled face and she squeezed the younger woman's hand hard. Elaine felt the slight tremor in the fingers and stroked them with her own absent-mindedly. She was talking almost to herself.

'I watched him on TV like you, Dorothy. He's so good at it now. Used to be terrible, if truth were told – shy and diffident, no idea how to handle the press or cameras. But I told him what to do, and made him practise. It was only a question of persuading him not to put up barriers all the time. Everyone else now can see the qualities I admire in him so much. He must be due for higher things, I'm certain. He's a man entirely without enemies: nobody has a bad word to say about him. And with many friends and allies. He needs me now like he needs a hole in the head. What am I to do?'

Dorothy waited. Elaine's face swam in and out of her vision, her voice alternately faint and clear. It would be a relief to go now. The whole journey was taking just too long: more than 103 years – crazy. She had not wanted to leave as long as life had been fun, but helplessness had eroded her sense of self, and once off her legs she had deteriorated quickly. Despite her upbringing she was not at all sure if there was any life afterwards. The possibility of meeting Oliver again made her groan. Then her little girl, so long dead, and her brothers, handsome dashing young men cut to pieces by the pounding guns, swam into her head. They seemed to be beckoning.

Elaine heard the groan. 'Are you all right? Shall I fetch someone?'

'No, no.' Dorothy was testy. No more poking about. She opened her eyes. 'You can't leave it like that, Elaine. I will not die in torment! What are you going to do with your Roger? Carry on, or stop?'

The younger woman spread her hands in a helpless gesture.

'Would *he* stop?'

'Him? No, I don't believe so. It doesn't matter so much to him, so he won't talk about it. That's what happens to all the blokes that get into trouble; their brains are not engaged. He really doesn't think it through.'

'Then you'll have to be the strong one, won't you?' Dorothy summoned all her own strength to stare challengingly at Elaine.

'I'm not sure I'm strong enough to do without him.'

'Stuff. You did all right before. Put your energies into your job. Nothing like work.'

Elaine shook her head. 'It's made worse, Dorothy, by the fact that my husband has left me and wants a divorce. It'll all come out soon – he's found someone else. Nothing to do with Roger – Mike doesn't know, I'm pretty sure. But it makes me feel very low. I am, for the first time in my adult life, horribly alone. If I stop my affair with Roger I should be manless for the first time in – oh, nearly twenty years. All right, the feminists would say I was man-free and should relish it. But all my working life I have used my husband as a prop – he took care of the necessity to earn a living, he provided me with respectability, even his name, he fetched and carried and paid, he was always great when the children were little, he comforted and defended and bedded me. I suppose I treated him much like my male colleagues treat their spouses – like Roger treats Caroline: distantly affectionate. Mike didn't interfere in my working life and expected relatively little in return. I couldn't even give him that. I feel such a total failure as a human being, as a woman. If I lose Roger as well . . .'

'You're thinking of yourself again.' The old woman's tone was severe.

'I'm at least good at that. Who else am I to think of?'

Dorothy shifted restlessly. 'Do you really love this Roger?'

Elaine thought for a long while. Then she nodded.

'Well then, silly young woman, you have your answer.' The voice was getting fainter.

'But what would I have left, without either of them?' Elaine wailed. 'Do you know the really daft thing, Dorothy? What makes me grind my teeth in despair at my own stupidity? Let me tell you. In trying not to behave as other women do I've succeeded only in falling into the same trap – needing a man, living through a man, feeling lost and helpless and terrified without a man. My God! I am a fool. And I never realised it, till now.'

The old lady's gaze was far away. Elaine doubted if she could still hear. Dorothy had made a much better fist of her life. Tied to a hopeless alcoholic, a husband who could fulfil virtually none of the obligations of manhood, this woman had clung with fierce determination to her home, her profession, her unique character and her family, who still adored her. Elaine leaned forward and spoke again. There had to be an answer.

'Tell me, Dorothy. I put so much energy into my love life that I took my eye off my political career. Now there's every likelihood that I will be stuck as a backbencher for ever – that's if I even manage to hold on to my seat. I have made a real hash of things! If I give Roger up, it won't be because I've stopped loving and needing him, but because I love him too much to risk putting him in any further danger. Yet what would be the reward for all this selfless devotion – what would I have left?'

The old lady stirred and smiled, as if she had moved a last chess piece into place. She raised her hand and poked an admonitory finger in the air.

'Ah! You ask me what you will have. What quality is it women have which keeps us going, despite all our trials? For if women stop, the world will come to an end.'

She chuckled softly, as Elaine's troubled face puckered into a puzzled frown. Dorothy beckoned her close with a gnarled finger and whispered conspiratorially. 'Pride, my dear. Pride.'

'What?' Elaine was not sure she had heard right. Dorothy's voice came in an angry sibilant hiss.

'Your *pride*! That's all you need, my dear. Now put it to good use.'

The door opened to admit Mrs Swanson with an anxious expression and a kidney bowl containing a syringe and ampoule. Ignoring Dorothy, who had closed her eyes, she explained: 'It's way past her time for an injection. Without it she won't sleep. Would you mind, Mrs Stalker?'

'Sleep long enough soon,' came the almost indecipherable mutter from the patient. Dorothy Holmes reached for Elaine's hand for one last squeeze and opened one eye – and winked, with what might have been a passing reminder of her old throaty laugh.

'Pride. Believe in yourself. If you don't, who will? At ease with yourself. Happy in your skin. Pride, it is. Don't forget.'

Part Four

CHAPTER TWENTY-SEVEN

Roger Dickson sipped his drink and looked around the White Drawing Room of 10 Downing Street with mild envy.

It was the smallest and least formal of the many public rooms of the Prime Ministerial residence and elegantly decorated in cream and white. Ceiling-to-floor windows were hung with red curtains, with plump inviting cushions on the striped red and cream silk of its two comfortable sofas. A coal-effect gas fire burned cosily in the grate; the Waterford glass chandelier twinkled in the January sun. On the mantelpiece were displayed Staffordshire figurines of Gladstone, Disraeli and Wellington, while the paintings were modest and dull. One, a dismal affair of browns and greens, was entitled *The Quiet Ruin*. Not appropriate yet for Number 10, Dickson reckoned. The overall effect was similar to dozens of country houses on show throughout England – smart but not sumptuous, comfortable but not casual. A perfect location for a quiet pre-lunch drink with the Prime Minister, the Party Chairman and the Chief Whip.

'I think it's settled, then. We go for it this year, and as soon as possible.' The Prime Minister pushed his spectacles up his nose. His strange vowels betrayed his nervousness. Other people found waiting dreadful: he preferred it, as a time of savouring options, of consideration, of not having to take any decisions. Now there would have to be a plan of action, against which future gains and disasters would inevitably be measured.

The Party Chairman agreed. 'You might want to use local elections in May as a rehearsal: summer elections have always been kind to us.'

The Chief Whip was of the same mind. 'We have to go to the country some time in the next fifteen months. Waiting till next year pushes us up against the barriers and reduces our room for manoeuvre. Nor is there any powerful reason to delay till autumn. The economy is likely to be much the same as now, and given the trouble in Russia everything could be much worse.'

'To be honest we're in a much stronger position now than we might have expected,' Dickson ventured, ticking items off on his fingers in unconscious tribute to a Prime Ministerial habit. 'We're not too far behind in the polls. Boundary changes will deliver us a score of winnable new seats. The last Budget was very helpful and seems to be working. The recession may have lasted too long but it is over, even if growth has been hampered by the downturn in the rest of Europe. I think the voters are sophisticated enough to accept that we have done everything possible.'

'The line will be that they run terrible risks if they vote for the other lot, then?' That suited the Party Chairman. All kinds of lurid monsters could be conjured up. 'Preliminary testing by Saatchi's suggests that's still our best ploy. Double whammies and all that, however much the *cognoscenti* recoil in horror.'

The Chief Whip smiled delicately. 'It worked last time. And the time before that.'

The Prime Minister drew the discussion to a close. 'We'll need a presentation by Saatchi's as soon as possible, Chairman. While you're at it, hint they might be a bit cheaper this time. It was over a year before we could afford to clear their bill after the last election, and if you ask me, for all the vast commercial benefit they get from our victories, they ought to be paying us, not the other way round.'

The four men rose and stood talking for a moment more, conscious that once the meeting broke up, for them at least the general election campaign would have started. Spirits rose and pulses beat faster as they turned to leave. For twenty years the party had been a superb machine for gaining and holding on to power, far outliving both predictions and governments elsewhere. There was every chance that the formula would turn up trumps again.

'Roger, just a minute.'

The Prime Minister laid a hand on Dickson's arm and motioned him back to the sofa. He waited till the door closed.

'Roger, as you will have gathered, I'd like you to be a senior member of our election team. You're a splendid speaker these days and much liked and admired in the party and in the country. There will of course be promotion for you after the election.'

Dickson grinned broadly. He was too close to the Prime Minister in background and outlook to bother demurring.

'Thank you, Prime Minister. I shall do my best. The department is busy but no doubt the junior Ministers will cope.'

'Ah, yes, I hadn't thought of that. Who's your Minister of State?'

'Lord Cairns – in the Lords. We don't have one in the Commons. It would be useful to promote somebody: that would release me for other duties.'

'I wasn't planning a big reshuffle before the election, but I can see what you are driving at. Are you thinking of Muncastle? But he had all that trouble last year.'

'Seems to have got over it. He and his wife are closer now, if anything. You might like to make the point that men who stay with their wives are to be rewarded.'

That was a cynical comment and the Prime Minister knew it. 'Given our keenness on family life and all that. I get it. Is he any good?'

'Excellent: reliable and competent. I've no complaints.'

'Right – leave it to me. And – Roger – thank you for all your help in the coming months. We have a lot to do. This election is not at all a foregone conclusion, as I am sure you realise.'

'They never are, Prime Minister. That's democracy.'

The Prime Minister had made no move to dismiss him. For a moment Dickson hesitated. Then he realised that, for the Prime Minister, the morning's decision might mean that his last days in power loomed ahead. He coughed discreetly.

'You have served us exceptionally well, Prime Minister, if you don't mind my saying so, in very trying times. Following in the footsteps of your predecessor was a tall order, and what with Europe and all—'

The Prime Minister cut him off with a wave. 'The trouble is, I shall have to behave as if nothing has happened for weeks yet. I'm off to Bonn this afternoon – more secret negotiations over the next EC treaty. It might well be a brilliant idea to get the election out of the way before Son of Maastricht hits the fan. What a business.'

Dickson commiserated. 'I wish our future was not so dependent on the German view, I must say.'

The Prime Minister chuckled. 'Do you know I owe my title to the Germans – indeed the very nature of my job? It all boils down to Walpole. The new king, George I, the first Hanoverian, spoke not a word of English. He tried to chair the Cabinet in Latin but that didn't work. So he asked his most distinguished Minister, Sir Robert Walpole, to take over. Caused a great deal of fuss and jealousy at the time. The traditionalists sneered that according to the constitution we could have no sole or *prime* Minister: it was a term of abuse then, you see. Nothing changes, does it?'

Roger smiled, but his leader was looking thoughtful.

'Was there anything else, Prime Minister?'

'Well . . . yes, really. Let me try out an idea on you. I have to start putting together the next honours list. I felt very badly when Nigel Boswood had to go. In the normal course of events I would be sending him to the Lords now. The way he was hounded out was dreadful, but I gather he's picked himself up and is helping our weaker constituencies up north. Financially he has put in quite a lot of money, and is advising candidates and so on. They all think the world of him. How would people feel if I gave him his peerage anyway?'

Roger looked at the tall man before him with new respect. 'I think that would be a splendid idea. He was kind to me and I am proud to have known him.'

The Prime Minister seemed to be waiting, his face inscrutable.

'It would, of course,' Roger continued smoothly, 'also make a point which would not be lost on the gay community.'

The Prime Minister relaxed with a wry smile. How nice it was to have these complex matters completely understood.

'Quite. My thinking entirely.'

Out in the streets of London the pace of activity began to increase. Those who had most to gain or lose from an election set their alarm clocks earlier in the morning and went to bed later. Holidays were cancelled or left unbooked. Large amounts of money were moved from one bank account to another, evading tax, purchasing influence, slipping into invisibility. In party headquarters activity was stepped up, with private polling, collation of secret reports, commissioning of party political broadcasts, speechwriters, research assistants, booking of halls and poster sites through nominees, rewriting of draft manifestos and the quiet suppression of anything which did not have success in the election as its objective. In television companies meetings were convened to discuss media coverage, and negotiations started with Sir Robin Day, Nicholas Witchell, John Suchet, Anne Diamond, who was pregnant yet again, and Selina Scott. Publishers hassled recalcitrant commentators to finish election guides and get them into bookshops in time. The *Guardian* decided to hold political debates in suitable venues around Hampstead, but not to invite Glenda Jackson this time. In departmental offices senior civil servants met after hours and arranged the writing of the black books: incoming administrations would receive a full secret brief on where the department's activities stood, geared up to their party's stated preferences and policies and election manifestos. Neither would ever see the brief prepared for the other side. If power changed hands the entire departmental file would be closed for twenty-five years and the newcomers obliged, to their fury, to start from scratch.

Down in the City of London a different war was waging, a war of faceless men in black balaclavas bent on death and destruction.

On Sunday 11 February the office of Alan's Cab Services in North London was phoned with a request for two minicabs for different addresses. In both cases two men with soft Irish accents got into the back of the cab carrying a holdall. The first car belonged to twenty-nine-year-old Ethiopian-born Mustafa Turkelew, who was told to drive his Ford Cavalier to New Scotland Yard. When he turned around he found himself staring at a machine-gun. As the destination neared the men jumped out and told him to carry on. He was warned he was being followed and would be shot if he called the police or disobeyed instructions. The Nigerian driver of the second cab, a blue Nissan, was dealt with in identical fashion. With a handgun at his neck and another a few inches from his chest he was told to drive to Downing Street. His passengers announced they were from the Sixth Irish Fighters and warned that the journey must be completed inside twenty minutes. They left him near King's Cross. Both men thus found themselves driving towards the nation's prime terrorist targets with a vehicle empty in the back, except for a bomb.

Soon after, security cameras in Bishopsgate picked up a large eight-wheeled tipper truck parked on double yellow lines. Two men jumped out and sauntered away in opposite directions. The video operator, thankful for diversion on a quiet Sunday afternoon, was puzzled that the men did not appear to have locked the lorry and had left its hazard lights flashing. Nor had they returned ten minutes later. He reached for the phone.

Meanwhile Mustafa was checking his mirror as if his life depended on it, as indeed it did. Within three streets the experienced cabbie was satisfied he was not being followed and pulled up. For what seemed like an eternity but was in fact only a few seconds he contemplated the holdall on the back seat. And then he got out of the cab and ran like a bat out of hell.

His workmate, an older man with three young children, had less time to think. The journey to Downing Street would have taken longer than twenty minutes. He had no doubt what he was dealing with. In any case, nobody who knows London would casually order a cab to go to Downing Street: for several years huge black iron railings have closed it off and access or even parking nearby is forbidden. He drove no further than Holborn and then, frightened and desperate, flagged down a bus to block the road. The bus driver needed no hints but used his radio to call the police.

Ten minutes later both cabs blew sky high and their cabbies were left shaking and staring at crumpled heaps of blackened metal.

When the lorry went off its ton of explosive lifted the whole street for half a mile in all directions and sent a gigantic mushroom cloud of debris high into the afternoon air. A crater twenty feet deep yawned where it had stood; shattered pipes and snaking underground cables in the broken roadway resembled a piece of mangled flesh with broken bones and tendons exposed. The lorry itself disappeared completely. A chunk of metal was hurled 200 yards down the road at head height before burying itself in a wooden panel near a popular sandwich bar. The big engine, the only part not to disintegrate, was discovered a hundred yards away smashed into a gent's outfitters, enveloped by the smell of singed cloth. As the road was broad and open, damage was widely spread, superficial but spectacular, with windows blown out in hundreds of skyscraper buildings, their shards of glass crashing through the air like propelled weapons. The underground car park of one company shuddered in the shock wave and the chairman's prized vintage Rolls-Royce, so carefully stored in security, was smashed beyond repair. The beautiful church of St Ethelburga built in 1470, where Henry Hudson and his crew received Holy Communion in 1607 before sailing to find the north-west passage, and which had survived not only the Great Fire of London in 1666 but the Blitz, was blown to smithereens. An angry fire belched black smoke as a gas main fractured. And hundreds of police and fire crews and ambulance men and women worked with grim faces and case-hardened professionalism to help the dozens of injured and tend the dying, all the while wondering if there might be a second bomb nearby.

As a prominent member of the backbench Northern Ireland committee Elaine was promptly contacted by the media and invited to comment. She accepted not least because her own disgust yearned for expression. By long-established precedent there would be no Commons statement, no ministerial remarks, no official outpouring of anger against the terrorists: all that would have given them what they craved, publicity.

'The IRA, and indeed all terrorists, should know that they simply cannot win like this.' Elaine stood facing the camera by the police line in Bishopsgate. Her hands were trembling but she held herself firmly. 'Everyone here will work to ensure that the disruption is kept to a minimum. The IRA must be told that these tactics are a failure. The United Kingdom is a democracy. They will not obtain by the bomb or the bullet what they cannot win by the ballot box. Don't they realise that by now?'

Overhead the chunter of police helicopters interrupted the recording and she was obliged to start again. The young broadcaster was obviously keen to get away from the area.

'Do you think this will have a bad effect on London as an international financial centre?'

This was taking unbiased reporting a little too far. Elaine glared at him.

'Of course not. Why should it?' she said, belligerently.

A breeze ruffled her hair, bringing an acrid smell to her nostrils. In the distance the Lord Mayor of London, wearing his chain of office, a business suit and a hard hat, moped disconsolately: and kept his mouth shut. No doubt the hand-wringing over the last time bombs hit the City had inspired the bombers to try again. Nor would their success today be the last.

Next day in the Commons security room Gerry Keown was conscious of an atmosphere. Fear and apprehension were natural; this was the front line in any attempt to undermine national order. Everyone was on their toes for, even though the video cameras had done the trick and the police had pulled four men in for questioning, there was no guarantee that the whole team involved was now in custody.

Angry looks greeted Keown as he walked in, hung his leather jacket on its hook and began to button up his uniform. He lowered his head and muttered a 'Good morning'. It was not clear whose voice returned the greeting with a sneer, the lilt exaggerated with loathing. Never before had he been made to feel so self-conscious about his Ulster accent. For a second his gorge rose and he contemplated having an argument; but he had to live and work with these men and it was unlikely they would ever understand the sectarian hatred which undercut the province's politics. He was not certain he grasped it himself, though he knew which side he was on.

A message was waiting for him in the control room, neatly addressed in a House of Commons envelope. It was from Karen Stalker, telling him that she was planning to come to help out at half-term, and perhaps at Easter too if Parliament were still open then, as a break from endless studying for her A levels. The word 'endless' was underlined, speaking volumes about the tedium of English examinations. If by chance he were still interested perhaps he would ring her. Dates and a phone number, which Gerry knew already, followed.

His spirits rose and he was able to ignore the unpleasantness for the rest of the day. By the following morning tempers had cooled and a gruff apology made. The view was passed around that Keown was a decent sort and it was not his fault he was born on the wrong side of the Irish Sea. The unpleasant incident was forgotten.

'You can tell the election will be soon,' commented Diane Hardy. 'The postbag's gone bananas. Every problem under the sun, but mostly hunting.'

Elaine looked up from the previous day's pile. Beside her the bin was overflowing. 'The economy is still under severe strain, there's bloodshed and mayhem in London and in the most God-forsaken places on the Russian steppes, and they're still going on about fox-hunting. Is South Warmingshire for or against?'

Diane flicked through the pile and consulted a calculator. 'Both,' she grunted. 'Hunting accounts for around twenty-five per cent of the entire month's post; it's running twelve point three per cent pro and twelve point two per cent against.'

'That settles it: I shall abstain.' Elaine chuckled wryly. 'What a daft country we are, more agitated about animals than any other issue. Yet we abuse our children and treat our old people with neglect and cruelty.

Which reminds me, we have a memorial service for Dorothy Holmes coming up I must attend. It turns out she was quite distinguished. Another vote lost – and I shall miss her.'

'Come back to bed.' The voice wheedled, but carried a hint of command.

Peter was standing at the dressing table, looking in the mirror. He was certain that there had not been that large freckle on his neck the week before. It was not a mole, and its faintly purplish colour was not pigment. He pressed it gingerly. It did not hurt; the colour faded under the pressure, then came back, a touch darker.

On the dressing table the short note from Hermann caught his eye once more. It was a while since Peter had used his German, but the simple words swam into each other until only one short phrase remained.

> Hello Peter! Wie geht's dir? Mir geht's jetzt gut, aber ich habe eine schlechte Nachricht für dich. Ich bin HIV-positiv. Es tut mir leid. Ich liebe dich noch sehr. Hermann.

'. . . eine schlechte Nachricht' – bad news. It was bad news, all right. HIV positive. It was all very well Hermann saying now that he still loved him. It was too late.

The man on the bed stirred restlessly. Lean and languid, he took pleasure examining Peter's girlish buttocks as the boy stood a few feet away, but he could not wait for ever.

'Come on, sweetheart, I haven't got all day. I'm supposed to be tying up a report on the latest hole in the ozone layer and I'd really like to explore your holes and protuberances a little more before I leave. I have paid for your time, you know, handsomely.'

Peter turned back to the bed with a practised smile which might have appeared warm and affectionate. Yet there was no light in the blue eyes, just bitter loathing, of this man, of all the men like him, of what they had done and what they wanted done.

'I'm out of condoms,' he lied. 'Does it bother you? You know me well enough now.'

'I don't suppose you can pop down to the chemist's looking like that,' said the client in a bored tone. 'Come on over here. We'll manage. Now, where were we?'

Clarissa Dickson held buttery toast with both hands and surveyed her father gravely. The youngest of the family and now seven, she was a pretty child with dark curls and huge brown eyes. She missed her older brother Toby who was away at boarding school, while Emma, upstairs

506

hogging the bathroom, was the worst kind of big sister possible. Yet it was Clarissa who ruled her father's heart, not least because her intelligence outsmarted everyone else in the household and because her spirit and beauty reminded him so strongly of the woman he loved, who was not her mother.

'Daddy.'

'Um?' Roger was deeply into the *Times* leader which was calling for elections before Easter. His preference was for after, though not long after, to take advantage of fine weather. People were more likely to feel good, and therefore vote—

'*Daddy*.'

The child leaned over and planted a sticky hand on Roger's shirtsleeve. It made a greasy mark, as she knew it would. He started up with annoyance.

'I'm sorry, Daddy, but I have to get your 'tention. Why are you so busy now? You never have time even to come and kiss me goodnight.'

Roger folded the newspaper and made to lift the child on to his lap. To his surprise she was too heavy.

'My, kitten, but you're getting to be a big girl. You've been growing up as my back was turned. I'm sorry I was ignoring you. I did kiss you goodnight last night, but it was after midnight and you were fast asleep. If you dreamed of a handsome prince it was me. But there's going to be an election soon, and I have a lot to do.'

'What's an 'lection?'

He thought for a moment. Outside the sleek shape of the ministerial Jaguar purred quietly into place by the front door. He heard the doorbell and Caroline's answer; Alec would sit in the car till he was ready. Damn and drat. It was all very well being part of the inner Cabinet, yet how cruel it was, how horribly high the price. His children were growing up and he was not part of their precious childhood, hardly at all. Not that he noticed it, most of the time.

'An election, my sweet, is when we choose our MPs. Do you know what an MP is?'

'Member of Parl'ment' – instantly.

'Correct. And what do Members of Parliament do?'

The child considered. What did her father do – actually *do*? She put her finger in her mouth and shook her curly head.

'Our job is to look after people – to attend to their problems. A bit like the doctor, but he looks after your body. I look after all sorts of things for people back in Warwickshire – getting their house repaired, helping them with their pension and so on, if they can't do it for themselves. Every so often we ask people if they like the way we're doing it and they choose. That's an election.'

'How do they decide?'

If he explained, he would be late for the first briefing meeting. That could mean going into a tricky negotiation sailing by the seat of his pants. The child was watching him.

'Don't you have school?'

'Not today. Teachers being trained – Baker day, they call it.'

Roger was looking at the clock. Conscious that she was losing his interest, the child hurried on: 'Mummy was going to take us to the Planetarium but I've been there and it's boring. She says we're too young for the London Dungeon but I like all the gory stuff and I'm not a bit scared. Can I come into your office? Or tea at the Housacommons? Please say yes. Can I bring my friend Minna? She's never been. She's American. Her daddy is *really* important. He draws the Simpsons on TV. But you won't know about the Simpsons, Daddy, because *you* don't have time to watch TV either.'

Clarissa was doing her childish best to look severe. Roger felt his gut contract and knew it would be a miserable day, not least because the child's reproaches would haunt and distract him when he ought to be concentrating on the latest ruling from the European Court of Justice. He rose heavily and ruffled her hair.

'Don't,' Clarissa said crossly. 'I'm too big for that now.'

'That's enough.' There was sharpness in his voice, and her lower lip trembled. Immediately he regretted his brusqueness. 'I'm truly sorry, sweetheart, but I'm tied up all day. Mummy can bring you into the Commons but I shan't be there. I'm not free at all till later this evening. Forgive me but I have a job to do.'

Before Clarissa could start again, or cry, or detain him any further, Roger Dickson rose quickly, and moved to the door. With a forced smile he waved and was gone.

Elaine wondered groggily how long the body could manage without quite enough sleep. Not the total sleep deprivation which results from not being allowed to close the eyes at all, but the insidious raggedness which comes from being an hour or two short night after night and never catching up. The debate the previous evening had finished at midnight – not too bad, considering – but the Opposition had insisted on separate votes on four different motions, requiring Members to traipse through the lobbies and hang around in the tea room. It was the second time that week and there was more to come as the legislative programme intensified. Eventually she returned home, eyelids drooping, after one thirty, then was up at seven for a radio breakfast show. Now it was almost nine and time to leave for the House again, when all she wanted was to go back to bed.

Karen was asleep in the spare room, which had rapidly been turned into a tip in classic teenager fashion. She had insisted on bringing a large suitcase and a carrier with her even for the four days of half-term, and now their contents were scattered all over the floor, on chairs and on every other surface.

Karen opened an eye. Her fingers emerged from the tossed sea of the duvet and she wiggled them in a wave at her mother.

'Hi, Mum,' she mumbled sleepily. 'You off to work?'

'Don't be so surprised, young lady. The question is, are you? Do you intend to show your face at the Commons before lunchtime?'

There was the suspicion of a guilty struggle on Karen's face. 'Oh, right. I'm supposed to be helping. Yeah, I'll be in soon, don't worry. Is it all right if I go out tonight? Gerry Keown has asked me out again.'

Elaine's glance fell on the lines of her long-legged daughter's body. The girl stretched, pushing her bare toes out of the bottom of the duvet in a natural relaxed move, like a lithe young cat.

'You be careful.'

'Oh, Mum, don't be silly. I'm sure he's all right. I'm not a little girl any more, remember? Eighteen soon.'

'I know he works at the Commons, but I don't know anything about him. I'm only concerned for your welfare, Karen.'

'You'll be wanting to vet all my boyfriends next. Don't lean on me, Mum, I don't like it.'

The girl's tone contained a hint of warning, the child challenging the authority of her elders, feeling her strength. Elaine checked herself. She was jumpy partly because of the long-term lack of sleep, but also because of the bombs, and because of the heightened political atmosphere once television cameras caught Maurice Saatchi sliding into Conservative Central Office. Not until elections were out of the way, which could be months yet, would matters improve. It was not worth having a fight with Karen: she needed all her energy for the campaign. If she did not hold on to South Warmingshire, which was looking increasingly unpromising, the future might be bleak indeed.

Then there was the nagging question of Roger. It was as if she and her lover were travelling in a car with faulty brakes, with an enhanced sense of danger and the madness of carrying on, unwilling to consider that round the next corner a juggernaut might be blocking the road. Yet if either of them jumped out and refused to go any further the fateful journey would come to an end, for them both, for ever. And that thought made her heart stop.

The worry and indecision were affecting her work. There were times when she could think of nothing else. She was no longer certain she knew what Roger wanted. A natural politician operating in a man's world, and thus not accustomed to considering anyone else's welfare for long above her own, she was utterly unprepared for the womanly dilemma, as to whether her man's needs should be best met by giving in or denying him.

'You still there, Mum?' Karen rolled over and sat up. Her dark hair stood up spiky and sleep-knotted around her head. She rubbed her eyes and grinned.

Elaine moved to the door. 'I'm just going. Leave the bathroom tidy and scrub the bath, will you? Life in close proximity with you, young lady, is like living with a grubby elephant at times. I bet your Gerry would not be impressed. I will see you later.'

The phone rang in his flat. Gerry Keown picked it up.

'Yes?'

He did not give his name. Hardly anyone knew his personal number, for security reasons. It might be his supervisor, needing a few extra hours of overtime. Or possibly his mother in Belfast, wittering on about the news and wondering if he was in one piece. But no friends or acquaintances: for them he had no phone, and the number did not appear in any directory.

'Volunteer?'

The voice was male, the accent harsh, guttural.

Keown swallowed.

'Yes.'

'Do you have your code word?'

Keown gave it. A boy's name, never forgotten. He let his mind roll back to the memory of the bullet-torn body of his twelve-year-old brother, shot one Sunday in Derry by British soldiers on the rampage. He had asked in his grief if there was anything he could do. It had been a long time, starting as a ward orderly, then training as a psychiatric nurse, then making the smooth transfer to Broadmoor, which was always short of male nurses. It had been his duty to stay out of politics, not join any organisation other than the Prison Officers' Association as did all the other uniformed staff. Never say a word.

The vetting procedure for the House of Commons had been the biggest hurdle. Asked about this brother's death, Keown had grimaced, looked at the floor and told the interviewers that it had put him off politics of all kinds and he never voted. Easy.

'Are you ready, Volunteer? We have a commission for you.'

He was ready. It was time to repay.

It was here somewhere. Betts began rummaging in his old desk in the untidy room adjacent to his bedroom. Nobody ever came up here apart from his landlady, who clucked and wiped and went away again. She was not permitted to tidy his papers and nothing was ever put away. That meant it was wherever he had put it, two and a half years ago. With an election in the offing he must find it.

At last it turned up inside a tatty dossier marked 'GOK'. That had been a joke from the *Liverpool Echo* days, an annotation for those miscellaneous or murky items which might someday earn their keep. The letters stood for 'God Only Knows'. But if he handled this delicate piece of business well, everybody would know in due course, and he would gain enormously in the sight of all those who mattered.

The problem was how to do it and avoid trouble at the same time. Betts considered, frowning, then tipped the folder out on the table.

There is was: the letter on House of Commons notepaper, written by Roger Dickson to Elaine Stalker, which Betts had obtained from Karen Stalker the night of – but he did not want to remember too much. The pieces had been torn, then carefully sellotaped together. The writing was still clear. It was obvious who it came from and to whom it was addressed. The tone was still warm and loving. It was still dynamite, whether the affair was continuing or not, though much better if the two were still bedfellows.

There was always the question of his source and her threat to see him in court if he divulged a word. But it was a long time ago. If her appearance at that by-election was any guide she was now a young woman with a light in her eye who might easily waver under hostile cross-questioning. It would be her word against his – with the obvious question put to the jury of why she did not report the alleged rape at the time. In any case, he might be able to use the letter to force a confession out of Dickson, or Stalker, without actually having to publish it. Then Karen would not feature at all.

He sat at the desk and pondered. Then he put the letter back in its envelope, placed it in his wallet and went out.

The last important vote would be at seven, then the evening would be clear. Men appeared in the lobby wearing dinner jackets and impatient expressions, as if there could be anything more important than the final version of the Shopping Hours (Amendment) Bill. The tea room was busy but the main dining rooms would be nearly empty, apart from the unlucky Minister who had drawn the short straw for the adjournment debate at the tail end.

In his comfortable office in the Department of the Environment, waiting for the division bell, Andrew Muncastle signed the last letter in his box with a flourish. Another two boxes awaited his attention but could be dealt with at home. The content of the boxes was much more interesting since his promotion to number two in the department, especially since the Secretary of State was so often on speaking tours up and down the country. Only the trickiest matters would be kept for full 'Prayers', which were now held only once a week. Roger was simply not available much of the rest of the time. To all intents and purposes Andrew Muncastle, Minister of State, four years an MP, was running the department himself.

He would have been the first to admit that he too had changed in the course of that four years. He recalled his terror at being the first maiden speaker of his intake and his certainty that he would make a mess of it. These days, offered the chance to stand out, he was no longer afraid or hesitant. He always prepared carefully and never strayed beyond his brief. In the Commons he turned in solid if unspectacular performances and had never once embarrassed the government while on his feet. He was not about to rush it: let others yearn for stardom. For him steady progress up the ladder was more appropriate and more sure.

The scandal had faded surprisingly quickly. Miranda had vanished to the other side of the world. He knew, should they ever meet again, that the greeting would be frosty. His conscience told him he had used her, yet it was easily salved by the reminder that it was she who had seduced him, that (at least when they started) she was the knowing, experienced partner and he a virtual beginner. It hadn't worked out, that was all. Now she was gone the press had lost interest. There were other scandals, other victims. Andrew's resolute dullness made it difficult to write any more, still less to make a fool of him. It helped not being a noisy self-publicist like David Mellor, not being well known. He intended to keep it that way for a good while yet.

Life with Tessa had also improved. She was stronger, less petulant, less dismal altogether, with more of the delicate prettiness that had attracted him in the first place. Her hostility to his marital approaches had subsided and now, albeit tentatively, he was welcomed to her bed. The years with Miranda had taught him one or two tricks of the trade, for that lady had enjoyed being caressed with the utmost gentleness in between bouts of rampant action. So too, it appeared, did his wife. Even so, the adventure with Miranda had awoken appetites he did not know he possessed. It was unlikely that he would only ever sleep with his wife between now and his deathbed.

For the time being, however, Tessa must be kept sweet. He could not afford a further bout of scandal. He reached for the phone.

'Tessa? Hello, darling. Have you had a good day?'

He paused and listened, doodling on a notepad.

'Look, I called to say we will be voting soon and then I'm free. How about dinner? . . . No, somewhere nice. The Gay Hussar is fun. Will you book a table for eight o'clock? . . . No, wear what you like . . . A dress, yes. See you shortly.'

There was a discreet knock on the half-open door. Fiona Murray came in, carrying a sheaf of papers.

'I am sorry, Minister, but these have just arrived. The Secretary of State has asked if you can give the Commons statement on controlling pollution on Thursday as he has to be in Glasgow. Hope that won't spoil your evening.'

Andrew was getting used to the fact that officials seemed to know everything about Ministers' movements. Not that Fiona had been doing anything as crude as listening on the other line without permission; but their information systems were nevertheless extraordinary. He looked at her with renewed respect. She was tall and slim, red-haired, self-effacing in the way of unmarried women civil servants, but with attractive eyes, sharp and intelligent and occasionally humorous. And, presumably, ambitious. Quite a tough cookie. He wondered, idly, if there might be an opportunity to find out more. Perhaps on the next ministerial two-day meeting in Brussels.

'No, Fiona, not at all. Would you arrange for a full briefing tomorrow? That would be most helpful. I am grateful to you.'

He smiled at her encouragingly. And Fiona Murray tilted her well-organised red head, just enough, and smiled back.

The Members' tea room was full, as MPs queued for coffee and a sandwich before starting the long trek home. Maureen, the cheerful Irish tea lady, wielded the pot with a flourish, while the West Indian boy made beans on toast to order. Outside was dark and damp and uninviting.

Elaine had deliberately donned a pretty dress to raise her spirits but the ploy did not seem to be working. She moved into line beside Freddie Ferriman, who was clutching a plate of sticky brown cinnamon cake and two Kit-Kats.

'How's it going down your patch, Elaine?' he asked affably.

They were surrounded by Opposition Members; she delayed her reply until they were seated at a table inside the second room, away from inquisitive ears.

'So-so. It could go either way, I suppose. Right now we're bashing away at local government elections. The results should be better than last time but that's not saying much. Most people won't vote, and many who do will cussedly vote the opposite way for the council, on the principle that we politicians must be kept under control. Divide and rule. Damned inconvenient.'

Freddie was flicking crumbs from his tie. He would much prefer a drink, but it was a long drive back through rain and heavy traffic to the constituency and not worth being breathalised, not with the big contest in the offing.

'What about your family these days, Elaine? I always think it's so hard on an MP's family, especially for a woman. I really don't know how you ladies manage.'

His plump face shone with insincerity. Elaine suppressed her annoyance. It was all very well being tired and anxious about the election, but she mustn't let prats like Freddie get her down.

'We manage just about the same way as you gents – with difficulty,' she replied. 'My daughter is almost grown up now – doing her A levels this summer, so if we have a June election she won't be able to help, much to her chagrin. She has offers from two universities provided she gets decent grades. So we both have our fingers crossed.'

'Oh, she'll get in,' said Freddie. 'They wouldn't turn the daughter of the famous Mrs Stalker down, now would they?'

'What do you mean? She has to go through the application system fairly like everyone else.'

Freddie leaned forward, a knowing look on his face. 'Nonsense. You know perfectly well what I mean, Elaine. The university authorities are open to persuasion. That's what happened with my son. All your daughter's effort is irrelevant, though I'm sure she's very clever, just like you. If she doesn't get good results you simply phone the vice-principal and ask him to fix it. He'll say yes. They always do – they need MPs to vote for their grant money, don't they?'

Elaine recoiled in anger. 'I would do no such thing. And I don't need to – Karen will be accepted at university on her own merits, not on mine.'

Freddie laughed uproariously. 'Wonderful! A clean politician! I should put that on your election address. Cleaner than the rest of us, eh? That's why you're so unpopular here, Elaine: you won't play the game. Never learned, have you?'

Elaine's eyes flashed. 'If that's the game—' she began, but Freddie was already leaving the table, a sneer on his face.

She was boiling. Under the table she clenched her fists, or she might have crashed one down and sent the teacups flying. *How dare he?* Yet Freddie's self-satisfied back as he waddled away told her his only intention was to rile her, and he had succeeded. If she lost her seat in the Commons at this election there would be certain distinct compensations: she would not have to put up any more with horrors like him.

It was seven o'clock. The vote was called and she trailed through the lobby feeling depressed. She had hoped for three things when seeking election to this place: that she might be useful; that she might achieve a position of some importance; and that she might enjoy the life, make friends, steeped in the ambience of the most ancient Parliament in the world. The first ambition, to a large extent, had been achieved, mainly by the steady load of casework in the constituency. As for importance: her continued links with Northern Ireland had presumably been valued and had led to several enjoyable trips to the province, but there was no doubt

514

that it would have been better right at the start to have involved herself with a more mainstream subject, such as environment or education. She had decisively missed out and was not sure she would welcome or accept the only possible prospect for promotion – to the Northern Ireland Office. Not that there was much chance of that happening. No woman had ever been appointed there by a Tory government; its activities were still, perhaps subconsciously, regarded as too dangerous for women.

Unreasoning anger rose again in Elaine, like bile. If Roger, or any of the other whips, had ever spoken up for her talents, as no doubt was done for Andrew Muncastle, who was walking nonchalantly ahead of her beside his boss, she would be at Roger's side instead, and doing a far better job than Andrew ever could.

Jealousy. She was jealous. That was unworthy – yet entirely understandable. Freddie was right: she had not played the game, had not known what the game was.

As she came to the clerk's desk she pointed at her name and ensured it was crossed off, then headed for the narrow gap between the two doors, bowed to the tellers and walked out into Members' Lobby. She had been surrounded by jabbering colleagues for six or seven minutes yet not one had addressed her. The merry companionship she had assumed would be automatic on her arrival had never materialised. That was what made it so hard for a woman: the sheer masculinity of the place. Taking up with the chaps, however, could either mean playing Ferriman's little games, or getting involved with somebody. As she had with Roger. Fat lot of good that had turned out to be.

She turned almost by instinct, to find his hand on her arm.

'Will you be in your room in a few minutes?'

She nodded. Nobody in the moving crowd had heard his question. She hurried back to her desk, opened the direct phone line, shut the door tight and pretended to be busy.

The phone rang. Just to show a modicum of independence, she let it ring four times before lifting the receiver.

'Hi. You were looking very attractive in the Lobby tonight – that frock suits you. But your face was downcast. What's the matter, pretty lady? Fancy a drink?'

'Yes, I would. I was feeling a bit blue, with the election coming up. Your place or mine?'

'Mine, of course. I have the ministerial drinks cabinet at my disposal. Wait till the coast is clear, then come on up.'

Roger's room was on the Upper Ministerial Corridor behind the Speaker's Chair. She paused at the door and listened. Had there been voices she would have disappeared to the ladies' loo ten yards away and waited. In earlier years there had been no cause to worry: an MP can talk to a whip, and may have ample reason to talk to a junior Minister. But

Cabinet Ministers were elevated creatures. Were she seen up here, curious questions might be asked, though she was ready with an excuse about asking Dickson to speak in her constituency.

The sound of classical music wafted through the door. She knocked softly, and was promptly invited inside.

The high-ceilinged room, painted a dingy brown and cream, showed few signs of its occupant. Ministers rarely bothered to decorate or personalise their Commons offices, for they spent most of their time in the departments which, under the guiding hand of the Private Office staff, gradually filled up with souvenirs, photographs of official events and presentation pieces. The Commons was old and dusty and almost impossible to keep clean. The room had the air of a monk's cell, enclosed and austere. Only a framed photograph of three laughing children, on a bookcase facing the desk, and another of Caroline on a horse with a rosette, made any statement at all.

Roger rose and took her hand, leading her to a leather sofa. His jacket was over the back of a swivel chair behind the desk, and his shirtsleeves were rolled up, showing his strong forearms. Not for the first time she marvelled that the rest of his body did not fulfil that promise but was white and almost hairless, vulnerable like a child's. There was the smell of soap about him; subject to five o'clock shadow, he must have quickly shaved before coming to vote, perhaps in the hopes of seeing her. That would be difficult with Karen at the flat. She would have to disappoint him, though the occasions when both were free were few and far between.

He poured her a malt whisky and regarded her frankly, with much appreciation. She was wearing a spring-like blue dress, gathered at the waist, which suited her and made a change from the uniform of padded-shoulder power suits.

'So: why so sad, Patience?'

'Oh, I don't know. Seeing Muncastle standing next to you and being consumed with envy, I guess. Most unworthy of me.'

'Ah, yes. But you probably have as much public sway as Andrew. You're much better known, for a start. People outside ministries think we're all-powerful, but we aren't. We can't budge without public opinion behind us. And that's where you come in, Elaine. Being on the box is just as important, in its way, as influential as having a red box.'

Her look strayed to the two open boxes on his desk and she raised a quizzical eyebrow. Their eyes met, and both laughed ruefully. He shut the lids with a flourish, as he was supposed to do if anyone else was in the room, for several of the papers were marked 'Secret'. To Elaine the gesture emphasised her exclusion from government. But at least she now had his full attention.

She sipped her drink. 'I think I may lose my seat, if the polls don't pick up.'

'What's your majority?'

'Four thousand-odd. Not enough.'

'Well, it's my job now to ensure you don't. There's plenty of good news in the pipeline. Is there anything in particular which might help you in Warmingshire?'

She considered. 'We're waiting for a decision on a new bypass. I've hassled the Transport Minister but it's like talking to a brick wall. Some Ministers forget who their friends are.'

Dickson scribbled himself a note. 'I'll see what I can do. Now then: are you going to ask me back for coffee later this evening?'

'Can't. Honourable apartment already occupied so honourable guest not welcome. My daughter is there for half-term. She knows about us, but I don't think it would be wise to be bouncing around regardless when she comes home from the cinema, do you?'

Roger's face was thoughtful. 'I agree entirely. Are you expected anywhere else for the next ten minutes?'

'No, I'm at your disposal, Secretary of State. How can I help?'

A veiled expression came over his face. He moved quietly towards the door, stepped into the corridor, looked both ways for a moment, stepped back, and then shut the door and turned the key in the lock. Motioning her not to speak he checked the curtains, then switched off the main lights.

The room was instantly transformed into a cosier, more intimate place. A kinder glow came from the green-shaded desk lamp on the edge of the leather-topped desk and picked up the dark red of the carpet. On the mantelpiece a wooden clock ticked quietly. Roger turned up the music slightly, until it covered the sound of their breathing. It occurred to Elaine that before her arrival he had tried the effect, and liked it.

'I have sat in this chair long nights, Miss Patience, thinking about you. Fantasising that you might walk in, as you have just done, into my world of rustling paper and hard boxes and file covers, and turn me once more into a human being.'

There was a wistful, sad light in his eye. She raised her glass to him gravely in mock salute.

'Had I known, I would have taken all my clothes off at the door, Secretary of State. Why have you never asked me up here before?'

'It's too dangerous. The bloke next door has sharp hearing and an even sharper nose for trouble. He's in Prague tonight. But I want to have a try. With the election looming we may not get another chance. I am off on a two-day speaking tour tomorrow and I'm feeling demob-happy. You game?'

That word again. She wondered what was coming. 'Ready for your instructions, sir.'

'Good. Stand up. Go and stand in front of the desk, your back to me.

Push the files out of the way. Don't look around.'

A large shadowy etching of Gladstone above the mantelpiece glowered down at her. She blew the image a kiss. Behind her there was the sound of fumbling, then she understood exactly what Roger wanted. Slowly, provocatively, moving her hips, she bent over the desk, shoving pens and notepaper out of the way until she was holding on to its edges with both hands.

'You brilliant woman,' Roger breathed. Quickly he lifted her skirt up and over her back and pulled down her panties just enough, exploring her with his fingers, then he entered her from behind. She parted her legs for him and pressed her cheek down on to the leather, holding on for dear life, suppressing a squeal as he got her exact measure and began to thrust hard.

And suddenly the room was going round, and the smell of old stained leather was in her nostrils, and she knew his power and manhood and the humiliation of women. Her breasts flattened painfully against the desk and her nails dug into the wood, while her spirit shouted angry protest at this brief moment of snatched, urgent relief. What ought to have been a singing exultation of their love was a tawdry incident that she would only remember for its rawness and pain, and the hopelessness of it. With a yelp of frustration she swept reports and confidential documents on to the floor; one of the boxes tumbled over with a dull thud, scattering its files across the carpet. How she loved and admired this man, how she wished this had never started, how she feared its end, as he rammed into her, again and again, till with a gasp of triumph and despair he was done.

It had not taken long. They were panting and flushed, and collapsed on to the floor in front of the desk, clothes awry, conscious of their shared defiance of propriety. Half apologetically Elaine fished around and began picking up folders. Roger put a steadying hand on her arm.

'Forgive me, Elaine, but I've always wanted to do that. You've no idea how erotic a woman is, bending over, and especially in a fusty old place like this. When I saw you wearing that full skirt in the lobby tonight I knew it was worth a try. Thank you.'

'Made it in the Minister's office. What's the point of having a great man for a lover if we couldn't do that?'

They laughed and clung together. He touched her face tenderly where the embossed leather had made a mark. Yet the bleakness of the event chilled her. Here, in a Cabinet Minister's room, bent over his desk, hemmed in by all the insistent paraphernalia of his life and hers, slotted in somehow at the dog-end of the day, with no time for foreplay, unable to offer him comfort or warmth or a gentle unfolding towards climax: instead, they had coupled like animals – caged animals. Long afterwards it would be this lovemaking, scrambled together among the documents and itineraries and reports requiring his immediate signature, which remained with her, and reminded her that their affair had no place whatever in his life or future.

The phone rang and made them start guiltily, as if it had eyes. Roger climbed to his feet and pulled his clothes back into place. He picked up the handset.

'Yes? Oh, thank you, Alec. About ten minutes. No, I will come down. Thank you.'

He bent and offered Elaine a hand, then watched admiringly and with a proprietorial air, arms folded, as she restored an element of decency to herself. She drained the whisky glass and placed it safely on the desk.

'God, I feel mad, or drunk, or something,' she said, shaking her head. 'I wish we were only starting instead of finishing, don't you?'

He nodded with a wry grin. His own feelings precisely. Her next words hit him like a double punch, though she had said them many times before.

'I love you, Roger Dickson, and I always will. Till the end of time. I mean it. Whatever happens, don't you forget that.'

His face clouded over and his voice was husky. 'I . . . I know. You'd better go, Elaine. It's not safe here. Take care. I will ring you.'

She squared her shoulders and walked a little unsteadily to the door, and, having checked that the corridor was still empty, slipped away. Roger stood silently for a moment, then set about clearing up, picking up papers and restoring them to proper order.

The most important paper in the room was not on the floor but locked in a drawer to which only he had the key. He had meant to show it to Elaine, but the moment had never arrived. He still did now know what to do with it. It was a photocopy of a letter he had once written, long ago, to her. It had come a few days earlier with a compliments slip from a journalist on a tabloid newspaper, asking if it was genuine.

CHAPTER TWENTY-EIGHT

Karen Stalker pretended to be asleep, half listening to the birds of Warmingshire singing outside her window. Through a gap in the curtains floated a single strand of light in which dust motes danced lazily. Sunday morning was inviting her to get up and greet it, and gradually, as the bright sliver of spring sun widened and moved soothingly over her limbs, the excuses for staying in bed began to slide away.

Nemesis beckoned, in the form of grim red revision files piled under the bed. How she wished she had studied science or geography or a straightforward subject where the only requirement was to learn and regurgitate, instead of literature, where she was obliged to come up every week with original ideas. Much of it, like the Eliot poetry, she enjoyed but did not understand, while her nascent pleasure in Trollope was spoiled by the excessive analysis demanded of her. Nit-picking, it felt like. The French was reasonably securely embedded in her head; Camus had even been fun. It was modern history which gave her nightmares, for unpredictable questions were liable to come up. She did not mind being required to use her brain: she did that working in her mother's office. But pleasing the examiners was not in the same league as satisfying her mother's constituents, not by a long chalk.

Her mother had seemed troubled and preoccupied in recent weeks. National polls which indicated only a tiny government lead made uncomfortable reading in a constituency like South Warmingshire, though sweet Mrs Horrocks was reassuring. Karen realised that she now knew quite a lot about modern politics through her involvement with her mother's work. What she had learned did not warm her towards politicians in general, though it helped her understand, even admire, her own mother. Maintaining integrity and some semblance of good nature at Westminster was a Herculean task, yet her mother managed it, more or less. Karen could imagine no occupation she would have been less likely to choose for herself.

She folded her arms back under her head and contemplated the ceiling. The room was becoming warm under the persistent assault of the sun. Only a few weeks left: the exams would start just after her eighteenth birthday on 1 June. That meant no birthday celebration till all her friends finished. The general election date had not yet been announced but a decision would probably be taken soon. Given that unemployment was still falling, the odds on June were shortening fast. Karen was pleased to think that the first time she herself would be voting it would be for her mother. Thus parent might be celebrating at the same time as child. All being well.

A familiar face, clean and free of make-up, appeared around the door. 'Morning, miss! It's a beautiful day out there. Are you thinking of getting up?'

'Thinking about it, yeah.' Karen grinned sleepily.

Elaine was attired in dark-blue tracksuit bottoms and a white T-shirt. 'I'm going for a run over the hill. Why don't you join me? It'll get the brain working much better.'

Outside the window a songbird was trilling fit to burst. Karen contemplated her mother's scrubbed shiny face for a minute. There was a great longing there; maybe Mum needed to talk. The girl threw back the bedclothes and swung her legs out.

'Yeah, why not? Nothing too energetic, mind. I'm not as fit as you. Can I borrow some trainers?'

In a few minutes they were on their way. Outside the wind was cool and whipped through their T-shirts, until a steady stretch of wordless jogging set the pulses thumping and brought a healthy flush to their cheeks. The morning sun fell on their shoulders as the two headed away from the house, up the road, past the village shop and the church, both open for business, and turned along a footpath which led across the fields towards South Warmingshire's largest hill, and thence down to the river. On the way they passed people in waxed jackets walking dogs or themselves, who clutched Sunday newspapers and ruminated on the ills of the world even while soaking up the peace and lush beauty of the English countryside on a fresh spring morning.

Elaine and Karen had been running fifteen minutes, not particularly fast. From time to time they were greeted by constituents and neighbours who turned in pleasure at the sight of the two handsome women, so obviously mother and daughter, as they trotted along the path. Elaine was well liked in the vicinity and most of those who saw her that morning would vote for her. Had the constituency been entirely composed of villages there would have been no problem. The opposition lay in the small industrial towns and the suburbs. In the former, socialism had found fertile soil ever since the Independent Labour Party was established a century before, while in the latter guilty consciences and a concentration of white-collar public-sector workers guaranteed a substantial Liberal Democrat vote. The split opposition had let Elaine win comfortably with less than half the turnout. Should one of those two not stand, or her own support slip, or should the electorate discover the delights of tactical voting, she would be in trouble.

The hill was less steep than it looked from below but its gentle slope took longer than expected to cover. Getting to the top without pausing became a small personal battle for Elaine, and she grunted and dug deep, her lungs filling rhythmically with the clean sweet air. Each weekend it was like this, as if this run were an analogue of the uphill battle she faced as the election loomed. Somebody had to be winner. She was not giving up yet.

On the crest of the hill a copse of old silver-birch trees waved graceful branches in welcome. The two slowed their pace and flopped in triumph against the crusted trunks, gasping and laughing.

'You'll kill me doing this!' Karen was panting hard.

'Nonsense!' Elaine puffed. 'The other way round. You have longer legs, you're half my age and you run much faster than me.'

'Must be mad.' The girl put her hands on her knees and bent over, trying to get her second wind. At last she stood up, hands on hips, and looked around appreciatively. 'It's great up here. I've never seen Warmingshire like this before. We are lucky living here, aren't we?'

'We are. I hope we can continue.' Elaine's tone was wistful.

'Oh, you'll be all right. You will win, won't you, Mum?'

Elaine leaned back against a tree. Her body felt free, lithe, young; every artery expanded, pumping heart deeply throbbing in her chest cavity. Exercise-induced endomorphins, those natural hormones so similar in action to heroin, were taking effect and filled her with a sense of physical well-being.

'I don't know, to be honest. Yes, if the swing is with us. No, if it isn't. This is a true marginal seat, and my personal efforts may make precious little difference. Last election we had a lot of help in the form of mutual aid from Roger's constituency workers, but I don't know if that will happen this time.'

'They would be mad not to vote for you, Mum.'

Elaine pulled a face. 'Thanks, but it doesn't work like that. Plenty of people vote not for a local MP but for the government, or for a fresh government, if that's their preference. What the Prime Minister and people like Roger get up to, that's what counts. I mustn't take it personally either. The day after, some biddy will come up to me in the market-place, win or lose, and tell me she didn't vote for me even though I did a good job for South Warmingshire, and ask me to help with a problem. She'll get quite indignant if I suggest she goes to talk to her new MP. There's one or two I won't mind telling to get stuffed, I can tell you.'

'I don't know how you put up with it at times. You could have done all sorts of things. What on earth made you go into politics?'

Elaine squatted down and picked at the grass. It would not do to spend too long chatting and getting cold, yet there were so few opportunities with her daughter away from the phone or homework or other insidious distractions. A nagging desire to clear her lines with Karen before it was too late had driven her into her daughter's room that morning instead of letting her slumber on as usual. She recalled out of the blue a song from years before, in which a man came from a long distance to explain himself to his son, saw the boy sleeping and left without saying a word. Paul Simon. Pop star, pop philosopher of her youth. *The nearer your destination, the more it's slip-sliding away.* That was it. It had made her feel very sad at the time.

'What made me do politics?' Elaine hesitated. The question was put to her so often by interviewers, or at Women's Institute meetings, but for Karen she tested the response slowly to see if it still worked.

'It all started when Jake was little, but perhaps the seeds were sown long before that. I don't like being told what to do, or what to think. I don't want somebody else taking my hard-earned money and spending it elsewhere, at least without my agreement to what it's being spent on. My freedom and my own judgement are very precious to me. I would be like that even if I were the only person in the whole world, but it's such a bonus to find I'm not alone. A lot of people have the same gut reaction in this country. That's why the British are so cussed, and why we've not been successfully invaded for nearly a thousand years. That's also why, to me, it feels such a privilege to represent them, to be an MP.'

'You would really mind, then, if you lost?'

Elaine nodded. Karen knew the answer to that one. 'And yet . . . I should mind that much less if we have a good clean fight, no dirty tricks, no slurs, just a cracking good argument on the issues. If there's a lot of unpleasantness and personal stuff I should feel that everybody had lost out. What matters in the end, Karen, is not the individual result, but that the system itself should be healthy. Democracy, I mean. That's how I might console myself, if I have to.'

It was simple language, but the sentiments were the more powerful for their simplicity. A breeze blew her damp T-shirt against her ribs and she shivered.

Karen listened carefully. It might all help for the exams. In the distance, screwing up her eyes, she could see their house in a clump with several others. The little development, outlined with fast-growing Leyland cypresses, stuck out into fields away from the village. No wonder there had been such a fuss when it was built, and why some locals said the Stalkers were demonstrating either ignorance or arrogance in choosing to live there.

'What will you do if you lose, Mum?'

'I don't know.' Elaine gazed down the valley as if the answer were written in the sprouting corn, so indifferent to her fate. 'I shall have money for a short while, though not enough for staff. I suppose I'll have to find a job of some kind while trying to get back in. It's in my blood now, and I doubt if I would be truly happy doing anything else.'

'If you win, can I come and work for you for a bit?'

Not for the first time, Elaine was startled at her daughter's directness. 'But what about university? You have offers for September. You're not going to throw all that up. I won't allow it. However dodgy my future might be, yours must be secure.'

Karen waved objections away with an airy flourish. 'I've thought about it, and this morning it's all come together nicely. If I get my A levels I will ask the university to defer entry for a year. Then I can spend my time in London, and go out with that nice docile Irishman Gerry, and look after you. The way you have been recently, Mum, so seedy, it's clear you need somebody. Your Roger seems to have been falling down on the job. Then I'll be readier to settle down to study, properly, next year.'

'And if it goes against us? There may not be any cash to spare, Karen.'

'Got that worked out too. If you're out, I will still take a year off, and we can go into business. Style advisers, or assertiveness trainers, or – or anything. I'll be your general dogsbody and you can pay me peanuts. If you lose, Mum, you will *really* need taking care of. Then we can make some money, you will find another seat, and I will go to college in a Ferrari. I fancy that.'

Elaine laughed despite herself and hugged her daughter affectionately. Without another word they moved off down the narrow path, skirting the hill and heading to the right, where the snaking silver of the river was visible across the fields.

But Elaine was grateful the girl had not pressed her on Roger. There were many more questions to which she did not know the answers: whether to finish the affair, and if so when, and how: and, worst and most worrying of all, in the heightened atmosphere of the forthcoming general election, whether it could be done cleanly and in safety, before they were found out.

Tuesday 8 May

The House was crowded, aggressive, at its bad-mannered worst. An exasperated Miss Boothroyd had spent more time on her feet yelling than she had been seated.

Roger Dickson had realised at once that in trying to perform at First Order Questions as if nothing else was in the offing he would be on a hiding to nothing. Naturally Andrew Muncastle had leapt at the chance to answer more questions than usual. Dickson excused himself on the grounds that his national party obligations had given him too little time for homework. However, even Andrew was unprepared for the barracking and noise which greeted his every word.

Andrew wrinkled his nose in disapproval. It seemed so pointless, all this screaming. Other parliaments were more decorous. Most did not have a Question Time at all, but listened respectfully when Ministers spoke, even applauded. The French National Assembly rose to its feet when the President made his infrequent visits. Elected Members around the world do not conduct themselves daily as if in a football stadium for the Cup Final or at the Roman games watching slavering lions heading for a hapless gladiator. Andrew's alarmed expression betrayed his dislike of the role of official pugilist, making his attackers go for him even more. Even his Honourable Friends felt obliged, such was the nearness of the election, to make infuriating remarks against which his usual parade of statistics was insufficient defence. The whole process was distasteful and unpleasant. Watching him, Dickson half smiled. Somebody had to take the flak. How beautifully Muncastle managed it.

The Prime Minister was not there yet. He was cutting it fine as the clock edged towards 3.14. He had to be ready, on his feet, on the dot of 3.15. Dickson allowed a frisson of professional annoyance to cloud his serenity. What on earth was the boss playing at? This Prime Minister had once said he loved politics because it was like playing dice: you never knew what turned up next. That casual, passive insouciance irritated. Leaving it so late did not give the impression of a great passion for the fight, a determination to get on with it, which should have been the hallmark of proceedings, today in particular.

A special Cabinet had decided the election date that morning, though speculation had clogged the front pages for weeks. The local election results had been at best equivocal. Council seats lost four years earlier had been won back, but not in great numbers. Mainly urban council seats had been contested this time in cities like Derby, Birmingham, Leeds. If progress could be made in such marginal areas then the election itself was worth trying. In any case, if the government were to act with increased confidence it needed a new mandate. Waiting any longer could erode rather than increase the thin 3 per cent lead the polls were now hinting at. The omens for administrations which clung to power, like Callaghan's in the late 1970s, were not good: the electorate did not relish such deliberate exclusion from the decision-making process, and were prone to vent their disapproval accordingly.

A great cheer, tinged with relief, went up from government benches as the grey head of the Prime Minister hove into view. Moving smoothly he settled himself next to Roger, behind and to the left of Muncastle, who was leaning over the dispatch box and shouting into the microphone, though nobody in the Chamber could hear a word he said. The timing in one sense was perfect. No sooner was Andrew perched back on the bench, red folder open in tense hands, ready for the next round, than the Speaker glanced at the clock and announced Prime Minister's Question Time.

'Question number one!' roared Freddie Ferriman, whose fortune it was to have come first in the ballot. Around him colleagues jostled excitedly, pretending to be intensely interested in the matter. Behind Freddie, where the cameras would pick up their earnest expressions, were poised five Members with highly marginal seats. The process was dubbed 'doughnutting'. Whether it would make any difference that they would be seen fleetingly on national television that night, and be recognised only by a few of their better-informed constituents who had probably already made up their minds, was a moot point.

There was no need to read out the question: it was identical to nearly all the others put to Prime Ministers in recent years, asking him to list his engagements for the day. That would enable a supplementary to be put on almost any subject.

'This morning I presided at a meeting of Cabinet and had meetings with ministerial colleagues and others. In addition to my duties in the House, I shall be having further meetings later today.' The standard reply, designed to be as boring as possible, revealed very little.

Ferriman knew what to ask next. He had been the proud recipient of a call from the Prime Minister's office that morning and it had taken all his strength not to breathe a word right through a very good and liquid lunch. Flushed with a second brandy, he stood as tall as he could and crossed his hands over his ample girth in what he hoped was a distinguished and impressive manner.

'And would the Prime Minister tell us', he intoned pompously, 'whether any decisions of significance were taken at Cabinet this morning?'

That was unfortunate. 'NO!' yelled the Opposition benches and then collapsed giggling at their own cleverness. Freddie held his ground for a moment, blustering, then gave it up as a bad job. He would have his moment of fame this evening, but not quite in the way he had intended.

The Prime Minister waited until the hubbub died down. Suddenly the House was silent, except for the shuffling of well-padded bottoms on well-upholstered seats. On the Labour benches Keith Quin shushed Janey Irvine and desperately longed to hold her hand at the historic moment. In the Strangers' Gallery facing the Speaker, Tessa Muncastle, warned by Andrew of the likely business of the day, smiled down on her husband. On the government front bench Johnson, now senior Whip, opened the whips' folder and wrote a crisp remark about Ferriman. Up on the highest of the back benches Elaine Stalker in her smartest suit gazed down on Roger's head and noted with proprietorial amusement that the silvered dark hair was beginning to thin on top.

'It may help the House to know', the Prime Minister continued with total solemnity, 'that Cabinet this morning accepted my recommendation that Parliament should be dissolved on 11 May, this Friday. I have accordingly asked the Queen for an audience tonight. If my request is granted, the general election will be on Thursday 7 June.'

The House erupted. This was the news they had been waiting for. Several jumped up quickly and left, heading for telephones. Others who had already announced their retirements sat quietly, hands clasped on knees, looking around the Chamber for perhaps the last time. Members who faced an easy election in safe seats considered which of their friends were worth going to help; those in marginals turned cold, their hearts no longer beating in quite the same way.

The remainder of Prime Minister's Questions was acted out as the start of the campaign, with energetic party points yelled across the Chamber, to the amazement of those seated behind Tessa in the Strangers' Gallery. A group of Japanese businessmen accompanied by their ambassador clung to simultaneous-translation headphones, expressions of puzzled despair on their faces, for the translator could not keep up with the rapid exchanges laced with idiom and abuse. The ambassador groaned inwardly and started making notes: it would take all through dinner to explain. The Press Association tapes began to clatter urgently, while on the Stock Exchange shares wobbled. Dealers busily hedged their bets. The polls were all over the place. It was impossible to read, this time.

'You must tell all your contacts,' the doctor said, with a practised persuasion which rang hollow in the windowless room. 'We have a contact-tracing service here and we can help you. It is in all their interests, you know.'

Peter touched the purple mark again. It was definitely growing, with a crust forming at the centre. He shuddered: in all his life there had never been a blemish, not till now. His mouth tasted foul, but the doctor had explained that thrush was not serious at this stage and could be controlled by antibiotics.

'Most of them are abroad,' he said dully. 'Only a couple in the UK and . . . most are OK, I'm sure of that.'

'You've been careful, then?' The doctor's insufferable niceness was stifling. He was young and moustached and earnest and probably gay. The man really wanted names and addresses for his wretched computer, gathering details to be turned into grim statistics, useful in the fight to win more money for his department. Peter was not minded to assist: except, perhaps, in one case. He reached for pen and paper.

'I only had unprotected sex with one man. He is married, so I don't want to give you his home address, but this is his office number. It will be quite a shock to him. Civil servant, rather high up. Expecting a long and distinguished career.'

It was on the point of the doctor's tongue to remark that, in that case, this chap – Mr Chadwick? – should have been far more careful. Mrs Chadwick would have to be tested as well, and told why. She would probably be quite upset. What a business.

Roger walked back into his office, closed the door, took the photocopied letter out and looked at it once more.

He had not replied, not acknowledged it in any way. But its sender would know it had arrived safely, for it had been put on the message board, marked 'Personal', so that his Commons secretary, trained to know what was not her business, had left it for him unopened. It was for his eyes only.

He read the words again for the umpteenth time. In themselves, there was nothing really incriminating. 'I am so sorry I missed you.' Anybody could say that. 'Do contact me.' Well, why not? 'Have a good trip' – no problem there. But it was the last phrase, scribbled as an afterthought, which made his heart thump: 'Thinking of you.'

Thinking of you – and why would a married male MP write that to a female colleague, also married, so affectionately, if there wasn't something going on? What a fool he had been. Then there was the whole tone of the note, so casual and intimate. He could well see the conclusions that a dirty-minded journalist would jump to, with his readers not far behind.

But could he stop it, or sue? He swallowed hard and allowed his imagination to run. A defending libel lawyer, waving that missive in court, would have a field day. Denial would not be credible, or at the least would dent his credibility. As if he didn't have enough on his plate.

He wondered how the note, written so long ago, had fallen into the wrong hands. Elaine would never show it around – might not even have kept it. He examined the photocopy carefully: it looked as if the page had been torn up and reassembled. Fished out of a waste-paper basket, then. A cleaner, maybe. But he was in no position to make a complaint.

What it told him, more than anything, was that somebody outside knew of the liaison. Not just his agent Tom Sparrow, who could be trusted, or Elaine's daughter, who might not understand but presumably would also keep her mouth shut, for her mother's sake. Someone much more dangerous, who was waiting for his response: who would telephone, or more likely confront him, and judge by his reaction exactly how big a story could be made out of it.

He shivered. He ought to warn Elaine – or maybe she too had received a copy. If not, she may well have forgotten all about that innocent-sounding note and deny its existence. That would be quite a story in itself. His head ached with the twists and turns, all of them fraught with danger. It felt like a devilish game, a punishment. Perhaps the true wages of sin were the fear of discovery, and of disgrace.

Wednesday 9 May

The *Globe* office was a hive of activity. Jim Betts sat hunched over a screen inputting prose as fast as his fingers would let him. A cigarette dangled from his lips, dropping ash softly on the grey keys. Above his head a screen was tuned to Sky's continuous new service. Life was a lot easier in the days before satellite TV; now the newspapers were in a constant struggle to keep up. When stuck, Betts would simply repeat what he heard broadcast. At least that gave his reports instant authenticity.

Nick Thwaite stuck his head inside Betts's door. 'When you're ready, conference, please, Jim. Tell the others.'

In a few minutes people began to gather outside Thwaite's office. Betts hurried up and ushered them in. He enjoyed being more important in the hierarchy, the sensation that some at least of the newspaper revolved around himself. Still there was something missing since his early days. The place was not as exciting now that Miranda had gone. The fashion editor in her elegant black shift dress and huge metallic brooch tried to take her place, but there was something about the too thin neck and bony knees that put him off. It was not simply that Miranda had filled all her clothes so well with that marvellous body: it was her personality, her love of life. By contrast, making love to the fashion editor would be like caressing a vase of brittle paper flowers. Betts ignored the woman and settled at the table.

'Right! General election time,' Thwaite announced, unnecessarily. 'No doubt the nation will get bored to tears with it all, just as they did before. But there's change in the air and I want to make sure the *Globe* reports accurately what is happening. We got it wrong last time, boys and girls, as did most of the other papers. So ears to the ground. Don't report what you don't hear. No writing slick pieces supposedly from the bar of the Lamb and Flag in Barham South which were really produced in your own little bedsits and are absolute rubbish. No announcing landslides in key marginals which then turn out to be rock solid. No writing off the Prime Minister – or the Leader of the Opposition, for that matter – until we are stone cold certain. Which way the paper will jump, how we advise our readers to vote, will be an editorial decision taken in the last few days before the poll, not now, and not by you. Till then we play it long. Am I making myself clear?'

There were nods all round. Thwaite consulted a list. 'Sports can look after themselves for the moment, though I'd like a piece on how the result might affect the Test series this summer. Part jokey – will they play better if there's a Tory or Labour government? – and part serious. Take a look at the parties' policies on sport, if they have any. And find out the party affiliations of the top players. Some will be only too happy to tell you.'

The sports editor looked up with a grin. 'We've done that already for the England football team playing in Turin next week. They've agreed to line up in blue and red jerseys for a picture.'

'Yeah – but just remind them they're there to beat the Italians to pulp, not each other.' Thwaite had a low opinion of the current team, with good reason. He turned to the fashion editor.

'Cherry, sweetheart, we need several pieces you can start on right away. What to wear on the campaign trail: smart outfits for both men and women hopefuls. Include underwear – you can make that a separate story. Can you get some of the MPs to do a bit of modelling? As long as they're not photographed in their constituencies we're within the law. In their undies is OK. One or two of the women are quite passable – try that Elaine Stalker. Offer money if necessary, but she'll be desperate for the publicity with a majority like hers. Freddie Ferriman might be game for a modelling piece too, or you could try Keith Quin, if you're trying to turn a sow's ear into a silk purse.'

The idea of the pompous Ferriman disporting himself in the latest from Gap struck Betts as highly comical.

Thwaite turned to him. 'We'll have plenty of political input, or at least all we can handle, from Andy Mack and our chaps up here, Jim. What I need from you is a thorough going-over of the main marginals. It only needs a handful to change and the government is out. Last time, however, the marginals held and it was the next lot – the ones regarded as safer – which fell like ninepins. So use your nose. You're on the road for the next few weeks, Jim: I don't want to see you back here till the

Monday after the election. Hire a Jaguar and enjoy yourself.'

Elaine looked in horror at the teetering piles of correspondence awaiting her signature. 'You've got to be kidding,' she said weakly.

Diane snorted and handed her three fresh Pentels. 'I am not. You can still use Commons notepaper and, more to the point, free postage, till the House is prorogued. Why do you think I stayed here all night clearing the outstanding stuff? We have to be out of here on Friday at the latest. Take the typewriter – it may be useful at home. I'll come in and collect the mail for the duration and send you anything useful.'

'It'll all go to the constituency office, won't it?'

'Oh, no. You'd be surprised how many people and organisations think everything carries on here as normal, as if the election is happening quite outside the political system. Heavens knows how this country survives as a democracy when there are so many stupid people in it.'

'We need some help up there. Is there any chance . . . ?'

'I'll come for a weekend. We're almost as pushed in Battersea. Why don't you ask your friend Roger Dickson?'

Elaine bit back an answer. Too many people seemed to know about Roger and herself. The press would be sniffing around, looking for angles, watching every senior politician with prurient intensity. She bent her head and began signing, setting up a production line as Diane expertly folded and slipped letters into envelopes. Slowly the pile ready for the post began to grow and the wall behind her desk, previously obscured, reappeared a few inches at a time. But the thought of Roger stayed with her.

She could not let it run on much longer. Exposure now would be a disaster. For a scandal to break in the middle of the election campaign would probably wreck her own chances in South Warmingshire; even Roger himself, despite his more comfortable majority, could find himself in trouble, particularly as he had been spending a great deal of time away from his seat. Disclosure would put him under huge pressure to relieve the Prime Minister of the need to defend him and he would almost certainly have to resign as a Cabinet Minister. His position in the party hierarchy and in the election war cabinet would have to be abandoned. It was worse than that. The whole campaign would be damaged, especially as the Prime Minister had been going hard for the family vote. In fact, if a whiff of the affair got abroad, everything both of them had fought for and believed in would be put at terrible risk. The end result of this parliamentary affair could be to destroy the government itself.

The phone rang. It was a woman journalist inviting Elaine to model knickers for the campaign trail for a two-page spread in a tabloid newspaper. The answer was a blunt 'No', though Elaine was surprised to find herself even considering the request. That was what hustling in a marginal seat was doing to her. The wheedling voice pleaded for a moment, then switched tack. Would Elaine be willing to model day clothes for the campaign, chosen by their fashion editor? Nothing too way out, but smart and attractive. Elaine reflected. This was not such a silly proposition. South Warmingshire voters were still intrigued by their woman MP, and a substantial proportion were immune to political argument. It could do no harm, might be fun, and it could help. She agreed. At the other end of the phone the journalist punched the air in triumph. MPs were such easy meat. Ask them to do something outrageous and they will refuse, mostly. Soften the request, make a different, apparently more reasonable suggestion, and vanity and need would oblige them to accept. It was an ancient trick which often worked. Now for fat old Ferriman.

The phone rang again. It had been going all morning, punctuating the women's dogged efforts with an insistent shrillness. Newspapers and radio stations and local TV, all wanting a comment or an interview, for Elaine's seat appeared on every list of contests to watch. Constituents rang, urgently requiring her assistance in return for their vote. Some threatened to withhold support unless she was for or against the issue closest to their hearts. Elaine readily argued with them all. The whole unreal business was acquiring a tinge of blackmail which she hated.

'Elaine? Roger. How are you?'

His distinctive voice could be heard clearly in the small room. Diane sniffed. She had thought her employer would have been wiser than to get embroiled in the most obvious cliché of all, with a fellow MP. Especially a prominent name, and married and likely to stay that way.

'I . . . I'm fine. Busy, clearing paper.' Suddenly, for the first time ever, Elaine wanted to tell him to go away.

'Are you free tonight at all, after the vote? I've something I wanted to show you. We may not get much chance from now on.'

She hesitated. Of course she wanted him; nothing had changed in that respect. And yet . . . Diane's disapproving face helped make up her mind.

'No, sorry, I can't. I have constituents in the gallery tonight and must take them for a drink.'

It was a lie. It was not a refusal, an ending: there would be other calls and at any time she could accept and fly to him. Yet something had changed. Her miserable face told its own story. Diane half smiled and turned back to her work, satisfied.

CHAPTER TWENTY-NINE

Monday 14 May

Campaigning started in earnest. Suddenly every news bulletin began with the daily doings of the parties' leaders and main spokespersons, however dull or predictable. Stunts and poster unveilings hogged the photo coverage, party-political broadcasts filled the airwaves. Martial music blared fitfully from loudspeakers; battle-buses were borrowed and plastered with stickers; village halls were booked and duly festooned with party colours, deposits were paid, signatures collected on nomination forms, appeal letters sent out; candidates fidgeted under last-minute haircuts and clutched lucky charms and umbrellas just in case.

At Conservative Central Office the mood swung between elation and despair, depending on the state of the polls and the points-scoring at each morning's press conference. The initial small lead increased at once to 6 per cent in the first days of campaigning and the pace turned to frenzy. Staff found themselves covering two or three press conferences a day. Dominic d'Abo slaved at his word processor until the early hours, or coaxed the printer back into life, or fed the photocopier, and bemoaned the feeling of writing press releases and speeches in his sleep, until he checked his diary and realised that to all intents and purposes he was.

The maddest events took on huge proportions. A pot plant arrived at Central Office ostensibly from an admirer, and turned out to be hosting a family of minute baby tarantulas. The police and RSPCA were called and the entire building had to be evacuated in case the mother spider was still there, hidden under a cupboard, waiting for her opportunity.

A few days later the Prime Minister found himself imitating his illustrious predecessor at an agricultural event, clutching a baby calf to his bosom to demonstrate solidarity with the nation's beleaguered farmers. On this occasion the beast, terrified beyond endurance by flashing cameras, let loose all over the Leader's best trousers. The farmers predictably thought this a splendid political comment, and nodded silent appreciation to the owner of the calf who had fed it thoroughly half an hour before the Prime Minister's arrival.

Saturday 19 May. Evening. D-Day minus nineteen

'How're you getting on, Jim?'

Betts raised the glass of red wine to his lips and leaned back on the propped-up pillows. Room service in British hotels was improving, even if West Country accents left him none the wiser.

'It's hair-raising down here, Nick. Not a Labour voter in sight but the government's running scared. They think they're going to lose a batch of prize seats to the Ashdown mob.'

'And are they?'

'God knows. You know what happens in a general election – at the last minute people turn tail and head back to safety. The polls suggest the government's in trouble, though.'

'Right. That early lead is slipping. Tomorrow's rush results suggest a gap in the government's favour of only 2 per cent – well within the margin of error. Careful how much weight you place on them, though, Jim. It's not over yet.'

Betts allowed himself a moment's thoughtful silence.

'Jim? You still there? What's on your mind?'

'I was thinking – I may have something that will put the kibosh on the whole government, if you're minded to use it.'

A decision of that magnitude would not be up to Thwaite, but he was not about to tell a subordinate that. 'Spill,' he commanded.

Betts invested his voice with all the portentous significance he could muster. 'Got something on a Cabinet Minister – *another* Cabinet Minister.'

Thwaite sucked his teeth. Betts's boasting was not always to be trusted. 'Have you, indeed. You ready to tell me the details?'

'Not yet. I may get a full confession out of him, which would be terrific. I think I'll confront him with what I've got – I'm in his area next week. Leave him to me for the minute.'

'Am I allowed to know who?'

Betts hesitated, then realised a marker might come in useful. He would then be sure to get the credit. 'Yeah – Roger Dickson.'

Monday 21 May. D-Day minus seventeen

In Milton and Hambridge a nervous Fred Laidlaw was attempting to pick up the pieces after the misery of the by-election defeat. With Mr

Bulstrode and Mrs Farebrother comfortingly at his side, and active if erratic support from his faithful Young Conservatives, the assault on the 5,000 majority had an uncertain if enthusiastic tone. There was every chance of winning the seat back, since jibes about a 'local' candidate could easily be met, but it felt like heaving the proverbial boulder up a mountain.

Fred had his traumas at the hustings, but his obvious youth and engaging friendliness slowly won supporters from among those who had recorded their protest at the by-election and now regretted being over-hasty. Some of the long terraced streets were a fruitful source of reconverts. He was, however, completely floored by one reluctant elderly female voter, who wanted to know whether he was in favour of joining the Common Market.

Fred, who was still in nappies when the Treaty of Rome was signed, was nonplussed. 'But we have joined the Common Market. A long time back. Over twenty years ago, in fact.'

The elderly woman eyed him with a pitying air. 'Nonsense,' she replied scornfully, 'you should get your facts right, young man. That was when we joined the Commonwealth.'

'Er, yes,' said Fred doubtfully. 'Anyway, I'm all in favour.'

That was clearly a mistake. 'Well, I'm not,' snapped the woman. 'So I shall be voting Liberal.'

In vain did Fred attempt to convince the voter that his opponent's party was vastly more pro-European than his own. He gave up and trudged with heavy heart to the next street.

He shared the story over a pub lunch with a sympathetic Mr Bulstrode, who reminded him with a kindly pat on the shoulder that, while people outside politics thought electioneering was fun or exciting, to participants it was simply bloody hard work, with an unpredictable outcome.

Tuesday 22 May. D-Day minus sixteen

Tom Sparrow sat down wearily and tried to work it out. This would be his fifth general election, with countless council and local elections thrown in. His fourth with Roger as candidate: all the more reason to hope for victory. He was unsure whether this one was proving unusually arduous, or if it was simply that his age was beginning, at last, to tell.

He would be sixty next year. Not officially his retirement date, but he could go then, if he wanted to. His plans had been to carry on for a while yet, maybe even see out the next Euro-elections in 1999. That date had an air of finality about it: end of the millennium, dawn of a new age.

He was startled at his own reverie. Never mind the next century – how well he remembered halfway through this one: the Festival of Britain in 1951 which he had visited with his father, the ending of the Attlee government when his mother had cried for joy to see Churchill once more Prime Minister. The Coronation and all its pageantry, when he was already sixteen and in his first job. He could dimly recall events even before that – the communist revolution in China, which had proved so much more durable than its counterparts elsewhere, then later the Mau Mau in Kenya, and Jomo Kenyatta languishing in a British jail. To so many people, including his own bright-eyed young helpers, those vivid dramas were dusty history. They became quickly bored if he tried to describe what happened and why it mattered. He felt out of time, disjointed.

Sparrow checked his list of reminders for the morrow. It would be a relatively quiet moment as Roger was campaigning up north. The following day, Thursday, would be busy, for there was a big rally in the nearby town, where Roger would be one of the stars.

Tom Sparrow made a decision, there and then. He would see this election through and Dickson safely returned; and then he would start making practical plans for his own retirement, and never fight another.

Wednesday 23 May. South Warmingshire. D-Day minus fifteen

For Elaine the campaigning had hardly ceased since the previous election which had started her parliamentary career. Much of the intervening period had been spent worrying where the next vote would come from. Her monthly diary had never faltered in its endless visits to schools, nurseries, factories, workshops, old people's homes, sheltered housing, working men's clubs, leisure centres and anywhere else the punters might be gathered in a sufficiently friendly mood to welcome her intrusion. Once the election was under way the whole business took on more focus and urgency. The change was not always for the better.

Canvassing was turning into a nightmare. Whatever unemployment figures might say, the bulk of the British electorate were out at work at every reasonable hour of the day, or even evening. Most women had part-time jobs. In Elaine's constituency and many others women now outnumbered men in the regular workforce. With a resigned sigh she realised that door-knocking on the two remaining Sundays would be essential, for no one was at home in daytime the rest of the week except elderly and housebound people who were less likely to vote, and the unemployed, who were best left undisturbed.

An opinion poll was published in the *Globe* covering thirty seats which must change hands if the government was to be defeated. Elaine was becoming accustomed to running her eyes down such lists to check where South Warmingshire was placed on each occasion. Even she, however, swallowed hard at the indication that she was 17 points adrift. Her own returns suggested that she and her main opponent were neck and neck. But supposing the research was accurate?

The phone rang; a reporter from a sympathetic local newspaper asked her views on the poll's findings. Elaine crisply informed him that only one poll counted and that was still a fortnight off, but that this one was a load of codswallop. He replied helpfully that the interviews were done to his knowledge in only one place in her constituency, in the market square of the main industrial town one Wednesday morning. The bias introduced by speaking only to the carless and workless seeking the cheapest shopping must have been obvious even to amateurs. The *Globe* reported it gleefully as gospel truth.

The doorsteps told a more cheerful tale. It was a cold damp evening when Elaine knocked on one door and found herself the object of a long harangue from a middle-aged man in a singlet, still grubby from work, who leaned forward aggressively, raised arm on the door-jamb, taking her to task for all the ills of the nation. At the end of the tirade he declared himself firmly a supporter of the other side.

Dispirited, Elaine tried to establish which, if any, of her opponent's policies particularly appealed to the householder, only to find herself interrupted by his diminutive curly-haired wife who popped her head under his arm.

'Mrs Stalker, is it? Good. Don't you worry about 'im, love. You'll not change 'is mind. But the rest of us in this 'ouse are with you. Come election day, we'll lock the old bugger in the pantry. You leave it to us.'

Thursday 24 May. The Midlands. D-Day minus fourteen

Jim Betts was enjoying himself. This was the easiest kind of journalism, buzzing around the country at his own pace, driving an expensive car, eating fine food and wine at others' expense, dictating pieces down the phone after lunch and leaving to the office the tedious tasks of inputting, spell-checking, word-counts and sub-editing. As long as he produced a thousand punchy words every day he was more than doing his job. What it was all doing to his constitution he would worry about later.

Now he was seated in the warmth of early evening in the cool lounge of a four-star hotel in Warwickshire, close to the constituency of Roger Dickson, Cabinet Minister and high dignitary in the Tories' faltering campaign. The evening paper showed that their original tiny lead had disappeared; the race was now too close to call. The Home Secretary was planning to join Dickson on the platform tonight at a big supporters' rally in the hotel. On the table before him Betts already had the main speeches, or at least published extracts, handed to him by a pimply boy from Central Office who looked like he needed a good meal and a sleep. Betts had been pleasant to the boy: might be useful for later, to find out what the atmosphere at headquarters was really like.

Betts was not a Labour supporter. He was not a supporter of any party and could readily turn his knife in any direction. If challenged he would have claimed to know too much about all of them to wish to vote for any. In truth, since he was on the road on election day, he probably would not be voting at all. What interested Betts was not who won but hard news or a good story. The consequences were of no concern to him, even though they might have a profound effect on the country. Arguments about policies left him cold. If taxes were increased, he would step up his efforts to avoid paying any. If they were reduced, he would be grateful, but not sufficiently so to cast his vote in that direction. Since much of the time he lived on expenses he was inured to the possible dangers of inflation. Politicians were all liars anyway, so what was the point?

On his lap lay a dossier on Dickson, filled with old press cuttings and an analysis from the *Globe*'s somewhat limited library. There was still an hour before the great men arrived. Betts considered, frowning, then reached in his wallet and retrieved what had been lurking there for the past month.

A letter. The letter. Enough to destroy a man, and his career; and his girlfriend's too, but she did not matter. And lose him his friends, in all probability. It would be a scandal to rival the Boswood business. The trick tonight would be to get his victim to admit his deceit, in public. Perhaps with a bit of violence thrown in – Betts was half expecting Dickson or a crony to take a swing at him, when the insistent query was put about how well he knew Elaine Stalker. A photographer was all laid on.

Betts's stomach rumbled. He was hungry and would need to eat before the meeting. There was only one way to find out if the two were still playing around, and that was to confront the man directly. Not before the big speeches; instinct told Betts that afterwards, when everyone was more relaxed and guards were temporarily down, might be better. It occurred to him that he should have taken a second photocopy, but that could wait. He folded the letter carefully and put it in the pocket of his mackintosh with a handkerchief, cigarettes and matches. Producing it with a flourish under his victim's nose would create a wonderfully dramatic effect.

First there was the question of food. He sauntered over to the reception counter. A plump young woman in hotel uniform with tumbling brown hair and a petulant expression was pushing buttons on a computer. A name badge announced 'Tracey'. She looked up.

'Can I help you, sir?' The accent was false and irritating.

'What time does the restaurant open?'

'Not till seven-thirty, sir. Would you like me to make you a reservation?'

'No – no. I wanted to eat now. What can you do for me?'

Tracey looked unsure. 'Chef's not in till seven, sir. We could maybe get you a sandwich . . .'

'Blast, I really wanted something hot.'

The receptionist made up her mind about him. He wasn't so bad, better than most of the loud-mouthed louts who caused trouble here every Saturday night. She leaned confidentially over the counter, and dropping the smart accent suggested that he head for Maggie's over the road, where if he was nippy the proprietress, who happened to be her auntie, would do him a banger and chips, double quick, and cheap at the price.

Ten minutes later Betts was seated at a plastic-covered table in the sticky fug of the smoky café, the last customer of the night, being catered for by Tracey's Aunt Maggie, a large, dumpy woman who seemed happy to have this young chap to fuss over, sent by her niece: maybe somebody special. The place was not very clean, but that did not bother him. Nostalgia took over as he remembered the down-at-heel cafés of his youth. The chips were undercooked and greasy, the sausages tough, but the fried eggs were runny and just as he liked them. A mug of fresh sweet tea and thick white bread and butter revived his spirits and prepared him for a long evening.

Tom Sparrow slowed the car on the main road, a hundred yards before the hotel, and turned to his passenger.

'It isn't going very well, Roger, and for all the reasons we have discussed. We seem to have upset too many of our own people – all the vested interests, solicitors, doctors, shareholders, pensioners, businessmen. All that stuff about "protecting the most vulnerable members of society" . . . In reality some of the most vulnerable were our own traditional supporters. We're meeting real resistance on the doorsteps, I can tell you.'

Roger patted his agent on the arm. 'After all this time in power, as the Opposition keeps reminding everybody, there can be hardly anyone we haven't offended at some stage. That's what government is all about –

taking difficult decisions without flinching. Look – the polls may have slipped a bit but they'll be up again, you'll see. It'll be all right on the night, Tom. It always is; it was last time.'

Sparrow was not mollified by being offered the same pep talk as every other worried supporter. He flashed his MP a sardonic look. 'I hope we're not expecting any more banana skins, that's all.'

'Such as?' Dickson allowed himself to sound cross. He expected reassurance from his agent, not criticism.

'You know precisely what I mean. I hear you on the phone. It really isn't on, Roger. You're putting everything at terrible risk. Don't you realise? It only needs one of those idiots to hear' – he gestured at the pressmen lounging in front of the hotel portico, awaiting their arrival – 'and we might as well all pack up and go home.'

'She's all right,' Roger said defensively, staring ahead.

'*She* may be. What you are both up to is not, emphatically, and you know it.'

Dickson was silent for a moment, then spoke quietly, slowly. 'She gives me – oh, a view of the world, and a way of thinking, that I can get from nobody else. I owe her my self-confidence, my ability to face all that rabble and everything they can throw at me. I know the dangers – better than you, at a guess. I am not going to stop, and you are not going to interfere, Tom. This is private business. Do I make myself clear?'

Dickson turned to face his friend, wearing his most stony expression. Tom Sparrow dropped his eyes. Wordlessly he opened his door and got out.

As they emerged from the Underground Karen slipped her arm through Gerry Keown's and smiled up at him. The evening was humid, with thunder in the air. In the distance came the sound of wailing sirens, then a police car surged past, blue light flashing, heading up Victoria Street.

'London!' Karen laughed uneasily. 'I'm glad I don't have to live here all the time. I don't know how people put up with it.'

'Some of us don't have much choice.'

His responses were always dulled by being obvious and Karen wondered why she didn't become more quickly bored in Keown's company. Perhaps because he was older than the lanky boys at college and was thereby harder, more mature. He was never aggressive or overweening, and never forced his attentions on her. That alone was a blessing. His manner was always pleasant, but reticent, giving a sense of considerable self-discipline beneath the surface. Karen wondered whether, if she treated him sweetly, he might eventually fall for her and lose that self-control. But in all the time she had known Gerry – three years in the autumn – that had never happened. Perhaps they were just good friends, or he was like a big brother. For the moment, walking away from the bright lights with Gerry tall at her side, she was grateful for the sense of security he gave her.

It had been quite an achievement to persuade him to try the theatre instead of his predilection for American cinema, as an early celebration of her birthday. A day and a half in London had been wheedled from her mother as a refreshing break from studying, though she had grimly kept a couple of books with her. Karen had responded to Elaine's hints about being surrounded by the world's greatest live performances in the English language and booked two tickets for *Return to the Forbidden Planet*, now in its seventh year. The more intellectual references of this noisy re-creation of Shakespeare's *The Tempest* had meant little, but the rock music, and the exuberance of a highly talented cast, had carried both away for an enjoyable couple of hours.

'Do you like working at the Commons, Gerry?' she asked, more by way of conversation.

He shrugged. 'It's better than parading the wards at the mental hospital, for sure.' He had not lost the soft Irish accent. 'Though the joke, of course, is that there is not much difference.'

Karen giggled. 'What do you think of the MPs – really, I mean? You see them every day. Do they impress you?'

Gerry shrugged. 'One or two. But the whole thing seems a sham, at times. Full of hollow men .'

'Really? "We are the hollow men / We are the stuffed men / Leaning together / Headpiece filled with straw."' Karen danced away from him, chanting. 'It's my A levels. Poetry. Fits, doesn't it? Especially when you think of those chaps in the Lords with their silly wigs. Heads stuffed with straw about sums it up.'

Gerry stopped, shaking his head, a half-smile hovering around his mouth, watching her. 'I never stayed at school long enough to take exams. Do you have to learn all that?'

'Oh yes. Great chunks of it. You know when the Speaker says, "The Ayes have it"? Try this: "The eyes are not here / There are no eyes here / In this valley of dying stars / In this hollow valley / This broken jaw of our lost kingdoms."'

It was sinister. This was almost exactly how he saw the brittle emptiness of his workplace. How others would see it, if those controlling his actions had their way. It would not be long now.

'Lost kingdoms? There were kingdoms in Ireland, once, too, you know,' he mused. 'All lost, but the legends live on.'

'Do you know all about Irish history?' Perhaps she could get him talking about something else which took his interest.

'A fair bit. Enough to make me . . .' He stopped. It had been on the tip of his tongue to say, 'hate the English'. At home it was a standard response, almost casual. The tension was getting to him. '... quite happy to be Irish,' he finished lamely.

He turned to her. 'Come on, I'll see you safely home. And before you leave, Karen, let me know. Don't just disappear, will you?'

At the door he shook hands formally and it was left to the girl to peck him on the cheek. Gerry seemed preoccupied. There had been modest clinches with him on the doorstep in the past, but he had always made excuses about coming in. Given her experiences last time a man had trotted up the stairs behind her, perhaps it was just as well.

'We have made *great* strides in law and order. The rise in the crime rate which *bedevilled* us for years in the 1980s has been brought *firmly* under control . . .'

Seated on an uncomfortable folding chair in the front row, Jim Betts ought to have been scribbling. The thoughts running through his mind should have been cynical and witty, along the lines of wondering who precisely had been in charge of the nation's well-being in the eighties. To hear the Home Secretary talk, it must have been a bunch of Martians. Any hint that those now so proudly disporting themselves on the platform might have been responsible, were in fact in office at the time, seemed wholly missing.

But the lines on his notepad were swimming in and out of focus and the pen was slithering uncontrollably all over the page. The room was unbearably hot and he loosened his tie. A sweat broke out on his face. He reached in his pocket to pull out his handkerchief and mop his brow, but no sooner was it done than he was sweating profusely again. With an effort he concentrated, screwing up his eyes against the television lights. He felt awful. At last the drone from the platform subsided and was replaced by solid if unenthusiastic applause from the large, well-dressed audience seated behind.

Now it was Dickson's turn. A prize specimen these days, Betts reflected, charming, smooth, pleasant-looking but without the oleaginous film-star veneer of a Parkinson in his prime. His trademark appeared to be his friendly, open smile which engaged the entire audience in personal contact, so that they warmed to him even though harbouring doubts.

Betts twisted around gingerly to look at the audience. It was not that the faithful gathered here were hostile: on the contrary, they wanted to believe Dickson's assertions that the election would certainly be won provided vigorous renewed efforts were made in the few days remaining, and were grateful for the sincerity with which he said it. In their heart of hearts, they hoped it was true.

He tried to concentrate his mind on the tall figure on the platform but a wave of nausea hit him. What on earth . . . ? He must have caught a bug, summer flu or something. What a bloody nuisance. It was not, however, going to stop him crowning his career on the *Globe* with the scalp of yet another Cabinet Minister. Dickson had only another half-hour of innocent freedom. Then he, Jim Betts, would confront him with the evidence of his long and no doubt passionate affair with Elaine Stalker. How the fur would fly. The headlines were forming in his imagination already. He licked his lips in anticipation.

Then the pain hit, as if a knife had been plunged into his guts, deep in, starting at his solar plexus, then twisting down, until with a strangled gasp he doubled up. The pen and notepad fell on the floor, but all eyes were loyally on the platform and nobody noticed. Again he reached for his handkerchief, but in wiping his face of its reamed sweat the smell of old cigarettes clinging to its grubby cotton made him feel suddenly terribly ill. He looked round wildly, struggling to regain control. The nearest EXIT sign was to his left, but over on the far side was a gents' toilet. He decided to make a run for the latter and rose unsteadily to his feet.

Halfway across the room, clutching his gut, he realised that he was about to be sick. A burst of applause gave him cover. With a wail of anguish he redoubled his efforts and pushed his protesting legs as fast as they would carry him, hoping to behave with more dignity once the door closed on him. But Jim Betts did not quite make it. No sooner did the door shut than he was on all fours on the tiled floor, vomiting copiously, a great yellow stream forming a growing puddle around him. He steadied himself as the first spasm passed, shaking off the lumps of gristle and half-digested chips deposited on his outstretched hands. Then his system shook and he retched again and again and again, until miserably he wondered if his very guts would come spewing out in their turn. Not until his body stilled did he react to the puddles messing his trousers. Then he had only a moment to struggle to his feet, reaching in his pocket once more for his handkerchief, before another seizure lower down in his abdomen threatened to tear him apart.

The meeting was drifting away. A large florid man came into the gents' talking busily to a companion. Their noses wrinkled in distaste at the appalling smell and they picked their feet carefully over the mess on the floor, heading for the urinals on the far side. Not until their own need was relieved did they turn and spot the prostrate body of Jim Betts, reporter *extraordinaire* of the *Globe*, sprawled on the floor, his stained backside exposed to the air.

Being men of generally seemly if not abstemious habit themselves, naturally their first thought was that the chap was blind drunk, and should be left to sleep it off in his own filth. But there was no whiff of

alcohol in all the pungent room. Consideration for others then took
hold. For a moment they debated calling for hotel staff to clean up and
have the man removed by the police. At last Betts's strange colour and
spasmodic twitching alerted the kindlier sides of their natures. While
one stayed behind, making soothing noises and ineffectually trying to
bathe Betts's face, the other headed quickly for the foyer. This was not a
joke nor a drunk. It was time to call an ambulance.

Twenty minutes later, as interest in the collapsed journalist waned, a
curious observer might have heard Tracey the receptionist cursing in a
most unladylike fashion as she took off her uniform jacket, rolled up her
sleeves, pinned an 'Out of Order' note on the toilet door, filled a bucket
and set to work clearing up. She had thought he was a better sort than
this and had even considered giving him her phone number. He must
have been drinking heavily on the side. It couldn't be anything to do
with her aunt's cooking; nobody had ever complained before.

   The pig had really left his traces. Not just vomit, but his coat and
trousers and underpants in a disgusting heap on the floor. Tracey
fetched a plastic binbag and donned rubber gloves to deal with the
soiled garments. The man must have been taken to hospital with his
shoes and socks still on but not much else below the waist. How
humiliating, but serve him right. She paused in her labours and
hesitated. Underneath the clothing was a handkerchief, a sodden
packet of cigarettes and some bits of wet paper. An envelope, it looked
like. Cautiously she stirred it with her toe; it might be important. Then
she made her mind up. Might have been once, but no more. Too far
gone to rescue now.

As soon as Karen Stalker was safely inside and he could hear her shoes
clattering on the stone stairs, Gerry Keown turned swiftly away. The
Tube took him back to Finsbury Park station, from whence it was a
short walk to the Portland Rise estate, opposite the park. The air in
North London was still, petrol-laden and humid and he was soon
sweating hard. In a corner house on the estate, in a back room, four men
were already gathered. The air was hazy with cigarette smoke. Lager
and Guinness cans littered the floor. As Gerry Keown was ushered in by
a blank-faced young woman there was another knock on the door. He
was not surprised to see hands move quickly, protectively, to back
pockets. He knew only one person in the room and then only by a first
name, though the voice was quite familiar, with an accent similar to his
own.

   When at last everyone was assembled, instructions were issued.

Gerry looked at his list, brooding, and was troubled to note that his heart was heavy.

He pointed at one name on the list. 'This one too?'

The answer was impatient. 'Yes, Volunteer. The lot. You have waited for this for a long time. Don't fail us.'

Back at the flat Karen Stalker undressed, still crooning the bleak poem to herself. The little room was stuffy and she opened the sash window as wide as it would go, hearing in the distance more sirens. The noise bothered her less, now she was off the street; it was amazing what a person could learn to live with. Instead, after an undemanding and relaxing evening, she felt more confident about the tests ahead.

As she cleaned her teeth and considered, she wondered if it was entirely spurious to find parallels between the Commons and Eliot's vivid word-pictures: 'In this last of meeting places / We grope together / And avoid speech.' Perhaps not, given that it was written so soon after the First World War when the complacency of both Houses of Parliament had pushed two million men to their deaths.

On a quick impulse she phoned her mother and regaled Elaine with a cheery account of her date.

'How's it going your end, Mum?'

'Diabolical. Door-knocking is like swimming through mud – heavy-going and dirty. We really could do with some help – not you; you stick to your books. But all the promises of mutual aid seem to have evaporated. It's every man for himself.'

Karen was feeling very grown-up. 'Your Roger should get his people to help. He should make himself useful, if you want my view, which you don't. Or leave you alone completely. Oh, you'll be all right, Mum. We both will be. I'll bring the post up tomorrow. See you.'

In bed, she gazed at the ceiling and breathed the lines with their rat-a-tat marching rhythm. Her eyes were closing as she reached the last few words:

> This is the way the world ends
> This is the way the world ends
> This is the way the world ends
> Not ... with a bang ...

Saturday 26 May. D-Day minus twelve

Bright lights, hurting his eyes. He twisted his face away with a moan, but the pain in his head tore through his eye sockets with fierce intensity.

547

His gut was worse – it felt as if it had been ripped out, leaving a gaping bloody hole, like in wartime. White ceilings. Tiles, reflecting the harsh light. Tubes, stands, trolleys. Metal clashing on metal. The smell of disinfectant and plastic. His mouth felt dry, his throat blocked: there was a tube in the way, making him gag and want to be sick yet again.

Jim Betts now knew what it felt like to want to die. He lay prostrate in the hospital bed, arms limp at his sides. Gradually he became aware of a young woman doctor standing at the foot of the bed examining his notes. She moved closer; a name badge identified her as Dr Martin. She eyed him thoughtfully.

'Back in the land of the living, are we? We thought you were a goner for a while. Nasty bout you've had.'

Betts croaked and pointed to his mouth. The doctor called a nurse and together they removed the tube, bathed his face and helped him to a drink of sterile water. Deftly the nurse checked the fluid-replacement drip in Betts's left arm.

'What was it – what have I got?' he asked feebly.

'Oh, you've been suffering from salmonellosis. We'll need you to think about what you ate before you went down with it – probably chicken, or possibly eggs.'

The doctor wondered why the patient seemed vaguely familiar. His name meant nothing to her; nor would hers to him, for she used her maiden name in the hospital. Betts had been taken ill in the Midlands but after a day in a coma had been transferred to a hospital closer to home. Thus he found himself in St Thomas's under the eagle eye of Marcus Carey's wife.

Betts looked at her beseechingly. 'When will I be out of here? I have a job to do.'

'Not for ages. The lab should be able to tell us in a day or two which particular little bug you acquired. Then we have to keep testing you till you're clear. That can take three months or more, twice a week clutching a little pot of sample. As an out-patient, of course,' she added hastily, as Betts reacted.

'God! Can't you give me something?'

'Not antibiotics, if that's what you mean. Antibiotics would only prolong the carrier state. You're on ciprofloxacin for the diarrhoea and fever, if you really want to know, and that'll have to do unless you get much worse. Otherwise you fight this one on your own.'

'Got to get better. Get back to work. They need me.'

'Really, Mr Betts, can't they manage without you? What do you do for a living?'

'Journalist. Senior reporter. The *Globe*. Very busy with the election. I can't be sick, d'you hear?'

The aggressive squeak exhausted him. He fell back on the pillows, face pallid and clammy. Alison Carey frowned and checked the name again. When she looked up there was a glint in her eye.

'Been on big stories, have you, Mr Betts? By-elections, political scandals, that sort of thing?'

'Yeah, all that sort of thing. I saw Sir Nigel-too-good-to-be-true-Boswood off. That was me.'

Alison felt herself go cold. She remained silent, nodding as Betts huskily explained his importance to the world of political journalism. She would not dream of breaking her Hippocratic oath for Mr Betts, star reporter: but the hospital policy of providing patients with lots of useless information offered an opportunity. Giving him a hard time would be allowable, even sweet revenge.

'Now then, Mr Betts. You should understand that you are going nowhere, not for the duration of the election or for at least a week or two afterwards. Your entire system has been badly knocked about. Even in healthy subjects – and I'm not sure you were a prime specimen before – salmonellosis may cause a wide range of very unpleasant side-effects. Blood poisoning is the obvious one, but there are well-documented cases of inflammation of the heart, neurological damage, reactive arthritis, ankylosing spondylitis and permanent damage to the small intestine and colon. You may suffer from diarrhoea for the rest of your life, and you may never be able to eat normally again.'

Betts's eyes widened in horror. 'Will I die?'

'Well, let's see. There are about thirty thousand confirmed cases every year in England and Wales of what you've got, of which around sixty are fatal. That's about one a week. Maybe it's your turn this week.'

Had Betts been able to focus better he might have noticed a satisfied gleam behind Alison's otherwise stern professional demeanour. He turned his face away in desperation.

'I thought we'd sorted it out. Thing of the past.'

'I'm afraid not. The figures are rising. If I had my way I'd make every member of the government suffer with it, one really bad dose just like yours. Then they might take it seriously and do something effective. Meantime, I don't think it's going to finish you off – but you are going to suffer instead. Sorry, Mr Betts. Not nice, is it?'

And Dr Alison Carey smiled sweetly at her patient, scribbled briefly on his notes and left him.

CHAPTER THIRTY

Friday 1 June. Morning. D-Day minus six

Gerry Keown had worked through the night, preparing and snipping and packing. House of Commons envelopes and wrapping paper and dark-green presentation boxes from the kiosk were scattered at his feet as dawn was breaking. There was no time for a rest, only for a shower, shave and change into his uniform. It was essential to be there early, as if on the first shift.

There was no problem parking his car in the deserted underground car park at the Commons; no difficulty choosing a spot where he was unlikely to be observed by the security cameras; no hassle leaving one small package tucked behind a pipe in a spot carefully researched weeks before. And no hesitation, setting the timer as ordered for 13 June, the day Parliament was to return.

The place was remarkably relaxed. He headed downstairs for the rifle range. He had thought about joining, but had refused the invitation of his original partner, Constable Robin Bell, who would have spotted instantly that he knew how to handle a gun. It was located under the Lords Chamber, in a scruffy and disorganised part of the Palace with plenty of hiding places amongst the jumble and cupboards. Everyone joked that it was here in 1605 that Guy Fawkes and his fellow Catholic conspirators had attempted to blow up the King. Keown's friends were not interested in the monarch – her death would be counter-productive, with world-wide revulsion. The new Parliament was a different matter, a legitimate political target, and a warning to the new government to get out of Northern Ireland. Perhaps this time, if enough of them got hurt, they would take some notice.

It didn't take much, not in a building like this. The main damage would be caused by collapsing masonry as walls caved in and floors fell through on to unsuspecting heads. The Commons was the intended quarry, but their Lordships had an added attraction that most were elderly and less likely to survive.

It was a bright sunny day as he headed for the Home Office and the Ministry of Defence, House of Commons packages under his arm stamped with the Speaker's stamp. That had been easy to reproduce with the help of a friendly office supplies shop in Finsbury Park. Now that Whitehall and Westminster were half empty, people's guards were down, the atmosphere casual. The Northern Ireland Office was always too careful to be worth trying, and the item put in the internal mail to Number 10 probably would get no further than the post room. Staff would probably congratulate themselves on finding it.

After depositing his parcels he made his way back to the Commons and delved in the boot of his car. The next placement required sleight of hand, good timing and a little luck. If he was caught, the rest of the operation would be aborted. That was why he had done all the other jobs first – or nearly all.

Keown walked through Speaker's Court and took the Ministers' stairs to the principal floor. In a moment he stood at the door of the Chamber, behind the Speaker's Chair, an item concealed in his hand. This was the trickiest, for guided tours were still under way. He chatted easily to colleagues, explaining that he had been called in to replace a man gone sick, who then felt better and turned up. As lunchtime loomed people and staff drifted away. Quickly he moved to the side of the Chair. Underneath were two vertical slots used for temporary storage of papers when the Chair was occupied. He bent quickly at the knees, reached behind, and stuck the tiny box on its pad of plasticine far back under the seat.

Even if all the items were found in time a powerful statement would have been made. Personal gifts, however, would be more likely to get close to their victims. Their timers were set for the following few days, and all were tamper-sensitive.

Once he had been tipped off that his call would come after all these years as a sleeper, Keown had made himself a familiar figure to certain Commons secretaries. He had dropped hints to the girls as he drifted in and out of their offices that he was secretly charged with keeping an eye on vulnerable personages. Many of the secretaries were still around. Keown checked the names on his list; several were approached successfully, delighted to pass on a small goodwill token to their employers. The chairman of the backbench Northern Ireland committee and its treasurer, the chairman of the House Select Committee on Northern Ireland and one of its most prominent members all now received gifts on behalf of the security staff. In that familiar green, gold and white livery, who could refuse a box of House of Commons mint chocolates? Especially if innocently presented in the Commons' own gift wrap, available only from the kiosk? That the boxes had not been screened did not occur to the women concerned. A member of the security staff: who would dream of suspecting?

Two of the names on his list were unreachable. The Paddy factor was at work: in wanting to make their point as close to the election as possible (as well as after), his controllers had forgotten that during the campaign period certain prominent people cleared off from the Commons entirely, taking their staff with them. They were not at their London homes either. On the offchance he substituted Lord Prior, a former Northern Ireland Minister, and Lord Howe, a former Home Secretary, leaving gifts in the lobbies of the apartment blocks where they lived. That would have to do.

One left. Kept to the end. He did not want to do this one, and it would have been easy to forget it, to say the task had been impossible. Yet had he not reacted at the mention of the name, when first her daughter had spoken to him? Hadn't he courted the girl initially as a potential entry point for him to her mother, who had spent almost the whole four years of this Parliament as secretary of the backbench Northern Ireland committee? Keown was unsure what responsibilities that entailed, but she was on the list and not yet crossed off. If she were omitted he would have some explaining to do when he got home. He doubted if the controllers would show any more mercy to him than to their other victims, especially if there were any hint he might regret his role and turn Queen's evidence.

The dead boy called to him, insistently, from beyond the grave. Time to repay. He steeled himself and picked up the phone.

'Karen? Gerry here. First of all, happy birthday, though I know you're not planning to celebrate till after your exams. Glad I've caught you. When are you off?'

Nick Thwaite sat in the chair at the side of the hospital bed and contemplated his snoring staffer. The smell of sickness wafted over with each breath. Thwaite moved his chair several inches further back out of the line of fire.

The sound of wood scraping on the floor woke Betts up. He opened one yellowed eye, cautiously. Seeing a friendly face he blinked and half sat up.

'Oh, it's you,' he said. 'I thought it was that doctor. Every time I have a relapse she looks pleased. Ghouls, the lot of them.'

Nick was amused. 'How're you feeling? I hear you've got salmonella. Is that right?'

'It is *not* funny,' Betts responded grumpily. 'I feel like death and my legs have gone. When I tried to get to the toilet by myself this morning I passed out. Going to take at least another week, they say.'

'Pity. The whole election's coming nicely to a climax. Polls all over the place – now Labour are two points ahead. I've let Cherry have a crack at political human interest stories, and she's having a whale of a time. Her approach is a bit trivial, but the readers approve. She recently pulled off an excellent interview with the Prime Minister's wife – lovely pictures. If she carries on like this, she won't want to stay with fashion – and McSharry will be thinking about promotions.'

Thwaite left unsaid the obvious corollary – that there might be demotions, or even vacancies.

Betts frowned. His mind was functioning only sluggishly. He put out a hand. 'Nick – I left some things behind at that hotel. Important things. Did they turn up?'

His companion shrugged. 'The stuff in your room, of course; I've had that taken to your place. Your sicked-on clothes were destroyed. Was there anything important?'

'My notebook – and a letter. It was in my pocket.'

'Letter? No, nothing like that's turned up. You did make a helluva mess, Jim. We're lucky the hotel didn't send us a bill.' Thwaite reached behind him and pulled out a brown paper bag. 'Anyway, I brought you a bunch of grapes. Get well soon.'

Betts regarded the green fruit gloomily. 'They look just like suppositories,' he muttered. 'Got them sticking out of my bum and coming out of my ears, it feels like. Thanks anyway, Nick, I'll give them to the nurses. I'm off fruit for the duration. Nothing but endless fluids and sweet things like custard. By the time I'm better I shall be a scarecrow. What have I done to deserve this?'

Karen Stalker and Gerry Keown stood awkwardly at the police post at Members' entrance by Westminster Hall, surrounded by visitors who emerged blinking into the sunshine at the end of their guided tour. Beside the girl a pile of carrier bags held the remains of the post; behind her the hands of Big Ben moved towards midday. She fidgeted, eyes downcast. If her mother lost the seat, she might not see Gerry again and felt almost sorry. Future boyfriends would have a hard task to measure up to his courtesy, consideration and quiet maturity.

'I shall miss you, Gerry. Will you still be here after the election, if my mother gets back in?'

'Of course,' he said, but knew it was untrue. Returning would not be safe. In any case, for all he was aware, there might be another sleeper placed in the Palace, much like himself, ready for next time.

'All the best for the exams.' He stumbled a little over the words. 'I've brought you . . .' He thrust the package in her hand. 'Just some chocolates. Not for you, mind. For your mother, to wish her luck in the election. Will you make sure she gets them?'

'I'd be glad to. Might even eat a few myself. How very thoughtful of you, Gerry. You're so sweet.' Karen stood on tiptoe, placed an arm around his neck and kissed him on the mouth. A policeman standing nearby chuckled, then winked at Keown. The luck of the Irish.

'Must go' – and she was off, arms loaded with carrier bags, heading under the colonnades towards Westminster Tube and the train up to South Warmingshire. Big Ben began to chime, slow, sonorous, timeless.

Gerry Keown watched her go and stood quietly for a moment. 'Have a good birthday, and be careful,' he whispered to her retreating back. He could have given her a birthday gift, a real one, but it had been beyond him entirely to wrap yet another parcel, this time innocently, in the murderous detritus of his room. His expression as he turned away was sombre.

On the train home, staring out of the window or trying to concentrate on French irregular verbs, Karen realised that she could kill two birds with one stone. It would not be far out of her way to go into Roger Dickson's constituency office. Officially she could ask if there was any chance of promises of help being fulfilled. And if the opportunity presented itself to tell Roger Dickson to lay off she would take it. This time, without tears.

Feeling like the original bag lady as she struggled with the street door, Karen managed at last to make her way inside past boxes of last-minute handouts, a stack of posters still to be erected and pieces of a broken public address system left on the floor. Three elderly ladies busy folding leaflets at a trestle table recognised her, for her resemblance to her mother, despite the different colouring, was unmistakable. The good women were happy to be diverted for a few moments and one helped her deposit her bags while another poured a welcome cup of tea. Mr Dickson was still in London, they informed her, and would be so sorry to have missed her.

Tom Sparrow spotted Karen and motioned her inside his office. Visitors who distracted his helpers working under a tight deadline needed discouraging. He suspected, however, that Miss Stalker had not come for trivial reasons.

Sipping her tea Karen outlined the problems in South Warmingshire. 'We have plenty of bods in the office. What we need are a few more energetic types fit enough to doorstep and willing to come out this last weekend.'

Sparrow nodded sympathetically. 'Don't we all,' he agreed. 'People these days don't relish red-blooded political argument face to face. They prefer it all pat on the telly.'

'Some people just don't understand. We had a very shirty phone call from a retired politics professor who has recently moved into our area, wanting to know why we hadn't responded to his offer of distinguished help. He's eighty-two, and all he wants to do is sit round in the office explaining the origins of the First World War. I told him we really needed a pair of good legs with a mouth on top and he put the phone down.'

'That was unkind, Karen.' But Sparrow couldn't avoid a chuckle. 'I'll send a carload of experienced people over tomorrow afternoon, if that will help. We've about finished here.'

He waited. Karen examined her fingers for a moment, then looked him in the eye.

'They're still at it, aren't they? Can't we stop them?'

'I have tried, Karen, believe me. I am not sure they realise the danger, not only for themselves but for the whole government.'

'I don't think my mum is that bothered for herself. She is worried, though, what would happen to Mr Dickson's career if he was found out.'

'Not to speak of his family, his wife and little children,' Sparrow suggested drily.

Karen pulled a wry face. She had never heard her mother agonise in those terms.

The matter was left there, with both feeling unhappy. In their world hangers-on did not count for much compared with the principals. Sparrow courteously escorted Karen out of the office; it was apparent to both that they had a great deal in common and would worry or suffer in unison, whatever the outcome.

It was not until Karen was safely on the bus home and Tom Sparrow had gone to the printer's to collect the last leaflets that one of the helpers noticed the Commons carrier bag, green plastic with the portcullis logo. Enquiries ascertained that it must have been left behind by Miss Stalker; easily done, for the girl was so laden. That was a nuisance but not a disaster, as a group would be heading in her direction the following day.

In order to ensure that the package was not forgotten a second time the distinctive bag was put on Mr Sparrow's desk. As an afterthought, since they would have gone home before his return, one of the ladies wrote a note in large capitals, and pinned it to the handle.

The evening news made gloomy watching with its pictures of war and starvation and mayhem from all over the world. It looked as if the bloodshed in former Yugoslavia would never come to an end, nor the cycle of famine and war that swept one African country after another. 'Where ignorant armies clash by night' just about summed it up.

Roger Dickson poured himself a drink, tried to recall the origin of the phrase and gave up. His political schooling had included little experience of foreign affairs. When he was a child, Dean Acheson's acute remark about Britain having 'lost an empire but not yet found a role' was quoted but not quite believed in Whitehall or Westminster. Successive governments of all colours had accepted the free-market elements of the European Community but firmly denied and derided any wider political influence for Europe. Nobody had figured out how to react when the

West won the Cold War; once America showed it was not prepared to be the world's policeman the ignorant armies could rampage without restraint. Dickson wondered how Clinton would fare in the forthcoming US presidential elections. His regime, like Jimmy Carter's, had been high on hope but low on substance and achievement. Maybe, in the closing years of the century, Europe would have no choice but to get its act together and impose peace on its near neighbours.

In a few days' time it could be his pigeon. The Secretary of State for Environment was due for a big move upwards, all being well. That environmental subjects were no longer a matter of political controversy was entirely due to Dickson's adroitness in winning a cross-party consensus on the main issues. Certain controversial ideas had been dropped long before any Commons row. Good intelligence, the fruit of those years in the whips' office, told him how many recalcitrants would vote against the government: if a measure could not be pushed through, however desirable, it was a waste of energy even to try. The Department had even cut its budget, gently, without too much howling, while the emollient style of Dickson and Muncastle had charmed hostile councillors across the country into relative quietude. In all, he was a considerable success.

Now, however, he would be moving to something much tougher. His next appointment could easily be the Foreign Office itself.

If he got that far, he would seriously consider appointing Elaine as his PPS. It was the least he could do. She had spent most of this Parliament fretting about her lack of preferment. It was safe enough now, surely; he was not climbing the ladder but close to the top. After four years of avoiding detection they both knew how to behave in public. Several male Ministers had women MPs as their PPSs and vice versa, all without comment or nuance. Nor was she a new star flashing gaudily across the sky. People had become used to her – there were even several imitations, pretty, blonde, tough Tory women on the hustings this time. And she was coming up to forty, hardly a chicken. It would be worth trying.

He stood in front of the television set, brooding. Several years in Cabinet listening to debates on overseas policy had given him general background knowledge. If, however, the UK under his guidance was to move into a different era, he would need an ear, a sounding board, he could trust. Elaine would not only be useful; for him, she would be essential.

And if the election were lost . . . Dickson raised the glass to his lips and took a long swallow. Then all bets were off. He was sure of his place as a prominent member of the front bench, one of the party's two or three leading names. There would be a leadership contest. His name would have to go forward: to refuse would be an abdication, with complete uncertainty about whether any other chance would ever present itself.

And he might win.

He had not started out, all those years ago, with the idea of becoming Prime Minister. Only prats did that, their prattishness proven by their telling everybody on the first train to London. He had wanted what then seemed an impossibility, a modest position of influence at the heart of British life. For a long while the whip's post had seemed to satisfy that need and he had thought no further. Then along came Elaine Stalker, with her insight and originality and confidence-building, her willingness to take risks, indeed to seek out those risks. It was not all that surprising that renewed ambition had awoken in his breast. Without her he would never have been able to charm a stranger or spin a tale or tell a lie so effectively. But with her . . .

Danger: there was danger all around. She was dangerous to him, and he to her. Especially if others knew. Instinctively he glanced over his shoulder, then pulled out the photocopied note with its compliments slip from the *Globe*. The scrawled signature of the sender was unreadable and Roger was not about to telephone the paper to enquire. It was odd, however, that no journalist had contacted him about it in all the weeks since it had arrived. The note had lain near his heart, an ever-present reminder of fallibility, a warning against complacency and arrogance, almost as when, in ancient times, the Romans sent a slave to follow heroes on their victorious tour of the city and cry to them: 'Remember – you are only human.'

Suddenly he knew what he had to do. If the note were as incriminating as he suspected then he would not harbour a copy of it, not for a moment longer. A scrabble in the drawer produced a booklet of matches from some long-forgotten dinner. He tore letter, slip and envelope into tiny fragments, dropped them into an ashtray, struck a match and set the shreds alight, poking awkwardly at the small flames until the evidence had disintegrated into ashes.

The thing had gone; but the worry would remain, and stab him in unguarded moments.

He wished she would phone.

Betty Horrocks was doing her comfortable best. The South Warming-shire constituency was perennially short of money and had never been able to afford a proper trained agent. In recent years Mrs Horrocks herself had fulfilled many of the necessary duties. Since the office was tumbledown and seedy it was now mainly used for storage, and most election activity took place instead in a large modern glass conservatory attached to her home, with views over the immaculate garden where an elderly gardener toiled three times a week. A coffee-pot and chocolate biscuits were permanently available. Mrs Horrocks presided with good sense, warmth and somewhat scatty organisation. All concerned were doing their level best to win, but if they were to lose it would at least be from mellow surroundings.

She looked up as Elaine entered. 'Phone's been on the go all day. *South Warmingshire Gazette* want your views on the proposal for a new sewage farm, for or against. Central Television want to come and film you losing on Thursday – I told them they'll be welcome, but disappointed. Diane is arriving tonight for the weekend. I've offered to put her up here – you've enough on your plate. Tom Sparrow at North-West Warwickshire will send a carload over tomorrow, so you'll have two strong teams of canvassers out. Karen I have fed and sent home, firmly: I gave her a record token for her birthday, as you never know what young people's tastes are these days. I hope that was all right.'

Elaine thanked her warmly as she glanced through a small pile of messages, cards and letters. One postmark caught her eye. She slit open the envelope to reveal a cheque.

'Well, I never,' she breathed. 'My former father-in-law has sent a donation. Five hundred pounds, the old darling. To be recorded as anonymous, please, Betty. He wishes us luck, and says not to tell "Mother". That's the old lady, who never approved of me.'

'Families do turn up trumps occasionally,' Mrs Horrocks remarked. 'You'll meet my brother-in-law on Thursday night – that's Johnny's younger brother, George. He was appointed Deputy Lord-Lieutenant last year and will be reading out your results. You'll like him. Not as daft as Johnny: a different generation.'

'You sound quite fond of him,' Elaine teased.

'Me? Oh, rubbish. Much too young for me – there were ten years between them. Not my type either.' She eyed her MP briefly and seemed about to continue, then stopped. Matchmaking was definitely not Mrs Horrocks's line, though she resolved to introduce the two properly at the right moment.

One other matter remained. Mrs Horrocks steeled herself. 'And please would you phone Roger Dickson right away, on this number.'

With a disapproving air she handed Elaine a piece of paper. The number was Roger's home in London. Elaine frowned. Caroline and the children would already be in Warwickshire for the weekend.

Without further comment, Elaine put the note in her pocket, picked up her papers for the evening's engagement and headed for the door.

Saturday 2 June. D-Day minus five

The last Saturday of any election campaign is always the busiest. It was not helpful that the morning dawned cool and changeable. Tom Sparrow cursed as he rose and quickly shaved. Volunteers did not enjoy dodging showers, while posters, already close to the end of their useful life, would become soggy and torn and need replacing in time for election day on Thursday. The radio news was not good: polls showed that Labour was now three points ahead. The gap was still well within the margin of error which even the pollsters would now accept, but it worried him more than he liked to admit. This time Labour had done nothing stupid, or at least not yet. The Prime Minister was no longer young and fresh and new, nor did anyone pretend there were easy answers to the nation's worries. This time he felt even less sure about the overall outcome than last time, and that had been nerve-racking enough.

There had been letter-bombs in London. One had gone off in the portico of Lord Prior's block of flats behind Westminster Roman Catholic Cathedral and blown chunks of masonry sky high. At least nobody had been hurt. Another had turned up at the Home Office. It was thought more might be found after the weekend. The item intercepted at Number 10 was not mentioned, for dodgy packages there were a regular occurrence: drawing attention to them might encourage every loony in the country. All participants in the election campaign were warned to be especially careful.

The office was briefly quiet and empty as Tom Sparrow let himself in and switched off the alarm. He pottered around for a few moments, shifting boxes, picking up bits of equipment to create a clearer passage from the street door to his own office.

On his desk were various scraps of paper with reminders from the day before. And a green Commons carrier bag, which, according to the note pinned to it, had been left behind by Karen Stalker. Curious, he tipped out its contents: various unopened letters addressed to her mother the MP, a magazine, a cotton sweater, and a parcel wrapped in House of Commons paper. A gift of some kind, possibly from Karen to her mother. She was a decent kid. Sparrow picked up the box and idly tried to guess what was in it. He shook it experimentally, then sniffed at it and noticed the faint whiff of chocolate.

And something else, the faintest possible chemical smell, which he had known before, in the army, long ago.

Delicately, not daring to breathe, he put the box down on the desk and backed away. He did not get far. With a great roar the bomb exploded, blasting air and heat at high pressure through the small room and lifting Sparrow's outstretched body into the far wall. The ceiling first moved upwards, then disintegrated into crazy paving which came crashing down, covering the desk, the filing cabinets, the phone, the piles of paper, the floor itself. In one corner a fire began to flicker. The remaining air space filled with choking white dust mixed with smoke. A second later, almost in slow motion, the main window of the shop blew out, shattering glass over the pavement and seriously injuring several passers-by.

It happened so quickly. Then all hell broke loose. The alarms of nearby shops began to ring shrilly. A woman was screaming, sitting on the sidewalk, her face covered in blood, as a terrified shopgirl tried to comfort her. A pensioner leaned against the wall, shaking uncontrollably, then sank slowly to his knees. A young mother stood rigid with horror, staring at the pram where her sleeping baby was covered in a shivering heap of plate glass. In whimpering disbelief a schoolboy rubbed his leg where a jagged piece of metal was sticking out. The police and emergency services were on the spot in minutes, blue lights flashing, doors slamming, radios crackling. And inside the shattered building, his face unmarked, a beam across his broken back, Tom Sparrow lay dead.

Tuesday 5 June. D-day minus two

There would be a memorial service later, but the funeral was best out of the way as soon as possible. Best, as well, before the election rather than after. Among the few differences remaining between the main parties was their attitude to the Prevention of Terrorism Act, which permitted the incarceration and questioning of terrorist suspects for five days. The Conservatives were prepared to accept limitations on civil liberties in the pursuit of long-term peace while the Opposition were not. The attack on the office of a prominent member of the Conservative campaign team, a member of the Cabinet, was clearly politically motivated. Any public sympathy which could be garnered should not be ignored; not with the race so close.

A large crowd of friends, colleagues and the curious turned out to pay their respects. The press were there in force. Considering the haste of the arrangements it was all beautifully done, the coffin draped with a Union Jack and a single wreath of white lilies, with an honour guard from his old regiment, fresh-faced Royal Fusiliers young enough to be his grandsons. The path from the chapel of rest to the graveside was lined with wreaths and bunches of flowers from all over the country. Roger Dickson was a pall-bearer, his handsome face dark and grieving. In the soft summer air a breeze blew through the tall trees of the well-kept cemetery. Mourners turned to each other for comfort, and found none, only the certainty that the fight must continue.

Elaine and Karen stood quietly at the back of the main group as the coffin was lowered into the ground. Beside them a senior police officer stood respectfully, leather gloves in hand, watching the crowd.

Karen was crying, very softly. After the morning's exam she had spent a long session with Superintendent Collis, the man at her side. It had started as routine; everyone who had been at the office was being interviewed. Under his gentle probing it had slowly dawned on her that the bomb had in fact been intended for her mother, and that she had been the unwitting agent of Tom Sparrow's murder. As yet the facts were being kept under wraps, as was the discovery of two more bombs, almost certainly delivered at the same time. The Superintendent had tried to cheer her up a little with the comment that it would be much easier now they knew what kind of packages they were looking for, but the thought that others might still face the same fate had caused her even greater horror.

Elaine moved closer and put her arm around her daughter's waist. She had heard only the briefest version of the morning's interview. That Karen was an entirely innocent party was not in doubt. Yet the girl's recent emotional history gave cause for alarm, should she feel in any way blameworthy. An official police note was to go to the examiners, explaining the situation, though Karen had already turned down being excused any exams.

'I'm all right, Mum.' The girl sensed her mother's anxiety. 'I'm so sad, that's all. What had Mr Sparrow ever done to upset anybody? He just wanted the election to go well. Those bastards! Why is it the good ones get hurt, and not them?'

Elaine shook her head. 'It mustn't stop us, Karen. Most of all, it mustn't stop us saying things which do upset somebody. Behaving as if we have a gun at our heads all the time would be worse. It would mean that the wicked had won.'

'After nearly thirty years of the Ulster troubles it makes you wonder what would stop them,' came a sombre voice at her elbow.

Elaine started. Roger Dickson loomed large in a black overcoat despite the summer warmth. His expression was drawn. Behind him a hand-held TV camera was shifted, adjusted, its small spotlight searching Elaine Stalker's face. She was glad of its presence, which would prevent any kind of intimacy. She spoke a few anodyne words to Dickson, then turned deliberately away, taking Karen's arm.

Under the trees, out of camera-shot, the two women paused. Karen blew her nose, then for a moment, to calm herself, leaned on her mother, touching foreheads. The girl gazed into Elaine's face.

'He wanted to talk to you. Did you answer his phone calls?'

Elaine waited until she had her voice under control.

'No.'

'Are you going to?'

'No, I'm not.'

It was as if the words came from far away, were borne to her on the quiet breeze, as if, for some remote, complicated reason, she owed it to Sparrow.

'Never again. It's over, though I don't think he realises yet.'

'Oh, Mum . . .' The girl wrapped her arms about her mother and the two rocked gently, wordlessly together, mother and daughter, flesh of flesh, experience and innocence, spirit and body and mind, past and future, beginning and end.

Thursday 7 June. Election Day

Lieutenant-Colonel George Horrocks, Blues and Royals (retired), a tall fair-haired man, not quite fifty, slid his regimental tie inside his grey City suit, tinkled coins in his pocket and thought what fun he was having. It was the first time he had ever attended an election count. As Deputy Lord-Lieutenant, appointed by the Queen to represent her in Warmingshire with the Lord-Lieutenant and other deputies, he was obliged to be above politics. Nor had it been his taste to get involved. The political chaps who sat on his company's board with their knighthoods and peerages had never impressed him enough to wish to join them; they always seemed to be drifters, half glad to be out of the hurly-burly of the Commons and relieved to be on the receiving end of decent incomes at last.

Yet here he was, and the electric atmosphere, the lights, the tension, the cameras, all struck him as quite marvellous. It was extraordinary: there was the feeling that here, in this draughty hall normally reserved for unemployed five-a-side, Asian women's badminton and wheelchair handball, a spirit was abroad, a heady mix of independence, principle, politicking, devotion and choice, which had underpinned the nation for centuries. No, that was taking it too far. The ability to choose was much more recent than that. A century only had passed since the will of the ordinary people could be expressed peacefully and made effective. Though Mrs Stalker, over there in the smart blue suit, looking a bit tired now as one might expect, would probably claim it was not until women got the vote in 1918.

Mrs Stalker was standing talking to his sister-in-law, Betty. He would have to be careful what he said in their presence: the sort of City jokes which went down well in the club would displease these two formidable women. Probably quite rightly. Since Monty's death some years ago his widow had shown a surprising strength of character, though on reflection perhaps she was always the stronger of the two. Army wives had to be.

George Horrocks strolled casually across the hall, introducing himself. He watched fascinated as official party observers settled down to serious checking. Sporting the biggest rosettes, with red roses turning limp on their jackets, the Labour candidate and his wife sat side by side at a long wooden trestle table almost nose to nose with the counters opposite, as the box from Whittington was emptied in front of them. Each batch of twenty-five, pulled at random from the pile, was eagerly assessed. Four, five, six out of each batch were recorded for Labour.

563

That could mean 20 per cent of the vote, or slightly less, in an area which was usually solid Tory. Yet the Liberal Democrat vote was similar. Elaine Stalker appeared to have won that ward hands down. The two moved on to another table where an urban ballot box was being tipped out. That gave a more promising preview, suggesting that there Mrs Stalker was in line for barely one vote in three. Yet in the Labour ward the turnout was well down, whereas the Tories had got their supporters out. *It was going to be close.*

Their Liberal Democrat opponent headed for the corridor, lit up a defiant cigarette and wondered what had possessed her to stand again. There had, indeed, been serious negotiations about this seat between party leaders. If one of the Opposition candidates had stood down it could have been wrenched from the Tories relatively easily. Yet her main backer, a local businessman, had been furious. It was not democracy, he declared, to deny the people their choice of candidates. She was to stand, and there would be more helpers: it would not be the shambles of last time. He was wrong, and it was, and she was angry, but still in a strange way she was glad they had not given way.

In the television studio in London, Lord Boswood pontificated happily, drawing his facts from thin air. With no results in yet it was impossible to tell what was happening. Exit polls were being offered only with the greatest caution. The boundary changes had proven somewhat unhelpful this time around, with good rural wards being withdrawn from marginal Conservative seats all over the place. Some seats would be lost; others might come storming through. He felt wistful, an old warhorse, out to grass.

At home Karen was tucked up in bed with a yoghurt and can of soft drink, a clipboard and newspaper listing at her side, watching the colour monitor on her dressing table. The deal was she could stay up until it was clear which side had won, but must switch off and slide into sleep by two in the morning, whether South Warmingshire had declared or not. Her mother had promised to come into the bedroom and tell her anyway, the moment she got home. Next day was the second Eng. Lit. exam, in its own way more important.

It was almost time. Elaine and Betty Horrocks exchanged glances.

All round the country candidates touched charms and whispered prayers.

George Horrocks eyed the hopeful anxious faces in front of the platform, shuffled the papers, checked that the TV cameras were ready, and cleared his throat. In a way, the result itself did not matter. What mattered was that democracy was alive and flourishing. He stepped up to the microphone.

'Ladies and gentlemen! May I have your attention please. The results in South Warmingshire are as follows . . .'